Ultimate Seven Sisters Collection

By

M.L. Bullock

Table of Contents

Seven Sisters

By

M.L. Bullock

Dedication

This book is dedicated to my best friend and sister Karena. Thank you for endless summer days on bicycles, for sharing your blanket and keeping our room tidy. You are the best non-speaking actress I have ever met.

"Many a night I saw the Pleiades
Rising thro' the mellow shade
Glitter like a swarm of fire-flies
Tangled in a single braid."
Alfred Lord Tennyson
"Locksley Hall"
1842

Prologue

Mobile, AL, 1850

Her white hand shone like bone in the moonlight. Shivering, she stood perched on the walkway that led to the Delta Queen. To the casual observer, she might appear to be a statue, standing perfectly still, leaning slightly against the shiny wood railing. No, she was not a cold, unmoving statue but a real woman alive and free for the first time.

Musical notes jostled with one another in the air, and the voices of spirited patrons rolled from the riverboat like waves lapping along the shores of the Mobile River. Above the glittering riverboat hung a clear, dark sky filled with heavy stars that shone with an unusual brilliance. She heard no familiar voice but to her, those stars, the Pleiades, shone their approval like a message from heaven. Her lips turned up in a small smile as she imagined her mother saying, "Run—be free. Be what I can never be!"

She raised her hand to her lips to calm her heart—it leapt like a calf! She turned her head slightly, her long curls brushing her bare back. Looking down the sandy, moonlit path, she gave a small wave and smiled into the darkness at the friend she left behind. Then she disappeared into the bubbling soiree aboard Mobile's most celebrated ship.

Once inside, the young woman was thankful for the music. She was sure that without it, all of Mobile would hear the pounding of her heart. Clutched at her side was a small satin purse, elegantly beaded and embellished with silk ribbons. She slid her hand into the purse and pulled out a small, leather-bound book, running a finger over the cover. The book had changed her forever. Inside were his words, which had opened her closed heart. Like Ali Baba whispering the words that had opened the enchanted door.

How beautiful and courtly were his words! How completely he had allayed her every fear. She had carefully gathered each letter and bound them in her book. They had given her the courage to forget the darkness that had surrounded her.

Suddenly, anxiety overwhelmed her. What if he no longer wanted her? What if she had been too late in her reply? Would she now pay for her aloofness? She could never go back! She had done the unthinkable. The die was cast.

Somewhere aboard the Delta Queen was Captain David Garrett, the gentleman who had liberated her heart. The riverboat would leave Mobile soon. She had seized her chance, a chance at happiness away from the ghosts of Seven Sisters. She would reveal her soul to him, the man who had proven worthy of her love and devotion. His writings had plucked at her courage, creating a crescendo of hope, love and desire that commanded release. It would be fulfilled by her spontaneous act of affection—her willingness to leave behind a world of favor and prominence for a more uncertain one as his bride.

She moved through the thick wooden doorway, humming along to the waltz that flowed out of the concert hall. A woman with vulgar red lips smiled up at a mustached man who held two glasses overflowing with some sort of dark libation. Callie's disgust shook her back to her task. She hated hard drink; it made good men evil.

Her green eyes glittered as she searched the hall for Captain Garrett's dark, handsome countenance. She had seen him less than a dozen times, but she had sketched his face perfectly in her mind and added details after each visit, like the curl of his hair and the dark fringe of his eyelashes. Always his hair curled around his crisp white collars. His wide, toothy smile and cleft chin made him look like an exotic Russian prince, she imagined. She would recognize those dark blue eyes in a crowd of a hundred men.

She moved amongst the partiers, touched and jostled by dancers and couples flirting. Such a different world from the ballrooms of the local plantations where elegant ladies prided themselves on navigating the crowd without crushing another debutante's dress! A few gentlemen tipped their hats to her, but she was largely ignored. Her coral-colored silk gown, his favorite, rustled as she continued her quest.

Again, those questions screamed like banshees in her mind. What if he no longer wanted her? What if she had been too late in her reply?

She could never go back to her unhappy life. The dark thing she had witnessed, the many dark things she had seen, made that impossible. Her desperation rising, she asked a short, officious-looking man where the captain was. He silently led her through a myriad of hallways with a slow gait that irritated her. He tossed her a curious look once over his shoulder, and then unceremoniously left her standing in the hall outside a wooden door with a bronze handle.

She fussed over her barrette and pinched her cheeks for some color, as her mother had taught her to do. She was no hothouse rose like her cousin, but the flush of warmth in her cheeks flattered her thin nose and unusually full lips. It gave her an added sense of attractiveness. She felt confident, beautiful and wanted by this man of honor and gentility.

She raised her hand to knock, but then changed her mind. Instead, she followed her inner streak of boldness, the same boldness that had led her to this place, to this moment. Smiling to herself, she swung open the door. "David," she called out softly, laughing joyfully at saying his name aloud for the first time. The intimacy thrilled her.

No answer came. She stood silent in the small parlor, embarrassed but determined to find him.

Soft moans and a shimmer of light filtered through an open door. She strained to hear the hushed voices. Frozen momentarily in the shifting light of flickering candlelight and a rising moon, her heart raced to keep up with what her mind already knew.

"David, David! Oh, yes!"

As quietly as possible, she delicately pushed the door open wider. Standing perfectly still, she said nothing. She did nothing. The forgotten book slipped from her hand, making an odd slapping sound as the leather cover hit a space of bare wooden floor.

Half-dressed, his body exposed, his normally perfect coiffure of dark curls unruly and wild, David Garrett stood to face her. Even in the dim light, she could see his blue eyes. How easily they reflected his emotions—a flicker of realization, regret, and then sadness. Had he ever truly loved her? He opened his mouth to offer her his words, a reproach, perhaps an explanation. But she raised her hand in protest, surprising him into silence for a seemingly eternal moment.

From behind him there was a shuffling of clothes, then a familiar face peeking around his legs, a round cherubic face. Callie's cousin rose from the small, rumpled bed and stood standing next to the half-dressed captain. Her skin gleamed with sweat, evidence of her extreme betrayal. A blue gown lay piled on the floor, one that Callie recognized as her own. The half-naked girl giggled again, wrapping herself around David. Then she stretched out her hand to Callie, as if inviting her to join them. The scandalous move seemed to bring the captain to his senses; he scolded her loudly for her vulgar gesture and tried to dress himself as graciously as he could with a sense of obvious urgency.

Lifting her skirts with one hand and pushing him away with the other, Callie ran from the room, leaving the muskiness of the betrayers' lovemaking and her childish dreams behind. She ran blindly down the long hallway, through the unfamiliar complex of passageways that were now filled almost to capacity. She made her way through the crowd, running when she could.

She was thankful for the tears that blurred her vision. She didn't want to see the faces, the witnesses to her great shame. She welcomed the deepening agony, the hurt of the betrayal, the overwhelming sadness. Behind her she heard someone call her name. She never looked back.

Before she understood what was happening, she felt herself falling, falling into the blackness of the river. Above her, his outstretched arms, a quiet scream, silver stars, welcoming warmth, and then—nothing.

Chapter 1

I climbed into my blue Honda, slipped it into neutral and slid silently down the driveway. I hated saying goodbye to the comfortable garage apartment that smelled like fresh paint and new wood; however, I felt an unusual call to leave for once. I had the courage to go. That Zen-like, "I'm starting over" spell comforted me on this unseasonably cool morning as I slid the last box of my belongings into the backseat of the car. The rest, a collection of CDs, memorabilia from a recent trip to the Bahamas and most anything that did not fall into the jeans and t-shirt category, I left behind in a small storage space about a mile away. I had paid for six months in advance but was already putting off the idea of coming back to Charleston.

I did feel a twinge of guilt as I put the car into gear. I had not even bothered to say goodbye to William, my friend and sort-of boyfriend. He was kind and good and understanding, but I knew that would never last. We were too different in too many ways to describe. Perversely, I liked leaving on a high note, without the nightmares and all the screaming. It felt like a personal triumph. I was being selfish, but I was okay with that. At least for the moment.

"Once I make up my mind, the die is cast," I said to no one in particular.

I muttered, "Well, if I am stubborn, I have had to be." I already loathed myself for traveling down this predictable mental highway, but what else could I do for the next few hours but drive and think? I hadn't "gone there" in a while, so perhaps a quick review would be healthy. I rolled my eyes at myself in the rearview mirror. I sounded just like my last shrink. "How can I help you if you won't share with me, Carrie Jo? Why won't you let someone in?" Feeling a softness that I rarely experienced, I had pulled back the cover and let the light hit my secret for the first time in a long time.

* * *

"I'm not trying to be difficult, but without significant personal discipline, I would have gone nuts—like my mother, a long time ago." Encouraged by the petite, smiling psychologist, perched in her overlarge leather chair, I continued on, "You see, Dr. O'Neal, I have a problem—I dream about the past. I'm kind of like a human DVR; my dream life is usually not my own. It belongs to whatever memory movie plays the loudest wherever I'm sleeping."

Dr. O'Neal had looked at me blankly, unshaken by my confession.

Okay, the young, pretty doctor has earned ten points for the poker face she's wearing, I'd thought wryly. Her focused attention encouraged me to ramble on.

"That's why I love my garage apartment so much. It is brand spanking new, with no movies, no memories. I sleep, and I dream my own dreams. My 'problem' gets even more complicated when I sleep with someone else. I can see their dreams too."

Luckily, there haven't been too many of them, I'd thought, but I hadn't felt the need to share my lack of a love life with the dainty Dr. O'Neal, new bride and smart career woman. Her fingers had flown across her notebook, her manicured hands busy recording her undoubtedly smart thoughts to form a brilliant pre-diagnosis. I'd discreetly peeked at the wedding photo perched on her mahogany desk. It didn't take a degree to see she was proud of her groom.

I hated the silent moments of this confession, so I blathered on, in a hurry to make my point and come to the reason for my visit. That was me: give it to me in black and white, and I'll do the same for you.

"You see, Dr. O'Neal, I have this great job offer—it's a once-in-a-lifetime gig, really. But I hate giving up my apartment. I just don't know what to expect. That's why my friend Mia suggested I come see you. And, well, here I am."

To her credit, the shrink didn't zero in on my "problem"; instead, she took a sidestep that I hadn't anticipated. "What about your current relationships? Didn't you say you were seeing someone?" Consulting her notebook, she pointed. "Yes, he's a 'fantastic' guy. Don't you find it odd that you're worried about leaving your safe apartment but not this 'fantastic' guy?"

I left her office feeling deflated, insecure and even more confused. Why had I mentioned William? Obviously, Dr. Happily Married was going to focus on the sex angle rather than the real problem. When she called a few days later to setup a dream clinic session, it was a moot point. I had already made up my mind. I was leaving, come hell or high water. I had to take a chance away from the safety and security of my little apartment. I had to go where the work was. And although I couldn't explain it, even to myself, I knew my destiny waited for me in Mobile.

* * *

As I zipped onto the highway and left Charleston behind me, a ball of anxiety settled in the pit of my stomach. What was I doing traveling into the unknown? What night terrors would I experience in Mobile? I had to admit this kind of bold, brash move was surprising, even for me. Still, like the proverbial moth to a flame, I drove down the slick highway, drowning out the voice of Cautious Carrie Jo with the hum of my old faithful car. I smiled at myself in the rearview mirror as a sort of encouragement.

Behind my oversize sunglasses was a pair of almond-shaped green eyes. I liked my eyes; they reminded me of my father. At least that's what I figured, since they weren't anything like my mother's. I had never met my father. That morning, I had quickly piled my mass of brown, curly hair on top of my head in a messy ponytail bun. A few brown strands whipped around my face like wildcats in the wind as I sang along with Natalie Merchant. I dug in my purse for my favorite coral-colored lipstick. The shade looked pretty and bright against my light olive skin. I smiled at myself again to make sure the lipstick hadn't smeared on my teeth. I rarely wore lipstick, but somehow I felt like I needed to today. I felt free and happy.

"Funny how I got here," I pondered absently, glad to let the mental review of my conversation with Dr. O'Neal fade away. A few letters, a polished phone call from an attorney. It seemed like something I had read or dreamed about, but everything checked out. The contract was signed, and I now had a nice deposit in the bank. Best of all, the contents of an antebellum home waited to be scrutinized, categorized and stored. I would finally put that history degree to good use. No searching frantically for summer work. No more manning small-town Sno-Cone stands while wearing a goofy paper hat. Actually, that had been a fun job. Kids were my weakness and I had met plenty of them while I shoveled shaved ice and flavored syrups into cups.

With an even bigger smile, I remembered turning in my notice at the funeral home. Working in the records office wasn't creepy, but I'd felt continually surrounded by sadness. I dozed off in my quiet office during one boring, rainy afternoon and surprisingly had not dreamed a thing. *I guess the dead carry no memories. They leave them behind for people like me.*

My cell phone jangled on the seat next to me, and I tapped the ignore button. I was ultra-cautious when it came to driving, at least with the phone. Without looking, I knew it was William, mad and hurt that I had left him without a word. My frustration rose. He knew I was leaving, and I knew he didn't want me to go. What else was there to talk about?

I turned Natalie up louder and sang "Carnival" with all my heart.

Chapter 2

I had gotten on the road early, but there was no way I was driving eight hours straight. I couldn't sit still that long. I planned to stop in Green's Mill, Alabama, at a brand new bed and breakfast called the Delight of the South. The hotel's newness did not guarantee I would have a dream-free night, but I had a backup plan. I dug around blindly in my purse for the sleeping pills Dr. O'Neal had prescribed me. I was glad I'd remembered them, but I hated taking them. I always woke up feeling stupid, and the pills did not completely stop the dreams from coming. If the dream was there, I would still remember flashes of it the next day. But with sleeping pills, the dreams, unremembered and unappreciated faded quickly and settled back into the darkness.

I remembered the first time I took something to sleep. I would wake up screaming; masses of slithering snakes struggled to choke and strangle me in my dream, all because my mother, in a daze of medication or occasionally alcohol, had climbed in the bed with me to sleep. I could feel her loneliness, her confusion, her anger as she snored. At times I felt sorry for her, but then the snakes came while she slept. And in the daylight hours, the softness was gone.

I had plundered my mother's medicine cabinet and stolen one of her Valiums. "They always put her to sleep, so why not me?" my preteen self reasoned. I lingered on the memory, standing guiltily in front of that vanity mirror for a moment. I remembered thinking, "What would Jesus think about me stealing pills and doing drugs?" Hot tears had slid down my young face as I took the pill, choking it down without water.

Momma thought I was crazy, but the feeling was mutual. When I was about twelve, I'd tried to escape her cold indifference for a night by going to a neighbor's sleepover. I had felt safe and warm snuggled up with my sunny, red-haired friend Virginia. That night, Ginny had dreamed of her stepfather slipping into her room, sliding into her bed, lifting her pajamas and...

I was seized by Ginny's terror. I'd even felt her physical pain and woke up bathed in tears and blood. I had uncovered a tragic secret that would cost me a friendship. Even after Ginny's stepdad was arrested, I heard nothing from her. The unexpected twist was getting my first period, which had both confused and offended me. And I had made another discovery—screaming woke me from the nightmares that I witness occasionally.

I had not come home to find a sympathetic, benevolent mother. The short version of the story was Momma told her insipid religious friends that "Carrie Jo was psychic," and her prayer group tried to exorcise me. "Carrie Jo is full of the devil," Momma cried to anyone who would listen.

Momma never could keep a secret, not even her own. And she had plenty of them, I thought with a defiance and bitterness that almost smothered me.

Eventually, I wised up and kept my mouth shut about the dreams. If Momma and I had not moved around so much when I was growing up, I probably would have put those dream "demons" to sleep a bit easier. Instead, I slept in a constantly changing environment that included trailers, cheap motels and run-down homes most of my life until I left for college.

I shook my head to snap out of my reverie. I hated thinking about the past, but it chased me so much. I searched for a talk radio channel just to give myself something else to think about.

* * *

At lunch, I carried the binder of notes I had collected into a diner named Sal's and reread what I had been sent about my new project, Seven Sisters. I ordered a grilled cheese sandwich but sacrificially ignored the fries that came with it. I felt fat in my white shorts. They were a size ten, and I didn't want to move up to a twelve again. I had spent a lot of time walking the track near my home this past spring. I wasn't a big health nut, but I did like walking outdoors and exploring new scenery.

I smoothed my hand over the glossy picture of Seven Sisters, examining the columned facade of the main house. The antebellum home, the brief read, was built in 1823 by a family who went bankrupt shortly after the work was completed. By 1825, the wealthy Cottonwoods had purchased the mansion, renaming it Seven Sisters. Looking back at me from the collection of papers was a young woman with big, dark eyes, wearing a full-skirted gown with lace trim. She was riveting.

From what I had gathered from multiple video conferences and emails with the owner's attorney, the goal was to make Seven Sisters a sort of museum for visitors to Mobile, but the current owner had enough respect for the home's history to want a proper catalogue of its antiques first. That earned them points in my book. Too many people forget the past—I never could; it wouldn't allow me to.

I was the chief historian assigned to the project. I much preferred working alone, but that was impossible on a job this size. Luckily, my dearest friend and fellow historian, Mia, would be joining me soon. She had recommended me for the lead position, despite her own qualifications. She was one of the few people who knew about my "dream catching," as she called it. She never stayed in one spot too long—she had spent a few months in Egypt, then travelled to the UK for a tour of medieval castles, and then lived in Paris with a friend for six months over a bakery. I loved her confidence, her zest for life and her ability to travel like a local.

Mia knew more about antebellum artifacts than anyone I knew, which was hilarious considering Egyptology was her first love. I hadn't seen her since Christmas; I was excited to catch up on her latest adventures.

Right after college, I had worked on a few estate projects cataloging for an auction house. I was sad to see each antique sold off to the highest bidder. For a few months, I had possessed them, lovingly working to establish each item's value and historical importance. How I cried when the Trevi figurine, "Genteel Boy on Rocking Horse," sold at auction. The company had moved to Tennessee, and I had turned down an invitation to relocate with them. I'm not sure why.

I couldn't wait to see what Seven Sisters and Mobile had in store for me. Comparable to Charleston, Mobile had its charms; at least that's what the brochures told me. Coming so late in spring, I missed the city's big Mardi Gras party, but I wasn't much of a partier. I preferred studying the belongings of people who no longer walked the earth to drinking and dancing with its current residents.

I passed on a second glass of tea, as I didn't want to make another stop before calling it a day at the Delight of the South, but I gave the waitress a big smile all the same. I had a soft spot for hard-working women, having been one for so long.

I tucked a defiant curl behind my ear and flipped through the brief again. I would be working with Ashland Stuart, the current owner. His attorney had mailed me his picture and a brief summary of his credentials. He was incredibly handsome, in a masculine, southern kind of way. (*Too perfect. He must be short.*) He had short, blond hair with expressive blue eyes and a slightly pink, kissable mouth. I knew I had been staring too long at the photo because the waitress (Susan, according to her pink nametag) said, "Wow! He your boyfriend?"

"Nope, just a business partner." I smiled and flushed.

"Lucky girl." She tossed her head slightly in the direction of an open kitchen window at a heavyset man sweating over a grill. "He's my business partner." I laughed along with her but decided that was my cue to leave. I paid the bill, gathered the paperwork and left a nice tip for Susan. After she caught me leering at the picture of a complete stranger, it felt like passing off hush money.

Naturally, I thought of William, and I welcomed the guilt that seemed to surround everything in our relationship—or whatever it was. While the car's interior cooled off, I rang him back. His voicemail picked up, and I was so surprised that I stumbled over leaving a message.

"Hey, William, I'll be in Green's Mill soon. I'm doing fine, and the car is great. I wanted to say, I mean...I'll try to call again when I get to my room. Okay? Okay, talk to you later. Oh, this is Carrie Jo." Yep, that sounded dumb *and* guilty.

Chapter 3

My drive into Mobile was uneventful. Like most downtown areas, the streets were narrow and lumpy, and the roadways were shaded by the oak trees whose branches obscured the light with its boughs full of Spanish moss. I found my new garage apartment quite easily and spent a few minutes getting to know my temporary landlord, Bette. I knew right from that first meeting that I was going to like chatting with her. She was amiable and helpful, and she seemed to have a tremendous knowledge about the history of the area.

I spent some time getting my room in order. Time wasn't on my side; I had to get ready for an afternoon meeting with the attorney, the contractor and, of course, Ashland Stuart. The apartment was new, clean and completely comfortable. I adored it. Bette told me that she had considered writing a novel or two a few years ago, with the apartment as her studio, but life had not slowed enough so far to allow her the luxury. There was a full-size bed, complete with a comfortable mattress and clean cotton sheets. The desk was perched near the entrance window, which overlooked the street below and gave me a wonderful view of downtown. I was happy to see a mini-fridge and a kitchenette; Bette had really thought of all the basics. I decided to explore more later. Right now, I had a meeting to prepare for, and I was nervous already—I was the boss. I couldn't believe it! A few changes of clothes and about 45 minutes later, I was walking up to Seven Sisters.

I began to rethink my choice of shoes for the evening as I walked up the broken brick sidewalk that led to the house. Seven Sisters stood at the end of a private road that needed a bit of upkeep. As I walked, I breathed in the purple wisteria. Bees hung around it, even in the late afternoon, and the flowers drooped in the humidity. Tough brown vines grasped at any growing thing they could reach. Masses of pink azaleas that someone, years ago, thought would add color and charm to the sidewalk crowded the pathway.

Hollis Matthews, the attorney who had originally contacted me about the research project, had warned me about this slight inconvenience. But I had not realized I would be trekking through a subtropical jungle—not in these shoes, anyway. Silently, I rebuked myself. This was the opportunity of a lifetime! Was I going to let a little humidity and some abandoned gardens prevent me from exploring this prize?

As I moved along the path, I looked back at my blue car sitting behind a shiny black Lincoln with a few other vehicles—all the cars looked much nicer than mine. It suddenly occurred to me that I could afford to buy a new car now. My current employer was paying me well.

I smoothed my skirt, admiring the tiny red rose pattern, and tugged at my short-sleeved red blouse. The sweetheart neckline made me feel pretty and didn't reveal my cleavage at all. I touched my hair absently. It felt soft, but I knew the night air would make it curl even more. I had left my hair down for the evening, but I did manage to straighten it. Sort of. I at least made the effort to tame my normally wild locks.

I looked down at my worrisome shoes, red sandals with a pretty wedge heel, with my red painted toenails poking out happily. I decided I looked great, and I squared my shoulders to boost my confidence.

It was dusk, and the lights from the house shone through the thick hedges. The flowers' fragrance set an irresistible ambiance for a romantic southern evening. "How often does a girl get to visit an antebellum home that has been hidden away from the world for the past hundred years?" I asked myself. I felt very lucky indeed.

As the path turned, I stepped out of the maze of flowers, surprised at the sight of Seven Sisters, with her faded white columns rising up like an ancient Greek temple from the dark woods that surrounded her. I blinked, letting my eyes adjust to the fading light. The surrounding foliage and wild trees seemed to make it even darker. I stood gawking at my new office and felt no initial foreboding, no warning, just a warm feeling of delight and excitement. (I would reflect on this later. Shouldn't I have sensed something?) Oh yes, this would be my home—at least until next spring.

Through the old, warped windows, I could see lights and hear music playing softly inside. I hated being late and last. The scene seemed so strange, the present imposing on the past. Seven Sisters stood tall and silent, enduring the "party" that had gathered under her roof. The quiet dignity of the house juxtaposed against the tinkling of laughter and the sounds of jazz music made the gathering seem like a group of naughty teenagers assembled to dance on a grave, disregarding all the lost life beneath their feet.

The warm feeling from just a moment ago disappeared as the fine hairs on my neck pricked up. Suddenly, I felt the air move slightly. I scanned the area around me but detected only an abandoned garden statue a few yards away. It was an odd—and disturbing—sight. The statue was a satyr pouring water over a nude girl. His tongue poked out at me, the one who dared invade his garden. His grotesque face, as well as the rest of him, was weathered green, evidence of his lengthy stay on the property. I laughed nervously, pulling my attention away from the leering creature. I paused on the sparse grass below the steps leading to the great house. A curious aroma of damp, old wood and leaves filled the air, and I could see that the promised repairs had begun with the wooden porch. Out of the corner of my eye, I detected movement. I turned quickly, my skirt swirling around my tanned legs.

A broad white smile and the handsome face of Ashland Stuart greeted me. He wasn't short—at all.

"Hey! I hope I didn't startle you." Ashland smiled even bigger, if that were possible. For some reason, I was not sure he was honest in his apology. He looked like someone who liked having the upper hand.

"Well, maybe a little. I didn't hear you pull up." I smiled back nervously and purposefully turned my attention back to the house, away from the man who had managed to sneak up on me. I needed a moment to compose myself.

"I'm Ashland Stuart, but I'm sure you know that—my attorney believes in bios with pictures. I recognize you from yours, Carrie Jo Jardine." I didn't know what to say; he seemed to know everything. So I gave him a slight nod. He stood close to me and turned his attention to the house. "First time here at Seven Sisters?"

"Yes. I regret that my maiden voyage had to be in the dark. Still, I'm glad to be here. Can I ask you a question?"

His white teeth gleamed at me; they shone in the fading light, making him look like something fierce. He had a wide, masculine smile, which I suspected he enjoyed flashing at all the women he encountered. "Any question at all."

I ignored his flirtatious invitation. "Seven Sisters—how did it get its name? It's easy to romanticize a name like that, so I figured I'd ask someone who probably knows rather than assume it was named after seven actual sisters or a family of tragic Greek goddesses. There were no real facts on that in the profile I received."

He laughed at that, and then it was my turn to smile at him. "Not a romantic, then? Actually, we're not sure and had hoped that our new historian would be able to answer that question for us in the fullness of time." He shot me another smile. "Family gossip suggests that the Seven Sisters are actually the seven columns that surround the house. But there are those who think it may be a clue to a lost family treasure."

"How interesting," I said sincerely, captivated by the notion of uncovering a family secret.

"One other older bit of gossip is that Seven Sisters is not this house at all but the name of the family house in France. That was the talk in the 1820s, anyway. Who knows? Perhaps you'll be able to settle it once and for all." I didn't know what to say, but I was intrigued.

He broke the silence. "It looks like we're both late. I've kept you to myself for too long." He stood so close I could smell his expensive cologne. It was worth the money. I had an urge to touch his creased cotton shirt. I snuck a peek up at him as he stood silently gazing at Seven Sisters.

I wondered what he dreamt about when he closed his light blue eyes at night. Would he see memories of a happy childhood, inspiring dreams tinged in a warm, honey hue, or would his dreams unroll endlessly like dark shadows leaking from a deadly, hidden personality? There was only one way to truly know, and I shuddered slightly at the thought of waking up next to this golden man.

He must have felt my movement as I sensed my own terrible vulnerability, standing in the woods, in the dark, with a man I did not know. He looked at me serenely, like another statue in the garden. Only he was much nicer to look at than the satyr. I felt like he belonged here.

"Shall we make a grand entrance?" He offered me his arm, as I suspected he had done with countless women before me. Feeling disarmed, as much by my own thoughts as by his practiced charm, I nodded courteously and looped my arm through his, trying to ignore his muscles. I shoved back conjured images of southern belles entertaining well-dressed suitors as they glided up these same steps together before walking through the massive doors of the house. (I wasn't a romantic, right?) My skin flushed slightly, and I didn't know if it was due to my nerves or the nearness of Ashland Stuart.

He rang the bell, and the door swung open. We were greeted by a tall, distinguished-looking man who I knew immediately was Hollis Matthews, Ashland's attorney. Before I could speak, Ashland said, "Look who I found wandering around the property." He gave me a playful grin as he strode down the hall, and I took a moment to admire his big shoulders. Matthews was a perfectly dressed gentleman, down to his blue suit with a subtle pinstripe, white pocket handkerchief and neat manicure.

"Not wandering, just walking up the driveway," I called after Ashland. I fought my natural tendency to get defensive when embarrassed. "You must be Mr. Matthews." I leaned forward to shake the attorney's hand, remembering to act like a professional. His skin felt cool and moist, and I wanted to snatch my hand away and wipe it on my skirt. With a tiny nod, he welcomed me inside the foyer of Seven Sisters.

I couldn't resist a good stare at my surroundings. I was delighted to see that repairs had begun in earnest, but there was much more to do. It was much as I expected: wooden wall panels hidden under peeling paint and misapplied wallpaper, and bare wooden floors that looked spongy in a few places. A sprawling staircase filled the center of the room, and off to either side, I could see many rooms with darkened doorways. A collection of boxes and crates lined the foyer, and I felt a flurry of nerves and excitement. I could hardly believe I was the boss. Well, the boss of the museum project, anyway. Something told me that the sleek Mr. Matthews may have been the true man in charge here.

"Miss Jardine, it's such a pleasure to meet you. I hope that driveway didn't give you too much trouble. We'll make it proper soon. Kindly step this way; I've got a few things for you to sign. I hope you like the arrangements we made for you. Our contractor has been working around the clock to get your rooms ready."

"I think there's been some kind of mistake. I did not plan on staying on-site. I've already rented a small apartment just a half mile away. I just have...I have certain..."

"Didn't you?" He slid his silver glasses down his thin nose and walked toward a small table and overstuffed chairs near a dusty fireplace. I followed him to continue my protest and immediately began a mental appraisal of the items in the room while he shuffled through a stack of papers.

"It's Carrie Jo, please." I took a step toward the cabinet, unable to resist a peek. "When will I be able to start?"

"Soon. First, I need you to sign this confidentiality agreement, the one we discussed on the phone. It's fairly standard, but please let me know if you have any questions. You can start as soon as you like. As soon as tomorrow, of course. With such eagerness to explore this mansion-sized time capsule, I'm surprised you wouldn't like to stay. Aren't historians slaves to history?" Without waiting for a reply, he continued, "We've arranged for you to have a room here, along with your team." Matthews slid the papers and a pen across the table and appraised me. He had slate gray eyes, almost as shiny as his glasses.

"I sure hate to inconvenience you, but I won't be staying on-site." I felt my backbone stiffen slightly as I sat opposite him, faking confidence. "I hope that's not a problem for you or Mr. Stuart."

"It's not a condition, of course, and we do realize you can't devote yourself to this project around the clock. The offer was meant to help you offset some costs and make things more convenient, but it's whatever you desire." He accepted my signed papers and passed me an envelope with a check inside. I slid the check into my red clutch without even looking at the numbers. Such a fastidious man. He would never miss a small thing like a zero.

He smiled and rose from his chair. "Well, Miss Jardine. That is, Carrie Jo. Let's take that tour. I'm sure you are eager to meet the contractor." He pointed me back toward the door.

I listened to him talk about the upcoming maintenance schedule as we walked down the hall to the back of the house. I wanted to yell "Stop!" at every door we passed, but I figured I could control my curiosity just this once.

"Mind your step on the..."

I felt a sharp, stabbing pain at the back of my head. Everything went black, then fuzzy, and then slowly the lights came on. It was as if someone had hit a dimmer switch. What had been there before, a dark, empty hallway with peeling paint and an inch of dust on the chair arms, had transformed. The paint looked fresh, a pale blue, and the wooden baseboards shone with wax. Fine wooden floors lined with blue floral-patterned runners looked vibrant and soft. A long table against the wall held trays of fresh fruit and hot foods. Lined up against the wall were three young black men holding trays and pitchers, wearing white collared shirts and black cotton pants. I drew my breath sharply, surprised by their frozen presence and glad they didn't seem to see me sprawled on the floor even though I was practically under their feet.

I realized that somehow, I was having a genuine Carrie Jo dream.

Chapter 4

The heat from Muncie's starched white collar comforted him on this unusually cool October evening. Seven Sisters was full of candles and laughter, and it smelled like a banquet, just like one he had heard about in a fairy story. In the distance, the boy heard the deep, booming voice of Stokes, the house man, announcing supper to the guests. Muncie held the silver tray tightly—a neat trick while wearing thick, white cotton gloves. All serving slaves wore white gloves. Mr. Cottonwood would be mightily embarrassed to serve his guests food that slaves had been dipping their hands in. Best to keep the gloves on to show you had clean hands.

It took skill to keep those gloves clean and white during service, to walk in the stiff shoes, to tote a tray without clattering a spoon. Muncie had kept Early and the other boys up half the night walking the space of their small room until Stokes poked his head in and told him to go to bed. He wanted to practice; he didn't dare trip and fall on his face.

Muncie's heart pounded in his chest, and his dark skin flushed with excitement. Stokes strode to the servants' hall, inspecting each of the gathered slaves. Muncie kept his eyes down respectfully, staring at his own reflection in the shiny tray. He bit the inside of his lip to stop himself from smiling. He hardly ever saw himself, except when he could slip off to the river. There were plenty of mirrors in Seven Sisters, but he could get smacked for looking too long in any of them. It was too late in the year to swim now.

His first night of dinner service seemed like a dream. Really, he was too young to serve, but he was tall. And Hooney, the missus' housemaid, said he was pleasing to the eye even though he was very dark.

Early hadn't lasted in service. Muncie didn't know if Early had clattered spoons or gawked too much at the guests or spoken out of turn. Besides the beating he took, the older boy seemed relieved to leave the dining hall. He had no stomach for killing chickens and wearing shoes. He preferred spending his time fishing with Mr. Cottonwood or traveling with him into Mobile. Early didn't care; he was happy. That made Muncie feel a bit better about taking his spot.

Tonight was a special night. A bunch of people he didn't know were coming to dine with the Cottonwoods. In this little corner of what Muncie knew was a big world, the Cottonwoods meant everything to the plantation families of Old Mobile. Mrs. Cottonwood lay upstairs in her birthing bed, where she would stay until the baby arrived. She had a kind face and soft hands and had soothed his head once when he was full of the fever. Even though that was many years ago, Muncie remembered her cool touch and kind care. Now his friend Calpurnia was mistress of Seven Sisters, at least until Mrs. Cottonwood had the baby, since Mr. Cottonwood was often away. Calpurnia meant the world to Muncie, but she was also old enough to get married. Some gentlemen, both young gentlemen and some older men, were coming now from miles around to take a peek at Calpurnia. He didn't know how he felt about that, but mostly, he didn't think about it. There was always something to do nowadays.

Tonight, Calpurnia's cousin Isla, her uncle Louis and a group of neighbors filled Seven Sisters to capacity. Calpurnia had told him that she didn't really want to have this party and that she'd rather stay with her mother. She was nervous about the whole thing, and he wanted to make her proud. He loved Calpurnia, not like Tristan loved Isolde but like she was his own blood, like she was his kin. The very thought made Muncie blush again.

Besides the chatting of the people he served, the house seemed quiet after the business of the day. A stream of slaves had flowed from the main house to the cook house like a line of busy ants. Some toted water for baths; others carried trays of fruit and bottles of wine. When the hot food came to the house, two small boys ran out in front, tossing balls of hot cornbread at the hounds, shouting, "Hush puppy! Hush puppy!" Those pups couldn't resist those treats. Once they gobbled them up, they were easily wrangled and taken away from the house before the dinner guests sat down. Nobody wanted to hear a pack of yapping dogs while they ate their dinner. That's what Stokes said, although Muncie knew for a fact he was fond of those animals.

Suddenly, the guests came flooding into the room like magical creatures on mists of perfume. The ladies, most of whom Muncie didn't recognize, wore dresses so big that the skirts swirled about them like colorful clouds. Some were made of colors he had never seen. He resisted the urge to touch the airy fabrics.

All of the gentlemen looked stiff and straight with high white collars and tapered cloaks, like the toy soldiers Muncie found stuffed in a box in the upstairs nursery a long time ago. Even Mr. Cottonwood looked clean and nice, like he'd been dipped in the Mobile River six or seven times. Tall Uncle Louis had white teeth that shone all the time, maybe because he smiled all the time. Muncie searched the crowd but did not see Calpurnia. He heard a nearby sniff and realized he was gawking. He didn't dare to look at Stokes, instead shifting his eyes downward to his tray.

Stokes strode past him and the other slaves and walked to the wooden double doors of the dining hall. Standing tall and straight, he announced in his deepest voice, "Ladies and gentlemen, I present to you Miss Calpurnia Cottonwood of Mobile and Miss Isla Torrence of Savannah."

Feeling safe with Stokes at such a distance, Muncie peeked at the door. The two girls strode into the room together, arm in arm like two roses of different colors. Isla turned her head to cast her broad smile around the room—a move that seemed bold, beyond her fifteen years. Her blond curls bounced like they were happy too. Perky dimples showed brightly in her soft pink cheeks. Muncie could see, even in the failing light, that her eyes glistened with pleasure at all the attention.

Muncie's heart sank when he saw his friend. Although she wore a small smile and tipped her head slightly at a few of the guests, her unhappiness was obvious to anyone with eyes. Taller than her cousin and thinner by far, Calpurnia looked like a queen, like Guinevere, without even trying. Her soft brown hair was piled high on her head with pretty combs tucked in the silky tresses. Coral earrings dangled from her ears; Muncie recognized them as Mrs. Cottonwood's.

The gathered guests clapped appreciatively, and the ladies took a turn around the room and were seated on either side of Mr. Cottonwood at the head of the table. When Calpurnia sat down, Muncie could see her cheeks flush under all the attention. He knew she would rather be in the library or tugging at flowers and weeds or at her mother's bedside—anywhere but there.

For the next hour, Muncie was too fearful to think of Miss Calpurnia, even though she was very close. He catered to Stokes' every need and snapped to attention when summoned. It took all the discipline he had not to look interested in the conversations that teemed around the table, although he and the other slaves were very busy. Occasionally, he tossed a suspicious, disapproving look at one tall, dark-haired gentleman sitting a little too close to Calpurnia. Captain Garrett was his name. He had been here before and had taken Calpurnia on an unchaperoned stroll around the side garden. He insisted on pouring her drink and asked her questions that didn't seem to be any of his business.

Muncie was relieved, for more than one reason, when the dinner service came to an end.

After dinner, the gentlemen would find a fine Kentucky whiskey waiting for them in the front parlor while the ladies would take lemonade, with gin if they chose, on the side porch. Musicians played softly in the background, and heaps of flowers on the mantelpieces and tables filled the dining hall with a heavy fragrance of magnolias, honeysuckle and beeswax.

Muncie wished he could pat Calpurnia's hand and assure her that she was lovely and perfect. She would agonize later over every detail. Trying to get to Calpurnia nowadays to speak with her or just be with her had proven difficult. Every time he tried to walk with her in the grove or meet her near the gardens, he had met Isla instead. She seemed to know his every move, and even now as she left the dining hall, he felt her eyes on him. He blushed against his collar, now wet with sweat.

Isla had been at Seven Sisters only two weeks, but she acted as if she were the lady of the house. According to Hooney, the girl was putting on airs because everyone, even the house slaves, knew "that she was just a poor relation of no true standing."

The day before the party, she had taken a fall near the fountains. At first, Muncie had felt alarmed when he saw her lying on the ground. She'd cried and cried, and he was worried that she had been hurt. But once he got there, he suspected she just wanted him to hold her. "Hold me, Muncie! No, don't leave me here," she had murmured like she was beginning to faint.

Normally, he wouldn't touch her, but he didn't dare leave her stranded in the yard either. As he had lifted her in his arms, she'd smelled like honeysuckle and stolen sweets. Feeling her soft little arms around his neck made him feel strong, like a man. But a greater, deeper fear gripped him inside. Instead of loving Isla, loving holding the frail little creature that clung to him too tightly, he couldn't wait to deliver his misbegotten goods to someone else. He had called out to the house as he approached, "Mister Stokes, Mister Stokes, sir!"

Isla had protested angrily, saying he was walking too fast, but he'd ignored the feeling of her frilly clothes crushed under his hands and her girlish voice. He'd held her like she was a snake, a dangerous snake—like one of those black snakes that chased you with all their might until you began chasing them back. In this case, that didn't seem like a good idea. He had done right in calling out, Stokes had said, but he must never again touch any of the women in the house. Not even if she fell down a well. Stokes had called him stupid, but Hooney had understood. Muncie hadn't told anyone else, not even Calpurnia.

Muncie relinquished his silver tray at the waiting station and dabbed his forehead and neck with a towel. His breakfast was long gone, and he heard his stomach rumbling. But he shuffled after Stokes in his clunky shoes, ready to serve the men in the study. Mostly, he was supposed to watch and learn, but he had to be ready to help out if called on. So far, nothing exciting had happened. Mr. Cottonwood and Captain Garrett talked loudly about traffic along the Mobile River while the Cottonwoods' neighbors, Mr. Semmes and Mr. Beauchamp, exchanged jokes that Muncie didn't understand and then slapped one another on the back. Captain Garrett laughed too loudly, and it seemed he liked pouring Mr. Cottonwood his whiskey.

A light tap on the door surprised Muncie, and he hustled through the opening to see who was beckoning to him. Moving as fast as lightning and waving to him was Isla. "Muncie!"

A jolt of worry hit his stomach, and this time he knew it wasn't a rumble of hunger. His brain yelled "Danger!" but he worried that something was wrong with Calpurnia. Against his better judgment, he slipped into the Blue Room, next to the men's parlor, behind her. It was dark except for a single candelabrum that shone like a faraway beacon near the window.

Before he knew what was happening, Isla melted her body against his and planted her lips on his dry mouth.

Her kiss was delicious and tasted like lemonade. She made a little groan against him, shaking him back to reality, and he pushed her, holding her at arm's length away from him. He didn't know what to say except, "Please..." In a second, her inviting lips curled tightly in a rueful scowl, and her body stiffened. She suddenly seemed tall and imposing, not soft and pliable as she had been seconds before.

With savage ferocity, she slapped him across the face, stinging his cheek and his still-warm lips. "I know the truth about you, Muncie! You don't think I see how you moon after Calpurnia like a whipped dog?" Her voice was a seething whisper. She stepped even farther away from him, peering at him. "She's no better than me, even though she has a rich daddy and an old name. You'll see, Muncie. You'll see who the real woman is." With that, she swished out of the Blue Room with a click of her heels. Muncie touched his hand to his cheek, still hot from Isla's vicious slap....

Chapter 5

"Carrie Jo! Can you hear me?"

"Miss Jardine, we've called an ambulance. They'll be here momentarily." Matthews spoke very close to my ear; his stale breath brushed my skin—too intimately for my taste.

I shook my head. "No, just give me a minute." My weak protest started a hushed conversation, but I was simply too tired to eavesdrop. Snippets of my dream—the crushed white magnolias on the mantelpiece, the coral earrings that hung from Calpurnia's slender ears—crowded into my mind. The scent of hot cornbread, the taste of lemonade on my lips and the warm aroma of clean beeswax lingered on and around me like an invisible cloud. As always, I was surprised no one else could taste and see these things. Unwanted tears slid down my cheeks. Muncie's hopeful face hovered before me. He was dead, long dead. He would never know that I had been there, witnessing a day in his private life.

"Here, put your arms around my neck. You can do that, right? You can't just lie here on the floor."

I slid my arms around Ashland's neck and laid my throbbing head on his shoulder. "But I barely even know you," I whispered.

He laughed softly and said, "You're going to be fine," as if his words would fix everything. He carefully positioned me on an antique settee near the window in the front room, where I had met Matthews earlier. "I'll be right back. Don't go anywhere," Ashland said with a smile.

I had to chuckle. *Here I am, lying helpless on a fainting couch.*

Matthews looked down at me with his piercing, gray eyes. "I've called the family's physician, Dr. Patterson. He'll be here in just a minute. No arguments on this. You'll understand that I can't have you knocking yourself out without some follow-up medical care."

I nodded and wiped away the unexpected damp streaks on my face. "Of course."

Ashland reappeared with some bandages. With a quick, "This might hurt," he pressed them to the screaming spot on my head. I focused on the darkness outside the window, dutifully accepting his attempts at healing. The doorbell rang, and the sleek attorney disappeared down the hallway.

"Looks like it stopped bleeding," Ashland said. "That's always a good sign." He pulled my hand up to hold the bandages in place while he cleaned up the paper wrappings.

"Good evening, Ashland. Miss Jardine, is it? Now let's take a look." Matthews was thin, but Dr. Patterson made him look muscular in comparison. The doctor probed my scalp with a bony finger, examining the wound without a lot of fuss. I bit my lip to stop from shouting during his inspection. He sat next to me, flashed a light in my eyes and checked my pulse. "So tell me about this fall. Was it from a great height?" Before I could answer, Matthews spoke. "Actually, she tripped over a bit of old carpet. No great height at all."

"Can you follow my finger, please?" Obediently, I followed the doctor's bony finger as he moved it back and forth in front of my face. "Well, Matthews, I think she'll be just fine. It wouldn't hurt to get a stitch or two, but you will certainly live." He stared up at Matthews, who said nothing. He peered at me over the top of his glasses. "Do you feel nauseous? Can you stand, Miss Jardine?"

I was determined to get on my feet. This couldn't be happening. "I feel fine, truly. Embarrassed, mostly. I'm sure I can stand up."

"Hold on. Take your time, darling. You don't want to get ahead of yourself. If you do feel sick or off-balance at all, go to the hospital. It's possible that a whack like that could cause a concussion, but I expect you're fine. Ashland, help her up, please." The friendly doctor watched me amble about for a moment before declaring me healed.

"Do you have a friend who can drive you home? I'd feel better knowing you were tucked in safely for the night. Is there some family close by?" The doctor removed his glasses, polishing them with a shirt sleeve before replacing them, without much improvement. He looked at me inquisitively.

"Uh, no, I've no family here. But my place is just a few minutes away. I'm really very embarrassed to have made such a scene."

"Well, accidents happen, and it's not surprising in a place as old as this. I'm sure there are all kinds of hazards around here." He looked at Ashland with a grin and said, "It's good that someone is going to restore her. Seven Sisters, I mean. She must have been a beauty in her day." Bag in hand, the doctor glanced around the room for a moment, then handed me his card. "Now you call me if you have any problems at all tonight. If I'm not in, my wife will take a message. If you folks don't need anything else from me, I'll be off. I do expect you to call tomorrow, perhaps when you finish here, okay?"

"Thank you, Dr. Patterson. I'll walk you to the door." Matthews led the doctor from the room, and I was left with my boss watching over me as I sat on the dusty couch.

Once Ashland and I were alone, my face flushed. I felt like an incompetent ninny falling down in front of the great football hero. What must he think of me? Why did I care? I felt raw emotions building just below the surface and knew I would need some privacy to recall what I had seen and experienced without the added embarrassment of an audience. Like a cornered rabbit, I was ready to run. It was always that way after a dream. It was almost like I had too many feelings; they piled up on one another in a big old heap.

"I think I'll go back to my apartment now. I've had enough fun for one night. I'm sorry I messed up the meeting."

"Don't worry about that. You heard the doctor, though. You shouldn't drive, Carrie Jo. I'll take you home. You say it's not far?"

"No, it's not far, over near Catherine Street, but I don't want to leave my car here. And I don't want to be any more trouble." I tried to think of a good reason to refuse but couldn't really find one beyond leaving my car behind.

"It's the least I can do. You did trip on my property. I'll take you home, and then either Matthews or I can bring your car to you later. Let's find your things. And I'll need those keys."

He sounded so assured and logical that I didn't put up a fight. I forced Muncie out of my mind and set about looking for my purse and keys. I found them on the desk in the front room with the check I had so happily received earlier.

The ride home was quiet and short, only three turns. On a sunny day, I could make the walk from Seven Sisters to the garage apartment in about ten minutes, I figured. I looked forward to that. The roads were uneven and dark, despite the many streetlights. Most of the downtown streets I had seen were shrouded in live oaks, giving the whole area a sort of otherworldly feel. *No wonder I'm dreaming of the old days*, I thought wryly. *I'm surrounded by history.*

I was thankful Ashland hadn't encroached on my silence. It took a lot of effort to not rewind the dream in his presence, slowly, carefully, reliving each detail. I wanted to remember everything, blurt it all out, but the wisest choice was to capture it all in my digital journal. I shuddered to think of how Ashland would look at me if he knew about my "dream catching." I didn't want to find out with this throbbing head. It would be a long night.

We pulled into the gravel driveway, and I fumbled for the apartment key. Without asking, he stepped out of the car, opening the car door without a word. I was relieved to find that climbing the stairs to the apartment went easily. No repeat performances; no falls.

"Thank you for bringing me home."

"No trouble at all. We'll bring your car back in a few minutes. I'll put your keys in the planter here." He looked at me steadily. "I'm sure you want to clean up a bit. Call Dr. Patterson if you have any problems at all. He's on call 24/7. Is there anything else you need? Are you sure you're okay? Do you want me to bring you some supper?"

"Thanks, but I'm not really hungry. I think I have something to snack on in the fridge. I appreciate you bringing me home. Thank you again."

Flashing his easy smile, he left me on the porch. I slid the key into the lock, and then I was finally inside, alone, leaning against the door. No brave face needed. Nothing to prove—and after all that, no flow of tears.

I pulled off the offending shoes and decided against tossing them into the trash can near my desk. They weren't to blame, although I doubted I would have the confidence to wear them again anytime soon. Locking the door and checking the shades, I tossed a scoop of bath salts into warm running water and soaked in the tub for the next twenty minutes. I carefully avoided putting pressure on my head; I leaned back into the water, feeling it soothe away the tension. After a few minutes, the details of the dream came back, slowly at first and then like a flood. From the yapping hounds to the feel of stiff cotton on my neck, I recalled the details with surreal clarity. Unwilling to lose even a snippet, I climbed out of the tub and wrapped myself in a cotton robe, half drying my tired body. I didn't want to peek at my head. I hated the sight of blood.

I took a bottle of water from the mini-fridge and went over to the laptop on the desk, flipping it on. My fingers flew over the keyboard as I wrote down my dream, scene by scene. Like a supernatural scribe, I obediently recorded all I had witnessed. It was a habit I had developed over the years, first in book journals and then on my computers. It was a weird sort of record, a kind of written proof that I wasn't crazy. It felt like I was collecting evidence for a case that I hoped one day to present to someone who might actually understand. As usual, I finished with a brief commentary of what I felt during the dream and after.

Hours later, I cried. Too tired to write anymore, I shuffled to the full-size bed. It took up half of the apartment, but I was grateful for the comfort. I slid out of the robe, tossed on a giant sleep shirt and peeled back the sheets. I reached my hand under the cheap bamboo paper lampshade and clicked the light off. Drained and tired, and finally empty of borrowed memories, I slept like the dead.

Chapter 6

I awoke later than I had planned, but I felt excited about the day ahead of me. My new landlord, Bette, had politely tapped on my door to invite me to breakfast, an unexpected perk that I sincerely appreciated. I stepped into the bright kitchen of Bette's home to eat a bowl of decadent cheesy grits and bacon. The smell set my stomach to growling. The kitchen had an old-fashioned but tidy floor and a vintage, chrome-edged table. A bowl of polished wax fruit decorated the tabletop, along with a pair of whimsical Campbell's Soup salt and pepper shakers. *This is what a home must feel like*, I thought happily.

"Ready to work on that big old house today?" Bette slid a small glass of juice and a cup of coffee toward me, and I gratefully accepted them.

"Yes, I think I am! It's going to be a lot of work, but chances like this don't come but once in a lifetime, really. Thanks again for allowing me to stay in the apartment."

"Oh, it's my treat. I like having people nearby, and frankly, I'm happy that Mr. Stuart has hired you. They needed to do something about that place. The Seven Sisters mansion is too beautiful to just rot into the landscape; we Mobilians need to have a bit more pride in our history here. We've got some real stories to tell. Did you know that the French settlers used to send little orphan girls over here to marry these backwoods French-Canadians? Poor little things. They called them the Pelican Girls because they landed on Dauphin Island in Pelican Bay. No, wait, maybe the ship was called The Pelican. Oh, I can't remember, but there are plenty of sad stories to tell. Not the least of which are the ones from Seven Sisters, but I guess you know all about those." Bette's short white curls framed her round face perfectly and shook with her expressiveness.

"I don't know a thing, really—only the facts from the brochures. I am intrigued, though." Then I thought for a moment and asked, "Are the Stuarts an old family here in Mobile?"

Bette smiled, then launched into her story. "Well, Mrs. Stuart was actually a Hunter. They were the ones who purchased Seven Sisters sometime in the 1960s. According to my friend, Cynthia Dowd—she's on the board of the Historical Society, and she has such lovely white hair—the families here were very excited when the Hunters purchased the property. There was a lot of work going on at Oakleigh, the antebellum over off Government Street. People had hoped that the Hunters would do the same thing with Seven Sisters, but nothing happened. Emily Stuart died sometime around 1985, I think. After that, things just quieted down. That was such a sad affair. That little boy, Ashland, was so brave. He didn't have a soul to depend on. Not counting all the family that came out of the woodwork. Imagine, so young and so much money, of course. Still he's got a good head on his shoulders. Cynthia has bent over backwards to introduce him to her daughter—poor cross-eyed girl. He's come to a few of our luncheons and talked about the old house. What a stir he caused. I can't understand why he's not married yet." Bette sipped her coffee from the chipped china cup and stood to look out the window.

Before I could ask anything else, the cuckoo clock on the wall signaled the half hour, kicking me into business mode. "I have to run. I can't be late, not good for the first day on a new job. Is there anything I can do to help clean up?" I rose from the vinyl-padded chair and carried my dishes to the sink. I wasn't used to anyone cooking for me, much less washing my dishes.

"Oh, no. I've got this little meal under control. I'll make biscuits tomorrow. Maybe you'll tell me what you find. I wish I could explore that old home. Such sadness, I bet."

I waved goodbye and stepped outside into the sunshine. I had dressed in comfortable, light clothing, just blue jeans, a new t-shirt and sneakers. That was a good thing. It was warm already, and I imagined it would get even warmer in the house. I managed to pull my hair back in a ponytail, partly because I wanted to hide last night's wound and partly because I knew I'd sweat.

Last night's accidental dream already seemed like a distant memory, but I didn't doubt that Muncie had lived, served and maybe died right where I would be working. Finding out more about him was added incentive to dig deep into the history of the old home. It felt good to have a purpose beyond cataloging antiques and paintings.

My phone jangled in my purse. I pulled it out and sighed. William. I couldn't keep putting off talking to him; it just never seemed like a good time. That described our relationship perfectly—off-balance and never right. I couldn't blame him entirely. He tried to make me happy, but I had to be honest. I didn't love him. With a sigh, I hit the ignore button. I found my car keys in the planter where Ashland had promised to leave them. I knew that he had driven my car home. When I opened the door, I caught a whiff of his cologne. Absently, I wondered if I would see him today as I eased out of the driveway.

When I arrived, I was on time but nearly last to the party. The small road that led to the house was lined with work trucks, everything from landscapers to a local computer setup team. It was weird knowing that many of these contractors waited on directions from me. I grabbed my laptop bag, along with my notes, and headed up the path. It was nice to make the trek in the daylight. (I intended on sticking my tongue out at the ugly satyr.)

Walking through the azalea-lined pathway seemed much less menacing with a blue sky trying to peep through. A squirrel squeaked and skittered in the underbrush, probably complaining at the cacophony of humans who disturbed his normally peaceful environment. "Sorry, little guy," I said with a shrug.

At the end of the path I once again faced Seven Sisters, my new second home, and the sheer size of the building set me back on my heels. The house sat slightly to the right of the path. I could plainly see the work that time had so mercilessly made of the house, the missing and hanging plantation shutters, the moss covering everything that dared reach up for the sun. Fruit and pecan trees that had begun as hopeful saplings now smothered the landscape, closing in perilously on the house. Off to the right of the path stood several statues, including the revolting satyr who had mocked me the night before. I spied a brick walkway under a collection of leaves. I was happy to see the landscaping company taking the initiative, cleaning up the limbs and leaves scattered on the ground. I gave a wave in their direction, mentally pledging to talk with them later.

I didn't stop at the steps this time but walked right in like I owned the place. I found Matthews, sleeves rolled up and sweat on his brow, helping a young man open boxes in the front room. "Good morning!" I said cheerily, my ponytail swinging as I jumped in to help. After a brief discussion, I persuaded Matthews to allow me to relocate the computers for the inventory system to the back of the house. I reasoned that it would be cooler and, since I would later be working on the back of the property, in various sheds and buildings, more convenient for my team and me. Less walking and hauling around expensive equipment, I said. Truthfully, I think I just wanted to be in the Blue Room. Close to Muncie.

I met the general contractor, Terrence Dale, who insisted I call him TD. He was handsome in an earthy sort of way. He had lively brown eyes and a natural enthusiasm about life that was infectious. He seemed as excited as I was about restoring the home. Both of us were young and ready to earn our place in our respective arenas. According to him, he had fought long and hard to win the contract. With the recommendation of the Historical Society, he ultimately dominated the competition. He was only a little older than me, probably not thirty yet, but he had already worked on several local projects. I liked TD immediately and was glad to work with someone so knowledgeable and amiable. My part of the remodel would be only as a historical consultant, which left me with plenty of time to stay focused on my task. I couldn't wait to get my hands dirty.

After hours of setting up passwords and permissions on the computer network, checking delivery dates and sending introductory emails, I begged off lunch and slipped away to take my own private tour of Seven Sisters, before the full team arrived and the hard work began. I wanted to feel the place, to reconnect with the past. Don't get me wrong—I'm not a psychic, but I don't claim to understand how my dream life really works. My goal wasn't just to give my client a catalog of inventory. I wanted to quietly honor and pay homage to the people who had once loved all these things. I'd already walked through much of the ground floor during the course of the day, including the Blue Room, the banquet hall, the massive ballroom and the two front parlors, but now I could take my time, free from questions and Hollis Matthews' invading stare.

Chapter 7

I had spent considerable time in the ladies' parlor the evening before. Like the rest of the house, it had high, smooth ceilings with intricate wood trim. A massive sliding wooden door, with a convenient keyhole peephole, separated it from the men's parlor. The peephole opened only from the men's side.

The men's parlor had a small fireplace and a wall lined with built-in bookshelves. If I closed my eyes, I could smell the faint aroma of pipe tobacco that had once, many years ago, filled this dark paneled room in celebration of Miss Calpurnia Cottonwood. I hoped that somewhere in the house, those books had been found. Both parlors had doors that opened to a wide porch. The sliding door that connected to the Blue Room was less impressive. The Blue Room was slightly larger than the other two parlors. During Muncie's time, the windows were hung with heavy blue curtains embellished with gold threads. Now they stood bare, naked. Despite the warm afternoon, I shivered. Walking to the alcove where I had witnessed the unwanted kiss, I amateurishly attempted to open myself emotionally to feel a remnant of life, to experience the boy's turmoil again. But I felt nothing, only sadness at seeing a veil of dirt on the wall and grooves in the wooden floor made by dragging heavy furniture.

According to TD, Seven Sisters was at first built in a T-shaped, Greek Revival style, perfect for keeping the home cool even during Mobile's hottest subtropical summers. Over time, rooms had been added, expanding the size of the home for entertaining. I longed to open the doors and windows and allow fresh air to flow through the home. I promised myself I would do that someday. I strolled down the hall to the room where I had witnessed the house slaves lining up for inspection. It was smaller than the rest of the rooms, and it also had a sliding door that connected it to the music room. Just beyond that, at the front of the house, was the banquet hall. None of the original furniture remained on-site, but I had some leads on the table.

My stomach rumbled, and I glanced at my watch. It was past one; Chip, the IT guy, the maintenance team and Hollis Matthews would undoubtedly be returning from lunch at Mama's, a nearby eatery on Dauphin Street. I secretly hoped that they had ignored my earlier protest and had taken the initiative to bring me back a snack, but I didn't count on it.

I felt in my pocket for my tiny but powerful LED flashlight and climbed up the wooden staircase. The contractor had assured me that the staircase was in good condition and could be safely used. The occasional twinge on my scalp hoped he knew what he was talking about.

I stepped lightly on the bare wooden floors, ignoring the squeaks and complaints of the old staircase. My sweaty ponytail hung limp in the stifling heat of the upper floor. TD promised that cool air would be flowing up here by tomorrow, and I hoped he was right. I couldn't ask my team to work in this oppressive heat. I quickly climbed to the top of the stairs and walked to the two large windowed doors that overlooked the back of the property.

I was surprised to find that the locks were modern, and I opened them without much fuss. I didn't feel brave enough to step out on the veranda; instead, I stood in the hallway breathing in the fresh but humid air and examining the forgotten gardens below. It was a dismal sight.

Forlorn rows of shrubby trees, half-hidden statues and a few small dilapidated buildings dotted the landscape. It looked less hopeful than the house. Large magnolia trees spilled white blossoms all over the ground and obscured what appeared to be a large sundial. *Not good planning there*, I thought. A massive wisteria vine crawled over whatever it could find, covering camellias with cascades of purple flowers and thick, brown vines. Was that a grave or a stump? I looked closer, keeping my sneakered feet safely in the hallway. Clustered in the center of the main yard was an abandoned rose garden with scrawny bushes and clumsy limbs. Despite the sound of a nearby car horn and the hum of the generator below, I felt very lonely standing on the second floor of Seven Sisters. A thick aroma of decay rolled up from the gardens, an unsettling fragrance of rotten leaves and wood. This was certainly not the pleasant view that the young woman in my dream had enjoyed. In her time, smooth lawns, flowering hedges and white-painted benches and lattice filled the landscape. It was disappointing that what was once elegant and ordered was now overrun and lost beneath a solid layer of chaos. Sadness washed over me. I couldn't help but think of Muncie, so young and hopeful despite his bleak reality.

With a sigh, I turned my attention to the stacks of boxes and plastic tubs that lined the walls and filled some of the rooms. Walking from room to room, I could see it was a work in progress, but TD and his crew were obviously talented. I loved the colors they had chosen. One of the bedrooms, the one closest to the left side of the stairs, was painted a vivid blue. The massive windows were surrounded with intricate wood molding, obviously new and painted a rich cream color. The floors were a dark walnut wood, and a chandelier sparkling with crystals hung from the ceiling. Of course, electrical lights instead of candles crowned the fixture. Except for allowances for modern building standards, it was as authentic as it could be.

I pulled on my cotton gloves and rifled through a few boxes. I unwrapped a fine porcelain piece, a perky bird resting on a branch. "This will look lovely on a mantelpiece," I said to myself. Wrapping it back up carefully, I put the lid back on the storage box. I rummaged around like a child at Christmas, careful not to undo the cautious work someone had done packing these precious artifacts. Each one had a story, a reason for being included in the collection. I continued my wandering until I came to a small box in a corner of a small bedroom. I had to prop the door open; it was heavy and wanted to swing closed. This was one room that had intact shutters, and there wasn't much natural light. I pulled my flashlight from my pocket and tossed the beam on the box. It was dusty and cardboard, and it didn't seem to belong with the neat plastic tubs and crates.

I pulled back the flaps and saw a box of papers. Digging through the box, I found letters from the late Mrs. Stuart to the Tennessee State Museum, inquiring after several items. I set the letters to the side and kept digging. At the bottom of the box were several leather-bound journals. I lifted one and rubbed my gloved hand across the cover. The engraving was worn away, so I couldn't read it in the low light. Suddenly, a shadow passed across the doorway.

"Hello? Hey, I'm in here!" I called out. I assumed it was Chip or maybe even Matthews. It was impossible to hear a car approach up here. I placed the book back in the box and stepped into the hallway. As I crossed the doorway, the door to another bedroom down the hall slammed shut. Surprised, I called again, "Hello?"

I took the gloves off and clutched the flashlight, then tried to walk quietly (and bravely) to the closed door. The creaking floorboards gave me away. I stopped at a loud creak and said a little more quietly, "Chip? Mr. Matthews?" Nobody answered, but I could hear the shifting of furniture and the soft jangling of music from behind the closed door. I took a deep breath and walked quickly to the door, turning the knob with force. It wouldn't budge. "Chip? TD?" I asked as I fought with the knob and tapped on the door. The music stopped, and suddenly the knob turned easily.

The room was bright and sunny but cool, cooler than the rest of the house. It was completely empty. I stood in the center of the room and spun around; there were no other doors except for the way I came in. "Okay, Carrie Jo, get real. It was a draft, or a crooked door that decided to swing closed." I breathed deeply and realized I was squeezing the flashlight furiously. I tucked it in my pocket, unable to fight the fear that crept up my spine. I felt the urge to leave, and quickly. I walked around the boxes, kicking a music box that was lying on the floor. The toy issued a few complaining strains and quit. I picked it up and turned it over in my hands. *Okay,* I thought, trying to calm my mind, *I must have left this out because I was just in here.* But I knew I had never seen it before. I set it on a nearby plastic storage tub and left, walking straight downstairs. I was happy to hear voices—voices of the living—in the foyer.

The incident upstairs shook me. I steered clear of the area for the rest of the day and worked on prepping some room layouts instead. By the end of the afternoon, I remembered the box with the leather-bound journals and (like a miserable coward) sent Chip upstairs to retrieve it for me. I declared it too heavy for me to carry and asked him to bring it to my makeshift office. He complied, happy to help with something besides computer work. He delivered it with a smile, obviously not chased by ghouls and goblins.

On an impulse, I took a journal from the box and decided to take it home with me. I was curious to read it but more than ready to go home.

Later, I took a walk and snacked on the stuffed fried shrimp po' boy I'd bought. As I walked, I felt a tinge of sadness. I had hoped that Mobile would be a new start for me. No dreams, no screams and no one to peer at me. I tried to shake off the feeling of regret, sure I was being too dramatic because I was tired. Certainly I had imagined half of what I thought I'd seen, right? I climbed the stairs to my apartment and waved at Bette (who seemed to witness all my arrivals and departures). On the porch was a box with my name on it. It was wrapped with shiny red paper and had a gold "Emogene's" sticker taped to the front. A card lay on top, with my name printed in large, scrawling letters. I picked up my package and went inside, thankful that I was able to shut the door behind me for the day. I slid the elegant card out of the crisp envelope. A whisper of expensive cologne told me who it was from before I read the card. The card read: "Good luck on the new project. I know Seven Sisters is in good hands." Instead of signing his name, Ashland had written a big, elaborate "A." I opened the box to find a bouquet of exquisite flowers including Indian pinks, Irises and sweet tea roses. I breathed in the fragrances with a smile, locking the door and tossing my purse on the desk. I looked for a vase and found an empty Mason jar in the kitchenette. I filled it with water (still smiling) and slid the bouquet in. It was a thoughtful gesture, and I tried not to read too much into it, but it was the first time in my whole life that I had received flowers from a man. I set them on my nightstand and headed for the shower.

I needed to wash away the fear and anxiety. "I was the right woman for this job," I told myself, wishing I felt as confident as I sounded. "Ugh, I hope I know what I'm doing." As I slipped on my nightgown, I did feel a little better. I turned on the radio and listened to music until I began to feel sleepy. That was sooner than I expected even though the room was getting warm. I flipped off the radio and stretched out, feeling frustrated in more ways than one, kicking away the comforter. I slept probably a half hour, but I tossed and turned frequently and woke with snippets of dreams rolling around in my head. Some were my own, some were just memories, and there were others still that I wasn't sure about.

Restful sleep eluded me. My cozy room was too humid and warm tonight. I flipped off the window air conditioning unit. It wasn't blowing cool air at all. I opened the windows, but the warm air hung like a wet blanket. I had a long, hot summer ahead of me in Mobile. Sleeping in a flimsy nightgown had not cooled me down. Maybe ice water would do the trick; I padded to the kitchenette to get a glass. On my way back to my hot bed, I picked up the book I had left on the desk when I came in. It felt cool in my hand. I rubbed the edge of the worn book, knowing I should wear gloves but unable to bear it in this heat. I flipped on the bedside lamp and sat on the bed. Reading by the dull moonlight that streamed in from the porch was impossible. Although some of the ink had faded, the writing was intact, with delicate letters. I could see the author's name penned in the upper right corner of the first page. The journal belonged to Calpurnia!

She was long gone now, like Muncie. I pulled the sleek brochure out of the folder that Hollis Matthews had sent me. This was her! She was Calpurnia Cottonwood, the girl on the cover. I looked at the picture closely under the lamp. It was certainly her. I would recognize those almond-shaped brown eyes anywhere. They had an innocent downward slant, making her appear even more youthful than she was. In the photo, which was obviously of an oil painting, her back was turned to the artist. She looked back with a slight smile. She held a book, but the print was too small to read. I studied the girl's face, amazed that I had seen it warm and alive, flushed under the attention at a candlelit dinner party. The photo was a near likeness, a shadow of the nervous girl who struggled under the weight of an intricate hairstyle, voluminous skirts and (I suspected) the heaviness of life. I tucked the photo back into the folder, like she was a hidden treasure. "Calpurnia," I whispered into the hot Alabama night. I wanted to devour the book, read it page by page, but I was suddenly very tired. Perhaps the humidity and heat had stolen my energy.

I remembered the oscillating electric fan in a nearby closet and placed it near my bed. I set it on high and pointed it in my direction. After pouring myself another glass of ice water, I went to bed with the book. Soon the fan had cooled me down, and I began to feel sleepy. I had no idea that in my hand was a key. A key that would take me back in time again, back to Seven Sisters, back to Calpurnia and Muncie. As I closed my eyes, I felt myself drifting to a different time and place. I did not feel afraid. Perhaps I should have.

Chapter 8

My face shone strangely in the mirror, like a disembodied head, floating in the amber light of my bedroom. I hated the coiled hair piled upon my head. I looked like Medusa, the disgusting Gorgon doomed to life without love; my braids like forbidding snakes, keeping everyone away. This is what Mother wanted. I stuck my tongue out at myself, screwing up my face in an ugly look, in a defiant protest against the universe. Of course, I was not defying Mother. I'd never defy her. She was the one who had insisted on this debutante charade.

"Calpurnia, every young lady sits for a painting at your age. You'll thank me someday. Why, you're in the rose of your youth, and you're so lovely." Mother had cradled my chin lovingly, speaking softly down to me as I sat pouting on the edge of my lace-covered bed.

Compared to my mother, I felt like an old spinster, although I was sixteen—well, almost sixteen. Mother was petite with delicate hands that she kept folded in her lap when she reclined. She had smooth, dark blond hair, lively brown eyes and a tiny mouth that wore a permanent smile, without an excess show of even, white teeth. Even now, with her swollen belly and red cheeks, Mother was the picture of feminine perfection. My figure, on the other hand, maintained its childlike shape, straight like a hickory branch with no curve at all.

Downstairs, waiting impatiently in the ladies' parlor, was the insipid Reginald Ball, aspiring artist and some sort of distant cousin on my father's side. Except for his limited enthusiasm for art, he was a bore with vacuous eyes who never wondered about anything beyond the arrival of the next plate of sweets. Still, I felt a tinge of sympathy for the rotund Mr. Ball. He would always be what he was now—the bumbling son of an elegant gentleman who made no secret of his disappointment in his progeny. At least Reginald Ball had given up his feeble attempts at courting me; now we observed an easy quiet during our sketching sessions. I was quite the better artist than he but was too much of my mother's daughter to tell him so.

In the beginning, before I met him, I had secretly hoped that I would like him, maybe even love him. But that was not to be. "Strange," I told Muncie later, "artists typically have an overabundance of joie de vivre. They're searchers of the beauty in the world around them, full of artistic curiosity." I suspected that Mr. Ball's sole interest in art was merely to make a living. Had he been full of turmoil or offered even a single controversial thought, I could have overlooked his swelling stomach, round face and piggish black eyes. Reginald Ball had truly been an intellectual and romantic disappointment.

After the convening of the first sketching, my hopeful mother closed ranks on me, discreetly asking for details of our conversation. (Heaven knows why she bothered to ask since Hooney, her servant, had sat watching over us the entire time.) The dark-skinned woman had absently plucked at the threads of the small pillow she was working on, presumably for the new baby, quietly clucking at me when I'd behaved rudely or indifferently toward the boring Mr. Ball. Exasperated, I told Mother, "He's a dreadful bore, and he licks his fingers after he eats."

My aloof father, during a rare moment of felicity toward me, had paid for the portrait in advance so that I might have all the advantages of my less wealthy but more socially skilled neighbors. Safely married and out of the way for the son he hoped he would finally have, I assumed. He brushed his sunburnt lips against my forehead after he bestowed his unwanted gift on me. I was careful not to make any gesture of unkindness toward him or to refuse him. I had sealed my heart off from my father many years ago. He was a cruel man who liked drinking corn whiskey, the spirits the slaves drink, and then lashed anything that got in his way, even Mother and me if we were unfortunate enough to cross his path.

If he had always been cruel, my heart would not struggle so, and it would be easy to keep him out. But I remember a different father. One who held my little brother with tears as he left us for heaven; a father who used to bring me soft rabbits for pets and trinkets from his trips to New Orleans. I don't remember the day that kind man disappeared, but it happened many years ago. That man was long gone. Happily, he rarely stayed at Seven Sisters, preferring traveling his properties; he said it was to manage our many businesses. He came home long enough to make my mother cry and to walk the pathways of the garden with his purposeful, no-nonsense stride. Then he was off again, leaving Mother and me the run of the house and the property for however long his latest trip would take him.

In the past two months, I had endured day-long sittings with the painter. As a quiet protest, I took particular delight in tormenting him by making slight modifications to my attire before each sitting. Changing my hairstyle or the silk coral dress with the fitted bodice and ribbon sleeves was out of the question with my observant mother. However, I did manage to make small changes, like exchanging my coral pendant on the gold chain for the jade choker or sliding a flower behind my ear. The awkward Mr. Ball spent a good half hour at the beginning of each sitting, fussing over his sketches before deciding how to best correct them. The results were predictable. Dead set on proving himself worthy of his subject, he behaved like a gentleman, never scolding me or acknowledging the changes openly. The game became boring over time. In matters of mediocrity and passivity, Mr. Ball had proven a winner.

Today, in honor of our last sitting, I wore the ivory combs with the painted roses in my hair—a gift I had received in the post a few days ago along with a note promising that by tomorrow evening, my favorite uncle would be here, at Seven Sisters! Along with the package arrived an assortment of trunks and boxes, much more than my Uncle would need during his stay. I suspected the trunks held gifts, perhaps mementos of his many adventures. Or maybe they belonged to an exciting guest.

Uncle Louis would be with us by dinner tomorrow and would stay with us for the rest of the summer. Perhaps this is why my father had decided to tour our land; he frequently and quite loudly denounced Uncle Louis, his wife's brother, as a proud man with more money than brains. Mother and Father had shouted loudly at one another before he had left again, this time taking only Early with him. I hated my father's petty jealousy over Uncle Louis. Tall with an elegant, pale radiance, my uncle towered over my father. He adored speaking French and frequently sent Mother and me books of poetry and collections of stories that we both relished. I had not laid eyes on my fair uncle for well more than two years. He was so busy traveling, acquiring new things, seeing new places. Oh, how I longed to leave with him, to see the world beyond the red dirt roads that encircled Seven Sisters—roads to my prison! I thought often that I would die here, finally stuffed inside the stone crypt along with my dead siblings. A quiet voice from deep within my heart promised that this would not be my fate.

With my chin lifted in faux confidence, I entered the parlor with a firm smile that I hoped masked my insecurity. Mother was in bed, where she would stay until the baby arrived—it was left to me to be the lady of the house to any guests, invited or otherwise. So far, I had received a local merchant, who had insisted on showing the "lady of the house" his latest collection of furniture samples, wooden miniatures that he insisted would be custom-made. How privately amused I had been when the rude fellow had managed to gain access to a mere sixteen-year-old girl with no authority to even purchase supplies for the pantry.

I also sat through an uninteresting tea with the birdlike Lennie Ree Meadows and her giggling niece. If they had held any disappointment at being entertained by me, they had hidden it very well. They were more interested in the condition of my mother and the whereabouts of my father than me. Feeling unusually generous toward our chatty neighbors, I dismissed their queries with benign and vague answers but rewarded (or distracted) the quivering Ms. Meadows with my happy news—Uncle Louis was on his way.

"Only just last week, we received the wonderful news that dear Uncle Louis is coming for a visit. He will stay for a few months before returning north to see his oldest sister, Mrs. Olivia Grant. We will be honoring him with a late spring banquet, and of course, you and your niece must come." As expected, this was the tidbit of gossip Ms. Meadows required. She quickly departed, presumably to boast that she had received a personal invitation to dinner at Seven Sisters. She would be the one to announce to the community that the elegant Louis Beaumont would once again pay a visit to Mobile. He was getting older but was undoubtedly still one of Alabama's most eligible bachelors. I giggled to myself thinking of my Uncle Louis married to the nervous Lennie Meadows.

Reginald Ball was, as I expected, pacing nervously waiting for me in the parlor, sweaty hands dipping into the sweet tray. If he had bothered to look at my hands rather than my nonexistent bosom, he would have noticed my permanently stained fingertips. Traces of my constant scribbling, as my mother describes it. "Mr. Ball," I said, smiling at him and stretching out my hand in an unfamiliar movement that I copied from my mother. "I do hope I haven't…"

Before I could continue, I met the eyes of the most beautiful man I had ever seen. He rose from one of the blue velvet chairs that faced the empty fireplace. He had a thick mop of dark, wavy hair that he wore slightly longer than the current style. He had dark blue eyes that were fringed with curled black lashes. His tanned skin was clear and warm-looking; I felt myself blush but managed a tense smile.

The stranger was half a foot taller than Mr. Ball, who was no short figure. Although his clothing clearly belonged to a gentleman, he appeared dusty and disheveled.

Mr. Ball cleared his throat. "Miss Cottonwood, I took the liberty of bringing this gentleman here, to Seven Sisters, as I found him in dire distress on the road. He says he was set upon by bandits, right on the road north of your home. We couldn't find his horse or belongings. I do hope you can assist him. I'd like you to meet, oh dear, I haven't collected your name, sir." The painter's face reddened at his oversight.

"Mademoiselle, sir, let me introduce myself. I am Captain David Garrett, at your service." He had a deep voice and a friendly manner.

We three stood looking at one another for a few seconds before I realized that I must take control of the situation. "Sir, you are most welcome here. If I may ask, how did this happen to you, Captain?"

"Blayliss and I decided to hunt for some rabbits this morning. Blayliss is a bit of a puppy but with a fine pedigree. The rabbit ran across the road in front of us, and we followed him. I rounded the curve, the one near that copse of trees, then two men stepped out onto the road. We exchanged greetings, and suddenly one of the men reached for my saddle. I began to ride on, but the two overpowered me." He paused here, no doubt feeling embarrassed. I said nothing, and he continued.

"The next thing I remember, I woke along the road with this good man standing over me. What would I have done if Mr. Ball had not found me?"

Hearing his part in the story, Mr. Ball practically glowed under the praise. "My dear sir, I venture to say you'd have found help here at Seven Sisters. However, it was my pleasure to help you in your time of need."

"Yes, indeed. Thank you, Mr. Ball." I smiled.

He turned to me. "May I thank your father or mother for your kind attention?"

"Neither is available to receive your gratitude at this time, but I will happily convey it to them. At present, my maid will show you to a room where you can change your shirt; she'll repair that tear in your shirt for you." I paused a minute before adding, "We would be happy to have you stay for dinner, sir. I'm sure by then the sheriff or perhaps my father will wish to speak to you."

"I am in your debt." His voice was low, quiet, almost intimate. But he made no inappropriate movement and did not leer at me. His perfectly masculine face was the picture of sincerity. With a nod, praying that I walked away without tripping over my ridiculously formal gown. I didn't look back but imagined the captain watching me as I left. I was pleased that I did not trip and also remembered my manners. I stopped to extend the invitation to my other guest, whom I had been warned not to forget. "Mr. Ball, of course, you must join us for lunch I think we must cancel our appointment for today, though. This is a very disturbing matter. I'm sure you understand." He nodded and giddily accepted my invitation.

My mind couldn't keep up with my heart. I barely remembered talking to Hooney and climbing the wooden stairs to my bedroom. I called out for Hannah, who sat in the hall outside my mother's door. I raced into my room and began to tug impatiently at the silk ribbons of my gown. My face looked pinker in the mirror, and I couldn't help but smile at myself. I felt the butterflies cavorting in my stomach. This was a new experience for me, and I wasn't sure how I felt about it. I stepped out of the coral silk dress and into the blue cotton gown with the purple stitching at the sleeves. It had tiny purple flowers stitched along the top of the bodice. It was my favorite gown. I had been saving it for Uncle Louis, but I felt pretty in it. I sat down at the vanity table and helped Hannah unwind the braid. "Are you sure, Miss? I like this braid on you. You look like a real lady."

Determined, I took the brush and pulled it through my hair, working out the braids carefully. "Yes, thank you." I pulled the top of my hair back away from my face and slid it into a barrette at the back of my head. I attached a blue bow and fluffed it with my fingers. Suddenly, I agreed with Hannah. I looked like a child now.

I traveled down the hall to see my mother, stepping lightly in case she was sleeping. I tapped lightly on her door before opening it. Sitting in the roomy, padded chair next to her sunny window, Mother put her book aside and welcomed me with her outstretched hands. "Well, why are you not dressed in your gown?" she asked quizzically. For the next few minutes, she listened, nodding and widening her eyes occasionally until all the events of the morning had come tumbling out.

Instead of sharing my excitement, my mother sighed heavily, her hands folded perfectly in her lap. Suddenly, I wished that I were a child again, that I could lay my head in that lap and feel her cool hands stroke my hair. "Of course, we'll have to tell Mr. Cottonwood. He needs to know these roads are not safe. We don't want anything to happen to Uncle Louis or any of our neighbors. Ask Stokes to come see me. Keep Muncie near you, would you?"

I hated that the peace of our home would be disturbed, as it always was with my father's arrival. I hated more knowing that, somehow, I had caused this disturbance. I felt guilty for feeling happy just a few moments ago.

"Now then, don't sulk, Callie. All is well. You have guests to attend to now, so off you go. Ask Hooney to set out the blue and white china and bring in some of the spring fruits. It's not every day we get the opportunity to entertain a Captain. And do be kind to Mr. Ball."

There was no sense in arguing with her or saying anything more. She was already reaching for her note paper. Before I joined the gentlemen downstairs, I visited my private library in the corner of my room and looked for a book. Obviously, anything written by Augusta Evans was inappropriate to share with mixed company. I finally selected Tennyson's Locksley Hall. I had nothing else really to talk about other than my books. I was no singer, and I had kept my love for drawing a secret from Mr. Ball, as a kindness. Sliding the book into the pocket of my blue dress, I walked slowly, as dignified as I could, down the winding stairs. My guests had made themselves at home on the porch where I had left them, and thankfully, our dinner waited for us.

In the distance, someone plucked on a fiddle. Pink azaleas lined the porch, which was cluttered with silky white camellias. We sat intimately at a round table set for three, positioned under a gnarly oak that bent graciously over us, protecting us from the beaming sun. Mr. Ball talked effervescently, snacking on sugared donuts, a generous slice of ham and a bowl of strawberries. Mobile had a new mayor, a Mr. Charles Langdon of Southington, Connecticut. Many Mobilians of Mr. Ball's acquaintance, namely his influential father, apparently had strong objections to the new mayor, which no doubt stemmed from his northern lineage. Still, he was a direct descendant of a notable hero who had fought in the Revolutionary War. I pretended to be interested as well as I could.

I pushed a strawberry around Mother's blue and white china and tried not to stare at Captain Garrett like a wide-eyed calf. I noticed he wore his own shirt; perhaps my father's wasn't a good fit for him. He was considerably larger than my father. I flushed thinking of David Garrett's arms. How would they feel wrapped around my waist? My mother was right—I was a silly girl.

Taking advantage of a break in Mr. Ball's oration, I took the opportunity to engage Captain Garrett in conversation. "Tell me, Captain, do you travel to Mobile often?"

Mr. Ball slurped on his lemonade and said, "Yes, we do want to hear about your travels. The Delta Queen, that's the name of your boat, correct?" His short dark hair stuck out above his ears, and his bald spot shone in the sun.

"I have been to Mobile many times, Miss Cottonwood. It is a city I have come to appreciate recently," he said with a smile. "I have thought many times that if I were to ever take leave of my boat, I would happily call this fair city home. How much more so now that I have found such fair and pleasant company?" He lifted his glass and tilted his head to both Mr. Ball and me.

"Ma'am, the sheriff is here to see you." Stokes stood officiously in the doorway.

"Thank you, Stokes. Just one moment, please, gentlemen." The men rose as I left the table.

A tall, lanky man with a bushy black mustache stood in my foyer. After a few pleasantries, I led the sheriff to the porch, poured him a glass of cold water and sat quietly as he interviewed our guest. He drilled through the formalities, writing down a few notes as Captain Garrett recounted this morning's misfortune. Satisfied with the interview, the sheriff mentioned that the captain's horse, a dappled gray, had been found already. The thieves must have gotten cold feet and left the horse after realizing what a shameful act they had committed. "Still, we're taking this very seriously. I have a few ideas about who these troublemakers are, but I can't be certain without more investigation. I'll do some checking around, Miss Cottonwood. In the meantime, if anyone sees the men again, please send for me immediately. Don't take them on yourself, although I can see that you're hardly alone here." I could sense that the sheriff didn't seem to approve of me. "Is your father expected to return soon?" I nodded dumbly. "Well, that's a good thing. Can't be too careful. Now, if you'll excuse me, I'd like to continue my search." As he rose with his hat in his hand, he added, "Sir, will you be available if I have more questions?"

"I am at your service, Sheriff." The captain rose to his feet and nodded slightly.

"Where can I find you? Will you be staying long at Seven Sisters?"

"No. Now that my horse has been found, I'll return to the Delta Queen before nightfall. You can find me there; I will be in Mobile for another month. I am scheduled to pick up a load of supplies and then head up the river."

"Mr. Ball, if I may have a word with you, sir," With a nod, the sheriff left with Mr. Ball, who was now fully sweating after his meal. I was relieved to see the sheriff go but felt immensely embarrassed by how my new guest had been treated.

"Miss Cottonwood, I apologize for all the trouble I've caused you. I should take my leave before you are further inconvenienced."

"Not at all, sir. I have enjoyed your company. I'm afraid Mr. Ball and I have little to talk about," I said honestly.

He laughed softly. "I can well imagine that."

I smoothed the skirt of my dress as I stood, my hand rubbing over the book in my pocket. I removed it and held it nervously. Books had always comforted me.

He smiled faintly. "Ah, Tennyson... Locksley Hall? 'When I dipt into the future, far as the human eye could see; saw the vision of the world and all the wonder that would be.' He spoke the words exactly as I had read them.

"Yes! You know Tennyson?" I held my breath.

"Well, there's not much else to do on a ship but read," he teased me.

"I would love to see your ship—I mean the Delta Queen. Maybe when my mother feels better, we can take a ride. Or when I get old enough, I can go myself. We rarely travel anymore, but my Uncle Louis, Louis Beaumont, frequently travels all around the world. I guess travel is in my blood, for I want to see everything!"

He stopped and looked at me. "Don't be in such a hurry to leave home, Miss Cottonwood. It's much safer to have an adventure in the pages of your book. Many scoundrels await inexperienced travelers, especially ones as lovely as you."

"Are you a scoundrel, Captain Garrett?" I asked.

He blanched slightly. "I suspect that the sheriff thinks so, and Mr. Ball likely does by now as well. Do you think I am a scoundrel, Miss Cottonwood?"

"If my maid reports missing silverware, I shall know that you are, sir!" He laughed heartily, so I did as well.

"You have a keen wit, Miss Cottonwood." I acknowledged his comment with a nod, just as I had seen Mother do, but I kept quiet.

Later that evening, I enjoyed a quiet dinner and watched my mother sleep before I scurried back to my bedroom to record this momentous day in my journal. My candles burned brightly into the night, and I ignored the cramping of my hands. I wanted to remember everything, every word, every gesture. I even mentioned Mr. Ball in the history.

I opened my bedroom window; the smell of gardenia filled my room in just a few minutes. Pale moonlight splashed on the walls, and I tossed and turned on my bed, thoughts of Captain Garrett filling my head and burning my heart. With tired eyes and numb fingers, I eventually slept, only to dream of my new friend riding his ship across a sparkling sea.

In my dream, I saw myself standing on the shore, watching the ship sail out of sight. And then, I saw Reginald Ball, walking on the water like Holy Jesu and waving a handkerchief furiously at me.

Startled, I woke and found my father standing at the foot of my bed. Even in the moonlight, I could see he was drunk, swaying under the power of his beloved corn whiskey. Like an angry demon, he cracked his belt at my legs while he grabbed and twisted my foot. I refused to scream. I did not want to satisfy his lust for terrorizing me, nor did I wish for my mother to be his victim. She would certainly try to come to my rescue, as I always tried to help her. The belt stung my leg through the thin cotton of my gown. He sweated and sputtered, calling me vile names and hurling accusations at me. I gathered from his violent diatribe that he had had a visit from the sheriff. I couldn't prevent the tears from filling my eyes, but I still didn't cry out. How many times before had I faced this blind fury that was once the father I loved?

He raised his hand over and over again, unleashing his fury on me. My gown ripped, and I could feel the blood rise to the surface. Suddenly, something welled up inside me, something different, a wild defiance, a strange rebellion. I didn't want to die; I didn't want to be punished. I wanted to live! Blindly, I kicked at him and landed a blow right in his slim belly. With the help of the whiskey, he toppled over, falling onto a wooden chair with a crack. He howled like one of his beloved dogs, but I raced from the room. I left him, running in the darkness down the stairs. Now sobbing, I ran out of the house, into the Moonlight Garden. I scampered through the familiar maze of marble statues almost to the back fence. I cowered under a tree, my legs tucked underneath me, carefully hiding myself from the revealing moonlight.

I cried and rocked back and forth, listening intently for any intruders into my garden.

Only one came. Muncie. He said nothing but climbed in under the tree with me. He put his arm around my shoulder and pulled me close to him. I cried until he tapped my shoulder. We heard the dogs barking and sounds from the house, but no one came. I was glad he didn't try to talk to me, except for when we prayed to the Virgin for protection. We stayed there until it was nearly morning; then we crept to the kitchen house where Hooney waited for me. She clucked at my wounds and said, "Child, child." She patted the raw, red stripes on my leg with a cloth dabbed with foul-smelling liniment. Unable to stifle my cry, I released a scream and welcomed the stars that clouded my vision...

Chapter 9

I was rudely awakened by the sounds of rapid-fire knocking at my door. "Hello? CJ, I know you're in there! Come on, girl. Open up!" I rolled over in a tangle of sheets that stuck to my sweaty body. Pushing a handful of curls out of my eyes, I peered at the clock. 7:15!

"Carrie Jo! Open the door, hon!" Once again I was forced to leave my dream world behind, plunged into the reality of today. I peeked through the thin lace curtain to see Mia standing on tiptoe, looking back at me on my small upstairs porch. She had replaced her Egyptian bob with a short shock of blond hair. I was surprised that she wasn't wearing her trademark black and white clothing. Instead, her curvy body was covered in a short, red and white polka-dot sundress. Her pale skin gave her an ethereal look, but her eyes, large and darkly luminous, were completely earthly and emotional. If I didn't know her voice so well, I would have never recognized her. Only Mia could so completely transform herself in just a few months.

That was one of the things I loved about her. She had an ability to become whatever she wanted and didn't appear to feel any pressure at all to conform to anyone else's idea of who she should be.

"Coming!" I shouted at the door. Except for some mysterious new tattoos on her arm, Mia looked like a cast member from a retro '50s television show, down to her red slippers.

I opened the door and welcomed her excited embrace. She hugged me, kissed my cheek and invited herself into my muggy apartment. She chattered away about the flight and about me not responding to emails. Finally she looked at me with her perfectly lined eyes and said, "You're not ready! Get ready! We have to go. I can't wait to see this house."

I stepped into the restroom for a quick shower, leaving the door ajar so we could talk. I hopped into the shower and waited for the water to warm while Mia came and sat on the floor. She talked away as I soaped and showered. I only half-listened. I wanted to linger over my dream, but I was forced to push it to the back of my mind. I didn't feel anxious this time; I knew that I would remember every detail, probably for the rest of my life.

I hated the idea of going to work with wet hair. It didn't seem professional, but time was not on my side and I had sweated through the night. I couldn't endure spending the day smelling sweaty hair, and what if anyone got close? Ashland came to mind, and I tried not to let my mind linger on his warm hands, his strong arms or his cologne.

Mia finally came to a stopping point in her monologue about her recent travels, which I would usually find fascinating. I was able to ask her a few questions. "So when did you get in?"

"Yesterday—I just told you that! I knew you were pretty busy, being the boss and all." She was kidding, but her tone irked me a little. "Alright, now. Don't start." I reached for the loofah. "Where are you staying?"

"Oh, you know me. I'm couch-surfing. I'll always be an anthropologist. I've got to check out the locals." I heard her rummaging in my medicine cabinet.

"Mia, are you sure that's safe? Do you know this person? Whose couch are you on? Where exactly are you staying?"

"Not far from here. I walked it, actually. Down off Royal Street. My host works at a nightclub down there, but he has fabulous reviews on the surfing site."

"Is that really a good idea?" I wasn't really surprised by anything Mia said or did. She was definitely her own person. She always had been since I'd known her. I simultaneously worried about and admired her.

"Oh, yeah, my host is pretty legit—and interesting. He works at Gabriella's. It's very exclusive, and it's beautiful inside. They completely restored the building. Love that brick."

"You've been inside?" I tried not to sound shocked.

"Stop worrying, Mom. Besides, Henri Devecheaux is absolutely fascinating, and he's very spiritual. He also looks great in a dress!" She laughed wickedly.

"Well, if you change your mind..." There was an awkward silence, and then came the question I was expecting.

"Hey, have you talked to William in the past few days?"

I wanted to ignore the question but felt obligated to explain myself since it was Mia who had introduced us. I had thought that at one time William and Mia could have made a go of it. They had spent a lot of time working together, huddling together on a private project, but apparently it was just work. I turned the oversize shower handles slowly, stalling for time. I reached my hand out for a towel, and Mia obliged.

"I've been meaning to call him, but I never do. I guess I don't know what to say. I mean, what we had was nice. He was nice... I just don't know. Something is just not quite what I need it to be." I squeezed the water from my hair and wrapped my body in the pink, fluffy towel. I pulled back the curtain slowly. "I really like him, but on so many levels we..."

"Oh my God! What happened?" Mia's dark eyes were fixed on my right foot.

I followed her gaze to a massive bruise on my right ankle. My tan skin was blue and purple and seriously swollen. Nausea swept over me, and I sat clumsily on the commode. I stared at the wounded area, then pulled up my towel to check for more bruising. I half expected to see welt marks along my legs. I stared at Mia. "I don't know..." I couldn't process what I was seeing.

"Don't give me that. There's no way you could not know. Look! It's obvious that these are fingerprint bruises. Who's been manhandling you? Was it William?" Mia's dark eyes flashed angrily.

"No! Never, he'd never. I don't really know..." I could feel swollen tears filling my eyes. I didn't want to believe that a "ghost" from the past could actually reach me, touch me.

"Does it hurt?" She lifted my foot and examined it carefully.

I pressed on the skin. "It's a little sore, but that's it."

"You want to tell me what's really going on here?" Mia looked into my eyes, laser-like.

I sighed. "Sure. But this may take a while. Let me get dressed. We'll grab some breakfast, and I'll tell you what's happened."

She nodded, and I left her to get dressed. I opted for some purple jeans and a casual red top. I wound my wet hair up on top of my head in a perky bun and took a minute to tap my lashes with mascara and dab on peach lip gloss. I scribbled a note for Bette, asking her to check out the air conditioner, and left it on her door. Thankfully, she wasn't home this morning. I would hate to refuse her company. I was relieved that she hadn't gone to the trouble of making those biscuits she had promised me.

We rode in silence to the Golden Egg, a tiny breakfast shop I had spotted on my drive into Mobile. Sliding into the vinyl-covered booth, I felt calmer, even hungry. We ordered some bacon and eggs and thanked our young waitress for the basket of biscuits and butter she cheerfully deposited on our table. Mia sat looking at me expectantly.

"I don't know what to say," I muttered with a shrug.

"Don't be shy around me. You know I'm jealous. I don't think you're crazy—just tell me! How many dreams have you had here?" She leaned forward.

I took a deep breath. "Here's how it started." I told her about my embarrassing fall my first night at Seven Sisters and about Muncie.

She broke in, "Well, that's it! That's how you got the bruises."

"Shh..." I looked around, embarrassed. "That's not it. Besides, that's the wrong foot—and there's more." Her eyes widened as I told her what I saw in my second dream; about the soft-voiced Calpurnia, the handsome yet suspicious Captain Garrett and of course, the cruel, larger-than-life Jeremiah Cottonwood. I was not surprised to see Mia pull a small notebook out of her purse and jot down some notes as I talked. When it was all over, she looked at me with her mouth open.

"Carrie Jo, this is amazing. All of this is simply amazing. Are you okay, though?" She paused, looking at me carefully, "Are you really sure you are okay? We could call Dr. O'Neal," she finished in a whisper.

"I'm perfectly fine. I just can't believe this is happening. These dreams are different than the ones I've had before. I can actually feel what she feels, what he feels. I know what they're thinking. I could smell the wisteria, taste the lemonade and see the clouds sailing by. I know it really does sound, well, crazy but it's like I'm them." My voice shook, but I was determined not to burst into tears in the middle of the Golden Egg.

Mia didn't say anything—she just watched me. Finally, she leaned back against the cracked vinyl seat and tilted her head. "Do you know how lucky you are? What I wouldn't give to experience just a few minutes of seeing the past, of being there? I love the past. I love history. You are a real dream catcher. The real thing, and you don't even see it."

I looked at my plate that I had barely touched, surprised at the scolding. The over-easy egg had congealed; the once creamy grits were stiff and unmovable. I felt a shift in the air. The uneasy "invisible" moved around me, and I shivered. I stared back at my friend and said, "Lucky? Is that what you think?"

I could feel her anger rising. "I just mean you have something that other people wish they had. It's not a curse, CJ. It's a gift," she said matter-of-factly and leaned forward to touch my hand. I couldn't help but pull away.

"Pardon me if I don't share your perspective. Where have you been the past ten years, Mia? You of all people know how weird I am, how different. You would really want to live like this? Afraid to lay your head down and close your eyes in a strange place?" I felt aggravated and a little mean. "I don't think you'd be doing much couch-surfing."

Her perfect red lips curled up in a rueful smile. "Ouch, okay. I'm sorry." She reached across the table once more with her manicured hand and tapped mine. "Tell you what, I'll tap into some resources and see what I can find on your cast of characters. I'll help you find answers, CJ. You aren't alone." With a squeeze of my hand, all was forgiven, at least on her side. And for Mia, I guess that was really all that mattered. Her indifference stung.

Before I could respond, she gasped, "Look at the time! It's 8:30!"

"Oh, Lord," I said as I scrambled out of the booth and threw some cash on the table. We didn't say much as we drove to Seven Sisters, and the silence continued when we pulled into the long drive.

"Wow," I heard her whisper.

"Uh-huh," I agreed.

Looking quite like a butler in his black dress pants, vest and white shirt, Matthews met us at the door. "This must be Miss Reed," he said jovially. He extended his hand to Mia, and the two chatted for a moment while I slipped past them. I took a moment to stop by the ladies' parlor. It was bare now, with only the makeshift desk, two dusty chairs and the reclining sofa. It was all wrong and missing so many details. I walked to the door that led to the porch and discovered that the old door wouldn't budge. Still, I could see the wilderness that was once a garden through the dirty window. I pushed aside the sadness and instead quietly pledged to make it right...whatever "it" was. "I will make it right," I whispered into the air.

"Hey, daydreamer," Mia teased, "Come show me the setup, then take me on a tour."

I laughed, my sadness forgotten. I left the stuffy room behind and took Mia on a tour of the house. We finished in the Blue Room, where we had installed the computers.

I found Chip, our IT guy, hunkered over his computer. He had short, curly hair, which made his ears appear even larger than they were. He gave me the usual nonchalant wave but perked up and sat a little straighter in his chair when Mia strolled in behind me with her red fingernails, retro ballet flats and vintage dress. I made introductions and listened to them chatter about the new program that he had designed for our "little" project. He clearly knew what he was doing; although he was no history major, the young man had more than adequate knowledge about networking, firewalls and password control. We'd be working with some expensive antiques, some that had been delicately restored. It was so important that nothing came up missing. Butterflies flipped in my stomach, reminding me that I would be the one responsible for anything that went wrong. Still, for a few minutes, I felt sane and happy and completely in control.

Ashland walked in with perfect timing. I was beaming from ear to ear, and he gave me an equally brilliant smile. He wore an untucked blue linen shirt with jeans. He looked comfortable and sophisticated, even with his tanned arms full of boxes.

"Oh, here, let me help you with that," I said with a laugh.

He looked as if he wanted to say something but instead looked past me. I turned to see Mia standing there, looking a schoolgirl holding a notebook and pencil to her chest.

Before I could say anything, Ashland spoke. "You must be Mia. I recognize your face, even though your bio picture looks very different. Can't change those eyes." He gave her a half smile and extended his hand for a shake.

She took his hand slowly and rubbed her pencil eraser against her lip. I felt uncomfortable, mostly for Ashland. With a grin and a low voice, she said, "I am Mia. I suppose you are the Master of this Plantation, Ashland Stuart?"

"I'm not anyone's master, but I am the boss."

Mia playfully slid on top of a nearby desk and tapped it with her fingers. "So, boss, is this where you want me?" I couldn't believe my ears or eyes, and I felt my face flush bright red. I had seen her use the direct approach before, but never on a client or someone she barely knew.

I jumped in. "Um, over here, Mia. This is your spot, I believe. Right, Chip?" Changing the subject and hopefully the trajectory of the conversation, I asked, "Chip, is the wireless printer online yet?"

"Should be, but let me print a test page just to be sure. If you and Mia could do the same from your computers, that would help."

I nodded, too embarrassed to look at Ashland until he tapped me on the shoulder. "Got a minute?"

"Sure, I can spare a few minutes. What's up?" I spun around in my chair to face him.

"I want to show you something, but you'll need to put your tennis shoes on. Did you bring them?"

I nodded and went to my desk for my gym bag. I pulled on some socks and my Nikes and was ready to go.

I repositioned my ponytail on the way out of the Blue Room, purposefully avoiding Mia's stare. *What just happened? Did Mia think Ashland would be won with a little awkward flirting?* He was certainly not her type. Usually, Mia's guys were quirky—sometimes handsome, sometimes plain, but always quirky. There was nothing quirky about Ashland Stuart.

He didn't mention Mia's show or what he thought about her, and I was too professional to bring it up. "Have everything you need? For the office?" he asked. "Matthews promises me that you do, but if you need something else, please let me know."

"Certainly, I will. I think, so far, we're doing all right. I expect this place will be like a beehive for the next few months with remodeling the house and setting up the museum."

"Yes, it will be, but that's the fun of the whole process. You know, I minored in history in college. I love the history of Mobile, but there is so much we don't know. I feel honored that I get the opportunity to help others remember it like it should be remembered." I didn't know what to say, so I just nodded.

"I have something to show you. I hope you're feeling better. How's that bump?"

"Great! Thanks again for your help. I can't believe how clumsy I was."

"As long as you're okay."

I felt a surge of happiness knowing that he cared. In the back of my mind, I heard Calpurnia's question: "Are you a scoundrel, Captain Garrett?"

Ashland continued, "I want to show you an interesting discovery. It takes a little walking, but it's nice out. And I think we'll have a clear path getting there. They've cut back some of the underbrush already. This find is truly amazing. TD found it this morning. That's why I was late."

He had certainly piqued my curiosity. "What is it?"

"You'll see, but wait; do you have your phone?"

I patted my back pocket to make sure. "Yes, of course!"

"You're going to need it." He laughed.

"How mysterious."

We jumped off the back porch; the steps were soft and spongy, too hazardous to use. I was happy that I didn't embarrass myself and fall in front of him—again.

"It's a ways ahead, past this small section, into the..."

"Moonlight Garden..." I blurted out.

"Yes, the Moonlight Garden. How did you know about that?" He paused on the pathway, looking like a Greek statue standing in a wild, green garden.

"I must have read about it someplace. I mean, I am a researcher." My excuse sounded weak. I knew about it because I had already been here, along with Calpurnia and Muncie, cowering under a sculpted fir tree. I had seen the two friends huddled in the wet rain, fearfully praying.

"Not many know about the garden. Even I'm not sure about the actual layout, and I own it. Still, it's not common knowledge that it's called the Moonlight Garden. Do you happen to know why it has that name?"

I felt my cheeks redden again. I wondered how much I should tell him, from what I had heard in Calpurnia's mind in my dream. How she had subconsciously named the statues as she wove through the complex arrangement of hedges and trees. The Moonlight Garden was a maze, with seven landmarks, statues of the demi-goddesses of the Pleiades or the Seven Sisters. They were Sterope, Merope, Electra, Maia, Taygete, Celaeno and Alcyone. Their parents, Atlas and Pleione, stood in the center. I decided not to tell him these details; how could I explain that? Instead, I said, "The statues of the garden were made of white marble that reflected the moon. During a perfectly full moon, the statues shone bright, like a Moonlight Garden. It's not as mysterious as you think."

"You seem to know a lot about it. I'm glad I hired such a good researcher." He led the way to the beginning of the maze. It wasn't nearly as beautiful as it had been, but I was happy to see that some of the important spots remained—a tree here and certain flowers there. I caught my breath just realizing how much I could remember.

"Well, I'm not psychic. I promise you that," I said, a bit tongue-in-cheek.

"What do you mean by that?" He stopped and looked at me sharply.

I couldn't understand it, but I knew that I had made him angry. The joy of the day drained away under the stare of his blue eyes. "It was a joke." I laughed nervously. "You know, that I'm not a psychic telling you these things. I'm just an average researcher."

His jaw popped a little. "It's not far ahead, just beyond the first two clumps of trees there."

For the second time that day, I had to ask myself, *What just happened?*

We walked a few more minutes, and I managed to avoid most of the sticker-filled dewberry patches but chided myself for not giving my skin a good douse of bug repellent before setting off on this journey. I tried not to be irritated by Ashland's unpredictable moods. He swung his machete at some branches and ignored me. And I returned the favor. I made myself a thousand promises to keep him out of my mind, although it was tough not to watch his muscles ripple under his blue linen shirt. But I silently pledged to speak as little as possible to him until we entered the clearing.

We stopped in a small clearing, and under a copse of oaks and pines stood a forgotten mausoleum with the name "Cottonwood" etched above the door. It was made entirely of hewn stone blocks that fitted together masterfully. The mausoleum doors were green, evidence of copper, with a huge keyed lock below the right door handle. It had a peaked stone roof that looked intact, down to the window grates. It stood about eight feet high and was large enough to hold a large family.

Large tears welled up in my eyes. I thought of Calpurnia's hopeful face, how she imagined a life in the world beyond her privileged prison. I wondered if she managed to escape, and if she did, was it to another pretty jail nearby? I slid my sunglasses down, over my eyes, quickly dabbing away the wetness.

"And there's more. We found a dozen small crosses over here, but there's nothing written on them. There's really no telling who else is here."

"This is pretty amazing. Let me grab my phone." I began snapping pictures and emailing them to myself so I could examine them later on my computer. I couldn't believe TD had found this.

"I wonder who we have here. I mean, obviously, someone in the Cottonwood family, but who? I suppose there are some records somewhere?" He seemed genuinely curious about who lay at rest on his property, and I couldn't blame him. I shuddered to think that Jeremiah Cottonwood may have been lying just a few feet away from me. The wound on my ankle twinged.

"Hmm...that should be easy to find out. I imagine Mr. Cottonwood and his wife and perhaps their children. What was the daughter's name? Calpurnia?" I snapped away with my phone, pretending I didn't know. I was not a skilled liar. I squatted next to the small white crosses, hoping my question didn't give me away.

"No, it couldn't be her. Probably her parents, though." His large hands touched the stone crevices, feeling where they met so perfectly.

Genuinely curious, I asked, "Why couldn't it be? Did she get married and move away?"

"No. She went missing—sometime in the 1850s, I believe." I felt liked someone kicked me in the gut, but Ashland didn't seem to notice. He continued, "It was a serious scandal for the time. They looked for her for years, even made some accusations, but no one was ever arrested. Lots of people have tried to discover her whereabouts; even my mother was obsessed with finding her. It consumed her life her last few years. I'm sure she often thought of her when she came out here."

I heard the sadness in his voice; this obviously touched him deeply. "It is a riveting story," I said. "Young heiress goes missing. She must have been something of a celebrity in her time."

He nodded. "I expect she was. And Miss Cottonwood wasn't just wealthy; she was extremely wealthy, the heir of two fortunes, the daughter of two established families."

Although standing in the woods with Ashland was many a girl's dream come true, all I could think of was getting back to the apartment to pore over the first journal, Calpurnia's journal. I had to know what happened to her. We stood looking at the mausoleum and the crosses. Except for the buzzing of mosquitos, all was quiet. "Thank you for sharing this with me, Ashland. This is an amazing find. I'll have to come back with a decent camera."

He wiped the sweat off his forehead with his hand. "You're welcome. We'd better get back. As hot as it is, it will probably rain soon."

As we trekked back to the house, my mind raced through the possibilities. I now had two missions: find both Muncie and Calpurnia. Where could she be? My mind naturally went to the most likely suspect, her father. I knew his brutality firsthand.

"Did you hear me?" Ashland asked.

"I'm sorry. No, I didn't. What did you say?"

He sighed a little. "I asked you to dinner."

I shrugged. "Sure, but I'm not much of a cook if it's potluck."

He laughed out loud. "What? Why would I ask you to dinner and ask you to cook?"

My eyes widened. "Oh, dinner...so, not for everyone...just me and you? I thought you...um..."

Ashland chuckled. "Wow, I feel like I'm in high school here. Listen, Carrie Jo, don't feel compelled to say yes because you work for me. And contrary to what you might think, I'm not usually this forward."

I felt my brow furrow. "I don't think anything at all. You just caught me off guard a little—I guess I was daydreaming. I would like that, but I have to do something first. Can I get back to you?" I smiled at him.

"Okay...are you seeing someone?" Ashland looked anxious, but I didn't want to explain that I needed to "break up" with William. Even though William and I had kissed just once, I felt like I owed him some honesty, if nothing else. Carrie Jo Jardine was not the kind of girl to two-time.

"No, it's not like that. Can I get back to you?" With that, we finally made it to the back door.

"Sure." He gave me a nod and didn't stay long after that—I hoped I hadn't scared him off.

Mia greeted me with, "Gee, you guys were gone for an hour," apparently forgetting her earlier theatrics with Ashland. Of course, I couldn't wait to show her the pictures. Her eyes lit up. "Ooh...that is so cool. Okay, I'm wearing jeans tomorrow, and you have to promise to take me out there. You know what, let me do some checking. I bet we can find out who's buried there."

I rubbed the sweat off my forehead with a paper towel. "What do you think about the little crosses? Children? Pets?"

"Probably children, but we may never know without digging them up. Hey, before I forget, don't make plans for tonight. I've got a surprise for you later." Mia pressed her red lips into a smug smile.

I chuckled. "Oh, Lord, I'm worried about what that could mean. Sure that sounds great." I was happy to think we could get our friendship back on track.

By the end of the workday, we had assigned furniture to three of the rooms downstairs, deciding that the Augusta Evans book collection would be perfect for the ladies' parlor. The men's parlor would house rare pipes and a small collection of pistols from before the Civil War. The future Seven Sisters Museum was beginning to take shape. It was a good feeling to see that, to be a part of the restoration. The following week, I would be meeting with someone from Mobile's African-American Museum. Ashland had made it clear that he wanted this important facet of antebellum life highlighted. We would have access to some photographs and artifacts, which I planned to distribute throughout the house and the other buildings that were to be reconstructed here.

* * *

Just a few hours later, Mia and I were walking down nearby Dauphin Street. Flickering gas lamps welcomed us into a candlelit restaurant called Bevere's. I loved everything about it, especially the high ceilings and proper linens. After some back-and-forth on what to order, I had to ask, "Mia, what happened today?"

She looked up from her shrimp cocktail. "What are you talking about?"

"I'm talking about what happened with Ashland. The whole 'You're the boss' thing. He doesn't seem like your type at all."

Her face was blank, and she said in a low voice, "He's Ashland Stuart. He's everyone's type. He's also the handsomest guy I've met in a very long time. Not to mention he's uber-rich. And what does that mean? 'He's not my type.' In case you haven't noticed, I don't have a type."

"I'm sorry, Mia. I didn't mean to embarrass you or hurt your feelings. I was just wondering."

She popped a shrimp in her mouth and chewed. "No worries, doll. I gave it a try, and it didn't work out. No biggie. Hurry up and eat, though. We have to be at our destination by 8 p.m. I know it's a Thursday night, and I promise not to keep you out too long."

We chit-chatted a little after that. I asked about her parents, and she confessed that she hadn't seen them in over six months. I missed them; I had spent a lot of time at their house during college. Thirty minutes later, we were standing in line at Grand Central Station, a bustling nightclub, waiting for a spot at the bar. It was hopping, even on a weeknight. Two spots together finally came open, and we slid onto vinyl-covered stools. Before I could ask what was happening, the lights dimmed, and a spotlight hit the stage.

It was William.

Chapter 10

The audience clapped and cheered, but I couldn't move. This certainly had been a day of surprises. William sat on a wooden stool in the center of the stage and pulled the mic close. He strummed his guitar and played "The Heart of Love," his most popular song. He had a brilliant smile that he used often, along with a perfect voice. And in just a few verses, the audience was in love. You could see it. Unfortunately, I wasn't. He was my friend but nothing else, no matter how badly he wanted to be—or Mia wanted him to be. I didn't understand why she was so invested in my relationship with him. I could feel her give me a sidelong look, but I refused to look at her.

The second song into his set, William spotted us at the bar. I gave him a weak smile, and Mia waved. He had the audience swaying in their chairs, especially the ladies, and why not? His shoulder-length dark hair and green eyes captivated many of them. Once his performance ended, William worked his way to the bar, stopping to talk to some enthusiastic fans along the way.

"Mia! Why didn't you tell me?" I whispered to her. This wasn't how I wanted to do this, face to face.

"I thought you'd like it."

"Hey! What did you think?" William hugged Mia and then me.

"You were brilliant, William. They love you, and we do too. Right, CJ?"

He smiled even more broadly, and I offered, "I love the new song, the one at the end."

"Thanks!"

After an awkward silence, I asked, "So, when did you get in?"

"I was going to call and let you know, but then Mia said we should make it a surprise. I got in last night, and I'm booked for the next two weeks. Maybe longer, if the Mobile crowd likes me. How's the house? When do I get a tour?"

Mia had headed to the dance floor, no doubt leaving the barstool for William.

"Listen, William, can we talk? You know, outside? It's kind of loud in here."

With a sigh, he agreed, and we walked out of Grand Central and down the brick sidewalk. To the casual observer, we might have looked like a loving couple, me in my summer dress, William looking smart in his crisp gray shirt and black dress pants. I couldn't remember seeing him dressed up before. "You look nice. I don't think I've ever seen you wearing something besides jeans."

"Well, whose fault is that?" A playful grin spread across his face and then quickly disappeared. "Uh-oh, you don't look too happy, CJ. What's up? I have a feeling I already know."

I stopped and just blurted it out. "William, you are a wonderful man, and I think of you as a friend, but..." I took a deep breath, "I can't say that I feel anything except friendship toward you. I hope that you didn't come all this way because of me. I am sorry."

William's green eyes flashed, and he looked like I had slapped him in the face. "You think I came down here for you?"

I sputtered, "I just assumed that you..."

"I told you months ago that I was sending some demos out. Thanks for listening. Look, I get that you don't like me like that, but I think I'll live." William had taken a step away from me. I'd never seen him angry with me before. "Listen, I have to go—the next set is starting soon. Let's just..." He raised his hands in the air and then turned and walked away, leaving me alone on the sidewalk in downtown Mobile at night.

Pausing for just a moment, I decided to walk home. Humiliation and confusion rose like waves inside me. Riding back with Mia wasn't a good idea right now, and she had coerced me to leave my car at home. The only other people I knew in town were Ashland, Bette and Matthews. It didn't seem appropriate to call any of them.

Eventually, anger fueled my stride. I didn't think much about walking by myself until I reached the end of the street. Dauphin Street had been busy and well-lit, but the surrounding side streets were lined with oaks that kept them shadowy. Discreetly, I slid my hand in my purse and felt for my phone just in case I needed it. But really, what was I going to do with a cell phone? Other than a catcall from a passing car and the occasional fellow pedestrian, nothing happened. I climbed the stairs to my apartment and unlocked the door. I was met with a blast of cool air. The new air conditioning unit was working beautifully.

My phone dinged—a message from Mia, but I didn't bother opening it. My heart said something was wrong, but I couldn't put my finger on it. Instead of checking in with my old "friend," I typed in Ashland's cell number and sent him a message with shaking fingers. It simply said, "How is your weekend looking?" with a smiley face. Not a minute later, he texted me back, "Great! Dinner tomorrow night?" I tapped in, "Sounds great. 7pm okay?" I got a smiley face back. "Oh, Lord, what am I doing?" I groaned as I threw the phone on the bed. "Am I actually going to date the boss?"

It was still early for me, and I couldn't go to sleep without investigating the journal I had smuggled from work. I kicked off my shoes, slid into my pajamas and snuggled into the soft cushioned chair next to my bed. It was deep and perfect for curling up in a ball. I flipped on the lamp and took the book in my hands. I examined it cover to cover. It was a leather-bound journal with an engraved monogram in the center. The letters were faded—might have been a "C" or maybe even an "O" or a "G," but I knew whose it was. I opened the cover and confirmed it: *Miss Calpurnia Christine Cottonwood.*

She had a neat, slanted penmanship. The faded letters looked light brown and were almost gone in other places. I thought about putting on my gloves, but I wanted to feel the book, feel connected to her. With a deep breath, I opened the book and walked into her world...

Chapter 11

April 20, 1850

Dear Diary,

Mrs. White had her puppies all over the bottom step of the staircase. I suspect she was trying to carry herself up the spiral staircase to my room but the climb was simply too much for her and her enormous belly. I am Thankful that it was Hooney who found the scattered litter and not my father or someone else who may have been tempted to drown them in the river. I am happy to report that the new family is safely ensconced in my armoire. What a sight to see all those precious, white faces in my old hatbox! I expect they will call the space home for a while, at least for a month or so.

Today, I prayed in earnest that Mother's baby would arrive soon. I'm loath to name the baby "sister" or "brother," as I hear from the slaves that this is bad luck. I prayed extra last night to break any curses I may have spoken over it in the past. How wonderfully entertaining it will be to have a sweet-smelling baby to sing to and share my stories with! (Hooney snickered at me and said, "Babies is a lot of things, but sweet-smelling ain't one of them." I rolled my eyes at her and got censured by Mother.) Honestly, the True and Genuine Reason for my prayer was for Mother. This will be her fourth try at having a son and Heir for my father, with thus far no fair results except for me. As I am surely to marry soon to whomever pleases my father's fancy, an heir will certainly be needed, and no girl either. Mr. Cottonwood wants a strong, strapping son to take the reins of Seven Sisters, not a disappointing, spinster daughter. So I pray and hope for only the best news that Mother will safely deliver a boy and that I will marry in the Fullness of Time; however, I am careful not to speak that aloud.

Dear Cousin Isla is a great comfort to me. She has a great wit and knows more dances than I and is a far better singer. She says things that make me blush and scolds the new upstairs house girl constantly. I do reprimand her, but sometimes I wish I could be more like her, free and unencumbered by worry and duty. She told me her father has been long dead but her mother is my own Mother's dear sister. I have never had the occasion to meet Aunt Olivia, but I'm sure that, like Isla, she is a great beauty. It is a boon to have someone to talk with, and I will forever be in Uncle Louis' debt for bringing her to me. How often of late I have poured my heart out to her. How comforting to be assured that all will be well, that a husband, handsome and charming, will be found for me, even if I am tall, flat-chested and not musical in the least. We have pledged to marry close kin so we could be near to one another for the rest of our lives.

I had hoped to spend time with Uncle Louis today, but again he's been riding with Father. They are taking a survey of the land, the improvements to the riverfront and the extended quarters for the slaves. I have barely seen my uncle on this trip, but he assures me we shall continue our conversation as soon as possible.

Mr. Ball came to give his regards to my cousin but could not be compelled to stay for lunch, strange as that may seem. I wondered that he did not, as I've never known him to pass by a plate or bowl without dipping his hand in it. I suspected that he may have had intentions to court my cousin, but as she had no one to whom he could present his request formally, he simply dithered about without saying much of anything before excusing himself. I suspect he will return at a later time. Isla says she would rather be thrown off the top of Seven Sisters than be courted by or married to Reginald Ball. I had to laugh, but of course I did scold her for such a foolish notion.

April 21, 1850

Dear Diary,

What a blissful, delightful day! This morning, I received three calling cards, one belonging to Captain David Garrett! How happy I am! Although I was not able to formally greet my guest, Cousin Isla assures me that he asked after my health and well-being multiple times. And since he "Could not speak to the lady himself," he chose to write me a note...

> *Miss Cottonwood,*
>
> *It pleases me to thank you once again for your kindness toward me during my hour of need. Truly I have not seen such great hospitality as the cordiality I received at Seven Sisters. I feel ashamed that you had to rescue me and that I was not rescuing you, dear lady. I pray that we shall meet again and soon so that I may properly show my gratitude toward you and your family.*
>
> *Your faithful friend,*
>
> *David Garrett, Captain*

Words cannot express the joy I felt receiving this note from the Captain. How I nearly fainted when I read it! Cousin Isla assures me that he trembled while he wrote, hoping to convey his deepest thanks without offending in an unseemly manner. She told me that she encouraged him to speak honestly, to confess his true heart in the matter. Although his written message was succinct, Cousin Isla assures me of the deep levels of sincerity he displayed. I feel sure that somehow, some way, I shall see the Captain again and give him my equally solicitous esteem. I took the liberty of returning his note with my own:

> *Dear Captain Garrett,*
>
> *Thank you for your kind words. You are most welcome for the care that we provided you. I encourage you to make yourself available to my father, Mr. Jeremiah Cottonwood, at your convenience, sir, so that we may talk further.*
>
> *Kind regards,*
>
> *C. Cottonwood*

How I labored over the note! I tuck it inside my gown every day, hoping for the opportunity to present it to my new friend, with all discretion, of course.

April 25, 1850

Dear Diary,

How can I describe to you the utter depths of my misery? All the joy of life has left us as the search continues for dear Uncle Louis. All of his effects remain carefully stored in his rooms, but alas, we have no word of his whereabouts since these many days past. What an event it had been, Father and Uncle Louis participating in loud and raucous debate, one that echoed through the house and even up the staircase. I had seen the horses ride up the dusty lane but thought nothing of it when another left shortly after. There was always a commotion when menfolk are about, and plenty had been around for days, except for Captain Garrett.

To listen more closely, I decided to peek out my door and found my mother swaying at the top of the stairs, looking as pale as a beaten sheet. "Mother, why are you standing here?" I said. "Come, dearest, you should not be here in the draft." I looked down to see her gowns stained red, and blood also dotted the carpeted floor. Her bleeding had come, and no one was to be found! I screamed to see the blood, so much blood. And in a flash, Hooney came upstairs to see what was amiss. She said something in a language I did not understand and ordered me to help her get Mother back to her bedchamber. I caught Muncie peering up the stairs, concerned for me, I'm sure, but I waved him back. Since he was a "man" now, my Father said, "He has no place on the top floor, and I'll whip the hide off him if he comes back." I believed him.

As much as we tried to coax her, Mother would not speak to us but only stared off into space, like someone who was locked in a dream. I cried, "Mother, Mother, what is wrong?" I patted her hands, rubbing them furiously, but she didn't see me. "Now, look," Hooney said to me in a stern voice, "You go down them stairs and tell Stokes to send for the doctor. He should never have left the other day—and then go tell your Father—or better still, your Uncle Louis—that Mrs. Cottonwood is in a bad way. Send one of them girls up here too—I need some clean clothes and water. Now, go on! Get going, Miss!" I did what I was told and scurried down the stairs like a madwoman. Unable to find Uncle Louis in the parlor or the Blue Room, I sprinted to my Father's study and told him the urgent news. He set down his whiskey glass and rushed passed me, looking like a ghost, his face drawn with concern and confusion. How I felt for him in that moment! I could not find Stokes, and I noticed that Early, my father's constant companion and slave, was also missing. But I did find Muncie, who nodded and left right away to request the doctor's presence. Dear Muncie!

That was many days ago, and I am sad to report that the baby quickly passed from this life on into heaven, where my other siblings waited for her with a pair of wings. At least that is what the priest told me. Another daughter, another disappointment for my father. I had not been present when she slid into this world, I imagine in a pool of deathly blood, but I had dreamed of a baby crying in the night. I was supremely surprised to learn that it had indeed been a dream, as the sound was very life-like to me. Mother was still not speaking; Hooney says she only grunted a little when the baby, I will call her Angelique, came forth. There would be no funeral for baby Angelique, only a quiet sliding of the stone door and a quick deposit of a tiny bundle of forgotten life on a cold slab.

To bring further sorrow, Uncle Louis remains gone from Seven Sisters. The Sheriff rummaged through all of his accoutrements, papers and personal effects but found no clue of where my Uncle may have ventured. Isla and I have been inconsolable, crying and praying constantly for his safe return.

I pray all day and night that my Mother will return to me. I miss her gentle hands and bright conversation. All our happy days together are too few, and I plead constantly with God to give us more. Why would she be in such a state? What horrible thing did she see or imagine that frightened her, down to her soul?

Oh, Diary, what shall happen to us all?

I wiped fat tears from my eyes, careful not to stain the delicate pages. I read the passages over and over again. There was more—much more—but I needed time to process all that I had learned. I looked at the clock; it was close to midnight. I uncurled in the round chair, slid the journal into a manila envelope and replaced it in my bag. I flipped off the light and slid into my cool sheets, thankful again for my kind landlord. It took me a long time to fall asleep, and when I did, I could swear I heard a baby cry.

Chapter 12

My day began with an impromptu breakfast with Bette in her comfy kitchen. My thoughtful landlady had prepared us praline-pecan French toast with fresh fruit and sausage patties. I have to admit that until I met Bette, I wasn't much of a breakfast girl. But she definitely made me a believer. I was glad I was starting the day so pleasantly, since I knew I had some unpleasant things ahead of me. At least I had a date with Ashland to look forward to and, of course, all of Seven Sisters to explore. Calpurnia was on my mind heavily; it was so tempting to spend all night diving into that journal, but I had to keep life balanced. It was dangerous to think about the past so much that it took up all my present. I had learned that lesson the hard way.

"Thank you for fixing the air conditioning. The new unit is working like a charm, and I slept great last night."

Bette smiled at me warmly through perfectly applied lipstick. She had a soft, ivory complexion and even whiter teeth. She was attractive, and I imagined she had been striking in her prime. "That's no problem, no problem at all. This isn't the old days. We can't sleep without air conditioning in Mobile. I don't know if it's gotten hotter or if we're just spoiled now. I remember when the only AC around here was at the library. I sure spent quite a few summers reading ridiculous love stories when I was young." She wasted no time serving me generous helpings of everything. "I know you have to get going soon, but I'm just dying to know how the restoration is coming along. My sisters and I, at the Historical Society, that is, are all atwitter about the commotion. I heard the grounds are looking better and better."

I nodded, unable to resist digging my fork into the fluffy French toast. "I wish I could give you the inside scoop on the remodeling, but Matthews has made it pretty clear that I have to keep quiet about the details." I felt genuinely sad about keeping all the excitement to myself, but I couldn't break the confidentiality clause in my contract.

She patted my hands; hers was soft and cool. "I don't want you to get into trouble. That Hollis Matthews is a strange bird, isn't he? Okay, okay, I'll tell the ladies they will just have to wait." She sipped on her coffee. I loved her coffee cups, fine white china with a gold rim. I appreciated that she brought out the good dishes for me.

Maybe I was just missing having a friend to talk to, but I felt like I could trust Bette. I blurted out, "I can tell you something, though, something we found that wasn't in the house…" I whispered, "We found the old Cottonwood mausoleum."

She set her cup and saucer down with a clink. "No…oh my goodness. That is something, isn't it? I bet it was hidden under all those vines and bushes right there on the property. There's no telling what you will find on that land." Her hand flew to her chest. "Oh, I wish I could see it!"

I remembered the pictures on my phone, so I dug it out of my purse and tapped the screen. "Here. I have a few pictures right here." I did not think it wrong to share with her the details I knew about the cemetery—that was public knowledge. Besides, I hoped that Bette might know something about Calpurnia, so I had to ask. "Ashland was telling me about that missing heiress, Calpurnia—the one who disappeared before the Civil War. Have you ever heard of her?"

Bette dug a pair of reading glasses out of a nearby drawer and was peering at the pictures attentively. She looked at me with wide eyes. "Oh, yes, most everyone in Mobile knows about her. But I imagine Ashland could tell you all about that. His mother was obsessed with finding Calpurnia Cottonwood. The late Mrs. Stuart was a very intelligent woman, something of a scholar before she married Mr. Stuart. But in the end, it became a kind of obsession with her. Some people say that the Cottonwood girl ran off with a military man. But I don't know, they didn't really do that sort of thing in those days. Others say that one of the slaves probably killed her and buried her on the plantation."

Bette looked up from the phone and put one arm of her glasses in her mouth, trying to drum up a forgotten thought. "Now, I've also heard that old Mr. Cottonwood did her in when he was drunk. That man, by all accounts, never passed up the chance to tilt a bottle. And he gambled his wife's money away...well, much of it, anyway. But that was so long ago, it's hard to know what the truth is and what is simply plain old rumors. You know what they say, 'Nothing makes a Southern story better than a stretch of time and a few glasses of gin.'" Bette pursed her lips and shook her head; her curls bounced around her face. She handed me back my phone, too polite to ask for copies of the pictures. I was thankful, as I'd have had to say no.

I asked, "Tell me about Mrs. Stuart. What was she like, and why did she become so obsessed with Miss Cottonwood's fate?"

"Emily was her name, Ashland's mother. She was from a very fine family from the northern part of the county. Remember? She was a Hunter, and later she discovered the Hunters were a part of the Beaumonts, one of Mobile's oldest families." After dropping that bomb on me, Bette kept talking. "Emily was tall and athletic; she beat me more than once in tennis, but she was very much a lady. I remember when she first got married—oh, she was the talk of Mobile. So lovely in that big old chiffon gown. You know, back in the '6os, it wasn't a wedding gown if it didn't have umpteen ruffles."

I nudged the conversation along. I would circle back to the Beaumont comment in a minute or two. I didn't want to be rude. "You say you two played tennis together?" I poured more syrup on my French toast; I wasn't really hungry any longer, but I desperately wanted this conversation to continue.

"Our husbands were members of the same country club; we played doubles a few times. His name was Gerald. I wasn't crazy about Mr. Gerald Stuart—he liked to talk over her too much. Sometimes I would ask her a question, about her son or something else, and he'd answer for her. That drove me crazy! She did love that boy, though. He was her everything."

I took a sip of my coffee and ignored the clock. It was getting late, but the conversation was riveting. "So is Ashland an only child?"

"Yes. I think she wanted to have more—she did love children, but he was the only one. When her husband died, I half thought she'd marry again. Mr. Stuart had a cousin that she seemed especially fond of—handsome man, can't remember his name, but nothing happened. However, Mr. Stuart left her an extremely wealthy woman, as well he should have, as unkind as he was at times. Drive through Mobile, and you'll see the Stuart name all over the place."

My phone dinged. I glanced at it and saw Terrence Dale's name pop up. I hit the ignore button.

Bette didn't let my interrupting phone stop her story. "When she bought Seven Sisters, we thought for sure she'd restore that place, but she didn't. I hate to speak ill of the dead, but I think the poor thing kind of lost her marbles. All that money and that sweet boy, and she spent all her time trying to find that girl who was long dead."

"When you say Beaumont, you mean that Emily Stuart née Hunter was a descendant of the Beaumonts. As in the family of Christine Beaumont, who married Jeremiah Cottonwood?"

"The very one!" She looked supremely delighted to be the one to tell me this news. "That means that Ashland is also related to the Cottonwoods." She smiled, rose from her chair and started picking up plates and dishes. I jumped in to help, wanting her to continue but not wanting to push.

"Oh, thank you," she said. "I'm sorry I'm dithering on. You'll have to excuse me. I'm just so excited that the big old house is going to get the treatment it needs."

"I'm happy to listen. It's nice to hear what the local community thinks and what stories you can share with me." I added warm water and soap to the sink. "I'll wash these while you put the food away. I don't know where anything goes."

"Thank you! I didn't invite you over to wash the dishes, but obviously you were taught manners growing up."

I smiled as I washed the glasses and cups. "You say she lost her marbles. What do you mean?"

"Well, she started hanging around a different crowd, a lot of psychics and mediums and such. She even tried to get the Historical Society to sit in on one of those séance things; you know to boost the energy or some such. I told her I couldn't do that, I was a Baptist!" She laughed heartily, and I did too. "I think my friend Cynthia Dowd did, but she didn't want to talk about it. Poor Emily gave so much money to those charlatans. In the end, all the money in the world couldn't help her find that girl. Anyway, Emily got pneumonia. Poor Ashland found her in the garden, nearly dead. She died just a few days later."

I felt a surge of sympathy for Ashland to have lost both parents so young. Still, he appeared to be coping with life fairly well. He was educated, committed to restoring important historical sites in the city and, of course, independently wealthy. That was the legacy his mother left him.

"When you can, Carrie Jo, when it's allowed...will you come speak to the Society? We would love to hear from you. Maybe tell us something about the process or how you got started in the preservation field?"

"Sure, I'd be happy to. It will probably be a few weeks before I can, though." I gave her a bright smile and dried my hands off. "Looks like I'd better go; time is getting away from me." I grabbed my purse and phone and said goodbye.

I left Bette's feeling happy, having found out a little more about Ashland and Calpurnia. Did I believe a slave killed her? No, but Mr. Cottonwood was certainly a likely suspect. The Hometown Donut Shop was on the way, and I decided to stop and pick up a few pastries for the crew. We'd have at least six of us working inside the house today, not to mention all those that would work outside. A couple dozen donuts would be a nice treat. I pulled into the packed parking lot, grabbing the last spot. Fortunately, the line wasn't long. I stepped up to the counter and ordered three dozen plain donuts and two cartons of orange juice.

The little diner was bustling; even the counter was full. I surveyed the crowd and locked eyes with William. He didn't say anything to me, but he raised a foam cup as a greeting and then quickly turned his attention back to his donut. *Hmm...I guess this is how it's going to be now.* The perky server brought me my order, and I clumsily stacked up the boxes and tried to get out the door without losing any. William was on his feet in an instant, pushing the door open for me. He followed me to my car and opened the rear door. I slid the donuts in and arranged the juice cartons on the floor. "Thank you."

"I want to apologize for last night." William ran his hand through his dark hair. "I was wrong to go off on you like that. I guess, well, I guess I was really hoping for a different conversation."

"I'm sorry too. I should have had this conversation with you before I left, but to be honest, I was a coward. I like you, and I value your friendship. I wasn't fair to you."

He tucked a wisp of my hair behind my ear to stop it from whipping my face in the morning breeze. "Always worried about someone else, CJ. It's okay, I promise." As I drove away, I wiped a tear off my cheek. *I did like him only as a friend. Right?*

The crews were working outside, setting the grounds free from choking vines and gnarly underbrush. Junk trees, like old "popcorn" trees, were being cut down. But of course, no one was touching the live oaks. Rotten wooden siding was being replaced, and I could see the beginnings of Mobile's newest living museum come to life.

I waved one of the crew over and handed off two of the boxes of donuts and one carton of juice. I headed indoors with the remaining goodies, feeling confident and happy. Inside were Mia, Chip, three interns from the University of South Alabama and, of course, Matthews. Somewhere in the house, I could hear TD working on wood. Except for the finishing touches, the Blue Room and a small side room were nearly completely restored and ready for use. The rest of the house would be restored in sections, with careful attention to detail. I could see TD had placed heavy plastic over the doorway to the Blue Room, since the door had not been hung yet. That would keep dust from collecting on our equipment. I was happy to feel cool air in our room. Someone had brought in a tower AC unit. *What a brilliant idea!* I was relieved to hear the upstairs was cool as well.

Seven Sisters was a unique project compared to the few others I had worked on. Those had involved off-site planning projects, and here, we had the opportunity to work right in the environment. I would be deciding on how the home would be restored and what we would be presenting to the public. I felt the weight of that responsibility even more now that I had seen firsthand what life here had been like. I took the donuts and juice to a little table we had set up in the Blue Room. I opened the box and set out some paper cups.

Matthews was the first to arrive at the table. "Thank you, Carrie Jo."

"My pleasure. Have you heard anything from C. M. Lowell on those mantelpieces? I know it's only been a few weeks, but TD is going to need to install them before they cut the molding for the rest of the room."

"Right. I'll put a call in to them this morning. I'd forgotten about that. I've got some leads on paintings for the two main parlors. One is pretty incredible; I emailed you photos of both of them. Don't forget, we've got boxes of paintings in the attic. And good news—we have air up there now, too. If you can't find what you want, there is plenty of room in the budget, but many of the local families are willing to allow us to use their pieces. With all credits, of course." I couldn't figure Hollis Matthews out: one minute he was cold and distant, and the next he was kind and friendly. One thing I knew for sure—he was always a man with a plan.

"Great. I'll check out those pictures and let you know. I've got some plans ready for the ladies' parlor, including a significant display of Augusta Evans books. I'll have those to you by the end of next week."

With a nod of his salt-and-pepper head, he walked away, probably off to call about those mantelpieces. I invited the interns to have a donut and took a few minutes to get to know them. There were two Rachels, Rachel Kowalski and Rachel McGhee, and James Pittman. All of them were excellent archaeological students who had earned their spots on our team. I'd Skyped with them individually before I came to Mobile, but this was the first time we'd met in person.

"Well, guys, are you ready for the grand tour? It's the same one visitors will take once the museum is open." We started in the ladies' parlor, continued on to the men's parlor and the Blue Room, and then went up the opposite side of the hall to the servants' waiting area, the music room and the ballroom. There were of course a myriad of closets and smaller rooms that wouldn't be shown to the public.

Chattering like the excited teens they were, they climbed up the spiral staircase. I stood in the hallway right where I had read about Mrs. Cottonwood bleeding over a century ago. I pointed to the bedrooms on the right and the guest rooms and private sitting room on the left. We walked through the rooms, starting with Calpurnia's, then on to the three other rooms on the same side of the hall. The hairs on my arm stood up in a few places, but I shook it off. I supposed that seeing the place I'd been reading and dreaming about was giving me the shivers. There were no strains of music or slamming doors. I breathed a sigh of relief.

"Okay, let's head back down and talk about what you'll be doing." In the Blue Room, Mia was printing off material and stapling papers together. We hadn't spoken, but I gave her a small smile and thanked her as she brought me the paperwork. "Rachel K., I've got you working on the ladies' parlor. I've sent you an email about it, but let me just show you what I want." We talked for a while, and then the interns were off to work on their tasks. I turned my attention to a more challenging task—repairing my relationship with Mia.

Chapter 13

"I know what you're going to say..." Mia immediately went into stress mode. "And you're right. I never should have interfered with you and William. I guess I thought I knew what was best for you."

We stood alone in the ladies' parlor. *How appropriate*, I thought ruefully. *The place where drama has unraveled for nearly two centuries.*

"You can't do that, Mia. You can't just apologize without hearing me out. You have to listen first. That's how friendship is supposed to work." She clamped her mouth shut and nodded as I continued. "I know I was a wreck in high school and even more of a wreck in college, but you have to stop. You can't fix me. You don't get to pick who I date. Besides, it seems to me you and William would make a better couple than he and I would—did."

"Don't you think I wanted that to happen? I was crazy about William, but all he wanted to talk about was you." Mia's eyes watered, and a tear slid down her powdered cheek. "I've liked him since freshman year, but he never so much as asked me out. We hooked up once, and that was just because he got drunk at Solomon's at the Ren Wrap Party."

"Mia..." was all I could say. I touched her arm and then dug in my pocket for a tissue. "Then why on earth would you try to get us together?"

"I wanted him to be happy. I wanted you to be happy. I don't know."

She started crying, and I hugged her. "I'm sorry. I didn't know, Mi. I wish you had told me so I could be there for you."

After a minute, Mia wiped the tears away. She jutted her chin out slightly and said, "I have something to show you." That was my friend, ever changeable. But I rarely saw her emotional.

"Sure, whatcha got?" I was happy to get off this heavy subject. I sensed that there were more feelings lurking under the surface of those pretty eyes and stylish clothes, that she still wasn't happy with me, but I wasn't sure. I *was* sure she would tell me if she wanted to talk about it.

I followed her back to the Blue Room, and she waved me over to her computer. I pulled up a chair and listened as she presented her findings on the mausoleum. "Did you know that there was once a garden here called the Moonlight Garden? Well, of course you do. You dreamed about it, right?" I made a gesture for her to lower her voice. She continued in a whisper, "Anyway, the mausoleum is located due north of the center statue of the Moonlight Garden. What's interesting is the white crosses you found around the mausoleum are arranged in the exact formation of the statues in the garden."

"So the crosses aren't grave markers?" I asked, curious about the connection.

"Could be." Mia shrugged. "But what are the odds that they would be in the exact alignment of the statues? I mean, exactly like the garden statues. Look. According to this old drawing a visiting author made here sometime at the end of the 1840s, this was the location of the Atlas statue, the god who was the father of the Pleiades. Just outside the garden was Pleione, the mother who protected the family. These crosses are all markers. I blew up the photos of the crosses you sent me. Did you notice the names engraved in them? Well, partial names. Most of the letters have been worn away." Mia pointed at the screen. "See, this is Sterope. This one is Alcyone…"

I just stared at the screen. "How could I have missed that? What does it mean?" I could see the names, but I wasn't convinced that it meant anything other than that the old Cottonwood family had an appreciation for Greek mythology.

"You're the historian," she said with a laugh. "I'm the anthropologist. You can't figure that out? It's obviously some sort of map… or something."

"I don't doubt you found something significant here, but I don't see a map yet. Tell you what, you keep working on this. Maybe later this afternoon, we can walk back to the mausoleum and take pictures of all the markers. At the very least, it would make a neat tidbit to share with visitors."

"Sure, sounds great." I could tell Mia was disappointed at my lack of excitement, but I had so much to do. Getting sidetracked by a hunch wasn't something I wanted to get mired in. I patted her on the shoulder and left her to work on her research, happy that at least we had a truce of sorts. I printed the layout proposals and went in search of TD. We needed to get on the same page with our remodel priorities. I had certain ideas and plans for the opening ceremony, which was scheduled to take place in six months. We had to make sure that at least these opening exhibits were ready to go.

The handsome contractor had been working on the ground floor earlier, but I couldn't find him. I went upstairs and saw only Rachel K., who was cataloging the contents of some of the boxes in one of the guest rooms. I waved at her and walked back toward the spiral staircase to continue my search outside, but I paused in front of Calpurnia's room.

The door was ajar and swung open easily with a gentle push of my fingertip. I stepped into the empty room and stared at the bare fireplace with the missing mantelpiece. I missed the elegant furnishings, including the armoire and mirror. I walked to the window that overlooked the driveway. In Calpurnia's day, it would have given her a lovely view of the carriageway. I touched the cool painted wall. TD had chosen a light peach for this room, which was close to the original color. The room had been an even lighter shade of pink. It was small in comparison to the others on this floor, but I loved it. I touched the window and felt the urge to sit in the wide windowsill. I closed my eyes and imagined Calpurnia sitting here, looking for some sign of David Garrett or Uncle Louis traveling up the driveway to see her.

I stayed still, half hoping I could conjure up images of the past, to see without dreaming here in this room, but it didn't happen. The chainsaws in the yard and the voices of the excited interns downstairs all traveled into the room, preventing my ears from finding the quiet they needed to truly hear. Suddenly, I could hear Rachel and James talking, and the conversation was amplified as if they were in the room with me. Rachel was excited that Professor Cooper was giving her four weeks of class credit for landing a spot on the Seven Sisters Project. James bemoaned the fact that no such courtesy had been extended to him. According to his professor, it was business as usual. And as a matter of fact, he was expected to deliver a report on his work at the mansion at the end of the semester if he wanted extra credit. I left my leather portfolio on the windowsill and crawled on the floor to the nearby cast-iron grate. It was like listening in on a telephone. I pulled my phone out of my pocket and used it as a flashlight, shining it into the dark vent. Something caught the light and glinted, but I couldn't reach it with my fingers. I made a mental note to come back with a screwdriver later. It was probably just a screw from the grate, I figured.

I wondered if this phenomenon worked in all the rooms. *Rachel and James must be below me...* I wandered from room to room, checking for sound from the grates. I heard music playing from the ladies' parlor, maybe Tori Amos. Chip was talking to someone on the phone in the men's parlor; it sounded like his mother again. Poor Chip. *No wonder he was always leaving the room to talk on the phone.* I could hear Mia and Matthews having a heated discussion from the grate in the Blue Room.

"Have some patience. If what you say is true, that she's dreaming already, then there's no reason to hurry. Let's wait and see what happens." I knew that angry voice; it was Matthews. The next voice was inaudible, but I could tell that he was talking to a woman. *"What does that matter?"* Matthews sounded aggravated. *"Who cares what he thinks? Listen, stick to the plan and stop improvising and scheming. Just do your job and keep your mouth shut. Too many people know about it already."*

"Don't think....because...I'm not one to...play with me and you'll be surprised." I was sure that was Mia's voice. My heart pounded in my chest. Somehow, some way, I was being betrayed.

"Carrie Jo, what about this?" Rachel K. was standing in the doorway, probably wondering what I was doing lying on the floor. She held up the music box that had played its strange solo the day before. "Looks like we need a key to play it. It wasn't in the box."

I got off the floor and dusted myself off. I faked a smile and took the box from her, giving it a cursory glance. "I'm not sure what to do with this stuff. Looks kind of modern. Thanks, Rachel. I'll figure it out."

"Okay. Are you all right?"

"Yes, I was just...yes, I'm fine. Thanks. Listen, don't forget to copy me on the list, okay?"

The perky intern bopped down the hall, her dark ponytail swinging. I decided to play it cool. Nobody knew that I knew anything. *Let's keep it that way. Put your game face on, Carrie Jo.*

I went back to Calpurnia's room to get my portfolio from the windowsill, but it wasn't there anymore. It was lying on the floor. The pictures had slid out of the unzipped book and now lay in an unorganized pile. I set the box down and squatted to pick up the papers, restacking them neatly.

From this angle, I could see into the vent. That was no screw from the grate—it was the key! The tiny silver key for the music box. How had it gotten in there? With a rush of emotions, I crawled to the grate and tested it by pulling on the edges. Nope, it wasn't going to budge. I felt in my pocket and found my small utility blade. I used it like a screwdriver. The screws came up more easily than I thought they would. In just a minute, I lifted the grate and reached for the tiny key. I shoved it into my pocket and replaced the grate, racing to get the screws in as I heard TD calling for me. I met him in the hallway, and we took our scheduled tour. I deposited the music box Rachel gave me on my desk and left Mia in the Blue Room without saying a word. I had a lot to think about and an endlessly growing list of mysteries to solve. To top it all off, I had a date with Ashland Stuart in just a few hours.

Like the girl from long ago who intrigued me so, I could feel the events of life swelling up around me. Destiny was unfolding its complicated pattern, and I was a mere thread in the tapestry.

Chapter 14

Ashland insisted on picking me up that night. As I carefully shampooed my hair (that bump still hurt) and later ransacked my closet for something suitable, I reviewed my trip to Mobile thus far. As it stood, I had a sore leg, a bump on my head and handprints on my ankle, and I had probably lost a good friend—no, two good friends—for an undetermined reason. One of those friends *might* also be betraying me somehow with a man I found repulsive and crafty.

On the upside, I was dreaming more clearly than ever before, I had the job I always wanted and I was going to spend some time with Ashland Stuart. I was looking forward to getting to know him better. He seemed intelligent and quick-witted, and he was of course very handsome. I suddenly regretted putting all my "date" clothes in storage in Charleston. In the end, I opted for white jeans, a blue and white striped top and navy blue flats. I looked at myself in the mirror. *Hmm...jeans aren't too snug. Okay.* I pulled my hair into a low ponytail at my left shoulder and dabbed on some makeup. *Well, he said I should dress casual, so I am!*

Ashland knocked on my door a few minutes early, but thankfully I was ready to go. As I climbed into his car, I waved goodbye to Bette.

"You look great!" He gave me an appreciative smile. I couldn't believe I was doing this, going out on a date with my boss. He was out of my league, really, but he had asked. I tried not to think about the why too much.

"Thanks. You did say casual. Where are we going?" I fastened the seat belt and put my small purse down by my feet.

"Do you like seafood?" The car slid through the tunnel that led to the causeway across Mobile Bay. "This area has some of the best. You'll never have shrimp like Gulf shrimp, I promise!"

My stomach grumbled, and I was happy to chit chat with him. "Oh yes, I love all types of seafood. Are we going to a restaurant?"

"No, I thought we could have dinner on my boat." The sun had fully set, and the stars shone brilliantly over the bay. I gasped as a meteor whizzed across the sky. "Look at that!" I squealed with delight, rolling down the window so I could see the sky better.

"See, I've even arranged for entertainment." Ashland laughed and rolled his window down too. A few more flew by—we were in a genuine meteor shower. We crossed the bay in a few minutes and pulled up to the Fairhope Marina. "I've never been on a boat before," I confessed.

"No worries. It's a big boat, and the seas don't look too rough tonight, so it should be pretty smooth. We won't go out far, just outside the bay, and then we'll have dinner. I've cooked something special for you."

"Gee, I hope you didn't go to any trouble, Ashland."

He looked at me thoughtfully. "That's nice."

"What's nice?"

"You calling me Ashland. I like that." He stepped out of the car and went to open my door. I was finding that he was a true southern gentleman. I liked *that*.

"Do you trust me?" He gave me a wide smile. *God, he's handsome!*

I nodded once, accepted his hand and stepped out of the car. I promised myself I would not trip this time. We walked down the planks to the boat, and my eyes widened. It *was* a big boat. As a matter of fact, it was the largest one in the marina, as near as I could tell. I could hear the tinkling of glasses and people laughing. Apparently lots of people had planned to watch the stars fall tonight.

I chuckled at the boat's name, "Happy Go Lucky." We stepped aboard, and Ashland gave me a tour. It had several rooms, an ample kitchen and a full-size bathroom complete with Jacuzzi tub. I felt like I was in an old episode of the Lifestyles of the Rich and Famous with Robin Leach. Well, okay, maybe not quite that luxurious, but it was close.

Ashland led me to the dinner table he had set up on the deck. I could see that he had a server waiting for us, who held out my chair and handed me a fine cloth napkin. Ashland's eyes twinkled as he opened a bottle of champagne. The server brought us covered dishes; with a flair, he removed the covers. They were plates of cold, boiled shrimp with cocktail and tartar sauce. In a few minutes, we were served West Indies Salad, stuffed flounder and cocktails.

"My compliments to the chef," I told the server. He looked from me to Ashland.

Ashland grinned. "I'm the chef."

"No! You can cook? Hidden talents. Thank you for going to the trouble of doing all this for tonight.... Oh, look; here comes some more stars..." We made a toast to the stars, and eventually neither of us could eat anymore. We washed our hands and settled down on a cushion at the bow to watch the skies. That night was the Leonid Meteor Shower. It would be ending soon, but I wanted our time together to go on and on.

Ashland sighed. "The stars are so beautiful tonight. You know, in the winter, you can see the Pleiades—the Seven Sisters—in the Northern Hemisphere. Actually, there are nine stars, but only seven can be viewed with the naked eye. They say they're dying stars and will fade away soon."

"Mia mentioned something about that to me the other day. She said she believed those white crosses we found were actually markers because they had the stars' names on them. They were pretty faded, though; I didn't even see them until she pointed them out to me. She's convinced it's a map to something." I sipped my cocktail absently, staring up at the stars.

"A map to what? Did she say?" Ashland was staring at me. I felt a surge of worry, but I wasn't sure why.

"No, she didn't. I told her those markers didn't mean anything. They could just be names of children who died at birth, or even markers for family pets. I mean, who knows, really?"

He looked serious; his jaw was clenched a little. He set his drink down on the side table. "I think it's time I told you a little about my mother and why I'm restoring the old house. You see, my mother's family were descendants of the Cottonwoods—and the Beaumonts, even though they later moved to the northern part of the county. My mother loved that old house, and she spent a lot of time there in her last years."

"Bette, my landlady, she's with the Historical Society, and she told me a little about that." I wanted to let him know he didn't need to dive into painful memories just to fill me in. I wanted to save him some heartache.

He smirked. "Well, people do talk."

"Oh, no! Bette isn't like that at all. She knew your mother, and she really liked her. She didn't say anything negative." *Except that she had lost her marbles.*

"That's good to know. You probably know that my mother was obsessed with finding the heiress, the Cottonwood girl. She did everything in her power to locate her, even hired detectives and researchers to follow the leads she uncovered. Nothing ever came to fruition. My mother's theory was that the girl was killed because of a treasure, a necklace that was worth a remarkable amount of money. Don't get me wrong; the Beaumonts and Cottonwoods were wealthy, at least before the war, but Mr. Cottonwood had made some bad investments and had done who knows what with his fortune. And he had his eye on his wife's. Mrs. Cottonwood's brother wasn't willing to see his sister's inheritance squandered by a man he hated. So, with her consent, he took her fortune out of the bank and put it all in a small collection of jewelry. She could keep her money in her own hands that way. It was the only way women back then could."

"Wow, that explains so much."

He looked like he didn't know what to make of that comment, but he continued. "According to the local historians, Mrs. Cottonwood invested the money in diamonds and sapphires. The largest piece in the collection was a necklace called The Seven Sisters. It was seven sapphires, with two diamonds, set in the swirling formation of the stars. It was quite the showpiece. She was never seen wearing it, but in her will, she left it to her only living heir, Calpurnia Cottonwood. It was my mother's theory that after Mrs. Cottonwood died, Mr. Cottonwood killed the daughter or sent her away so he could get his hands on it. At least, that was her theory."

I didn't know what to say or think for a minute. I said in a quiet voice, "Is that why I'm here? You want me to find this treasure?" I felt a keen sense of disappointment. Had I been wrong to come to Mobile? Had I been wrong to accept his dinner invitation?

"Oh, no, not at all. I'm just telling you about the 'treasure' because I felt like you needed to know. Please believe me when I tell you that I didn't hire you to find a necklace. I want to build a museum, one that helps the city and the region remember its past. I feel like I owe that to my mother, to my family. I don't want you to find the necklace, but I am asking you this: help me find out what happened to Calpurnia. I can't explain it, but I need to know."

He reached out and covered my hand with his. The stars fell around us, some skidding across the sky like quiet angels falling into the faraway sea. Others simply appeared and disappeared, leaving nothing behind but a moment of awe and brilliance. Ashland leaned toward me, one hand on mine, the other on my cheek. I closed my eyes as he kissed me. And I kissed him back. His lips were soft and warm, and I could have stayed like that forever.

As I pulled away slowly, I whispered, "Yes, I'll help you find her."

Chapter 15

We spent hours talking about the house. How we would move the flow of traffic through the home, what rooms we should include on the tour and how much parking we could accommodate. We talked about the mantelpieces that were finally delivered and when we would begin reconstruction on the kitchen house. We didn't kiss again, but we held hands and watched the stars. Eventually, I looked at my watch. "Oh my goodness, it's after midnight!"

"I'd better get you home. I had no idea it was so late. Hold on just a minute." After he left, I walked along the boat and watched the moonlight dance off the water. This had been the perfect date—stars, water and Ashland's sensual kiss. I ignored the nagging, suspicious voice that said he was just using me. That he really did want me to treasure-hunt for him. *Shut up! Is it so hard to believe he likes me?*

In a half hour, we were driving back across the causeway. Jazz played quietly on the radio. "Thank you for a lovely evening, Ashland. It was breathtaking to see those stars falling."

"The evening isn't over yet, is it?" he asked me playfully. I blushed, glad that he couldn't see me in the dark. I didn't know how to answer him.

We exited off the interstate and on to Government Street. I was taking mental notes, learning how the city was laid out. Government would take us right to my apartment. From the exit, I looked down over the city and easily spotted Seven Sisters lit up like a Christmas tree.

"Ashland? Who's working at the house tonight? TD or Hollis Matthews, maybe?"

"Nobody that I know of. Nobody's supposed to be, anyway."

"Well, someone left some lights on. Can we stop by real quick, just to check it out? We just got that shipment of Pena ceiling medallions in, and I would hate for anything to come up missing."

"Yes, we'd better." We turned on the private road, surprised to see three cars lined up in the driveway. I recognized one of them.

"What the hell?" Ashland was clearly not amused.

"Hold on, that's Mia's car. I didn't give her permission to be here. What in the world is going on?" Maybe she came to see the mausoleum in the middle of the night, but I wished she had told me she was going to be here.

It was eerily quiet, and fog was rolling up from off the river. The house sparkled with light against the murky backdrop of mist.

Before I could say anything, Ashland was on his phone. "Matthews? Call me when you get this message." He then called the police, who told him to wait for an officer to arrive.

Ashland and I looked at one another, and it was clear neither of us wanted to wait. We got out of the car and headed for the house. The path to the front door was much easier to navigate now that the azaleas had been cut back and thinned. But the sidewalk was broken in some places, and I nearly tripped over a crack. Ashland reached out to steady me and didn't let go. The satyr leered at us as we passed, his tongue poking out perpetually, mocking the unwanted visitors to his lost garden. I shivered.

"Do you hear singing?" I asked Ashland as we climbed the steps, still holding hands. He nodded but didn't say a word. I could see he was angry. I wondered if he knew who the other cars belonged to. What could they be doing here at one in the morning? Yes, someone was singing softly, a chant or something. A soft female voice whimpered and cried. It was coming from upstairs.

We stood at the bottom of the stairs, and I had a mental flash of Muncie peering up the spiral staircase and Calpurnia waving him away. "Go back," she had mouthed to him. *Is that what we should do?* With a wave, Ashland told me to follow him. We walked upstairs, unable to avoid the squeaking and complaining wood that echoed after every few steps. But nobody came out to see what the noise was.

The light at the end of the hallway was on, but the singing—no, the chanting—was coming from the first room on the right, Calpurnia's room! The wooden door hung open, and from the slit of light we could see three figures sitting on the floor of the mostly empty room. There were candles burning, and I could smell incense.

Ashland was ready to storm into the room, but I held him back for a moment. I heard a girl's voice whimper and cry, "*Mon dieu, aidez moi.*" She repeated the phrase over and over again.

Then I heard Mia's voice. "What do you need help with? Who are you?"

"*Mon dieu, aidez moi!*" The girl's voice was more intense, getting louder.

Ashland looked at me, his blue eyes dark and furious. "There's a child in there!" My eyes widened with surprise. I followed him as he pushed the door open. "What the hell is going on in here?"

A breeze blew past me, sending chills down my spine, and the candles flickered and shook. Mia sprung to her feet angrily. "Wait!" she cried out. She was with a large black man in a gray suit. I didn't know him. Unfortunately, I knew the other man with them.

"William?" I nearly shrieked. He looked away, ashamed, and I saw a tiny smile on Mia's lips.

The man in the gray suit said, "I am Henri Devecheaux. I am here at the request of Mia. I do hope that is all right. It was not my intention to break any law." His voice was deep and rich.

"Where's the child?" Ashland demanded.

Mia laughed at him. "What child? There is no child here—well, not anymore."

I stepped forward. "Who was just here? We heard a child crying." She didn't say a word and just stared at me. "Is this some sort of game, Mia?"

"This was never a game to me, Carrie Jo. Never, not for one minute. You know why I'm here. Don't pretend you don't." Her voice was calm.

"I have no idea why you're here, Mia. I never gave you permission to be here. I don't even know how you got in." Ashland watched us carefully; I supposed he was trying to figure out what was going on. So was I.

"Does your date know about your secret power? Does he know how you communicate with the dead?" Her lip curled. I couldn't believe what she was saying. "Does he know what you really are?"

"Mia! Why are you doing this?" I felt confused, angry. I wanted to strike out at her, but I didn't.

From the window, I could see police lights below. I took a deep breath. "I suggest you go downstairs and explain yourself to the police." My hand was shaking as I reached for the nearest candle and blew it out. William paused when he passed me but wouldn't look at me. Henri excused himself and apologized again, but Mia said nothing as she left us. We were left standing in the room with a few candles and some chalk drawings on the floor. I grabbed a nearby work cloth and wiped them away.

It felt wrong in here now. Not peaceful or happy, just wrong and troubled. Like Mia. What had happened to make her hate me so?

"Carrie Jo? What was she talking about? Didn't you hear a child in here?"

I knew I would have to tell him everything, and soon. I just didn't think I could do it tonight.

"I did hear a child's voice, but it was probably one of them," I explained away. "Trying to have some fun with us. They must have known we were climbing up those stairs because they squeaked so bad. I don't know what's happened with Mia." My hair stood on end. I was pretty sure we had heard the voice of a child, one who had lived here long ago, but I knew that it was not Calpurnia or Muncie.

"What was she talking about? Are you some sort of psychic?" He spit the words out; I knew how much he disliked psychics.

"No, I'm not psychic, not at all. I never asked her to do...this, whatever this is. And I promise to tell you everything, but let's talk to the police now. I need to get any keys she may have stolen and change computer passwords before we leave." I paused at the door. "I'm sorry, Ashland."

He put his hand on my shoulder and pulled me to him. We stayed like that for a moment, remembering how perfect the evening had been before all this. "You do know we have to fire her, right?"

"Let's go do it now."

The police asked us a few questions, but Ashland did not want to press any charges. He wanted to keep the incident out of the papers. I pulled Mia aside. "I don't know what kind of stunt you were trying to pull, Mia, but it has gotten you fired. I hope it was worth it."

Her dark eyes were full of emotion, but I couldn't fathom what she might be thinking. She left with William, and Henri made it a point to personally apologize to Ashland again for the intrusion. He handed me his card and left us to finish up the police report.

Once we were alone, we went from room to room, checking closets and doors. I think Ashland needed to make sure there really was no child here. I didn't need to look. It was after three now, and the stillness outside began to creep indoors. It was the sort of stillness that promised lurking danger. I don't know if I was just tired or if I was seeing things, but the shadows began to move erratically. I heard every creak in the old house. I didn't like it.

"Ashland, let's go. Will you take me home?" Fear crept over me. I had the overwhelming sense that we weren't alone in the house, that someone or something was watching us. I wanted to run away. Far, far away. I walked out on to the porch, feeling some relief. Ashland flipped off the last light and joined me.

"Well, this will be a date you'll never forget." I laughed at that but quickly walked to his car. I wanted to go home and climb into my bed. I wanted to forget Mia and William. Forget the uneasiness I was feeling.

"I know I said I would tell you everything, but it's really late—or really early, depending on how you look at it. Can we talk tomorrow? Maybe have lunch or something?" I needed to think about what I would say to him, and I was so tired that I might not make sense. This was going to sound crazy enough as it was.

"Yes, that would be great. I'm exhausted too." He started the car. "I just need to know...can I trust you?"

I looked at him squarely in his handsome face. "Yes, Ashland, you can trust me." We didn't talk on the ride home. Three turns, and I was at my front door. I waved goodbye and stepped inside. I kicked off my shoes, locked the door and stripped before climbing into bed.

* * *

My phone was ringing. I ignored it, but it rang again and again. Finally, I crawled out of bed and dug for it in my purse. It was Ashland. *What time is it?* I saw that it was 8 a.m. I was exhausted; wasn't he?

I yawned and answered the phone. "Hey! Good morning. You're up awful early..."

"Come to the house. I'm sorry to wake you up, but I need you to come over." The urgency in his voice was palpable.

"What is it? Is everything okay?" I stood, my body tense. Did they vandalize the place? What mischief was Mia into now?

"TD called me this morning. He found Matthews. He's dead, Carrie Jo."

I sat on the edge of the bed, barely able to process what I had just heard. "What? How did he...I mean, when did he..."

"I don't know anything. But because of the report we made, the police want to talk to everyone who was there last night."

"Of course. I'll be there in fifteen minutes."

"Thanks, Carrie Jo." He hung up, and I scrambled to get dressed. I couldn't believe this was happening.

Since I began working at Seven Sisters, I've lost my best friend, who appears to have some serious unexplained issues with me. I've lost a sort-of boyfriend but found a guy I really like. I've met several "ghosts" and have had a lapful of mysteries thrown my way. Am I now going to be a murder suspect?

I didn't know what to think about all of it, but there was one thing I did know. Seven Sisters was a place where life and death happened, where fear and hope resided—a place where things were lost and things were found.

I wondered what today was going to bring...

~~*

Moonlight Falls on Seven Sisters

By

M.L. Bullock

Dedication

To my husband, Kevin, the world's most devoted collector of ugly shirts. Thank you for all the plot twists, endless cups of coffee and those long back-road drives. Let the adventure continue. At last....

I saw the Pleiades through branches bare,
And close to mine your face
Soft glowing in the dark;
For Youth and Hope and Love and You were there
At our dear trysting-place

Arthur Henry Adams

Excerpt from "The Pleiades"

Chapter 1

I swung my Honda into the long driveway that led to the antebellum home, doing my best to navigate the maze of police cars and emergency vehicles. It was an odd sight: the swirling red and blue lights cast against the fading white columns and the green-gray mold that covered the chipping paint, evidence of many wet, humid Alabama seasons gone by. It was just a little after 8 a.m., and it had been a long night with too little sleep.

Ashland met me at the car. His drawn face and clenched square jaw were evidence that he was angry and disturbed. Hollis Matthews, the attorney who had hired me, had been found dead somewhere in the building. "Hey, thanks for coming over so fast. Listen, the police want to talk to us about last night, but don't go in yet. They are about to take him out."

I stepped out of the car, suddenly aware of how wild my wavy, long hair must look. I gathered it up in a ponytail holder and searched his blue eyes. "Are you okay?" I had not been a fan of the fastidious attorney, and I wasn't sure how close he and Ashland had been, but it was upsetting no matter what. Especially since foul play was suspected.

"I'll be fine." He led me by the elbow to a police car. "This is Detective Simmons. She will be investigating the... she's in charge of the investigation." Detective Simmons looked to be in her late 40s, with bright red hair and a freckled complexion. She was tall and pale, and she looked like she knew what she was doing.

I put my hand out. "Hello, Detective. I am Carrie Jo Jardine. I'm part of the research team here."

"Thanks for coming, Ms. Jardine." After a quick handshake, she got down to business. "What is your connection with the folks that were here last night? I understand that the woman," she said as she consulted her notebook, "Mia Reed, worked with you here? How long have you known her?"

"Um....yes, we went to school together. I can't believe Mia would be involved with this, but...then again, I've discovered recently that I don't really know her like I thought I did."

"What do you mean by that, Ms. Jardine?" The detective shielded her pale green eyes from the sun that was rising, along with the heat.

I thought about the conversation I heard the day before through the cast-iron floor gates. It was Mia and Matthews, plotting about something, something that I was pretty sure concerned me. Was I sure it was Mia? I decided against sharing what I heard. I didn't hear everything, and Ashland was standing next to me. I didn't want to look like a backstabbing friend, even though I wasn't. "Well, when we caught her up here with her friends, she tried to say that I gave her permission to be here, but I never did. I think they were having a séance—or something. I would never have agreed to that."

"You say she was having a séance? Who were these other people?" Detective Simmons pursed her dark red lips as she waited for my answer.

"I don't know exactly what they were doing. There was a lot of chanting, and it was just plain strange. Her friend was Henri Devecheaux, a local guy. He gave me his card." I felt my pockets, but the card wasn't in these jeans. "It's at my apartment. I can call you with the information later. The other guy was William, William Bettencourt. He was a mutual friend of ours from Charleston." I hadn't yet told Ashland that William had been my sort-of boyfriend, and this was certainly not the right time to share.

The officials were carrying out Matthews' covered body. As they passed us, I shivered and looked away, at the ground, at the sky, anywhere else. I had never seen a dead body before, at least not in my real life.

"Let's go inside and get out of the sun," Ashland offered. I followed him, and the detective walked behind me, but I was nervous about going in. I didn't know how he had died and where. I didn't want to be disrespectful.

From the way that police were moving up and down the hall, I could tell that whatever had taken place here had happened in the Blue Room. Many tragic events had played out there, against a timeless backdrop of beauty and perceived elegance. In the current restoration project, the Blue Room was ground zero for our operations. It was our computer center, where my team and I worked to produce layouts for each of the rooms and gather the antiques and supplies needed to set them up as a living museum in honor of Old Mobile. It was my temporary workplace; when we completed the project, our work area would be moved off-site, but this was how Matthews had wanted it. He wanted us to work here, in the house. I didn't know why, but I was happy to oblige—this was a once-in-a-lifetime gig. Now the gray-haired lawyer with the cold gray eyes was as dead as those buried in the mausoleum just a few hundred yards away.

"Can you tell me if anything is missing from the house?" the detective asked. "I mean, I know it's a big one and you've got a lot of boxes here, but could you and Mr. Stuart look around and tell me if anything is gone?"

I nodded, and Ashland and I walked around, careful not to touch anything. I was happy to note that whatever fear had struck me the night before, whatever creepy apparition I had believed I had heard, was gone now. The warmth of the day and the cheery sunshine had pushed the shadows away, taming them back to the darkness where they belonged. We walked through the downstairs, except the Blue Room, and didn't notice anything out of place. The detective followed us around as we did our inventory. The mantelpieces were there. The paintings from the LeMans family, very expensive paintings of antebellum pets, were still leaning against the wall, wrapped in paper. They had been Mia's find.

Finally, we climbed up the wooden spiral staircase, and I followed Ashland as we toured each room. The first room had once been the guest room, and all was in order. We surveyed each room with nothing to report. The door to Calpurnia's room was standing open, and the chalk markings were still on the floor, evidence of Mia's amateur séance. I shivered again, remembering the anguished cries of *Mon dieu!* Ashland put his hand on my shoulder.

"Nope, nothing missing here either," he said. "The only room left is the Blue Room. Is it possible for us to go in there, or should we wait?" I could hear the strain in his voice. For the first time, I noticed that he hadn't changed since the night before. He looked crumpled and tired.

Detective Simmons nodded. "Sure, let's go see if they're finished." She walked down the staircase ahead of us.

I grabbed Ashland's hand. "Do you want me to go in? I mean, you don't have to right now."

He gave me his best college football star smile. "No, I'll be okay. I know he wasn't a friendly guy, but he helped me through some rough times. I need to see what happened. Let's go." We headed to the Blue Room, now empty of emergency workers, except for a few stragglers talking quietly in a corner near the printer.

Immediately, my eyes were drawn to my desk. The music box was gone! The one that one of the interns had handed me the day before. I had set it on my desk when I came downstairs. Now it was gone.

"The music box is gone." I walked to my desk and looked underneath it. "Can I pull out the drawers?"

Detective Simmons looked at one of the other officers. "Yeah, we're done in here," he said. The pair left us with the detective. I opened the drawers on the off chance that I had stuffed the box inside one, but they were all empty.

"What did it look like?" Ashland asked.

"It was about eight inches long, maybe five inches wide, rectangular. It had an ornate domed lid, probably made from ivory with enamel and wood inlays. There was a dancing lady on the top—Rachel Kowalski brought it to me yesterday. I set it here." Puzzled, I stood up and tapped my desk. I looked again and again, and it was certainly gone.

"Was this item valuable?" Detective Simmons stood across the desk from me. "Maybe valuable enough to kill someone over?"

"It's valuable in the sense that it has historical value; it is an antebellum music box that actually works, which makes it rare. But as far as killing someone for it... I don't see that happening. I mean, look around. If you were here to rob the place, wouldn't you take a computer or some of the other equipment? You know, equipment that you could pawn or sell to someone? What are they going to do with a music box?"

The detective gave me a crooked smile. "That's the question, isn't it? Listen, do you have a picture of this box you could send me?"

"No, I hadn't photographed it yet. It wasn't really a part of any of the exhibits. I guess I could find a photo of something similar to show you. Might take a while, though."

"That's fine. We've got plenty to work on here. I guess that's it for now, then. You plan on staying in Mobile, or are you going back to Charleston?"

"I don't have any plans to leave, Detective."

She flipped her notebook closed. "Good. That makes my job so much easier. Mr. Stuart, I will be in touch." With a curt nod, she left Ashland and me alone.

Except for a few spots of blood on the carpet, there was no sign of a struggle or even a crime. Ashland sat in Mia's old chair, leaning his elbows on his knees and holding his head. "I can't believe this. Who would want to kill him? And why would they do it here?"

I pulled up a chair close to him and put my hand on his arm. "Does he have any family? Someone we should call?"

"I've got my office taking care of that. He had a sister, I think, but he never talked about her. I don't even know her name. He said she was sick, and that was it. I guess I'm the only family he had besides her. I know he was distant, but he believed in this restoration as much as I do. As a matter of fact, it was Matthews that pushed me toward completing my family's legacy. If it weren't for him, I don't think I would have even started this. But now that it has begun, I have to see it through. I couldn't help my mother, but I can restore this place for her, and for my family, for the people who lived here—and died here." He added the last with raw sadness.

"Listen, do you want to take some time off the project, at least until after the funeral?" I wanted to help him, but I wasn't sure how yet. This was a way to start.

He gave me a weak smile. "No. We're going to stay on schedule. That's what he would have wanted." He put his arm around me and hugged me. I hugged him back. He stood up, and we began walking to the door. "Going forward, I'm going to need more of your help with things around here. I am counting on you to bring Seven Sisters back to life."

"I'm here, Ashland. I'm not going anywhere." I could see the tears in his eyes. I pulled him close and kissed him. We stood together at the foot of the stairs, our arms around each other. From upstairs, I could hear movement, and then it stopped. Ashland didn't seem to notice, but as we stepped apart and turned to leave, I heard a soft sigh.

It was probably just the house, the wood expanding from the heat of the day, the metal shifting along the porch railing. Maybe it was a draft blowing through some silk curtains.

Whatever it was, I wasn't afraid. I had Ashland by my side.

Chapter 2

I heard some of the locals refer to summer days in Mobile as "slow as molasses," but at Seven Sisters they were anything but. A few weeks after the murder, our contractor, Terrence Dale, was finishing up painting the last of the downstairs rooms as large pieces of heavy wooden furniture began to arrive. For now, we carefully wrapped and stored the pieces like the paneled armoire and the round entry table with intricate magnolia details in the music room. I felt like we were making significant progress, but there was a problem.

"You know I am on your side, TD, but this is not the right color. This is a red-based burgundy—we need a blue-based burgundy."

He stared at me as if I had two heads. He was smart and talented, but he was wrong on this. Obviously, I could not tell him how I knew he was wrong, that I had been in this room almost 200 years ago. *Yeah, that would sound crazy.* I slung my hands in my worn jeans pocket, determined to have my way. I didn't know why TD was giving me such a hard time. I had practically given him free rein over the Moonlight Garden. I did not argue when he wanted to place mirrors in the reflecting pool or decided to suspend white cast-iron chandeliers in the trees or brought in truckloads of white gravel. Why was he being so obstinate now?

"Carrie Jo, this shade has Historical Society approval and is as authentic as you can get. I know you want historical accuracy here, and you're getting it, but don't you think you're splitting hairs?" TD took off his hat and wiped his forehead.

"I'm sorry, TD, but we have to change it. I know it seems like a small thing, but I must insist. I realize it will take time to get the room redone. Do whatever you have to do to make it happen." Sometimes being the boss sucked, especially when I had to tell my team something they didn't want to hear. This was one of those times.

TD looked at Ashland for backup. He didn't vocalize his request, but I could tell he wanted it. Ashland gave a nervous laugh and put his hands up as if to say, "I'm out of this."

"Come on, guys. You're killing me here. I can't bring just anyone in here for this job; the Motre Brothers are the best in Mobile County, and they have a really tight schedule. You know it takes specialized painters who know how to cut in around all this molding, and the paint has to be applied with specific materials...I don't even know if I can book them again right now." TD had a solid argument, but I wasn't going to give way. Calpurnia and Christine Cottonwood deserved to have their home restored correctly. It was my turn to look at Ashland for support.

He gave us both an uneasy smile. "You two work this out. I'm just the guy who writes the checks."

TD slid his hat back on his sweaty head and pulled it down snugly. He crossed his arms and stared at me. I had to do something to sweeten the pot. "I'll help, TD. I know how to paint, and I have some experience with places like this. I don't want you to get behind schedule...and...Ashland will help too."

"Hey..."Ashland said with a laugh, pretending to be irritated that I had drafted him for this time-consuming task. We had barely spent any time together recently. Maybe this would be a way we could rekindle that spark we shared that starry night on Mobile Bay. "Sure, I'll help. But it has to be soon, like tonight or tomorrow night. I have to go out of town this weekend."

I smiled at TD and stood next to Ashland. The contractor gave in to my request with a regretful grin. "Fine. If you two are willing to help, maybe we can get it done in a reasonable amount of time. I'll still call the Motre Brothers and see if they can take care of it."

Ashland eyed me suspiciously, "You know, you sure are being a stickler about some paint. Is there something I should know?" I had promised him before Matthews was murdered that I would come clean about my "gift," but there never seemed to be a good time. Now Ashland had all the responsibilities that Matthews had managed, plus his own, and I had a living museum to reconstruct. Besides a busy schedule, Ashland seemed to be taking Matthews' death pretty hard.

I shook my head. "No, it's just the wrong color. You want it to be right, and so do I." I smiled innocently, hoping to satisfy his curiosity. He looked at me intently but thankfully didn't push me further. I was afraid that if he latched those vibrant blue eyes on me for too long, I would tell him everything. I wasn't ready for that. Inwardly, I cringed at the idea of revealing my secret to him. I knew Ashland didn't care for psychics. Although I wasn't one, he might think there wasn't much difference between me and the charlatans that took his mother's money.

Fortunately, he didn't press me. Instead we talked about Maximillian's Chandelier—or the copy we had managed to procure. The replica of the massive legendary fixture was created using the original from the Hopkins County Museum. We would have loved to have had the original, but the Hopkins board said no way. Getting this replica was an achievement begun by Matthews, but Ashland's charm had made it happen. It would be on display in the ballroom and wired for electrical lighting. The lighting company that created the piece had done a magnificent job of hiding the fact that the lights weren't candles but tiny light bulbs that flickered just like the real thing. A special switch would allow us to select the amount of light and flickering that we wanted for the occasion. Proud of himself, Ashland opened the crate like a kid unwrapping a new toy. How was it possible that this guy could love history as much as I did? For Ashland, this wasn't just about Old Mobile history; this was about his mother and her legacy. I respected that. I felt a twinge of sadness thinking about my own mother before quickly pushing it down as I had learned to do over the years.

"Help me get this open."

I laughed. "You don't want to wait for TD to come back?"

"No way, I want to see it now. Besides, I'm not talking about hanging it by myself, just opening the box."

Uh-oh. I must have taken a whack at Ashland's ego. I grabbed a nearby flathead screwdriver and a hammer; we pried the lid off and stood staring at the reproduction. It was ridiculously decorated with crystals and gold-toned chains—it was perfect. The floor was not complete in the ballroom, so it would be some time before it was hung. From the beginning of the project, the hanging of the chandelier was to be the last thing on the very lengthy to-do list, the crowning moment of the new museum. I sighed just looking at it. Of course this was only "Phase One," getting the house and grounds ready. The more detailed work, like finessing the displays, would take time too. But I felt a kind of sadness just thinking about leaving Seven Sisters.

We pulled the paperwork and inspected the chandelier, then Ashland signed off on the receiving invoice and sent it back digitally with his phone. "Let's get something to eat. Are you hungry? I skipped breakfast this morning, and my stomach is growling."

"Sounds good. Let's check with the two Rachels and Chip and James to see if they want to tag along." Ashland looked disappointed; once again, I had misunderstood him. I quickly added, "Or I could just see if they want me to bring them something back."

"Okay, why don't you do that, and I'll go find TD and see if he got in touch with the Motre Brothers. I don't mind painting, but that might mean moving my schedule around a little."

I gave him a guilty grin. "Yeah, I guess I should have asked first. Sorry about that."

"It's no problem; I said I wanted to be hands-on around here, didn't I?" He strode out the front door, and my pulse quickened just watching those big shoulders under his cotton polo shirt. Ashland Stuart was the handsomest man I had ever known. I couldn't understand why some talented southern debutante had not scooped him up yet.

I went to the Blue Room first, expecting to find Chip there manning the phones or hunkered over his computer, but the room was empty. I tried not to look at the floor, at the spot where Hollis Matthews' body had lain, but I couldn't help myself. Perversely, I wondered if he was still there, not him but an echo of him, something I could see in a dream. Had Mia killed him? I had heard them argue, but not clearly—not clearly enough to tell the cops about it. I missed Mia, but everything about her confused me. I lost my best friend, and I didn't even know why.

I peeked in a few more rooms, but I could hear voices upstairs. I stood at the bottom of the staircase and called up. "Rachel K! Chip?" No one answered. I climbed the stairs, my hand sliding along the polished oak banister; it felt as smooth as glass under my fingertips. I wondered how many hands had done the same thing since it had been built. Hundreds?

The second floor, now empty of most of the boxes and completely painted, looked as if some loving family was about to move in. The white molding along the ceiling and floors looked crisp and clean. The reproductions of the original runners and rugs had not yet arrived, but the floors looked as smooth and even as one could expect. Sunlight streamed through the windows at the end of the hall, casting the area in a warm, golden glow. Despite the cheeriness of the sunlight and the warmth of the summer day, I felt a chill as I stood on the upstairs landing.

All the doors had been left open, except the one that led to Calpurnia's room. Further down the hall, in the master bedroom, I could hear James' high-pitched voice. He was an entertaining young man who talked nonstop, and the team liked him despite his tendency to be pessimistic. Since he could work while he talked, I didn't mind too much. I heard Rachel laughing along with him. "You guys..." I called out to them, a little irritated that they hadn't responded. "I've been calling you!" I started to walk down the hall and invade their party, but I heard furniture scraping in Calpurnia's room. I stood outside the door, my hand on the knob. Even though I was the boss, I tapped on the door, giving whoever was unnecessarily scraping the floors a chance to stop before I gave them a piece of my mind. The sound continued, like heavy wood being dragged across the floor. But no furniture was in the room yet, except the mantelpiece. I stepped back, my heart fluttering in my chest. I could see shadows moving under the door. I knocked again, this time the sounds of scraping and the moving shadows stopped. I turned the round knob; it was cold and the lock felt sticky, but I pushed the door open.

My mouth fell open. I had been wrong—the place was full of furniture. To the left was a four-poster bed; to the right, a long dresser with a vanity table in the center and a dim oval mirror on the wall behind it. Against the far wall stood a cedar armoire, not exactly like Calpurnia's but very near the same style with delicate floral scrollwork at the top and bottom. To the far right was a hope chest sitting under the window, just as Callie had placed hers. The only thing missing was a desk, the small writing desk and chair that went on the opposite side of the bed.

"Hello? Rachel?" Nobody answered me but I wasn't surprised, I knew no one was in the room. Just to make it official, I slowly walked to the armoire and tugged the door open. The antique door swung open smoothly, the scent of cedar filled the room, and of course there was no one inside.

"So you like it?" Startled, I turned to see TD leaning in the doorframe.

"Yes, you did a marvelous job with the choices. Just what I was looking for, TD. Thank you." *Okay, breathe now. You were just hearing things, obviously. There was no one in here. That scraping was something else, probably the kids down the hall.*

"I'm glad I at least got that right."

"I know I was a pain about that paint, but I never said you weren't gifted. This looks awesome. Thanks again." I walked to the doorway, smiling at him.

"You know, if you wanted the furniture moved, I would have done it for you. Geesh, you are such a perfectionist, Carrie Jo."

"What are you talking about?"

"The furniture. This isn't how we arranged it this morning. Ashland and I had the vanity and dresser combination piece over by the window, thinking it made more sense that whoever lived here would want to have better lighting when doing her hair or trimming his beard. The bed wasn't there either. We put it over there."

I stared up into his brown eyes. "I didn't move a thing, Terrence Dale, I swear."

He looked at me and then at the room. "Well, then who did? Because this isn't how I left it."

"Beats me, but it wasn't me. I did hear something, but when I opened the door, there was no one in here."

"Maybe Ashland did it. In the future, if anyone wants to move stuff, let's make sure we don't scrape the floor. Look at that." He pointed to a definite groove in the wood near the armoire.

"Ah, geesh. Yeah, I will tell the rest of the team. These really are perfect for this room."

He stood with his hands on his hips, staring at the floor. "I think I can get that out. By the way, it's like I thought, the Motre Brothers are booked solid through the first of the year. It will have to be us, so are you ready to paint tonight? I'm picking up the material this afternoon."

Still trying to process what had just happened, I nodded. "I'll be here. Six works for me. I have some progress reports to type for the board."

"Yeah, that's great. See you then." He knelt down and looked at the long scrape, and I left so I didn't have to hear him swear. It just wasn't his day. I walked down the hall and found all four members of my team unpacking tchotchkes from boxes and placing them on tables. They had taped a room name on each table and were sorting through potential display pieces. I saw that even Chip was in on the action; obviously, the friendly Rachel

McGhee was the true attraction. For someone as socially awkward as Chip was, he didn't let that stop him from trying. First Mia, now Rachel.

"Hey, guys. TD is on the warpath because someone moved the furniture in Callie's...I mean the front room up here and scraped up the floor. Who did it?" It was my job as the boss to get to the bottom of this mystery. The four stared at me blankly, looking at one another. "Come on, no one is getting sent home. I just need to know."

Nothing but crickets.

Finally Rachel K. spoke up, "Honestly, Carrie Jo, we've been in here the whole time. I didn't even know that there was any furniture in that room. I saw that the door was closed, but I didn't go in. Did any of you?" Everyone shook their heads and stared at me.

"Are you kidding me? Ashland and TD put that furniture in there this morning to surprise me, but it is now arranged differently and the floor is scraped up. Are you telling me that it did it by itself?" I tried not to think about the sounds and the moving shadows.

"Maybe the ghost did it?" Rachel M. offered. "I mean, I've never seen it, but I heard this place is haunted." Now it was her turn to get stared at. She laughed nervously. "I didn't say I believed it. That's just what they say."

I put my hand on my forehead and rubbed it. This was too much. "Okay, besides a ghost, is there any other possibility? Did you see any workmen up here, moving things around?"

Everyone shook their heads again, and Rachel M. said, "No, Carrie Jo. Nobody has been up here except us this morning."

"Well it must have been one of them. If you see anyone up here, you tell them they need to check with me before they touch anything—even a light fixture. Oh, and Ashland and I are going out to grab a bite for lunch. Do y'all want us to bring something back?"

James shook his head. "Thanks, but we're going over to the Spot of Tea for lunch. Rachel M has never been, and I thought it would be fun. We will be back by one, though."

I looked at my watch; it was 11:30. "Go on, take some extra time. See you back here at 1:30." Excited, they thanked me and left me alone on the top floor of Seven Sisters. I walked back to Callie's room, but TD was gone too. I sat on the padded hope chest and surveyed the room.

What had I heard? Had it been Callie, unhappy with the arrangement? Other than the fact that she was presumably dead, it made sense. The room was now exactly like it had been during her time here—from the mirror on the wall to the armoire positioning. Did she know I was here? I didn't feel afraid sitting in the sunshine. I felt excited. Happy. Yes, this was the way it should be.

"Okay, you can have it your way but don't scrape up the floor again." I left the room, closing the door behind me as if to give her some privacy. I paused on the top step, hearing no more scraping, no more sounds. I half expected to hear a sigh, a rustling of taffeta, but nothing...

I walked down the stairs to find Ashland.

Chapter 3

Ashland and I stepped out the heavy wooden front doors of the house into the cool shadows of the columns that lined Seven Sisters. "I'm sure those kids are just pranking you. Who else could have done it? I mean, I haven't seen anyone else inside this morning, have you?" I had to admit that I hadn't, but I did not believe they were lying to me about it. Ever since Mia's unannounced séance, Calpurnia's room had become an uncomfortable place to hang out in. The feeling of "wrongness" remained, and I didn't know how to fix it.

I shrugged. "Maybe you're right. What else could it be?" I took a deep breath, leaving the lingering doubts on the porch, ready to enjoy my time with Ashland. It was so encouraging to see the front lawn taking shape, the trash, limbs and leaves hauled away, the rows of oaks lining the property more clearly visible now. Even the ugly satyr looked as if it belonged in the lush landscape; it had been properly cleaned, and the vines that had risen up to strangle it were gone. I looked forward to the day when the outside of the house would receive the kind of love that the interior had. However, the repairs to the wood and the replacement of missing ornamental pieces were evidence that a complete paint job was soon to follow. According to our shared calendar, TD had the week of July 4th marked off for the massive job. I felt for the guys who would have to paint in the unforgiving Alabama heat.

Ashland talked like an excited schoolboy—he had scored a meeting with the city council to talk about changing the zoning to accommodate his plans to make the house a museum and came away with everything he wanted. I never doubted he would succeed. If his shocking good looks and confidence didn't get you, his intelligence would. I liked him more each day, but I was careful to keep our relationship as professional as possible, except when he flirted with me in his sweet, southern boy way. I learned from the Mia episode that Ashland liked taking the lead.

I was looking forward to this lunch—I hoped maybe it would be a precursor to an in-depth conversation about how I knew the things I did about this house. My plan was to talk about my childhood experiences and gauge his reaction. If he balked at that or called me crazy, I'd leave it alone. If he didn't, I'd tell him what I knew. He'd asked me to help him find Calpurnia, right? Between the journals and the dreams, I felt confident that I could bring him some type of closure, maybe even vindicate his mother.

As we stepped off the porch, I smiled up at him, shielding my eyes from the sun. He wanted to know what I thought about partnering with the Exploreum, another museum in the heart of downtown Mobile. Before I could offer an opinion, we were interrupted. "Hey, Ashland. I hope I'm not catching you at a bad time."

We had been so immersed in our conversation (and I in my thoughts) that I had not seen the attractive brunette approach. Always the gentleman,

Ashland smiled at her and said, "No, of course not. Hi, Detra Ann. How have you been? I thought you were still away at Auburn. Oh, where are my manners? Detra Ann, this is Carrie Jo Jardine. Carrie Jo, this is Detra Ann Dowd."

Dowd, Dowd? Where have I heard that name before? Oh yeah, Bette. Is this tall, pretty woman Cynthia Dowd's daughter? She doesn't look cross-eyed to me. "Hi, nice to meet you." We exchanged pleasantries as expected, then Detra Ann turned her attention to Ashland.

"Nope, I'm all done for the semester with just one more to go. Then I will be ready to take my place at 3D Public Relations." She smiled proudly and then looked from Ashland to me. I guessed she thought I was going to get lost, but I stayed by his side. I wasn't going to miss out on our lunch date. Detra Ann was taller than me, but she had a toned, curvy figure. She had long dark hair, blue eyes and full, pink lips. In her pale hands she held a picnic basket. It didn't take a rocket scientist to figure out why she was there. "Are you one of the decorators, Carrie Jo?"

Ashland answered for me. "No, Carrie Jo is the project's main historian. She's done a wonderful job bringing this house back to life."

Detra Ann's eyes widened in surprise. "Oh, that is good news. I would love to take an unofficial tour to see what you've done so far."

Too polite to refuse her, Ashland said, "What do you think, Carrie Jo? Can we give an unofficial tour?"

"If she doesn't mind stepping over boxes and paint supplies, sure." I tried not to pout about having my lunch date delayed. If Detra Ann could offer some public relations ideas that would put Seven Sisters back on the map, then why not? Ashland curled his hand around Detra Ann's elbow and led her into the house, sharing points of interest along the way. I followed the two beautiful people like a middle school tagalong. He began the tour upstairs, and Detra Ann asked intelligent questions about the original owners and how Ashland planned to advertise his new museum when the work was complete. I didn't contribute much to the conversation except when asked, which wasn't often; I might as well not have been there at all. The tour ended in the ballroom with a peek at the new chandelier.

The pretty brunette caught her breath at the sight and practically squealed. "This is a sign, Ashland! You'll never believe why I came today. I wanted to talk to you about having a Christmas ball at Seven Sisters for the Historical Society. This would be the perfect venue for the event—and think about what it would mean for your advertising efforts. Why, everyone in the state will want to attend!"

Ashland eased the heavy wooden lid back on the chandelier crate and asked, "Hmm...What did you have in mind?"

A smile crept over Detra Ann's face. She knew he was interested, and so did I. But to me, the idea of a hundred modern-day debutantes and their dates traipsing through Seven Sisters seemed somewhat sacrilegious. Would Ashland so easily forget all of our hard work? What about Hollis Matthews? Surely Ashland, an old-fashioned southern gentleman, wouldn't dream of having a celebration here now?

"I'm thinking of a ball, right here in this room, with a silent auction to benefit the Society. Maybe if the grounds were ready, we could offer a Christmas fireworks show too. Those are just a few ideas I had to get you started. Think about what this could mean for Seven Sisters—it would be like she was taking her place again in Mobile society. And of course, you'd be helping an old friend get established in her new career. You know, I would give this project—and you—everything I had." She smiled at him and looked around the room appreciatively, probably planning on where to nail up some garland and station Santa.

"Wait—what are you talking about?" I interrupted, surprised at the turn of the conversation. "There's no way the house will be ready by December— that's just six months away, Ashland. Some of the floors still have to be refinished, the ceiling of this room hasn't been completed yet, the square medallions won't be here for weeks, then there's the painting on the outside..."

"That's plenty of time to get ready for an event that, like you said, is six months away. You've seen how quickly TD can work—I think this might be a good goal to work toward. And she's right; it would be the perfect event for putting Seven Sisters back on the Mobile scene."

My face must have turned two shades of red because it felt hot and splotchy. "Are you forgetting that Mr. Matthews died here not long ago? Would it be right to have a party in the house so close to his...demise?" I could see that struck a chord with him. He needed to think this through before committing the house to a party.

"Hey...I'm not agreeing to anything yet. I just want to hear what she has to say and keep our options open. What about joining us for lunch, Detra Ann? We could talk more then."

She lifted her basket in her hands as if she were offering a gift to a Greek god. "I've got that covered. Is there a good place to eat in here, or should we lunch out on the porch?" She paused and with an insincere smile said, "I think there is enough for three here, if you like fried chicken and fruit salad."

"Actually, I've got something I need to do," I said, ignoring Ashland's surprised look, "but thank you for the invitation." I forced a smile on my face and walked out of the ballroom, down the hall and out of the house. I was furious—furious that Ashland would even consider having a ball here without talking to me first. Furious that Detra Ann had interrupted our lunch date and that once again, I would have to delay my confession to Ashland. It was enough to make a nice girl swear.

I left Seven Sisters, walking down the broken sidewalk that led to the main road. I could have driven to nearby Joachim or Dauphin Street for lunch, but I wanted to walk. I heard a vehicle behind me coming down the drive; it was TD in his big, blue Dodge truck. "Hey, you want a ride? Car broke down?" He slid his sunglasses up to the top of his head, his brows furrowed with concern. I walked to the open window. "One of these days you'll have to say goodbye to that old eggbeater you call a car."

"Ha! I'm in no hurry to do that. I'm going to get some lunch and thought I would take a walk and enjoy the nice day. Where are you off to? Still mad at me about the paint?"

"Nope. I know how temperamental you historians can be—I've worked with enough of them. I knew I should have shown you the color before I had them put it on the walls. Oh well...live and learn." He smiled good-naturedly and unlocked the door. "Hop in. I'll buy you lunch."

I thought about his proposal—it couldn't hurt to spend some time with Terrence Dale. He had gone the extra mile for me so many times in the past few weeks, and I did want to get to know him better. "I can't convince you to walk?"

He laughed at that idea. "When you walk as much as I do, you'll ride every chance you get. Tell you what, I will take you to lunch and you can walk back. I have an appointment in about an hour anyway." He slid his shades back over his eyes and smiled. He really was a handsome man. Not in the obvious, otherworldly Ashland kind of way—he was the boy next door, friendly, with a nice body and useful hands. *Good Lord, CJ. Calm down. Must be the heat...*

"Okay, that sounds great. Let's eat somewhere close, though—I have a history with dress shoes. I'd hate to trip and sprawl out across a downtown street."

TD grinned. "I know the perfect place. I bet you haven't tried it yet."

"Well, now I'm curious."

As we drove, TD took the time to show me some points of interest—things he loved about his city. He was from a southern part of the county called Grand Bay, but he'd been living in the downtown area all his adult life. Instead of turning right onto Dauphin Street, TD took us left on to Royal. "There's a great spot called the Joe Cain Café at the Renaissance. It's an easy walk back to Seven Sisters."

Stylish and modern, the Renaissance loomed above the Mobile landscape. It wasn't the tallest building, as that honor went to the RSA Battle House Tower, but it was in the top three. Fortunately, the Joe Cain Café was on the ground floor and the line to get in wasn't long. TD ordered a prime rib wrap—it sounded delicious, so I ordered the same. We took a seat next to a window, which would be good for people-watching.

"Tell me about the garden, TD. I saw the crate of mirrors come in." I was ready to think about something other than Detra Ann and her picnic basket. "Explain to me again how you plan to illuminate the garden? How do the mirrors fit in? I have heard of capturing the sunlight but never the moonlight." I assumed part of the reason behind his irritation with me about the paint job was because he wanted to focus on this particular garden.

"The house originally had three gardens: a rose garden, an extensive herb garden and of course the massive Moonlight Garden. The latter had been a wedding gift from Christine Beaumont to Jeremiah Cottonwood, but it later became a major attraction. Countless parties were held there, and it was the talk of the county. It was a large garden, which featured a maze, at least nine statues and copious amounts of white flowers that shone in the moonlight. Unfortunately some of the varieties aren't even available anymore."

I knew most of what he was telling me, but I let him tell me what he knew. Recreating the Moonlight Garden had been TD's special project. From the beginning of our partnership, he had taken a keen interest in making it come back to life. Since it was such a unique feature, it would be a standout addition to his resume. Only a handful of qualified contractors could say they had rebuilt a "moonlight" garden. This would be a nice addition to TD's already impressive list of accolades. Before I ever had a dream about Seven Sisters or the people who lived there, I had never heard of "moonlight" gardens, but now I found the idea fascinating. Still, I couldn't tell TD about my nocturnal experiences. I let him explain the concept, with some careful nudging.

"How does a 'moonlight garden' actually work? I mean, does that mean it could only be used during certain times of the month, when the moon was up?"

"Essentially, yes, but life was different then—very much dictated by the phases of the moon."

"What do you mean?" I asked between bites. The wrap was delicious, and I ate it with abandon.

"Well, the people needed to know when the tide would come in, being so close to the Mobile River, and they would want to know the most fortuitous times for planting and harvesting. All those things are determined by the moon. It made sense to consult the lunar calendar for special parties too. Many a tale has been told about the debauchery that occurred on those moonlit nights behind Seven Sisters." I gave him an unbelieving look, and he grinned. "I'm not kidding! Not to mention that this family, at least on the Beaumont side, had ties to France where these types of gardens were the settings for secret society rituals. To have a garden was a luxury; to have a moonlight garden...that definitely gave you bragging rights. From the historical record here, the Cottonwoods and the Beaumonts had plenty to brag about."

"Yeah, I guess you're right. Those paint colors can attest to that. Only the wealthiest Mobilians had painted walls. The velvet curtains with the gold thread are another clue that they were ridiculously wealthy." TD's puzzlement reminded me to keep my inside information to myself. "Something I read. Anyway, it sure wasn't about simplicity. The Cottonwoods were very concerned about displaying their wealth and influence." I let him eat some more before I asked him another question. It was warm by the window, but I loved the Alabama sunshine. Strangely enough, being in Mobile felt like home—like I belonged here. Maybe it was just me being sentimental.

He gestured a bit with his sandwich. "You know we won't get the bright solar light, more a kind of white glow from the moon, with those mirrors. Like the original designer, I plan on placing the mirrors in the garden to discreetly bounce the light around. For instance, the mirrored panels I ordered will go in the largest fountain, the Atlas fountain. Instead of lying flat, the mirrors rest against marble wedges hidden in the pool. These wedges prop the mirror up to a 30-degree angle so it catches the light and throws it back. When it is done correctly, it will look like the fountain and the garden are glowing."

"Wow! That sounds incredible!" I was genuinely impressed with his ingenuity. TD knew his stuff—that was for sure!

"It is the easiest thing in the world to shove some solar lights into the ground and install some lamps in a garden, but I find what the designer— Chaveux—did was simply amazing. Now, of course we can have those gas lamps if you want them, hidden discreetly in the greenery if you like..."

"No way. I like your idea. Hey! You know what? We should celebrate when you complete the project! Let's do that. I wonder if my calendar has the lunar cycle on it." I dug in my purse for my mini-calendar; I had not brought my day planner with me.

"Really, could we? That would be great. Let's see, it's going to take me..." TD stared off, probably counting days, trying to figure out when he'd be through. "Okay, I have repair work on half a dozen statues, replacing the fountain at the Atlas location, and then laying the white stone for the walkways...I'm thinking I could be done in two weeks. When is the next full moon?"

"That works out great! The next full moon is August 8th. We'll have some cocktails and enjoy the Moonlight Garden, but let's keep it small—just the team and some of the guys who helped you."

TD gave me a smirk. "So no Historical Society folks, then?"

"Please don't make me comment on that." I shoved the calendar back into my purse and cleaned up my mess. I'd eaten the whole wrap, and now I felt fat. Thank goodness I was wearing a dress.

My lunch partner chuckled. "I don't think you have anything to worry about. She's not his type."

I felt my face warm. "Who? What are you talking about?"

"Oh, come on. I'm not blind, you know. Everyone knows Ashland likes you. He doesn't make it a secret—I don't know why you're trying to."

"I'm not! ... What do you mean?"

"Do you want to keep what's happening between you and Ashland a secret for some reason? Maybe you don't like him as much as he likes you?"

"TD, I don't think I should be talking about this because he is my boss. But no, that's not true. I do like him just as much."

He smiled and sighed. "I knew it. An old country boy like me never had a chance, did I?"

"Stop that!" I shot him a look of exasperation.

"I'm just kidding, CJ—lighten up. I'm in love with my work, and that's all I want right now."

"I'm glad you are—I couldn't imagine restoring Seven Sisters without you. Let's get back to work. You've got just a few weeks left and I have to go make sure Detra Ann hasn't talked Ashland into hosting a Christmas ball."

Chapter 4

I must have jinxed myself extolling the virtues of my eggbeater car because at the end of the day, it wouldn't turn over at all. *Turn the key, click. Turn the key, click.* I laid my head on the steering wheel and halfheartedly prayed before I tried it again. *Turn the key, click.*

Everyone else had gone. Ashland had left as I pulled up with TD after lunch, but there was no sign of his friend Detra Ann. He had given both TD and me a nod, and that was it. *What's wrong with him? I bet our painting date is off too.* TD had just glanced at me and shrugged.

For the rest of the afternoon, I had focused on computer work. I was behind on emails—that had been Mia's job, and now I had dozens of inquiries to follow up with. When it got to be 5:30 and neither Ashland nor TD had shown up, I assumed we weren't painting and headed out to my car. What was Ashland's problem? Surely he didn't think that TD and I had something going. What kind of girl did he think I was? *Oh, to hell with him. I can't think about that right now.*

I had planned to go by the grocery store to stock my mini-fridge and then go home and dive into Calpurnia's journals, but that wasn't going to happen without a car. I sat in my dead car, swearing softly under my breath. I looked up at the house and thought about going inside and calling someone, but who? Ashland left without saying goodbye and blew off our painting date, and TD had made it clear that he was exhausted. The only other person I might call would be Bette, but I was too tired to chat with her. I liked her a great deal, but she definitely had the gift for gab. My inner voice told me to walk away, go home—now. I listened.

The weatherman had finally got one right—the dry ground appeared as if an invisible painter were carefully sprinkling drops of liquid on a blank canvas. I wrapped my raincoat around me. Bette once told me that if you don't like the weather in Mobile, just wait a minute—it will change. She was right. It was warm and balmy earlier and now cold rain had come through to cool everything down, at least for a few minutes. There was nothing I could do but walk home in the rain. I wished I'd thought to bring an umbrella.

As I walked, I remembered what TD and I had talked about on the way home from lunch. "TD, I want to ask you a question," I'd said. "But don't freak out on me. I promise I'm not crazy."

"Color me intrigued." He had grinned as he turned on to Royal Street; he wanted to show me more of the city. "Shoot, I won't judge—promise!"

"Do you think the house is haunted? Is Seven Sisters haunted? Have you heard anything, or maybe felt something?"

I thought he'd give me his typical chuckle or his deep, throaty laugh, but there was nothing. He was so quiet. "TD, did you hear me?"

"Yeah, I heard you. I'm just thinking."

"Oh, okay." So I waited.

About five minutes later, he spoke. "Yes, I think it is haunted, but probably not the way you might think. I believe it's just packed full of mysteries, mysteries it wants to tell. But so far, we haven't been smart enough to figure them out. I think it is haunted by the sadness of a family who never knew what happened to their daughter; I think it is haunted by the hopelessness of the slaves who lived there, for surely that must have been what they felt. I think it is haunted by the emotions of those who lived there, but do I think ghosts are haunting this place? No, I don't. I've never seen anything that couldn't be explained some kind of way."

It was my turn to be thoughtful. I had no idea TD was such a deep thinker. "What about the furniture being moved around? Nobody confessed to doing that—and there's another thing..."

His warm brown eyes were fixed on me. "Yes? Did you see something in the house, Carrie Jo?"

"No, not exactly but the night that Ashland and I found Mia and her friends upstairs, we heard something—and later I felt something. I do think that someone is there."

He didn't laugh at me, but I could tell he wasn't convinced. "As far as the furniture goes, are you sure those kids weren't playing a joke or something? Anyone could have done that."

"Yes, but I was on the other side of the door when the furniture was being moved. I could hear it scraping, and the door wouldn't open," I said in a furious, desperate whisper. "When it finally opened, all the furniture had been moved, and there were scrape marks on the floor. You saw them yourself. How do you explain that?"

"Well, for starters, you don't know what you were hearing since the door wouldn't open. Secondly, have you checked the room for a hidden door or a false wall? I mean, the place is full of them. It's possible that we missed one."

I felt a little relieved. "Yes, that's possible. It's better than the alternative."

"What would that be?"

"That an unhappy ghost didn't like the way the furniture was arranged in her room." We stared at one another, wide-eyed, and then TD laughed.

"You historians—such imaginations. Well, if you do find any unhappy ghosts, ask them if they know where the missing statues are—I'm pretty pissed that someone would steal them." The subject had changed and I pretended to listen, but I couldn't help but think about Calpurnia being unhappy with the furniture arrangement.

Calpurnia! Is it you? Where did you go? Where are you now? Let me know somehow! She stayed on my mind as I walked home, leaving my broken old car behind. I definitely had to buy a new one. *I'll have to make the time, I suppose.*

The grey sky above me grew darker, and lightning flashed in the distance. Not a great time to go for a walk, but in a weird way I liked it. My hands ran along the fleur spires of a decorative gate in front of a friendly-looking Victorian. I bet that house had a story or two to tell. A territorial Yorkie barked at me across the green lawn, and I waved my fingers at him. The smell of camellias filled the air, and a pre-storm breeze shook the white petals off the overgrown bush, sending a shower of silken petals onto my path. I stopped to pick one up. Enjoying the sweet scent, I rubbed it between my fingers to stir up more of the perfume. Suddenly, an aggressive breeze tried to lift my skirt, but I held it down as best I could. I crossed the street carefully; the rain was really coming down now. It didn't take long for the streets to fill up from the sudden downpour. Try as I might, I couldn't avoid stepping into pools of cold, clear rainwater. With every step, I felt colder, stiffer. I could feel my headache returning and I was ready to get home. Just one more block now.

I walked past St. Ignatius, the big Catholic church. I wasn't a Catholic myself, but I loved looking at their statues, especially the faces. It always intrigued me how artists could capture and recreate the faces that they "saw" in their minds. I secretly wondered if maybe they weren't just "dream catchers" of a sort, zipping through time to see the faces of dead saints, then zipping back to the present to give us a glimpse. I could certainly have done that, if I'd been any good at drawing or sculpting or painting. I wasn't.

Last block! The rain slid down the collar of my raincoat and down my back. I shivered and flipped the collar up tighter. It did little good. I rubbed water from my face, and my hair hung around me in heavy tendrils, all the curls made straight by the driving rain. Finally, I saw my apartment, the desk lamp shining through the flimsy curtain. I climbed the steps and reached in my pocket for the key. "Oh, hell!" I'd left my house key in my car. Why hadn't I put it on my key ring? I stood staring at the door. I halfheartedly turned the knob just to be sure it was locked—it was. I had two choices, walk back to the car or ask Bette to open it for me. I hated to bother her, but I could see the light on in her kitchen.

I carefully walked down the steps, cold and shivering. I knocked on her door, and she opened it in less than a minute. "Goodness gracious, come on."

I shook my head. "I'm soaked and I don't want to get water all over the linoleum. I need a favor. I left my house key at Seven Sisters. Could I borrow yours, or could you open my door?"

"Sure I will. Let me grab my umbrella. I'll go with you. I don't mind you taking the key, but I need to talk to you anyway." She scrambled off and came back smiling through her perfectly applied bright orange lipstick. She held a huge umbrella, big enough for two. She dangled the key and said, "I've got you covered." We stepped outside; it was a driving rain now, falling so hard that you couldn't talk over it. It was kind of silly for me to get under an umbrella now, because to say that I was drenched was an understatement, but she insisted. We walked up the steps together, and she opened the door for me. Without waiting to be asked, she went to the bathroom and grabbed an armload of towels. I took off my jacket and accepted one. I wrapped it around my hair and pulled off my raincoat. Suddenly, I sneezed loudly and repeatedly.

"Oh, that's not good. Sounds like you might have a cold coming on. Why don't you hop into a warm shower and let me bring you a pot of soup up. Do you like tomato or chicken noodle?"

"I don't want to be any trouble," I said, pulling off my soaked wedges, feeling cold and uncomfortable—and very tired.

"I insist. I'll be back in about 30 minutes with something delicious."

She left, and I stumbled to the shower, stripping off my wet, clingy clothing as I went. Bette must have forgotten that she had something to tell me. *Oh well, I can ask her when she gets back.* I caught a look at myself in the mirror—boy, I looked terrible. No wonder she wanted to make me some soup. I climbed in the hot shower and let the water do the work. I glanced down at my ankle; the bruises were nearly gone now, the fading evidence of a dream encounter. I shuddered, remembering Jeremiah Cottonwood's cruel belt striking my skin—Calpurnia's skin. I'd never experienced a transfer like that. I hoped that wasn't a new, permanent development. What would happen if I witnessed something worse? I refused to think about it, but my mind stayed on Callie. I planned on digging into those journals that night. I had found a few more in that dusty old box and planned on reading them all as soon as possible. I lathered up and rinsed, taking my time and enjoying the steam. I felt almost normal, except for what was obviously a cold. I heard the door slam and hollered out, "Is that you, Bette? I'm almost done."

I turned off the water and slung the shower curtain back all the way. I stood peering through the steam. I didn't hear Bette, so I called out again, stepping onto the plush bathroom rug and closing the door partially. "Bette?" I wrapped a towel around my body and stopped. Nobody answered. Even though it was damp, the hair on the back of my neck began to rise; I could sense the shifting of the air, and the inexplicable feeling that I wasn't alone overwhelmed me. I reached for another towel and patted my hair with it, trying to behave as naturally as I could.

"Bette?" I called a little more softly, stepping out of the bathroom into my bedroom/living room. Nobody was there, no one I could see with my naked eye, but I knew someone had been in the room. My desk drawers were open and the papers disorganized. Instinctively, I reached for the first thing

I could: my hairbrush. *Smart, CJ. What are you going to do? Brush them to death?* I held it like it was a deadly weapon. I saw a shadow on my doorstep and swung the door open with a "ha!" only to find a startled Bette grappling with an oversized umbrella and a crock of steamy soup.

"Oh my word, are you okay? Can you grab this crock? Be careful, it's hot—use the handles. Boy, she left out of here fast. Did you two have an argument or something?"

I took the crock and set it down on a nearby table. "Did you see who it was?" My eyes must have been as big as goose eggs.

"Yes, but please sit down before you fall down. You look very pale, Carrie Jo. That was your friend, the girl that looks like Marilyn Monroe. Well, she doesn't now, her hair is black, but that was her. I wonder why she changed it; she looked so much better the other way. Are you okay?"

"No, I'm not. I think you're right, I should sit down. I should also tell you that my friend, or former friend, didn't have permission to be in here. Did you know the police are looking for her? They think she might have had something to do with Hollis Matthews' death. I better call Detective Simmons and let her know. On top of all this, I feel horrible."

"You sit—I'll bring you the phone. As long as you leave the lid on that crock, it will stay nice and hot."

"Would you hand me my purse, please?"

"Surely! Here you go." She passed me my phone and purse and started tidying up the desk.

"You better wait, Bette. The detective will want that left undisturbed so she can examine it."

"Oh my goodness, that's probably true. Oh dear, I better put on some coffee." She went into my kitchenette and quickly had a pot of coffee going. Somehow, the smell soothed me, and I dialed the detective's number.

It went to voicemail so I left her my information and hung up. She called me back in less than two minutes, and I happily accepted a cup of black coffee from Bette. "Yes, Detective, it's the same address, the one I gave you. I'm in the upstairs studio, and the porch light is on. Yes, she's here. Okay, see you soon."

I hung up and looked over at Bette. "She asked if you could stay and give a description. They really want to find her." I sipped on the coffee, but my stomach growled. I decided to get a few spoonfuls of the soup in my tummy before Detective Simmons arrived.

"I had no idea that she was a suspect. I swunny! I would have thrown my umbrella at her if I had known."

"I'm sorry, I try not to gossip about what goes on up at the house. Actually, I have a hard time believing she could do such a thing—I don't think she did, honestly, but she must know something. Why else would she disappear like that? Mia has been my friend for many years—I spent all of my college holidays at her home with her family. They are good people, very loving and accepting, but something has happened to my friend. She's not the same anymore. I don't know why or what it is. Anyway, one night Ashland and I found her and a few others having a séance at the house. Well, naturally, we had to fire her. She couldn't just bring people into Seven Sisters like that. When she left, Mia was furious, angrier than I had ever seen her. The next day, Mr. Matthews was dead. The police think she did it."

Bette said, "Oh my word," repeatedly during the course of my story and finally sat staring at me. "I wonder what she wanted today. She was after some papers, it looks like. For what purpose, other than to cause you some heartache?"

"Well, I think I know what she is after." I reached inside my purse and grabbed my crocheted change purse. It was the only thing my mother had ever given me. I unzipped the ragged container and pulled out the silver key, the key to the music box.

"Hmm...what does it go to?" She turned the key over in her plump hand. "Looks old and very delicate."

"It is very old. It is the key to a music box, one that came up missing right after Mr. Matthews' died. You can't play the box without the key, and I think this proves that Mia has the box." I walked over to my small jewelry box and removed a silver chain, one with a lobster claw clasp. I fed the chain through the hole in the key and put it around my neck. It might be safer if I wore the key rather than leave it in my purse, especially now that Mia was so desperate that she'd risk being seen to get it.

"All this to play a music box?" Her eyes narrowed a little, and then I saw her face light up. "Oh! Unless there's something else about this box. Maybe it has a secret compartment?"

I smiled at her sadly. "That's what I am thinking, but now it's gone. I didn't check it while I had it. I don't know if we will ever find it."

"Sure you will. I see car lights—that must be the detective. She's a woman—how interesting." Bette opened the door and waved. I put the lid back on my soup crock and suddenly realized I was still wearing towels.

I grabbed some jeans, a sweat shirt and some underwear and ran to the bathroom to change. My hair was a lost cause; wild curls were already popping out, so I just gathered up the damp mess in a ponytail on top of my head. I brushed my teeth and walked out to find Detective Simmons looking over my desk with a cup of coffee in her hand.

"Hi, Detective Simmons. Thanks for coming. I'd like you to meet..." Before I could finish, I was sneezing my head off, excusing myself again. I returned to the bathroom, blew my nose and washed my hands. I caught a quick glimpse of myself in the mirror. *Yep, this cold is going to be a doozy. Darn!*

Detective Simmons did not have too many questions for me. She asked if I had heard from Mia recently, and of course I hadn't. I showed her the key. She offered to put it into evidence where it would be completely safe, but I wasn't willing to part with it.

"Okay, so here's what we've got. Mia Reed has a new look, short, dark hair, and she was wearing black clothing. Are you sure it was her? I mean, it was rainy."

Bette nodded vigorously. "No doubt it was—I have never seen anyone with a tattoo on the back of their hand like she had—it was the sun, I think. That was definitely her, and she looked right at me. Heifer! I should have smacked her."

"No, please don't confront her if you see her again. She's a suspect in a murder investigation—it is safe to assume that she is dangerous. If you see her around here, call 9-1-1 and then call me. Are we clear?" The redheaded woman stared at both of us and added, "I don't want either of you acting like Nancy Drew—or Jessica Fletcher. Got it?" We nodded. Detective Simmons left us alone, and we looked at one another.

Bette said, "Well, my goodness! I don't think you look a thing like Angela Lansbury." We laughed, and I finished my soup. Then she left me alone to rest, and I certainly did. I had every intention of calling Ashland, but this cold had gotten the best of me. I passed out on my small, uncomfortable couch, waking up around 11 p.m. I got up to check the locks and turn off the lights. I peered out the windows, saw nothing and then climbed into bed. I didn't even remember covering up.

Chapter 5

Before my feet hit the floor the next morning, Bette was tapping on the door. I could see through the sheer white curtain that she had a tray of food for me. *So thoughtful.* I padded across the floor, blowing my nose before I unlocked it. "Sorry, this cold is kicking my butt."

I flopped in my desk chair, accepting the food that my kind landlady offered me. "This is so thoughtful, Bette. I can't believe you would do this for me. Thank you." The neat little Formica tray was a vintage piece, probably a genuine butler's tray from the 1930s. I appreciated the historical touch. Bette brought me a small bowl full of fresh fruit, including watermelon (my favorite), a glass of orange juice and a heaping bowl of her decadent grits. On top of the quickly melting pat of butter were bacon bits and plenty of shredded cheese. Sitting on top of that were three decent-sized shrimp, arranged neatly in a swirl. She had even included a folded linen napkin, salt and pepper shakers and a vase with a single pink flower in it.

"That flower came from my garden, right there on the side of the house. But if it makes you sneezy, you just stick it in the refrigerator. It will keep in there for a few days. Maybe you will feel better by then and you can enjoy it. Do you have everything you need?"

I nodded, sipping on my orange juice. "Thanks again. I can't believe this wonderful breakfast. I appreciate your...your..." I sneezed again, and I was suddenly grateful I had not eaten a big spoonful of grits. That would have been embarrassing.

"Maybe you should stay home today. Do you have any sinus medicine or cold medicine in the bathroom?" She didn't wait for an answer; she went to my medicine cabinet and announced that I didn't. "You know, living in Mobile, you need a few things, including sinus medicine." She laughed heartily and said, "Tell you what, since you feel under the weather, I can go into town for you, pick up some juice and some good meds. What about that?"

I knew she was only trying to help me, so I tried not to interpret her offer as pushy. I wasn't used to being fussed over, and she obviously enjoyed having someone to take care of. I felt too groggy and snotty to argue, but I still intended to go into work. "No, I can do it when I go out this morning. I only plan to stick around for a few hours, just long enough to see them get started repainting that room and finishing the floor in the ballroom."

Bette smiled at me, showing off her impossibly perfect lipstick application. "I think you might be pushing yourself too hard, but I'm not your mother—I can be a bit bossy at times. Just want to make sure that you are taking care of yourself. That reminds me, I won't be home this afternoon. I've got some errands to run, and I have a date tonight, so don't wait up for me. You think you'll be okay?"

"Yes, I'm sure I will. I hope to hear more about your date later." I grinned despite my runny eyes and nose.

"You shall, my dear! Hey, I have a great idea!" *Uh-oh, I wonder what this is.* "I think you should ask Ashland to stay for a while tonight—I know you're worried about how it looks, but I'm more worried about your safety. I bet you didn't even tell him about Mia being here, did you?"

"I passed out last night. By the time I woke up, it was too late to call. And I was too tired to text. I'll tell him this morning." I scooped up the grits in my silver spoon. They smelled so delicious I couldn't resist them. I popped them in my mouth and waited for the cough. Nothing happened so I took another bite. Maybe I was going to be okay after all. Not as sick as I thought.

"Uh-oh, no need to worry about that, dear. It looks like he knows already. Maybe Detective Simmons called him last night or something." Bette peeked through the curtain at the car pulling into the driveway. "That is one handsome fellow." She opened the door and waved at him. "Well, Ashland Stuart, come on in here. So nice to see you again!" Before I knew what was happening, the always elegant Ashland Stuart was inside my over-the-garage apartment, completely busting me in my pajamas, wild ponytail and runny, red nose.

"Nice to see you too, ma'am. Are you two all right? Did Mia take anything or harm you in any way, Carrie Jo?" He seemed genuinely panicked; somehow he had the idea that I was in trouble. I looked suspiciously at Bette as she slipped out the door, closing it quietly behind her. Surely she hadn't called Ashland on my behalf.

"No, I'm fine—we're fine. Mia was looking for this." I showed him the key on the silver chain.

He reached out and touched it, holding it in his tanned hand. "That? What is it?"

"It's the key to the music box, the one that came up missing from the house after Mr. Matthews died." I started to say more but I sneezed, luckily, I covered my face just in the nick of time.

"Are you feeling okay? Should I call Dr. Patterson?" He pulled up a chair from the dinette and sat next to me. I smiled weakly. His thoughtfulness was touching, but again I wasn't used to anyone caring about me. Now I had two people looking out for me.

"Oh no!" I suddenly felt sick and took off for the restroom. My grits and juice hadn't stayed down very long. I couldn't believe I'd just thrown up with Ashland in the other room. Now I really felt like dying.

Ashland called Dr. Patterson as I dragged myself to bed. "Sorry you had to see me like this. So embarrassing."

"No reason to feel embarrassed. It happens. I'm just glad it's just a virus or something. When I saw your car had been left there overnight and all four tires were flat, and then Detective Simmons and Bette called, I was sure something had happened to you."

"What? My tires are flat?" I sat straight up in the bed, but only for a few seconds. Dizziness overtook me, and I flopped back on the pillow. "What the heck? When I left there yesterday, the car wouldn't crank, and now I have four flat tires? Somebody, probably Mia, has been trying to make a point. But I'm not sure what it is."

Ashland chewed on his pink lip. His ridiculously blue eyes were thoughtful. "Should we call the detective again? Let her know about the vandalism to your car?"

"No. Without anyone seeing it, it would just be a guess, not actual proof of wrongdoing. Damn, she's desperate to get this key. We need to get that box back from her. There's something special about that...that..." *Achoo!* I sneezed again, louder this time. *Oh my God! I sound like a donkey!*

"There's no way you are going anywhere for the next day or so at least. I'll make sure that room gets repainted and check with TD about the flooring. Actually, I think TD can take care of all that. I just need to call him. I'd like to stick around for a little while, if you don't mind." He handed me the nearby tissue box. My lungs were threatening to sneeze again. *Nope, false alarm.* I kept the tissue handy just in case. I didn't know whether to throw up or sneeze.

"I don't want you to see me like this. I'll be fine once the doctor gets here."

"There's no one here to take care of you, so I'm staying. At least until you go to sleep."

I didn't argue; I was too tired and too sick. I kind of nodded and rubbed my nose. "Listen, Ashland. I'm sorry about yesterday. I got a little snippety with your friend, and I know that was wrong. It's just that I feel very...."

"Passionate about the house? I get that. You are a historian, so it only makes sense."

I rubbed grits out of my hot eyes. *Man, they get everywhere!* "I was going to say 'protective' of the house, but yes, passionate is a good way to describe it too. You see, yesterday I wanted to talk with you about something, the thing I've been promising to talk to you about for a while now. And then Detra Ann and her picnic basket showed up and that got postponed. Later you left without saying goodbye. I guess I'm just a big ol' ball of mixed-up right now. Should we just be friends, coworkers? I don't want to get into something complicated. You know, if you have a past with her or something like that, I don't mind stepping back. I mean, it's not like we're boyfriend and girlfriend, right?"

Ashland stared at me, then laughed. He reached over and placed his cool hand on my forehead. "Good Lord, Carrie Jo! You've got quite a fever because you are talking crazy."

"Could you please drop the temperature on the air conditioner? I'm hot, now that you mention it. I guess that could be a fever." A sharp rap at the door let us know that the skinny doctor had arrived.

"Good morning to you both," he said. "Let's see, you definitely have a fever, but how high?" He opened his old-fashioned leather bag and took out a thermometer. He slid a plastic cover over it and told me to lift my tongue. "You know the drill. No biting, and keep it under your tongue, okay?" I did as I was told, leaning back on the pillows with my eyes shut. I felt like I had stayed there forever when the thermometer suddenly beeped. The doctor peered at it, lifting his glasses up to get a good view. "Miss Jardine, you can't go to work today. And if this fever doesn't come down, not tomorrow either. Look at that, son, it's 102. Someone will need to stay with her here, or she can go to the clinic to be monitored. But either way, we have to take her temperature every hour. If it spikes, take her straight to the emergency room."

He looked inside my ears and down my throat. "Very red, very swollen. Probably strep but we won't know for sure without a throat culture. I can do it here and take it to my lab for testing, or you can come in."

"I want to stay home if that's possible, and I don't need anyone to babysit me. I'll be fine, I promise." I smiled as sweetly as I could to show them how well I was. They both frowned at me. I guess my appearance accurately portrayed how I really felt. I opened my mouth, and Dr. Patterson efficiently swabbed my throat.

"Once I get the tests back, I can write a prescription for an antibiotic. Okay? I'll have my nurse bring it over later this morning. In the meantime, give her this fever reducer every six hours, Ashland. Are you feeling nauseous, Miss Jardine?"

"Only from here to here." I pointed to the top of my head to my feet. He laughed at my answer. "Well, I'm going to give you some Phenergan to stop the vomiting. It will make you sleepy, so absolutely no driving. Sleep is the best thing for you. Here we go." He handed me a small white pill. I swallowed it and accepted the paper cup of water he handed me too. "All right, well, don't forget. Ashland, take her temperature every hour until it gets below 100. That's an order." Ashland closed the door behind the doctor and locked it.

Ashland turned back toward me. "Here, do you need an extra..." He didn't have the chance to finish his sentence because I pushed past him like a madwoman, headed for the toilet. Hot and rancid-smelling orange juice came back up, thankfully into the bowl. I shook after I vomited. It always did that to me. I would have made a lousy drunk.

"I have to take a shower." I held on to the doorframe, certain I looked like something the devil spat out of hell. "Could you do me a favor? I need some clothing. Top drawer, underwear and a big t-shirt." My internal gauge warned me that I was beginning to feel worse. I needed to hurry up and get still. But I wouldn't get any rest smelling like vomit, and I knew a cold shower would cool me down.

"Is this okay?" He handed me what I asked for.

"Yes, thanks, Ashland. I'll be right back." I carefully stepped into the shower and stood under the cool water. I washed my hair but didn't bother conditioning it. I'd be sweating for a while, and I was sure I would need another shower pretty soon. I wrapped the towel around my hair, slid on my yellow cotton panties and pulled my old Tweety Bird nightshirt over my head.

"Oh well, if he's one of those guys that likes watching 'angels' in lingerie, he'll definitely be disappointed," I said to no one. A matching bra and panty set was about as "sexy" as I got, and that sure wasn't going to happen today. I was a "slow mover" when it comes to guys. I didn't feel compelled to sleep with someone just because we went on a third date. Ashland and I had been on only one date, but it was a magical night. I would never forget the stars zinging across the open water of Mobile Bay. Feeling wobbly, I reached for my toothbrush and brushed my teeth. I left the bathroom feeling better but sleepy and kind of goofy-headed.

Ashland rose from his chair and stood still. I could almost hear his thoughts. "So what are the protocols here? Should I stay? Should I go? What do I do?"

"I think you should go; I'll be okay," I answered him.

"What?"

"Didn't you just ask me what the protocols were?"

He froze and stared at me like he'd seen a ghost. "Are you kidding me? I must have been talking aloud."

"I guess so, right? I think I will be okay now." In my hazy state, I was oblivious to what had just happened.

"Do you need some water?" Ashland still looked bewildered.

"No, I'm good. Thank you for being here with me."

I plumped my pillow and lay back slowly. It felt good to lie down. My brain felt fuzzy and kind of "floaty." It was a nice feeling—so much better than throwing up. *Oh my God! I threw up with Ashland here. Now he will never want to kiss me again. I wish he'd kiss me now.*

Ashland pulled the sheet up over me. "So you are a psychic, just like Mia said," he whispered, sounding serious and kind of sad.

"Oh no, I'm nothing like a psychic. I'm a dream catcher. Way different than a psychic. At least I think so, anyway." I rubbed my itchy nose with the back of my hand. I wished I had dried my hair first.

He sat in the chair next to my bed, the half-round chair that I liked cuddling in to read. "Tell me all about it. What do you mean you're a dream catcher?"

I guess it was the medicine, because I told him everything. I couldn't stop my mouth from talking, and eventually I passed out.

Chapter 6

My eyes opened slowly; I felt like I had one heck of a hangover. I blinked against the failing light, surprised to see Ashland sitting in my chair, poring over Calpurnia's journals. His sleeves were rolled up, his leg was crossed over his knee, and he looked as serious as I'd ever seen him. He heard me stirring, closed the book and said, "Hey, you slept a long time. How do you feel?"

I pushed my wild brown curls out of my face and sat up slowly. My stomach felt sore. I still felt warm but not as warm as earlier. "I'm okay, I think. You been here the whole time? What time is it?"

He looked at his gold watch. "Almost 5. Yes, I've been here—I've been reading." He leaned forward, his elbows on his knees, the worn journal in his hand. "Why didn't you tell me you had these?"

"Do you mind if I go to the restroom before we get into that?" My mouth felt gross, and I really wanted to tidy up. Also, I needed some time to think about how I was going to answer that. I should have already told him that I had found the journals; they were his property after all.

"Sure. Sorry to seem anxious, but I'd really like to talk to you. You dropped quite a few bombshells on me before you passed out."

I swung my legs off the bed and stared at him. "Oh no. Did I say something crazy? I'm so sorry. I don't take drugs very often, and they make me loopy."

"It wasn't the drugs, Carrie Jo, and I'm glad you told me the truth—about everything."

Darn, that doesn't sound good.

He stood up and walked to the edge of the bed, helping me get to my feet. "We can talk about this when I get back. I have to run a few errands. The nurse came by and brought those antibiotics. You need to take those. Dr. Patterson says the strep test was positive, and you probably have a viral infection on top of it that's upsetting your stomach. I'll bring back some ginger ale and crackers. Those work for me when I'm sick. And then we can talk more. Will you be okay by yourself?"

"Yeah, I think so. Believe it or not, crackers and ginger ale sound good." Ashland smelled so good. I leaned on his arm and walked to the restroom.

"I'll see you back here in about thirty minutes. I am locking the door, all right?"

"Sure, I'll be fine." I didn't feel fine, but I had been needy enough for one day. This was truly so unlike me. I cleaned up and got dressed. No more wallowing around in my pajamas; I put on blue jeans and a cotton shirt. I swallowed the antibiotics with a few sips of water but didn't bother taking the Phenergan tablets. "Never again."

As I brushed the snarls out of my hair, I had plenty of time to think about my confession. I couldn't really remember much, but I had the feeling I had told Ashland much more than I wanted to. *Oh God, please tell me I didn't say something like "I love you."*

I sat in my favorite chair, running my fingers along the edge of the journals. I absently rubbed the key around my neck, thinking about Mia and her quest for the box. True to his word, Ashland returned with the promised goodies. I opened the door and helped him carry the bags in. "Did you buy the whole store?" I inspected his purchases, pulling out cans of soup and other treats.

"I got hungry, and you didn't have much in the pantry. Besides, you'll need all this to get better." My head spun, and I held on to the kitchen counter. "Hey, go sit," he said. "I think I can figure out where this stuff goes. Do you want to try some soup now or just the crackers?"

"Just the crackers and that ginger ale you promised." I watched him arrange the cans neatly on the shelf. He really was too good to be true. Handsome, thoughtful and single. That couldn't be right. Ashland must have had some deep, dark secret—something that would explain why some girl like Detra Ann hadn't scooped him yet. I smothered a giggle thinking of Detra Ann catching him with a hunting net and a stun gun. *Am I still feverish?* Ashland poured us both a glass of ginger ale and handed me a sleeve of crackers. I took them gratefully and sat on the floor in front of the bed. The shag rug was comfortable, and there wasn't much seating in my apartment. I needed a change of scenery.

I tore open the crackers and snacked on a few quietly. I could tell he wanted to talk about the journals or maybe something dumb I'd told him while I was enjoying my pain-killer. I couldn't take the silence anymore. "Ashland, I'm sorry I didn't tell you about the journals—it's just that so much happened so quickly. I never meant to keep them from you, I promise."

"Yeah, it has been a crazy month or so."

"I found a collection of them in a box upstairs before the air conditioners were put in. Some old letters from your mother were in there. That led me to believe that she knew about these books, and I thought you did too. I guess I was wrong to assume that." I pulled a spiral of itchy hair out of my face and put it behind my ear. "What else did I tell you?"

His pink lips curled slightly. I could tell he was enjoying this moment a little too much. "Quite a bit, actually, but we can talk about that later."

I buried my face in my hands. "I apologize for anything dumb I may have said. Like I told you, I don't take medications very often."

Ashland laughed and agreed with me. "I don't guess you remember this but you told me you were a dream catcher. Can you tell me what that means?"

I swallowed the mouthful of crackers I had and took a sip of my ginger ale. "I know how you feel about psychics—but I'm not a psychic. What I have, what I do, it's different."

"Really? Because I could have sworn that you read my mind this morning." His bright blue eyes darkened a little, like he didn't know what to think about me. Neither did I.

"That was some kind of coincidence—I've never done that before. I'm not a psychic! Sometimes I dream about people and places, but not always. It's something that started when I was a kid, and it is definitely not something I asked for. It's cost me a lot in the way of friends, relationships—you name it."

"You told me about Ginny."

"Did I?" My heart felt heavy thinking about my childhood friend.

Ashland rubbed his hand through his hair and nodded. "How does it work? Do you know? You must know something about it."

I felt my glass sweating in my hands, so I set it on the nightstand. I had to explain this cautiously, and I was a hand talker when I was stressed. "I'm not really sure." I clenched my hands together. "If I walk into a room while I'm awake—even one with lots of history in it, I can't see or hear a thing. However, if I go to sleep in it, the past comes to life. It doesn't happen every time, and I can't pick which part of the past I see, but it just happens. Until recently, I thought I had it under control. But then I came to Mobile and well, I started dreaming again. Mia used to call it 'dream catching'."

"Have you dreamed about my house, about Seven Sisters?"

"Yes, I have. It happened the first night, when I fell on the carpet. I dreamed about a slave—a sweet boy named Muncie." My voice shook as I thought again about the boy's anxious face, his kind thoughts. "He was smart and full of life; he was Calpurnia's friend. I just had to know what happened to him. That was before I promised to help you find her, find Calpurnia. Then when I brought some of the items from the house here, those journals, I dreamed about her. I have never had that happen before. I've never had a dream triggered by an object. I don't understand what is going on. I'm sorry I didn't tell you about all this to begin with, but I didn't think it would be an issue. And after I knew how you felt about the supernatural, I didn't want to. If you remember correctly, I didn't want to stay on the property. It was Mr. Matthews that wanted me there." I quietly added, "I think he knew about me, about my ability." My head throbbed just thinking about it all. *Would it be rude to crawl back in bed and take another nap?*

"What? How would he know about you?"

"Mia. Before he died, the day before he died, I heard the two of them arguing. It was about me—I'm sure of it. I think they were after something, plotting something. Maybe all of this was about the necklace that you mentioned."

"I can't believe it." Ashland got out of his chair and walked to the window, his hands slung in the pockets of his khaki pants. "I want to believe you, but this really makes me uncomfortable. I don't like this kind of stuff at all and... it's not just about my mother." He turned around and leaned against my desk, his back to the window. I didn't press him, but I knew he wanted to tell me something.

"It's okay if you don't believe me." I got on my feet, feeling tired and wobbly again. "I promise you that I am a damn good historian. I love the house, and I don't intend to quit."

He put out his hand to quiet me. "I never doubted that. It's just—man, this is hard to talk about. I almost don't believe it happened."

I sat on my unmade bed, sensing the importance of the moment. This wasn't about me. This was about Ashland. "What is it? You can talk to me about anything."

"Man, I never thought I would talk about this." He paced the floor, rubbing his hand through his hair. "People talked about my mother. They said she was crazy, and I know they were right for the most part. When she got really sick, I mean mentally, after my father died, Mother did some crazy things, like talk to the house plants and even to people that no one else could see. I always thought that when my dad died, she'd be happy; he was not a nice man. He didn't care what I did, but my mother, she had to toe the line. Behave a certain way, be the perfect wife. She couldn't do it. She was different. Don't get me wrong, my mother was strong, but there are many different kinds of strong. She was beautiful and sensitive to the unseen world. After he died, she began hanging around people like gurus, mediums—you name it. Whenever there's money involved, people come out of the woodwork. It's not an exaggeration to say that every single one of them were frauds—except one."

"What happened with the one who wasn't?"

"My mother had a séance at the house, kind of like Mia did, but she held hers downstairs in the Blue Room. I remember her cousin, Robert Matthews, that was Hollis' brother, chewed her out for that. He loved my mother and tried to help her, but she insisted on spending money on anyone who promised to contact Calpurnia Cottonwood. I'll never forget that night. It was so foggy that you couldn't see out the windows. Cousin Robert didn't want to stay, and I didn't want to be there either—I was just a little kid. Cousin Robert tried to take me with him, but my mother wanted me to stay. Her friend Madame Farouche said I was a sensitive; my presence could boost the spiritual frequency at our séance."

I could tell it was a stressful memory for him; Ashland was paler than usual. He sat in my favorite chair and continued, "The séance started, and

Ultimate Seven Sisters Collection – Moonlight Falls on Seven Sisters

it was nothing special. Round table, fluttery tablecloth, crystal ball, lots of candles and some incense." His lips curled up in a rueful smile. "It was everything you'd see in a bad movie. You remember those old black and white movies with gypsies and a gray moon?" He chuckled. "For about thirty minutes, Madame Farouche talked in a 'fake' voice, pretending to be Calpurnia. I knew it was all fake the whole time, but my mother believed every word of it. I felt so angry about being there—I'll never forget that. Then suddenly the atmosphere in the room changed. The rest of the group didn't notice that the fog outside was moving and that there were even lights in it. Don't ask me to explain that. As a kid, I thought it was part of the sham—part of the act, but all the grownups had their eyes closed, calling out to the dead people in the house. I had been sitting on the floor playing with my cars when the room temperature plummeted—it was in the middle of summer and there was no draft, not even a door open. I felt the sudden urge to run, run as far away as I could. I did! You've heard of 'fight or flight', right?"

I nodded, my eyes wide, my stomach rumbling from the crackers.

"Well, it's definitely a real thing. And how was I going to fight a spirit?"

I pulled the desk chair next to his chair and took his hand. "It's okay. Tell me what happened. You're not crazy, and I swear I won't tell a soul. I understand how personal this kind of stuff is, Ashland."

"Thanks, Carrie Jo. I ran down the hall—that same hall you tripped in." His bright blue eyes were wide with the sudden realization. "I didn't really have a plan. I just wanted to run out the back door. But I couldn't. A girl was standing there, an older girl in a big blue dress. I saw every detail of her perfectly. I wasn't scared at first. She had blond curls here." His hands motioned to the sides of his face. "She had a face like an angel, pale with pink cheeks and lips. Cherubic is a good way to describe it. Her. Her arms were pale, and she reached for me and blew me a kiss. When I first saw her, I wasn't fearful—not at all. Surprised, curious but not afraid until I saw that she floated above the floor. The edges of her blue gown faded into nothing, no feet, no shoes. She floated there for a second and then hovered outside the door, beckoning to me with her hands. Still beautiful and floating, she smiled and whispered something to me, but I couldn't hear what she said. I didn't answer her, I couldn't. In a split second, that sweet-looking face shifted into a snarl, and she came at me with a speed I've never seen before. I froze but screamed my head off."

The hair on my arms stood up just hearing his story. He continued on, his voice wavering, "It tasted—I could taste lemonade, but I didn't enjoy it. I felt like I was going to die. I screamed and screamed and screamed until I couldn't scream anymore. Cousin Robert came busting through the door and grabbed me. And from that day forward, I stayed with him and never returned to the house, except for the day I found my mother almost dead in the Moonlight Garden. I took her to the hospital; she was diagnosed with pneumonia, but she had been sick for so long that she died in just days."

My hands were folded over my mouth, my eyes wide with fear. "I'm sorry that happened to you. I know that had to be terrifying, especially for a child."

"I haven't seen a thing since, and I never told a soul except Robert about what I saw. My mother begged me to tell her what I saw, but I wouldn't. I knew what would happen; she'd want to do it again. She would think I had seen Calpurnia and would make me try it again. Honestly, I don't know what I saw. I suppose it could have been my imagination or maybe some kind of drug Madame Farouche slipped me. Robert said I probably fell asleep and dreamed it all. I can still taste the lemonade on her lips." He rubbed his lips absently with the back of his hand. He looked more uncomfortable by the second. It had to have been hard for him to share—I wondered if he'd ever told anyone else besides his cousin.

Rain had begun to fall again, splashing lightly against the windows. I loved the way that you could smell the rain before it arrived in Mobile. I had never noticed that before, not in Charleston and not in Savannah. Here, in the Heart of Dixie, you expected to smell the rain long before you saw it. I didn't care for the mosquitos afterward, but the rain? I loved it, even when I got caught in it. "I think I know who you saw that night at Seven Sisters— the girl in the blue dress. That may have been Calpurnia's cousin, Isla. As a matter of fact, I am willing to bet that it was. Have you read about her yet in the journals? How far did you get?"

I stood to pick up a journal, but I got up a bit too quickly. Ashland's compelling tale had held me spellbound until the nausea reminded me that I was sick, truly sick. *Steady, girl. No vomiting right now.* I took a deep breath and padded to the bathroom, mumbling an "Excuse me" as I went. Fortunately, I wasn't sick this time. I washed my face and felt compelled to scrub the cracker crumbs out of my teeth. *You look horrible, girl.* Well, there wasn't much sense in dolling up this face now, was there? He'd definitely seen me at my worst, hadn't he? *Oh Lord. I hope so.* I prayed that I had not slept with my mouth open and that I didn't snore.

When I came out of the restroom, Ashland was gathering up his things. I was sorry to see him go, but I also welcomed the time alone. I wanted time to think about what he told me, how it fit into the narrative I'd been developing during my journal readings. "Sorry about that. I'm getting better, but I'm definitely not 100 percent yet." I leaned against the doorframe to steady myself. Oh yeah, it was almost nap time again. "Hey, thanks for taking such good care of me, Ashland. Maybe someday I can return the favor."

Ashland flashed his best football star smile and kissed me on the forehead. "Oh, I hope not. I definitely snore louder than you do." He smiled and walked out into the rainy Mobile night.

Chapter 7

Long after Ashland left, I felt his kiss on my forehead. After I watched his car lights swing into the misty fog of the Alabama night, I clicked off the bedside lamp and snuggled in my bed. I thought about the first time I saw Ashland, how he had appeared without a sound, confident, handsome and playful. Somehow, we had managed to connect, both witnessing the unusual events that continued to center around his family home. I felt like death warmed over, but my heart felt happy because of my luck to meet a guy like Ashland. A guy more like me than I had ever imagined.

Are you sure about this?

I fell asleep and dreamed normal dreams, honey-hued, warm, slow-moving—all about Ashland. His hand was at my waist, and we danced without touching the ground in the Moonlight Garden. Terrence Dale appeared, playing the violin, pulling sentimental strains from the strings. More dancing couples swirled around us—Calpurnia and Muncie, Mia and Hollis, Isla and David Garrett.

The honeyed background faded, and the garden became as black as the inside of a mausoleum. I heard voices. They whispered to me, calling my name. I groped in the dark for Ashland, but he wasn't there. I felt hands on me—I screamed and brushed them away furiously.

I woke with a start to find a big orange tabby nuzzling my chin. "Well, hello," I murmured. "How did you get in here?" I heard humming in the kitchen, and my first thought was Mia. But why would she let a cat in?

As quiet as a mouse—a very sick, coughing mouse—I walked into the kitchen. "Bette?"

"Good morning! I brought you some breakfast. Sorry I didn't cook, though. I was out late. I picked up some fresh croissants, butter, strawberry preserves. But I didn't get any juice. Have you ever had coffee in a French press?"

"No, I haven't. Thank you for all you've done, but you didn't have to do this." Still, my hungry stomach couldn't wait to dive into the spread. I sat in the green vinyl chair of the dinette; the tile floor felt cool on my feet. The orange tabby followed me into the kitchen, rubbing against my legs. "I think your cat likes me." I reached down and patted his big head. Normally I preferred dogs, but I might have to change my mind if all cats were as friendly as this one.

"Let me introduce you to Bienville—I also had Iberville, but he's my ghost cat." Bette smeared butter on her pastry and poured us both a cup of coffee from the French press. The aroma of coffee whetted my appetite further.

"What?" I laughed at the idea of Bette believing in a ghost cat. "What do you mean? Is he white like a ghost?" Surely that was what she meant. *Well, who am I to judge? I'm the queen of weird.*

Bette laughed with me. It was a pretty sound, light and lilting like a young girl's laugh. Her head of white curls didn't bounce today, evidence that she'd sprayed her coiffure with hair spray before her date last night. Of course, her precise lipstick application put my best attempt to shame.

"Well, I had two cats. They were my LeMoyne brothers—you know who they were, being a historian and all. They founded many of the cities along the Gulf Coast, including Mobile. I think there were five LeMoynes, but I only had two cats. Well poor Iberville ran into the street and was dead, deader than a doornail. I tell you I know he was dead because I buried that thing myself right in my backyard garden near the purple azaleas. A couple of days later, who did I find sitting outside my kitchen window. Iberville! He walks a little funny now, and his meow has changed, but what can you expect? He died, didn't he?"

She looked at me and smiled hugely. "I'm kidding, of course! That's what we Mobilians call a tall tale!" Her laughter gave away how much she'd been pulling my leg.

I couldn't help myself and laughed too. "Where I'm from, we call that a lie!"

Bette put her hand on her chest in mock indignation. "Here in Mobile, we're too good-mannered to call anyone a liar—even our politicians. It's tall-telling, and it's practically expected."

"That's good to know," I took a bite of the fresh croissant, and it was light and delicious. Just what I needed.

Bette reached for another croissant with her well-manicured hands. "I swunny, he is like a ghost, though. Just when you think he's gone, he pops up again. Now, that one—he's a friendly butterball. Since he knows you like him, he'll probably pop in again. But you don't have to let him in." She noshed on a pastry without so much as a lipstick smudge.

"Tell me about your date, Bette."

"Oh my, you know a lady never kisses and tells. But do you remember an old actor named Steve McQueen?"

"No, I'm afraid I don't."

"He was a handsome rascal back in the day. Big dark eyes and a head full of lush hair." She shuddered in appreciation. "He was quite a looker. One of my favorite films with him in it, Le Mans, had him playing a race car driver with a limp."

"And? Your date looked like Steve McQueen?"

"No, but he had a limp." She broke into giggles and for the next thirty minutes told me about her date night, although she left out the juiciest details. Then she excused herself to let me continue recuperating.

With a full belly and another piping hot cup of coffee, I sat at my desk to read the journals in the bright sunny light. I pulled out a pair of white cotton gloves from the drawer, a voice recorder and a notebook. If I was going to find Calpurnia, I had to get serious and approach the mystery like a historian. She couldn't have just disappeared—she wanted to be found, and I had promised Ashland that I would. I grabbed my phone and dashed off a text to him: *Feeling better today. I'll be ready for work Monday. Thanks again!*

Just a minute later, my phone dinged with a reply: *That's great! I need your keys. Tires are fixed. I'll drop it off for you.*

What a nice thing to do. I hadn't even thought about my car. *Okay, I'll be here. Thanks for fixing them. I look forward to seeing you.*

Looking forward to seeing you too. Call Rachel K. Found something.

I dialed Rachel's number. "Hey, Rachel. Ashland says you found something?"

"Oh my gosh, yes! It's beautiful—a painting. I emailed you a photo of it. It's a portrait of Calpurnia Cottonwood. And according to the date on it, it had to have been painted not long before she went missing. I don't know how anyone missed this. I'm thinking it will go perfectly on one of the mantelpieces, maybe the one in the ballroom."

I knew exactly which picture it was although I'd never actually seen it. "Does it have an artist's signature at the bottom?"

"Yes, but it's kind of blurry, hard to make out. I plan on getting on that, though."

"I'm pretty sure Reginald Ball is the painter. He was a local man, one of the gentry here back in the day."

"I've never heard of him. Are you sure?"

"Pretty sure. Thanks again for emailing me, I'm pulling it up now. You guys have done a great job. Keep up the indexing, and I will see you all on Monday."

We said our goodbyes, and I flipped open my laptop. Rachel's email was at the top of a ridiculously long list of unanswered messages. I clicked on it and held my breath as the attachment loaded. It was Calpurnia. She wore a coral-colored silk dress with coral lace at the elbow sleeves. Her brown hair was piled on her head, just like it was the day she met David Garrett. I squinted at the picture—no, her eyes weren't brown but that odd hazel color that could be brown or green depending on what she wore. In this portrait, they were green and lively. Despite what Callie thought about Reginald Ball, he had managed to capture many of the unique things that made the young woman so lovely. Her soft skin, the slope of her long neck, the nervous smile on her full lips. He must have loved her, in his own nervous, inept way. I felt a twinge of sadness for him, knowing that she'd never have willingly married him despite his best efforts at courting her. I left the portrait up while I began my research. This was long overdue. I sipped my coffee and opened the book, searching for the last entry I'd read.

Chapter 8

Dear Diary,

No well could ever be as deep as the Sadness that fills my Soul. All the happiness of life has disappeared into the Endless Black Night, and I wonder every minute how much longer I must endure the cruel barrage of slanderous names my Father casts upon me. Now that Mother has slipped into Heaven and taken her Lovely Face from me, I have no one to help. I am kept like a prisoner here. I cannot accept callers or well-wishers—not even Reginald Ball can see me now. Father says that idle tongues have spoken ill of my Virtue, and I of course deny all these charges while knowing that I have indeed given my heart to Someone Special already.

Father vows to protect me from the Ardent Affections of any man unworthy of my name and pedigree, including Captain Garrett, whom he says is no true captain but only a poor boat captain with a mercenary's heart. The Sheriff continues to visit, looking for clues to find Uncle Louis, but no man or woman has seen him. Who else can be taken away? All that is left to me now is Cousin Isla, and she is ever changeable in her moods— one minute I believe she loves me as a Sister, as she often declares herself to be, but then without an explanation she shows a depth of cruelty I never believed possible in one with so lovely a face.

Last night, in a drunken rage, Father tore the gardenias—Mother's gardenias—out of the ground, the ones that grew under my window. Someone had told him that the white flowers put off a scent that made men sick for love. I swore that no man had climbed up the lattice to my bedroom window, but he would not relent, convinced that I behave like a common woman whenever I am given the chance.

Some days, even Cousin Isla is forbidden to see me and I am forced to remain in my room with only the comfort of my books and drawings. Once I dreamed about dying, letting my Father find me pale and dead in a pool of crimson, but I have neither the courage nor the heart to do such a thing. For I know that if I did, I would never be permitted to enter the Gates of Pearl. I cannot stand to think of living an eternity without Mother, Baby Angelique and all my other siblings. Perhaps Uncle Louis is with her too, but I wondered if I would ever know.

Although my door is locked, Isla often comes and sits outside it to talk to me. The other day, she told me about all the calling cards I have received. She said Stokes refuses everyone, but she greets them for me and keeps the cards in the hopes that one day I will see them.

I sat on the wooden floor, my head against the door, and asked if any of the callers know I'm being held prisoner in my room. She responded that Stokes tells everyone I am recovered from the Fever that has ravaged the city. But she mentioned that a few callers are persistent, returning frequently to check up on my health, sending flowers—even a note.

I caught my breath when I heard that, but I did not dare mention the Captain's name. I asked who comes so frequently.

She thought for a moment and said, "Well, Reginald Ball, of course. And I am surprised that your father will not permit him entrance. He is your Cousin also, isn't he?"

Unsatisfied, I pressed her for more names. She paused. "Why, the Captain, of course," she said. I could hear the smile in her voice. She told me he suspects that something is amiss and he's been all but forbidden to court me. She has taken him for walks in the Rose Garden to entertain him, and she told me that from their conversations, he seems determined to see me.

I thanked her for caring for the Captain, even as my heart Ached at the thought of him being here and not seeing him. I dared to ask if he had left anything for me on any of his visits.

She lowered her voice and said, "Yes, he did. A note. I'll ask Hooney if I can bring your supper tray up. If she says yes, I'll slip the note under your plate."

I nearly cried for Joy. I thanked her fervently and begged her to talk to Father for me. I vowed I would not misbehave or shame him.

I could hear the sadness in her voice as she said, "I will tell him, but you know your Father. He is a most obstinate and unyielding man." She heard someone coming and admonished me to be discreet with these correspondences from the Captain. If anything were found, she would also be punished. She bid me Goodbye, and I heard the rustle of her dress and her footsteps running away from the door.

After she left, I looked at myself in the standing mirror. I appeared a pitiful sight, sitting on the floor in a heap of dirty muslin. I hadn't bothered to dress beyond my nightgown—I'd been in this room for nine days without an attendant. I had not bathed, and I had no one to help me with my hair so I'd left it down. The long tresses hung like brown ropes around my head. Enough rope to hang myself.

I heard someone climbing the stairs, heavy iron keys jangling, and my heart beat in my chest like a snared bird. Like a maniacal whirlwind I scooped up all my books and papers, tossed them carelessly in the floor grate and pulled the rug over it. My father flung the door open and stood in the doorway, glowering at me. The evil brown leather belt was missing from his hands, but that meant very little if his mind swam with whiskey. After a few steps into the room, I could see that he was not impaired, but he looked as furious as I have ever seen him.

I prayed: Oh Sweet Jesu, Father has a Dark Soul. Please save me from Death This Day.

"Where is it? Where did Christine hide it?" His deep voice rumbled through me like a wave of hatred, threatening to toss me upon perilous rocks.

"Where is what, Father?" I asked. I leaned against the wooden bedpost, trying to step out of his way as quickly as my feet would allow me. He paced through my room, pulling open drawers, tossing my carefully folded clothing haphazardly on the floor. He tore through my armoire, snatching my gowns from their hangers. I could hear the delicate fabric rip. Swearing, he emptied my hatboxes and shoe boxes into a storm-swept pile on the floor. Truly, he was a madman. I cried, gasping at the sight of the destruction of my possessions. I silently prayed that he would not look in the grate and discover my most Prized Treasures.

He ranted about my Mother plotting with her brother, my dear missing Uncle Louis, and accused me of keeping secrets from him. Then he grabbed my bare arm with a forceful grip and pulled me to him. *"Where is it?"* he demanded.

I promised I did not know what he meant and begged him to stop hurting me. He ignored my cries and dragged me out of my room. I nearly tripped twice, but he didn't slow his gait. He dragged me down the long hall to my Mother's room. Isla peeped out her door but did not attempt to interfere. I sobbed, feeling raw abandonment. Did no one care that I might die at the hands of this Madman?

Obviously Mother's Bedroom had been previously plundered, her boxes and drawers ransacked—a Mighty Search had been launched here, and there was no doubt that Father had not yet found Satisfaction for his Efforts.

He shouted, *"Where is it, Daughter? It is mine, and I want it now!"* He released me, and I tumbled to the carpeted floor, where I stayed with my eyes downcast. Out of the corner of my eye, I could see Hooney outside the doorway, waving her hand to let me know she was there. *"Help me,"* I said in my mind, but what could she do? Father tore through Mother's belongings again, searching for something, something important. The sight of it, the blatant disregard for the many things she had touched, the heirloom items she had loved—that belonged to me now—made me cry even harder. I ignored Hooney's yellowed eyes and warning gestures. Father had to cease this destruction.

"Please stop!" I lifted my hands above my head to protect it from the expected blows. At that moment, I did not care. *"Don't do this to her things! Please, just tell me what you're looking for!"*

He ceased his searching and stood over me victoriously, his chest heaving with anger and exertion. *"If I discover that you know where it is, that you have hidden what belongs to me, I will beat you."* I knew that of all the things he had ever told me, this was the truest.

I stared at the dusty toe of his black leather boot, praying that it wouldn't kick me. "Please, Father, I don't know what you want."

He did not speak to me again but walked out of the room at a furious pace. I heard him yelling at the bottom of the stairs, calling for his horse and his slave, Early.

Hooney rushed to my aid, murmuring that she would take care of me, help me bathe and fix my hair. I heard her say, "Don't you dare faint on me. You know I can't carry you. I'd have to call Stokes."

I didn't want to go back to that room. I needed to breathe some air. I begged her to let me stay out a little while, but she was adamant that I needed a bath. She shouted to Hannah to bring some water, then patted my arm with a cool hand as she led me back to my room. She promised me I could go for a walk outside and get some fresh air after I had bathed and eaten, and I do not remember ever being more Grateful for anything.

The warm water washed away the grime, but my heart will be forever changed by my experience in confinement. Later, as I walked through the Rose Garden with Hannah by my side, I swore to myself that I would leave this place—while I lived and breathed.

I heard a voice behind us. "Miss Calpurnia! How it blesses my soul to see you looking so fine!" It was Reginald Ball, practically running toward me with hearty bowlegged strides. I stopped to greet him, waiting beneath one of the hearty oak trees. My confinement had made me sensitive to the bright sunlight, but I welcomed the warmth.

I greeted him and thanked him for his kindness in visiting me. He told me he had offered to bring the doctor, which of course my Father refused. I was gladdened by his thoughtfulness and assented when he asked if he could walk with me a while.

I accepted the parasol Hannah handed me. It matched my dress, the lavender one with the blue flowers. Mr. Ball and I strolled past the pink Bourbon roses with their round blooms and bright green leaves. They were sensitive things, those roses, prone to shedding their flowers at even the slightest cool snap. Who would care for them now that Mother had left us?

Mr. Ball looked at me and said earnestly, "Miss Calpurnia, I feel that because of our Long and Continuous Friendship, I may speak frankly with you. With all Courtesy, of course."

I encouraged him to speak his mind, as I had no fear that my Distant Cousin would behave inappropriately. In all things he'd proven to be a careful observer of decorum.

He began by apologizing for bringing up such matters as he was about to discuss, and then said he suspected that those who manage my affairs do not have my best interest in mind. He rang his hands as he talked.

I had never received an apology before an offense! I spun my parasol, worried about what he might say, and begged him to speak plainly before I fainted there in my Mother's Rose Garden.

He confided to me that my Father had amassed a great deal of debt, so much so that the local bank was selling a portion of his property to offset the losses. Having depleted the Cottonwood Fortune, it seemed my Father wanted to take for himself the Beaumont Trust. That inheritance had been reserved for me, he told me. And if my Father managed those funds as ineptly as he had the preceding trust, I would have nothing.

I froze in my tracks, surprised at the frankness of this conversation. As a rule no one spoke to me about finances, my inheritance or any such thing. I had never even considered the subject on top of everything else I worried over with faithful fervency. I somehow found my voice to say, "Nobody tells me these things. I don't know what to say."

He asked me whether my Mother had ever spoken with me about it, and I shook my head, my ear bobs bouncing lightly. I stared at the thick green grass as we made another turn around the garden spot. "She did not."

He gave me a sad smile and said, "The elegant Mrs. Cottonwood was far too much of a lady for such crude conversations, I am sure. Still, you should know that the Beaumont Fortune is not in a bank—at least not anymore. Your Uncle Louis removed it before he arrived at Seven Sisters, undoubtedly to protect his sister's interests—and yours. Now it is nowhere to be found."

I reached out and held onto his arm to steady myself, the panic rising. I asked desperately what would happen now. Mr. Ball suggested that I search in my Mother's belongings for some clue. Suddenly my Father's anger, his maniacal searching of my room and my Mother's, made so much sense.

Mr. Ball said in a low voice, "You need a Protector, Miss Calpurnia. Someone who will assure that your interests have the utmost Care and Concern." He smiled through crooked teeth, and perspiration popped up on his brow; he sopped it away with a dingy handkerchief.

"Like a Solicitor?" I replied.

Bemused at my ignorance, he answered me with surprise, "No, my dear. Not like a solicitor—a husband. Surely you can see what I am suggesting. If you and I were to marry, all things would be well." He held my hand as if it were a delicate porcelain teacup that he feared he might break. "You would have my name and my protection, and I would have the pleasure of your company."

I stared into his sweaty face and pulled my hand away in surprise. How could I answer this now, when my heart is so full of grief for my Mother?

He assured me he would not have broached the subject if it were not Urgent and said that if I would trust him in this, he would be the Happiest Man Alive.

I felt I could not bear one moment more. I hastily bid him farewell, blaming my poor health, and left my would-be suitor standing in the Rose Garden in the sweltering sun. My Mother would have been appalled, but I needed time to think about all that I had heard.

Chapter 9

True to his word, and his chivalrous nature, Ashland popped by for the car key and soon returned with my Honda. I smiled, seeing it safely delivered in my driveway, better than new with four brand new tires. I wondered how much that would set me back, then remembered that I made excellent money—I could certainly afford tires if I wanted them, or in this case needed them. I waved down at TD, who was giving Ashland a ride back to Seven Sisters in his big blue pickup truck. *Hmm...maybe I should buy a truck.* I was a southern girl, wasn't I?

Ashland ran up the stairs with a carton in his hand. "This is for you—an excellent wonton soup from the China Room over off Joachim. I think it will help you feel better. We need you well so you can get back to the house! We've got deliveries everywhere."

It smelled delicious! "Thank you, for the hundredth time—you are full of surprises! I guess you took me seriously on our date when I told you I can't cook." I grinned playfully, accepting the warm container.

"Never doubt a lady. Call me before you go to bed, okay?" His hand touched my cheek. I thought he would kiss me, but TD honked his horn at us, then laughed. "Oh my! Bette will be out here in a second. I know I've said this a dozen times, but thank you again. I hope you didn't spend too much on those tires. I plan on selling her soon. I'll bring you a check Monday."

Ashland scowled, shaking his head. "No! Those are on me—it happened on my property, after all."

"Yes, but it was my psychotic friend—I think. Anyway, I insist."

This time, he did kiss me quickly. "We will argue about this later, lady. I have to go finish painting a parlor pink."

"Send me pictures!" I called after him as he climbed into the truck.

They both answered, "No!" and drove away.

I stood smiling on the balcony. It was broad daylight now, simply a beautiful day. I was going to have to get a sun lounger so I could lay out and get some sun on my off days. Bette's car was in the driveway, but I didn't see her kitchen light on. I thought that was odd but decided I wouldn't bother her. I would make sure she was okay later on.

I took my soup to my desk, fetched myself a silver soup spoon and sat down to enjoy my lunch. Calpurnia smiled back at me from the computer screen, and I stared at her. "Where are you, Callie?" I nearly jumped out of my chair when Bienville meowed outside my door. I had not seen the big cat climb the stairs, but there he was, peeking through the screen, no doubt wanting to cool off. I laughed at the fat little thing and opened the door for him. He came in and sat beside me at the desk, lounging happily on the area rug. I rubbed his fat tummy and turned my attention to the book. I remembered my antibiotics and took them with a bottle of water. I loved the soup—once again, Ashland had come through for me. *You know, I should do something nice for him. Maybe cook him something. I can't cook, but Bette could probably teach me something—something simple— like spaghetti! Yes, that's it!* I got so excited about the idea that I almost left immediately to go see her.

I finished off my soup and cleaned up my mess. It was time to read again. I was getting closer to the truth—I just knew it! I settled down for a few hours of work. Classical music played softly in the kitchen, and I closed my eyes, enjoying the peacefulness in my apartment. I felt peace seeing my old blue car in the driveway. There was nothing like freedom—and that's exactly what Calpurnia didn't have. I sighed and turned to the next page.

Dear Diary,

Father's absence brings hope and peace. He takes with him the Shadows that Steal the Joy from Seven Sisters and all those who call her home. Oh, Sweet Mary! Is it wrong to pray for my tormentor's death? I dare not ask Father England, the priest who came to visit, although he is a kind man who was genuinely fond of my mother. Once, Father England served this family exclusively, but not so anymore. Father refused to support the work of the ministry or provide him with any recommendations into our society.

"May that priest be damned for lying to us all!" he had shouted in a rage after the death of his son. Now the small chapel, the one with the stained glass windows, stood empty and forlorn, like my Father's broken faith.

Once my Father had cut a handsome figure in his coat and tails, but now his bitterness, his unrelenting anger with God, stole that away from him. He was gone now—and he had taken the storm with him. The slaves whispered about him, although they would not dare do so to me. I was his daughter and heir to this place. This trip, so the story went, was an effort to collect the many debts he was owed from renters and sharecroppers. Their debts to him would be paid by their blood if they did not deliver what he wanted. Before his departure, he crept up and down the halls of the house looking like a wild man, Early ever beside him. Father tore apart nearly every room looking for my Mother's Fortune, which I pretended to know nothing about. Ignorance and ignorance alone had previously saved me from his wrath; why should now be any different?

I would take this time to find that treasure, if it was the last thing I did, but I needed a companion, someone I could trust to keep my secret and help me cover the grounds. Of course, my mind first turned to dear, sweet Muncie, my Only True Friend, but nay. I could not place him in so grave a danger. He could die for helping me! It would be the same for Hooney, and she was old and more my Mother's slave than my Father's property. By reading a few of my Mother's papers, I had discovered that all the house slaves now legally belonged to me. I could do with them what I wished, once I was married. How ridiculous a law it was! A woman could own a house or a slave, but she had to have the permission of her husband to manage either of them. I prayed that one day I would be free of such selfish laws, but I didn't know how that would come to pass.

There was no getting around it—I would have to marry, but it would not be to Mr. Reginald Ball. I had my heart set on another man, one whose dark good looks and explorer's soul were surpassed only by his ability to write directly to my heart. Dear Diary, remember the letter Isla promised me? The one she was to put under my supper plate? I received it just the other day, and you will marvel at the words. Oh, how my heart sings his name, though I dare not speak it aloud—not even to Isla who insists that he loves me with all his heart, soul and mind!

"My Dearest One,

The days that have passed since I laid my eyes on your Exquisite Face might as well be a thousand, for one day is like a thousand when I am away from you. I stood on the deck of my ship tonight, planning my trip up river, my heart breaking; it is breaking because I will leave you behind once again. Why? Why have you not written to me, Dearest? Have you cast me out of your heart, perhaps in favor of another? With all that has come between us—these Herculean obstacles—I do not blame you, Sweetest, Daughter of the South. Do you remember sitting under the tree with me, the one that bends a little like a green bower from the Song of Solomon? I do. I dream of it. You put your gloved hand in mine, and you allowed me to carefully remove those pink kid gloves so that I might touch your hands with my own. Oh, how that delighted my soul!

Now I must leave, My Darling. Once more I will speak to your Father and Request the Hand of His Daughter in Marriage. I fear that Once more he shall Refuse me and Rain Down his Cruel Words on me, but I am not Afraid. What are Words, Dearest? Nothing that can harm us, surely. I pray that one day we shall say the words we long to, speak the vows that our hearts have ached for. For now, I must say Goodbye, Dearest. I shall write again soon. Write me your heart and leave it with Cousin Isla, for she knows how to find me.

Your Most Faithful Admirer,

Captain David T. Garrett

Oh, Diary! As always, I copy the letter here so you may read it, but I have tucked his letters in my leather book. It is my one Book of Love, and one day it shall set me free. One day, I will lay them at his feet and show him how he gave me courage with his sweet words. How they strengthened me as I searched day after day for the treasure that belongs to me. For with That, I Shall be Free and have the Thing which I Long for the Most.

Dear Diary,

I plundered my Mother's things, grabbing bits of ribbon and her handkerchiefs and stuffing them in my drawer. I pray that Father will not demand that I return these items, as they are Precious to me. I found her music box and listen to it daily, when Father is not home, of course. The tune is a curious one, but I like it. I keep its key on a ribbon tied about my neck as a kind of talisman against my father's hatred. He doesn't know I have it, and I don't think he cares any longer. He's stopped searching for her Fortune and almost completely ignores me now. Instead, he stays away with Early, selling bits of our land to keep him in whiskey and clothing and gambling money. I wish he would die before he steals everything from me! Father English would be so ashamed of me, of that I am sure.

With much convincing, I have persuaded Dear Isla to take up my cause. Somewhere, my Mother has set my fortune aside for me, and I must find it! I must have my freedom—even if I must buy it from the one who says he owns me. Like one of his Slaves—he says he Owns my blood and body. Father remains away, and I pray to God every day that he shall continue to do so. Together, my cousin and I search everywhere in Mother's Chifferobe, but we searched high and low and found nothing. Also, my Sweetest Friend Muncie searches too, whenever he has a moment. He plunders the hothouse and the gardens for any signs of a new burial spot or anywhere my Mother may have hidden her dowry. I believe that one day we shall find these things and I, as Mistress of my Own House, will set my friends free! Stokes has become suspicious, and I must be the perfect example of carefulness or else he will hasten my father's return.

Oh, Mother! Please speak to me. Speak to my heart and tell me what I must know. I need you to guide me.

Reginald Ball has not returned to see me, nor has the Captain. Alas, he has traveled up the dark waters of the Mobile River.

You must keep a secret, Dear Diary! I saw him sail away! My Dear Cousin alerted me he was leaving and told me where to meet him. She gave me a flask of lemonade and ordered Muncie to attend me on my journey. "Dare I do such a thing, Isla?" I asked her.

"Yes, Dearest," she said. "You must see him off!" I took the flask and promised to drink from it when I got thirsty.

My Dark Captain never knew I was there! How it thrilled me to see the boat's wheels begin to turn! Muncie and I stood and smiled at one another in the moonlight.

"One day, Muncie, I will ride that boat away from here."

"Me too, Calpurnia, I'm going too! Which way you go—that's where I go. Wherever you go, I go too! You can't leave me here, all right, Miss?" I

hugged him, and we held hands running up the woodsy path back to the house. We had to hug the tree line until we made it to the very back of the house. When we came to the back of the maze, we stood panting, trying to catch our breath. Just this small escape off the grounds near the river had thrilled my soul. I could be free! How delightful it is to run across the grass and breathe the night air! I drank all of my lemonade and enjoyed the feeling of joy it brought me!

The Moonlight Garden shone like an otherworldly heaven on earth. The moonlight bounced off the Atlas Fountain and then from statue to statue. I remember how when we were young, we would play in the fountain, dancing and spitting water like mystical water creatures. Even the copious white flowers of the garden shone like tiny ghosts. They waved at us as we traveled past them, caught in the midnight breeze. I danced around the fountain, feeling happier than I have in a long time. I danced, spinning around and around in my white dress. I was like another flower in the Moonlight Garden. Someday I would float away on a breeze. I laughed, and Muncie laughed with me. He snuck quietly into his rooms to avoid getting caught by Stokes. I was about to do the same when it started to rain. I went back into the garden and danced, dancing, spinning, moving, circling the many statues and hedges. I can't explain how it made me feel. It washed me clean of all my worries, all my fears. They were gone, drenched now, washed away by the tears of the angels. For a while, I felt like a madwoman—I cried and laughed at the same time. Remembering the pain of the loss of my mother and laughing with the joy that filled my heart when I thought of leaving Seven Sisters behind.

I was completely drenched and dead tired when Hooney found me lying on a bench in the garden. She crossed herself when she saw me—Hooney, like my Mother, prayed to the Virgin for mercy and help. I laughed at that too.

She said, "Child, you'll be sick now. Sick like a dog out here in this rain. Whatcha think you doing out here in this wild place? This ain't nothing but a wild place. Devils dance in here! Don't tell Hooney you've been dancing with the devils tonight, Miss Calpurnia. Oh Lord!" she shouted out loud, shocked by my laughter. We walked into the house, and I leaned on her arm, still laughing. She called out for the doctor, Isla and Stokes, muttering that I needed a warm bath and some sleep. She crossed herself again, and I heard her say something about how I'd lost my mind.

I vaguely remember getting in and out of the tub. Finally, I was dried and my gown slipped over my head. Hooney and Hannah rubbed my feet with special oils that they hoped would keep sickness away. When I awoke the next day, I was indeed as sick as one could be. The doctor said it had been brain fever, although I did not have a fever at all. In a few days I was better, but I was forever changed by the experience. I hoped one day that I would again experience such freedom.

Chapter 10

I marked my spot in the diary with a silk ribbon, closed the book and set it on my desk. I paced the floor, thinking about what I had read. *Callie never knew about the fortune—the Beaumont fortune—until Reginald Ball told her about it. He wanted to marry her because he A: wanted to protect her or B: wanted her money. There might be a C too: he wanted both. Callie didn't want to marry him, so she decided to find the treasure herself with the help of her friends.* I walked to the coffeepot. This was going to require more brain juice!

"What I want to know," I said to a bored Bienville, "is did Isla spike that lemonade hoping that Muncie and Callie would get drunk and do something more than take a trip down to the river? What did she want to happen? Did she want Callie to fall in the Mobile River and drown? Did she want her to make a fool of herself onboard the Delta Queen, or did she maybe...." I tapped my chin with my finger. "Maybe she mistook Callie and Muncie's friendship for romance and just assumed that the two would at least kiss."

I didn't trust Isla, and it was plain to me that Calpurnia was far too trusting of her. *I wouldn't be surprised if...no, I'll think about that later.* It was dark out, but the light of the full moon danced in the trees. I looked at Bette's two-story house and saw nary a light on. I wondered again if she was okay. Her car was there, right where she had parked it the night before. Suddenly, I got that creeped-out feeling and decided to go check it out. She had to be okay, right? "Come on, fat kitty. We need to go check on your Momma."

I walked down the stairs and across the stone steps that led to her back door. I rapped on the door and called, "Bette!" but heard nothing. I knocked louder this time and still nothing. Suddenly, I felt uneasy, as if someone were watching me. The oversized tabby launched himself out of my arms, scratching me from fright as he ran into the nearby shrubs. "What is wrong with you, Bienville? You're going to feel mighty silly in a minute when you see nothing is wrong," I grumbled, rubbing my arm.

Just then, Mia stepped out of the shadows. She'd transformed herself again, back to her black Egyptian bob and dark eyeliner. She wore a black dress that hugged her curves and black leggings with a big, satin bow headband. She looked like an evil preppy. I began to think quickly. *Okay, if I scream, she'll lunge at me. What's in her hand?*

"I didn't think you'd ever come check on that old lady. What took you so long, CJ? She's inside—you should go see her," she said, laughing at me. "She squealed and squealed when I stuck her with my little blade."

"What? Oh my God, is Bette okay? What did you do?"

"Just enough to get your attention—is it working?"

"Why are you doing this, Mia? Why? Don't you know how much I loved you and your family? You were like my own sister!"

"Those days are long gone, 'sister.' You can keep your love—I want that treasure. I want Seven Sisters!"

"You think Ashland is just going to sign over his house to you? Why would he? You murdered his friend and then attacked me. He's never going to forgive you for that."

"Oh no, don't tell me you two are in love. That's hysterical. The wealthy Momma's boy and the weirdo bastard hooking up. Someone call Maury!" She spun the knife like a pro. Then she put her free hand on her hip. "You are colossally stupid, CJ, and that's always been your problem. Can't see the forest for the trees—or the tree for the forest, however it goes. Seven Sisters isn't just a house, it's a treasure. And it's *my* treasure!"

"What have you done to Bette?" I was practically screaming now.

"Give me the key, Carrie Jo, and I will go away. Give me the key!" She spoke calmly as if she were reasoning with a child. "I deserve this—if you only knew!" She laughed maniacally. "Seriously, I'm going to count to three, and you better hand it over. I want that key." She stood even closer. "I will have that key. Give it to me now! It's mine—it's my birthright!"

"I'll never give you that key, and Bette had better be okay. Or I'm going to kick your ass, Mia!"

She charged me with the short dagger, but she never had a chance. Iberville, the Ghost Cat, pounced on her from the kitchen window, scratching her arm and making her drop the blade. I snatched it up off the ground, and she took off running behind the house and into the neighbors' backyard. I didn't care! I would have to deal with her later.

I broke the window above the kitchen doorknob and frantically undid the lock. "Bette! Bette! Where are you?" I heard a sound in her living room. I held my breath and found my friend tied to a chair. She had a gag in her mouth and looked terrible. "Oh my God, Bette! Oh my God! I am sorry! I'm calling 9-1-1 now, okay?" I cut her loose with the dagger, made the call and then helped get her to the restroom before the EMTs arrived. Once they arrived, I called Ashland.

He picked up and said playfully, "Are you calling to tell me good night like you promised?"

"What? No, Ashland. I'm calling because Mia assaulted Bette. I'm at Bette's now, and she won't go to the hospital."

"I'm on the way. Stay there, okay?"

"Okay." I hung up and stayed with Bette. I couldn't convince her to take a trip to the hospital, but I did talk her into calling a relative to come pick her up. She wouldn't be safe at her house, at least not until the police caught

Mia. And what was the holdup on that? Five minutes later, police cars were everywhere. *Better late than never, right? Well, well. Speak of the...* "Good evening, Detective Simmons. Have you caught her yet? Mia Reed?" I walked with a purpose. Someone had to take this seriously. People's lives were at stake.

"No, I'm still gathering the facts on this case."

I stared at her. "Are you seriously going to tell me that no one thought she might come back here? This is bad, Detective. Bette should never have been at risk. Will you please take this woman seriously? She's not going to quit until she gets the key!"

Ashland had come up behind me and put his arms around me. "You okay? No cuts or bruises?"

"I'm fine, and please don't baby me!" I was shaking all over with anger. I picked up the dagger off the living room table. "This is what she came at me with," I said fiercely to Detective Simmons. "If it hadn't been for the cat, I would be dead right now!"

I gave the knife to her and said to Ashland, "She's obsessed. She thinks that Calpurnia's treasure is her birthright—somehow she believes she is entitled to it. She says she won't stop until she gets it!"

"Okay, we will talk about this later. Let's make a report and then go home. You come stay in my guesthouse tonight. Then we'll talk about finding you somewhere else to stay, just to be safe."

"No way! I am not leaving my friend here to fight that crazy girl by herself. She needs me."

He nodded. "I know Bette is a friend—she's my friend too. But tonight she's going to stay with her son, and you will stay with me. We will all get together tomorrow and talk about this more, okay? Now let's do this report and go pack your stuff. You still have the key, don't you?"

I touched where it hung around my neck. "Yeah, I still have it."

"Where is she supposed to go to do the report?" he asked Detective Simmons.

"I think we can wait on that report. Get her somewhere safe. We've got plenty of time to work on that."

"Great. Thanks, Detective," he said.

I made sure Bette left safely and then walked upstairs to pack a few things. The first thing I stuffed in my overnight bag was Calpurnia's journals, my laptop and then a change of clothing and other necessities.

I didn't cry one drop. I wasn't afraid—not fearful at all. I was pissed off! The seriousness of what was happening was finally clear. Mia had been right about one thing—I was colossally stupid when it came to understanding anything. If I didn't take this seriously, start uncovering the truth, Ashland could be next—or any of the people I cared about who worked with me on Seven Sisters. This wasn't what I had planned for when I signed on for this project, but here it was. The disappearance of Calpurnia Cottonwood and her fortune wasn't merely an entertaining story. Discovering the whereabouts of the heiress and her jewels was now my highest priority, above everything else. This had to end, before anyone else died! I thought of all those who had touched this fortune and then died unnaturally. Christine Beaumont Cottonwood, Louis Beaumont, Calpurnia Cottonwood and Hollis Matthews, and who knew who else?

I grabbed my bags, keys, purse and jacket and left the apartment with every light burning. I didn't have much for a burglar to steal, and if Mia decided to come back, I wasn't going to make it easy for her to hide in the shadows again.

I climbed into Ashland's Benz, and we drove away. I dreaded sleeping in a new house, but I had a plan. I had the silver key around my neck. I was going to see if I could replicate the transfer I had gotten before. Dream catching with an object was new to me, but it had worked. If I could just remember how I had done it. Ashland patted the seat, and I slid closer to him. We could very easily cross a few lines at his place, but did I want to confuse things more?

Country music played quietly on the radio, and I watched the dark scenery as we drove. It didn't take long to get to his large home in Midtown Mobile. It was off the road a ways and surrounded by a passcode gate. He tapped the numbers on the screen, and the black cast-iron gates opened slowly. I sang a spooky tune and smiled at him.

He laughed. "There's no fog tonight. It's only scary-looking when it's foggy out."

We drove up the long, straight drive lined with palm trees. In front of the house, there was a circular driveway. I looked up at the massive two-story home with smooth stucco and plenty of Spanish details. "This looks like it belongs more in Florida than in Alabama."

"Watch out, now. Alabama has plenty of beaches too. I like it. I feel like I'm at a resort every time I go home."

I laughed as I grabbed my bags out of his trunk. "I guess so! This is amazing. Wait. Where's all the staff? Aren't they supposed to come out and greet us?"

"All right, stop that now. Let's get inside before the fog really does roll in here. Besides, I only have a housekeeper and a landscaper. That's it!" He grinned at me.

"Well, you're my boss. I guess I could put on a maid's outfit."

He just smiled slowly and took my hand. We walked into the house together and out of the dark Alabama night.

Chapter 11

The guesthouse looked like something out of a swanky coastal magazine. It was joined to the main house by a stepping-stone walkway lined with a few palm trees and interesting concrete statues of flamingos and dolphins. It was kitschy in a cool way, and I loved it instantly. I had never stayed at a beach house before. Mia and I went to Spring Break at the beach once, but we had stayed in a condominium. *Mia...what had happened to her?*

Ashland said, "So, this guesthouse is only a few months old. As far as I know, you'll be the first one sleeping here, unless the housekeeper took an unauthorized nap." He sat on the bed and bounced on it a little to demonstrate its newness.

"Hey, get off there! I can't have you messing up my bed." I put my laptop and journals on the lovely white painted desk in front of the window and the rest of my things on the floor. I had a sudden thought. "Are any of these items antiques?"

"Nope. Nothing significant. Most of this is brand new. You should be safe here, Carrie Jo. I want you to get a good night's sleep."

"I plan on that. So why don't you take me on a tour, or do guests only get to see the guesthouse?"

He held my hands and kissed them. "I don't know what I would have done if something had happened to you tonight. I want you to promise me you'll be careful. No chances at all."

"Scout's honor," I said, but I had my fingers crossed behind my back. "Okay, let's walk and talk. You lead the way."

Ashland's home was remarkable. He had a leathery "man cave," with ridiculous overstuffed leather chairs and a massive television. I expected that, but he also had a gorgeous kitchen and a beautiful pool table. My eyes lit up when I saw it. I loved playing pool—it was the one sport I could win at. "Want to play?" I asked. He cast me a disbelieving look. "Oh, don't look so surprised. I'm good at quite a few sports," I lied. It was mostly pool and poker.

"Sure, rack 'em up." He grinned at me. "But I warn you, I'm pretty good."

"No, it's your table—you do the racking. Let's see how good you really are." He gave me a mock bow and racked up the balls.

"May I ask you something?" I reached into the netting to retrieve some of the balls and slung them his way.

"Yeah, sure. I'm an open book." He jostled the balls into the rack, tightening them and setting them on the mark. We perused a collection of sticks on an elegant wooden rack. Choosing two of the most beautiful, we walked back to the table. He racked, so that meant I got to break. I lined up the cue ball on the opposite dot and had my eye on the 7 ball. I took aim at the 2 ball. I liked breaking left of center—it worked well for me. I had distributed the balls well with that first shot.

I shook my head. "There's something I can't figure out. Why did Mia believe she had a right to any jewelry that we might recover? I mean, she wasn't interested in stealing it—she really believes it belongs to her. Why? Do you know something about that, or is this another mystery? Like we need one more."

"I was surprised to hear that. I have to be honest, though; people file papers all the time claiming to be related to me somehow. I am extremely wealthy, and people are extremely greedy. If they can find a way to relieve you of your cash, they will do it. If she was making a claim that she was a relative, and went the legal way, there might be paperwork on it filed downtown. Hollis used to take care of those things for me."

"Hmm...it might be worth looking into. She's not the kind of girl to make something up like that." He looked at me with raised eyebrows. "Okay, yes, she did try to kill me and she held Bette hostage, but she's not a liar. Somehow or another, she's got it in her head that she's entitled to it."

"I'll check that out in the morning. Your shot. Hey, how far did you get in the journals?"

I told him what I had read, and his eyes got big. "Are you kidding me? She did that? You think she spiked the lemonade? For what purpose?"

"Because she's a schemer. But what she's scheming on, I don't know. I can't understand why Calpurnia would trust Isla. How could she have been so blind?"

"That's a very good question. I guess we can both attest to the fact that sometimes you can't see what's right in front of you. Most young people weren't as sophisticated back then. Not socially, anyway. Someone like Calpurnia wouldn't know anything about the ways of the world. I suspect her cousin knew a little more."

"Hmm...a whole lot more, from what I gather."

"What's that mean?"

"Oh, nothing. Your shot!" We played until I won. "I told you pool was my game."

"I believe you!" He laughed, raising his hands like he was surrendering. I took the bottle of water he offered me. Absently, I wondered what two regular people would be doing in this situation, but we weren't two "regular" people. We were both careful and cautious, and we'd had to be— for very different reasons. Ashland had had to think about his wealth, his family name, his future. And my gift for dream catching demanded that I live a certain way. There were no sleepovers for me. I could dream what he dreamed; if those night visions were full of Detra Ann or some other woman, I would be devastated. His hand touched my cheek, and I tilted my face towards him. "Kiss me," he whispered. I nodded. He half smiled and leaned down, then kissed me like he meant it. *How weird is it that I feel like I've known this man all my life? Okay, okay. Calm down. You don't believe in that kind of stuff, do you?*

When he gently pulled away, I put my arms around his neck and his went around my waist. He held me close, his head on my shoulder and mine on his chest. Finally, he let me go. We didn't say anything else, and I walked away with a smile. I walked down the hall and through the French doors to the stepping-stone walkway. I practically hopped across each one, thrilled to be here with Ashland. I realized how lonely his life must have been. Sure, people would always be around him, but he must always wonder what they want from him. That had to be a lonely way to live.

I got ready for bed, pulling down the window shades and checking all the locks. I mean, who could jump the fence, really? The whole place was fenced, but just in case. I wanted to be safe. I slid on my pajamas, skipping my shower until morning. I know it was silly, but I just didn't want to wash his kisses away. I could still smell his cologne on my skin. I picked up my phone and texted him.

Thanks for letting me stay here tonight.

In just a few seconds, he wrote back.

My pleasure, and I can't wait to cook breakfast for you.

Sounds yummy. Goodnight.

Night, CJ.

I closed my eyes and pulled the key out of my nightgown. I stared at it and rubbed it. I thought about the house and about Calpurnia. I went to sleep praying that I would see what I wanted to see. Many hands had held this key over the years; I wondered whose hands I would see when I finally stepped into the dream, if I dreamed at all.

I thought about Ashland and what the future might hold. I thought about his beautiful face, his soft lips, his kind ways. People had no idea how kind he was....soon I was asleep and dreaming.

A pink painted fingernail spun the key on the black dining room table. The music box sat in front of her, and she slid the key into the slot. She turned, turned and turned until the music began to sing. It was a melancholy tune, one that haunted her at night, but she couldn't help herself. She could almost imagine Calpurnia singing this tune, humming it while she combed her hair or wrote in her diary.

"Mommy! Mommy!" A little boy with pink cheeks and a shock of white-blond hair ran into the room with a wooden car in his hands. "Look, Mommy! Look what my cousin gave me."

A dark-haired man smiled from the doorway. She smiled back, yet she had questions about him. Unanswered, dangerous questions. Did he really love her? Or was he only getting close to her so that he could take her son away for his own nefarious reasons? She laughed at herself. Surely, she was being paranoid about her cousin Robert. He'd never been accused of such things. It was her mind, as always, playing tricks on her.

"Mommy! Isn't it wonderful?"

"Yes! Yes, it is. Now put your car down and dance with Mommy." The little boy did as he was asked. He put the car on the table and walked back to his mother. He gave her a little bow and began to waltz with her. She laughed with delight, and he smiled up at her.

"Oh, Ashland. I love you, son."

Ashland? I woke up from the dream, sitting up straight in bed, sweating and breathing fast. That was Ashland and Emily! Poor woman. Her mind had been a fog of uncertainty—fear and curiosity. Poor Ashland—poor kid. I tried to calm my breathing and clear my mind, but it wasn't working. I decided to take a quick shower, desperate to wash away the memory of that disturbing dream. In just a few minutes, I was standing under the warm water, letting it beat down on me. Then I slid on my nightshirt and towel-dried my hair. I climbed back into the bed, purposefully banishing Ashland from my dreams. I rubbed the key and thought about Calpurnia dancing in the garden. I thought about how she felt when Muncie held her hand, how she loved to hear her mother sing those French lullabies, the ones from her childhood.

Again, I fell asleep.

A smile crept across my face when I turned back to look at the pale faces watching me from behind the lace curtains of the girls' dormitory. I didn't feel sorry for any of them—all of those girls hated me. They thought they were my betters because they were orphans and I was merely the accidental result of my wealthy mother's indiscretion. I couldn't understand why they felt that way. As I told Marie Bettencourt, at least my parents were alive and wealthy. Hers were dead and in the cold, cold ground. "Worm food now, I suppose." Her big dark eyes had swollen with tears, her ugly, fat face contorting as she cried. Mrs. Bedford scolded me for my remarks, but even that did not worry me.

I had a tool much more effective than Mrs. Bedford's threats of letters to the attorney who distributed my allowance or a day without a meal. Mr. Bedford would defend me—for a price. I would have to kiss his thin, dry lips and pretend that he did not peek at my décolletage a little too long. Once he even squeezed my bosom ever so quickly with his rough hands but then pretended it had been an accident. Mr. Bedford never had the courage to lift up my skirt or ask me for a "discreet favor," as my previous chaperone had called it, but I enjoyed making him stare. It had been great fun for a month or two until I saw how easily he could be manipulated.

And now my rescuer had come at last, a man, Louis Beaumont, who claimed to be my mother's brother. I had never met Olivia, my mother. Not that I could remember, anyway, and I assumed I never would.

Louis Beaumont towered above most men, as tall as an otherworldly prince. He had beautiful blond hair that I wanted to plunge my hands into. It looked like the down of a baby duckling. He had fair skin—so light it almost glowed—with pleasant features, even brows, thick lashes, a manly mouth. It was a shame he was so near a kin because I would have had no objections to whispering "Embrasse-moi" in his ear. Although I very much doubted Uncle Louis would have indulged my fantasy. How I loved to kiss, and to kiss one so beautiful! That would be heavenly. I had never kissed a handsome man before—I kissed the ice boy once and a farmhand, but neither of them had been handsome or good at kissing.

For three days we traveled in the coach, my uncle explaining what he wanted and how I would benefit if I followed his instructions. According to my uncle, Cousin Calpurnia needed me, or rather, needed a companion for the season. The heiress would come out this year, and a certain level of decorum was expected, including traveling with a suitable companion. "Who would be more suitable than her own cousin?" he asked me with the curl of a smile on his regal face. "Now, dearest Isla," he said, "I am counting on you to be a respectable girl. Leave all that happened before behind in Birmingham—no talking of the Bedfords or anyone else from that life. All will be well now." He patted my hand gently. "We must find Calpurnia a suitable husband, one that will give her the life she's accustomed to and deserves."

Yes, indeed. Now that this Calpurnia needed a proper companion, I had been summoned. I'd never even heard of Miss Calpurnia Cottonwood until now. Where had Uncle Louis been when I ran sobbing in a crumpled dress after falling prey to the lecherous hands of General Harper, my first guardian? Where had he been when I endured the shame and pain of my stolen maidenhead? Where? Was I not Beaumont stock and worthy of rescue? Apparently not. I decided then and there to hate my cousin, no matter how rich she was. Still, I smiled, spreading the skirt of my purple dress neatly around me on the seat. "Yes, Uncle Louis."

"And who knows, ma petite Cherie, perhaps we can find you a good match too. Perhaps a military man or a wealthy merchant. Would you like that?" I gave him another smile and nod before I pretended to be distracted by something out the window. My fate would be in my own hands, that much I knew. Never would I marry. I would make my own

future. Calpurnia must be a pitiful, ridiculous kind of girl if she needed my help to land a "suitable" husband with all her affluence.

The coach and four turned down the red dirt road that led to the mansion. Seven Sisters, Uncle Louis had called it. Massive dark oaks lined the wide, dusty lane, so massive that I could not see the building until we were very close. When we cleared the trees, I gasped at the sheer size of the house. Seven towering columns lined the front porch, reaching up, up, up like an ancient Greek temple shining white in the glorious sun. Children and house servants scurried about to greet us, and even a couple of old hounds barked a welcome. I squealed with delight, clapping my hands. I'd never seen anything so fine in all my life. I wanted this. This was who I was, where I belonged! I was no poor relation, no orphan. I was Isla Beaumont! I deserved this kind of life, didn't I? The coach had barely stopped before I got out, excited to arrive at last.

I was disappointed that my cousin had not greeted me herself. How important was she that she could not afford to take a moment to show her "poor" cousin a kindness? When I did finally meet her, I was astonished. Taller than me by six inches, she moved with natural grace and had a quiet manner. She would never squeal with delight or misbehave as I did...as often as I could. Calpurnia was easily the prettiest girl I had ever seen, and I didn't count myself the least of those. Uncle Louis was obviously besotted with her and forgot me instantly. The two beautiful ones left this mere mortal behind, slipping away for a private chat in one of the many gardens surrounding the plantation. Again, I felt my heart harden and my hatred grow stronger. In Uncle Louis' heart, I would always be second. Well, that was no matter to me. I could play this game as well as any woman could. They did not know how smart I was, did they? I could sing, read, do figures and speak French, a little.

The servant, Hooney, didn't like me. I knew that from the moment she laid those wise, yellowed eyes on me. That made me hate her too, but I smiled as if I were as sweet as honey. It didn't do any good; she didn't tolerate foolishness, even if she was a slave. I played the game, pretending to love my cousin. But all the while, I wished she were gone from here, leaving me as the heiress. Wasn't I a Beaumont? That was far better than being a Cottonwood, surely. Perhaps I should remind Uncle Louis of that.

Hooney let me know that Christine Cottonwood did not want to see me now, that she was ill and in bed ready to have a baby. No matter to me; I hoped she would never get out of that bed. She could die there, like Marie Bettencourt's mother. "Worm food now, I suppose." I laughed at the memory.

After a few days, the newness of my surroundings began to fade, and I began to explore beyond the house. This time, no one stopped me. No one said a word to me. Where I had been a prisoner before, I now was free! I was the friend, nay, the cousin of the heiress. I was given free run of the *house. Unfortunately I could not find a single man to kiss or any place where I could have fun. One day I quietly watched some of the slaves bathing in the river. I'd never seen a naked black man before. I climbed up into a live oak and nibbled on a biscuit as I watched them. I did this many times, enjoying the games they played as they splashed in the water. I wondered how shocking it would be to climb down the tree, step out of my dress and jump into the water. Would they catch me? Would they caress my white, wet skin? Would they make me their woman? I would rise out of the water like Venus emerging from the sea, my long blond hair plastered to my naked breasts. They would worship me.*

Ah, only a fantasy. Even I knew that black men never touched white women—not if they wanted to live beyond the touching. Still, it must be wonderful to be had by one of these magnificent men. It was the boy Muncie who spotted me. I saw him when he did it, telling the other boys to put their clothing on. Oh, Muncie! You infuriate me! You of all people should hate Calpurnia—she is your master, your mistress. I knew he loved her in a way that he should not. I smiled at him and slithered down the tree like the snake did in the Garden. I munched on an apple and stared at the surprised boys. I took a bite and then shoved the apple into one boy's open mouth before turning and walking away. I heard them whispering behind me, some of them praying, others talking fearfully. That had not been the way I wanted that to go, but Muncie had thwarted my plans. Very well, I would hate him too!

The longer I stayed at Seven Sisters, the more people I found to hate. Reginald Ball, a cousin of Uncle Jeremiah Cottonwood, was one such person. Another man infatuated with Calpurnia, who I had decided was no great beauty after all. She had that mulatto eye color that shifted from brown to green, and her neck was far too long. I also hated Uncle Jeremiah, for he had slapped me when I tried to kiss him. I couldn't understand why he would refuse me a kiss—but when I followed him around a bit, the answer became apparent. Uncle Jeremiah had another lover—and not another woman. No, he'd chosen for himself a boy, a lovely boy with light skin, white teeth and a handsome face. His name was Early, and I believed that slave boy fancied himself in love with his Master. It made me laugh and laugh when I saw the two of them slip off into the Moonlight Garden together. What they did there was less amusing to me; I didn't care. After my spying, I'd walked back to the house smiling. The people in this house had so many secrets—secrets that would smother them. I laughed again.

I walked up the stairs to my room, wanting to think some more about this house of secrets, when I heard someone speak to me. "You seem to be enjoying your stay here." I turned on the third step, pressing my bottom against the railing, and looked into the face of a man who seemed to know me. "Have we met, sir?"

"I should think not. I have come to pay court to Calpurnia Cottonwood. But as I do not find her about, you shall do nicely."

I walked down two stairs and leveled my gaze at him. "I don't play seconds to my cousin, good sir."

"Well, had I known that you were here, I would have courted you first. How can one love a moth when such a butterfly is fluttering about?"

"You talk like you know poetry, sir. Are you a well-read man?" I stood on the step above him, and we talked in whispers now.

We talked for another hour, taking a stroll in the rose garden while Calpurnia ministered to her mother, who had taken a turn for the worse. At that first meeting, my words were careful and well-chosen. But after three such walks, we discovered that we were after the same thing—the vast riches of Calpurnia's fortune. The word was out that Christine and Louis had converted the fortune into a collection of precious jewelry pieces and that they planned to hide them from Jeremiah. The man had become a drunk and a poor manager of the Beaumont-Cottonwood estate. At least, that was what the jeweler had told Captain David Garrett while aboard the Delta Queen for a night of cards and bad behavior.

I wanted to be free, and that would take a fortune so I could live like the lady I was. David wanted to go with me; we would travel the world, first in the Bahamas, then on to Paris and then to Greece. Oh, to travel! I had kissed David impetuously in the rose garden that day, but he barely responded. His beauty attracted and stirred me as no other had. He gently pushed me away and whispered an apology, but that only made me want him more! Eventually I knew why he was so hesitant to kiss me, court me, and make love to me—because he secretly hoped that he and Calpurnia would marry. He would be the rightful heir to the fortune. I had a choice to make: stand aside or work my magic on David Garrett. If I wanted to keep him, I could. I knew enough tricks to please a man for a hundred years. But did I want him? That was the question. I couldn't make up my mind—until I saw the way Calpurnia looked at him. Her lips parted, her face tilted up, listening to his every word, her hand worrying over her intricate coiffure. Yes, it was clear she wanted him.

I went to bed smiling; now the snare could be set. I would have those jewels and David Garrett too. I had been there only a few weeks, and I already knew all about my cousin. I knew her weaknesses—those damn books of poetry, the ones that talked about love, falling in love, being in love. That's how we would do this. We would write notes; he would woo her into trusting him, and I would pass them on to her, both of us laughing at our craftiness. From time to time, he appeared to feel guilty. When I saw his resolve relaxing, I would win him over again with the tricks I'd learned with the General and his friends.

One dark night, a storm settled over Seven Sisters, and it seemed determined to tear the place down. Lightning popped around the house, snapping trees, sparking around the ponds and fountains in the Moonlight Garden. Was God punishing us for all the evil we had done? I didn't know, but I prayed for the first time in a long time. "Dear Lord, I hate Calpurnia Cottonwood. Please strike her with lightning so I alone will be the heir to the Beaumont fortune." He did not answer me, nor did my cousin die that night. Still, it did get me to thinking about the baby that Christine carried. I had heard the nurse say it was a miracle he had lasted this long; perhaps the thing would die and I wouldn't have to take care of him. I had no taste for murder, although murder had happened here, not so long ago.

Uncle Louis—beautiful, perfect Uncle Louis—was dead, buried behind the mausoleum, if those yapping dogs had not dug him up and eaten him by now. I'm sure I should feel sad about it, but I do not. Early, the slave who loved Mr. Cottonwood, had done the deed. The tall Frenchman had wandered into their trysting place (someone may or may not have told him where it was) and discovered their lovemaking. Drunk on corn whiskey, Jeremiah swore at the man but didn't do anything else. Early ran after him, his half-naked body exposed as he smashed him in the head with a garden curiosity, a concrete ball that rested atop one of the many fountains. He smashed him over and over; Uncle Louis had not made a sound from the first blow to the last. When he was through, Early put the ball back on the fountain and the waters turned to blood. I laughed quietly at the biblical allusion from my hiding place in the maze.

Thinking that Mr. Jeremiah had done the killing before he passed out, Stokes helped Early hide the body, burying it where it lay. "Worm food now, I suppose," I whispered to myself. "Oh no, dear Calpurnia. What can you do? Uncle Louis is gone. Who will protect you now?"

I spent the rest of the evening with Calpurnia, pretending that I had not seen a thing. We danced to the tune of the music box, and I pretended to be a doting cousin. It was an easy charade. Muncie came to serve us our dinner, and I teased him a little by asking him to join us. Calpurnia scolded me for it, but before I could make a sound against her, Stokes came in and announced that Mr. Louis' horse had returned but our uncle was missing. This news greatly alarmed Calpurnia, but I smirked. I knew! I knew what had happened! Calpurnia sent Stokes for the Sheriff and went downstairs to arrange the staff to go help look for him. It was believed at that time that he had fallen from his horse and may be in dire need of help. As the staff—even Hooney—clambered into the foyer for instructions, I silently walked towards Christine's chambers. She was asleep when I went in, but she woke up and inquired about my health. I did not offer her sweet words or hedge about my business. I began speaking in a whisper, like I was casting a spell—I told her everything that I had seen, everything I had done before I came to Seven Sisters. And when that was through, I told her what her husband was doing and who he was doing it to. I told her things you would never tell a genteel lady. I shocked her over and over again, her heart breaking with each word. She cried, but no one could hear her now that the search had started. I stood before her as she clutched the wooden bedpost, leaning against it for strength. "Louis is dead, dead, dead now. Gone. Worm food now, I suppose." That phrase had worked on Marie Bettencourt, and it worked on a fine lady like Christine Cottonwood too. She let out a heart-wrenching cry and fell to her knees holding her belly, weeping. Before I left her, I said, "You will die too now, and that baby will die. You will all be together as worm food. And when you are dead, they will put you in that cold, cold mausoleum alongside the other dead ones." She didn't answer me but stared off into space, not crying, no longer moaning, saying nothing. She finally stopped crying and sighed a little.

I squatted down beside her and held her face in my hands. I kissed her, but she was no longer with me. She stared off into the distance; her mind had closed her off from the trauma. "If you can hear me in there, Christine, don't worry. I will take care of your daughter too. You won't be alone for long." She did not respond but merely kept staring. Oh yes, this was far too easy for a girl like me, a talented girl, a girl with a future.

Chapter 12

I woke up screaming. Thankfully, no one could hear me in the guesthouse. When I realized I was awake and it had all been a dream, I put my hand over my mouth to stop myself. I had learned that trick before, to scream when I wanted the dream to end. Somehow it worked, when I remembered to do it. I got out of bed, the darkness of Isla's life weighing me down. I had seen what she had seen, done what she had done. I went to the restroom and brushed away the tastes of lemonade and gin and all those unhappy kisses. I got in the shower to wash it all away, checking my body for bruises as I scrubbed. Happily there were none. My mind rocked with all the information I had collected. When I dried off, I decided to immediately record what I had witnessed.

I flipped open my laptop and began to type like a crazed scribe. From the first moment to the last, I wrote down every thought I could remember. Now it all made sense! Oh, Captain Garrett, how could you? Calpurnia had loved you so and now, to discover it was all a ruse, it made no sense to me. I had cried more over the past couple of weeks than I had in my whole life, but I couldn't help it. My heart broke for so many of these people. I knew them. I knew even Isla in a way she would never approve of. I felt sorry for her, which she would reject immediately, but she too had been a victim at one time. Of course, she had certainly done her share of victimizing others too.

As I wrote my thoughts, feelings and dream-catching experiences, my email dinged. Once I got to a stopping place, I clicked it and was surprised to see an email from Mia's parents. My shaking finger wavered over the key for a minute before I opened the message.

Dear CJ,

I hope this letter finds you well. I was wondering, would you mind asking Mia to call us, please? We have not heard from our daughter in six months. We understand that she is busy but if you could, would you tell her? Thanks so much!

When are you coming to see us again? We miss you too!

Love,

Alice and Myron Reed

I read the email again and again. I couldn't believe what I was reading. They had no idea where their daughter was? That was heartbreaking. That meant I would be the one to deliver the bad news to them. This was so unfair! I began to type a response, but nothing came to mind. I closed the laptop and finished getting dressed. I would have to think about what I would say.

I needed to talk with Ashland about the dream. Would he believe me? He had to, didn't he? The alarm went off on my phone, reminding me that

TD's Moonlight Garden presentation was that night. An involuntary shudder went through me. I packed my things and went in search of Ashland, my mind still swimming over the dream, the email and everything in between.

I found him in the kitchen, preparing breakfast as promised. I watched him quietly, waiting for the perfect time to share with him what I knew.

"Are you okay? You seem kind of quiet this morning? Trust me, I'm a great cook, and Eggs Cathedral is my specialty. Okay, it's the Spot of Tea's specialty, but I copied it."

"I had a dream last night, Ashland."

His beautiful blue eyes widened, and he set down his orange juice. "Really? Who did you dream about? I thought that only happened in historical places."

"Apparently not in Mobile. All I have to do is think about them before I go to sleep and have something they touched. It doesn't always work perfectly—I mean, sometimes you don't dream about who you intended." I thought about Ashland and his mother dancing, about her mind wandering into dark places. I decided not to tell him anything about her. I wanted to spare him that. "I intended to dream about Calpurnia, but instead I saw Isla."

"Tell me everything." He pushed his plate aside and leaned on his hands. I don't know what he expected to hear, but obviously it wasn't this. "I can't believe it. She was a psychopath or something, wasn't she? She's the reason Christine went catatonic. Oh my God!" He got up from the table and pulled his phone out of his pocket.

Sensing his mood, I panicked. "What are you doing? You can't help them—they are all gone now, Ashland."

"I'm calling TD. I am going to ask him to dig behind the mausoleum. If Louis Beaumont is there, he deserves a better resting place than that." I listened to him talk to TD. He gave a few orders but didn't tell him what he'd find. When he hung up, he said, "Beaumont might not be there anymore; no need to get TD stirred up without a reason." I didn't blame him. TD was an excitable guy, especially if he was being taken off his tight schedule. Ashland looked at me suspiciously, and it saddened me. "I don't envy you your gift, CJ. Are you okay?"

"I'm fine, Ashland. Listen, maybe I should go. I have yet another bad situation happening. Mia's parents emailed me—they haven't heard from her in months, and they want me to call them or have her call them. I've got a lot to think about. I don't want to just tell them that their daughter has lost it—that she's killed a man and tried to hurt me. What do I say?"

He just said, "Tough break. I think the best thing to do is tell the truth, no matter how hard that is."

That was easy for him to say. I cared about the Reeds and knew just how much telling them the truth would hurt. "Well, I better go. Can you give me a lift home?"

"Sure, let me get my keys." Neither one of us was in the mood for breakfast now. I knew what I had to do, and it didn't involve Ashland. "Listen, I'll be at the house in a while, but I have something to do first. I need just a few hours, if that's okay."

"Please tell me you aren't going to talk to Mia." He seemed genuinely aggravated with me. I guessed my dream had put him in a sour mood. But what was I supposed to do? I knew he didn't like my gift, but he did want my help finding Calpurnia. Didn't he?

"No, I'm not. And besides, where would I find her? I have no idea where she is." Okay, that wasn't completely true; I at least knew where I could find a lead.

By the time we reached my place, Ashland was a little more himself. He kissed me before I got out of the car, but it didn't cheer me up much. I waved at him and walked up the steps to my apartment. I liked the little place, despite the excitement of the night before. Bette's car was still gone, and I hoped she would stay away a little longer. I had something to do. I looked through my desk drawer. There it was! I held Henri Devecheaux's card and dialed the number with shaking fingers. I muttered under my breath, "What am I doing? Detective Simmons was right. I am acting like Nancy Drew." I lost my nerve and hung up. No. If I was going to do this, I was going to do it face to face. I grabbed my purse and keys. His club was on Royal Street, which wasn't that far away. Mia had mentioned that he lived in the small building next to Gabriella's. That's where I would go.

I tried not to think too much about what I was doing. I thought about Calpurnia and Isla—and what a fool Calpurnia had been. But hadn't I been a fool too? I had been blind to Mia's scheming, her jealousy of me. How odd it was to see this familiar tragedy play out again. Only this time, I was in the middle of it! I pulled onto Royal Street and stopped in front of Gabriella's. The building was closed, and all the lights were off. Obviously, it wasn't a daytime establishment. I could see a few buildings surrounding the club, but I wasn't sure which was Devecheaux's place. I wouldn't find out from here, would I? I put the car in park, got out and locked the doors behind me. I walked down the sidewalk and stood in front of an arched gate with elaborate spires on top. I pushed the gate open and walked across the brick and up the concrete steps to the big wooden door. There was a large glass window in the center. I peeked inside and saw no one, so I took a deep breath and knocked. Nothing. I knocked again. This time I heard a dog bark, a tiny dog with white fuzzy fur and a protruding lower jaw. What kind of dog was that? He was cute and ugly at the same time.

I saw Henri Devecheaux pause in the hallway. As if to say, "I'm not here to harass you," I gave him a friendly wave. He wore a gold silk robe, which he tied a little closer as he walked toward me. He opened the big door and smiled suspiciously. "Good morning, Miss Jardine. How may I help you?"

"I wanted to talk to you about Mia if you have a minute. I wouldn't bother you if it weren't urgent." I smiled nervously.

"It's no bother at all," he said in a raspy voice. "I'm sorry. I sang my heart out last night, and my voice is shot. Come on in the kitchen, and we'll talk." I followed the big man as he sashayed into a stylish kitchen decorated in a rich New Orleans style with copper pots and plenty of fleur-de-lis embellishments. "Would you like a cup of tea?"

"No, thank you."

He poured himself a cup and invited me to sit with him. "How may I help you?"

"As I mentioned, this is about Mia. She's still missing. I know the police are looking for her, but that's not why I'm here. Her parents are worried sick— they've emailed me, asking about her. Do you know where I can find her? Off the record, of course. I'm not here to spy or get you in trouble. I want to help Mia. I think she needs it." There, that was the truth.

Devecheaux took a sip from his blue teacup and set it down. He inspected me, still suspicious. "I really don't know anything, Miss Jardine."

"It's Carrie Jo, please, and any detail could help."

"She contacted me when she first came to Mobile, wanting a place to stay. She found out I was interested in the supernatural and told me I could visit the house in exchange for her staying here. I jumped at the chance, of course. Who wouldn't? Big, mysterious house, rumors of murders, interesting story. I had no idea that I wasn't supposed to be there. She told me she was the boss, and she had a key and everything. It wasn't until you broke in on us that I knew something was wrong—horribly wrong. I never meant to break the law, you know."

"I'm not here to accuse you of anything, Mr. Devecheaux."

"Please, if I'm calling you Carrie Jo, you call me Henri."

"Okay, Henri. I'm not here to accuse you of anything. I just want to find my friend."

He took the last swig of his tea and gave me a sad look. "I'm sorry, but she's not here. I think she went to stay with her musician friend, Bettencourt. They were pretty hot and heavy when she left. I wish I could tell you more. I suppose the club where he works might be able to tell you where he's at." He rubbed his baby-smooth face. "May I ask you a question? I know it's kind of personal..."

"What is it?"

"Have you had any experiences in that house?"

"What do you mean?"

"You know what I mean, Carrie Jo. Experiences, with the afterlife, ghosts, haunts—anything like that."

I stood up from the table, ready to leave. Maybe he didn't know anything after all. "I think all old houses have imprints of the past, Henri. Don't you?"

"When we were there that night, I swear there was something—someone—there. I think it was a woman or a girl. Like I say, I have an interest in these sorts of things. I have a website; would you like to see it?"

Curious, I followed him to what looked like an office or a small production studio. He walked behind a desk, and I followed him. He kicked his foot to close the bottom drawer, but not before I caught a glimpse of the music box. My heart was pounding, but I pretended to focus on the computer screen. "Oh, that is interesting," I forced myself to say. Henri Devecheaux had the music box! What did that mean? He must have believed that I missed his sleight of hand, or foot, because he began to show me the features of his website—photos, videos of supposed ghosts, links to other sites.

"So, you see, I have Oakleigh and the Bragg Mitchell Manor on here—both with their full permission, of course. They let me come in and set up my cameras, I record for twelve hours, then I publish what I find here. It's kind of a hobby. But look, I have over one hundred thousand followers. People love Old Mobile history, and they love the supernatural. It's the perfect combination for an aspiring businessman."

"That is interesting. You have done a great job with the website. A hundred thousand people? That would be great advertisement for the museum. You know, when we get it up and running."

His eyes narrowed. "That's an interesting necklace you're wearing." I hadn't realized that when I leaned forward to see his computer, the necklace with the key fell out of my shirt.

I quickly tucked it back in and smiled nervously. "Yeah, it's pretty old. Thanks for sharing your website with me. Let me talk to Ashland and see what he says. Despite what Mia told you, he is the boss." I walked toward the door without waiting. He was right behind me but hadn't tried to stop me so far. "Thank you for your help, Henri. I hope I can get Mia the help she needs."

He smiled as he opened the door, but it didn't give me any comfort. I stepped out, feeling safer by the second but not by much. He said, "If I were you, Carrie Jo, I would leave that girl alone. She's not all there, and she sure doesn't consider you her friend anymore. She's obsessed with you, with that house and with...well, let's say she's a girl of many interests."

"Thank you. I will remember that." I walked down the steps as quickly as I could. My hands shook as I got into the car. This was too much! Devecheaux had the music box. I could see him watching from the doorway. I wanted to call Ashland, but I had to get out of there! I drove like a madwoman to Seven Sisters.

There were only a few work trucks on the property. The unveiling of the Moonlight Garden was that night, and it was going to be a small affair, mostly for the team and a few other folks. To my surprise, Detra Ann was there, talking with Ashland and TD. The brunette seemed about as happy to see me as I was to see her.

"Ashland, I have to talk to you."

"Okay, sure. Let's go out back. I have to tell you something anyway." We walked down the long hallway to the back door. This was the very hallway where Ashland had seen Isla as a child and she'd kissed him. "Listen, I told TD to hold off on digging right now. I was thinking that Louis Beaumont has rested this long, and one more night isn't going to hurt. And we've got people from the Historical Society coming to this tonight. It's not unusual to find skeletons on an old property like this, but not usually when the locals are visiting. What do you think?"

"Ashland, I found the music box. It's at Henri Devecheaux's."

"What? Really? That's where you went this morning? Why didn't you tell me? I would have gone with you. Do you know how much danger you put yourself in?" He ran his hand through his hair, and his jaw popped tensely. *Was he angry with me? When I was trying to help him?*

"I'm fine! I'm telling you I saw the music box—but I didn't get it. It was in a drawer in Devecheaux's office. And I think he saw this..." I showed him the key on my necklace.

"That's it! We've got to call Detective Simmons and tell her what you found out. Someone has to protect you!" He slid his phone out of his pocket.

"No, we can't do that! You said you wanted to wait on exhuming Beaumont's remains because you didn't need the bad publicity right now, but won't calling Simmons in to get the necklace do the same thing? I don't think Devecheaux knows I saw the box, so we should be okay. Let's wait until tomorrow and take care of all this nasty business at once. I'd hate to see TD's big night ruined."

"You're probably right, but I'm not happy about it. And I'm not happy you went over there alone to confront that man. He's twice your size, Carrie Jo. What would have happened if he had decided to take that necklace from you? You couldn't have stopped him."

"He didn't, and I'm fine. Stop worrying. We have a party to prepare for, don't we?"

"I don't think you and I have much to do. Detra Ann and TD seem to have everything covered. Let's get out of here a while. I'm starving—I missed my breakfast because an obsessed historian wanted to go play Sherlock Holmes. What am I going to do with you, CJ?"

"I don't know. Kiss me again?"

Chapter 13

That afternoon, I made it a point to buy a white dress. It was the one request TD had made: everyone was to wear white—I guess so we'd all "glow" in the dark. I wasn't a shopper. I liked buying online, but there was no time for that. In the end, I had to go to Hermes Bridal. I found a dress I loved; it was sleeveless with beadwork and a fringed hem. It was kind of a flapper style, and I thought it was perfect for a summer garden party. It had a steep price tag, but it was worth it. I looked wonderful in it.

As I shopped for shoes, I thought about my brunch with Ashland. We'd stopped by Bienville Tea Emporium and ordered mimosas and some of the best food, apart from Bette's, that I had ever tasted. It was nice to be in the moment, not stuck in the past. So much sadness there. The past is where all the regrets go. Regrets don't live in the present—they always trail behind you, tap you on the shoulder and say, "Remember me?" I didn't want to live a life of regrets. I wanted to always think of the present moment. I couldn't do anything about my dream life, but after spending a significant amount of time in Isla's "skin," I knew how dangerous that could be. Always thinking of the past. Counting regrets. Using pain as fuel for life. So toxic and deadly. How easy it would be to do just that.

At nine o'clock, I drove to the house, pulling in behind Ashland's sleek Mercedes. My Honda looked out of place, even with four new tires, but here I was. It was pitch black out, and I could see the moon rising high above us. No clouds, no hint of rain. It was the perfect night for this, I supposed, even though Louis Beaumont's body was probably just on the other side of the maze, behind the Cottonwood Mausoleum. A shiver ran down my spine. I remembered the first time I walked up this sidewalk, the first time I stood before the columned porch of the house. How different it looked now, yet so much the same. The painted white columns looked almost blue in the moonlight. Two newly installed gas lamps flickered at the bottom of the steps, lighting the way for visitors to the great mansion. Thankfully, the satyr fountain, an addition that had arrived sometime at the turn of the century, had been relocated somewhere less frightening and offensive. I couldn't have been happier about that decision.

Light poured through the windows, and soft music played, the piano player warming up for the soiree. What had begun as a small event for the team had somehow evolved into a party of fifty, complete with live music, champagne and appetizers. I knew who I could thank for that—Detra Ann. *What's your problem, CJ? You're jealous of nothing. She and Ashland are just friends. Come on now, be nice.* I wasn't normally a jealous person, but I couldn't deny what I felt. It was this house, I reasoned, feeling the cold chills shimmy down my spine.

Speak of the devil, it was Detra Ann who greeted me at the door. "Hi, Carrie Jo! You look great! I think Ashland is in the Blue Room."

I smiled, determined to overcome my own pettiness. Tall and athletic, Detra Ann was a pretty woman, and the white handkerchief dress she'd chosen showed off her toned curves and exquisite tan. I strode to the Blue Room, where I found Ashland sliding a box on my desk.

He turned around when he heard me come in. "Hi! Wow, you look great!"

"You sound surprised," I teased him.

"Nothing you do surprises me. Remember the first night we met? You fell in my arms?"

"That's not how I remember it. I fell on my head—you carried me in your arms." I stood on tiptoe and kissed him. "What's that?"

"A delivery for you, but that can wait. Let's go find TD and let him know we're here. According to Detra Ann, he's a nervous wreck. You know, I think those two might have something going on."

I raised an eyebrow. "Really? Well, she's done a great job decorating for the party. I think maybe we should think about having that Christmas ball after all—if you're still interested. Might be fun."

He smiled and said, "Let's wait and see how many more bodies turn up around here. We may not be able to get anyone here for a ball, except a few ghosts."

"Don't say that." I was dead serious. The ghosts of the past were always listening. "Please."

"Okay, okay. Come on, I need a drink or two. Let's put on our happy faces."

We found our way to the bar that had been set up in the ladies' parlor. The two Rachels, their dates, James, Chip and Chip's mom were already there. I hugged everyone's neck, and Ashland and I posed for photos with our group. We wandered around, talking to the visitors and sharing stories about the renovation process. One thing I could say about Mobile was that it was full of interesting characters—that included the wealthy and elite of local society.

At ten o'clock, TD finally appeared, welcoming us to the opening of the Moonlight Garden. He gave a brief history lesson on how the garden worked and then pulled aside the heavy dark curtains that covered the back doors. He and Detra Ann opened the doors, and the sight was nothing short of amazing. Moonlight bounced off the statues, the white flowers, the bleached walkways. I caught my breath at how perfectly TD had managed to recreate the garden that I knew from my dreams. I held onto Ashland's arm; he looked down at me, searching my face, but I nodded at him. "I'm okay," I whispered. The hedges were intact, although not as tall as they had been, and a few of the large trees were missing, but everything else was in place. I walked down the back steps and stood on the pathway. I could close my eyes and completely believe that Muncie or Calpurnia was very near to me.

"Ladies and gentlemen, I present the Moonlight Garden. Please take a tour and enjoy the grounds. Detra Ann has kindly provided a basket of flashlights if you need extra lighting. I'll be here if you have any questions."

The excited gathering filled the garden, some taking flashlights but most opting for the "natural" tour. It was a sight to behold. "TD, you have done a wonderful job. You can't possibly know how accurate this is to the original. It is simply breathtaking."

He hugged me and shook Ashland's hand. "Thank you for allowing me to be part of this. This has been a real labor of love. Now go take the tour and tell me what you think."

I wiped a tear or two from my eye, chose not to take a flashlight, and walked into the Moonlight Garden with Ashland. The house disappeared behind us, swallowed up by the massive gardenias that TD had so carefully planted and manicured. It was as if they had been here all along, hiding, waiting to be recognized again. The garden path veered to the right from the entrance, leading visitors along the hedgerow, where it turned to the left. I didn't need anyone to tell me where to go, because I'd already been here. The path led from statue to statue to the back of the property. I looked up at Ashland, and his blond hair made him look like one of the statues shining in the moonlight. His dazzling smile only added to the effect.

Suddenly a scream filled the garden, and Ashland and I rushed toward the sound. We didn't have far to go. Chip's mother lay on the ground, her flashlight beside her. The skinny young man with the oversized glasses tried to help her up, but she screamed again.

"No, let me sit for a minute, boy, or I might hurt myself worse. Oh, my ankle!" Chip shrugged and stood helplessly over his mother.

Ashland squatted down beside her. "Are you okay? Should I call an ambulance?"

She smiled, and her hand fluttered to her neck. "Oh no, I'm sure I will be okay. Maybe you could help me up? I just need to get off this ankle. I stepped wrong, is all. I won't sue you or anything," she said with a giggle, putting her arms around Ashland's neck. "Wait a minute. You're Ashland Stuart, aren't you? I thought that was you. I'm Arnette, Chip's mother."

"Nice to meet you, Arnette. Let me help you up." Ashland and Chip awkwardly got her to her feet, and she held onto both of them.

"I just need to rest. Oh, oh, it hurts."

I smiled at Ashland. He had his hands full, and I was more than happy to let him handle it. "I'll see you in a few," I said. I hated that we wouldn't be walking through the garden together, but I felt compelled to continue the tour. I could hear the others laughing and joking about the dark, and someone even howled at the moon. I walked on, passing first Alcyone, the statue of the sister who was seduced by Poseidon. Next came Sterope, who had been ravished by Ares, then Celaeno, Electra, Merope and Maia, each statue representing in some way the tragic figures of the Pleiades or the Seven Sisters. Finally, the path took me to Taygete, the last of the statues before the Atlas Fountain, and to me the sweetest. Taygete had a long, graceful neck and elegant arms that she waved above her head. Her foot was placed on the back of a deer's head, a hind sent by Artemis to wing her away from Zeus' unwanted advances. Around Taygete grew a myriad of white flowers. I plucked one from a bush; it looked like a star. Some species I didn't recognize, but I saw some flowers that I did know: the Oxeye Daisy, Hepatica, devil's trumpets. I also noticed that TD had placed mirrors about the garden to bounce the light around, creating an unexpected glowing effect. Taygete's feet flowed in the dark like an unearthly spotlight. In my dreams, the garden was much darker, but this was lovely beyond words. I felt as if I had stepped right into another world. I stared at Taygete again, wishing Ashland could be here, when suddenly I got the feeling I was being watched. I wasn't alone in the garden anymore.

Creak, creak, creak. I froze after getting to my feet, the flowers in my hand. *Creak, creak, creak.* "Who's there? Is that you, Rachel? Detra Ann?" Nobody answered me. The garden was so quiet that even the crickets had stopped chirping. It was as if I had entered a vacuum. I didn't hear the voices of the partiers, and even the moon seemed different. I stepped into a clearing, feeling disoriented and slightly nauseated. *Must be the champagne. I must have had too much.* I leaned against the Taygete statue, trying in vain to catch my breath.

Then I saw her—standing in the moonlight, in the gap between the two hedges. I blinked, staring into the night, still shocked by what I saw. It was Isla, stone-faced, her hands folded in front of her in her skirt. She saw me but said nothing, just backed away without turning, disappearing into the hedge. My first thought was, "Run! Run now!" but I heard the sound again. *Creak, creak.* I had to know what I was hearing. The white flowers slid from my hand, and I stepped as quietly as I could down the path to the spot where she'd disappeared. Suddenly I saw a gap in the hedge, which I was sure had not been there before. I held my breath and stepped across into another small clearing. An old oak tree towered above the clearing, preventing the moonlight from falling fully on the ground below. Instead, it shone in splotches, here and there. Under the tree, a rope swing with an old board for a bottom swung back and forth as if someone had just leaped out of it. I walked to it, stilling it with my hands, the old ropes creaking as I did. That was the sound I'd heard. I touched the wood; it felt real. *This was real, right?* Again my senses were pricked by the feeling that someone was watching me.

Isla stood behind me. I knew without looking. I turned slowly, trying to prepare my mind for what I was about to see. It didn't do me any good. She was about six feet from me, looking as real as anyone I had ever seen. Her hair was carefully curled and pinned up, spirals of golden hair dangled, covering her ears. A green jade necklace hung at her neck, and she wore a black and grey dress with billowing sleeves. Her young face stared back at me; it appeared twisted with anger, her fury ready to be released upon me. I was not wanted here! A breeze began to blow through the clearing, a swirl of air that tossed flower petals to the ground and moved the heavy tree limbs as if they were touched by giants. The air became wintry. Isla suddenly smiled, turned and stretched out her arms, welcoming an invisible stranger to her secret garden. As he came closer, a faint image appeared, the outline of a man. His long, dark hair and white collared shirt were unmistakable—it was David Garrett. He was heartbreakingly handsome in a storybook sort of way. He whispered in Isla's ear like a caring lover would, playfully touching her curls. He smiled down at her and slid his arm around her small waist, and the two walked away to the entrance of the clearing. The captain was fully visible now but still unaware of my presence. Before the couple disappeared, the girl looked back at me with a bottomless stare. I stood by the swing, closing my eyes to avoid seeing everything swirl into blackness.

I woke with Ashland on his knees next to me. The Taygete statue towered above me, and the evening was warm and balmy. No more coldness—no more Isla. "What happened?" I asked him.

He laughed nervously. "I could ask you the same thing. Did you fall or decide this was a good place to take a nap?"

"No." I sat up, shaking my head. I felt okay, no bangs or bruises, as far as I could tell. "I walked through the clearing over there and woke up here."

"What clearing?"

"The one over there." I stood, knocking the fallen flowers from my skirt. I walked to the hedge, but the opening was now gone. My guess was it had never been there, at least not in recent years.

"What happened, CJ? Did you see something?" His eyes searched mine. I hated seeing that desperate look on his handsome face. He had looked up at his mother like that, wanting to rescue her, save her. I didn't want that. At that moment, I wanted him to see me as normal—I wanted to *be* normal. Maybe I would tell him later, but not now. He'd had enough for one day.

"I don't know, really, but I feel fine now. Can we go back to the house?"

He nodded. I knew he didn't believe me, but he was enough of a gentleman not to press me. We walked back holding hands. Once in a while, I couldn't help but look back. I didn't see anyone other than the invited, living guests.

"Let me get you some water."

I smiled at him. "That sounds great. I'll be hiding out in the Blue Room for a few minutes."

He laughed, and I strolled down the hall, closing the double doors behind me. I leaned against the cool painted wooden doors. What had this house done to me? Did I really want to stay here? How much more could I see? How much more could I take? I sighed and walked to my desk. There was the forgotten box. I read the return address—it was from H. Devecheaux. I reached for the letter opener and cut through the tape. On top of a wad of tissue paper was a note.

Dearest Miss Jardine,

I humbly ask your forgiveness for my involvement with Mia Reed and her schemes. I am returning this music box to you in hopes that, in some way, doing this might make amends. She left this item with me when she moved and asked me to keep it for her. Even though I didn't want to, I did as she asked because Mia can be a dangerous, demanding woman.

I cannot tell you how I worry for you, as Mia thinks of nothing else but reclaiming a lost treasure that she is convinced you are keeping from her. Please be aware that she is a danger to you and to anyone who stands in her way.

As for my part, I regret the night at Seven Sisters. I regret calling up those old ghosts, for ever since that night, I have not had a decent night's sleep. I cannot shake the feeling that I am being watched and that death hangs close to me. Perhaps when this box is returned, I shall finally have some peace. I am leaving Mobile. I do not plan to return. Please express my sincere apologies to Mr. Stuart, Detective Simmons and everyone else I have hurt.

Yours,

Henri Devecheaux

I tossed the tissue and note aside and stared at the delicate-looking music box. My hands shook as I removed it from the box. I set it on my desk and slipped the necklace off my neck. Somewhere on this box was a hidden keyhole, the keyhole that operated not only the music but also a hidden compartment. Again I felt that someone was watching me. I rubbed my fingers over the enamel figurines, the dancing couple caught forever in a waltz. At the base of the podium that held the couple, I spotted a smooth piece of brass. I carefully slid the brass piece away. The hinge moved easily; someone else had found the spot recently but could get nowhere without a key. With shaking hands, I slid the key into the slot and turned it, hearing it click. The top of the box opened up to reveal a bright red, velvet-lined interior. Inside was a folded slip of paper. With trembling hands, I removed it without unfolding it. The lettering on the outside was perfect, like someone had written it yesterday.

"Here's your water...is that the box?" Ashland's face went white, and he froze.

I nodded up at him. "I found the compartment. It was in the base, and I found this note there. Ashland, I think you should be the one to read it. I suspect it is from Christine."

He put the water on the desk and accepted the note. He carefully unfolded the stiff paper, spreading it out on the table in front of me. "No, let's read it together."

Dearest Daughter,

Find your True Self, and you will Find a Treasure!

All my Deepest Love,

Christine Beaumont Cottonwood

I blinked, staring at the page. *True self, true self. Where had I seen that before?*

"This is impossible. I don't get that at all. What does this mean? Was she out of her head when she wrote this?" Ashland's discouragement didn't bother me. I was a historian—solving mysteries was my job.

I frowned at him. "Let's think about this for a minute. It's a riddle meant to confuse anyone who doesn't have any business reading it. Like you and me. Wait a second. You read most of that diary, didn't you? How did Calpurnia always describe herself? Her true self. She was a girl who liked literature. She would have identified with a heroine, a character, maybe even a... oh my gosh!"

"What is it, CJ?"

"Her neck, she hated her neck. Even Isla mentioned that Calpurnia had a long neck. That's it!" I stood up quickly from the desk, the rolling desk chair flying away awkwardly. I know where it's at!"

"Are you serious?"

I grinned and nodded, as excited as a kid running to the ice cream truck. "We will need a shovel, though."

"A shovel? If this requires digging anywhere around here, we'd better wait until after the party. Only thirty more minutes. Can you wait that long?"

I pretended to bite a fingernail. "I can if you can."

~~*

Shadows Stir at Seven Sisters

By

M.L. Bullock

Dedication

This book is dedicated to my father, Jerry Patrick. One day I will get the hang of identifying trees and plants. Until then, I look forward to our next walk together. And if I never learn, I'll still know you loved me. Thank you for everything.

Speak Forever

Speak forever, childlike virgin;
like a divine power,
tear out from my bleeding heart
the thorn,
And you will see a poor infant crying!

Speak forever, and the storm
that is going to batter my youth,
will stop and carry its rage
far from me,
As soon as you will tell me:
"For you, my word!"...

Camille Thierry (1845)

Chapter 1

What would Detective Simmons think about Ashland and me digging in the garden of Seven Sisters on a moonlit night? She'd probably raise a ginger brow, lick the lead of her pencil and waste no time whipping out her notebook. Yet here we were, dressed in white like two ghosts, slinging dirt from a hole we dug in front of the Taygete statue. We'd been digging for ten minutes—the adrenaline was beginning to wear off now, and I was starting to worry that my hunch had been wrong. Dead wrong. That nagging voice in my heart that only spoke when something was going horribly wrong began whispering in my ear. *I can't believe you didn't take the time to do some research first!*

I leaned against the shovel, trying to catch my breath. The sweat that covered my face and neck was like sweet nectar for an irritating chorus of Alabama mosquitoes. They apparently couldn't resist it. It didn't matter that it was coming up on midnight. It was still hot out. "Ashland, maybe we should come back in the daytime, bring a metal detector or something."

"Are you saying you were wrong? Could we be looking in the wrong place?" He leaned on the rusty handle of his shovel.

I frowned. "No, I don't think I'm wrong, but I want to be absolutely sure before we tear up all of TD's work."

"That only seems fair!" Ashland and I looked up to see our contractor, Terrence Dale, standing just a few feet away. He watched us with his hands on his hips, a cross between amused and aggravated. "May I ask what the hell y'all are doing? Ashland, I know I just work for you, but this was my project. Why are you digging holes in the...." A sudden realization hit him. He knew what was happening. "What exactly are you looking for?"

Ashland gave him an apologetic smile. "Sorry, TD. We didn't want to do this in front of you. I know this sounds ridiculous, but Carrie Jo thinks she knows where the Cottonwood treasure is located. We have good reason to believe that it's here, under or around the Taygete statue. I promise I'll get the garden looking like it's supposed to again if it takes me all week."

"Why here?"

I swatted away mosquitoes and explained to him what I knew: in some of Calpurnia's journals she referred to herself as T, which I believed stood for Taygete. I repeated her mother's clue, *Find your True Self, and you will Find a Treasure.* Taygete was Calpurnia's "true self." She was a character that Calpurnia identified with, a doomed young woman with a long neck and an unkind father.

"That makes sense, but I hate to tell you this—I moved the Taygete statue. It was over there," he said as he pointed to an old hedge, "but to me it made more sense to put it here instead, more like the star alignment."

"So you're telling me we're digging in the wrong place?" I panted, tossing aside another shovelful of dirt.

"That's what I'm telling you. The original location was in there." He pointed beyond the massive hedge, where I had seen Isla Beaumont meet Captain David Garrett. There had been a swing and maybe a statue or a fountain; I had not been paying attention—my eyes had been fixed on the ghost of Calpurnia's cousin as she waited for her lover. She hadn't wanted me there, that much I knew. I felt her presence again, on the edge of the garden, approaching slowly to see what the interlopers were up to. Maybe I was imagining things. I wasn't a psychic—just a dreamer.

I shuddered and thought of that old southern saying the old-timers used when hit with a sudden case of chills, *A rabbit ran over my grave!*

"Come on," TD said. "If you're determined to look for something, don't tear up the entire place. That hedge is pretty old, but if we go around to the other side, I can show you how to get in there." We followed him through the thick bushes, forcing our way into the hidden clearing.

There I was again—only this time I hadn't slipped through a supernatural door. Only a broken stump of the old tree remained; the statue was gone, and no swing hung from the branches. *I had touched that swing! I heard it creak, right?* There was no scent of magnolias, just the heavy odor of dead leaves and dirt. I could feel her even closer. "Ashland, we're not alone here." I was talking about Isla, but that was before I saw someone step into the secret garden with us—it was Henri Devecheaux.

"What are you doing here, Mr. Devecheaux?"

His eyes were wide with fear as he stared at me. He didn't say anything, then suddenly let loose a blood-curdling howl and fell to the ground as if he were dead. I tossed down the shovel and ran toward him.

Devecheaux lay like a dead man on the thick green grass of the Moonlight Garden, but it was clear he was very much alive. His dark pupils were encircled with white, staring up into the vastness of the starry Alabama sky. Crouching near him, I put my head on his chest just to be sure—his heart was slow but steady.

"We need to get him to a hospital, but I'm afraid to move him!"

Suddenly the leaves in the garden shook loose from the oaks and magnolias that encircled the hidden clearing, pelting us with flowers and painful seed pods. The silky magnolia blooms blanketed everything with an unearthly white glow. I cleared the flowers off of Devecheaux's face and said, "Mr. Devecheaux! Henri! What happened? Why are you here?"

Through clenched teeth he said, "She's coming!"

"What? Who's coming?" Ashland's blue eyes were wide, and his hands shook. He got on his feet and looked around, unable to detect the intruder. But I had no doubt who was coming—and why.

"We've got to find that treasure. It's the only way to stop her!" I shouted at him over the sounds of rustling leaves and breaking tree limbs. My heart pounded in my chest, and I could hear an eerie buzzing in my ears like a hundred voices trying to speak at once. I let out a little sob but bit my lip, refusing to let fear paralyze me.

"CJ! We have to get him out of here!" Ashland held his hand up to his face, trying to protect himself from a barrage of heavy foliage.

"She's not going to let us—we have to find the treasure, now!" I turned to TD, who appeared as frozen as the statue. He seemed completely unable to process what was happening. I felt sorry for him, but there was no time to explain. "TD! We have to dig! We have to find whatever it is that's buried here. Please help me!"

Digging into the ground like a madwoman, I tossed dirt as quickly as I could. This was a long shot, wasn't it? How would we know where to dig? I had to go on blind faith, praying silently, hoping that God was listening and willing to help us.

TD shouted, "Over here! I think I hit something!"

Just as suddenly as it had started, the blowing leaves stopped. Everything went completely still, and the air around us took on a honey hue, just like when I had walked into the clearing before. I looked at the spot where the opening had appeared in the hedge, and there she was—Isla. "Ashland, get over here! Now!" I pointed at the phantom visitor, screaming at the top of my lungs.

Ashland looked and then scrambled to his feet, dragging the big man with him. Isla hovered above the ground, and the edges of her dress hem faded into the grass. She wore a blue gown, and her hair fell in perfect ringlets across her shoulders. Her eyes were on me, full of ferocious hate. TD had stopped his digging; even he could see the ghost watching us. "For God's sake, TD! Keep going!" I shouted. I ran to his side and began helping him pry a small wooden box out of the ground. I forced my shovel blade into the dirt, grunting with the effort, and eased the box up. TD reached down and grabbed it, brushing the dirt off. The lid had elaborate fasteners and a metal nameplate. He rubbed at it and read aloud, "CBC!"

"Christine Beaumont Cottonwood!" I took the box and held it tightly. I wanted to open it, but I knew I shouldn't. This wasn't my task—Ashland had to do it. He had to claim what was his, what had rightfully been Calpurnia's. That was the only way to break Isla's claim on the thing she'd wanted so badly. She'd plotted and schemed for the treasure, willing to destroy whomever or whatever got in her way. Even death had not stopped her hate for her cousin.

Ashland and Devecheaux stumbled toward us, and Isla glided behind them unblinking. I helped Devecheaux sit on the ground; his breathing was fast, and I imagined his heart pounded in his chest as mine did. All of a sudden, she stopped and raised her face so we could see her fully. Her skin was gray, her lips bloodless, her eyes dark, not blue as they had been in life. She extended a hand to Ashland, giving him a dead smile, an invitation to...something. A kiss? To think that face had charmed Captain Garrett into doing the unthinkable. Ashland took a step back, almost walking into the hole before TD stopped him.

"Ashland," I said, "you have to open the box, now!" I passed the dirty container to him.

Isla ignored me, her skin no longer gray but vibrant. I caught my breath at how alive and beautiful she appeared; except for the faded hem and invisible shoes, you would have sworn that she indeed lived and breathed. She gave him a sweet smile and slid closer. "Darling," she whispered.

"Ashland! Don't look at her. Open the box!"

He tried to work the latch, but his fingers wouldn't cooperate. "It's locked!"

"Bang it with a shovel or something!" TD yelled at us desperately.

"No, wait. Try this!" I slid the necklace from around my neck. It had fit the lock in the music box, so maybe it would work here too. Ashland took the key and slid it into the rusty lock. At first it refused to open. Isla inched forward again, just a few feet from us now. The soft, yielding look was gone from her face, and her jaw was tight. That soulless buzzing filled my ears again. Ashland jiggled the lock, and the lid opened. He pulled a velvet bag out and let the box fall to the ground. I grabbed his hand, and together we stood holding Christine's lost treasure.

"Is that what you want, Isla? You can't have it! It doesn't belong to you—it never did! This belongs to me and Calpurnia—not you, never you! Now leave us—leave Seven Sisters! You have no claim here anymore!" he shouted at her.

Her face contorted into a scream, but no sound came. Her skin faded to gray again, her blue eyes turned black, then gray, and the bright yellow color seeped from her hair. She didn't flee but simply faded into nothingness, taking all the warmth from the air around us. She was there, and then she wasn't. The buzzing stopped, and the air was still. The honey hue had changed back to muggy darkness.

"She's gone," I said. "She's gone." I smiled with relief, but it faded when I looked at Ashland. He was as white as his shirt. TD was on his knees near the hole he'd dug, and Devecheaux lay on the ground, now truly like a dead man.

I prayed that he wasn't.

Chapter 2

Ashland and I trailed the ambulance all the way to Springhill Memorial Hospital. Neither of us spoke during the frantic car ride. We were too busy trying to navigate the traffic. The clinking of the flashers was the only sound. *Did that really happen? Did we just experience the supernatural? Had we really found a treasure?* My dirt-stained dress and my dirty legs and fingers all attested to that.

Even though Ashland was dirty from head to toe too, his blond hair glowed in the moonlight. His hair was quite like Louis Beaumont's, but Ashland was tan. He was not the tall, luminous figure that his great-uncle (times eleven?) had been. The Stuart blood ran strong in him too.

Yes, it had happened. The black velvet pouch lay tossed in the backseat, untouched and unopened. Ashland swung behind the emergency vehicle as it parked. "I'm going to park around here somewhere. Why don't you walk in with Devecheaux? I'll meet you inside."

"Okay." I stepped out of the car and watched him drive away. The hospital workers lifted the gurney out of the back of the ambulance. There was the big man wrapped in white sheets, trying to talk but only mumbling.

"We're sorry, sir. We can't hear you. Who's that? Who are you looking for? Someone named... No, I can't understand. It's okay, Mister...."

"His name is Henri. It's Henri Devecheaux."

"You a family member? Wife? Girlfriend?"

"No, just a friend. He came to my party tonight. Is he going to be okay?" I attempted to follow him into triage but was blocked by an unsympathetic nurse.

"Ma'am, you'll have to wait until the doctor assesses him. Why don't you follow me, and we'll fill out his paperwork. Do you know if he has insurance?"

"No, but since he had his heart attack or stroke or whatever this is on the property of Seven Sisters, I'm sure my boss will want to cover the hospital bills. I can give you that information easily."

"That sure is nice of your boss. Who are you working for?"

"I work for Ashland Stuart, the owner of Seven Sisters. We had a garden party tonight."

"Huh. I didn't know anyone was living there."

"Not living there—just a party. It's kind of a museum now." Answering all these questions was aggravating, but I had to keep my cool.

"Let me look at you. Are you injured?" She appraised my outfit with an unbelieving eye. "You sure you two weren't in a wreck?"

What was I going to tell her? That we'd done war with a ghost? "I'm fine. And yes, I am very sure. No wreck."

She raised her ultra-thin eyebrows but didn't challenge me. It certainly didn't help that Ashland walked up completely filthy too. "Yeah, I'm sure y'all had quite the party over there at that big house."

She left, disappearing behind the door of the triage room. After about fifteen minutes, it was clear she was in no hurry to come back. I whispered, "Nobody can know what happened in the Moonlight Garden tonight. Who would believe it, Ashland?"

"They'll just have to believe it. I know what I saw—it was Isla there. We all saw her. I think she wanted me to kiss her or help her or...I don't know. It's weird because I knew what she was trying to do. Isla wanted to trick me into taking her place. Somehow, I knew that. Could you feel that? Like you said, though, when I pulled the bag out of the box, it was all over with."

As he spoke, I began to feel the same kind of "wrongness" I had felt in the garden. Not nearly as strong, but there it was. Hoping, looking for a way back in. I knew what we had to do. "Oh my goodness, Ashland. This feels wrong. There's still a chance something...that she could.... You've got to look at it—to see it." I was almost in tears. "You need to touch it, take possession of it. Let's go now. Follow me. You do have it with you, right?"

He nodded, wide-eyed, and followed me to the ladies' room. I checked the stall—no one was inside. We were alone. I locked the door and stared at us in the mirror. No wonder the nurse thought I was crazy. I was covered in dirt from head to toe. I wanted to wash my face, but more than anything, I wanted to look inside the pouch. What treasure could be so precious that a soul would defy Death to retrieve it?

Isla had not been clever enough to solve the riddle herself during her lifetime. Poor Callie didn't even know about it, really. The young heiress hadn't discovered that the box held a clue, a precious clue that would eventually lead us to the right spot to unearth the hidden prize. Now here we were—dirty and disheveled, hiding in the ladies' room on the ER floor of Springhill Memorial Hospital. At least the bathroom was clean.

"Are you ready to look?" I whispered to him hurriedly.

"Definitely. Let's see what all this has been about."

I heard a soft buzz again, but Ashland didn't react. I must have been the only one who heard it, but I knew she was lurking about, watching.

He pulled on the strings of the dry-rotted bag, loosening them with shaking fingers. Without looking inside, he plunged his hand into the bag and removed a heavy necklace loaded with sapphires set in gold and silver. Their brilliance had not lessened with time. I held my breath as he passed them to me, thinking of who must have held them last. Had it been Christine Cottonwood or Louis Beaumont? Or perhaps someone else?

Carefully, Ashland dumped the remaining contents into his hands. There were ten gold coins, the likes of which I'd never seen, two sapphire earrings encrusted with diamonds, gold and silver, and lastly a bracelet with hundreds of diamonds shining brightly under the fluorescent light.

The bad feeling began to fade slowly, and then she was gone. She'd seen that we'd found her treasure, or what she had believed was hers. She had seen, and now she was gone. I prayed that I would never see or feel her again.

Someone knocked on the door, and we quickly stuffed the items back into the bag. Ashland put it in his pocket, and we went to the sink to clean up. We scrubbed up with soap and water, washing our arms and faces. The knocking persisted. "Just a minute, please," I called to our impatient visitor.

Once we'd finished our "birdbath," we walked out together, our heads held high. We'd done nothing wrong. Let her think whatever she wanted.

"You found the treasure, and the spell is broken, Ashland. She's gone. Can't you feel it?"

He smiled sadly. "Yes, but tomorrow, I will have to answer some questions. People are going to want to know how I found these and where."

"So you'll tell them. No biggie. Just don't tell them the supernatural stuff. People don't believe in that, you know."

"Yes, I do know." He still looked sad, obviously remembering that he had been one of those people just the day before.

"Are you worried about Mr. Devecheaux?" I asked. "I'm sure he will be okay now that he's here."

"I need to check in with TD. He didn't take any of this well at all. He'd been so adamant about the house not being haunted. Definitely a nonbeliever in the supernatural, and now his world has been rocked. I'm sure he'll have some questions, and I hope I can answer them." With a thoughtful look, he added, "I'm thinking of Uncle Louis too, murdered and buried in an unmarked grave. I have to correct that. To think, Isla knew what happened to him but refused to tell anyone. What kind of sick family do I come from?"

"Not sick. Just a family with secrets. They just kept too many secrets. Let's go see Mr. Devecheaux."

"Shouldn't we wait until they call us?" he asked, his hand on his pocket protectively.

"Hell no! You're Ashland Stuart, for goodness sake. Use your clout for once. Pull some strings. Get us back there!"

He grinned. "You're right. Be back in a minute." And in just five minutes, he was back with a big smile on his face. "Come on, I'll take you to his room."

"He has a room already?"

"He does now. He's up on the third floor. Here's the elevator."

I smiled at him, put my arms around his neck and hugged him. "We found the treasure, and now we have to find Calpurnia. I promised you I would, and I mean it. We will find her and bring her home."

"The more I think about it, the more I wonder if that's what she would want. She spent so much time trying to escape Seven Sisters; it might be too ironic, too cruel to bring her back here. If she ever left. Still, I want to know where she is—what happened to her. Did Isla know that too? Someone knows. She deserves to be found, CJ. I'm glad that you're committed to this. Tell me...is life always like this with you?"

I thought of what Isla had said in my dream: *Worm food now, I suppose.* What had happened to the enchanting girl with the elegant neck, beautiful hair and unassuming, sometimes nervous smile? "No, my life was pretty normal, minus the occasional dream, until I met you. Or maybe it's the house? Maybe it's Seven Sisters that's bringing all this out."

We stepped off the elevator and onto the third floor, which was apparently the cardiac unit. The doctors must have thought Devecheaux had indeed had some type of cardiac event. That didn't bode well. *Please, God, help him.*

I hoped He would listen. We pushed the door open to find Devecheaux quite alone. The mocha-skinned man's only companions were some noisy machines that dinged every so often. I walked softly to his bedside and held his hand. "Mr. Devecheaux. Henri. Can you hear me?"

At first he didn't respond, but I tried again. "Henri, can you hear me? It's me, CJ. And Ashland is here too."

He opened his eyes and looked at me. I saw a tear slide down his cheek. "You're okay," he whispered, then looked at Ashland. "And you're okay. Thank you, Lord."

"Yes, we're fine. What about you? What does the doctor say, Henri?"

"I don't know. I can't remember. But you are okay, so that's all that matters. Did we stop her? Will she come back?"

The sound of his weak voice, cracked with desperation, broke my heart. I didn't know Devecheaux well, but I knew he usually had a deep, booming voice. He'd made a mistake participating in that séance at Seven Sisters, but he'd tried to make amends, hadn't he? He had sent the music box back to us. Buffeted by Isla's angry spirit, he'd fought against her to come to us, to warn us, to help us. That's what I wanted to believe. I hoped it was true.

People were still good, right? Some of them, anyway. *Oh Mia, why did things turn out like this?*

I smiled down at him. "No, Isla won't come back. Her power is broken, Henri. She has no more hold on us. We found her secret and exposed it. Tomorrow, the rest of her secrets will be exposed too. People will know what she did, who she really was. Louis Beaumont will be given a proper burial. It's all okay."

"Thank the Lord. Oh goodness, I can't believe this happened to me. I've never had to battle anything like that."

Ashland said, "Mr. Devecheaux, I'm going to have to ask you to please keep this off your website. CJ told me that you have some kind of supernatural website featuring old houses in Mobile, but I don't want what happened tonight to show up there. Please. Getting rid of Isla was a step in the right direction, but I have a feeling that's not the end of the story. Somehow I know we haven't met the most dangerous thing yet." He paused and looked at me, his eyes wide at his own confession. This was all new territory for him. "I've got to find a missing girl, and sharing this all over the Internet won't help me. If you agree to keep quiet, I'll reward you for your trouble."

I just looked at Ashland. Even though I knew he was concerned for Seven Sisters, I was surprised he was even raising this issue. But I kept my mouth shut and just listened to the conversation.

The big man smiled. "That's mighty kind of you two. I appreciate that, and you can count on me. I won't tell a soul. Not even Mia, if she ever came around again."

"Thanks, Henri. Why don't you get some sleep...we'll come see you in the morning."

"That will be fine, but I have to tell you what I saw." He reached for my hand with his own cold, clammy one. He rubbed the back of my hand and closed his eyes for a minute.

"It was Isla that led you to the Moonlight Garden, wasn't it, Henri?"

"She did, CJ, but that's not everything. I saw a man there too, a handsome man with angry dark eyes, dark hair, a fancy hat and a white collared shirt. He watched us from the edge and didn't come close. He watched Isla. When he saw she failed, he turned and walked away. Right into the mist..."

"Must have been the captain. Captain David Garrett. What else did you see?"

"I saw the young lady, Cal...Cal..."

"Calpurnia?"

"Yes, she was standing beside Ashland in the garden. She was smiling and clapping when he opened the bag, and then she disappeared."

I smiled at Ashland too. The old Ashland would have stormed out of the room and run away from all this, but this was not the old Ashland. He had a new respect for the supernatural, I imagined. I suspected he had some abilities too, although he probably wasn't ready to talk about them yet.

"Thanks for telling us." I squeezed Devecheaux's oversized hand, ready to leave him to rest. He was going to need it.

"Now wait! I saw someone with you too."

I froze. Who would be following me? My father? I'd never seen him or met him, and I didn't know if he was dead or alive. I didn't even know who he was. Did Devecheaux mean my mother was dead? We never talked, and I was fairly sure she didn't love me, couldn't love me...mental illness was so cruel. But I had always imagined I would know if she were dead.

"I saw a young man, about as tall as you." Devecheaux smiled like he knew a secret. An amazing, happy secret. "A fine figure who wore black trousers, a black vest and a billowing white shirt. He had dark skin, very dark skin, and short dark hair. That boy had intelligent eyes and full lips. I didn't catch his name—I think he is known by a few, if that makes sense."

"It's Muncie." Tears filled my eyes. I supposed he was there to be close to Calpurnia. He was her closest friend, and she was his. "Was he with Callie?"

"No, he was with you, always staying close to you."

I blinked tears out of my eyes, not understanding what he was saying. "That's got to be a mistake. He was Calpurnia's dearest friend. He must have been there to watch what was happening or at the very least protect her from Isla."

Devecheaux's face fell. "I know what I saw. That boy was there protecting you, just like Calpurnia was watching over Mr. Stuart. When you hunkered down beside me, he was there too. He had kind eyes, full of love and sympathy." He contemplated me for a moment and said, "There's nothing to be ashamed of."

I turned beet red and said, "I'm not ashamed of Muncie; I just don't understand. I just assumed...I mean...Callie is related to Ashland, but could I be related to Muncie? I don't know much about my own bloodline, so it's possible, I suppose." I couldn't understand what he meant, but the man was sick. Maybe he just needed to rest. I squeezed his hand. "We can talk about this tomorrow. Now get some rest."

Ashland and I lingered by the door, whispering to one another. It appeared that Devecheaux had finally fallen asleep. I was glad. Suddenly, I had an idea. "I need to sleep with those jewels."

"What?" he said with a laugh.

"Seriously, I need to sleep with them to see who I dream about; it might help us find Calpurnia. Look, I'm not going to steal them."

"I didn't say you would." Ashland shook his head, rolling his eyes.

"Well, we need to find Calpurnia, right?"

"How do you know that will work? You said so yourself—that's not a sure method. What if you end up dreaming about another murderer or something? Carrie Jo, you have no idea what doors you'll be opening, and I can't go with you. I hate to think of you fighting with the ghost of Jeremiah Cottonwood alone!"

"Well, I'll amp up the power, then. I plan on dreaming in the house."

"No way!" he nearly shouted. "That's not going to happen. You can't sleep on the property; you'll dream the whole time. Something significant is always happening there."

"Come on, Ashland. You want me to find Calpurnia just as much as I do. This is the way to do it."

"This is the wrong way. No cheating. I want you to find her the regular way, like a historian. And you're an excellent historian. Promise me?"

"I know this will work if I do it correctly. I'm getting better at it."

"No!" It was Devecheaux's rough voice pleading with us from his hospital bed. "Please don't do whatever you're planning, CJ. You should know—Isla isn't the only ghost in that house. There are other things left undone, other secrets that you don't know about. Sometimes it's better to leave some things in the dark. Promise me?"

I could hear his heart monitor beeping fast, then faster and faster. I felt compelled to agree. "Okay, okay, I won't. For now. Goodnight, Henri. See you in the morning."

"I'll see you then. I promise you, I'll be right as rain."

Chapter 3

By nine o'clock the next day, an archaeological dig began right behind the mausoleum at Seven Sisters. It wasn't a coincidence, but we had to give Louis Beaumont a proper burial, hopefully with as little police involvement as possible. The less the police department knew, the better. It was easy enough to tell Detective Simmons some family legends about a lost uncle who died on the property sometime between 1830 and 1850. The coroner came out to take a look at the bones and agreed with Professor Wachowski of the University of South Alabama; the remains were of a man who died from blunt force trauma to the head almost two hundred years ago. The plan was to allow USA to do a full examination of the bones, and then we would place Beaumont inside the mausoleum next to his beloved sister. Things moved smoothly, almost too smoothly to be believed.

I stopped by the hospital before I went to Seven Sisters, but to my surprise Henri Devecheaux wasn't there. According to the nurse, he checked himself out without leaving a note, a phone number or anything. I felt a deep sense of loss—I barely knew him, but I liked him. I think he'd been caught up in the whirlwind, an unexpected near-casualty of the machinations of a malevolent ghost. I hoped he would be safe, no matter where he went.

The weeks went by, and I was soon distracted with a dozen tasks. I began to notice that the house had quieted somehow. The frenetic excitement that had vibrated right underneath the surface during our initial months of restoration had vanished. The house felt empty, but somewhere in the wings, something waited—some pending experience that hadn't manifested yet. Or maybe it had happened but was doomed to repeat itself. I shivered. *Doomed.* Why would that word come to mind?

I watched TD walk from room to room with his clipboard, writing furiously on his many checklists. I didn't bother attempting to engage him in conversation. He barely spoke to me anymore, or to Ashland. He had made it clear that he wanted this job to be over and never wanted to come back here again. Privately, I had talked to Ashland about letting TD go because he couldn't handle what he'd witnessed. But Ashland had refused, even though TD wouldn't talk to him beyond a "yes" or "no." I thought the three of us had been not just colleagues but friends. Now the closeness we'd developed during the restoration had vanished—another unfortunate casualty of the supernatural activity that seemed to ooze from the house.

He was aloof with Ashland and me, but he'd gotten quite close to Detra Ann. She stopped by frequently to bring him lunch or a coffee in the morning. As the old southern belles would say, "she'd set her cap for him." He didn't mind, apparently; just a few days after the lunch deliveries, I spotted him kissing her in his truck. *Good for you, Terrence Dale! Back to the land of the living, I see.* I waved at them as I walked to my car at the end of the day without waiting to see if they waved back. I didn't want to know.

On the other hand, my whirlwind romance with Ashland had come to a screeching halt. He'd developed a new habit—daydreaming. It interrupted everything: staff meetings, one-on-one conversations, even his interactions with vendors and subcontractors. I had no idea what was going on in his head, and it didn't seem like he wanted to share it with me. That stung, but I had some processing to do too. At least Calpurnia's treasure had been recovered; all the pieces now were in the safekeeping of a trusted local jeweler who would attempt to appraise each item. I'm sure his findings would be staggering—even for Ashland, who was no stranger to wealth. Somehow, Ashland had managed to keep the news of the discovery under wraps, but I knew that wouldn't last long. People always talked, didn't they?

The month had slipped by, and now we were in the dog days of August. I looked forward to September when we might get a reprieve from the unbearable heat. I'd spent one Friday afternoon working in the glass case in the upstairs hallway. I was so proud of the unique collection of hand-painted fans we were displaying. They had come from local families anxious to be a part of the Seven Sisters story. Even after all these years, the house was still a landmark, an enduring part of local culture. I closed the case with a sigh of pleasure.

When I left Seven Sisters that day, my goal had been to quietly slip out with another treasure I had squirreled away in my purse. Rachel K. and I had dug through the last remaining trunk, an extremely old one with a cracked leather lid, and it was there that I found the treasure hidden. It was an old schoolroom book with brittle paper and faded ink. The inner pages displayed beautiful penmanship and some painfully long sentences. Nothing like what you would see students using today. I didn't know whose book it was until I started scanning through it. And then there it was: "My name is Monticello..." I held my breath as I read the next few paragraphs. Some pages were poems that he'd copied, probably at the behest of a teacher like Christine or Calpurnia. This was no journal—not intimate details about his life—but it was proof that he'd been here. Now I had something I could dream with! More than ever, the idea of hiding out in my comfortable apartment for a session of dream catching appealed to me. I'd fallen out of the habit in the past few weeks and for some reason hadn't cracked open any of Calpurnia's journals. It was like a quiet voice inside my head said, "No, not yet."

Bette was going on a long weekend trip with her beau. She was so excited about the excursion, and I couldn't help but grin thinking about her bouncing curls and big smile. That meant it would be Bienville and me, but if I decided to slip away, there was always something to do in Mobile—a music festival or some kind of food fest happening. I absently thought of William. I supposed he'd gone back home by now or moved on with his tour. Despite how things had turned out, I believed William had liked me in his own way. But Mia had fallen for him hard...unbeknownst to me, of course. I shook my head and slung my purse strap over my shoulder. *Think of something else!*

I hoped Ashland and I could connect again somehow. My feelings for him hadn't changed, but I was a bit more cautious now. No matter—at least not this weekend. I intended to focus my energy on learning more about Muncie. I thought of the young man, his vibrant brown eyes and soft voice. I wondered if perhaps we were connected somehow, by spirit if not by blood. It was a nice thought.

I knew things about him. I knew Muncie's secret: he could read brilliantly, write well and work basic math equations, thanks to Christine Cottonwood and her daughter. I remembered that he felt very smart for knowing all these things. Above everything else, though, he had one burning desire—he wanted to go home.

Home for him was not the faraway land of Africa, like it was for so many slaves who arrived in Mobile. His home had been Port-au-Prince, Haiti. An uncle had waited until his mother had left the house, lied to the slavers and claimed that the little boy had been his slave. Too small to explain himself to the English-speaking slavers, Muncie had been stolen from his mother, who would cry for him every day, beating her breast with her fist and praying for her boy's return.

I couldn't explain how I knew all this. Perhaps from the dreams, or maybe I had read it in Calpurnia's journals, but I knew it. I reached into my purse and touched the fabric-covered book, feeling comforted. This book could be the key to so many secrets. I didn't need to sleep at Seven Sisters; I might be able to see what I needed without putting myself in danger.

"Hey, Carrie Jo! Do you have a minute?"

Rachel sounded like she had something on her mind. It seemed I wasn't going to get away so easily. "What is it, Rachel?"

"I've heard...I mean, Detra Ann told us that something happened here the night of the Moonlight Garden tour. That a ghost showed up afterward. That can't be true, right?"

I couldn't tell if she wanted it to be true or not, but I knew I had to be practical—and as honest as I could be. "Have you ever seen a ghost here?"

"Well, no, but there are times I feel creeped out. Like someone is watching me or something. I even thought I heard someone giggling once, but there was no one there. I've never actually seen anything, though."

"Well, it is a very old house. Which is why we are all here, of course!" I chuckled, and then gave her a comforting smile. "I did see something that night, but it's gone now, and I don't think it will bother anyone again. You don't have to be afraid."

She gave an audible sigh of relief. "Oh, good, because I don't think I could handle that."

"If you ever do see something, feel free to talk to me, Rachel." I smiled and waved goodbye to her as I got into the car.

Well, talk was bound to happen. Detra Ann was full of information, wasn't she?

I decided not to worry about it. I couldn't stop people from talking. Right as I swung into my empty driveway, my phone rang. It was Ashland. "Hey, what's up?"

"Does something need to be up?" He chuckled softly, sounding happier and more relaxed than he had in a long time. "What are you doing this evening?"

"What time?" I felt conflicted. I had Muncie's book to go through, but it was hard to say no to Ashland when he was ready to spend some time with me.

"Around sunset?"

I looked at my watch. It was five, but the sun didn't go down until sometime around seven in the middle of the summer. "I don't know. I planned on sitting in front of the television with a bag of Doritos. Why, you want to join me?"

"That doesn't sound like you at all—I have a better idea. Let me pick you up, and we'll take a walk along the beach on Dauphin Island. Afterward, maybe we'll go to Barnacle Bill's for a quiet dinner. What do you say?"

I smiled as I turned the car off. "I say yes. That sounds nice, Ashland. What time will you pick me up?"

"In about thirty minutes? It will take us another half-hour to get to the island, but I think you'll love it."

"Great! Sounds perfect."

"All right, see you in thirty."

My heart fluttered with anticipation. I hurriedly went through my scanty closet looking for appropriate clothing. Fortunately, I'd recently purchased some nice clothes at University Mall, but I wished I had taken the time to do laundry that week. *Oh well.* I reached for a pretty lilac handkerchief skirt and a cream-colored peasant blouse, and then I haphazardly ripped off the tags. I had some strappy tan sandals that would work well with this ensemble. *Perfect for strolling down a beach with Ashland.*

I heard scratching at the door and found fat Bienville looking forlorn and hungry. "Come on, chubby. You're on your own tonight, though. I have a date!" Then I spotted Iberville at the edge of the porch. The white cat was perched on the railing, his tail flicking. I called to him, hoping to pet him as a thank you for saving me from Mia, but he chose to ignore me again. That was okay. I could love him from a distance—I'd seen those claws in action. I put some water in a dish for Bienville and headed to the bathroom to get ready. My phone rang again, and I picked it up laughing, thinking it was Ashland. It wasn't. I heard Alice Reed's voice on the phone.

"Carrie Jo? Is that you? This is Alice."

"Hello, Mrs. Reed. Yes, this is Carrie Jo." I sat on the side of the bed, holding my breath. What would I say? *Just tell the truth, CJ.*

"I'm sorry to call like this, but we need your help." I could imagine Alice's stiff bouffant hairstyle shaking as she spoke. She and Myron were good people, always kind to everyone. "We are in Mobile, at the Battle House. We have talked with Mia. Carrie Jo, she is willing to turn herself in, but she wants to talk to you first. I know it won't matter much, and I know she's done wrong. But she's pretty insistent, and I'd like to talk to you too." Her voice lowered, and she spoke in a careful, respectful way. "My daughter isn't well, Carrie Jo. She hasn't been for a long time..."

She seemed well enough when she attacked me, I thought, but I didn't say that. I respected Alice too much. "Is she sick?"

"No. Well, yes, but not physically. It's another kind of sickness."

"Oh." I had firsthand knowledge of the other kind of sickness. My mother had battled mental illness all her life. How had I handled it? By avoiding her, giving up on her. Running away as often as I could. Mental illness was a cruel disease, but there were times I was sad and ashamed about the way I had handled things. Had I really done all I could for Momma?

"There's more to it than that. Anyway, may we please meet with you in the morning? Just me and Myron and then Mia? I feel like we owe you an explanation."

"You don't owe me anything, Mrs. Reed. You were always good to me, but Mia has tried to hurt me, twice. I hope she does get help. Believe it or not, I care about her."

"We know you do. When she comes back to herself, she will remember that too. May we meet with you in the morning? Here at our hotel? Say about 8 a.m.?"

"Sure, I'll be there. Actually, 9 works better if that's okay with you. What room?"

"Yes, we can do 9. We will meet you in the lobby—we can talk there. Thank you, Carrie Jo."

I hung up the phone, feeling relieved that they'd found Mia, spoken to her. I hoped she would turn herself in. Perhaps since Isla's "spell" was broken, it was broken over Mia too. I could only hope. Maybe things were going to be okay with her after all. I stroked Bienville's orange fur and then went to take a quick shower. I needed to rinse away the sweat. No matter how cool it was in the house, just stepping outdoors for a second made me feel like a wilted flower. I wouldn't have time to wash my hair, so I pulled it up into a ponytail on top of my head and put on a shower cap.

For the first time in a long time, I sang in the shower. It felt good to tap into my inner diva, but I was thankful no one could hear me except Bienville, who hopped up on the counter to listen to the free concert.

He didn't stay long. I didn't take it personally.

Chapter 4

Always on time, Ashland didn't disappoint. He arrived just when he said he would. But I didn't run out of the house like a teenager when he pulled up. I let him come upstairs first. I'd learned a thing or two from Calpurnia—ladies didn't run down the stairs and jump in cars or carriages. I was glad that Ashland had the manners of a true southern gentleman. I peeped at him as he walked up the stairs. I loved the color of his hair and how soft it looked. Make no mistake, though. Ashland wasn't anything but manly. I recognized his blue linen shirt, and my mind wandered back to that hot, sticky day when we walked to the mausoleum. The color matched his eyes, and I loved that shade on him. He wore casual khakis and a copper and leather bracelet. I was glad we were on the same wavelength as far as the dress code. *I think I got this outfit right.*

After he knocked politely, I opened the door, welcoming him with a smile. "You look great," he said, smiling appreciatively. "But then, you always do."

"Thanks, Ashland. Come on, Bienville. You can't stay in here by yourself. I don't know what you'll get into." The orange tabby flopped down beside me in a sign of protest. "No, I'm sorry. Those are the rules. No kitty home alone here." I scooped him up and carried him outside. Ashland locked the apartment for me, and I set Bienville free to play with his brother.

Ashland took my hand and led me down the wooden stairs into the warm afternoon. His hand felt warm and comforting. I hadn't realized how much I liked holding hands until I met him. We exchanged a few small smiles as we made our way to his car. He opened the car door for me, and I hopped in as elegantly as I could. Ashland took the wheel, and soon we were driving to the southernmost part of Mobile County.

He grinned at me. "Well, history lover, you will find the island fascinating. I know I do. The rumors are that DeSoto explored the area sometime around 1540, but it was the French that officially claimed the island in 1699. It's much smaller than it was once—it is a barrier island, but there's still some of the original topography left. A half dozen hurricanes have changed the island's shape several times, and pirates even razed it in the 1700s, but it's still a beautiful place. Serene, with sandy white beaches."

"Sounds like my kind of place. Do you come down here often?"

"Honestly, not as much as I used to. My mother and I used to stay at an East End beach house every year for a month or so. We'd come down, dig around for shells, visit the mounds, snack on shrimp. Those were nice summers. I didn't come back after she passed, not right away anyway. When I was a teen, I spent most of my beach time at Gulf Shores. That's where all the action is—lots of clubs and restaurants and girls in bikinis." He grinned at me, blushing slightly. "Dauphin Island is much more laid back than the panhandle beaches. No big buildings except for a condo or two, and definitely no teen clubs."

"Sounds like heaven. I was never one to frequent teen clubs." I laughed at the idea. My ultra-religious mother would have never gone for that. "Thanks for giving me the island tour. Dauphin Island sounds like an intriguing place to visit. I admit that I haven't been a very good tourist, but I love Mobile. It's a friendly place. Good vibes here. Mostly," I added quickly.

"That's good to hear. I was afraid that you'd be ready to leave as soon as you could." The concern in his voice sounded genuine. I hated to hear that he had doubts about my fortitude; honestly, I hadn't even thought about leaving Mobile or Seven Sisters. But then again, I wasn't your average girl.

"I have no plans to leave, Ashland. I'm still committed to finding Calpurnia. Aren't you?"

His handsome face relaxed a bit, and he gave me a wistful smile as we crossed the bridge that would take us to the island. "More than ever. I'm happy to hear that. I was hoping Terrence Dale would change his mind and stick around, but I'm afraid he's not going to. He won't say it, but I know it's about our garden visitor. I don't blame him, but he's the best contractor in Mobile—actually, the best contractor on the entire Gulf Coast as far as I'm concerned, and they aren't in short supply around here. Losing TD is going to put us behind on the opening at the very least."

"Maybe we could talk to him, together. Try to explain what happened. Well, not explain it...I mean, who could explain that? But maybe start a conversation about it." I gave him a nervous smile. It couldn't hurt, could it? It hadn't seemed right to force TD to talk to me, but now I guessed we had to. Ashland had every reason to be concerned, and we couldn't lose him if we could avoid it. He knew so much about the house and preservation, and besides, I liked him.

"Let's do that. I think with any luck, Detra Ann will help us." Ashland turned right on Bienville Boulevard, the island's main road, and I couldn't help but stare at my surroundings.

Dauphin Island had lots of pines and a few hearty palm trees. I'd been to Pensacola Beach once; it was nothing like this place. Despite the scattered beach houses and the massive water tank that greeted us as we drove onto the island, it had a sense of wildness. Yes, lots of history had happened here. I could feel that. What had those first settlers thought when they walked the beaches for the first time? We drove past a few seafood shops, more beach houses and a few duplexes. I spotted the wooden sign that announced the public beach. We drove down Bienville Boulevard to the West End.

"The public beach isn't as nice as the West End Beach. Won't take but a few minutes to get there—just in time for the sunset." Ashland smiled at me, his hair catching the fading sunshine like a golden halo. "You'll notice that there's no cell signal out here on this end of the island. Not much of anything except a long stretch of beach."

"So I'm going to be sitting on a beach watching the sunset with a handsome man and with no cell phones to interrupt us? Sounds perfect." I wasn't too good at flirting, but I must have done it right. It gave me butterflies to see him blush. A few minutes later, we pulled into a small parking lot; there were only two other cars there, but there was plenty of evidence the beach had been busy earlier. An abandoned floatie lay in the sand, tire tracks were everywhere and a lone lifeguard was closing his shack for the day. "You folks stay out of the water. Rip current this afternoon," the young man called to us.

"No problem. We don't plan on swimming," Ashland called back to him, giving him a friendly wave. He walked to his trunk, popped it open and took out a comfy-looking blanket, presumably for us to sit on as we enjoyed the scenery. Sunset was only minutes away now. We wore shades, but I had fun imagining his sexy blue eyes behind those stylish frames.

I slid off my shoes and enjoyed the warmth of the sand under my feet. It must have been a scorcher in the afternoon, but the evening ocean breeze cooled everything down. Happy with the spot he found, Ashland awkwardly spread out the blanket. I helped, and soon we settled down to enjoy nature's display.

"I'm surprised you didn't want to take the Happy Go Lucky out. I bet sunsets from the boat are real showstoppers."

"Yes, they are, but we wouldn't have had time today. I hope this is okay?"

I slid my arm through his and inched a little closer. "This is perfect."

Ashland leaned in, his lips almost touching mine. I closed my eyes behind my sunglasses, preparing for a kiss that didn't come. Then I opened them again and found him looking at me with a confident smile. He'd removed his sunglasses and was sliding mine up to the top of my head.

"I want to see your lovely green eyes. I love those eyes, Carrie Jo. May I kiss you now?" I nodded, and our lips met softly. His hand cupped my chin, and his thumb rubbed my jaw. I leaned even closer and curled my arms around his waist. He held me after I pulled away gently, and we stayed like that for a few seconds before he whispered, "Look at that." I turned to see the orange sun low on the horizon, seeming to dip into the ocean. The dimming orb left traces of red and gold in the sky. A few clouds lingered on the horizon, black and purple against the fading brightness.

"Wow, that's amazing. Thank you for this. I needed this moment." I squeezed his hand, wanting to kiss him again. I liked kissing him, that was for sure, but I had to keep it together. *Too late for that, CJ. You've already kissed him a half dozen times. Why stop now?* It had been so long since I'd been intimate with someone, and I found the temptation to succumb to my own needs difficult to resist. And the longer we sat there, the harder it was. Even if his intentions were as pure as the driven snow, mine weren't. I'd always prided myself on being a "head over heart" kind of girl, but what I felt for Ashland was unlike anything I'd felt before. I couldn't explain it.

Slowly, we leaned back on the blanket, his arms around me. I could hear the waves crashing nearby, but my thoughts were completely on the man beside me. I never dreamed I'd be lying on a blanket at the beach with Ashland. Who was in control of my life?

My hands ran instinctively up and down his arms...I loved the feeling of his muscular body. We kissed more deeply, and my hands curled in his hair. When I heard him murmur my name in my ear, the electricity was palpable. *Oh my God, I can't do this!* I pushed away gently—I had to catch my breath. His blue eyes were intense and full of passion. I felt the same way, but we couldn't do this here, not now. I leaned back on the blanket and closed my eyes. I felt Ashland lie down beside me. If we lingered on the beach much longer the sky would be full of stars.

"I'm sorry, I didn't mean to get carried away."

"Stop apologizing for everything. You didn't force me to kiss you." I punched his arm playfully and sat up, looking down at him.

He reached up and touched my hair, twisting a long strand around his finger. "You make me crazy, Carrie Jo. What am I going to do about you?"

"I guess you'll just have to love me." *Oh my God, I just said love. Get me out of here.* I stood up and pretended to dust sand off, avoiding looking at his face. "Why don't we take a little walk? I could use the exercise. Let me help you with that blanket." He seemed surprised but got the hint; I helped him fold it, and we strolled down the beach toward the very tip of the island.

"So how are *you* doing? We talked about TD, but what about you? We haven't talked much since that night in the garden." A sensible change of topic was in order.

He stuffed the blanket under his arm and slung his hands in his pockets as we walked. "Carrie Jo, you know I have never been a fan of the supernatural, but what happened with us in the garden made me a believer. I guess I haven't wanted to talk about it because I didn't know what to say. I saw Isla with my own two eyes, felt the wind ripping through the trees. We even found the family treasure, but admitting the reality of it all has been extremely difficult. That might make me sound stupid, but it's the truth." As we walked on a little more, I breathed in the ocean scent and savored being here with Ashland. "It didn't seem to faze you at all. I mean you acted like you knew exactly what was happening and how to handle it. How do you live with your...well, for lack of a better word, your powers?"

"Are you kidding me?" I gave him a wide-eyed stare. "That was the scariest thing that ever happened to me. Everything I did—I played all that by ear. I have no experience with ghosts at all. Except in my dreams, and normally they don't try to hurt me." *Except that time Jeremiah Cottonwood left a welt on my leg.* "Not to mention, I think we had help. Remember, Henri said that Calpurnia and Muncie were there too."

"And you believe him?"

"Why wouldn't I? Henri has nothing to lose or gain by telling us what he saw." I chewed on the inside of my lip. "I hope he's okay. I mean, I pray that she left him alone."

"Me too."

"You didn't answer my question, Ashland. Are you okay?" We had walked a long stretch down the beach, and the sand felt a bit cooler. He took my hand and we began to walk back to the car.

"I have to be. I'm Ashland Stuart, former football star and heir to the Stuart fortune, which is substantially more now than it was six months ago, thanks to you." He grimaced. "Am I okay? I'm sleeping again now and not jumping at every noise I hear, but something else has happened to me."

I froze in my tracks, curious to hear more. "What is happening?"

"I am remembering things, things from my childhood. Things I don't want to remember. I sound like a basket case, huh?"

"Hardly a basket case, Ashland. You have a long way to go before I check you in somewhere. Oh, sorry." The look on his face reminded me that this kind of talk was no laughing matter. In some ways, Ashland and I were more alike than I had first believed, at least concerning our families. "What do you mean, remembering?"

"I've been accused of having an active imagination, at least when I was a kid. Mostly by my cousin Robert, who passed on his loathing for the supernatural to me, but it wasn't always like that. I swear, and this is the crazy part, I remember that I saw Calpurnia. I'd forgotten all about her, but I did see her once. It was during those days in the garden, the Rose Garden. I always hated going into the Moonlight Garden, and now I know why, but it was different in the Rose Garden."

"Did she say anything to you? You weren't afraid, were you?"

"No, she didn't say anything. To be honest, she didn't seem to notice me at first."

"Really?" I put my hand on his arm. "What happened?"

"Mother was trying to prune some of the rose bushes, and I was sitting on the grass by a concrete bench reading a book. I didn't notice the visitor at first, but I kind of felt the air shift and knew someone else was there. I looked up, and standing a few feet away was a young woman, very slender and tall, with an elegant hairstyle on top of her head. She knelt down beside me to peek at what I was reading. I know now that was Calpurnia. I mean, I've seen her picture before in the brochures, but I never put two and two together. At least not until recently. I clearly remember that she smiled at me, and I wasn't afraid at all so I smiled back. She showed me her book: it was small, a little larger than her hand, and it had a leather cover. When she opened it to show me what was inside, it wasn't a regular book, just a bunch of folded notes tied together with a purple ribbon. I guess she wanted me to see that she was reading too."

We started walking again. I whispered, "I've seen that book before, I think. Did it have an engraving on the cover—a bird sitting on a branch?"

He thought for a minute. "Yes, I believe it did, right in the center of the cover. Do you know what book it was?"

"Yes, oh my gosh. I think I do!" He put the blanket in the trunk, and we got into the car. I could feel him watching me in the near dark. "That's the book she kept the notes in, the ones from the captain."

"I don't understand. Why would she keep Captain Garrett's notes in a book? I've never heard of that."

"I saw her father search her room once, but I got the feeling that he'd done it before. He looked through everything: her clothing, her hatboxes, everything you could think of to find Christine's treasure. What would he have done if he'd found those notes? It wasn't a clue to the treasure, but it would have put her in a dangerous position, especially with Mr. Cottonwood's pride. She was a clever girl. Hiding them in plain sight, in a hollowed-out book, would be the smart thing to do. The question is why did she show you the book? What was she trying to say?"

"I don't know, CJ. So I'm not losing it?"

"No, you saw her all right. You don't have any reason to be afraid of her. She'd never harm you, but I think she wants you to know something." A shiver ran down my spine.

"It's getting cool out here. Let's go eat at Bill's. They close up the sidewalks here around nine, so we better go if we want a seat. No more talk of ghosts tonight. Let's talk about living."

I was disappointed not to hear more but happy that he'd confided in me at last. It had been quite an evening already.

"Find us something good on the radio," he said with a soft smile.

"I can do that." I flipped the channels in search of a good song, and we talked about practical things like his upcoming speech at the Historical Society and the custom-made, very expensive velvet curtains for the Blue Room.

In the back of my mind, I knew what I had to do. This was going to be a late night.

Chapter 5

Strange music, a kind I'd never heard before, plunked from a piano on the boat. I knew it was a piano because Mrs. Cottonwood often played the big shiny black one in the ballroom, but this music was different. No long strands of silver notes here or heart-aching songs of love, but plunking notes that piled up together and made your feet want to move.

I never touched the big black piano, but I had wanted to. What if there were silver notes in my fingertips too? Shouldn't I let them have their song? Mrs. Cottonwood would probably never have scolded me—that gentle lady would never harm a fly—but Stokes would have beaten me with a hickory stick. I got smacked once for looking too long in a mirror. I missed the lady—she'd been nice with soft hands and a softer voice, but her death had not surprised me. Mr. Cottonwood was a cruel man, especially when he had turned up a jug a few times, but no one had suffered more from his words and hands than Mrs. Cottonwood.

How many times had I wanted to grab his arm or take a lash for her? But fear kept me from doing so, my completely miserable and undeniable fear. Hooney had warned me to stay out of the reach of the Master's strap. Once he started swinging he wouldn't stop, not until he passed out. She should know—she'd been at Seven Sisters for ages, longer than anyone except Stokes, but she'd only been beaten once. One stormy evening when we huddled around the kitchen fire for warmth, Hooney told me the story of Ann-Sheila, a pretty slave who had belonged to the Beaumont family before Mrs. Cottonwood came to Seven Sisters.

Like me, Ann-Sheila was an island slave, a free woman before someone snatched her away from her home. Hooney said she was the most beautiful girl she'd ever seen, and she was smart too—way too smart for a slave. Ann-Sheila loved Mrs. Cottonwood, not like a slave but like a sister or a good friend. Stokes and Hooney said that was wrong, wrong to think a slave could be the friend of a free person, especially a white person. Ann-Sheila could read, like me, and sometimes the Missus would ask her to read aloud from one of the many books in the library.

One evening, after Mr. Cottonwood had been in town for a few days of gambling, he came racing his horse down the lane, his anger stirred up from corn whiskey. They say he must have heard some bit of gossip in town, something about the Missus or Ann-Sheila or maybe both. He was powerful offended by gossip and had a great deal of pride for his family name. I don't know what the gossip was, but Mr. Cottonwood went looking for Miss Christine with murder on his mind. He found her in the nursery with Ann-Sheila and the baby Calpurnia, and in his rage had struck his wife and daughter. Ann-Sheila slapped the belt from his hands, but she should never have done that. No, she should never have done that.

The Master took Ann-Sheila to the slave quarters and made all the folks come out to see what he was going to do to his wife's pretty young friend. He'd summoned the sheriff, the nasty one with the greasy black mustache, to deliver the punishment. The Master shamed Ann-Sheila by taking her clothes off and forcing her down on one of the big wooden tables in the middle of the quarter. He didn't actually do the bad deed—the sheriff did that—but the whole time the sheriff was doing what he wanted, Ann-Sheila cursed him and Mr. Cottonwood until Mr. Cottonwood ordered Stokes to put his hand over her mouth to stop the curses. After the sheriff did what he wanted to do, Mr. Cottonwood made some of the slaves do the same thing. Some was old men and some was just boys. Everyone did what they was told, and even today nobody talks about what they did to Ann-Sheila. They turn and look the other way when passing the table, making the sign of the cross if her name is uttered, but nobody much utters her name in the quarter. You won't find nary a slave at Seven Sisters sitting at that table either.

When the deed was done, they say she crawled off the wooden table and started screaming and talking to people that weren't there. People say she cursed the Master in her island language, and other people say she cursed everyone that did the bad things to her. Hooney said she had blood all over her because the Master whipped her to the ground after the deed was done. It was all too horrible to think of. Ann-Sheila walked down to the river, and nobody stopped her. The Master laughed and laughed with his belt in his hand, mocking her, calling her names and such. When she got to the water, she threw her bloody self in with not a stitch of clothes on and floated away. Sometime later, some slaves pulled her out, and Hooney said that there was nobody ever been more dead than Ann-Sheila. The Master had her body put on a pile of wood, and he burned her up. "First that long dark hair caught fire, then the rest of her," Hooney whispered, her large eyes looking even more huge and luminous. "And the Master made the Missus watch too. Poor lady. She couldn't speak for days after that, but eventually she came round again. Horrible, horrible day. A cursed day." She'd finished her recounting with the sign of the cross and a few other signs that I didn't recognize.

Now here I was doing the same thing as Ann-Sheila, helping someone escape the wrath of Mr. Cottonwood. And not just anyone but the Master's own daughter! I stood on the bank of that river, trembling in my uncomfortable shoes and talking to God, telling Him why I wanted to live another day, but I was sure I wouldn't. I had nowhere to go except into the river. Tears streamed down my face like two fountains of salt water. Hooney's warning rang in my ear: "You knows too much—too much for a slave. You thinks too deep to live too long. You a dead man, Muncie, if you don't stop thinking. You a dead man." She'd prayed, sometimes for me and sometimes against me, twisting the worn edge of her white apron. I

*wanted to yell at her, "That is not my name! I am no dead man!" but I
never did.*

I hunkered down in the scratchy reeds and stared at the big boat. I would
wait right here until I knew she was gone, safely away. Then I would run
to the Mobile Bay Port, not the river port but the big one with the big
ships. I would find a way to steal aboard a ship, and maybe that ship
would take me home and once again I would be who I really was—I could
have my name again.

I guessed if the dogs came for me, those snarling hounds of Jeremiah
Cottonwood's, I'd do like Ann-Sheila—I would jump in the river even
though it wasn't a smart thing to jump in the Mobile River at night. There
was snakes in that river—cottonmouths that could kill a man with one
bite. If the snakes didn't kill me, perhaps the alligators would. Me and
Early saw one snap a raccoon right off the shore one day. We were little
then and weren't serving in the house yet. The two of us snuck off to
splash and swim, and when we were finally tuckered out we sat on the
bank to catch our breath before heading back to the quarter. All of a
sudden that gator raged up and out of the water, snapping that coon, and
then slid back into the black depths. Early had screamed, but I'd taken off
running.

I thought about my choices, snake bites, alligator bites or dog bites. Those
dogs were nothing but mean. I remember once they'd gotten into the
rabbits—Calpurnia's pet rabbits—and left nothing behind but torn bits of
fluff all over the ground like a furry hailstorm of death and guts and
blood. I had to clean it all up and gagged the whole time. But even with all
the dangers around me, I couldn't leave. Not without knowing for sure
that she was gone, safely away from the hands of death that reached for
her from Seven Sisters. I didn't want her to die like Miss Christine or
disappear like Louis Beaumont. She must live because I loved her.

I stood in the tall reeds without moving, like one of those statues at Seven
Sisters, frozen in time forever. I heard a limb snap and looked about me,
half-expecting to see Isla standing in my hiding spot. It was unearthly
how she moved about without anyone hearing her—like a Haitian demon,
one that played tricks on naughty, unsuspecting children. Some demons
could come up through the floor of a house, grab you from a tree or get
you any number of ways. My mother told me that you could summon one
up just by thinking about it or saying its secret name too many times. I
believed whether she was a Haitian demon or a plain old Alabama devil
in pretty white skin, Isla lived to torment me.

One morning, I woke up and she was on top of me, straddling me like she
was riding a horse. She was light as a feather; I suppose that's why I
didn't know she was there until her lips were on mine. She wore nothing
but her thin petticoat—too thin for my tastes. My eyes flew open, and I

stared into her blue ones. Like two pools of clear blue water they were, but empty, without any life in them. Startled, I pushed her to the ground, and she fell on the floor with a scowl, mustering up a scream at the sound of Stokes' heavy footfall approaching from the hallway. As his dark frame filled the doorway, he threw her a disdainful sneer and stepped out of the way, pointing to the door. "You shouldn't be here, Miss." When she left he struck me to the ground with his oversized hand.

"You stupid boy. Put your shirt on. I told you to stay away from her." I didn't argue with him or try to defend myself—he knew the truth. He was just afraid like we all were.

That same day, Calpurnia had searched me out. Her eyes were red from crying; her hair looked unbrushed and hung free down her back. She'd passed me as I pumped water from the well, giving me the hand signal that meant "Meet me in the greenhouse." I delivered the buckets of water to Hooney, looked over my shoulder a few times to see if the blonde devil dogged my heels and took the long way around to our meeting spot.

Calpurnia's thin arms were around my neck before I had closed the door good. She clung to me like I was the last breath she could take and she wanted to hold on to it. She'd gotten thin—too thin; I could feel her bones beneath the silk of her dress. "Calpurnia, what has happened to you? Are you hungry? You know we can't be here—your cousin, she's always following me. She might tell Stokes or Mr. Cottonwood." Her eyes were green that day; sometimes they looked brown, but that day they were full of heartache. I knew those emotions—fear, hopelessness, grief. They were all I knew for many years, but Calpurnia had helped me. When I cried for my Momma, Calpurnia read to me, sometimes about faraway places with coconut trees and colorful birds—like the ones I left back home.

"I don't want any food. I have to think. I'm sorry for calling you here, but what do I do? What can I do?" She shrugged her scrawny shoulders at me and handed me a piece of paper. "Look at this—it's a letter from Lennie Ree Meadows. She wants to help me with my wedding because I don't have Momma."

I took the paper and pretended to read it, anxious to see how I could help her but even more anxious to get away. I loved her, but after that morning's encounter with Isla, I had an uneasy feeling that something bad was going to happen. It hung in the air over me like a sword on a string, just like the story of Damocles. Any moment the string would snap, and the sword would come crashing down on me. That would be much worse than getting slapped by Stokes. I heard Hooney's warning ringing in my ears: "You a dead man, Muncie." I loved my friend, but what would happen to us if I was caught in here now?

"What does that mean? Who are you marrying?"

"No one has proposed to me, but Mrs. Meadows seems to think differently. She says my father has made arrangements for me to marry and he didn't bother to tell me. He wants me gone so he can have it all, all my fortune. It's mine because I'm a Beaumont! I know the truth now; Mr. Ball told me, but I can't find it! Mother hid it somewhere, but I don't know where." She rubbed her forehead with her bony hand and kept talking, "I bet half of Mobile thinks I'm going to marry that man. And if they didn't before, they do now! If Mrs. Meadows knows, every gossip in Mobile County knows. What am I going to do? I cannot marry him. I will not!" She snatched away the note and walked up and down the length of the greenhouse talking to herself, her hands on her hips.

"Who is it you're supposed to marry?"

"It's the mayor, that old man, Charles Langdon—the one from Connecticut. He came to my Cotillion Ball, but you probably wouldn't remember him. He's not a remarkable man except that he's old and likes licking his lips. What shall I do? I'd rather marry Reginald Ball than Charles Langdon, but it's too late. The die is cast."

"Surely she's wrong, Cal. Maybe she's wrong."

She shook the letter at me. "No, she's not wrong, but I'm not going to do it. I won't do it. I'll walk off into the river like Ann-Sheila before I do that." We heard a voice, Isla's voice, calling Calpurnia's name in the distance. It sounded like she was in the Rose Garden. I ducked down, and she squatted with me. "If I go away, please don't worry about me. I will be all right. Promise me you will not worry over me."

"No!" I whispered furiously. "You can't leave. What would your Momma say if you left here with no chaperone and no one to watch over you? I have to go too."

"Don't bring Mother into this. She's gone, and she left me here! I have to go, and I think I know someone who can help me. If I took you with me, it could mean the death of you. I couldn't live with that." She reached out and squeezed my hand. "I love you, Muncie," she said, her voice breaking.

Isla called again, and I could tell she was closer now. So close that I knew she'd find us in just a minute. Calpurnia stuffed the note in her dress pocket. I wanted to argue with her, remind her that I could die either way, whether I was with her or without her, but I didn't have much time. "You can't leave me here. Promise me you'll take me too," I pleaded with her, my heart jumping like a rabbit in my worn cotton shirt.

She sighed but smiled. For a second, I could see her as she used to be, happy, beautiful and full of life. The beautiful storyteller who dreamed of traveling the world with her uncle. "All right, but we have to be careful.

Nobody can know, not even Hooney. Now I have to go. My cousin will find you in here in just a second."

"Miss...don't trust her. Don't tell her nothing! She's not got a good heart like—she's not good."

"Stop that, Muncie. She's been through so much. You don't understand."

"No, you don't understand, Miss. She's trying to get me into trouble. I can't tell you how many..."

"Shh! Here she comes. I'll go so she won't find you here." She got up and yelled, "I'm in here, Cousin. I'm coming." She walked out of the greenhouse, the rickety wooden door slapping behind her.

I sat on the floor, feeling hopeless. What had I done? What had I agreed to? Mosquitos swirled around me, the angry black insects biting me until I got the courage to slip out of the greenhouse.

If Isla knew anything at all about Calpurnia's plans, it was bad—this would all be bad. Every bit of it.

I woke before the alarm clock and reached over to turn it off. I had an extra thirty minutes to think about what I had dreamed. I closed my eyes and thought of Muncie's strong heart beating in my chest. I remembered the utter desperation on Calpurnia's face. I could see the plants in the greenhouse, smell the fresh earth and hear the buzzing of bees.

I sat up and slid Muncie's workbook out from under the pillow. It had worked, just like I had expected it to. I ran my hand over the cover and flipped my hair back out of my face. I would try it again tonight—I had to know what happened to Calpurnia and Muncie.

A smile crept across my face. That wasn't his name, not his "true born" name. The Master had called him Monticello, and his only friend and her mother had called him Muncie, but these weren't who he was.

He was Janjak.

Chapter 6

I drove down Dauphin Street in my blue Honda to the Battle House Renaissance Mobile Hotel or, as the locals and I preferred to call it, the Battle House. According to local lore, Stephen Douglas spent the night here the very same day he heard he'd lost the election to Abraham Lincoln. It also served as a military headquarters during the War of 1812. I had never stopped to check it out, but it was certainly on my "must do before I leave Mobile" list. Battle House was an eight-story building with Tuscan columns along the portico. I knew some of the history, and under normal circumstances I'd check out every nook and cranny, but not today.

I pulled into the parking lot across the street, slid my phone into my pocket and walked to the hotel. When I pulled open the big glass door, I immediately felt underdressed. Why had I worn blue jeans and a casual shirt to such a beautiful place? I gawked up at the domed stained glass ceiling and the luxurious surroundings. This wasn't where I expected to be, nor was it where I expected to find Alice and Myron. They seemed way too frugal for a swanky place like this, but here we all were. They stood up, spotting me at the same time I saw them, and I took a deep breath and walked toward them. I looked about covertly but didn't see Mia. I slapped a friendly smile on my face and reminded myself that these people had been good to me. It was time to pay them back.

"Carrie Jo, thank you for coming down. We know how busy you must be, and we would never take up your time if we didn't have to."

"It's okay, Alice. I'm glad Mia has agreed to get some help." I hugged her neck and then Myron's. It felt like going home except for Mia's absence.

"Well, Myron? Should you tell this story, or should I?" Alice turned to her husband, who sat quietly on the couch next to her, his grief-filled eyes huge behind thick eyeglasses.

"No, dear, I'll let you do all the talking. As a matter of fact, I think I should like a cup of coffee. Would you two ladies like something?"

"No, thank you," I said with a small smile. Myron walked away stiff-legged. They weren't getting any younger, and I hated that they had to come all this way from Savannah.

"Carrie Jo, you have to forgive Myron. This really hurts his heart, and he's as ashamed as I am about Mia's behavior. I don't know what's gotten into her. Well, maybe I do." Alice didn't beat about the bush—she never had as long as I'd known her. I sat back in my seat and listened. Alice had a thick southern accent but spoke perfect English, except for the occasional "y'all."

"When Myron and I first married, like many young couples we expected to have a large family. We do love children so, but after a few years of marriage we began to suspect that was not going to happen for us. I went to our family physician and then other doctors, including some fertility specialists, and they confirmed our fears. Having a baby would be medically impossible for us." She tapped her manicured fingernail on the arm of the couch, taking a moment to think about what to say next.

"I cannot describe how difficult that was to hear. But we did not allow it to dissuade us from parenting and decided to adopt Mia. Carrie Jo, she had such a sweet little face and a big laugh that filled the room and our hearts. We instantly fell in love with her. She was so young when we took her home, barely two years old—we had every intention of telling her about the adoption when she got older, but the day never came. We put it off, making excuses, and then she got sick. Mia had come home from Egypt with some kind of fever. As she got sicker, her organs began to fail. The doctors recommended a blood transfusion. Healthy blood would boost her immune system, so naturally they came to us for blood donations. We couldn't donate. Mia has a rare blood type, and we couldn't help her. Anyway, it all worked out. They found the blood they needed, and Mia got better. But of course she had questions."

"I never even knew she was sick."

Alice lowered her eyes and shook her head. "She did not want anyone around; that was especially true after she found out she was adopted. I cannot be sure, but I think that whatever illness she contracted in Egypt—and they were never sure what to call it—affected her thinking. She was not the same girl she had been when she left. The sickness made it worse. Then we had to tell her the truth. She did not take the news well. She called me names, names I had never been called before. It was like someone flipped a switch inside her head. We tried to get her help, but she could not wait to leave us. As soon as she got healthy, she moved out of our house and barely spoke to us. She even began calling us Alice and Myron."

My heart broke for Alice. Why was Mia being so unreasonable? Her adoptive family was kind and loving, even if they hadn't been able to tell her the truth sooner. "I'm sorry, so sorry."

"I am not exactly sure what she did after that, but she mentioned in one of her few emails that she intended to come to Mobile and that you would be here. I was happy because I thought perhaps she would talk to you."

"She never did, Alice. I did not know any of this." But I began to put two and two together. Mia was the best researcher I knew. She would have found out her parentage in less than a month. The girl had connections everywhere. She must have believed, somehow, that she had a right to Calpurnia's fortune. She had said as much the night of the attack.

"Knowing Mia, she'd want to find her birth parents. Did she say anything about them? Has she found them?"

"I do not know, Carrie Jo. Obviously, all of this has her unhinged. Now she has attacked you, and you were her best friend. Please forgive her. Forgive me." Alice stifled a sob, and I flew to her side and put my arm around her.

"It's going to be okay, I promise. Mia will get the help she needs now." I squeezed her shoulders to reassure her.

"Miss Jardine?" I looked up to see Detective Simmons standing nearby. "I'm here to take Mia Reed into custody. Got a call from Myron Reed. Do you know anything about this?"

"Hello, Detective. This is Mia's mother, Alice Reed. She and Mr. Reed have convinced their daughter to talk to you. I don't know if questioning Mia right now will help you with your investigation. It appears she has some type of mental problem, something that wasn't there before."

"Be that as it may, I've got no choice but to bring her to the precinct, at least to get her picture and fingerprints. After that, it's up to the district attorney where she goes. Where is she, ma'am?"

"My husband is bringing her down now. But please, do you have to handcuff her?"

"Yes, I'm afraid I do. I'll be as discreet as I can, though."

I heard the elevator ding and saw Myron step out holding Mia's hand. She looked deflated, empty, her vivacious personality hidden beneath a layer of dark depression. I had known her since school and had never known her to go a day without makeup. But her hair looked oily, her pale skin sickly. I saw a spark of anger when her dark eyes fell on Alice, but she smiled when she saw me.

"Carrie Jo? What brings you down here? Couldn't wait to see me in handcuffs? That's rich. Real rich since I did what I did for you. That lawyer wanted to hurt you, CJ. I saved you. End of story."

"Mia Reed? You are under arrest for the murder of Hollis Matthews." Detective Simmons snapped the cuffs on a passive Mia. She led her outside and placed her in a waiting police car. Alice began to cry, and Myron put his arm around her.

"I'm sorry, dear. Oh my, I'm sorry." He blinked back tears. "If you will excuse us, Carrie Jo, I think I will take her back to the room, maybe get some rest."

"Of course. I'm just a phone call away. Please call me if you need me." He nodded and led his sobbing wife from the lobby. It was so odd seeing her cry. Alice Reed never displayed emotions like that in public; she was always such a refined lady, so cool and restrained. Mia had broken her heart. I left the lobby behind with a tear in my eye as well. The police car drove down Water Street, and Mia never looked back. As she promised, Detective Simmons didn't turn on her lights or sirens. It was a quiet end to a bad situation. At least I hoped it was. I walked across the street to my car and called Ashland.

"Good morning," he answered warmly.

"Good morning. I've got some news for you. Good news, I think, even though it doesn't feel that way." I told him about Mia's arrest and the events surrounding it. I hadn't realized how sad I was about it all until that moment.

"Well, maybe she will at least get the help she needs and Hollis' family will have some answers. Are you okay?"

"No, I'm not. I think I'll take a couple hours off this morning, maybe go to the library or take a walk. I don't think anything is pressing at the house at the moment."

"That sounds like a good idea. I've got some things to attend to across the bay, but if you need me…"

"I don't. I mean—I need you, but not for this." I cringed as soon as the words were out of my mouth.

Ever the gentleman, he simply said, "If you change your mind, call me. Take all the time you need. Talk to you later."

"Thanks, Ashland." I sat in my car and stared at the Battle House. Such a beautiful place, such a sad day. My phone rang, and I looked down at the screen. It was William. I snorted and tossed the phone on the seat. I had nothing to say to that betrayer. He must have known that Mia was mentally ill, yet he hadn't done a thing to help her. I had no time for him. None at all.

I drove past Cathedral Square and decided I would go to the library. Melting in my car in this impossible heat thinking about the past wouldn't help me understand any of what had just happened. I didn't need to guess; I needed to catch up on my history. Mia knew something I didn't. And as recent history had shown, that was never good. She had a reason to think she was a potential heir to Calpurnia's fortune. I needed to know what that was.

I pulled into the back parking lot of the library and grabbed my purse and research bag. Maybe some answers could be found here. I walked in and savored the smell of old books and the comfortable coolness of effective air conditioning. As they say in Mobile, "Today was hotter than dirt."

Blinking to adjust my eyes to the lighting, I went up the stairs to the reference section. I set my purse and bag on a back table, away from a cluster of college students whispering about a group project. I remembered those days. *Mia, what happened?* My phone rang again, and I scrambled to find it. I'd forgotten to put it on mute. I saw that it was William again and tapped the ignore button. The voicemail notification dinged, and I slid the phone back in my pocket and began walking down the reference aisles. Archived newspapers and perhaps shipping records would be a good place to start. I spotted a nearby kiosk and began to type.

Let's see, the Mobile Press Register—that's what I need. Hmm...year? 1850. I scanned the headlines. This wasn't going to work. Then I remembered reading that Calpurnia had disappeared in September. I clicked on the month of September and didn't have to click too much more. The first few headlines read, "Officials Search for Missing Heiress," "Cottonwood Girl Disappears" and finally, "Sheriff Fears Missing Debutante is Dead." I read the first article.

Mobile, AL

September 13, 1850

Saturday night, Sheriff Samuel J. Rice visited local plantation Seven Sisters and took account of a missing girl, Calpurnia Cottonwood, daughter of Mr. Jeremiah Cottonwood and the late Mrs. Christine Cottonwood. Miss Cottonwood is sixteen years of age, approximately five feet seven inches tall with brown hair. She may be in the company of a dark-skinned Negro that goes by the name Monticello or Muncie. A reward of $1,000 is being offered for the return of both Miss Cottonwood and the runaway slave. Please contact the sheriff's department with any information about their whereabouts.

That's it? The articles after that one didn't tell me much more. It was as if she really did disappear into thin air. I spent the next couple of hours scrolling through the articles, still not finding much of anything. I decided to switch gears. I began scanning through dozens of bills of lading. I had no way of knowing the exact date Muncie—Janjak—had arrived in Mobile, but I could guess. He probably arrived between 1838 and 1840. These records were heartbreaking. One that really stood out was a bill of lading from the William and Ivy Slave Trading Company of Virginia. Six slaves, including four children, and one free man—all with proper English names like Richard and William. No mention of Monticello or Muncie. Certainly nothing about Janjak. I leaned back in the chair. *Why am I here? I have at least one journal that I haven't read yet, and trying to find Muncie here is like looking for a needle in a haystack.*

Still, there was one more thing I could look up. I typed "slave ships" and "Haiti" into the library's search engine. *Wow! Quite a few hits.* I narrowed it down to the years I thought might be correct. There were four ships that had arrived from Port-au-Prince, and each listed children on the bill of lading. My heart sank. Such sadness. I sat back in the chair again, wondering what to search for next. I flipped through my notebook. I'd written myself some questions a few weeks ago. Now was as good a time as any to ferret out some answers. I scanned through my handwritten list.

Search the obituaries for Jeremiah Cottonwood, Christine Cottonwood, Isla Beaumont and Louis Beaumont.

I could scratch off Louis Beaumont. Poor handsome, honest Uncle Louis. He hadn't deserved his fate, but we knew what had happened to him now, sadly. I was looking forward to seeing him laid to rest properly.

I typed in "Jeremiah Cottonwood" and "obituary."

August 23, 1853—Died at Seven Sisters on the evening of the 23rd, Mr. Jeremiah Cottonwood, aged 52. Mr. Cottonwood succumbed to death after an accidental fall from his horse on Conception Street. His remains will be interred at the Cottonwood Mausoleum August 27th at 12 o'clock noon. Friends and members of his extended family are respectfully invited to attend the burial service by Rev. England.

I scribbled furiously, making note of the day and time. As we suspected, he was buried on the property in the mausoleum we'd discovered and just three years after Calpurnia disappeared. Excited now to have some progress, I typed in "Isla Beaumont" and "obituary." Nothing. *Okay, try again.* "Isla Grant" and "obituary." Nothing. I was surprised...Isla was an unusual name, even for the 1850s. I typed in "Isla" and "obituary." Nothing except a baby who had passed after a few days of life in the 1870s. So our Isla hadn't died in Mobile. A young woman like Isla would have found a husband, right? Maybe Captain Garrett?

I stared at the screen for a moment and then typed in "David Garrett" and "obituary."

June 4, 1860—Died in this city on Tuesday evening last, of a gunshot wound in the back, David M. Garrett, Captain of the Delta Queen. He died in what is regarded as good health. Captain Garrett was an explorer and businessman and was attended to the grave by members of his crew and other friends. He was a gentleman of talent and a citizen of commendable habits and propriety of deportment. Though no relative was near to mourn at his grave, he was not alone or laid to rest with strangers. Warm friends attended him, in heart-felt sorrow, to his last resting place at Magnolia Cemetery.

My heart fell in my chest. He'd proved a villain, or at least a betrayer, but I was hoping for a mention of a wife or a female attendant, just on the off chance that Calpurnia had left with him as Muncie had hoped. *Where are you, Callie?*

One more time. I typed in "Christine Cottonwood" and "obituary." Immediately, an entry appeared.

April 7ᵗʰ, 1850—Died on the 7ᵗʰ, Mrs. Christine Beaumont Cottonwood, wife of Jeremiah Cottonwood and daughter of Robert and Marie Beaumont of Birmingham, at 32 years of age.

Mrs. Cottonwood was a lady of many attractive graces and worthy virtues, remarkable for the earnestness of her friendships, her kindness to her fellow citizens and her large circle of kindred, whom the loss most affects.

She leaves behind a devoted husband and a loving daughter. Mrs. Cottonwood was laid to rest in the Cottonwood Mausoleum in witness of her family.

No mention of the baby Angelique? I scribbled down some notes and stuffed my notebook back in my research bag. I walked back out into the sunshine, contemplating all that I'd just learned. It wasn't surprising that they all died comparatively young. People did die younger in those days. Still no Calpurnia, but I'd done enough for the day. I remembered what Ashland had said about TD, about needing Detra Ann's help in mending fences.

It was time to eat a little crow. I sat in my steamy Honda, waiting for the air conditioning to offer some relief from the wilting heat. I dialed Detra Ann's number and crossed my fingers as the phone rang.

"Hi, Detra Ann? This is Carrie Jo Jardine. I was wondering, are you free this afternoon or maybe tomorrow? I'd like to talk to you about Seven Sisters."

"Oh. Hi, Carrie Jo. Yes, I'm free this afternoon. Around 4:30? Should I meet you at the house?"

I looked at my watch. That gave me a few hours. "Yes, that's perfect. I'll see you then." I hung up the phone and drove to the mansion. *This should be interesting.*

Chapter 7

My knees wobbled a bit as I reached above my head to straighten one of the crystals on the chandelier. Being on a ladder was not my favorite activity—I hated heights—but the possibility that TD's crew would lift this chandelier into place without fixing it drove me crazy. Under normal circumstances the contractor would have spotted the problem immediately, but he wasn't around today. Not that we talked much anymore. If I knew anything about contract labor, it was not to take anything for granted when the boss was away. As cautiously as I could, my shaking hands unwound the strings and the shard dangled free. I breathed a sigh of relief and prepared to ease back down to the safe ground.

"What are you doing?" The ladder shook under me. I froze and gasped for breath, as if that would steady me. "Oh my God, I didn't mean to startle you. Here, let me hold the ladder." It was Detra Ann, a bit early for our appointment.

I climbed down as quickly as I could with a nervous laugh. "You move like a ninja! I didn't hear you come in, and normally every sound in this room echoes; it's such a huge space."

"I'm really sorry about that. I have on heels; I would have thought you'd heard me coming in." She laughed, and I could tell she was nervous too.

"No problem. I guess my concentration was focused on getting that crystal untangled. I didn't hear a thing."

She looked around in awe of the room. "It's looking amazing. I have to say that I'm really impressed at how much you all have accomplished in just a few months. This is simply amazing."

"Thank you. We do make a pretty good team. Ashland has the brains, TD has the know-how, and I know the history. It's all worked out, thankfully." She nodded in agreement.

"You said you wanted to talk to me. I'm hoping that means you've changed your mind about having a ball here?"

"Nothing is off the table, Detra Ann, but I'm surprised that you'd still want to have a ball here after all the rumors you've likely heard about ghosts. That hasn't put you off?"

"Oh, come on now. In the world of marketing, having a ghost or two is only a plus. And you don't have to pretend with me; I know something happened here. Is anyone ever going to tell me what that was?"

I didn't know what to make of that. From what I had heard from Rachel, Detra Ann had told the interns about what TD saw that night, but maybe she didn't know everything. I had no idea. "Now who's pretending? Surely TD told you everything." I couldn't explain it, but I suddenly felt the hair standing up on my arms. I looked around the room, thinking someone had joined us. There was no furniture to hide behind here in the ballroom, but no doors had opened either. If anyone was here, I couldn't see them. Detra Ann looked around suspiciously and then stared at me. She was probably thinking I was crazy or at least melodramatic.

"Can we just talk without all the snark? For whatever reason, I do think we got off on the wrong foot. I'm Ashland's friend, but it is Terrence Dale that I am interested in. I'm not your competition. So can we try?"

Detra Ann's directness brought me back to reality, but my need to leave the room grew by the second. "Sorry. Sure, let's talk about it. I think I know the perfect place." I cast a worried eye around the room and led her to the Rose Garden porch. It was another scorcher out, but there was plenty of shade on the porch and an oversized ceiling fan with blades that looked like palm leaves. And it would get us out of the house.

We sat at one of the tables, and I turned the fan on high. Detra Ann looked so neat and polished in a light pink summer suit, and I felt underdressed in my white capris, blue and white checkered top and white tennis shoes. Her long dark hair was perfectly brushed and captured in place with a clear ponytail elastic, and her hairstyle put my sweaty, messy bun to shame. "I wanted to talk to you because I've come to a dead end, historically speaking. I agree, we did get off on the wrong foot, and that was at least partly my fault. I am sorry for that. I would like to be friends, and I think we can do some good here at Seven Sisters."

"I am so happy to hear that." Her hand flew to her chest and she smiled. "I agree. I know I come off as pushy sometimes, but I have five brothers. I guess being pushy and outspoken is a learned behavior."

"Wow, five? That must have been an interesting childhood."

"Oh yes, indeed. But thankfully my mom and I were very close, and I have a ton of girl cousins. There was no end to girly activities for me to participate in." We talked a little more about her family and her interest in promoting Mobile businesses. She didn't ask me about my family, and I didn't offer.

"So what did TD tell you about the party? He had to have told you something—one of the interns said you asked her if she'd seen a ghost."

Looking relieved, Detra Ann leaned forward in her cushioned chair. "I can't tell you how shook up TD was that night. He came to my house at two in the morning, and he must have drunk a six-pack before he drove over because he was loaded. At first, he couldn't stop talking about the Moonlight Garden, about you and Ashland, but he wasn't making much sense. He said something about the wind and a secret place in the maze, but when he sobered up the next day, he didn't want to tell me anything. I've never seen him so emotional. Restoring the Moonlight Garden had been such a dream for him; he had put everything into it, and now he barely talks about it. It's like he wants to forget it completely. I asked around because I wasn't getting any answers from TD and I knew better than to ask Ashland. He's never hidden his disdain for the supernatural. I have to admit that I'm happy we're talking about this now. Will you please tell me what happened? I'd like to be able to help the man I love."

My sympathetic heart decided then and there that I would tell her the truth and let the chips fall where they may. She needed to hear it if she was going to help TD recover. If it were Ashland, I would want to know. "All right, but some of what I'm going to tell you might sound incredible—even impossible. I'll tell you what I can, but I'm not an expert in ghosts or anything."

"From the little that TD told me, I thought you were some kind of ghost hunter. Did you see them before coming to Seven Sisters?"

A nervous laugh escaped my lips, "Uh, no, I'm not. At least I wasn't before I got here. I've had a few dreams over the years that were about certain places, but I don't have psychic powers or anything like that. There are times when I feel things, like just a few minutes ago in the ballroom."

"Oh, I felt uncomfortable too. But I didn't see anything, did you?" Her blue eyes were wide.

"No, like I said, I don't normally see anything, at least not when I am awake. But that night in the garden was different. We all saw her, the ghost—even TD. You see…" I related the story as best I could to her, and her plump pink lips parted in amazement as I told her about our furious dig and the discovery of the lost treasure.

At some time during the story, she'd kicked off her shoes, and her feet were tucked underneath her at an angle. We looked like two sorority sisters sharing secrets on the porch of Seven Sisters. As I recalled the supernatural experience, I remembered how cold I had felt, how the evil wind had disturbed the fallen leaves and flowers. In my mind's eye I could see Isla appearing alive except for her missing skirt hem and feet. I could easily recall her losing all color of life and turning ash-gray like one of the statues in the garden. I shivered.

"And you swear this is the truth—you aren't pulling my leg at all?" Her eyes narrowed suspiciously, and I didn't blame her. I'd be suspicious too if I didn't know what I knew, hadn't seen what I'd seen. I left out the part about Henri Devecheaux; there was no sense in bringing him into my story unless she asked. I had a warm spot in my heart for the bumbling ghost hunter. He'd disappeared, probably in an effort to distance himself from the house and all its occupants.

"No, I'm not. Everything I have told you is the absolute truth. I hope you believe me."

"I believe you, Carrie Jo. I believe you saw what you say you saw. I believe TD saw her too." Detra Ann chewed on her lower lip, thinking deeply about what she had just heard. "I have to admit that I'm glad I left early. I would have screamed my head off if I'd seen anything. I'm kind of a wimp when it comes to stuff like that." In a quieter voice, she asked, "Have you seen anything else since then?"

"Nothing like that night," I said. "Still want to hold a ball here?"

She laughed nervously. "Well, if we did, I don't think that's the story I'd tell."

I breathed a sigh of relief. "Thanks for not laughing at me or saying you don't believe me. This is so crazy, who would make that up?"

"Girl, I'm a true Mobilian. We don't hide the skeletons in our closets, and we don't laugh at the idea of ghosts. It's just not good manners."

"Thanks, Detra Ann."

She leaned forward spontaneously and squeezed my hands. "However, I don't think TD is as willing as I am to accept the fact that the dead sometimes aren't all that dead. He's really struggling, but at least I know what I'm dealing with now. I have an idea that might help him."

"Really? What's that?"

"I'll take him to church."

"What?" I laughed.

"No, really, I think it will help. TD is a solid guy; he just needs to get grounded again. I'll take him to my church, Cottage Hill Methodist."

"You think a church visit will do it?"

"Not just a visit. It might take a while, but yeah, that's what I think he needs. Don't worry about TD. Leave him to me. I'll get him back on track."

I totally believed she was committed to helping him, and as I'd suspected, she had designs on him. She had even said she loved him. Terrence Dale may as well surrender now and come peacefully because when a woman like Detra Ann sets her mind on something, she gets it. I admired her, and I was glad to know that he had someone in his corner. Regardless of how things had gone with us, I hoped for the best for him.

"That's great to hear. I've been worried about him."

"Well, he's going to be okay. Thank you for telling me the truth. Now what can I help you with? You said earlier that you were at a dead end. What can I do?"

Thankful that we were working together at last, I said, "I promised Ashland that I would help him find Calpurnia Cottonwood, the missing heiress who used to live here. My research led me to a steamboat captain named David Garrett. There was some evidence that he might have been involved in the girl's disappearance. I was hoping that maybe you'd know something about this Captain Garrett. I think his boat was the Delta Queen, used to run up and down the Mobile River in the 1850s, delivering cotton, and there was some gambling on board too. Have you ever heard of him?"

"Ever heard of him? My stars! My mother is an expert on David Garrett—I heard plenty of stories about him growing up. She even has a small oil painting of the captain, or so she believes, on her mantelpiece. As far as Calpurnia Cottonwood goes, I've never heard anything that put those two together, but I wouldn't put it past him. The captain had an eye for the ladies, especially wealthy ones, according to the reports. Is it any wonder that he was shot in the back by a woman?"

"It was a woman who shot him? Do you know who she was?"

"No, I don't recall her name. She was arrested for it but somehow got away. She disappeared, and nobody ever heard from her again. Nobody made much fuss, though. Who's going to cry for a guy who made a career out of deflowering debutantes and scamming their families for money to keep it quiet? If he hadn't been so ridiculously handsome and charming, they would have strung him up after the first time it happened."

"Who was that?"

"One of the Bellingrath girls, the middle one. That was before they moved to Mobile from Castleberry. She was the mother of Walter Bellingrath, the gentleman who created Bellingrath Gardens with his wife. Now what was his mother's name? I can't remember, but apparently she caught David Garrett's eye during a picnic lunch by the river. He bounded off the boat and eventually right into her heart, but not before her father did his best to prevent those two from getting too close. Old Mr. Bellingrath knew a scoundrel when he saw one. He was a tough old dude—he fought the Indians in Texas when he was a young man, and he'd made quite a bit of money through trading in the territory. That's the Louisiana Territory." I nodded, hoping she'd quickly get to the point. "Well, anyway, by the time he figured out that Captain Garrett had been shimmying up the trellis into his daughter's room, it was too late. The deed had been done. In those days, it was perfectly legal to have a man arrested for taking such liberties, but that almost guaranteed that the young woman and her family name would forever be tarnished. Of course, Garrett offered to marry the girl if Mr. Bellingrath paid him the dowry he was asking for, but the old man blew the roof. He wasn't going to give Garrett a fortune after he'd dishonored his daughter. Garrett supposedly laughed in his face and said, "I'll just take the money, then. I'm sure your daughter will find a suitable replacement for me when I'm gone.""

"You're joking! What a horrible thing to do!"

"I know. Aren't we all glad that we don't live in the 1850s? So Mr. Bellingrath gave up his fortune, but he didn't give up his daughter. Unfortunately for him, Sharon—that was her name—couldn't keep a secret. She cried and cried and blamed her father for sending her sweetheart away.

Eventually word got out, and the family moved back to Castleberry for quite a few years. Sharon supposedly later married a clerk who worked in one of her father's businesses, but no marriage license was ever found. Now we have found a birth certificate, and of course the baby was Walter Bellingrath, who eventually moved back to Mobile and established Belle Camp with his wife. Later it became Bellingrath Gardens."

"So Walter Bellingrath could have been Garrett's son?"

"Possibly, quite possibly."

"Could she have shot Garrett? Is that what happened?"

"No, I don't think so. Sharon Bellingrath didn't do much socializing after her public shaming, but the captain kept his game going. She was definitely not the only one. There was a young opera singer named Trixie Cartwright—a stage name, I'm sure—that he fancied for some time, but I don't know much about her."

My mind swam with the information she'd shared with me, but there was still nothing about Calpurnia.

"Oh, there is one more thing. He had a sister...wow, her name escapes me at the moment. She was a younger sister that he was quite devoted to. She didn't live with him; she had some kind of illness that kept her in and out of the hospital. But he saw her every time he came to Mobile, brought her gifts. My mother has a copy of a letter he wrote her. Would you like me to email you a scan later?"

"Yes! Would you? I would love to see that. And if you know anything else about Calpurnia—anything at all—please let me know. I'd like to find her before my work here is done. I can't even imagine leaving this place without knowing what happened to her."

"It's been quite a mystery for so many years. I honestly hope you do find her, but don't get your hopes up. So many people have searched for her and have met with sad fates. You're such a nice person, and I'd hate for something to happen to you."

Suddenly, the fan that spun above us stopped. The blades didn't just slow down, they came to a screeching halt as if an invisible hand had grabbed them and held them still. Both of us looked up. Detra Ann's eyes were wide with fear, but to my surprise, I was just mad. "Whatever," I said to the empty air above me. "I'll walk you out to your car, Detra Ann." We didn't go back through the house but hopped off the porch and walked down the driveway.

"Oh my God. What just happened?"

"I couldn't tell you," I confessed with a shrug.

"But I thought the ghost, Isla, was gone."

"Me too, but we don't know that was a ghost. And if it was, we don't know it was Isla."

"So there's more than one now?"

"I wouldn't doubt it. Please don't let word of this get out. It would ruin Ashland's dream of bringing his family home back to life, and I think if we found Calpurnia it would end. Don't ask me why, but I truly believe it would. That's why I have to."

"Yes, I can see that. Okay, I'm going to get all the info I can. I'll email that over ASAP. Is your work email the one I should use?"

I nodded. "That's perfect."

"I'll send anything else I find too. You have my word that I won't mention any of this, but you have to do the same. TD doesn't need to know about what happened with the fan or anything else. It would just freak him out worse."

"You've got a deal." I reached my hand out to shake hers, but instead she hugged me and smiled. "No handshakes! We hug in Mobile. You might as well get used to it. You're one of us now."

"Well, for a little while," I said.

She smiled. "I have no supernatural powers, but this I can predict—you're utterly and completely hooked. And not just on the house. You're a part of the story now, Carrie Jo. Part of Ashland's story, and a part of Mobile too. Once Mobile gets in your blood, you'll never be the same." She tossed her briefcase on the passenger seat and got into her light blue Mercedes.

I smiled at her and gave her a little wave as she drove away.

I knew she was absolutely right. I was part of the story now, but how would it end?

Chapter 8

Going home, I had so much to think about. I left Seven Sisters with an incomplete checklist of daily tasks, which I hated, but there was always tomorrow. As I drove down the bumpy road in my faithful Honda, I thought about my conversation with Detra Ann. I couldn't be happier that we were working together, and I couldn't wait to get that email from her. Off in the distance, grayish-black clouds hung heavy in the sky, rolling in from Mobile Bay. The threatening puffs looked impressive against the bright green leaves of the trees.

I planned on getting into the last of the journals and taking some notes that night. I felt like we were teetering on the edge of the truth, but that truth—in whatever form it would come—had not yet manifested.

I turned right into the driveway and waved at Bette, who was at her kitchen sink washing dishes. She waved back with a gloved hand. I made a mental note to make some time for my friend as soon as possible. Bienville didn't greet me as he often did, and I assumed it was because Bette was home now. That was okay. I liked having a part-time cat. I was in no way responsible enough to have a pet of my own.

A crack of thunder hastened my steps up the wooden staircase, and I looked out over the tree line below, again impressed with the sights and smells of the impending storm. Oddly enough, I loved storms as long as I didn't have to stand outside in one. Once inside, I unplugged my laptop to prevent an unwanted shock. I had so much material saved there, and I couldn't afford to lose it from a random lightning strike. I opened it up to check my email. Nope, nothing yet. But it hadn't even been an hour. *Be patient, CJ.* I hung up my purse and kicked off my shoes. I'd get a shower after the storm, and I didn't have to go out for supper. I had leftover wonton soup in my kitchenette. That would be the perfect dinner for an evening of reading, researching and hopefully some dreaming.

I had just pulled an oversized t-shirt over my head and slid into some yoga pants when someone knocked on my door. Puzzled, I paused before walking to the window and peeking downstairs. I saw Ashland's car and couldn't help but smile.

"Hey, come on in before you get caught in that storm." As if God were emphasizing my warning, lightning streaked across the Mobile sky, and I could see the rain approaching in the distance. He stepped inside, looking distracted and wet. "Oh no, I didn't even notice. You're drenched already! Let me get you a towel."

"That would be great," he said with a chuckle. "I'm obviously not as fast a runner as I used to be."

"Where are you coming from? The boat?" I called from the bathroom as I dug for the last clean towel. I'd have to do laundry ASAP. I padded back to him and handed him the towel. His blond hair was dripping wet. "Or maybe you swam from the Bay?"

He laughed. "I sure look like it, don't I? No, I've been downtown at Matthews and Ladner."

"Oh, good. Did they finally give you all your files?" I knew he'd been after the law firm to turn over everything that pertained to him. They were hesitant at first, and Ladner, the surviving partner, didn't even want to work with Ashland's new attorney. But naturally, Ashland persisted and got what he wanted.

"Yes, I got most of it yesterday, but I just got the last pack of paperwork this afternoon. You won't believe what I found." He was holding a folder, and his smile was almost electric.

"Here, sit on a barstool in the kitchen and tell me about it while I dry your hair. Were we right? Did Hollis know about the necklace?" I rubbed Ashland's hair vigorously with the towel and then rubbed his strong, broad shoulders in an attempt to dry his white button-down shirt. It wasn't working, but I enjoyed every minute of it. Finally, I tossed the towel over a chair and sat down. "What did you find? I can tell you're dying to tell me, and I'm dying to know! I heard something pretty amazing today myself."

He ran his hand through his messy hair and sat at the table with me. "Some of this might be hard to believe. But once you know everything, I think you'll have to admit I did pretty good."

"Okay, okay. You're the king of research, now spill it."

He opened his sheaf and pulled out some papers. Most were copies, old copies, from the look of it. I flipped on the light because the storm had made the room as dark as midnight.

"How many living children did Christine and Jeremiah Cottonwood have?" he asked. "Just the one, Calpurnia, right?"

"That's right." I didn't know where he was going with this, so I listened as patiently as I could.

"Take a look at this." He slid me a copy of a marriage license, dated March 13, 1867, in faded ink. The text read: "The State of Alabama and the County of Mobile Probate Court. To any of the State Judges or to any Licensed Minister of the Gospel or to any Justice of the Peace of the said County. Know ye that you are hereby authorized to join together in the Bonds of Holy Matrimony..." I peered closer to read the names, "Edward H. Tulley and Karah Lahoma Cottonwood."

"What is this? Some cousin of Calpurnia's? Maybe Jeremiah's brother's child?"

"Nope. She's not." His face beamed with excitement.

"Well, who is she?"

He dug in his folder and pulled out a photo of the couple, seated in a studio. A tall young man stood behind a couch, unsmiling, with perfectly smooth dark hair and dark eyes. Seated on the couch was the bride, her hair piled on her head, the dress collar cinched around her long neck, a hint of a smile at the corner of her lips.

I stood up and carried the photo into the living room, turning on the desk lamp. I ransacked the desk drawer for the magnifying glass. Oh, that familiar smile and the shape of the neck! Even her piles of hair made me think of Calpurnia. It wasn't her, but the resemblance was striking.

"What? Who is this, Ashland?"

"Meet Karah Lahoma Cottonwood Tulley, of our Cottonwoods. I think she's Calpurnia's long-lost sister."

"But how can that be? I mean, there's no record of a living child other than Callie."

"No, but unlike the other children, there are no death records, not even a mention of her death in the family bible. Don't you think that's kind of suspect? I do believe this is the baby that Calpurnia heard crying the night her mother died. Remember, she was surprised to learn that the baby died because she'd heard it crying sometime late that night. Somebody must have taken the baby away."

"Or been ordered to remove it. I wouldn't put it past Old Jeremiah to want to get rid of her. He didn't want another girl, and he sure didn't want to share that fortune, even if he couldn't find it."

"Yes, but from what you say and what I have read, it's more likely that Mr. Cottonwood would have wanted the baby dead."

"Ah, yes, but Jeremiah was a coward, except when it came to abusing his wife and daughter. He would have never done the deed himself. Just like Ann-Sheila."

"Who?"

I shook my head, thinking of the poor slave who drowned herself in the river. "It's not important right now. I'm just saying that he would have ordered one of his slaves to do it, probably Stokes or Early." I paced the floor, the wheels turning like crazy in my mind. "But Hooney, she would have intervened. I'm sure of it. She cared about Christine. It would have been easy for her to have that baby hidden away somewhere."

"It's hard to imagine how it all happened, but this photo seems like good proof to me. Somehow that baby lived. I wish we knew more."

"Well, there's nothing to do but have a nap. Maybe a nap with that photo will trigger something. It's hit or miss, but it's worth a shot."

"No way, CJ. I won't let you do that. It's too dangerous, especially with all we know now. I've only scratched the surface of what my supposed friend, Hollis Matthews, knew. I don't know how far down this rabbit hole goes."

"Literary references are appreciated, but you can't stop me from dreaming, Ashland." Lighting popped near the house, and the lights went off. Thunder shook the dishes in my kitchen cabinet. We both jumped and then nervously laughed at ourselves.

He said, "I'm not trying to stop you from dreaming. I just wish you'd dream about me once in a while." He stood close to me, his face the picture of seriousness, his shirt and hair almost dry now.

"Why should I dream about you? You're here, right now, aren't you? That's better than a dream." I reached out and touched his chest, putting the palm of my hand over his heart. Through the thin cotton shirt, I could feel his heart beating strong and evenly.

"Yes, I am here," he answered in a hoarse whisper.

I stepped closer. We were so close now that there was barely any space between us. My breath was coming faster, my heart pounded, my pulse raced. With a tilt of my head, I gazed into his blue eyes and whispered, "I am here too."

He took my face in his hands and kissed me. This was no "Bye, see you later" kiss. We weren't two teenagers parked in the woods after the prom but two adults who, until this point, had managed to keep our hands off one another. We kissed again, and I felt the weight of my hair fall around my shoulders as he slid my hair out of its ponytail. I got the feeling that Ashland wasn't leaving, and I didn't want him to. He paused and looked at me; his eyes sparkled with desire, his unspoken question obvious. I didn't speak a word but instead replied with a kiss. Yes, I wanted him to stay.

And he did.

Chapter 9

Neither one of us fell asleep, but we lay in the dark together for a long time before Ashland slipped away. He took his stack of paperwork with him except for the photo, which I convinced him to leave behind. I posted the picture of Karah next to Calpurnia's on my dry-erase board and sat in my curved chair clad in my t-shirt, my body half-wrapped in a sheet. The nearby streetlight cast a strange yellow glow on the board. I stared at the two faces looking back at me from antiquity. They wouldn't pass for identical twins—Karah's eyes didn't have the downward slant of Calpurnia's—but I could well imagine they might be sisters. Definitely related in some way. Their eye color could be similar. It was hard to tell with just a copy of an antique black and white photograph and a photo of an oil painting. I looked more carefully, taking note of the differences and similarities.

Their lips, full and bow-shaped, the same. Both had high cheekbones, but Karah's forehead was wider, like Christine's. Similarities were there, but it would be hard to know for sure without solid evidence. Here was another question: if Karah knew she was a Cottonwood, as the marriage license seemed to suggest, why didn't she come forward and claim her birthright, claim Seven Sisters? What had kept her away? I sighed. *Another mystery, like I need another one. Okay, no more distractions tonight.* I had to get my mind back on my task here—finding Calpurnia. Last I knew, she confessed to Muncie that she wanted to leave. But to where and with whom?

I picked up the journal and hunkered down in the chair. Thankfully the power had flickered back on, and I switched on the lamp. I ran my fingers over the cover of the journal and opened it to my bookmark. *Talk to me, Calpurnia. Give me some kind of clue! Where are you?*

I sighed, closed my eyes to quiet myself and began to read...

Dear Diary,

Pichon's Emporium delivered new dresses to the house today; some were mine, and the rest belonged to Mother. How easily I can call to remembrance her laughter when ordering those items. She'd given Mr. Pichon's unfriendly daughter her measurements with a smile, promising me that she would indeed regain her trim figure after the baby arrived. I didn't care what size her waist was—Mother's beauty was impossible to hide, and I had told her so. Now those dresses would never be worn, although Cousin Isla would undoubtedly ask me for them. My Cousin has a Persuasive Manner, and Truthfully I rarely refused her, but on this subject I would be unmovable. Nobody would wear Mother's dresses, not as long as there was breath in my body. I could not bear to see Isla preening about in them as if she were truly the Lady of the House. She's already taken to ordering our meals, even purchasing supplies, and she recently had the houseboys rearranging the furniture in the Ladies'

Parlor. These privileges had been given to her by my Father, I supposed, and I did not challenge her.

For these things I care not, as I do not plan to remain at Seven Sisters. Let Isla have her little victories over me, like telling Hooney I had not eaten or mentioning to my Father that I had not accepted Mrs. Meadows' call. I had long abandoned the idea that Isla held any love for me. She was not a True Friend—like Muncie.

But she will never wear Mother's dresses!

How oddly reassuring it had been to receive the packages, when just a few weeks ago I could have never dreamed that I would welcome such a delivery. Indeed to receive such an intimate package would have sunk my soul like an anchor into the depths of darkest despair. But this had not happened.

As I opened the box lid and lifted away the tissue paper from the cream and peach dress, it was as if my Own Dear Mother had sent this gift to remind me to remain strong and hopeful. I had ignored Hooney's yellow-eyed stare and removed the sumptuous fabric, hugging it as if it were my Dearest One. I spread it across the pillows of my bed and lay beside it, rubbing the fabric with my fingers. I hummed "La Mere," feeling sleepy but happy. Hooney murmured a prayer, most certainly about me and my Addled Mind, and left me alone to my musings.

Mother could never escape Seven Sisters now. I could not help her, but she wanted me to be free. She wanted me to run, as far and as fast as I could. That was the message I received from her dress box. I love you, Mother!

Now, I have taken Great Care to behave as if All is Well again. I ordered a bath and asked Hannah to fix my hair. I greeted my Cousin with a smile and even inquired about her health. She chattered like the day we first met. My Cousin considered herself to be Crafty and Intelligent, but she had no idea what I had planned. I smiled through her retelling of a bit of gossip she had picked up from our neighbor and her friend, Ocie Chastang.

"How amusing," I commented as she continued her tale. Apparently some newcomer to the Mobile Social Scene discovered that the local "parlor fan language" was quite different from the fan languages used in her home parish. Miss Louise Holcombe had made a fool of herself in front of an entire new crop of debutantes visiting from Jackson County. Isla laughed and laughed, and I did my very best to echo her amusement.

She cajoled me to come out and accompany her and visit with Ocie. She told me I looked lovely in my new dress and remarked, "I am sure that all the Gentlemen in Mobile County will be heartbroken when they discover you are to marry Mr. Langdon." She leaned back against the upholstered chair, her blue cotton dress—my blue cotton dress—surrounding her tiny frame like a blue cloud. She told me she was Quite Jealous that I should marry and move away, leaving her in this Great House by herself. "How will I ever manage?" she said with a pout. She feigned sadness, but she did not fool me. I knew that she did not feel it. I suspected that Isla Beaumont had never felt sad a day in her life. She never cried. Not for her Mother or mine. Not for Baby Angelique. Not a tear for Uncle Louis beyond dabbing a handkerchief to her dry eyes the day he disappeared. Muncie had tried to warn me, but I had refused to listen. Now I knew.

At the very least she had kept my Great Secret and never revealed to Father that I had spirited away a Collection of Letters from My Captain. Yes, at least there was that.

Tonight, as I prepared for bed, I examined again his latest letter. How his written words tug at my heartstrings like a violin master plucks at his instrument! Apparently some fiend—some Agent of Low Caliber—has shared the news that I am to marry. Read his words to me...

> Were I not a Gentleman of the South, how rudely I would lambast Your Proposed Husband to his Bride, but Alas, Madam, I am such. Inasmuch as it Pains My Heart, I release you from any Inclinations or Dispositions in regards to myself, knowing that I could never attain the Stature of the Man you are soon scheduled to marry. Forgive My intrusion and think kindly of me, Friend. I will Treasure Our Memories beyond a mere tomorrow.
>
> With fondest farewell,
>
> Captain David Garrett

My hand shook so when I sent my return. I assured the Captain that I had no desire to end our Friendship, that I considered him an Excellent Man and a Dear Friend. I refused to say goodbye, writing this...

> Now, my Friend, accept my heart-felt assurance that I continue to Value Our Amiable Acquaintance. That in truth, I have no designs to abandon you. Nay, how much more will I rely upon your Companionship as I navigate these Unknown Waters? I look forward to the Good Day when I may see you Face to Face. I pray that when that day arrives, I will have the Courage necessary to speak my True Heart.
>
> Yours in Friendship,
>
> Calpurnia Cottonwood

My note is winging its way to the Captain now. I pray that I may hear a return soon. What will I say to him? I am determined to speak my heart at last. I want to be His Wife and the wife of no other. For freedom—no, for his Love—I would gladly shed all my earthly trappings, pay whatever price, even lose my inheritance to be by his side. Oh, to see the world! To explore the sights and sound of life beyond my white sepulcher! One more word of encouragement, and I shall run to him with all my strength. I *pray that it is soon—Isla tells me that the Delta Queen shall leave Mobile soon, probably for the rest of the season. He must write to me! I will wait for him!*

How will I pass the time?

Chapter 10

I woke up with a weird startled feeling hanging over me. My phone buzzed on my nightstand—it was Ashland. It was never good when he called before 8 a.m. I pushed my unruly curls out of my face and answered the phone, trying not to sound like someone coming out of a love hangover from a night of passion.

"Dreaming about me?" His question caught me off guard, and I couldn't help but smile.

"Of course, Ashland," I started to lie but added, "well, kind of. I dreamed about Callie." Naturally, he wanted to know all the details, so I relayed what I saw, from the dresses to the notes. He prodded me with questions, and by the end of the conversation, I felt sort of sad. Not about the dream, but about Ashland and me. What would happen to us when the mystery of Calpurnia's whereabouts was solved? What if we never knew what happened? Nothing would be sadder than to discover that Ashland and I truly had nothing in common except for a love of old houses. I finished the conversation with, "Will I see you later?"

"I'm thinking about driving up to Fayette. That's where Karah was from, according to what I've found. It's about four hours away. I was thinking we could ride up and spend the afternoon exploring the library records, stay overnight, come back some time on Sunday. How does that sound?"

I waved my hand in the air in frustration—mostly at myself. My heart said, "Go! Go! Go!" but my brain was shouting, "Not so fast!" I won't even mention what my other parts were saying. "I wish I could say yes, but I better not."

He laughed nervously. "I guess that doesn't sound like much of a date."

"That sounds like the perfect date to me. It's just that I'd like to visit with Myron and Alice before they go home, and I need to do a few things around here that I've been neglecting." Like my laundry, I thought. "How about a rain check?"

"Sure, but I don't know when I'll be driving back to Fayette, Alabama, population 2,400 again."

"I'll take my chances. Besides, I have confidence in you. Keep your eyes open for anything you think might be relevant, and let's talk tonight. I'm dying to know who this sister of Calpurnia's is."

"Yeah, me too."

The pause in the conversation grew. It felt like Ashland had something to say, but he never said whatever was on his mind. "You still there?"

"Yes, I'm here."

Suddenly I regretted my decision. Maybe I should change my mind, pack a bag and head to Fayette for the weekend. But before I could, Bette tapped courteously on my door, giving me the excuse I needed to end the awkward phone call. How could this be? Ashland and I had finally shared an amazing intimate evening, and now I wanted to run the other way. What the hell was wrong with me?

"I better go. Bette's here. Have a safe trip, Ashland. Call me later?"

"Yes, I'll call before bed. Talk to you later."

"Bye." I hung up the phone, trotted to the door and opened it with a smile. "Bette! I feel like I haven't seen you in forever. How are you?"

"I'm very well, thank you! Listen, I brought you a crock of hot cheese grits with some bacon sprinkled on top. I would invite you down to the kitchen, but my gentleman friend decided to sleep on the couch last night. I had extra and I wanted to share. How's my Bienville been behaving?"

"Thank you for the grits!" I accepted the crock, grateful for the worn potholders she passed me with it. Naturally, they were Campbell's Soup Kids quilt blocks. I adored Bette's kitschy kitchen. If I ever had a real home of my own, my kitchen would be every bit as tacky and comforting. "Come on in, Bette." I padded into the kitchen and set the crock on the small table. "He's been a perfect gentleman. He comes and goes, but I forgive him because he's so huggable."

"That sounds a lot like my gentleman friend." I hoped she hadn't noticed that Ashland had stayed longer than normal last night. That would be almost as embarrassing as hearing about Bette's beau "sleeping on the couch."

"Do you plan to do laundry today? I'd like to use the washer and dryer if you don't mind. I'm running out of socks and underwear."

"Sure, you go right ahead. I'm not doing laundry today. Oh, I heard they arrested Mia. Any word on what's next? I figured they'd lock her up in some nuthouse somewhere. The poor girl is delusional, don't you think?"

"Yes, I do. I hope someone helps her, because she's a danger."

"To you, she is. Please be careful, Carrie Jo. I don't want anything to happen to you. You're like another one of my kids—or grandkids. I have gotten attached to you being here."

"Me too, Bette. Thanks for your hospitality and your friendship."

She sniffed and walked to the door. "Have a nice day, dear. And if you see a short, balding man with a noticeable limp leave, please don't judge me." She giggled and waved at me as she walked down the stairs.

I loved Bette and her quirkiness. She was a nice lady. I was happy to see her looking so perky. Not long ago we were fighting for our lives; Mia probably would have killed us both and now it was as if none of it ever happened. What a difference a short time makes!

I poured a glass of orange juice and sat down to enjoy my grits. These quiet moments made everything feel right again. I didn't normally "work" at my kitchen table, but I grabbed the laptop and began typing frantically into my dream journal, recording everything I could for posterity's sake. Of course, I didn't know if I'd ever have a future generation, but just in case. I shivered uncontrollably, then decided to get some coffee. I drank it black; I needed the energy boost, not extra calories. I removed the lid from the thick creamy grits and enjoyed the aroma: butter...cheese...a touch of garlic powder. That was the secret!

Gobbling them as quickly as I could without burning my mouth, I filled up my tummy with cheese grits. Sure, no extra calories there. I put the dish in the sink and ran some water in it. Grits were like wallpaper paste once they dried, impossible to remove without power tools. I scrolled through my phone's contact list and tapped on Alice Reed's name.

We talked for a half-hour. Alice was friendly, but I could hear the sadness in her voice. I understood that. Having a loved one with a mental illness was a heartache that one couldn't explain to anyone who hadn't experienced it. Apparently the Reeds had Mia settled into Mobile Mental Health for the next four weeks for various evaluations. The couple had returned to Savannah to put their house in order. They planned on moving back to the area to be near their daughter during her recovery. As she was technically in the County's custody, she could not leave the state until she went to trial for the death of Hollis Matthews. No way were they going to leave her to fight this battle alone. I admired their fortitude and prayed that one day Mia would come to realize that Alice and Myron were more of a treasure than any sack of jewels or old house could ever be. Alice ended the call by asking me to go see Mia when I could.

"You would be doing us a favor, and I know she wants to see you—you are all she talks about."

I gave her an indefinite maybe before wishing them well.

I took a long, cool shower because the day was shaping up to be another warm one. East Coast living was hot—Mobile had to be the humidity capital of the U.S.—at least of Alabama. I turned on the radio and sang along with Joan Jett. I screeched, "I love rock 'n' roll! Put another dime in the jukebox, baby..." When my concert ended, I dried off, dressed and began sorting my dirty laundry. Luckily for me, the washer and dryer were downstairs so I didn't have to carry everything too far. I put the first load in, tossed in some detergent and walked back upstairs with my empty basket.

My phone was ringing, and out of habit I picked it up without looking at the screen. "Hello?"

"Hey, CJ?" I spun around again, waving my hand at myself in frustration. *What do I do? What do I do?* I didn't want to talk to William. What would I say to him? Besides call him a few choice names. I banged my hand on the counter.

"Yes, this is CJ."

"Don't hang up on me! I've been trying to call you for days. I have to—"

"Whatever you want to say, I don't want to hear it, William Bettencourt. You were my friend, and you betrayed me, just like Mia did. I trusted you, and you plotted with her to betray me! Why would you do that, William?" I could hardly believe all the anger that I heard in my own voice. I really felt these emotions—in a hard, bitter and surprising way. Maybe William had meant more to me than I had thought.

"Don't hang up! Please, can we meet? I need to talk to you. You don't know everything. Mia is a dangerous woman, and I didn't betray you—I didn't dare leave her alone. By the time I knew she was serious, by the time I knew she was coming after you with a loaded gun, I couldn't leave her. That would have sent her over the edge!"

"You should have called me or called the police. How dare you call me now! I cared about you. Did you ever really care about me?" Tears slid down my cheeks. William had been my friend for three years. We'd flirted, tried to date and kissed once or twice, but it never worked out. He didn't answer me right away. Finally he asked, "Are you still a horrible singer?"

"What?"

"I said are you still a horrible singer?"

"Hell, yes I am. But what does that have to do with anything?"

"It's still me, CJ. It's William. I know you. And I have to say this—I've been dying to say this. I love you. I made a mistake by not telling you that. I made a mistake not telling you that I suspected Mia had a problem, but I am telling you now. Are you listening?"

"Yes, I'm listening."

"Mia thinks she's related to the Cottonwoods. Something about some guy named Jeremiah; she's related to him some kind of way. Anyway, she's been taking some kind of medication or a drug—I don't even know if it's legal. It's supposed to help her...what's it called again...'dream catch,' kind of like you. She's been sleeping with all kinds of things around her bed, but mostly she would just wake up screaming and cursing. She could do what you do, and it drove her crazy. She said she saw pictures and blurs of color but nothing clear and nothing that made sense. All she could do was feel things, feel the anger of Jeremiah."

"Are you joking? Is this part of some new scam, William?"

"Shut up and listen." He sounded as serious as I had ever heard him. "I'm not scamming you, CJ. She's going to try and come at you again. She hasn't given up. This is a ruse for her to get close to you. Don't go see her, no matter how much her parents beg you."

"Next you'll be telling me that Alice and Myron are in on it." He didn't answer me, but I wouldn't let it go. "Is that what you're saying?"

"I don't know for sure, but I think they could be. Just let the law handle Mia. This place they have her in—it's what it is known as a low-security facility. That means without much effort, Mia could be out of it in no time. If she can get to you, she will."

"But why? To what end? The treasure has been found, William. And Seven Sisters belongs to Ashland, not me. Why would she come after me?"

In a steely, serious voice, he said, "I think she wants to kill you, Carrie Jo. She has this idea in her sick head that if she kills you and does some kind of ritual, something she learned in Egypt, she can have your powers after you die. I know it sounds crazy. I didn't want to believe it either, but there it is. I am telling you the truth. Please listen to me. Keep your friends close to you. Keep the doors locked. Don't let your guard down for a minute."

I sat on the floor, closing my front door with shaking hands. I could hardly believe what William had told me. What did it all mean?

"Carrie Jo, please. Can I come over? I'll keep watch with you. I want to keep you safe."

"No, William. I don't want to see you. Thanks for calling me and telling me what you know. I thank you for that, but there is no way I am going to trust you again. At least, not right now."

"I want you to trust me, CJ. I do love you, as I always have. You know I have. What I said to you that night on Dauphin Street, it was a lie. A big lie! I did come down here to be close to you. I came down here because I wanted to have more than a kiss with you. I love everything about you. Your smile, your horrible singing, your beautiful face. It's you I want. Why else would I still be talking to Mia? I had to watch over you the best way I knew how. Please say you'll give me a second chance."

"I'm seeing Ashland, William. I'm not the kind of girl to date two guys at once. I do thank you for calling me."

He sighed, sounding defeated. "Well, I wanted you to know. My best to your boyfriend, and please tell him what I told you. Stay safe, Carrie Jo."

"Thanks, William." I hung up the phone. I lay on the area rug and stared up at the pristine white, glossy ceiling. What just happened? How did that monkey wrench get tossed into my plans again?

I thought for a few minutes, then I got to my feet. When William and I were dating, I ended it because I realized I wasn't in love with him. No matter what he said, he couldn't talk me into being in love. It just wasn't there. Still, I felt grateful for the phone call. I tapped on the phone screen again, ready to call Ashland to fill him in.

"No, I better not," I said to no one in particular. If I called him, I wouldn't have the opportunity to do what I planned to do later.

Tonight would be the night. It was now or never. I would finally sleep at Seven Sisters. I hoped I knew what I was doing, or this might be the last nap I ever took.

I kept my eyes peeled for petite lurkers wielding knives or guns in the hedges as I went back and forth to the laundry room for the next few hours. The more I thought about it, the more ridiculous it all seemed. But I did my research. Mobile Mental Health was indeed a low-security facility, so that much was true. As for William being in love with me, that wasn't something I could help.

About 11 a.m., Detra Ann's email pinged my inbox. I clicked on the attachment and studied the letter that appeared on my screen. I was surprised to recognize the handwriting. David Garrett's. I'd "read" many of his letters to Calpurnia while I dreamed about her, so I'd seen that script before.

Dearest One,

It pains me to hear such disturbing reports about your behavior while I'm away. My sincere hopes had been that you would stop fighting me at every turn and allow the physicians to provide you with the ministrations you need to overcome this serious malady. Perhaps reading this note will put you in remembrance of the promise I made to you. "Never will I leave you, nor forsake you, not for a thousand treasures or for Aphrodite herself." You are my own Dear Love; have I not proven such?

Stop believing the things your eyes see, because we know they cannot be trusted. Do not listen to the things your ears hear, because I shall always love you, no matter what others may say. I desire only your happiness and peace.

I will return to you as soon as I land in Mobile. I have something to show you, something that may pique your interest. Wear the blue gown for me, Dearest One. How I love to see you in your finery once again! No more black.

With much admiration and love,

David

The back of the letter listed her address as Dauphin Street Hospital, her name, Iona Garrett. That was it. I sat back in amazement. No matter what I thought of the captain, I had to at least give him credit for coming up with the sister cover story and trying to get Isla some help. Not that it ever worked. I printed a copy of the letter and forwarded it to Ashland, who immediately wrote me back, "Wow! That's amazing. Must be Isla, right?"

I sent back a smiley face and agreed with him. I folded my clothing and kept my doors locked. Despite what William told me, I still intended to do what I had planned.

I would sleep at the house and no one, alive or dead, would stop me.

Chapter 11

Sitting in the driveway of Seven Sisters, I talked to Ashland. I prayed that an ambulance wouldn't go whizzing by and bust me. As far as he knew, I was safe at home in my apartment. I still hadn't told him about William, and the guilt was beginning to weigh on me. "Yes, I am turning in early."

"Hoping for some good dreams?"

"You know me. That's what I do, right?"

"No, that's not what you do. You are a researcher—a historian. This dreaming business, this is just extra. One day, when these mysteries are solved, you'll be able to turn them off, right?"

I sighed. "I hope so. I have never dreamed so much in my life, and I have never been so emotionally invested with a group of people who haven't been alive in well over a hundred years. I'm hoping this goes away. After this, I look forward to sleeping in a brand new house far away from downtown Mobile."

"I see. I'd like to get to know that girl, the one that doesn't dream and sleeps in a new home away from Seven Sisters. And I've been thinking..."

"Long trip? Nothing better to do?"

"Hey, cut that out. I think all the time, not just on long, boring trips."

I chuckled, grateful that he had a sense of humor about the whole thing. "So what have you been thinking?"

"I've been thinking that we need to set a deadline. If we don't know something by Halloween, we let it go. We can't let this absorb our lives. I don't want it to do to you what it did to my mother. Me either. We have to live a real life with birthday parties and spaghetti dinners. We have to be real people, Carrie Jo. I need to be real."

"I am so glad you said that." Happy tears filled my eyes. This was exactly what I had been feeling when we spoke last, but I couldn't articulate it like he had. "I love you, Ashland Stuart. Not your old name or your money. Not your football trophies or your amateur detective skills. I love you."

"And I needed to hear that. Thank you, Carrie Jo, for not laughing at me and for taking on my family mystery like it was your own. I don't know any other woman that would have done as much as you have. I love you too."

I smiled into the phone. I took a deep breath and stared up at the house in front of me. Seven Sisters practically glowed in the moonlight. Purple shadows flitted across the colonnade; they looked like fleeting dark spirits, but it was only the wind moving the branches off nearby trees. "I better go now, Ashland. I'm getting ready for bed. See you in the morning?"

"You know it. I know I said this once, but I love you, Carrie Jo Jardine."

"I love you too. Goodnight." I hung up, trying not to feel guilty about lying to the man I just declared my love for. This wasn't what I wanted. I grabbed my purse and my bag and locked my car. I parked it out of the way and out of the obvious view from the driveway, but I didn't park around back. That would be admitting guilt for sure.

I walked toward the house. It looked so different at night and felt different too, now that I was alone. The pots were the same, each filled with various flowers like hydrangeas and hibiscus. I stood on the porch, pushing my key in the door, and I immediately went into wariness mode. I had no intention of being surprised by Mia with a weapon.

I wasted no time getting inside; at least I didn't have to look at the ugly satyr this time. I tapped in the alarm code, disarming the building, and then re-entered the code to arm it again. I checked the lights; all were lit and shining red. That meant locked down, right? I hoped so. Chip or Ashland normally handled the alarm system, but I thought I had done everything right. I didn't dare use a flashlight. Instead, I used my cell phone as a light as I walked across the foyer toward the spiral staircase. Calpurnia's room was upstairs, the first door on the right.

I climbed the creaking stairs, hoping I could avoid the usual squeaky spots with a little light footwork, but to no avail. *That meant that any mice who might be lurking about would know I was coming*, I thought in an attempt to amuse myself. *There was nothing hiding in the darkness here, right?* Bienville would be mightily ashamed.

Without pausing to think or worry, or look for unusual shadows, I pushed open the door. I had just been here the night before in my dreams, watching Calpurnia bathe in her gown. What a ridiculous custom that was! How happy was I to have a shower and the cultural permission to shower nude!

Still using my cell phone, I walked around the room and closed the blinds. I had pine- and cedar-scented candles in my bag, wanting to shed some needed light in the room. I had even brought a thrift store plate to put under them to catch the melting wax. I wanted to sleep, not wake up screaming in a dark room, but I didn't want to attract any attention. The heavy velvet curtains were drawn now, so it would be impossible for anyone to see candlelight. I hoped.

The bedroom was still arranged the way it had been after the supernatural activity there. I tried not to think about the sounds of scraping furniture and the sighing. I so wanted to believe it was Calpurnia who had moved her furniture around. When I closed the door, the sight of the lock made me sick to my stomach. It wasn't the original lock to this door, but it reminded me of all the times Mr. Cottonwood had locked his daughter in the room as punishment for one thing or another.

I set the candles on the nightstand. I lit the candles, and it immediately made the room look and smell happier. I stared at the door and knew I had to put something against it. I grabbed the desk chair and leaned it against the doorknob to prevent human intruders. What would I do if a spirit intruder arrived? I wouldn't think about that.

I left my clothes on, removing only my shoes and socks and tucking them in my bag. I pulled back the covers on Calpurnia's bed and lay down. It felt wrong being there, like I was an intruder in the girl's room, but maybe that was just me being me. I opened the last journal and began to read the next page.

Dear Diary,

Last night, as I waited to hear word from CG, I re-read the poetry book Uncle Louis last bought me. This poem, "The Will and the Wing" by Paul Hamilton Hayne speaks such stirrings to my soul! Listen to this, Dearest Diary...

To have the will to soar, but not the wings,
Eyes fixed forever on a starry height,
Whence stately shapes of grand imaginings
Flash down the splendors of imperial light;

And yet to lack the charm that makes them ours,
The obedient vassals of that conquering spell,
Whose omnipresent and ethereal powers
Encircle Heaven, nor fear to enter Hell;

This is the doom of Tantalus – the thirst
For beauty's balmy fount to quench the fires
Of the wild passion that our souls have nurst
In hopeless promptings – unfulfilled desires.

Yet would I rather in the outward state
Of Song's immortal temple lay me down,
A beggar basking by that radiant gate,
Than bend beneath the haughtiest empire's crown!

For sometimes, through the bars, my ravished eyes
Have caught brief glimpses of a life divine,
And seen afar, mysterious rapture rise
Beyond the veil that guards the inmost shrine.

Oh yes, to have the will to soar but not the wings! What sheer agony that would have been! Not I! I have both the Will and the Wind! My Will is my own, but my Wind, that will toss the sails and push us together toward our destiny.

Tonight, my Own Dear, tonight I confess my heart to you, for I know you have long waited to hear me say these words. I shall surprise you! I shall surprise you indeed, and you will welcome me into your strong arms and promise me that all will be well, yes, all shall be well.

The house is quiet tonight. Isla has left for a night of fun and foolishness with Ocie. I bid her good riddance. May she be as happy here as I was! Muncie waits for my instructions. My dark blue cloak and hood are already stowed in the barn in my horse's stall. I have shoved several coins into my change purse. I liberated twenty such coins from my father's purse easily enough. He was stone drunk on corn whiskey. Now the coins are in my purse, tied to my wrist. This small fortune would take care of us for an entire year at least, surely. I have no head for figures. I have given up on finding Mother's Treasure, but at least I will have her name, for that will be the name I travel with. I am no longer Calpurnia Cottonwood but Christine Beaumont. Once I marry, I will be Christine Garrett, wife of Captain David Garrett.

I have everything planned out. I have been sending Muncie on false runs into town. Actually, he has been racing the horse down to the river to the Delta Queen. He's gotten the time perfect now, and we are almost ready to run. Tonight will be the night! The steamboat will leave the dock at 8, and we don't want to arrive too early. It would be best if we were puffing up the Mobile River before my father discovered I was missing. As much corn whiskey as I fed him tonight, he may never wake up again. Forgive me for hoping so!

Here I am now, tapping my foot nervously. I've paced the floor. I've taken great pains to hide my journals in the floorboards, in case things don't go as I have planned. My book of notes from my Captain I have tucked inside my purse. And you, my Dear Diary, I shall truly miss. I write to you hastily now because you too must be hidden from prying eyes.

Au Revoir, Dearest Diary! When next you hear from me, I shall certainly be Mrs. David Garrett, world explorer and woman of the world!

I closed the book and closed my eyes and soon drifted off to sleep. I imagined Calpurnia kissing the book and hiding it. She no doubt wore her coral-colored gown because as Garrett had written in one of his notes, that was his favorite dress of hers. Then I felt myself sinking, sinking into the world of the past...I whispered to myself, "Captain David Garrett," over and over again. I had to get this right.

I lay there for what seemed like hours, but sleep didn't come. I swore under my breath and eventually just got up. This had been a stupid idea, anyway, hadn't it? Might as well go home and get some real sleep.

Before I blew out the candles, I walked to the mirror. My face wasn't staring back at me—it was Calpurnia's. She didn't seem to notice that I was there at all. I said something to her, and I saw her shiver and look about her. She ignored it, dabbed perfume on her wrists and neck and poked a few more pearl-tipped pins into her hair. I breathed slowly, reminding myself to watch only, not interfere. My job was to watch and learn.

It couldn't hurt, could it?

I slid my feet into the satin shoes with the low heels and walked out of the room. Hooney caught me outside. "You going somewhere, Miss?"

"Why yes, Hooney. I'm going to visit with Ocie. I won't be gone too long. Oh dear, is it that late? Well, then I won't be back until morning, I'm afraid."

"What about your Father? Mr. Cottonwood will be fit to be tied if he finds out that you..."

"Now, no worrying. You let me worry about him. It's only for a late supper and some quilting. I am sure Father wouldn't mind that. I am going to be an old married lady soon. I hope he understands that ladies like to spend time with other ladies before they marry."

"Oh yes," she said with a chuckle, "you should do that. You need that now that your Momma is gone, God rest that Angel's soul! You go on and have a time with those ladies. I'll send Stokes for the horse."

"No, Muncie will take care of it all. He knows which my favorite is, and I would like him to serve me." I didn't make eye contact but pretended to smooth my dress and hair as Hooney called for Muncie.

"Now, boy!" Muncie arrived just as we planned and I climbed up on the horse to ride sidesaddle supposedly to Ocie's.

"Here, let us get the carriage, ma'am. How will you ride home?" Hooney called up, looking worried and suspicious.

"Ocie's father will allow me to use his carriage, I'm sure. Now I must go. Time is wasting. Goodnight." I whispered into Muncie's ear, "Get me out of here."

We rode down the lane at an easy gallop but stopped once we left their sight. He handed me my cloak and hood. Where we were going, nobody needed to know that it was me—until I was ready to reveal myself. I wrapped the cloak around myself, and he lifted me back up into the saddle.

"Thank you, my friend. When you leave me, I want you to go right to Reginald Ball's camp. You remember the one, it's on the other side of the river. The one the Cottonwoods use all the time. Father rarely goes there anymore, but Mr. Ball says he paints there when he wants peace and quiet. Tell him what I have done, and give him the letter I wrote for you. As a married woman, I can grant you your freedom, and I know my husband will approve. You will be a free man, but get to Reginald. He is a good man. He will help us free you. I want to protect you from my father's whip. You will remember, Muncie?"

"Yes, I'll remember. Let's ride now so we don't miss the boat."

"Yes, let's ride." I clung to the horn of the saddle for all I was worth, the blue cloak swirling around me. We passed only one other rider, and he barely acknowledged us or looked in our direction.

At the dock, we pulled the horse into some woods and tied him to a tree. I removed my cloak and straightened my coral gown and patted my hair. Muncie's worried face gave me pause. I couldn't bear it if my friend were to suffer on my account. I wrapped my arms around his neck and gave him a quick hug. "Thank you for everything. I will write to Reginald, so please let him know where you shall be. I want to stay in touch, Muncie."

He just nodded and stared at the ground, surely at a loss for words. I knew he was the kind of boy—no, man—who had deep feelings for his friends. I knew he that was worried for me and that he loved me as the true friend he was. Still, I couldn't linger, I walked along the gangplank, pausing as I did. Here it was. The night I had been waiting for! The night where all things would become possible for me. With a sweet smile and a tiny wave of my fingers, I said "Goodbye" to him, maybe for the last time.

The picture began to fade into the distance, and I could hear someone screaming, screaming my name. "Carrie JO-O-O-O!" I shook myself awake, angry that the dream had broken at such a crucial moment. But then my anger was quickly replaced with fear. I was more than startled to see Mia sitting on the edge of the bed with a black leather strap in her hands.

"My, my, my. What a bit of a pickle you've gotten yourself into, CJ. Bit of a pickle, bit of a pickle, bit of a pickle." She was laughing wildly, and I sat up cautiously. "Doesn't that sound funny? So funny."

"Mia, what are you doing here? You shouldn't be here. How did you escape the hospital?"

"How do you think? I had help, of course. You are far too trusting, Carrie Jo. Far too trusting. You'll never believe who's been helping me. Are you ready for this? Give me a drum roll, please!" I just stared at her; I certainly wasn't going to give her a drum roll. I was thinking about how I could get out of this room without getting smacked with that belt.

"Well, I'll save that for later. For now, you might be wondering how I got in here, right?" I nodded obediently. "That secret door there, dummy. You never were much of a researcher, were you?" She laughed again at my perceived stupidity.

"Sugar is sweet and so are you. Sugar is sweet and so are you, CJ." She swung around the pole of the four-poster, obviously under the influence of some kind of drug. And armed. "Oh so sweet. I hear you and Ashland have been kissing in a tree, K-I-S-S-I-N-G! I knew it right from the beginning that you had your eye on him, but who can blame you? That guy is hot—and loaded, don't forget loaded!" She laughed and laughed as if she couldn't help herself.

"What do you want, Mia? Why are you here?"

"Oh, why am I here? Why are *you* here?" She cracked the belt by her side. She didn't hit me, but I could see where the tail of the belt had left a welt on her hand. A thin trail of blood appeared, but Mia didn't even seem to notice. "When I came up here to play around, you had me fired. That was rich, wasn't it? Now you know you heard Isla's voice in here, but you just couldn't stand that I might have more powers than you. You took Seven Sisters away from me—and Ashland too!"

"No, I never did!" I got out of the bed, wishing there was some way I could get to my phone without her seeing me. "I didn't ask for this, Mia. It's not something I prayed for or did some kind of spell to get. It just happens. You know that!"

"You *know* that!" she repeated, mocking me to my face. "Stop whining, girl. I hate hearing you whine constantly about dreaming. What great irony God has—if there is a God! Someone who doesn't want to see the past is a dream catcher, while someone who would give her soul for the ability can't have it. But I *can* have it and I will! I never wanted any damn hidden treasure. That was Isla! I never wanted Ashland either! You have the treasure. It's inside you, just waiting for someone like me to come scoop it out." Mia dropped the belt and slid a knife out of her pocket. She flipped it open, the silver blade shimmering dangerously in the candlelight.

"Mia, you don't know what you're saying. I'm your friend, remember. It was you and me and William. We're your friends. He called me, told me about how worried he was. I am too. Please let us help you."

She laughed again, an ugly, low sound. "William told you what I told him to tell you. That is all. As a matter of fact, why don't you meet our special guest tonight? Come on out, baby. She knows you're here." Mia snatched the chair away from the door, sending it to the ground with a crash. She turned the brass key and unlocked the door. I peered into the blackness and saw no one.

"Come on, baby. Don't be shy."

William stepped into the doorway, a devilish grin on his face. He didn't look at me, just Mia.

"Say hello to our guest, baby."

"Hello," William whispered. The small grin remained on his lips, and his dark eyes sparkled with amusement. He'd betrayed me again, and I had believed him. If I weren't in fear of being stabbed to death by Mia's blade, I would have fallen to the floor.

Chapter 12

Mia paced the room, waving her blade as she talked. "You know, I see things too. You aren't the only one with special blood and powers. But I can be stronger, much stronger than you, CJ. Then we can go anywhere, and I can dream about the ancient times, in faraway places. I will do it, and you will be dead. How does that sound?"

"It doesn't sound very good, Mia. Please, stop this." I tried to think of something to say that would keep her busy, but nothing came to mind. My eyes searched the room. How would I get out of here? William blocked the door, and Mia stood between me and the secret passage.

"I'm going to give you a choice, CJ. We can do this the easy way or the hard way; which way do you prefer?" Her finger touched the tip of the knife, and I could see the blood drip as she cut herself. "You can lie down like a good girl and go to sleep, or we can take out what we need while you kick and scream. Which would you like?" She took a step toward me.

"Mia, don't do this," I said, gasping with raw emotion. "Please!"

"Uh, uh, uh. That's not the right answer. Try again. Will you cooperate, or shall we have a bit of fun?" She swung her blade at me and laughed. William stood in the doorway, not moving, just watching the drama unfold.

"William, how could you do this?" I yelled at him. "Are you just going to stand there and let her murder me? You told me you loved me, remember that? Did you ever love me?" I saw something flicker in his eyes. Regret, maybe?

Mia growled with anger. "He never told you he loved you! He's never been yours, CJ. He's mine!" She took another two steps toward me.

"No, Mia! Don't do this!" I put my hands up above my head, waiting for the knife blade, when suddenly the air shifted and I could feel a vibration. In a split second the candles sailed through the air, pelting Mia with hot wax and flames. She screamed, and I climbed over her and then took off running with all my might toward the secret door. Out of the corner of my eye, I saw William race toward me, then a surprised look crossed his face as a ghostly hand crashed something that looked like a wooden stick down upon him. I screamed and ran pell-mell into the darkness.

"Oh God, oh God, oh God! Help me!" I ran, wondering who or what was following me. I had no idea where I was going, and I gasped in panic as I navigated the small space.

"CJ! Wait, I'm on your side!" It was William, and he wasn't too far behind me. "Please wait. I love you, CJ!"

I kept running. I turned left, then right and then left again until I came to a dead end. My hands flew over the dusty wall, looking for a lever or a brace of some kind. I couldn't die here, not inside the walls of Seven Sisters where no one would ever find me. I didn't cry out or scream, and the darkness hid me. I gasped to keep the scream suppressed and pounded on the wall, hoping that I might trigger something.

All of a sudden, William stood beside me. I could see his outline in the darkness. "William, don't hurt me. Please, don't."

His voice was soft and reassuring. "I would never harm you, Carrie Jo. I am here to protect you, remember?" His hand reached out, and I thought he was going to touch me, but he reached past me high on the wall. He pulled a hidden knob and opened the door to Louis Beaumont's room. The room was bright from the moonlight streaming in through bare windows. I could see William smile down at me. Could it be true?

From behind him I heard another growl. Mia thrust her blade into his back, and I could see the shock cross William's face. He fell to his knees, and Mia wore a triumphant smile behind him. "Traitor," she declared over him. "Well, it looks like you weren't the only fool in this game, CJ."

"Oh no, William! Mia, what have you done?"

William slid to the floor and didn't move. The dark red blood oozed out of his back and onto the floor. She stepped over him and lunged towards me.

"Now where were we, CJ? I remember! You were about to die, and I was about to get your powers."

"We need to help William, Mia. Stop this!"

"No, William is beyond help now. He's a betrayer. He betrayed us both. I guess that makes him a double betrayer. Those are the worst kind. Now lie down here and let's get this over with."

I moved away, walking backward so I could keep my eye on her. "No, Mia!" I picked up a cordless phone and threw it at her. I grabbed whatever I could off the desk and sent it sailing her way. She laughed and dodged everything easily, never ceasing her pursuit.

I reached for the doorknob, only to discover the door was locked. Who had locked it? I tugged on it and fumbled with the latch. Mia was right behind me; I turned to look into her crazy dark eyes, to face my death with my back against the door. *What next? What do I do next?* Mia raised the knife above her head and suddenly, a shot rang out.

Her arm fell, and she stood swaying on her feet. She looked confused, and then a strange blankness crossed her face. Before she crumpled to the ground, she said, "CJ?" I looked beyond her and saw William lying on the floor with a gun in his hand. He had shot her and saved my life. I ran to him, picking up the phone I had thrown along the way.

"William, stay with me. Okay? Stay with me!" I pulled off my shirt and pressed it against the wound on his back, trying to stop the bleeding. With shaking fingers I dialed 9-1-1 and gave our information. "William, I have to go unlock the door. You stay awake and hold this phone. Hold this phone, and don't you dare go to sleep! You got it?"

"Yes," he whispered.

I raced to the door, disarming the alarm and unlocking the bolt. I left the door wide open and ran back. Nothing to fear now; the evil that had chased me was now dead in a heap on the floor. Mia's eyes stared into nothingness. I knew she was dead, I could feel it.

"William! William Bettencourt! Don't you dare go to sleep! I'm here. I'm with you!" I wanted to cry, to scream for help, but I knew help was on the way. I feared it would be too late.

"Carrie Jo, I'm sorry. I tried to help. Everything I do is wrong."

"Stop talking. You need to be quiet. Listen, the sirens are getting closer. Can you hear them?"

"I love you, Carrie Jo. I always have."

"I know, William. I love you too. It's all going to be all right. You'll see."

William smiled, and his eyes blinked and lowered—the smile still on his face.

"No, no. William, please don't leave me." I began to cry, I held his head in my lap and smoothed his dark curls. I watched as his life slipped away from him. *What do I do now?*

Suddenly, in a rush of activity, an emergency team was in the room, pulling me away from him. They worked on William for a minute, then hastily transported him to the ambulance. Someone handed me a jacket, and I remembered I was wearing only a bra. My bloody shirt lay wadded on the floor. Another team worked at reviving Mia, but to no avail. She was gone. Dead right here in the room where she herself killed Hollis Matthews.

I sat on the floor, unsure of what to do. Go with William? No, he was gone now. I could hear the sirens wailing down the driveway taking him to the hospital. I looked up to find Detective Simmons staring at me.

"So we meet again. What is it about this house, Miss Jardine? Or maybe it's not the house but something else." She squatted down beside me.

I knew what she meant, but she was wrong. It wasn't me. It wasn't the house, either. It was the past—it was a bevy of spirits struggling toward their desired destinies even beyond life's allowance of years. But I couldn't tell her that. I didn't bother.

I stood up. "I'm going to the hospital with my friend. We'll talk later, or you can follow me there."

I walked out of Seven Sisters for the last time.

I would never return to the house. It had taken too much from me. Too much had been lost. How they had all struggled against it, Christine, Louis, Calpurnia—even Ann-Sheila. In my own time, Hollis, Mia, William, and TD. I had done all I could do to prevent those old spirits from forcing their way into our lives, but they had done just that.

From now on, I would no longer welcome the past into my world. I would do my best to shut it out, to refuse it access. I could no longer give my life away just to peer into theirs. Ashland had been right. This had been a bad idea, and now William had paid for my foolishness.

I was done with dreaming. Or so I thought.

Epilogue

Before my mind knew what I was doing, my heart had plunged me into the cold river. We'd had a cool snap recently, and the chill had settled in the water. I dove into the dark water, praying all the way. I saw her frail body crash into the black, her bright dress sink below the water, the weight of it pulling her down, down, down to her death. I rose once to breathe and could hear people on the boat shouting, but I didn't care. I dove down deeper, struggling against the current. It ran strong and fierce tonight, although you'd never see that from the surface.

I came up for air once more, then dove again, this time following the current. Thank goodness the stars shone bright and the moon glowed that night or I would have never seen her. She hung in the water like a magical hovering creature, still and unmoving. Her body traveled past the boat almost to the other shore. I swam to her, ignoring everything else—all my fears of snakes and gators. I surfaced once more for air, glanced at the boat and saw Mr. Ball pointing into the water.

I dove again and grabbed Calpurnia by her narrow waist and hoisted her to the surface. The gown indeed weighed her down but there was nothing for it. I struggled with all my might to get her to safety. Behind me there were a half-dozen splashes in the water, but I didn't look back at a single one of them. I swam to the shore and shoved her onto the muddy banks. There were no lights here, nothing to help me see her, but I laid her on her back. She wasn't breathing, and her face was white as a sun-beaten sheet.

I shook her and said her name over and over. She didn't speak or move or flutter an eyelash. I remembered seeing this before, so I turned her on her side and patted her back to ease the water out of her. At first nothing happened, but then I heard a strangling sound and Callie began to retch river water out of her body. "Oh, thank you, Lord. Thank you, Lord."

I continued to pat her until she had spewed up all the water. I heard a horse approach, and my mind said, "Run!" but my aching body could not comply. The horse came to a stop, and I looked up at the rider walking towards us. It was Reginald Ball, the gentleman who had painted Calpurnia last spring. He squatted down beside her and lifted her up.

"Are you alive, Miss Cottonwood?"

She nodded, coughing some more but never speaking.

"That was a very foolish thing to do. Very foolish indeed, but there is nothing to be done now. We must...um...I know where we can go. Muncie, can you walk? I don't think the three of us will fit on my horse."

"Yes, sir. I can run if I have to."

"You may have to because I can hear the dogs now. Let's go to my camp and get her tended to. Help me put her on my horse."

We lifted her together, but she still didn't speak to us. Finally, Calpurnia was atop the horse, with Mr. Ball holding her. I did as I was told, running after them in wet shoes. We traveled about two miles into the woods to a small cabin. I was never so glad to see a place as I was now.

"This your place, Mister?"

"Yes, no one will bother us here. Help me lift her. That's it. Thank you." I took her in my arms and carried her into the camp house. I laid her on the bed, and Mr. Ball fussed about lighting a lamp, finding blankets, patting her hair dry. He tried again to talk to her, but she wouldn't respond. I wasn't sure she could see us; her eyes looked as if she could see something we couldn't, something faraway and sad.

"Please, Miss. Talk to me." She said nothing. Once in a while her eyes would look at mine, but she didn't see me. Or anything, not the dirty lamp, not her rustic surroundings.

She never spoke. Not that day or the next. Mr. Ball left us alone that night and one more but returned the day after with food, water and some money. He looked worried and tired. I quietly repented for everything I had previously thought about him. He had proven to be another true friend and a good man. It was nice to know that Calpurnia had two people who cared about her.

"Everyone is looking for Miss Cottonwood, but I haven't the heart to send her back to her father. If anyone knew that I have aided her or helped a runaway slave, I would be in jail. Yet, I cannot sentence her to die. He would kill her if she returned after shaming him in such a way. Poor girl. I think I can make him see reason eventually, but it will take some time. We need to find a place for her, far away from here."

"What do you mean shame him? She would never do such a thing."

He nodded at me to follow him to the other room. "Apparently she threw herself at the captain. She wanted to marry him, but he was already entertaining another lady. So heartbroken was she that she ran slap off the boat and into the water. Poor girl. I always knew that man was a dishonest sort of fellow. And after all that she's been through already. How I wish she had married me when her mother was still alive."

"But he was to marry her. That was the plan. Can't she marry you now? She's a good girl, and you could protect her."

"Look at her, Muncie. She's in no condition to marry anyone. And as I said before, her father is in no mood to entertain new suitors, or anyone at all for that matter. He's as furious as I have ever seen. And the captain, Mr. Cottonwood beat him within an inch of his life. It was a sight to see, and how the cousin wailed. I wonder if I should talk to the sheriff and ask him to intervene on Miss Calpurnia's behalf. This has all been a mistake, a ruse played on her, obviously for Garrett to lay his hands upon her

fortunes. Oh, how foolish! I tried to warn her, but she wouldn't listen. Still, Mr. Cottonwood cannot be allowed to harm her."

"No! You can't call on the sheriff. He's not a friend. He punished Ann-Sheila, did things to her that no man should do to a woman. No, please, we cannot call the sheriff." Then I did something I never did. I reached out and took his hands, squeezing them. "Please." He didn't push me away.

"You've been a kind friend to our Calpurnia." He patted my hand and nodded. "Very well. I will not, but we must think of the way forward. Where could I send her? If she tries to go anywhere now, she'll be spotted. We'll have to travel by night, wherever we go."

We talked into the night, Calpurnia never moving, not even to relieve herself or take some food. We let her sleep, but I promised myself that I would have her eat that night no matter what.

It was decided that Calpurnia and I would travel by ship somewhere, the destination to be chosen another time. She had to get well before we could take her anywhere. A black man, a slave, couldn't go around carrying a white woman in public. She would have to walk and talk and be sensible. "In the meantime, keep her warm and comfortable. Get her to eat." Mr. Ball rose from the wooden table and smiled at me. "It's going to be all right, dear boy. We shall get through this. I still think I should notify the authorities, just to be on the safe side."

"No! You can't! The sheriff is a friend of Mr. Cottonwood, and he won't care if he kills her. Don't do it, Mr. Ball, please." He looked less sure of his promise, but there was nothing else I could do to convince him. I could see his commitment wavering.

"Very well, I shall come visit tomorrow after dark or perhaps the following day. There is plenty of food here and fresh clear water in the spring behind the house."

"Thank you. Thank you, Mister."

He gave Calpurnia a sad look, put his hat on and walked out. I heard the horse ride away and turned to my friend. I had to break through to her. We couldn't wait for Mr. Ball to return. We had to leave as soon as we could! I would take her home, to my home. I would be Janjak again. Momma would help us. I know she would. My heart raced in my chest.

"Callie, Miss...please, wake up." She stirred a little but never woke. Calm, keep calm, I told myself. Let her rest, and then you will talk. Explain to her everything that has happened, and then run, run for your lives!

All through the night, I slept on the floor next to the fireplace, but I didn't dare to start a fire. What if someone saw the smoke? About the time morning cracked the sky, I heard her voice, "Muncie? Where are we?"

"I'm here, right here. We are in Mr. Ball's cabin. He has helped us." I came and sat beside her.

"Oh, I remember now. Oh, my God. I remember. I think I am going to be sick." I helped her out of the bed and to the front door. She threw up water and bile, off the side of the porch.

"I'm okay, I am fine. I can do it." She walked back inside like a brand new baby calf. I tore a piece of bread from the loaf and handed it to her.

"This will help you. Eat it."

"I don't want to eat."

"You don't have any choice. We have to leave here and soon because I think Mr. Ball will bring the sheriff here. If you don't eat, you won't have the strength to go. And we have to go."

"What? He's going to bring the sheriff? Why? I have done nothing wrong."

"I suspect that the law would say otherwise. You are a runaway, and so am I. The whole city of Mobile is looking for us, right now. Mr. Ball is trying to reason with your father, but he's not having any luck. I think he's ready to give up, and it's only been a few days."

"What's he trying to do?" Calpurnia munched on the bread and stared at me.

"He wants to marry you so he can protect you and I can be free."

She stopped in mid-bite and swallowed. "No! I will never marry him nor anyone! No! I have to go!" She tried to leave but began to cry. "I shall never marry. I will die in that house. I know I will."

"No, no, you won't. Listen, you get strong. Eat your food. Tonight, after the sun goes down, we will go to the shipyard ourselves. Maybe I can trade some labor for passage. We can go to Haiti, to my home. I have people that will protect us there. My Momma and her brothers will protect us from harm."

"Yes, Muncie. I will eat and we will go, but you don't have to do labor. I have money, here." She felt her skirts, locating a hidden pocket and pulling out a purse. With shaking fingers, she opened the purse and dumped the contents onto the small bed. Coins bounced around, and a small book plopped on the ground. It was still damp from the river. I suspected that those pages were ruined now. I reached down and handed it to her. She accepted it and stared at it.

"You don't know what this is, do you?"

"No, I don't. What is it?"

"It's a book of lies. Lies a man told to a stupid girl. I swear to you, Muncie. If there were a fire in that fireplace, I would throw it in there and burn it *from my memory. I am not going to die this way." She flopped on the bed and stared at the empty fireplace. "He never loved me, and I loved a dream. When I opened the door, he was with her. He was naked with her. It had all been a game to them."*

I knew who she meant without her saying so. I sighed sadly. "Some men don't deserve happiness, and with her he will never find it. She is no man's woman but every man's. She will be the death of him, as she intended this to be for you."

She shoved the book into her bag and counted the coins, refusing to say more about it. We huddled in the cabin, hearing the dogs twice. But they never came close, not yet. It would only be a matter of time, though, before they discovered our hiding place. We were like the rabbits, waiting to be eaten. After the sun went down, we traveled through the woods. I knew the way. I knew how to read the moon and the stars and seek them for direction. This I learned from books. After midnight, we could see the port and the lights shimmering from the ships.

I held her hand. "Are you ready?"

"Yes, I am ready. Come what may, I am ready." We stepped onto the shell-covered road and walked toward the Harbormaster's office. Now was the moment of truth. We would live or we would die, but at least we would be together.

I woke to the low hum of the airplane's engine. I sat up and lifted the window shade. As we flew over the vast blue ocean, I wondered when we would make our descent into Haiti. Ashland was rereading the school's brochure, as he'd done a hundred times already. This was Janjak's school, or at least it had been founded by him. Now we were going to see it for ourselves, and Ashland had plans to make a sizable gift to the organization. We would walk where Janjak had walked and would at long last see the final resting place of Calpurnia Cottonwood. She'd died on the island, but much later. She'd lived a good life teaching and exploring the islands. Who knows what kind of happiness she found, but at least they were free—both of them.

"Not dreaming, are you?"

"I'll never tell," I purred, cuddling up to his arm.

"Then go back to sleep. We have a few more minutes before we land. You didn't sleep much last night." He kissed my forehead and leaned back in the seat. Once again I cuddled up next to him and dreamed, but not about the past this time.

No, this was different. It was bright and warm, this was a dream about the future—my future.

I looked down at my hands and noticed my perfect manicure and an heirloom wedding ring on my finger. I walked through a bright and airy room, hearing the soft cry of a baby, waking up surprised to find himself alone. "Now, now, I hear you, little man."

I pulled back the bassinet cover and smiled down at the round-faced baby with big blue eyes. For a moment, I felt them beside me, but I felt no fear. I didn't need to look. I knew who they were.

I hoped Calpurnia knew that the curse had been broken and that we were all free now. Free from all the dark shadows of Seven Sisters. We'd given the house to the City of Mobile. It was no longer ours. Our family was free forever.

I hoped Janjak knew that love, true love, always triumphs and that because of his selfless love, we were all here today, happy and safe and alive.

"Thank you," I whispered in my dream as I reached down and gathered my son—our son—in my arms.

~~*

The Stars that Fell

By M.L. Bullock

This book is dedicated to Lula Mae, a true Southern lady—strong, gentle and always believing the best in all those you love.

Though my soul may set in darkness, it will rise in perfect light;
I have loved the stars too fondly to be fearful of the night.

—Sarah Williams, 1868

Prologue

Mobile, Alabama, 1851

Hoyt Page never wanted to become a physician, but his family's good name required him to take up a respectable occupation. Since he loathed the prospect of a lifetime of military service or the pretense of local politics, medicine appeared his only option. To his and his family's surprise, he excelled at his craft.

Generally, Hoyt did not care to engage people in conversation unless the topic touched on a subject he held an interest in, like astronomy or pedigree horses. Too many times, he stood awkwardly through sessions of idle chitchat only to excuse himself before he made the unforgivable mistake of yawning. However, people in pain—that was quite another story. Those he could speak with all day, listening to their list of symptoms, offering comfort and wisdom. Hoyt found he had a mile-wide streak of compassion for the sick and infirm. He himself was a healthy man and had been a healthy child, but his concern for the sick was real and nothing he intentionally cultivated. Hoyt was committed to his work and did not mind the midnight calls, the long rides and the bone-aching weariness. Even those terrifying moments when he left a home feeling powerless to heal— yes, even in those moments, he knew he was walking in his unique purpose.

Just like tonight. He left Seven Sisters with his stiff black hat in his hands, his bag feeling unusually heavy. Every step he took away from the mansion brought him both relief and extreme regret. Jeremiah Cottonwood was an evil, reprehensible man, probably the angriest man Hoyt had ever known. Even Hoyt's father's temperament could not compare to Cottonwood's. The man married Christine Beaumont, the most beautiful woman in the state, but had that satisfied the arrogant bastard? Had her wealth and quiet beauty calmed his rambunctious spirit? No, of course not. Jeremiah Cottonwood had used her with hopes of getting a son—the son he needed to maintain control of his wife's extraordinary wealth. Hoyt's own cynicism surprised him. He shuddered and stoked the fire, which had died hours ago in his absence.

How many times had Hoyt visited the sheriff to voice his concerns over the treatment of Christine and her daughter Calpurnia? At least four now, but nothing had changed. What could he do? With a grimace, he recalled the conversation he'd just had with the sheriff of Mobile.

"Come now, Dr. Page. You should leave the gossip to the ladies. It's not seemly for a man in your position to engage in this kind of speculation," Sheriff Rice had said as his deputy and oldest son had snickered and leaned back on his dirty boot heels. Hoyt had cast a glance at the deputy over his shoulder but continued undaunted, determined to help Christine. "Do you have any proof that Mr. Cottonwood has abused either of them?" the sheriff had asked.

"What kind of proof do you need, sir? I know starvation when I see it. The girl is nothing but skin and bones, and her skin is sallow—both obvious signs of starvation. Her mother can't even speak—she's catatonic, unable to do anything by herself. Something is going on in that house."

"Did they complain to you, doctor?"

"No," Hoyt had said with a surge of desperation, "but I want it on record as the family's physician that I made a formal complaint. I cannot sit idly by while the man starves his daughter to death. God only knows what Christine—Mrs. Cottonwood—has had to endure. Have you ever known me to gossip about a patient or any family that I have cared for? Won't you at least investigate what I am reporting?"

"Surely you understand how sensitive this type of matter is, Dr. Page." Rice had stroked his greasy black beard like it was his favorite cat. His dark eyes were steady and fierce; they seemed to bore into Hoyt's soul. Hoyt had been unnerved that he couldn't read him.

"I am not asking you to arrest anyone. Just investigate. Please, sheriff. I would consider this a personal favor." Hoyt understood what that meant. The next time another fool deputy shot his toe or another one of Rice's relatives developed syphilis, Hoyt would offer his care for free—until Rice said otherwise. *No matter. It is worth it if it helps Christine!*

Sheriff Rice's wooden chair had squeaked as he'd sprung to his feet and offered Hoyt his hand. Hoyt had shook it tentatively and thanked him. "If it will ease your mind, Dr. Page, I will do it. If I see any cause to intervene, I will. You have my word."

With a nod, Hoyt had left the office, hoping to make it home before the rain began to fall. That was earlier that evening—it was now near midnight. It was a fortunate thing that the sheriff had been in his office. He had felt hopeful at first, but it hadn't lasted.

Knowing the sheriff's character, it was doubtful that Christine, Calpurnia and now the new baby would receive any help at all. He sat at his writing desk, wondering to whom he should write—who would help him? There was a judge, Judge Klein, who used to serve as a circuit judge. But what influence would he have here now? He sighed again and reached for the small cedar box hidden in the secret drawer of his desk. Not even his sister knew of his personal treasure trove.

Dearest Dr. Page,

Against the desires of my own heart, I have consented to marry Jeremiah Cottonwood. As this pleases my parents, it also pleases me. Had my father not suffered so extreme a shame at the hands of my sister, Olivia, I may have better resisted his pleas. Olivia has brought a cloud upon our name, and I dare not speak her name in public, not in the presence of a living soul.

Even Louis agrees that my marriage to Mr. Cottonwood is the wisest course of action for our family, although he continues to respect and admire your noble character. Truthfully, he does not express much care for my intended but assures me that he will remain by my side to guide me in my new role as the lady of Seven Sisters.

My friend (I call you this because you are still my dear friend despite this troubling news), you cannot imagine how unhappy I am at the possibility that I will no longer receive your Kind and Enjoyable Favor.

Please forgive me,

C.B.

He had not written back. In fact, it had been a full year before he saw her again. It had been at the Ferguson-Mays Christmas Ball at the Idlewood Mansion. He closed his eyes and remembered that night. The Greek revival home had been full of Mobile's elite....

***

Fragrant greenery decorated the balustrades and mantelpieces, and white and red candles flickered everywhere. The dark wooden panels of the parlor gleamed, and even the servants wore fine cuffs and tails.

Snow fell for the first time in a decade, and the gentlefolk spent a great deal of time gathered at the massive windows, watching the sparkling snow and dancing flakes in the comfort and warmth of the mansion. Two young cocker spaniels leaped up on the back of one of the couches and began barking excitedly. The partiers laughed at the entertainment, and this was the scene to which he entered. With the recent surge of influenza and other illnesses, it was a welcome picture of joy that he rarely witnessed. He handed his hat and coat to a servant and politely nodded to those who greeted him.

Immediately, his eyes fell upon Christine. Her dark blond hair no longer hung prettily down her back in carefully combed tendrils; instead she wore it in an elegant swirl at the back of her head, as a respectable married woman would. Delicate pearls dangled from her pretty ears, and she wore an expensive dark red dress. Some women could not wear such a shade without looking pale, but Christine's beautiful shoulders and bright skin made her look like a crimson angel. Hoyt drew himself up straight, suddenly proud of his height—he was well over six feet and easily one of the tallest men in the room. Although he was thirty, he maintained a trim physique and a healthy metabolism. Some women found him attractive, he gathered, but he considered his brown hair and hazel eyes rather plain.

Hoyt stared—he could not help himself. That he had thus far managed to avoid socializing with Christine had been nothing short of sheer luck. Now that he stood so close, he felt his heart melt. Yes, she had chosen Jeremiah Cottonwood over him, but how could he blame her? She, the obedient daughter of the Beaumonts, could do nothing but obey her father's wishes. Strangely enough, that made Hoyt love her more. Her sense of duty was as fierce as his own. All this time, he had asked himself if he had really loved her, and now he knew the answer. Indeed he had, and he loved her still.

Hoyt silently prayed that Christine would look in his direction, but she was engrossed in a conversation with one of the Maples twins. The hostess of the ball, Margaret Ferguson, suddenly stepped into his line of sight. "I am so happy to see you, Dr. Page. It has been far too long since you stepped foot in Idlewood. How long must it be? Two years? And how is your sister? Still not well? I miss my friend."

Returning Mrs. Ferguson's smile, Hoyt offered Claudette's formal apologies. "Alas, Mrs. Ferguson, she hasn't the strength right now for a night of dancing. But I feel sure another few weeks will have her right as rain. She asks that you excuse her just this once, and she promises she will return to your side in time for the church auction in January."

Her smile deepened, and she gave him a courteous nod. "Of course I excuse her, poor thing. This year's flu has wreaked havoc here too. Almost all my servants have succumbed to it, and now our boy is sick...."

"I pray it leaves your household soon, ma'am." Suddenly, he could hear the swell of violins and the sliding of the wooden panels that transformed the front parlors into a spacious ballroom.

Mrs. Ferguson leaned toward him and whispered, "Would it be vile of me to ask you to check on my Charles before you leave? My husband does not trust physicians, I am afraid; however, I would value your opinion. I cannot imagine what I would do if..." She sniffled as she confessed her greatest fear to him.

"I will be happy to examine the boy, but I am afraid I left my bag in my coach."

Her nervous smile reappeared. "I will ask Daniel to bring the bag up to you. Would it be possible for you to visit Charles now? That way my husband will not suspect anything. I do not think he knows yet that you are here."

"Of course, as you wish."

"His room is up the stairs, to the right. I will go find Daniel now."

"Leave him in my hands. All will be well."

"Thank you so much, Dr. Page."

Although with all his heart Hoyt wanted to greet Christine, he went up the stairs just as Mrs. Ferguson asked. He walked with his hands clasped behind his back, and his stiff collar felt hot and uncomfortable on his skin. He pushed open one door and found a young black woman busily folding linen. "Excuse me," he whispered as he closed the door behind him and continued to the second door. There was a low lamp lit on a desk in the second room, and Hoyt could discern the shadows of furniture, toys and books. *This must be the nursery.* A light glimmered on the other side of the room, and he could hear a child coughing.

He walked quietly through the nursery to the child's room and noticed a draft. He made a mental note to mention that to Mrs. Ferguson. The boy rolled over in his bed and looked up at him.

"Hello, young sir. You must be Charles. Your mother asked me to come see you. I am a doctor. Would you mind if I took a look at your eyes, nose and ears?"

The child said nothing, but his dark eyes had a shadowy, sickly look. Hoyt's heart went out to the poor little fellow. As he sat on the bed, a young man came into the room with his bag. Absently, Hoyt thanked him and opened the bag, looking for his liniment. He felt the child's head—he had a fever, and a high one. Fevers were child killers. He moved the lamp closer to the child's face and examined his eyes. The pupils were dilated slightly, and his throat felt swollen. "Oh, yes. That hurts, doesn't it?"

The frail boy nodded, and Hoyt continued his examination, peering into the youth's red ears and inspecting his runny nose. Fortunately, the mucus was clear with no obvious signs of infection. Either the boy's case was early in the going or this was not the flu. A sharp knock on the door grabbed the pair's attention. Hoyt stood quickly, wondering what he would say if Lane Ferguson came barging in wondering why Hoyt was examining his son. The door opened and Christine entered, her soft red dress filling the small room with happy color. Hoyt's heart leaped in his chest.

"Who are you?" the boy whispered, his voice sounding scratchy and hoarse.

"Why, I am Christine. I am Dr. Page's nurse."

"You don't look like a nurse, ma'am. You're too pretty to be a nurse."

"How charming you are, sir," she answered with a smile. "How is the patient, doctor?" Her dainty hand grasped the post of the twin bed as she smiled down at him.

Hoyt's mouth was as wide as the child's astonished eyes. He could tell that the young boy was quite infatuated with Christine, but who could blame him? His heart beat fast in his chest, and he felt a smile stretch across his lips. "Our patient will recover as long as he gets plenty of rest and drinks all the soup his mother brings him. Can you do that?"

"Yes, I can do that."

Hoyt stuffed his tools back in his bag, tousled the lad's hair and walked toward the door. What should he do? What should he say now?

"Goodbye, nurse. I hope you come see me again."

"I shall, I promise, young man. Good night." She walked out of the drafty room and Hoyt followed her, his bag in hand. They walked into the nursery, where several tiny lights bounced and shimmered; she must have lit the candles before she entered the bedroom. Swells of music rose from the lower floor, and candlelight sparkled from the greenery-decked mantelpiece. Christine took Hoyt's hand and led him to a tufted couch at the corner of the room.

Hoyt's hands were freezing, and panic gripped him. *Should I take her hand or refrain? Should I...what should I do?* He stared at her, not daring to touch her or ask why she had come upstairs. Just as he summoned the courage to touch her cheek and speak his mind, Christine turned her attention to the window. She made a comment about the snow—how beautiful it was, how quickly it would be gone—but Hoyt barely listened. The small talk made him impatient, and he rose to join her. Standing behind her, he quietly examined her hair, her elegant neck, the milk-white skin of her bosom. None of these had he ever had permission to touch or appreciate. How he'd fantasized about her hair falling through his fingers, her upturned face tilting toward his. Christine spun around, the silk of her dress rustling as she did.

Here was the moment he had been waiting for! He grasped her thin arms, pulling her close to him. He wanted to rail at her, yell at her for leaving him, but he couldn't. Her sweet lips beckoned him and he kissed her, softly, chastely at first, then more ardently.

"What if your husband..." Hoyt couldn't help himself. The unwanted words came tumbling forth.

"No! Do not mention his name! Don't spoil this, Hoyt! Let this moment be for you and me!" The two embraced, uncaring that anyone could enter the room and find them. In a ragged whisper she said, "All I need is this moment. That's all I need. Then I can go on."

There was a message in her confession—a desperation that made Hoyt both protective and angry. He felt it with every inch of his being.

Before he could seek the source of her anxiety, she whispered, "Come to me at four o'clock tomorrow, Hoyt. If you don't come, I don't know how I will make it. I need your strength. You have always been my friend and...even more. Promise me you will come."

"Where shall I meet you?"

"Come to Seven Sisters. Ann-Sheila will lead you to me."

"What of Cottonwood? Won't he be suspicious to see me calling upon you?"

"He leaves in the morning. Tell Stokes you've come to check up on Ann. She's been ill recently. He won't suspect anything."

"I will come, Christine."

"I had better go now, before someone misses me. Until tomorrow." She squeezed his hand and smiled at him.

Hoyt's heart banged happily in his chest as he watched her leave the room. He tried to gather himself, wandering around the room and pretending to be interested in the impressive selection of children's fairy stories on the shelf next to the couch. As patiently as he could, he forced himself to wait. No one must know their intentions. Mobile society was unforgiving when it came to infidelity, but was this truly infidelity? Weren't they meant for one another? Besides, Hoyt knew the secrets of just about all these old families—including his own. After what seemed like a lifetime, he walked out of the room and discreetly passed his bag to Daniel, who took it to his carriage.

Hoyt danced a mere four times, drank two hot whiskeys and discreetly excused himself far earlier than his sister would have liked. The entire night, he did not speak to Christine—it wasn't seemly to dance with a married woman unless she was a cousin or a sister-in-law. He could not bear to think he might bring her scandal or heartache.

Jeremiah Cottonwood greeted him during the course of the evening, preening like a peacock and showing everyone the gold chain and watch his eminent father-in-law had given him. After a few drinks, he began to share bawdy jokes. He was careful not to speak ill of his rich wife, but Hoyt was sure he was tempted to do so. As far as Cottonwood believed, he was the luckiest man in the room—twice as wealthy as anyone there and four times as wealthy as his hosts. But that did not humble the man at all. Hoyt considered it a pleasure to leave his company.

He spent a restless night in his modest two-story brick home, tossing and turning, wishing sleep would come and make the time go faster. The next day, he went out for a haircut and a shave, purchased a new shirt and came back home and watched the grandfather clock move ever so slowly. At three, he saddled up his horse and rode toward Seven Sisters. With any luck, Cottonwood would not be home and Hoyt could spend time with the woman he loved.

Ann-Sheila, Christine's constant companion, greeted him at the door. That was highly unusual, as Stokes was such a fixture there. Hoyt was so surprised that he inquired about Stokes' health, but Ann-Sheila assured him he was well and only away on business for Mr. Cottonwood. He knew her; she had been always present during his attempts to court his beloved. With a perfect smile and natural grace, she welcomed him into the plantation. It was a marvelous place with dark plum settees and plush carpets, the likes of which he had never seen. The only problem—it belonged to Cottonwood. Ann-Sheila led Hoyt to the ladies' parlor and began to give him a list of her false symptoms. Eventually the two were alone and the young woman leaned forward and whispered into his ear. "She's waiting for you in the Rose Garden. Out the side entrance just there."

Unable to wait any longer, Hoyt handed her his hat, bag and riding crop. He scrambled out the French doors, his steps hastening him to his deepest desire. The hedges surrounding the garden grew thick but were well-manicured by obviously talented gardeners. Hoyt had never been in this garden, but his beloved left clues for him along the way. A glove here, a book there, and finally he found her.

She sat under a wisteria-wrapped oak, her pale, perfect hands resting peacefully in her lap. When she spotted him, she rose and ran toward him, her eyes never wavering. "I wasn't sure you would come."

"How could you wonder?"

Her arms went around his neck, and they kissed like they were always meant to—with complete and utter abandon. Finally, when he couldn't stand the tension anymore he asked her, "Where can we go?" Taking him by the hand, Christine led him out of the maze to a sandy, narrow path. He could hear water rushing nearby, perhaps the Mobile River. Hoyt never questioned her; he followed obediently until they were alone in a small white cottage. How hurried they had been, that first time together! That stolen hour had been too brief but so passionate. They didn't talk about Jeremiah; in fact, Hoyt rarely thought about him except for on the few unhappy occasions he had to face him.

The following year, Hoyt had the pleasure of helping Christine bring their child into the world. It was an experience he had never expected, and it moved him deeply. He never doubted that the child was his—Christine confided in him that Cottonwood rarely sought her bed, and when he did his drunkenness made it impossible for him to perform his duty; however, she always left him so that he believed he had done the deed.

* * *

Hoyt took a swig of his brandy—it had been a gift from his sister. How close they used to be. How could he tell her about his secret life? Like their mother, Claudette would die of shame if she knew about his love for Christine. He poured another drink and thought about how wretched his situation had become. That night, he had held another baby; looking down at her sweet face filled him with joy, but even that had not roused Christine. His beloved was unresponsive, even when he whispered to her. Hoyt never claimed the child—that would bring Christine to ruin. But what should he do? He must take action! Surely he must! Regardless of the cost to his reputation or that of his family. But for now, he would wait a little bit longer. There was always hope that Christine would arise from her bed, her mind refreshed. Then what would she say to him?

Hoyt loved Christine as if she were his own wife, as she rightfully should have been. Now, they had delivered another one of their children into this world, only Christine could not see the baby, or Hoyt or anyone she had loved. Ann-Sheila, Christine's faithful friend, had been killed years ago, and since then, his sweetheart had been a broken person. Now here was his child, *their* child, yet he could not claim her. This was a sacrifice he must make—for his beloved and their children.

After Calpurnia was born, he and Christine experienced loss after loss, their children dying after a few days at most. Now tonight, another baby, likely their last, was born. Christine was now catatonic from some unknown, unspoken suffering, obviously at the hands of Cottonwood. If he could get his hands on that bastard just one time, he would show him how it felt. How often he fantasized about killing the man—how easy that would be! Cottonwood was a known drunk, yet he had powerful friends, including the sheriff and a few notable politicians.

With a surge of anger, he sent his glass crashing across the room, the warm liquid streaming down the carefully painted gray wall. Finally he cried, collapsing on his couch, the complete powerlessness overwhelming him at last. It was there where he slept until an urgent rap at the door woke him. He'd been dreaming—something vile, something horrible.

He woke in complete darkness, the fire almost gone and the room as cold as death. He squinted at the grandfather clock, but he couldn't make out the time without his glasses. The knocking continued, and he could hear something else...the sound of a baby crying.

Exhausted but curious, he walked to the front door. It was raining—he could hear fat droplets splashing against the windowpanes in the parlor. Lightning cracked across the sky. Hoyt opened the door and blinked against a nearby burst of bright light. His natural instinct was to insist that the young woman at the door come inside out of the rain, but he could not do so yet. It was illegal to give aid and comfort to a runaway slave, and he couldn't be sure she was here on behalf of her owner. She slid back her cloak so he could see her anguished face. Hoyt could tell that she had been crying, perhaps as much as the baby had.

"What are you doing out here with the baby? With Mrs. Cottonwood's baby? Have you lost your mind?" Then the thought suddenly came to him. *What if she was here because of Christine—what if his love had died?* "Has something happened to Mrs. Cottonwood or Miss Calpurnia?"

"No, sir. I mean, I don't know of anything. I'm here because of the baby."

"What? Why would you bring the baby out in a thunderstorm, Hannah? That's your name, correct?"

"Yes, sir, that's my name." Another pop of lightning lit up the narrow lane. Hannah gasped, and the baby began to cry in earnest. "But I had to come, lightning or no! The master said this baby is dead. You have to take it!" She handed the writhing bundle to him.

Puzzled, Hoyt stared at her. "What? She's alive! I hear her crying! Take her home."

Hannah screamed in agony, "No! No, Dr. Hoyt! Please don't send the baby back. Please listen! Hooney told me to come—the master says this baby is dead."

Still stymied, Hoyt pressed on. "Come inside, Hannah, and warm yourself by the fire. Let's figure out exactly what you are saying."

"No, I can't go in there. Hooney said I was to come right back because Miss Calpurnia would need me. The master told us, 'The baby is dead.' He don't want no dead baby! We was to get rid of it."

Awareness rose like a black sun in Hoyt's mind. Would Cottonwood murder a baby? A baby he believed was his child? Hoyt snatched the bundle away from her in desperation. The baby's cries were now more pitiful and heartbreaking. Crying loudly herself, Hannah ran from Hoyt, no doubt back to Seven Sisters.

Hoyt stood in the doorway as the enveloping darkness swallowed Hannah's tiny figure. She was gone from sight in seconds. He brought his daughter indoors and found a warm blanket to wrap her in. As she cried, Hoyt stoked the fire, his mind working to figure out what he should do next. What did this mean for Christine? If it weren't for the baby, he would have driven the carriage back to Seven Sisters right away—thunderstorm be damned!

Leaving the unhappy baby crying on the settee, Hoyt ran to his neighbor's door and banged on it until she answered. He managed to acquire a pint of milk without giving too many details about why. Mixing a little sugar in the milk so the child would sleep better, he fed his hungry daughter until she fell asleep, satisfied at last. He arranged her on his bed, wrapping her tenderly in the soft blanket. He left her only long enough to raise a warm fire in the bedroom fireplace.

For the first and last time, he slept peacefully beside his child, knowing in his heart that tomorrow he must let her go. He had to protect Christine. Let the world believe the child was dead—he knew that she wasn't. She was beautiful, perfect and alive! As he lay in the dark, smelling her hair and allowing her tiny fingers to wrap around his finger, he cried. At least he had this moment—it was more than he deserved. He prayed for Christine and asked God to forgive him for all their trespasses.

He knew what he had to do. He could not keep his daughter, but he had to take her somewhere safe. No foundling hospital. He remembered the young couple on the other side of the county, the Iversons, who owned a small store. They had lost a baby two weeks ago. Surely, they would welcome a child of their own now. But for now, he held his baby close. Staring at her in the dim light, he could see Christine's perfect bow lips, his own eyes and his beloved's tapered, elegant fingers. He lingered in the moment, knowing it would disappear with the rising of the sun. His life had been unconventional, not at all the way he had envisioned, but it was his. Soon he fell asleep, dreaming of nothing and no one.

Sometime during the night, he felt a draft blow through the room.

He smelled roses, the sweet, large blooms of wild roses that grow only on vines. Those had been Christine's favorite. He must have been dreaming— what a pleasant dream! Hoyt whispered her name and felt her cool hand upon his brow and then his cheek. He attempted to rouse himself, but the brandy and the weariness of the day made it impossible to move even his arms. She was near him, somehow, watching over him and their daughter. She kissed his forehead and Hoyt opened his eyes to smile at her. He felt peace and then surprise when he saw that she wasn't there at all. She had been there—he could still smell the roses—but now Christine had gone.

Yes, now she was gone.

Chapter 1

I hadn't had a dream in six months, but I couldn't worry about that right now. Seventy-five of Mobile's most elite and notable women had gathered at the Bragg-Mitchell Mansion to hear me speak about my work at Seven Sisters. I was sure some had come to hear about the crystal chandeliers, the antique ceiling medallions and the expansive Moonlight Garden, but most probably wanted to know how I had "landed" Ashland Stuart. A few others likely wondered if the rumors they had heard about ghosts and such were true. To this crowd of local nobility, I was a nobody, at least in the genealogical sort of way. Even though most Mobilians, the average Jane and Joe, didn't give a hoot about these kinds of things, they really mattered to the old families. For Ashland's sake, I wanted them to accept me on some level.

I had arrived thirty minutes early, and a throng of excited women greeted me at the massive front doors of the mansion. Most were polite, but there were a few unfriendly faces in the crowd. Fortunately, the unspoken rules of polite society did not allow the more curious of my greeters to simply jump in and ask me pointed questions, although it was plain that many of them wanted to.

"You are so lovely! No wonder *our* Ashland was so taken with you," one woman said. She introduced herself, but I instantly forgot her name. I was not too good at remembering the names of the living.

"She certainly is, Margaret! How Sheila cried when she heard Ashland had run off and gotten married!" I wanted desperately to roll my eyes at the idea of Ashland and me "running off" together like naughty teenagers, but I slapped a smile on my face instead. *How do I respond to that?* For the moment, I didn't have to. The ladies remarked on my hair, my pink sheath dress and my fitted green jacket with the three-quarter sleeves.

Is that a Bobbie Brooks dress?

Who does your nails?

Love those shoes! Are they Italian?

I nodded through more introductions and politely smiled as each shared some detail about Ashland with me. Naturally, or so it seemed to the women gathering around me, the conversation steered around to my family name. One lady emerged as the unofficial leader of the group. She was an older woman, my height, with a slim figure and a suspiciously wrinkle-free forehead. She wore pale pink lipstick and expertly applied brown eyeliner that flattered her brown eyes. I couldn't remember her name.

"You from New Orleans, darling? I knew some Jardines from New Orleans once. The family had a delicatessen and muffaletta shop down on Toulouse Street, but it got washed away when the storm came through." The five women surrounding her paused their mini-conversations and observations to listen to my answer. It was unnerving to say the least. *What am I doing here? I almost failed public speaking in college!*

Like a white-haired angel, Bette came to my rescue. "That was Hurricane Katrina," she offered politely. My friend tried to run interference for me, bless her. After all, she had insisted months ago that I come speak about the old house, and I couldn't really refuse her. Bette and I had been through a lot together—we both survived Mia.

"Yes, that's the storm I'm speaking of, Bette." My interrogator continued undeterred, "So you say you're from New Orleans, Miss Jardine—I mean Mrs. Stuart?" She sipped from a white china teacup with a gold band around the rim and an elegantly scripted "B."

"No, I didn't say that. I may have family there, but my mother is from the East Coast."

"Your mother? What about your father? Isn't he a Jardine? Or is that your mother's name?" The older redhead with the perfect afternoon chignon raised her eyebrow as if she had discovered something shocking. I knew my mistake immediately. I wasn't supposed to admit that I didn't know my father or have his last name. *I knew I would screw this up.*

Bette's delighted squeal broke the silence. "Oh look, there is Detra Ann! I am sorry to steal Carrie Jo from you, Mrs. Betbeze, but I have to deliver our speaker to Miss Dowd. No doubt y'all will speak again." Without waiting for a dismissal, Bette gently steered me by the elbow toward a busy Detra Ann, who was greeting a few stragglers. Bette whispered to me as we walked across the perfectly polished wooden floor. "Don't you let that old bat bother you. I have seen her drunk as a foreign sailor and doing the bump at the Mystics Mardi Gras ball, and I swunny! If you shook her family tree, there's no telling what would fall out! Did you know she has an albino sister that nobody sees?"

"Thank you for stepping in."

"No problem. She's as mean as a snake! A snake in designer clothing! The only claim to fame that family has is Yolande Betbeze. She was Miss America in 1951 and, by all accounts, quite a beautiful young woman. Holliday Betbeze needs to get over herself—1951 was a long time ago. Though there's quite a story about Yolande."

Bette always made me smile. I had no idea what "doing the bump" meant, but I laughed thinking about Holliday Betbeze drunk at a ball. "It's okay. It's not like I can hide who I am. You'll have to tell me all about Yolande Betbeze sometime."

"Actually, I was hoping to talk to you later." We stopped about ten feet shy of Detra Ann, who still had not spotted me. "A lot has happened since you've been gone." She dropped her voice and looked around the room before continuing. "I think I found something you should see."

"Really? I'm intrigued." I wanted to know what she was talking about, but it was clear that she was not going to divulge the information with so many ears perked up around us.

As Bette squeezed my hand, her clunky costume ring dug into my skin, but I didn't complain. "You have a special gift, Carrie Jo, and you're not afraid to use it. I admire you for that. It must be hard to dream about someone else's life all the time. Anyway, I won't get into what I wanted to talk about now, but maybe you could come by later this week?"

I nodded, but I felt like such a fake. What would Bette think when I told her the truth? *I don't dream anymore.* What could I say to her? *Sorry, I burned up all my "magic" beating the ghosts of Seven Sisters.*

My dreaming dry spell had me questioning everything. What did it mean? Was it natural? Had I really short-circuited my "power" trying to defeat Isla? I had no idea and knew no one who could mentor me. Funny how you don't appreciate something until you don't have it anymore. I spent so many years trying to pretend that I was normal, and now I would give anything to see Calpurnia and Muncie again.

"Carrie Jo! It's so nice to see you. It has been too long! You look lovely and so tanned—looks like married life has treated you well." Detra Ann had colored her hair during my absence, and the change only made her look more attractive. I could never go blonde—I'd had a bad experience with Sun-In when I was in middle school, and I was sure bleaching my hair would only be worse. The leggy blonde had an angular, beautiful face, and she hugged me as if we were old friends.

At one time her mother had hoped that she and Ashland would hit it off, but fortunately for me, it didn't happen. Detra Ann had fallen hard for Terrence Dale, a talented contractor who worked with us at Seven Sisters. Well, until the supernatural activities weirded him out to the point that he quit. Who could blame him? I sure didn't. I liked TD. We had hit it off from day one. I liked Detra Ann too, but as friendly as she was at this moment, she was changeable. I think Detra Ann primarily did what she wanted to do. As far as marketing went, she was a whiz—but as a future BFF? Probably not. Besides, I had trust issues. My longtime bestie had turned out to be a crazed killer. Apparently, I wasn't too good at judging someone's character.

"I'd say so! Good to see you too. How are things going at the house?" I did not regret our decision to give the house to the City of Mobile, but I did miss it. I longed for the coolness of the Blue Room. I missed the fragrance of the magnolia petals in the Moonlight Garden—I even missed the squeaky stairs and doors. I remembered the first time I walked up the staircase, the cool, smooth wood felt familiar under my fingers. How that first view from the top floor of the grounds below astounded me! It had been love at first sight. Then to discover that I had a heritage there, in a roundabout sort of way, well, that was just incredible.

I did miss it. Even after all the sadness, murder and mystery, I missed Seven Sisters.

"Quite well. We've been packed since the doors opened—people love it, Carrie Jo. You and your team did a remarkable job—you really captured the spirit of the house."

I must have turned a few shades of red because she quickly added, "You know what I mean. We are a month away from Halloween, and we're finally having our first ball." She smiled politely, but Detra Ann was well aware that this subject had been a source of contention between the two of us. When we first met, hosting a ball at Seven Sisters seemed somewhat sacrilegious to me. After all, the ghosts of the past were lingering, unwilling to let go of their lives and their agendas. But that was then—perhaps they'd put all their old bones to rest now. I wanted to believe that, but I knew it wasn't true. Something was undone. Something wasn't right. I could feel the supernatural approaching again, like a lone drum beating in the distance. And just as before, it filled me with anxiety.

Masking my thoughts as well as I could, I smiled at the beautiful, blue-eyed blonde.

"You know it wouldn't be right to have our first ball without you and Ashland in attendance. Would you consider coming?"

"I'll talk to Ashland. He's been so busy with the Dauphin Street project I barely see him. I guess the honeymoon is over now." It was intended as a joke, but it sounded harsh and unhappy.

Bette chimed in, "Now, don't you get discouraged. It takes some adjustment being married. I think you'll find he will come around. He'll balance things out soon. Ashland has a strong work ethic."

Detra Ann chuckled. "He's all work, that's for sure. Please let me know if you can come to the ball. I'll save two tickets for you, just in case. Bette has promised to come—and bring a date."

"Wow, Bette. I'm gone for three months and you find Mr. Right." She chuckled but didn't offer any more information about her mystery date. I wondered if it was her "Steve McQueen" she'd been so crazy about before. "I will do that, Detra Ann. I know that Seven Sisters is in good hands if you're there." I meant it. Like Ashland, Detra Ann loved Mobile and the house. I had no worries that those hallowed grounds would be mistreated.

My heart hurt—I wanted to go home.

"We're offering nightly tours all October, did you hear? Rachel is the best guide—you'd be so proud of her." I smiled thinking of Rachel Kowalski be-bopping from room to room, explaining to the tourists how we acquired the mantelpieces and where the Augusta Evans book collection came from. I wondered what else she might tell them. *"Here's where Hollis Matthews was murdered by an insane historian...and over here, we found the body of Louis Beaumont."*

"I am sure I would be. Rachel is very passionate about local history. I am glad she stayed on with you. How is your mother? Recovering okay?"

Detra Ann frowned and gave an exasperated sigh. "Driving her friends and her nurse crazy. You would hardly know she had surgery; she is on her phone and laptop all the time, still working on behalf of the Historical Society. No way she will be out four more weeks. My guess is she will be back in two, tops. I can't say I'll be sad. That means I can move back to my place even sooner."

I had heard rumors that she and TD had been "playing house" as Bette called it. I was not judging her, but I was curious to hear how he was doing. "I am sure TD will be glad to have you back home."

Her beautiful smile disappeared, and she glanced at Bette reproachfully. "I, uh, TD hasn't been well. He took a trip up to Montgomery, but I think he's home now." She glanced at her watch and promptly changed the subject, "Oh, we better get started." Detra Ann walked away and left me standing by the open French doors.

"Bette? Is TD okay? I get the feeling I said something wrong. What just happened?"

"He left her high and dry." She froze and pressed her lips together thoughtfully. "All men get a little crazy now and then, but that I didn't figure. From all accounts, he's not doing too well. I hear he's had some sort of breakdown."

"Breakdown? What kind of breakdown? Like a mental breakdown? Oh no, this is all my fault."

"No, no, no. Don't take that on yourself. We better head to our seats. My table is right at the back if you need anything." She half hugged me, and I obediently walked toward my seat at the front. I wanted to fuss over my hair and clothing but refrained. My heart sank at the thought that TD was hurting. I remembered seeing his face in the garden the night we fought Isla. He'd dug the hole like a furious dog, trying to locate the box. We'd found it, but at what cost?

I sat in the chair, staring at my empty teacup and saucer. Trays of sweets and sandwiches decorated my table, but I didn't sample any. *Focus on the moment, CJ. You can find out more about TD later.*

I scanned the room as Detra Ann called the meeting to order. Thankfully, most of the tables and guests were behind me so I didn't have to stare at all the faces. Instead, I took in the details of the mansion. This shindig was in one of the front rooms. This particular room had lovely high ceilings, cheerful yellow walls and tons of white molding, decorative columns and a shiny white mantelpiece. A carved marble mantelpiece—in the Federal style, I guessed. The event planner had opted for an intimate setting; there were at least a dozen round tables covered with white linen tablecloths and matching wooden chairs. If I hadn't been so heartsick about TD, I would have cherished every minute of this experience. The Bragg-Mitchell Mansion wasn't as fine as Seven Sisters, but it was one of the loveliest antebellum homes I'd seen in Mobile.

"Now, please make welcome this month's speaker, Carrie Jo Stuart." People began to clap, and I clumsily rose from my chair. Why had I worn heels? Had I learned nothing from history? I was a historian, for Pete's sake.

Carrie Jo Stuart. I still wasn't used to hearing my new name, and I could not help but smile at the friendly applause. I thanked Detra Ann and stood behind the podium, clumsily arranging my notes. My throat felt dry as I stared out at the anxious audience. More than anything, I wanted to jump into the details about our most prized acquisitions. The amazing sculpture in the men's parlor—the delicately carved cherub faces on the mahogany mantelpiece that TD placed in Christine's room. But I didn't.

I decided I would start things a little differently.

Might as well give them something to talk about.

Chapter 2

"Ashland! Are you up there?" I scampered up the stairs to the second floor of our two-story Victorian searching for my husband. According to Ashland, purchasing one of the old homes on Anthony Street was nothing less than miraculous. People loved these homes, and I can't say that I blamed them. From the smooth white exterior to the black cast-iron details, it was a lovely place. Naturally we had worked our magic on the inside, replacing the horrible windows with double-paned Victorian reproductions. This house—Our Little Home, we called it—was indeed little, but it had some historical importance. It was once home to an inventor and author, Mills Broughton. Still, it just didn't feel like home yet.

What did I think? That I would spend my days swanning down the staircase of Seven Sisters, greeting callers in the Blue Room?

"In here!" Ashland called from one of the guest rooms. The soft blue carpet runner felt luxurious underfoot. I pushed on the half-open door and found him rummaging through the closet. "How did it go?" he asked without looking up from his task.

"I nailed it—no tripping or stuttering."

He gave me a disbelieving look.

"Okay, I did get tongue-tied once or twice. Honestly, I am fine." He grinned at me and, as always, I felt my heart do somersaults. He continued to rifle through my carefully stacked closet. I paused to add, "I may have shocked them just a little." I suppose I needn't have told them about my life in Savannah, my brief stint in foster care and how much Mobile felt like home.

"What do you mean? I am sure you were great." His distracted attitude hurt me a little.

"I mean, I told them that I didn't come from an old Southern family. I was just Carrie Jo, historian and researcher."

"Nobody cares about that, CJ. Just you. If you give people a chance, they might surprise you." His voice sounded tired, and I could tell he was in one of his quiet, sulky moods. I wasn't the kind of person to push someone into talking, as I hated that myself, but there were many times in our short history when I wished I knew what he was thinking.

He finally pulled a suitcase from the closet, which triggered a landslide of boxes and bins down on top of him. Laughing, I helped him pick up the books that tumbled out of a blue plastic tub. "We've really got to think about getting a bigger place. Or at least put some things in storage."

"Or you could get rid of some of this stuff. I think most of these are full of your old books and papers."

"I don't have all that much, and I need those for my research. Remember I am supposed to be consulting on the Tillman House. These are important for that project. What about you? I had no idea that you were such a pack rat. You have boxes of baseball cards taking up half the closet." I didn't mean to complain—and I wouldn't have if he hadn't said something first.

"Me? At least I confine my items to the closet. The whole dining room table has become your research center." He frowned, tossing the suitcase on the down coverlet of the queen-sized bed.

Wow, that stung just a tad. His junk didn't really bother me, but I sensed he was angry about something—something about me. "Okay...well, I will do my best to finish my office and keep things off the kitchen table. Um, I'm going to change my clothes—maybe get a shower."

"No need to rush," he said with a sigh, his hands on his hips. "I have to go to New Orleans for a couple of days. I should be back on Sunday."

My shoulders stiffened and my chin jutted out. No way on God's green earth was I going to ask him where he was going. Now I didn't really care! "Two days should be enough time for me to get my office in order. Have fun on your trip."

"It's not that kind of trip—it's mostly for work. I've got to see some people. You can tag along if you like."

"No thanks. Tagging along isn't my style, and I have an office to organize." I strolled out of the room, my hands curled into angry fists intended to keep me from crying.

"Wait. I'm sorry, Carrie Jo. Come back." He shoved a tennis racket and a box of miscellaneous items back into the closet and closed the door. "I didn't mean that crack about your stuff."

I nodded and said, "Okay," leaving the room before he saw the tears in my eyes. It wasn't just this incident—it was where we were now. Like two unhappy strangers forced to live away from home. I walked away, closing the bedroom door behind me, just to let him know that I wanted to be alone for a little while. I knew whatever had ticked him off was not my office.

Everything had been fine during our months in Haiti and the Bahamas, and even afterward when we spent some time on the Happy Go Lucky, Ashland's boat. But those three months were gone, and real life piled in on us. I couldn't help but think maybe we just weren't meant to be together. Perhaps we had rushed into things; the supernatural drama of Seven Sisters forced us to move too fast, too soon. I wondered if that could be true—I suspected he did too. We were from two different worlds. His was respectable, full of tradition, and he was from a family of wealth and means. The world I stepped out of had none of those things. Everything I'd ever had, I had to work hard for, harder than my peers did.

Despite my momentary anger, divorce wasn't a consideration—not for me. I loved Ashland, and I would do my best to make it work, but no way did I plan to be a pushover. *Tag along? What was he thinking?*

Let him go to New Orleans—I could use the time to myself anyway. I stepped into my closet and looked for something to wear. I reached for a pair of old jeans and a soft grey V-neck t-shirt, then went to turn on the shower. As I chewed my fingernail nervously, I heard my phone whistle in my purse. I walked to the dresser and dug it out. It was a text from Ashland.

I'm a jerk.

Walking back into the bathroom, I turned on the shower and stared at the phone. I tapped in my response. *What do you want me to say? That you're not?*

That would be nice.

Sorry. I'm all out of nice.

I threw the phone on the bed, stripped off my clothing and stepped into the warm water. It felt good to be mean for a moment. I typically wasn't very good at mean, but I found married life made me better at it. Not that Ashland wasn't wonderful, thoughtful and completely patient, but living with someone was a new thing for me. I barely had roommates in college because I so treasured my privacy.

When he didn't text me back after a minute or two, guilt washed over me. Maybe this was a good time to test out that old adage that making up was much more fun than breaking up. I wondered how he felt about taking an afternoon shower with me. Before I could call out to him and ask him to join me, I heard the front door slam closed. *Oh well, there goes that idea.*

I rubbed my body down with a thick, soft towel and shimmied into my panties and blue jeans. I pulled on the t-shirt and tucked it into my jeans. I wrapped my waist with a luxurious black leather belt and opted for some black sandals. I pulled my damp hair on top of my head so I could focus on putting on makeup without fighting my wayward wet curls. I laughed when I saw myself in the mirror. I looked, as they sometimes say in Mobile, like a "hot mess." Nothing like Calpurnia and her carefully coiled braids. How times had changed!

"I miss you Calpurnia. Muncie—Janjak, I miss you so much! I hope you're happy where you are," I said to the air around me. I didn't expect to hear anything, and I didn't, but I sensed they were with me still. That both comforted and troubled me. Why weren't they at rest now? For the second time that day, I felt that nagging feeling, like I'd left the water running or the oven on. Something missing, something forgotten—something disturbing.

Putting down the mascara wand for a moment, I closed my eyes. *What is wrong?* I listened to my heart, hoping it would give me a clue, but I heard nothing but the birds chirping outside my spacious bathroom window.

Talking to the air around me I said, "You know, if you're unhappy, all you have to do is tell me. But please—no scary stuff." My phone rang loudly beside me, and I jumped up and out of my vanity chair. "Oh my gosh! You guys have a sense of humor, don't you?" I stared at the phone and picked it up. When I read the screen, my jaw nearly hit the floor. The call was from Terrence Dale!

"Hi, this is Carrie Jo."

"Can you hear me?"

"Yes, I can hear you. How are you, TD?"

"Fine. I need to talk to you—face to face. Can I come by and see you? Or maybe you could come to my place tomorrow? Around four? I should be home by then."

"Sure, I can do that. I'll come to you. Are you still over off Clairborne Street?" I smiled into the phone. I was happy to hear from him.

"Yes, on the corner. I think you've been here once before to pick up something."

"That's right. I'll be there. Would you like me to bring Ashland too?" Reuniting the friends would be a dream come true.

"If it's okay, I'd like it to be the two of us." He didn't offer much explanation, but I chalked it up to male pride. Southern male pride at that. Whatever he wanted to talk about, he didn't want Ashland to know about it.

"I'll see you at four tomorrow."

"Sounds great. Thanks for taking my call."

"Happy to hear from you."

TD hung up the phone, and I walked to the big window that overlooked the backyard. The garden was in a sorry state. The gardenia was overgrown and wilting in the heat, and riotous weeds overran the walkway stones. I couldn't help but think about the Moonlight Garden and how proud TD had been when he finished that project. It had been a thing of beauty—until the three of us tore it up digging for lost treasure.

I held the phone in my hand and pulled up Ashland's name from my contact list but then changed my mind. Why should I tell him about the phone call? He wasn't in an all-fired hurry to tell me who he would see this weekend. Besides, this was just two friends meeting to talk. What was the harm in that?

I felt guilty, even though I had done nothing wrong. Did I really want to start keeping secrets from the man I loved? I walked down the stairs, shocked to see that the front door stood wide open. Crunchy fall leaves had blown in and were strewn down the hall. Piles of them were heaped on the hallway floor as if someone had raked them into a tidy piles. I didn't remember it being so breezy out.

"Ashland?" I stepped out on the porch, past the cheery pumpkins and potted mums. It was only two o'clock, but it was getting cloudy and dark. I could smell the rain on the wind. Looking up and down the sidewalk, I didn't see a soul. Ashland's truck was gone. I walked back inside and called again. Nobody answered. I locked the door and pulled on the knob. I'd have to deal with these leaves but right now, I just wanted to think. I pushed on the door again—now it was closed tight, without even a draft of air around it. I flipped on a light and leaned my back against the door. I coached myself, "Alright, don't be a baby. He probably didn't close the door properly. There's no one here."

Just to be sure I wasn't lying to myself, I walked through the house. Like a teenage girl, I opened every closet just to make sure I was alone. When I had satisfied my overactive imagination, I turned on the radio to a local jazz station. It was too early for wine, but I did help myself to a glass of the peach iced tea Doreen had made us earlier. I had never had a housekeeper before, and the idea had made me uncomfortable at first. But Ashland assured me that he paid Doreen and the rest of his staff well.

Hmm...maybe Doreen had popped in while I was in the shower. Yeah, that was probably it. Anyway, no harm, no foul.

I pretended I didn't hear the faint sound of giggling.

Chapter 3

By six o'clock, I had made a significant dent in the chaos. The built-in bookcases in my office, gifts from Ashland, were full of my research books and a decent collection of leather-bound classics. I arranged them by color first, then changed my mind and lined them up by author. When I was finally satisfied with my library, I turned my attention to the various papers, pictures and other materials I had collected over the years. Ashland had also surprised me with a custom-made desk, deep enough to allow me to spread out my papers but not so long that it hindered access to the French doors leading to the private backyard garden that would one day spring to life. I did love this room; it reminded me of a study in an old 1940s movie, like *Rebecca*, down to the small fireplace on the outside wall. I imagined spending long days here, happily buried in forgotten manuscripts. I wanted to continue working simply because I loved it. That was one reason why I volunteered to help Roz Tillman organize her family's estate. What else would I do with my time if I wasn't working?

One day, Ashland and I would raise a family—I believed that—but now wasn't the time.

Sipping my iced tea, I walked to the window and pulled back the white linen curtain. The sun was sliding down the sky. It would have been the perfect sunset to watch on the Happy Go Lucky. I had meant to catch the sunset earlier, but time had gotten away from me. The jazz station played something by Etta James, which made me miss Ashland all the more. I had stopped checking my phone half an hour ago. He would probably be in New Orleans by now. Maybe I should have tagged along after all.

I opened the door and breathed in the fresh air. The gas lamp kicked on, its amber light casting a few fall shadows in the baleful garden. The all-too-brief rainstorm earlier had blown through, taking with it all the warmth of the day. I closed my eyes and enjoyed the coolness. I toyed with the idea of abandoning my office project and maybe grabbing a bite to eat somewhere—I'd made so much progress already—but then my neighbor stepped out on his porch. I couldn't see him, but I could hear his very private phone conversation. Closing the door as discreetly as I could, I stepped back inside. I turned the lock and nearly jumped out of my skin for the second time.

Someone walked past my door quickly and without saying a word to me.

"Doreen? Is that you?" Setting the glass down on the corner of the desk, I walked into the hallway. "Doreen?" I froze—the front door was standing wide open once again. More leaves were in the hallway, as if someone had deliberately brought in baskets of shriveled leaves and scattered them on the hardwood floor. My half hour of work sweeping them all out earlier had been for naught. I turned off the radio and called again, "Doreen? Ashland?" Chills ran down my spine. *I know I saw someone!* I walked to the front door and closed it again. *And I know I locked this door!*

I didn't bother calling again. Something was happening, but the ghosts of the past were silent, at least the ones I knew personally. The urge to flee was overwhelming. I ran back to the dining room and grabbed my keys and purse off the sideboard. Just as I turned to walk out, I noticed a fat, worn envelope resting on top of a stack of unopened envelopes. As frightened as I felt, it caught my attention. I didn't remember ever seeing it, and I had been working in this room and the adjoining one all afternoon. It was addressed to me with no return address, but that didn't matter. I recognized the tight, controlled handwriting.

This was from Mia! Had she been here? Had she escaped from the facility?

I stared at the return postmark. It had arrived a month ago—no wonder I hadn't seen it. Ashland and I had been gone for months. Why would Doreen set this here and not where she put the rest of the mail? That familiar, unsettled feeling began to creep over me. No, I didn't want to be here anymore. Not right now. Taking the envelope with me, I left my Victorian home behind. I pulled onto Government Street and headed to Bette's house. Anywhere would be better than here, and I could use some comfort and advice. As I closed the door behind me, I heard a stifled giggle. It was her—Isla was here! In my house!

Stopping at the red light just past my house, I reminded myself to breathe. My knuckles were white—I had a death grip on the steering wheel. This was no time to freak out. Surely I was wrong. We had defeated Isla, right? Breaking my rule about using my phone while driving, I dug in my purse. I had to talk to Ashland, now! Trying to beat the light change, I tapped on the screen and called my husband. "Hi, this is Ashland..." Voicemail. Rats! How would that message sound? *"Honey, please come home. I think the ghost is back."* I tossed the phone back in my purse.

Focus on the road, girl! It was a pleasant drive for a Friday night. Not a ton of cars out on the normally busy street, and many of the old houses along Government were decorated for fall. The sight of porches full of pumpkins and the trees draped with goofy sheets meant to look like ghosts helped calm my nerves. Still a bit panicked, I pulled into Bette's driveway. From the road I could see that she wasn't home, and my heart sank in my chest. Her light blue convertible, a gift from Ashland and me, was gone and the house lights except the side porch light were off. I pulled into the driveway just to have a place to think for a minute. I checked my phone again but Ashland hadn't bothered to call me back. *What was going on with him?*

Glancing up at my old apartment, I wished I could barge in and make myself at home. That's where my life here in Mobile had begun, in Bette's over-the-garage apartment. I missed that place. Bienville, Bette's orange tabby, was nowhere to be found. I spied Iberville, his less than friendly brother, staring at me from the gardenias that grew beneath Bette's kitchen window. Now what? My appetite had disappeared, but I didn't want to go back to the house right now. I tore open the package on the seat next to me.

All that was inside was a scrap of paper and a worn leather-bound book. With some trepidation, I unfolded the note. Yes, this was from Mia.

Nothing I can say will ever make up for what I have done. However, after reading this, maybe you will understand.

–M

Refolding the note, I examined the unusual book cover. The leather cover was embossed with the image of a peacock showing his feathers. Flipping on the map light, I studied it closer: *The Stars that Fell* by E. Halderon. I didn't see anything that jumped out at me as I leafed through the pages, just faded letters on delicate paper. I closed the book and slid it back in the envelope. Now wasn't the time to read an old book from a former friend. Lightning cracked across the sky in the distance. I had to go somewhere—I couldn't just hang out in Bette's driveway all night.

Seven Sisters! Detra Ann mentioned that they were having nightly tours during October. I put the car in reverse and made the quick trip to the plantation. It had been three months since I had stepped foot on the property, and the thought of returning thrilled me. Maybe my former intern and fellow historian Rachel Kowalski would be there. I turned down the long drive that led to the house. Someone had trimmed back the hedges, and I could see the top floor of Seven Sisters shining brightly all the way down the driveway.

It was barely dark, but there were half a dozen cars in the driveway, presumably to take the Halloween tour. I was thankful there were no inflatable cartoon witches on the lawn or plastic bats hanging from the live oaks. Detra Ann and her crew had lined the pathway to the house with hurricane glasses that held white flameless candles. It was lovely and simple, evoking a certain understated magic.

I parked the car, stuffed Mia's envelope in my purse and followed the sidewalk to the massive front steps. I paused at the bottom, remembering the first moment I stood here, the night I met Ashland. He had emerged from the overgrown brush like a phantom, but his easy smile had won my heart.

Standing near the front door was a perky young woman, an Azalea Trail Maid, according to her massive purple antebellum dress. The gown moved as she waved to me and walked to the porch edge. She handed me a tour brochure. "Hi! The next tour starts in 30 minutes, but you can step into the foyer and enjoy some refreshments."

"No, thank you. I am not here for the tour. Is Rachel around? Rachel Kowalski?"

"Um, I'm not sure. I don't really work here, but the lady in charge, Miss Dowd, is inside. Maybe she can help you."

"Alright, thank you." I smiled at the teenager and walked through the open door. How different it was now than the first moment I saw it! No more lumpy carpet and musty rooms. The walls were meticulously painted, and hardwood floors shone brilliantly throughout the house. Someone had placed a round table in the foyer, covered with more brochures and information about local historical landmarks. I didn't like that, but the house wasn't mine anymore. Not that it ever really was. It had belonged to Ashland's family, but now it was just another historical property owned by the City of Mobile. Nobody greeted me in the lobby, so I made myself at home. I walked first to the ladies' parlor, where everything was exactly where I left it. As I looked around the room, scenes from my dreams played out in my head. Over by the fireplace was where Calpurnia had first laid eyes on David Garrett. It was such a sad room, really. The side door was closed, but I could hear voices in the Rose Garden.

"I'm sorry, ma'am, but the tour is in the Moonlight Garden now. Just out the back door. Oh, Carrie Jo! I didn't know you were here." It was Detra Ann, surprised but polite.

Suddenly, I didn't know what to say. "I was just in the neighborhood. I mean, I thought I could..."

"No need to explain. Come on into the Blue Room. We can chat in there unless you prefer to sit in here."

"No, the Blue Room is fine." I followed behind her, anxious to see what my old office looked like now. The walls were still painted a cool blue. Calpurnia's painting hung over the fireplace, as it should. All of our desks and equipment had been removed, replaced with period furniture. There was a modern piece, a small love seat, by one of the tall windows. Detra Ann and I sat, and I fumbled for what to say. I needn't have worried; she was still the take-charge kind of gal. *Like I used to be before all this. What happened to me?*

"What can I help you with, Carrie Jo?"

"I, uh, I just wanted to come by and see the place. It feels like forever since I walked these halls."

Detra Ann sat with perfect posture on the couch beside me. I felt an awkward smile stretch across my face. She gave me a sweet smile of her own in return. "I understand that. This place must feel like home. You are always welcome to stop by, Carrie Jo. You know, you're kind of a legend around here. Chip and Rachel just adore you."

"That's sweet to say. Those two were hard workers, and I am glad that at least Rachel is still here. I guess Chip got the job at the Mobile Museum?"

"No, he didn't. To his credit, there was some stiff competition. He has been lurking around here, mostly to see Rachel, I think. He spends a lot of time working with his professor in the northern part of the county. Some project trying to find the old fort, Fort Louis de La Louisiane."

"That's interesting. Wow, if they found the actual location—that would be such an important find." She nodded and then we sat quietly again, the sound of the clock ticking on the fireplace filling the emptiness between us. Seven Sisters still had the comforting smell of wet paint and fresh wood. Maybe we had done something good after all, Ashland and I.

Detra Ann's blue eyes scrutinized me. "I know why you're really here, Carrie Jo."

I caught my breath. "You do?" *You know that I'm hearing and seeing things again? That I'm not dreaming and that my husband barely talks to me anymore?*

"Yes, you're here about TD. Aren't you?"

I didn't know what to say. *I came here because I think Isla Beaumont is in my house.* "I won't deny that I am curious. What's actually going on, Detra Ann? Bette mentioned he had some sort of breakdown?"

She leaned back against the love seat, her posture collapsing under the obvious weight of their relationship. She slipped off her heels and sighed. "You could call it that. All I know is that things were going along fine, and then the incident in the Moonlight Garden happened. Everything went downhill after that. He tried to get over it—I tried to help him—but it didn't happen. He had nightmares, bad nightmares. He'd wake up screaming."

I hadn't known that. How would I have? "Did you ever get him to go to church? You mentioned giving that a try."

She nodded. "He went, but I guess he never found the answers he was looking for. Honestly, I don't know how to help him. I am crazy about him—as you well know—but I am not going to date a man who refuses to work and mopes around all day. Have you seen him lately?"

Now was the time for some honesty. I couldn't keep it from her. "He called me earlier. Says he wants to talk. I am supposed to meet him tomorrow afternoon."

"Carrie Jo, I know you have a big heart, and I care about TD too. But he's not the same guy you remember. He is angry all the time. The littlest things set him off. I mean, I do not think he would harm you, but then again, he is not the laid-back, sweet person we used to know. He is moody and..." Her pretty freckled nose crinkled. "He drinks a lot. One of my brothers is an alcoholic. I know the signs, and I refuse to enable TD."

"I owe this to him. I feel responsible for what happened. If it were not for me, for my dreaming, we would have never been in that garden digging around. I am the reason he is drinking. I have to make it right."

Detra Ann reached across the love seat and took my hand. "You can't help who you are, any more than I can or anyone else can. You did not make TD drink. He fell apart on his own." I nodded, but I was not convinced. "Look at all the good that has happened, Carrie Jo. Now we know what happened here. Calpurnia can rest now. All of them, they can rest because we all know the truth. That's no small thing."

"No, it's not," I agreed. *But they're not all resting!*

Chapter 4

"Detra Ann, I have a huge favor to ask you. You do not have to say yes, but I need to ask it anyway."

"Okay, what is it?" She looked at me intently, waiting for me to spill the beans. Would she think I was crazy? Until this conversation, I would never have believed that Detra Ann cared about how I felt, not one bit.

"First, I promise you, I will help TD. Whatever has passed between you two, I know you belong together, just like Ashland and I do. I can't explain it, but I know." She gave a tiny smile. "Fight for what you have—what you want, Detra Ann. Pray for it. Be patient...he's going to come back around. Whatever is bothering him, we'll uncover it, but I need you to help me."

"What do you mean? I don't understand."

How to explain when I wasn't sure myself? "TD had a part in what we uncovered. He helped us—he's probably experiencing the same kind of resistance we have."

Her big blue eyes widened. "You mean like spiritual resistance?"

"That would be my guess. Now you see why I have to help him—I know Ashland would want that too. Honestly, ever since that night, nothing has been the same. Not for me, not for Ashland. Obviously not for TD."

Detra Ann's eyes betrayed her feelings. She was telling the truth: she didn't understand, and she was definitely afraid.

"You have to keep fighting. There's nothing anyone, dead or alive, can do to keep you apart—not if you were meant to be together!"

At that moment, a glass figurine from a nearby side table, one of the less expensive ones in the arrangement, flew off the mantelpiece and shattered on the floor at our feet. Both of us jumped up, careful to avoid the glass.

Detra Ann clutched my hands, and we just stood there and waited for more strange activity, but nothing happened. Detra Ann breathed a sigh of relief. "What just happened?"

"I'm not really sure, but someone or something did not like our conversation. That means we're going the right way! That's where I need your help."

"Anything. What is it?" Still looking around the room nervously, Detra Ann slipped her heels back on.

"I want to spend the night here, in Calpurnia's room—no, wait. In Christine's room. I won't harm anything, and I can't really explain it, but I feel compelled to stay. You see, I know I missed something. A piece of the puzzle is missing. When I find it, all will be well."

"You want to dream, don't you? I don't know. What would Ashland say about this, Carrie Jo? He loves you so much. If you were hurt, or if something happened to you, he would never forgive me."

"Nothing is going to happen. I am going to sleep with the lights on, but I need to try and dream here. I can't help but feel that I left something undone. I missed something. We missed something. I have to find out what and make it right. Worst of all, Isla is still wandering around. Although I haven't seen her yet, not fully, I know it's her. I need her to be gone! Please, let me stay just this one time."

Detra Ann smiled. "Okay, on one condition—no, two conditions. First, I stay with you, and second, you come to the Halloween Ball here. Agreed?"

"That's not necessary. I can stay alone. I swear I'm not afraid to be alone."

"I am sure you aren't, but you won't be. That's the deal, take it or leave it." She wasn't budging, and strangely enough, I was glad. I hated the idea of taking part in a ball. I was the worst dancer on the planet! But if it meant I could stay at Seven Sisters, I would just have to put on my dancing shoes and a smile.

"Fine, agreed, but we can't sleep together." Her look of surprise spoke volumes. I chuckled. "No! I mean in the same bed. You see, when I dream, there is a chance I can transfer and see your dreams too. I don't want to know what you are thinking when you are dreaming. That's an invasion of your privacy. You can stay in the other room or set up a cot in Christine's room. But are you sure you want to do this?"

"Yes! I want to see a real dream catcher in action! This is all new to me!"

"Well, I'll go call Ashland. I hate to go back to the house tonight. It's getting late."

"No worries, I'll call my housekeeper. She can bring us both some clothes and toothbrushes and toothpaste, whatever we need." We made a little list, including some food, and waited until the guests left. At about 10 p.m., we walked up the stairs to go to bed. My call with Ashland didn't happen. I did get a hold of him once, but the music in the background was so loud that I couldn't hear him. Angry, I hung up and put my phone on mute. I didn't want to hear it if he called me back. I had to focus now. I had to rein in my emotions and focus on Christine.

Maybe that's what I'd missed! What happened to her? To her baby? That had to be it!

I opened the door to Christine's room. I loved this room—it never got a ton of sunshine during the day, but it was bright and had a serene view, even in Christine's day. After I changed into the pinstriped capri pajamas that Detra Ann brought me and we chitchatted a while, we lay down to sleep. I took the bed, which wasn't the original but was in the right spot in the room. We'd brought in a rollaway bed for Detra Ann. She moved it to the corner of the room and made it up neatly with pink sheets.

She piled her blond hair on top of her head in a ponytail and looked at me expectantly. She didn't look a bit tired. "I'm nervous as heck. What do I do?"

I smiled at her. "You don't have to do a thing. I might read a little before I go to sleep. Sometimes it helps me relax."

"Listen, do you really think this will help TD? You weren't just putting me on?"

"I would never joke about this kind of thing, but it's just a hunch. You see, we all had a connection. Ashland was connected to Calpurnia, I was connected to Muncie, but TD...I'm not sure about."

"I see."

"I sound like a crazy person, but all I can tell you is what I think and feel. There are no books I can read that teach me about all this stuff. You know, growing up, I never considered myself a spiritual person. But I guess I am. Weird how that works."

"No, I get it. I've never seen anything. Except that fan stopping on the porch and the figurine crashing earlier. And both of those things happened with you around."

I hadn't thought about that before. She had a point.

"Another thing. If everyone involved is connected, who was Mia connected to?"

"That's what we need to figure out—and what happened to Christine. That's important, that much I know."

We chatted some more until Detra Ann began to yawn. "If you don't mind, I'm going to plug in my headphones and listen to some music. It's kind of my nighttime routine. I love sleeping to music. It drives TD crazy, but it helps me sleep."

"Sure, go ahead. Is this light going to bother you?"

"Not at all. I don't have a problem sleeping with the lights on. In fact, it might help because I admit I'm a little freaked out. Not because of you— because of what happened earlier."

"I get that. Me too, but I don't feel any sort of presence right now. Thanks, by the way. I appreciate you allowing me to do this."

She was quiet for a minute. "I have never known anyone like you, Carrie Jo. Before I met you, I thought that supernatural stuff was nothing but hokum—just shills trying to make money on whoever would believe them.

But you're not like that. You're just a real person. Have you always dreamed about ghosts?"

I had never thought of it like that, and I admitted it to her. "I always just thought of it as dreaming. When I was a kid, I thought everyone did it, but I learned the hard way that I was wrong. Completely."

"What did your parents think? Are they supportive about your...powers?"

"I would hardly call it a power," I said with a laugh, "but I can see why someone would think that. Until I came to Seven Sisters I considered it more of an impediment. It used to drive my mother crazy. I don't think she knew what to do with me. She never quite got it. She thought I could turn it off, like I was having these dreams on purpose. It upset her to think I could see people's dreams."

"So she wasn't a dreamer? A dream catcher?"

"If she was, she never told me."

"What about your dad? Did he dream?"

"I don't know. I never met him."

"Oh, I'm sorry."

"It's okay. You can't miss what you've never known, right?"

"I guess that's true. Well, Ashland sure loves you." She stretched out on the rollaway and smiled. "I've known him all my life and have never seen him fall in love before—ever. Don't get me wrong, there have been plenty of girls interested in him, but he's always been kind of standoffish. Never committing to anyone. I am so glad he has you."

I was curious to hear about my husband from someone who knew him better than I did. "Bette told me that your mother used to hope the two of you would get together."

She chuckled. "My mother is a control freak. Ashland and I kind of got one another—we left each other alone. He was always talking about what he'd like to do for Mobile, how he wanted to restore his family's name. I was always talking about leaving this city. Little did I know I would end up loving it too." She chewed her lip and added, "Everyone in Ashland's world wanted something from him. Hollis wasn't the only one who wanted his money. I felt sorry for him—he got used a lot. Our senior year, we used to skip school together and go to the beach, but I swear nothing ever happened. We didn't like each other that way."

I smiled. "I'm glad he had a friend."

"What else did Bette tell you about me?"

"Nothing bad. Well, except that you were cross-eyed. Imagine my surprise when I met you and you were just drop-dead gorgeous."

"Ha! Don't I wish!" She laughed aloud. "I had a lazy eye for like one summer, but the eye doctor corrected it with a patch. What an amazing summer that was—me wearing a patch for three months, all the guys running the other way. It did do one thing, though. It made me more sympathetic toward people with physical challenges."

"Yes, I guess it would."

She yawned and smiled. "I guess I'm going to try and sleep. If you need me, I'm right here. Kick that fan up a notch, will you?"

"Sure." I slid out of bed and turned up the oscillating fan. It was comfortable to me, but then again this old house didn't have central air and heating. Before I got back into bed, I dug the envelope out of my purse.

Detra Ann had her back to me; she was playing on her phone listening to music. I examined the envelope again and sighed. Why was I doing this? Could I trust anything that Mia might tell me? What did I care about her reasons for trying to kill me—and William? She did kill Hollis Matthews and God knows who else.

Nothing else to see, just my name and new address and a crumpled envelope. I pulled out the book inside and held it under the yellow lamp light. It was apparently the first in a collection of biographies of actors and actresses. The words *THE STARS THAT FELL* were embossed with gold, or they had been. I could see a just fleck or two of gold now. I ran my fingers over the peacock and opened the cover.

Published in 1921 by the Nelson-Howell Publishing Company. Well, so what? What did this have to do with Mia? Another delusion?

I leaned back against the pillows and closed my eyes for a minute. Mia was crazy—there was no doubt about that—but she had been right about so many things. When it came to research and hunches, she was the best. I felt a twinge of sadness. Mia had been the first to discover that the Beaumont treasure was real and the first to have an idea of where it might be. She was right about the fact that the statues were a map, a map that was echoed with the markers in the Cottonwood cemetery. She knew, even before I did, that Calpurnia had never found the treasure.

I held the book to my chest and took a deep breath. I guess it was time to know what else Mia knew. I hoped I wouldn't regret this.

I probably would.

Chapter 5

I could tell the book was old by the font and the page layout. And I recognized that "old book" scent, probably one of my favorite smells in the world. The book began with a note from the author and some commentary about his subjects, which included a woman named Delilah Iverson.

Dear Reader,

I am not merely an author but a collector of unusual lives. THE STARS THAT FELL is a representation of my life's work. Many of you, no doubt, will recognize some of the more famous names like Delilah Iverson, Nate Daniels and Edwin McCarthy.

I must confess that it took some convincing on my part to compel my first subject, the talented Miss Iverson, to agree to speak to us concerning personal matters. In the end, she graciously yielded to my pleas and allowed me that privilege. As I have such great respect for the lady and consider her a dear friend, her story begins THE STARS THAT FELL.

Your Faithful Scribe,

Ernesto Halderon

I flipped to the first chapter and read the first few sentences. Nothing unusual yet. I sighed and hunkered down in my bed, reading by the dim light. A light pattering of rain began tapping against the window. The house was quiet except for the occasional squeak of wood, which one would expect in a house as old as this.

Dear Ernesto,

What should I say? So, you wish to hear my story? I am willing to tell it, but I insist on doing the telling. Perhaps if you knew how crowded my mind would become with the faces of those who are gone, those I have loved and lost, you would forget this idea, have mercy and find a more worthy muse for your book. Yet I can see by the anxious look on your face that you will not allow me to depart without first having told all.

For myself, I cannot imagine that any intelligent person would care to read about my life, for I have not found it so unusual or interesting. Surprising? Yes! But it was my life, and I have enjoyed every sun-filled and rainy day included within it. Even when the storms came and the war rolled over the South like the devil drove it, I wanted to live! I guess you could say that I have a strong will to live. As I am now seventy, this I certainly have proven.

Where shall I start? Should I tell you all my secrets? Whom I have loved and whom I have hated? Should I tell you about the stolen kisses, the promises we made and the inevitable betrayals? Should I tell you about the time I missed my happiness by mere minutes? Oh, but those were the times when I felt the most alive, alive in my pain! If it's a tale you want, then a tale you shall get.

Hmm... I liked her already.

***

My life began quite happily, dear Ernesto. I was not born with a silver spoon in my mouth—quite the contrary! At an early age, I learned the value of hard work, and it is not a lesson I regret having learned. Yet we had fine things when it was possible. Hard work has paid me well, as you can see by my many achievements here. But things were different then.

My parents, Jacob and Katharine Iverson, owned a sundries shop in downtown Mobile, Alabama. My father was also a master carpenter, and his fine Norwegian workmanship was always in high demand. Our shop was right on Conception Street, across from the Irish church that rang bells for matins and whenever a good Catholic child was born in the parish that surrounded it. Near our shop was the dress and hat shop where I later went to work. Our home was above the sundries shop. It was nothing large, but I had my own room, which was quite a treat for the time.

My brother and I spent many happy days there until right before the war. My parents loved America, but my father had no desire to take sides in a war that would divide the great country he so passionately loved. My parents weren't quite Southerners yet, although they loved living in Mobile. My mother always said that Norway was the most beautiful place on Earth but Alabama was certainly the warmest. She liked that. She told me on many occasions that the cold hurt her bones.

My brother had other ideas. Neither he nor I remembered Norway, although he was born there. I was four years younger than Adam, and we were very close, as close as a brother and sister could be. I was born an American, born at home in Mobile. Although he had been born in Norway, Adam was a Southerner through and through. I still remember him young and happy. He had the blondest hair; it always fell in his eyes. Mother would say, "Delilah, cut your brother's hair. He looks like a sheepdog." We would take the chair out behind the shop, and I would cut his hair as best I could. He was kind to me, even when I cut gaps into his hair or made him look like a beggar boy. He would say, "Yes, this is what I wanted, thank you, Delilah." I would smile, and he would give me a coin, just like I had been a true barber. He always had a way of making me feel special.

When other young men his age began to sign up to serve in the Confederate Army, he felt it his duty to do the same. Mind you, we were not slave owners; my parents abhorred slavery, but they equally abhorred the heavy taxation by the Northern states—it was a concern for all local businessmen and indeed businessmen everywhere I would imagine. For many men, that alone was enough reason to go to war. They were fighting for their wealth and happiness. There were plenty of raw materials in the South but no way to manufacture anything. All those factories were up North. Mobile was the Cotton Queen, but she had nary a one cotton processing company.

What arguments my father and Adam would have on this subject! That was a difficult time for all of us. I was only fifteen when the talks of war turned serious; Adam was nineteen and a young man—ready to prove himself as such. My Uncle Lars wrote us inviting us to travel to Canada until the war was over. That idea didn't sit well with my brother; he knew that the local families would call our father and him a yellow coward.

"It's always better to fight," Adam would say to Poppa. Then Poppa would speak Norwegian, and Adam would join him. I couldn't understand a word they were saying. I always regretted that. Eventually, it would become clear that Adam had lost the argument. At the request of Uncle Lars, we prepared to head north to Canada to ride out the war. I didn't want to leave my hometown, but I also didn't want to see the city destroyed. It surely would be—and to some degree it was! Adam was angry, of course. As a grown man, he could make his own decision. I knew he wanted to leave us. I couldn't let him go!

I had followed Adam that afternoon. I watched him walk into the military station and talk to the sergeant. He had not yet signed up, but I knew he was intending to do so. That evening, when Poppa put the violin away and Mother finished the dinner dishes, I ran upstairs and went into Adam's room. He was in bed, wearing his nightgown, his hands behind his head. He stared out the far window, looking at the moon.

"What is it, Lila?"

I sulked toward him and crawled in the bed with him. "You cannot leave me, Adam. You would send me all the way to a land where I know no one. All the way to Canada."

"Hush now. You want me to be a kid forever. It's only for a little while, and then I will be home with my jacket full of metals and ribbons."

"That's not what will happen, and you know it." I held him tight as if it could really be the last time I saw him. He held me too.

"I don't know anything of the sort." He rubbed my hair playfully. "Wouldn't you feel proud to have a brother who served in the war? Wouldn't you want me to show them that I am not a coward?"

"Yes, you could show them, but then I would lose you. That's not fair, Adam. You would do this just to show off?" I sat up, my dark curls falling around my face.

Adam took my hand and kissed it. "You'd better go to bed, Lila. Tomorrow's going to be a big day."

I walked slowly to the wooden door, my lower lip quivering. "Please don't do this, Adam. Will you make me a promise?"

He rolled back over to face me. "What is it?"

"If it is raining in the morning, you will stay with us. If it's sunny, you will go. Isn't that fair?"

"Really? That's the deal you want me to make?" He smiled sadly and covered back up. I was an excellent deal maker—just ask anyone who came to the shop. "That's too easy. You know it's going to rain tomorrow."

"Okay then, let's say that if you see a rainbow in the morning sometime before 8 a.m., you will stay." Even as I said the words, I could see Adam actually seeing the rainbow and then looking at the clock. My mother called it intuition; I mostly kept my knowings and seeings to myself, but that day was special.

Adam laughed at the idea. "Not giving yourself much of a chance to win, Lila. You do like these silly tests, don't you? Okay, I agree. If I see a rainbow tomorrow before 8 a.m., I will stay with you and our parents. We will go to Canada. If not, I go to join the Army. That is a deal. Now go to bed."

"Thank you, Adam!" I slipped out of his room feeling as if I had won the argument. Somehow I knew that God was on my side. Adam would see a rainbow, and he would be okay. Best of all, we would be together.

Little did I know he would hate me for it later.

Chapter 6

Closing the book quietly, I placed it on the nightstand. I didn't want to sleep with it. She wasn't the girl I wanted to see right now. Her story was beginning to intrigue me, especially in light of the fact that *THE STARS THAT FELL* was on Mia's required reading list.

The truth was I wanted to see Christine, to dream about her. Strangely enough, I felt complete peace. I knew I was doing the right thing. I felt no fear that I would see snakes or be chased by horrible monsters. I simply whispered "Christine Beaumont Cottonwood..." quietly until I slipped into my dream.

The air around me moved fast at first, and then suddenly it stopped. I was in Miss Christine's room, standing at the end of the bed. I was standing behind the doctor who was sweating so hard he asked me to wipe his brow with my apron. I did as I was told. My name was Hannah, and I was new to Seven Sisters. I came from some place called Philadelphia, a long way from here. My former mistress, a woman who ran a house of ill repute in the Blue District, lost me in a card game to one of her rich lovers. It had been a joke to her, sending me away from the only family I had ever known. How she laughed and drank and laughed some more that night. Fortunately, my new master was a nice man who taught piano. He moved to Mobile, but he died quite suddenly from pains in his chest.

I come upstairs to bring him his morning cornbread and milk mush, and the old man was cold dead. I didn't know what to do, so I sat down, ate the mush and then walked down to the sheriff's office to tell him the news. Soon, I was sold to another family, and some folks say I was very lucky to get to work at Seven Sisters. It was a grand place with many rooms and plenty of food to eat. But it was full of sadness. Everyone here was sad. At least at Madame LaMont's everyone was happy, but that was probably because they were always drunk. Here, in this big fine house, it was like they was all under some sort of magical spell, the kind that slowly crept in and couldn't be removed no matter how many prayers you say.

The baby's head began to show, but Miss Christine never made a sound. She tried to sit up a few times but refused to speak. She just stared up at the ceiling. Her mouth was slack, and Hooney had to wipe it often. "Miss Christine, please try. Push that baby out, Miss Christine. You'll feel so much better if you do." Hooney pleaded with her kindly, but the woman was gone. She was like the living dead. It broke my heart.

"Hannah, come up here for a minute and let me come help the doctor. You stand right here and wipe her mouth when she needs it. And talk to her kindly. Help her remember who she is and what she is doing. We need her to push that baby out, or the doctor here might have to cut her open."

Hooney's voice was dead serious, and I didn't want that to happen to Miss Christine. She had been a nice lady. She'd given me a new cotton dress and apron when I got here. She'd even made sure that I found a pair of secondhand shoes that fit me well.

"Miss Christine, please wake up." *Hannah patted my face with her hand and suddenly....*

I wasn't Hannah anymore. How weird was this? My gift was changing, and I didn't understand it at all.

Now I was Christine.

I feel warm, like I have too many clothes on. Oh, to be alone and naked with Hoyt! I would take a thousand beatings for him. How I love that man! When will I see him again? Look! There's our daughter! There's Calpurnia, over there in the corner. Why does she look so sad? Don't cry, Callie. I have something for you. I know you will find it.

I wrote you a note, dearest. "Find your True Self, and you will Find a Treasure." I hope you understand. You are our treasured daughter, our daughter. I wish I could tell you...

Oh...why does my stomach hurt so badly? I scream and scream and scream, but nobody hears me. Whose dark face is that leaning over me? I want Ann-Sheila! Where is my friend? No, she's gone. Like Louis.

Louis! Louie! Come back to me!

Look, there's baby Calpurnia trying to walk in her new shoes. How proud I am! My daughter! How she would hate me if she knew my secret! Oh, the pain is excruciating! Why can't someone see that I am in pain?

My Mother used to say that pain was proof that you were alive. That pain was essential for living. Once we stopped hurting, we stopped living. I want you now, Mother! How you would disapprove of Hoyt and me, but he is a good man! I married the man Father wanted me to marry, and see what it has brought me? Nothing but sadness and ruin. Mother, Mother, please don't go. Take me with you.

I try to sit up and follow her, but she leaves the room, a swirl of blue silk behind her.

I see another face now...Isla! NO! NO! Get her away from me! So much like Olivia but so evil! She is my tormentor. The things she told me! I feel the darkness surrounding me!

The lies! Oh the lies she tells me, Louis! My beautiful brother! It cannot be true!

Hoyt! Hoyt! I hear your voice. Help me, please, my love! My own darling! Help me. Please watch over our children. They need you—I need you. Maybe the day will come when you and I can be together truly. How I long for that day. No more sneaking to the cottage, hoping and praying that no one catches us! I would do it all again, all for love, all for my family!

What lovely roses! Who so kindly brought me roses? May I smell them? Bring them closer.

Again, the dark-faced girl is leaning over me. I barely see her smile as she shows me a baby. Is that Calpurnia? I feel a surge of wetness between my legs, but the pain has gone. What has happened? The room has darkened! It is too dark, and I hear voices that I cannot understand.

No, the voices have stopped. All is quiet. All is quiet. A little rest now...

What is that sound? It is the sound of thunder—it is Jeremiah! Make him leave, Hoyt! You do not know how he beats me. How he hurts me. If only you could hear me. Where am I?

I am coming, Calpurnia. My child is crying. Mother is coming now!

Hannah wiped at Christine's face again.

Wait...Christine saw me! I saw her look at me! She saw me! *Who are you?* her mind asked. Her face did not move.

I am a friend, Christine. I am here to help you.

Are you an angel? Are you here to take me to heaven?

My heart melted in my chest. How could this be happening? She couldn't really see me, could she?

Before I could answer her, I was Hannah again.

"Get that baby out of my sight!"

I winced at the master's anger. He would never hit me with his leather strap, but he had beaten many others at Seven Sisters. He leaned over the bed and yelled at Miss Christine, who could not hear him. I muffled a cry as I watched him.

"You were supposed to get me a son, wife! Not another daughter! A son! You have failed me for the last time! Everyone out!"

The doctor stood to face him, his face wet with sweat or tears or both. "No, sir, I shall not leave my patient, even if you beat me with an inch of my life. Your wife has wounds that will kill her if we leave them like this. I will not allow you to harm her!"

"Damn you too, Page! You nosy bastard! Always here sniffing around, sniffing at the skirts in this house. You do what you have to do, then you get out of here. Or I will call the sheriff to come and drag you out. You forget your place, sir."

"On the contrary, I forget nothing." Dr. Page stood up and tossed a bloody cloth to the ground, his hands clenched in angry fists.

With a grunt of disapproval, the master left us alone, at least for a little while. The doctor finished his ministrations but lingered at Miss Christine's bedside. He held her hand and spoke to her quietly, but the missus never looked his way. I thought maybe I saw a hint of a smile on her face, and then nothing but emptiness. Hooney stood on the other side of the bed, sniffing and wiping tears from her face. She whispered prayers, the kind of prayers the missus often said, and made the sign of the cross.

The doctor gave Hooney instructions on how often to give the medicine he was leaving. "I shall be back in the morning to see her. These drops will only help with the pain, nothing else. She needs to be in a hospital. I'll see what I can do to make that happen. In the meantime, you keep him away from her."

"I don't know who can stop him if he means to get to her. All we can do is pray."

"Well, don't defy him, but at least send for me. Surely you can do that. I will not stand by while he kills his wife. The lady needs to rest if she's ever to come out of her sickness."

Hooney promised and put the sleeping baby in my arms. I peered down at her face: she was peaceful, unaware that her Daddy was evil and that her Momma had lost her mind. I wondered what kind of life she would have.

A few hours later, the doctor was long gone and the master was deep into a bottle of corn whiskey. He came staggering back up the stairs, yelling for his wife. Instead, he found me in the nursery with his baby daughter. "That baby is dead," he growled, wavering on his feet.

"What? No, sir. She's not dead—she's sleeping like an angel. She is a beautiful little girl." I smiled, but my insides were frightened and my alarm was screaming at me to run.

"I don't think you heard me right, girl. That baby is dead. You hear me? Dead! Now get rid of it. I don't want no dead baby around here stinking up the place."

I stared at him, blinking wildly. What should I do?

Mr. Cottonwood cast an evil grin. "Want me to show you it's dead?" He reeled toward me but I stepped back, avoiding his snatch easily. The baby began to stir and fuss.

"No! Please! I understand, sir! This baby is dead. I will get rid of it right now." I ran out of the room before he could change his mind. The master shouted something at me, but I moved too quickly to hear but a few words. "Oh Lord, Jesus, Mary and Joseph! Help me!" I whispered as I practically flew down the stairs and out the front door.

"That baby is dead, you hear me!"

I cried as I ran, and Hooney ran after me. "Wait, Hannah! Where you going?" I paused, but only for a moment. I wept as I told her what happened.

"Did you hear him, Hooney? He says this baby is dead. I think he is going to kill her."

"Nothing you can do but take that baby away. The master says that baby is dead, it's dead. Take her somewhere where he can't harm her. I know where you should go—to the doctor! Quick, go now! Follow the road until it forks, then go left like you're going to town. It's the yellow house with the green windows! Go, Hannah!"

The master yelled again, and his voice sounded closer and closer. Oh Lord, he's like the devil chasing me! What will he do to us if he finds us, baby child?

The rain began to fall, but I did not let that slow me. I kept my eyes slitted against the raindrops as I flew down the red clay road. I had to get the baby to a safe place. I had to, for Miss Christine! Imagine someone wanting to kill an innocent baby!

Not tonight. Not if I had anything to say about it!

Chapter 7

"CJ—Carrie Jo! Wake up! Carrie Jo! Now!" Detra Ann's concerned face hovered over me as she roughly shook my shoulders. "Hey, are you with me, girl?"

"What? Is everything okay? Was I talking in my sleep?"

"Try screaming! You almost gave me a heart attack," she said with a nervous laugh. "I thought the boogeyman was chasing you and..." her voice dropped to a whisper, "I thought I heard something downstairs."

Her cool hands grabbed mine, and I could see in the dim light that her eyes were wide and fearful.

"I'm sure it's nothing. Just me scaring up some nightmares. I apologize, Detra Ann. Let's try to get some sleep. I'll keep quiet now, I promise."

She nodded but didn't move. She was convinced she'd heard something. I glanced at my watch; it was 4:30. We remained quiet, holding hands, waiting for any sound. I felt the hair on my arm prickle up in alarm and anticipation. Yep, something or someone was with us at Seven Sisters.

After a minute, I asked in a whisper, "What did it sound like?"

"Kind of like..." Before Detra Ann could answer, I heard a loud thump coming from the bottom floor. "Like that!" The willowy blonde froze, unsure what to do.

"I heard it too this time." The thump was a footstep. Someone was walking—no, stomping—up the wooden staircase. *Stomp, shuffle, stomp, shuffle...*

"What do we do?"

I slung the covers off and ran to the door as quietly as I could. Yes, I had set the lock, but I was not leaving anything to chance. "Hand me that wooden chair!" Detra Ann did as I asked, and I slid the chair under the doorknob hoping that would protect us.

Stomp, shuffle, stomp.

"Is that Ashland? Is this some kind of joke?"

"What? No!" I whispered furiously. "He doesn't even know we're here—nobody does!" The stomping continued, and the sound was very close to us now.

"Oh my God! It's at the top of the stairs now! What do we do?" Detra Ann was nearly in tears.

I grabbed my phone off the nightstand and dragged her by the hand to the far corner of the room, nearest the window. It was too late to call anyone—the intruder was here with us. The fear mounted as the stomps sounded louder and more threatening. Suddenly, the sound stopped, and I squeezed Detra Ann's hand as fiercely as she squeezed mine. I watched in terror as the doorknob began to turn ever so slowly. I heard Detra Ann gasp. The doorknob turned easily now, more quickly. I was just about ready to call out, to scare away whoever stood outside the door, when I heard a voice growl, "Christine!" I knew that voice—it was Jeremiah Cottonwood! There would be no reasoning with him—not in this life or any other.

"Oh, hell!" I began to pat the wall frantically. I shoved the phone in the pocket of my pajama pants and searched in the near dark.

"What are you doing?" Detra Ann exclaimed, nearly frightened out of her mind.

"Looking for a door! There has to be a way out of here!"

"There is! Move that picture!"

I lifted the heavy-framed picture off the wall and set it on the floor. The ridge was discernible now, but only barely.

"Christine!" the voice insisted, angry that he could be denied access. The doorknob continued to rattle until the door opened a tiny bit. I heard the wooden chair crack and creak. The phantom paused his assault, and it seemed I could hear him breathing. *But that can't be true! He can't breathe! He's been dead for over a hundred and fifty years!*

"Here!" Detra Ann pushed on the corner of the hidden door, and the latch gave way. A small door, just big enough for one person at a time to fit through opened, and she scurried through. I climbed in behind her, closing the door furiously just in time to hear Christine's bedroom door, the chair or both splinter behind us.

"Run, Detra Ann!" I yelled at her.

I heard her sob, "I can't see!"

I stepped in front of her. "It's okay. I have my phone. Follow me." We began to move quickly. The dust under my feet felt sticky and thick. I held her hand and turned on the flashlight app on my phone so we could work through the stuffy labyrinth. Finally, we came to a short set of stairs. We almost fell down them, but we managed to control our fear long enough to get downstairs without killing ourselves.

Above us, we could hear the stomping grow louder. Thank God, the malevolent ghost of Jeremiah wasn't in here with us. Detra Ann sobbed again, and I tried to comfort her. "It's okay, I promise. We'll be out of here soon."

"If we leave our hiding spot, won't we still be in the house with that thing?"

"Just stay close." At some point during our frantic escape, I hit my mouth. My lip felt swollen, and I could taste blood. Still, I was alive—we were alive!

The air smelled stale, but I forced myself to breathe as normally as I could. We walked past another hidden door; I could see an unearthly light shining from behind it. I thought about pushing it open, but a fleeting shadow passed across the light. Nope! Not this one! I couldn't tell where we were— probably somewhere behind the dining hall wall. In the distance, I could hear what sounded like a piano crash and the furious stomping became louder, so loud that it sounded like a freight train. Forget controlling my breathing—it was so hard that my chest hurt; sweat dripped down my face and neck. I dragged Detra Ann behind me and ran on into the dusty darkness. She stumbled as I came to a stop. I flashed my light against the wall. It had to be here somewhere! It had to be! Suddenly, the door popped open without any help from us. We froze on the spot, neither of us breathing or moving. Nothing came. I pushed it open.

We couldn't stay trapped in the wall all night. At any moment Jeremiah Cottonwood could decide to appear, and who or what could stop him? "When we get out, run to the right to the back door. You ready?"

"I don't know, but let's do this." Even in the shadows, I could see the determined look on her face. "Don't you dare let me go!"

"You either!"

I pushed the door open wider. It struck a small side table, slinging picture frames and porcelain pieces to the ground. We were out of the wall and didn't waste time dawdling in the dining room.

"Christine," the disembodied voice growled at us from somewhere near. We couldn't see him, but it was as if he were everywhere at once. Suddenly, the stomping above us stopped but there was another sound coming from the window. A windstorm blew outside, and the branches of the live oaks were slapping at the windows viciously as if they would whip us too. For some reason, it entranced me.

"Don't stop!" Detra Ann yelled at me. It was her turn to drag me now. She ran toward the open door; her ponytail had come undone, and her blond hair flew behind her. I held onto her hand for dear life.

"Christine! You are mine!" I heard the voice yell—Jeremiah's anger was palpable. I slid on the freshly waxed wooden floor of the hallway that led to the back door. I ungracefully sailed against the wall and crashed to the ground, and my knee crunched as I landed. Detra Ann struggled to help me up, and I yelped in pain.

"Run, Detra Ann! Go!"

"I'm not leaving you, so get your ass up—now!" Her adrenaline surging, she practically jerked me up off the ground, snatched my arm and slung it over her shoulder. The green potted palms begin to move under the influence of the unearthly wind. The brochures and flyers that had been so neatly arranged on the welcome table were now scattered about the room. I heard a distinct giggle—a familiar giggle. Then whispered words sent chills deep into my soul: "You'll be worm food now, I suppose!" *Isla! They were both here!*

The massive double doors that led to the back garden seemed so far away, but we awkwardly ran together. I ignored the pain, determined not to hinder Detra Ann from escaping Seven Sisters.

"Oh God—oh God—oh God!" she whispered like a chant. We could feel the supernatural presence surging, swelling behind us like a cloud of evil that threatened to overwhelm us and steal our warm bodies from the land of the living. If we turned to look, I was sure we would see something awful, something we would never forget. There wasn't a chance that I was going to look behind me. I closed my eyes and ran for the door on my damaged knee.

"Keep moving!" I shouted to myself and to Detra Ann, and then my phone began to ring in my pocket. Only it wasn't my ring tone that played—it was the tune from Christine's music box! No way was I going to stop to look and see who called me.

It was my turn to panic. "Oh God!" Somehow, we made it to the back door. I hung on Detra Ann's shoulder as she flipped the dead bolt. This time I did look—I saw Isla hovering against a wall, floating above us, grinning as she watched us fight for our lives. I did not see Jeremiah Cottonwood, but a solid black cloud was moving toward us from the stairway. He was coming! My phone rang nonstop in my pocket; Christine's song played at an unearthly decibel. Suddenly, Detra Ann swung open the door and everything stopped. Isla and the black cloud disappeared. The stomping, the laughter, the wind—it all stopped.

"Come on, CJ! No looking back. Let's go!"

I don't know how we managed it, but we made it to the first cast-iron bench in the Moonlight Garden. It was pitch-black out. The skies were clear, with no storms at all, but the stars had begun to fade. The sun would make its appearance soon. I leaned on Detra Ann's shoulder, trying to catch my breath.

"We're okay. We're alright," she panted, her voice filled with relief. She hugged me and began to cry.

I patted her back to comfort her and finally whispered, "Yes, we are." *Please let this be the end of it!* I reached in my pocket and pulled out my phone.

The message on my screen read: *You Have 2 Missed Calls!* Curious to see what it would say, I tapped on the screen. *Unknown Caller at 5:00 AM.*

We sat staring at the open door, but nothing ever emerged. I didn't know what Detra Ann was thinking, but I was ready for this dream catching experience to be over. My knee was screaming, and my blood was still pumping furiously from our unexpected run through the house.

"Is it always like that?"

"No, it's not, I promise. Or I would lose my mind."

"I'm not sure I haven't lost mine. I don't know how you live with this. Now I see why TD is having such a hard time dealing with his experience."

"It's a rare thing, but it is disturbing when it happens. Something happened tonight, something triggered Jeremiah Cottonwood's anger. He didn't like us in his wife's room."

"Maybe he's worried that you might find another treasure?" I could tell she was doing her best to reason away the spirit's attack.

"Maybe he was—but I don't think so. He wasn't after the treasure; he wanted Christine, remember? He kept calling her. I don't know what just happened. I need time to think."

"So do I! I'm ready to go, but my keys are upstairs. You need to go to the hospital."

"Not me. I'm fine. What about you? " My knee was throbbing, but I didn't want to go anywhere until I was sure we were safe.

"Well, there appears to be only one thing to do."

"Detra Ann—you can't go back in there!"

"No worries, girl. I don't plan on it! The police will be here soon. We tripped the silent alarm when we walked outside without entering the code in the keypad."

"Oh, thank God. Then maybe we can go home. I have had enough fun for one night." I put my arms around her and hugged her. She'd said she wanted to hang out with a dream catcher. Well, be careful what you wish for. Sometimes the dream sticks around and follows you home! I hoped Jeremiah would stay within the confines of Seven Sisters and not show up at my new place as I suspected Isla had been doing.

There had to be something I could do—then I remembered something Henri Devecheaux once told me. "Spirits don't come unless they are welcomed, and they only stay when they have a claim to something. You want to keep a spirit away? Don't welcome it, and don't give it a claim on anything you own."

That might be easier said than done, though. I was beginning to think Isla had her sights set on Ashland.

And alive or dead—she never played by the rules.

Chapter 8

Thankfully, it wasn't Detective Simmons who responded to the alarm. It must have been too early in the day for her. No doubt if she had heard the call, she would have been here, ready to lick her pencil and give me unbelieving stares. We'd certainly given her enough to think about. That reminded me—I needed to call her about Mia. I felt sure that the woman who tried to kill me shouldn't know my new address, and she sure as heck didn't need to be writing me.

During our ten-minute wait, Detra Ann and I concocted a story to explain why the house was in such a state and why we didn't want to go inside. We'd say a squirrel found its way in the house and we ran out. That might also explain why it looked like a tornado had blown through the downstairs foyer. The officer, an older gentleman, didn't doubt us—he seemed happy to "rescue" two pretty young women from a dangerous rodent. He did a search of the house and declared that whatever animal it was must have made a break for it because the house was all clear.

"That's great, but I'm not staying. If you wouldn't mind, we'll just grab our things and leave."

Officer Thornton looked tired after his sweep. "I can't understand why you were here to begin with. This isn't a residence, is it?"

"We were working late getting some things ready for the Halloween Tour and figured we'd just spend the night. Then that rowdy squirrel came in and liked to have scared us to death." Detra Ann was doing a marvelous job playing her role as the helpless blonde who needed a big strong man to rescue her. I found it funny to say the least.

"Oh, I see. Ended up scaring yourselves silly, did you?"

I could tell by the way Detra Ann's back stiffened that she didn't care for his tone. I smiled and said, "Well, you know how it is in these big old houses. Give us just a minute." We walked up the stairs and gathered our stuff.

"What a jerk!"

"Let's just get out of here. I guess we should change first. I can't drive through Mobile in my pajamas. People think I'm nuts anyway."

"Only Holliday Betbeze," Detra Ann said with a giggle as she pulled on her jeans. "That was quite a speech you gave at the Historical Society. I can't believe you told those women your mother was mentally ill."

"They would have heard about it eventually. I figured why put off the inevitable? I believe in taking charge of my life in every way possible." We didn't bother making the beds or cleaning up the foyer. The clock said 5:30—still too early to be up. I wanted nothing more than to go home and climb into bed with Ashland, but he wasn't there. I didn't want to be alone again, not right now.

As if she'd read my mind, Detra Ann asked, "Want to grab some breakfast? I don't think I'm ready to go home right now."

"Me either. That sounds wonderful." We thanked Officer Thornton, and Detra Ann locked up Seven Sisters again. I wondered what her employees would think when they saw the mess we'd made.

Still a bit jumpy, I rode in my car alone—I refused to leave it on the property. I turned the radio to a boring talk radio station. Just something to keep my mind busy, make me feel normal again. With a sigh, I followed Detra Ann, wondering what we would talk about over breakfast. I didn't know where she was going, and I didn't really care—I just wanted to get away from Seven Sisters. I kept hoping to see the fat orange sun climb above the Mobile Bay. I wanted this night to be officially over! Instead, steel gray clouds shielded the sun, so I was left listening to WPMX for comfort. Mike and Dave were no less boring than usual. I needed boring at the moment.

I turned up the volume, listening to Mike extol the virtues of the new roundabout that the city had installed on Old Government Street. He was making some good points when the radio began to distort. I hit the tune button, but to no avail. "Well, rats." Watching the road with one eye, I tapped on the radio buttons in search of another channel. I felt tired and still a bit freaked out. I switched from the FM radio to the satellite radio, and still nothing. *What? How is that possible? Something should be working.*

Stupidly, I turned up the volume as if that would help.

Help me...

Help me...I can't see...

The voice was faint, almost indiscernible. I turned up the volume again but heard nothing.

"Hello? Is someone there?"

You...help me... You saw me...

Suddenly and with perfect clarity, I knew who was talking to me. It was Christine! We had connected in the dream—somehow, she had seen me. Now here she was being spooky in my radio. Out of sheer fright, I turned off the radio. The light changed and Detra Ann was making a right turn into By the Bay Bed and Breakfast. I pulled into the spot beside her and put the car in park.

What had I done? Why had I gone back to Seven Sisters? Ashland warned me to stay away, but I didn't heed his advice. Now my radio was talking to me and angry ghosts chased me out of the home I'd loved. I laid my tired head on the steering wheel, but I didn't cry. I was too tired to cry.

Detra Ann opened the car door, squatted down beside me and patted my back. A few moments later, she said, "Let's go have some coffee. Hardly anybody comes here, and I know the owner. We can sit on the back porch and look at the water. We don't have to talk if you don't want to. Sound good?"

"Sure." Coffee sounded really good right now. I grabbed my bag and followed her to the back porch dining area. There was an old man sitting at a faraway table reading his Mobile Press Register and drinking coffee. He politely raised his cup to us and then went back to his paper.

A middle-aged woman wearing a Smuckers jam apron walked out on the porch with a pot of coffee and two cups. "Good morning, Detra Ann. Y'all having coffee this morning? You're up awful early."

"Good morning, Gloria. Yes, ma'am, and a basket of biscuits too, please."

"Sure thing. You want those with fig or peach preserves?"

"How about both?"

Our friendly server smiled as if she'd just been told she won the lottery. "Wonderful! I'll be right back." She laid a small laminated menu on our table along with the coffee and cups. Detra Ann poured two steaming cups of black coffee and placed one in front of me.

We sipped for a minute, and the silence was wonderful. Gloria came back with the promised hot biscuits, and I helped myself to one. They smelled buttery and delicious—how could I resist? This was normal, this was what I needed, to drink coffee with a friend. She was a friend, wasn't she? I placed an order for scrambled eggs and bacon, and Detra Ann asked for grits and eggs.

"I heard a voice on the radio," I confessed.

"What? Like a talk show?" Her tired eyes were apprehensive. She had to be thinking I was nuts.

"No, not like a talk show. Something happened in my dream tonight, something that has never happened before. Christine saw me. I think, no, I *know* she knew I was there! She asked me who I was—she thought I was an angel come to take her to heaven!"

"What? That's impossible, CJ."

"No more impossible than dreaming about the past and going back in time! No more impossible than a dead man chasing us out of his house!"

"Don't get mad. This is all new to me. What happened? I mean, how does it normally work? Is it like a vision?"

"I transferred tonight—I saw from different viewpoints. That means instead of being just one person, I was two. There was a girl there, Hannah—she was a young slave. At times, I was looking through her eyes, and at other times I was Christine Cottonwood. It seemed that when they touched, I switched viewpoints, like I was watching a movie. That's never happened before. I wonder what it means."

"I'm dying to know, what did you see?"

"I saw Christine giving birth to a baby, and she didn't even know she was there. Her mind was so fragmented, so fragile. Isla really did a number on her, and so did Jeremiah. I think he'd been abusing his wife to the point that when she heard Louis was dead, she checked out. But that's only a guess right now."

"Checked out how?"

With shaking hands I put another biscuit on a china plate and buttered it. Ooh...I felt dizzy. I realized it had been way too long since I'd eaten.

What a pretty pattern! Blue butterflies dancing around the rim, such a happy dish. I loved butterflies. I had forgotten how much...

"Carrie Jo?"

"What?"

She laughed nervously. "Checked out how?"

"Oh, when I was her, she went from one thing to the next, with no logical train of thought. One minute she was seeing Calpurnia dancing in the corner of the room, and the next she was walking through a garden with her brother. She couldn't have been older than twelve. Next she was... oh my gosh!" I took a sip of my coffee, hardly believing what I was remembering. My brain felt tired—no, sticky, as if there were some type of residue left over from my dream catching. I felt off—weird.

"Christine was *avoir une liaison* with her doctor, and it wasn't just a one-time thing. She was in love with him—she thought of him as her *vrai mari*. Christine loved him more than anyone, except her daughter."

Detra Ann laughed again. "I didn't know you spoke French. You are a girl of hidden talents, Carrie Jo." She smeared peach preserves on a biscuit and popped a piece in her mouth.

I stared at her like she'd slapped me. "I don't speak French. I never have."

"Surely you must. You just spoke it perfectly. Maybe you took a high school or college course?"

"I didn't take French ever. I took Spanish and Latin." We stared at one another.

What a pretty lady. Such vibrant blue eyes, trustworthy eyes. Louis says the eyes are the windows of the soul. Such a poet he is!

What was happening to me? I clutched my napkin like it was a life preserver and I was drowning.

"Well, you must have heard Christine speaking French and the words stuck in your brain. That makes sense—well, as much sense as any of this does. Hey, are you okay?"

"I...uh...yeah. I'm fine."

"So Christine and her doctor? That's kind of scandalous, especially for those days. Tell me what you know."

Hoyt! Where are you, Hoyt?

Oh my God! I am going nuts! I should have listened to Ashland. I should never have gone back to Seven Sisters. What was I thinking? ...Hoyt?

I practically leapt out of my chair. "Detra Ann, thank you for breakfast, but I think I better go home. I'm tired and my mind is racing..."

"Aw, but we're just getting to the good part."

I reached for my bag. She was chewing on her biscuit, and I could see our food approaching. I couldn't stay—I couldn't have a meltdown here in the middle of this nice bed and breakfast.

"I'm sorry. I'll call you later." I stumbled trying to get off the porch but I kept on walking. *I have to go home...take me home!*

Detra Ann followed me to the car. She was talking to me, but my ears weren't listening. I felt tired, ready to go to sleep. *Yes, maybe a nap would calm my nerves. Calpurnia...come lie down with Mother.*

"Carrie Jo? Let me come with you. You don't look well."

"Je vais bien," I lied with a smile, feigning happiness, "really I am."

"But you just..."

"Please, let me get some rest and I will call you later. I promise." I closed the door and pulled out of the gravel parking lot. As I turned on to the side road, I glanced at myself in the mirror. Yes, I was still Carrie Jo Jardine Stuart, but there was something else going on behind those green eyes. I couldn't see her, but I knew she was there.

Now it all made sense. Why Jeremiah chased us through the house! Why he tried so desperately to stop us from leaving! She had made her escape through me! She had been with us the whole time, and her husband knew it.

Somehow, Christine Beaumont Cottonwood had returned, but why? And for how long? How would this end?

This time, I really had gone too far.

Chapter 9

Carrie Jo drove away, kicking up rocks from the back tires of her tan Cadillac. She sped out of the parking lot without even a courtesy wave. *Ashland is going to kill me!* I walked back to the porch and made excuses to Gloria about why my friend took off so suddenly. "She's not been feeling well. This looks delicious!" I smiled and Gloria walked away, happy that at least I was staying to enjoy her home-cooked breakfast.

I took my phone out of my purse and stared at it as I poured myself another cup of coffee. What was I going to say to him?

Sorry. I had a sleepover at Seven Sisters with your wife, and now she's gone a little nuts.

No. That wasn't true. She believed what she told me about her dream catching. That much I was sure of. CJ had her secret power, but I had one too. Well, a couple actually. I was a human lie detector. Whenever someone lied to me, big or small, bells went off. Carrie Jo didn't have an inch of dishonesty in her—not until she told me everything was okay. In general, she had a unique honesty about her, but now my "bells" were ringing like crazy. She wasn't okay, and that was partially my fault.

Ashland had asked me to befriend his wife and help her get to know our circle of friends. But with everything going south with TD, and with the added responsibility of my sick mother, I just hadn't gotten around to it. I'd had every intention of hosting a party for the new couple or something, but then I got started on the Halloween Ball. At least Carrie Jo had promised to attend. That would be the perfect time to present her to everyone...if we got that far. I wasn't sure she'd ever want to step into Seven Sisters again—me either for that matter. I didn't know what happened with her dreams, except the little she told me. But what happened afterwards, that was completely real.

In just about an hour, I would call Rachel Kowalski and give her a heads up on the mess we had left behind. I planned to use the invading squirrel defense, the same as we had with the cop. Hopefully she wouldn't ask too many questions.

It was early, but I called Ashland. He needed to know what happened. I figured I might as well fess up and get it over with. "Hey, did I wake you?"

"Of course not. What's up?"

"It's Carrie Jo."

"What is it? Is she okay?" I could hear the desperation in his voice, which made me feel even guiltier. What kind of friend was I? So far, he'd proven to be a better friend to me than I had been to him. I would never forget what he did for me—how he stayed by my side after Fred Price assaulted me. He was there every step of the way, and I could never repay him. I had five brothers, but Ashland had proven to be a better brother than any of them. It was too bad we didn't have romantic feelings for one another. According to my mother, we should have skipped the love part.

"Love can come after marriage, Detra Ann," she'd said. "Compatibility is much more important to a happy marriage."

I had replied, "Not for me. One day, I'll fall madly in love and that will be it." I knew the truth—she wasn't actually concerned about my happiness. The only thing she truly cared about was where our family ranked on the city's "Most Wealthy" list. My marriage to Ashland Stuart would have permanently secured for her the top spot, right over the head of Holliday Betbeze. *Sorry, Mom. I'm not going to use my friend to help you get a better parking spot and boost your ego—or your bank account.*

"Yes, she is fine—at least I think she is. She came to the house last night, Ash, to Seven Sisters."

"What? Why?"

"I think she wanted to talk about TD, but then I made a mistake. Don't be mad, but I let her stay there last night."

"Are you crazy? That's the last thing she needs!"

"For the record, you never told me to lock her out! Besides, I was with her. As much as I love you, I'm not your wife's keeper!" The old man across the porch gave me an irritated glare and then turned the page of his newspaper, pretending that he wasn't listening.

He sighed heavily into the phone. "What makes you think she's not okay? What happened? She had a dream?"

In a whisper I told him, "Yes, but the real strangeness didn't happen until after she woke up. I think she brought something back with her. We got chased out of the house this morning—whatever it was nearly tore the place up. We got out okay, but it was the weirdest thing I have ever experienced. This ghost—this entity, it was after us, Ashland. After her, I think. I thought she was handling it all well. I mean, I'm the one that should be freaking out—I had no idea this would happen. But then it just went wrong. I took her to breakfast, and that's when she went all strange."

"Strange how?"

I gestured wildly with my hands, as if he could see me. "All daydreamy and confused. And another thing...does she know French?"

"No, I don't think so. We were just in Haiti, and she never spoke it there."

"She's speaking French."

"What?"

"I can't be sure, but I think she's kind of losing it, you know, mentally. Did you know that her mother is mentally ill? She told the entire Historical Society, Ash."

"I know all about Carrie Jo, and she's no crazier than you or I. Where is she now, Detra Ann?"

"I took her to breakfast at Gloria's place, but she went home before our food arrived. She should be there now. You should call her."

"I've been trying! Now I know why she hasn't been answering. I need you to go there and stay with her until I get home. Please don't leave her alone. If you can't go, then I can call Bette. I'm on the way, and I can be there in an hour and a half—two at the most."

I poked at my eggs with my fork and leaned back in the wicker chair. "Fine. I'll go, but I'd like to go home and change first. And when you get home, we've got to talk about that house. How am I supposed to go back there now?"

"Don't wait, please. I need you to go now."

"What am I supposed to say to her? 'Please let me in—your husband sent me over to spy on you?'"

"No, but you can tell her that I heard she wasn't feeling good and that I asked you to come over. It's the truth—she hasn't been taking my calls, and I *am* worried about her. We've not been...well, we have had some problems lately."

My heart sank a little. Carrie Jo had hinted at this. I wanted Ashland to be happy—I knew he cared for Carrie Jo a great deal—probably more than anyone else I'd seen him with. For goodness' sake, he married her.

"Okay, I'll do it. Be safe. I'll see you there."

I hung up and finished off my breakfast. I sent Rachel a super long text about the "squirrel" and explained that I would be coming in late. She sent back an "Okay" and that was that. I was sure she'd light up my phone after she saw what had taken place inside. Then what would I say?

Yeah, sorry about the mess the stark-raving ghost left us. Try not to upset him, and don't mention the name Christine.

Gloria picked up my plates, and I gathered my belongings. I paid the bill and drove to Carrie Jo's house. Unfortunately, I was behind a street cleaning truck that refused to get out of the way. I knew he saw me waving at him, but he still didn't budge.

"This is just great," I complained to the truck. My phone rang and started singing "Thank God I'm a Country Boy." I knew it was TD. I couldn't dig the phone out of my purse fast enough. We hadn't spoken in weeks, and our last conversation wasn't anything nice. I'd given him an ultimatum and he gave me his answer—I came home to find all his things gone. I'd cried all night but hadn't called him. He had not called me either.

"Hey!" I said as casually as I could while juggling the phone and the steering wheel. *Keep your game face on, girl, and don't get wimpy!*

"Hey, beautiful." I loved his warm voice, and I especially loved it when he called me that. He had a delicious Southern accent that made him sound uber-sexy. His accent was distinct and fine in a way that set him apart from the other guys around here. He could talk excitedly about projects and buildings, but when it came to him and me—he was slow and on purpose. I'd loved that.

"Good to hear from you, TD. How have you been?" *Be cool, be aloof!*

"Things are good and getting better—especially now that I am talking to you. I have so much to say to you, beautiful. I was hoping we might have coffee this morning—if you'd be willing to see me. I know I have been wrong about so much—I would like to apologize and talk about our future—if you think we might have one."

Uh-oh, something doesn't feel right. Probably just some apprehension left over from last night. So why is my "lie detector" going off like crazy?

"I would like that, but I have to visit a sick friend this morning. I am going to go check on her now. I'll be available in a few hours. Is that okay?"

"Yes, we could meet later this morning, if you have some time for me."

"Are you sure you are okay, TD?"

He chuckled. It sounded insincere, kind of forced. "Never better! Just can't wait to see your gorgeous face." *He was lying to me—but about what?*

"Alright... so where should we meet?"

"Why don't you come to my place? I would like to talk somewhere private, talk things over, see what I can do to make it up to you. I know I've been a jerk."

Nope. This is a bad idea.

"I think I would like to take things a bit slower. Can we meet at Starbucks, the one on Airport?"

"Alright. I'll be there. See you at ten?"

"Okay, I'll see you then."

"Detra Ann?"

"Yes?"

"Thanks for agreeing to see me."

"See you later, TD." I hung up the phone, caught a break in the traffic and whizzed around the truck. If I weren't such a lady, I would have given that guy a piece of my mind—or at least an ugly gesture. When I got to Carrie Jo's house, her shiny new car was in the driveway. I pulled the BMW up behind it and wondered what I would say to her.

Why am I here? If something creepy is going on, I'm out of here. I can't take another creepy thing! I don't even believe in ghosts!

I dropped my keys in my purse and slung it over my shoulder. I hoped this wouldn't take too long. All I had to do was check on her and ask her to call Ashland.

"Oh no," I said to myself when I walked up the sidewalk. The front door stood wide open, and dead magnolia leaves from the front yard had blown into the house. This didn't look right—not one little bit. I stood on the pavement wondering what to do next. Visions of my own attack five years ago flashed in my head. I practically ran to the open door. "Carrie Jo?" There wasn't a sound in return except the sound of rustling leaves. I hadn't noticed the breeze until now—it picked up a swirl of dry leaves and tossed them around the foyer. She wasn't answering, and I couldn't leave here until I knew she was okay. I just couldn't.

I stepped into the foyer, a layer of leaves crunching under my feet. I continued to call her name, when I heard a sound from upstairs and froze in my tracks. Oh my God! What if someone else was here—an attacker like Fred Price? I dug in my purse for my tiny pearl-handled gun. I wasn't taking any chances. This could be a dangerous area at times—I mean, I loved Mobile, but we had our share of violent criminals. I walked through the entire lower hallway and checked all the rooms as if I were a rookie police officer.

"Carrie Jo?" I said again, this time in a whisper. I heard another sound—definitely coming from upstairs. She could be hurt up there; I had no choice but to climb those stairs. I left my bag on the lower steps and began to work my way up. *Thank God I'm not wearing my usual high heels today.* Between the leaves and the wooden steps whoever was up there, if anyone at all, would know I was coming long before I got there.

I called her name again. This time I plainly heard a door close. The sound wasn't too far away either. I gritted my teeth and kept moving up. I was just three steps from the top now. *Not too late to change your mind. Go outside and call the police.* I stopped and lowered my gun. Maybe that was what I should do. What was I thinking? How was I qualified to do this? Just because I had once been a victim didn't mean I was now an expert. Before I could sneak back down, the door closest to me opened and out walked Carrie Jo in a terry robe with a towel wrapped around her head. She jumped back in surprise, and suddenly I felt a cruel punch in my gut. My gun flew out of my hand. I could hear the sound of the shot.

I screamed as the sensation of falling overwhelmed me. My arms reached out for something, anything, to help me stop my fall, but I couldn't grasp a hold of the rail. I heard a loud pop, then a thud, and everything went dark.

Chapter 10

"Detra Ann!" I screamed in horror as I scrambled down the stairs after the fallen blonde. Blood poured out of her side, and the smell of gunpowder filled the air. I hadn't touched her but she'd fallen somehow. "Detra Ann!" I screamed and ran to her side. I squatted next to her in the blood and felt for a pulse. She was alive—at least for now.

Doreen walked inside and stifled a yell behind her hands. "Oh my God! Oh my God!"

"Doreen! Call 911, now! Please!"

She dropped her grocery bags on the floor and ran for the phone. "Yes, we have an emergency." She handed me the phone and ran to get towels for Detra Ann, who was still unconscious.

"Yes! I need help. My friend fell down the stairs. She was carrying a gun, and I think she's been shot. Please come! She's bleeding pretty bad. Please help us."

"Okay, ma'am. They are on the way. It won't be but a minute. Is she breathing? Can you see?"

"Yes, but it's shallow."

"Okay, now you say she's been shot?"

"Yes, oh my God! Please hurry!"

"Where has she been shot?"

"In the side, around her waist. I think she lost control of the gun as she fell. I don't know! Oh my God! She's my friend, but she's not supposed to be here. I came out of the bathroom and she was here."

"It's okay. Don't worry about that right now. Let's see if we can stop the bleeding. Do you have some towels?" asked the friendly dispatcher.

"Yes, I do now."

"Fold a towel and press it to the area where's she been shot. That should slow down any blood loss."

"Make them hurry! She's bleeding through the towel. Please, Detra Ann. Don't you dare die!"

I could hear the ambulance tearing down Government Street. Doreen scrambled to her feet and opened the door and then ran to the laundry room.

"Detra Ann, stay with me! Can you hear me?"

Her dark eyelashes fluttered, but she never opened her eyes completely. I saw her body sag just as the EMTs came barging in the front door.

"What happened?"

"I don't know. I think she tripped and fell—her gun went off. I didn't even know she had a gun! She's been shot." I got out of the way as the two young men squatted down beside her.

"What's her name?"

"Detra Ann. Please, is she going to be alright?"

"We'll do our best to help her."

I watched as they assessed her quickly and prepared her for transport. They braced her neck and expertly moved her body to the gurney.

"Here, ma'am. I got you some clothes." Doreen handed me a tote bag with a shirt, jeans, underwear and sandals.

"Thank you. Please call Mr. Stuart for me. Tell him to come to the hospital."

"I will!"

I followed the men to the ambulance and didn't wait for an invitation to join them. I climbed inside and sat out of the way on the only available metal bench. While working furiously to stop the bleeding they asked me questions about allergies and blood type. I didn't know what to tell them—I didn't know any of these things. The sight of Detra Ann near death, her normally tanned face pale and lifeless, sent shockwaves through my psyche. What had she been doing in my house? How did she get in, and why did she have a gun? I couldn't answer any of those questions but whatever the answer, I prayed that she would live. The rest of the ride was a blur. When we arrived at the hospital, I ran after the gurney. The EMTs paused in the ER hallway only long enough to call for a doctor. "She's bleeding out! Code Six!" They whirred past me through a set of self-locking doors. I wanted to chase them into the operating room, but a sympathetic nurse blocked my way.

"I'll meet you at the registration area in a couple of minutes. In the meantime, you can change. There are some scrubs in here," she said kindly, pointing to a nearby closet.

"Thanks, but I have clothes. Is there a bathroom I can use?"

"Right through there." She hurried away, following after Detra Ann and the team that had assembled around her. I couldn't stop shaking. I stumbled into the bathroom and changed my clothes quickly. Fortunately for me, Doreen had enough foresight to include my cell phone. What a relief!

With shaking fingers, I called Ashland. Strangely enough, he was already on the line. He'd been trying to call me. I let out a sob. "Baby? Are you there?"

"Yes, Carrie Jo. Are you okay? Doreen called me. What have they told you about Detra Ann?"

"I'm fine. I'm at the hospital, Springhill. They haven't said much yet. They just took her back. Are you on the way?" I was in full-blown crying mode now.

"I am—I'll be there in about an hour. Do you have someone with you? Maybe Bette?"

"No, I'll be fine." I scurried out of the bathroom and went in search of the nurse at the registration desk. "I have to go. The nurse wants to talk with me. I don't know what to tell her."

"I'll call Cynthia and tell her to get down there. She can answer their questions. Just take a deep breath, and I'll be there soon."

"Ashland?"

"Yes?"

"Hurry, please."

"I will. I'll talk to you soon."

He hung up, and I stood at the registration desk waiting for the nurse. When she didn't return I called Terrence Dale. He didn't answer, so I left him a message. "Hey, this is Carrie Jo. I'm calling because Detra Ann is at Springhill. She's had an accident, and I think it might be a good idea for you to be here. I'm in the emergency waiting room. Bye." Fifteen minutes later, I took a seat in the waiting room, hoping that the nurse would come back eventually.

The first person to arrive was TD. Detra Ann was right, he did look different. He was thinner now, and his silky brown hair brushed his shoulders. Not an unattractive look, just different. Even his clothing style had evolved. Now the young contractor wore torn blue jeans and a vintage t-shirt with the emblem of an old rock band on the chest. No more khakis and polo shirts, I supposed. "TD!" I said, throwing my arms around his neck. He tentatively hugged me and awkwardly stepped back.

"What's happened?"

"I'm not sure, really. I came out of the shower, and she was there on the stairs with a gun. I don't know if I startled her or what, but she fell and the gun went off. Now she's shot! In the side! I'm waiting and waiting, but nobody will tell me anything."

"She tried to shoot you?"

"No! I don't think so—I don't know what she was doing, but she is hurt really bad. I witnessed the whole thing, but it all happened so fast. I can't tell you much about what happened."

He hugged me again and helped me find a seat. He said, "Wait here. I'll go see what I can find out."

I watched him chat with the receptionist. She nodded and smiled at him, and he waved at me. "Thank you," he said to her when she pressed the button to let us back. "She's in surgery, but they're allowing us to sit in the surgery waiting room. The doctor will come speak to us when he's finished."

"Oh God! Ashland is on his way in from New Orleans. He said he would call her mother. I haven't heard anything else." We shuffled through the bleach-scented halls of Springhill Memorial until we came to the surgery waiting room.

"Yeah, she knows—she called me too. She was in Foley—she'll be here in about 45 minutes." He plopped down beside me. "The woman hates me. I can't say that I blame her. Detra Ann was way too good for me. Damn— that's her calling me now. Excuse me." He stepped just outside the door and took the call.

With a growing numbness, I sat in the smaller, colder waiting room. There were only a couple of people there. I stared absently at the muted television and waited for TD to return. He came back looking somber—it had been a long time since I'd seen him smile.

"I was supposed to meet her this morning. She said her friend was sick— she was going to check on her and then meet me afterwards. I can't believe this." His head was in his hands, his shoulders slumped. "I've been such a jackass," his voice broke in a sob.

I must have been the sick friend she was referring to. Still, that didn't explain why Detra Ann was in my house with a loaded gun. I knew I had locked that front door, but the hallway was full of leaves again. *I wonder if...I can't figure this out right now!*

"I'm listening." I put a hand on his back as he cried. This was what he needed—he needed to talk. "It's okay—Detra Ann is strong. She'll survive this."

After a few minutes, he stopped crying, and a kind nurse stopped by with a bottle of water and some tissues. "Anything yet?" he asked. "The patient is Detra Ann Dowd."

"No sir. She's still in surgery, but the doctor will come right out when he's finished. If y'all need anything, I'm right outside."

"Thank you."

"TD, I know this is none of my business, and you can tell me to shut up if you like, but what happened? With you and Detra Ann? She's just crazy about you."

"She didn't tell you?" I could see the shame in his brown eyes.

"Well, I heard a little, but I'd like to hear it from you."

"I really don't want to talk about it."

"We don't have to. I'm sorry I asked."

Leaning back in the plastic chair, he sighed. "No, I said I wasn't going to do that anymore. I'm facing my demons. I promised Detra Ann that I had changed. I can't drink away what I saw—what I know I saw." He rubbed his eyes and looked at me. "For a long time I hated you and Ashland—you know, for that night. It was like from that night forward everything went wrong, and I do mean everything. I couldn't focus—tools came up missing—I even got robbed. I lost jobs—I think I lost my mind for a while—a long while."

"I'm truly sorry, TD. I never meant for any of that to happen. I guess I—we didn't count the costs before we went looking for Calpurnia and the treasure. I really am sorry."

"I believe you. I meant to tell Detra Ann something today, but I guess it's not her I'm meant to tell. It's you."

I turned sideways in the chair, my arm on the back, my hand under my chin. "What is it?"

"When I was in high school, my sophomore year, I was in a car accident on I-65. I'd been dating this girl—Ashley Dubose was her name. Sweet girl. We hadn't been dating long, but I was crazy about her. You know, like you are in the tenth grade. One Friday night, we drove downtown to the Saenger Theater to see *Gone with the Wind*, her favorite film. She lived in Theodore, so after the film I took the interstate to get her home faster. Her dad was strict about her curfew, but I didn't mind. I liked her a lot. Everything was great. She was chattering on about Scarlett O'Hara—I was half listening when she kissed my cheek to thank me for taking her. I half-turned to kiss her and took my eyes off the road for only a second. That split second changed everything."

"What happened?"

"A truck sideswiped us and we went spinning. Ashley died. I walked away from the accident with just a scratch on my arm."

"I'm sorry. That must have been so difficult to process."

"It was, but it only got worse. For the next six months, I saw Ashley everywhere I went. Not like a face in a crowd or someone that looked like her. It was her, bleeding, with her empty eyes that stared through me—just like she looked in the car, you know, afterwards. I felt like a crazy person. Imagine sitting in economics class and your dead girlfriend is standing in the corner of the room. Only no one else can see her—just you. Just staring and bleeding. It happened every day for months."

"That sounds horrible. How did you cope?"

"My parents tried every way they could to help me. They're nice people. Medication, grief counseling, therapy—nothing worked. Finally, one afternoon my grandmother picked me up. It had been a rough weekend—it had gotten so bad I didn't want to leave the house. Not even for school. Anyway, Granny Kaye came over one day—she knew all about what I'd been going through. She didn't tell me where we were going or anything. We pulled into the parking lot of Valhalla Cemetery, and she grabbed my hands and started praying for me. When she was done, she handed me a note card and a pen. She told me to write Ashley a note. I thought that was a crazy idea, but she was adamant. I wrote five words: *I'm sorry. I loved you.* We took the card and some flowers to Ashley's grave." He took a deep breath and continued, "She told me to read it out loud, and I did. I cried the whole time, but I read it. I left the card and the flowers on the grave, and I didn't see Ashley ever again after that. Granny and I never talked about it for the rest of her life, but I will always be grateful for what she did."

"Wow, that is incredible. It must have been so terrifying to see her over and over again like that. I'm glad you had some resolution, though."

"I did until that night in the Moonlight Garden."

"Oh my gosh! You mean she came back?"

"No, it was the other one that I saw, the one that was reaching out for Ashland. Isla, I think her name was."

I shivered and nodded. "You saw her? Where?"

"Everywhere. And worse. Sometimes..."

"What? What is it?"

"Sometimes I'd wake up and she'd be on top of me. I'd scream, and she would disappear. I think I scared Detra Ann to death. She thought I was having nightmares, but they weren't like nightmares. CJ—they were real. She visited me, and I didn't want her to. She was really there, just like Ashley. Only I could smell her, feel her...even taste her. And when I fought her, she would change and I would be kissing a dead thing. I wanted to die. My soul was dying. Anyway, that's when I started drinking. I thought if I was drunk I wouldn't see her. It worked for a little while."

"I am so sorry. I had no idea that you were going through that." Impulsively, I put my arms around his neck and hugged him.

"The problem is I am still going through it, and I don't know what to do."

"Why didn't you tell us? We're your friends, TD. We care about you. Ashland and I would never let you fight her by yourself."

"What does she want? I don't have Granny Kaye in my corner this time, unless you believe in heaven and such. I know she did. She was a praying woman, and I've never been much for faith and prayer. Detra Ann tried to help me, just like Granny Kaye, but she couldn't. She didn't know what to do, and she has no idea about Ashley..." His voice dropped to a whisper. "Or that Isla is lurking around. I can't blame her for dumping me. I am a mess! I don't blame her, and I don't blame you, Carrie Jo."

"Now I know, and together we can fight her. We will figure out why this is happening! Believe it or not, I think I've seen her too." I admitted to TD something I hadn't been ready to tell my own husband. *What am I doing?* "I think she's been at my house."

His brown eyes widened in surprise. "What do you mean?"

"Well, I found this package in my house. It's Mia's handwriting. It was in my house for a month, and there is no way that Ashland or I would have missed it. Isla made sure I found it. I guess it was her. Something did, anyway." I chewed on my lip remembering the shadow that sailed past my door. "I opened the envelope, and inside was a small book—a collection of biographies, but the main story was about an actress named Delilah Iverson."

"I've never heard of her."

"Me either. I haven't finished reading it yet, so I'm not sure how it fits in. That's the kind of thing Isla would do. Death hasn't slowed her down. But besides that unexpected package, I keep seeing someone move out of the corner of my eye. If I am alone in my house, she sails past my door and I hear her giggle. It's bone-chilling." I shivered with the memory.

"I know that feeling," he said. "Yes, it is."

"She's been leaving my front door open and scattering leaves everywhere too. I don't know what to do about her. When Ashland comes home, I guess we'll all be having a 'come to Jesus meeting' because *she* is affecting us all. And there's more..."

Before I could tell him what I knew about Hoyt and Christine, we were interrupted.

"Isn't this cozy? So happy that you two found my daughter's surgery so unimportant that you can't behave respectably."

"What?" TD and I stared at Cynthia Dowd in surprise. She didn't elaborate on her accusations.

Ignoring TD, she addressed me coldly, "How are you, Mrs. Stuart? How is your mother? I hear she's ill."

The gossip from the Historical Society luncheon had traveled quickly. Well, what of it? I had nothing to hide, and I wasn't going to be cowed by my friend's overbearing mother. Before I could open my mouth to speak, the ginger-haired Detective Simmons joined us. She was dressed in a poorly fitting pantsuit with a gaudy pin at the lapel and wore no makeup except some feeble attempts at mascara and an overabundance of lipstick. She was a sharp contrast to the well-dressed Cynthia with her perfect bob cut, Mary

Kay makeup and a trim yellow suit. If the difference in statuses bothered the detective, she didn't show it. As usual she pulled out a notebook and a small pencil.

"Just the person I was looking for—Mrs. Stuart. May I talk to you for a minute?"

"Can't it wait, Detective? I am in the middle of a conversation here."

"Suit yourself. We can either talk here or talk down on Government Street in the squad room." She wasn't messing about today. It was her way or the highway apparently.

"Fine, if you'll excuse me, Mrs. Dowd, TD." Only TD acknowledged me.

I followed her down the hall and saw that she was intending to walk out of the hospital. "Where are we going?"

"To my office. Like I said, we need to talk."

"You gave me a choice—I chose to talk to you here. I have no intention of leaving Detra Ann right now. She had an accident, in case you didn't know." I didn't mean to sound snappy, but the abrasive detective had caught me at the wrong moment.

She turned around and stared at me, her pencil in her hand. "In your house! You think I don't know what happens on my beat? I know everything. Would you care to tell me how she got shot in your house?"

"I don't know exactly, or why she was even there. As far as I knew, she had stayed behind to finish her breakfast at By the Bay Bed and Breakfast. I hadn't invited her over."

"So she just broke in and shot herself?" Simmons said with a smirk.

"No, not exactly. After I got home, I went upstairs to take a shower. I needed to relax. When I walked out of the bathroom, Detra Ann was walking up my stairs with her gun drawn. She lost her balance, fell backward and down the steps. As she fell, the gun went off. That was it. That's all I know."

"That seems a bit farfetched, don't you think?"

"I can't help that, Detective. It's the truth."

"You say this woman is your friend?"

"Yes, she is. We've been—we've been working on a project together. I like her, and I am sure the feeling is mutual. She isn't dangerous!"

"You have a hard time keeping friends from killing you, don't you?"

"What?" I stared at her incredulously. I knew what she meant. Mia had tried to kill me, so why not Detra Ann? But I knew Detra Ann would never harm me. Even if we weren't besties, she loved Ashland—I was sure of that.

"It's the truth. People you hang around have a nasty way of getting killed, Miss Jardine—I mean, Mrs. Stuart. Now I want you to come downtown to take a test."

"What kind of test?"

"The kind that tests your hands for gunshot residue. That way, we'll know what happened. It would be a good way to clear your name, ma'am." She raised an eyebrow and scrutinized me.

"What's going on here?" I looked over to see Ashland beside me. I could smell his expensive cologne and felt his warm hand rest gently on my shoulder. "My wife isn't taking any kind of test unless our lawyer says so. Here's her card. Now if you'll excuse us, we have a friend who needs us."

I wanted to kiss him for being there, for coming to my rescue, but I had no reason to run. I knew I was innocent—if I could quickly prove it, why wouldn't I? "Wait, Ashland. I don't mind taking that test. I never fired that gun. I never touched it. If it will clear me, I will do it."

"That's not necessary, CJ. You don't have to do it."

"No, I want to. If it helps the detective, I don't mind. May I come down after I see Detra Ann? She's in surgery right now. I don't know how long that will be."

She nodded begrudgingly. "Sure, that will be fine." She scribbled something on a piece of notebook paper and handed the note to me. "Present this to the officer at the front desk when you get there. They'll get you to the place you need to be. Just walk in and take the test. They wipe your hands with a special cloth, and you wait for the results. They'll know if you fired a gun. If you fired that gun or handled it after it was fired, you will have residue on your hands. If that's the case, you will be arrested."

"Hey..." Ashland started to protest. "She's cooperating, detective."

"No, it's okay. I haven't done anything. I didn't touch that gun! Not before—not afterwards—and sure as heck not during! I will come down soon, Detective. Thank you."

"Fine. Since the patient is in surgery, I can't interview her, but I will send the team to check her hands too. Y'all have a good evening now."

We shook our heads as she left. "What is she thinking?" Ashland asked. "That you would try to kill Detra Ann? What kind of theory is she working? If she had bothered to ask, she would know that I sent Detra Ann to the house. She'd called me and told me you were upset."

"Really? But why did she have her gun out?"

"I don't know. She must have thought something was going on inside—she must have thought you were in danger."

I thought about the door standing wide open. How many times had that happened in the past twenty-four hours? And Ashland didn't even know about it. I decided right then and there that I was going to come clean with him as soon as we were alone. He needed to know that I hadn't been dreaming, until last night, that I'd been seeing Isla and that TD had seen her too. This wasn't over—it seemed the house wasn't through with us yet. But for now, I had to push it aside.

"I don't know, but I am so glad you are here. TD is here, and so is Detra Ann's mother."

"Detra Ann told me what you two did. That you stayed at Seven Sisters. Is that why you weren't answering my calls and why you kept hanging up on me?"

"I only hung up once, and that was because I couldn't hear you. I didn't know you called me."

"How is that possible? I called you like six times, Carrie Jo."

"I don't know what to say except I never got a call from you."

We walked back in silence toward the surgery waiting room. More and more I believed that something was trying to keep us apart—trying to destroy us all. *Oh my God! I am crazy like my mother!*

"When did Mrs. Dowd get here?"

"Just a few minutes ago. I gather she thinks I am involved in the shooting. She made some snide comment about my mother. I guess she heard about my speech at the society lunch."

"I've been meaning to talk to you. You know, your family history is your own business. Why did you open yourself up for ridicule like that?"

"I don't know. Because they are a bunch of busy bees that love to gossip? I figured they would find out the truth anyway, so why not be straight about it. Holliday Betbeze led the pack on that. I'm sorry if I embarrassed you."

"Stop that, Carrie Jo. It's like you don't even know me. I never said you embarrassed me. You've seen how warped and twisted my family is—haven't you?"

"Ashland, I wasn't raised in your kind of world." We stopped in the hallway outside the waiting room. "Where I come from, you tell it like it is. There's no sense in prettying things up. My mother is mentally ill. End of discussion. They kept poking me about her, and I told them. That's it."

He sighed and went in the waiting room. I followed behind him and tried to hide my frustration. *We really are in trouble, aren't we?* Well, at least he came. He was here with me. Or maybe he just came to see Detra Ann. No matter, he was here. And that meant the world to me.

The pieces were beginning to fall into place. Isla was on the move, and she wanted something from TD. I wondered what the trickster had in mind. And I wondered if, once and for all, I could actually defeat her.

Chapter 11

When we left the hospital a few hours later, Detra Ann was sleeping peacefully. The surgeon said she had been very lucky. The bullet had missed her major organs, and there were no fragments left behind. However, she had to be watched the next twenty-four hours. She had lost a lot of blood and had a history of bad reactions to anesthesia.

Mrs. Dowd had appeared genuinely happy that Ashland had come to see her. She'd tolerated TD and me, which was fine with both of us. Ashland tried to include us, but Cynthia had made up her mind to hate us, at least for the moment. After a while, none of us spoke. We sat waiting and staring at Detra Ann, who slept through the whole uncomfortable exchange.

We said our goodbyes, and TD promised to call when she woke up. Ashland still didn't want me to take the gunshot residue test, but I had to. I was innocent! I wanted to prove them all wrong. The faster I was cleared, the more quickly Simmons would start looking at other scenarios. A dull worry began to creep up within me...what if Isla was responsible? I knew she had been there—the open door and the scattered leaves attested to that. Who would ever believe it? The only person who could tell us what really happened was Detra Ann, and she wasn't awake yet.

We drove in silence down Government Street to the Mobile Police Department Headquarters. The only sound was the radio playing softly.

Wait, I know that voice. It was William Bettencourt singing "The Heart of Love." I couldn't help but smile. He deserved the break. I was happy for him. I hummed along to the tune.

"Seriously, CJ?"

"I'm happy that he got his big break."

"Thanks to you. He almost got you killed. I'm not convinced he was so squeaky clean. If he hadn't gotten his name in the papers..."

"That's completely unfair. He saved my life, Ashland." Neither of us moved out of our seats. "I love you, Ashland Stuart. Not William or anyone else."

"I love you too. You ready?" Ashland appeared nervous, unsure. I hoped that his doubts weren't about me. Surely he didn't believe that I actually shot Detra Ann.

"Yes, I want to get this over with and go home. It's been one heck of a day."

"You know I can call our attorney and have her down here in no time."

"I don't need an attorney, Ash. I haven't done anything wrong."

"That doesn't always matter. We have been on the local authorities' radar recently, what with Hollis' murder and Louis Beaumont's body in the backyard. They aren't exactly in our fan club."

I knew it was true, but we were innocent of wrongdoing. We parked, put some change in the meter and walked in, hand and hand. I explained to the on-duty officer why I was there and showed her the written order from Simmons. She led us to the lab and there we sat, taking in the stark ambiance until the lab tech and a uniformed officer appeared. I couldn't help but notice that the police officer had his cuffs handy. True to her word, Simmons wasn't taking any chances. If she could arrest me, she would— she'd promised me that. Now it was my turn to look at Ashland nervously. I gave the tech my name, and then they proceeded with the test. Unsealing the small damp cloth from the package, she rubbed my hands vigorously, both tops and bottoms.

"I'll be right back," she told the officer. He let her pass and stood by the door, his arms folded across his chest. We didn't make any small talk with him or even with each other. It was a nerve-wracking experience to say the least.

"She's clean. Not even a trace." She wrote something on a piece of paper and handed it to me. "Detective Simmons will be in touch with you soon. Keep this for your records."

"That's it? I can go?"

"The detective may have more questions later, but we're all done with you today, Mrs. Stuart."

"Okay."

"If you all would follow me, I'll lead you out." I had had no idea that the entry doors had been locked behind us. Suddenly, the whole thing seemed surreal. Actually, the past forty-eight hours had been surreal. We walked back to the car and got in. I leaned back in the seat and let out a sigh of relief. Lightning cracked over the bay, and the sky darkened ominously above us.

"Take me home, Ashland." I felt so tired. The anxiety from this morning, the strangeness, was creeping back into my mind. "I'm ready to go home."

"Home where? Our new home or Seven Sisters?" I didn't know if he was joking or what, but I wasn't in the mood.

"*Notre petite maison.* I just want to be with you." I sighed and closed my eyes.

"What did you say?"

"I said I want to go to Our Little Home. Not Seven Sisters."

"No, you said '*notre petite maison*'. But you don't speak French. What's that about?"

I felt the blood drain from my face. *What was going on?* I smiled awkwardly. "Maybe I heard that somewhere."

He frowned and eyed me suspiciously. "Let's go, then. I'll cook us something, and we can talk."

I nodded my head against his shoulder. "I would like that." *I have so much to tell you.* When we arrived home, thankfully the front door was neatly closed and there were no leaves on the porch and sidewalk. Doreen's car was gone, but she had left the house neat and tidy. Lightning cracked again, and this time the rain began to fall, heavy, soaking drops. I tossed my purse on the foyer table under the gilded mirror and stared at the stairs. Doreen had dutifully cleaned up the blood, and you'd never know what had happened earlier. I was glad for that and happy that Simmons hadn't taken the liberty of wrapping yellow tape across our front door. Wouldn't the neighbors have loved that?

Ashland wrapped his strong arms around me, and we kissed like we hadn't kissed since our honeymoon. He led me gently by the hand to the bottom of the stairs, but my feet wouldn't let me go up. I couldn't go up there, not right now, but I wanted him as much as he wanted me.

"No, I have a better idea." We had a barely used guest room on the other side of the kitchen. I smiled and pulled him in that direction. Ashland's sexy grin told me he liked the idea, and he followed me into the room. It felt cool and fresh—and presumably free of lurking ghosts and unhappy entities. I liked this room. We fell on the soft down comforter together and spent the next half hour lost in one another's arms. How wonderful to be with the man I loved! We needed this. I needed him! I loved him with every fiber of my being.

"I love you, Ashland Gregory Stuart." He showered my neck with kisses, and I laughed as his lips whispered across my skin.

Hoyt! Hoyt, I love you! Christine's pleading voice whispered in my head. I smothered the urge to spring up from the bed. Instead, I closed my eyes and forced myself to focus on the moment—this moment, in this lifetime. I was alive and here with my husband.

What do I do about you, Christine? What am I supposed to do? Ashland stroked my cheek with his finger and I whispered, "Hold me tight, Ashland."

"I love you, my wife. Are you hungry yet?"

"Starving! Are you sure you want to cook, though? You've had a long day already."

"I like cooking for you. And believe it or not, I couldn't find a decent meal in New Orleans."

"I do find that hard to believe!" I said with a laugh. "Okay, well, at least let me chop up some vegetables or toss a salad or something."

"That's a deal." We kissed and got dressed, and then I padded off to the restroom to work up a decent-looking ponytail. I took a ponytail holder out of the bathroom closet and checked my hair in the mirror. I didn't mind a sloppy ponytail, but my curls could look crazy if I didn't have a care for the finished product. Unhappy with the ponytail I'd made, I took it down and tried again.

Can you hear me? I know you can hear me. Please help me!

This couldn't be happening! *Go away!*

Suddenly the mirror began to reflect a smoky image. I looked behind me, but there was nothing. I stumbled back against the wicker hamper and stared at the mirror. I didn't speak, I couldn't! All I could do was gape at the outline of a woman's face struggling to appear in the smoke.

"Christine?" I gasped at the apparition.

"Hey, did you hear me?" Ashland barged into the bathroom, and I turned my attention from the mirror for a second. Even the voice had quieted in Ashland's presence. "What is it, Carrie Jo? You look like you've seen a..." His smile disappeared, and he pushed the door all the way open.

"I think I have."

"What? Here?"

I reached for his hand, and he pulled me out of the bathroom. "Okay, let's forget dinner. We'll order out—we have to talk."

"I agree. And I need a drink. How about you?"

"Yes, please." I followed him into the living room and flopped on the suede blue leather couch. I couldn't stop shaking. I wasn't necessarily afraid of Christine, but encountering ghosts or whatever that was always set my nerves on edge. It wasn't a natural thing. Not at all.

Help me.

Unleashing my wild hair from the ponytail holder, I accepted the small snifter of brandy that Ashland handed me and moved the pillow so he could sit beside me. "I don't know where to begin."

"When did all this start? Have you been dreaming about the house again?"

"That's the thing. I haven't been dreaming. In fact, until yesterday, I haven't had a dream in about three months. But I've been so happy with our new life and all, I haven't thought much about it. Then I started to experience this feeling, like something was...what's the word I'm looking for?"

"Undone?"

"Exactly. Undone. Like a wrong note played in a song you know or a whisper that you can't quite make out."

"I've felt the same thing. I thought it was just me."

I squeezed his hand, and we sipped our drinks. "Do you think we missed something?"

"Maybe. I'm not the expert, though."

"I'm sure not either," I said wryly.

"What else? Tell me what else has happened?"

"That feeling I described, it got stronger as the weeks went by. Then when you left for New Orleans, I felt like a jerk. I went downstairs to catch you before you left and found the door wide open. Not only that, but there were piles of leaves all over the place, like the door had been left open for days. That happened a few times. Including this morning, when Detra Ann got shot. And that's not all."

"Yes?"

"She's here...Isla. I've heard her giggling."

"Are you sure?"

"Well, I can't say a hundred percent, but I am pretty sure. The day you left I was working in the office when she went sailing by my door. She's back, and that can only mean one thing—we missed something."

He swirled the amber drink in his glass and downed it. "Damn," he muttered, setting the glass on the coffee table. "I wonder what it could be."

It was my turn to down my drink. "More, please." Ashland took our glasses and refilled them. A branch began to tap on the window; the storm outside had kicked up the evening breeze and the rain continued to fall.

"After that, I decided to get out of the house as quickly as I could. I drove to Bette's house, but she wasn't home. All I could think was to go to Seven Sisters. Detra Ann told me at the luncheon about the night tours, so I thought I might see Rachel and kill some time until I felt brave enough to come back here."

"You should have called me. I would have come right home, or you could have driven to New Orleans."

"Really? Because when you left I wasn't getting that vibe from you at all. It felt like you wanted to be alone, so I left you alone. For the record, I did call. You were at a party."

He laughed. "I wasn't at a party, CJ. I was at a supper club, Henri's club in New Orleans. I didn't tell you because I didn't want you to worry. I guess I was just trying to protect you."

"You saw Henri?" I couldn't help but smile. Even though he'd been caught up in Mia's web, at least at the beginning, he'd proven to be a worthy friend to Ashland and me. He'd left Mobile after the incident in the Moonlight Garden. I didn't blame him. Not one bit.

"I did. I haven't been completely honest with you. I've been back to the house too."

"What? Why?"

"That same feeling that something was off. Detra Ann called me a few weeks ago and reminded me that I left a few crates there. I should have told you, and I'm sorry I didn't. I admit I was happy to get the call—that was my excuse to go back. Especially after all the fuss I made about deeding the house to the city. I loaded up the crates and then took a walk around the property."

"And?"

"And nothing—not at first. There were tons of visitors there, walking through the house and the gardens. It was so crowded." I could tell he was pleased about that. I was too. "Re-enactors were scattered around the property, talking to guests and pointing out some of the architectural details and the 'acceptable' history. It was exactly as we hoped. The people love it, CJ."

I smiled, happy that he was happy. Restoring Seven Sisters had been a real dream of his. "You knew they would."

"I hoped. You helped make that happen." He sipped his brandy again and continued, "I walked through the gardens toward the back of the property, where it meets the Mobile River. The grounds team that TD hired did a remarkable job of cleaning it up and bringing it back to life. I decided to walk down to the riverbank. It was a good hike, but I wanted the time to think. I felt like I was being watched, but I kept walking. I wasn't sure where I was going, but then I saw a woman peeking out from behind a tree. She wore a full-skirted gray dress with black lace trim. I thought for a minute she might be one of the re-enactors from the house, but as I got closer, I knew she wasn't."

"What did she look like?"

"Attractive, but not beautiful like Calpurnia. Sweet. She had a sweet, round face. She was about your height, maybe an inch shorter, and looked to be in her early thirties."

"Okay. What else?"

"Thinking she needed help, I shouted to her, 'Are you okay?' She stepped on to the path and faced me—she was about fifty feet away." Ashland took another sip of his drink. Anxiety crept over me—what happened next? I didn't rush him, but it took great restraint. "She raised her hand above her eyes, like you do when you're trying to block the sun. But the weird thing was, the sun was behind her. She called out, 'Hoyt! Is that you?'"

The hair on my arms began to crackle. I froze—my eyes widened at hearing someone else speak that name. "Oh, no," I whispered.

"I said, 'No, ma'am. I'm Ashland. May I help you?' Without a word, she ducked back into the woods and ran from me. I called after her, asking her if she needed help, but she didn't answer. I could hear the leaves crunching under her shoes and the swishing of her skirts, but when I made it to the point in the path where she had stood, she'd disappeared. But there was no pathway. And she couldn't have run through that section of woods, too much underbrush. No way she would have made it with those skirts. I ducked through, trying to look for any trace of her, maybe a footprint or a bit of cloth, but I didn't find anything."

Peering into the brown liquid in the glass, I asked, "Didn't you recognize her, Ashland?"

"I don't think so. It wasn't Calpurnia. I know her face. And it certainly wasn't Isla."

"No, it was neither one of them. You saw Christine, Calpurnia's mother, and she's looking for the man she loves—she's looking for Hoyt Page."

"Hoyt? Who's Hoyt?"

"He's the man she should have married. I believe he is Calpurnia's father."

"What? Who is he?"

Taking my drink with me, I walked to the back door and pushed open the curtain. The rain still streamed down, and the gutters were full of water; they poured off the side of the house. Somewhere, a cat begged to come inside. I touched the crystal glass to my lip. The scent of brandy comforted me.

Hoyt! Where are you?

For the next hour, I told Ashland everything. About the dream. About connecting with Christine. About running from Jeremiah. He didn't question me or interrupt me. It felt good to tell it, to tell it all.

"That's it. We have to find this other daughter, the one that's missing. Christine needs to know she's okay. Right? Is that what this is about?"

"I don't know. I would think so. At least, it's a place to start."

"But where do we start? Have you seen this girl?"

"I haven't...but I think Mia has. She sent me this book, that's the book I found the day you left for New Orleans. In the note, Mia says that once I read it, I will understand why she did what she did. I don't know if that's true or not, but I think there could be something significant in there."

"Well, we don't have any other clues to go on. Sounds like you, Mrs. Researcher, will be doing some research." Suddenly, Ashland laughed. It was a strange sound after everything we'd talked about. "You know, if this historian thing doesn't work out for you, you could open a detective business. Mysteries seem to follow you, Carrie Jo."

I raised my eyebrows and shook my head. "No thanks. I prefer dusty old books to voices in my head and bad dreams. Thank you, by the way, for believing me."

"Of course. If you're crazy, I'm crazy too. I've seen a few things myself, remember. I hope I never see Isla again."

"That's another thing. TD has seen her and is scared to death."

"Why would she show herself to him?"

"Why not? When she was alive, she was quite lovely. And if she thought she could use him for her own means, then..."

"That doesn't sound right. We found the treasure—why is she hanging around? Where are Calpurnia and Muncie?"

"I'm sure they are resting, Ash. Their part in this craziness is over, at least I think it is, but Christine's isn't yet. As long as there are secrets, Isla will have some measure of power."

"Great. That's just great."

"I think you're in the clear. You stood up to her. But we have to help TD. She's terrorizing him, Ashland, and he doesn't know what to do. Instead of doing this by ourselves, we have friends who will help us. We just need to come up with a plan."

"Then it's a good thing I went to see Henri."

"Why do you say that?"

"Because he's willing to help. Because he knows more than we do about all this stuff. And because, like you, I trust him."

"I think you should call him and ask him to come back to Mobile." Despite all the supernatural storytelling, I felt warm and comfortable now. Maybe it was the brandy or just being with Ashland. The rain had begun to slack now, and we cuddled up together on the couch. Neither of us was ready to break the mood.

"I will do that. You ready to go to bed?"

We'd forgotten all about eating, and I was too drowsy to think about it now. "Can't we sleep here tonight?"

His arm was behind his head, and I was lying on his chest. Sometime during our chat, I'd grabbed the chenille throw off the back of the couch and covered us with it.

"Sounds perfect," he said, kissing the top of my head. Smiling, I snuggled up to him and listened to the sound of his heart beating. I loved him so much. I couldn't believe how lucky I had been to find him. I wished Christine had had a happy ending. How many times did she lie on Hoyt's chest and listen to his heart beat?

Christine, I'm sorry for what happened to you.

I fell asleep and stepped into a dream, but it wasn't mine.

Chapter 12

"Calpurnia, dearest. Come show Mother what you found. Oh, look at this, Hoyt."

The little girl danced in a circle, swirling her skirts about her. The tiny ladybug on her finger refused to fly.

Screwing up her face, she stared at it. "She won't fly, Mother. Why won't she fly?"

"Maybe she needs a rest, dearest. Proper ladybugs rest in between flights."

"Is that true, Dr. Page?" With an untrusting look, the four-year-old tilted her pretty head and questioned her mother's friend.

"Yes, that is quite true."

Christine plucked at the petals of the white daisy she held. How childish to play games like "He Loves Me, He Loves Me Not." Even her soul knew that Hoyt Henry Page loved her beyond reasoning—as much as she loved him. What a picture the three of them made! Quite like a happy family enjoying a summer day by the water. But that was only a picture—an ever-fading dream buried in her heart.

Calpurnia spun around again, trying in earnest to force the bug to fly.

"Your sister came calling yesterday, Hoyt."

"Claudette? I suppose she came to bring Calpurnia a birthday gift?"

"No. In fact, she did not mention her at all."

Hoyt rose from his reclining position. He dusted the elbow of his sleeve and looked at her. He didn't dare hold her hand or touch her in public, but he had the sudden urge to do so. Christine knew this, and it assured her of his love.

"What then was her business?"

Christine tossed the now-bare flower aside and smiled at him. "She requested a meeting with Mr. Cottonwood. When I pressed her, she implied that it was business, but I know better."

"I see. What did Claudette say that would lead you to that conclusion?"

Christine raised her hand to her eyes to shield them from the sun. "Calpurnia! Come back this way. Stay away from the water!"

Frustrated, Hoyt scolded her, "Christine, you're being evasive."

"My daughter is perilously close to the river, Hoyt. Calpurnia!"

Hoyt stung at the phrase "my daughter." It was just the two of them. Couldn't Christine even then say "Our daughter?"

He brushed off her concern and tried not to appear hurt. "She will come to no harm. See? She's just spinning about. Now tell me what troubles you about my sister's visit?"

"It was a pretense, Hoyt. She has no real business with Jeremiah, none at all. She came to tell him. About us. I am sure of it."

He laughed. "She knows nothing. I have told her nothing. She has seen nothing." He tossed his hat on the blanket beside him and secretively reached for her pale hand. Such a lovely hand. Well-sculpted like a Grecian statue. "For the record, Claudette has a keen business sense. She handles all my finances."

Christine pulled her hand away in frustration. "Always willing to defend her. She knows, and she will make sure that my husband hears her out. Why has she never married? Perhaps if she were married, she would be less prone to interfere with matters that do not concern her."

"That is just her way, Christine. I promise you that I will speak to her this evening and see what is on her mind. Do not worry so."

Her heart felt instantly lighter but before she could thank him, a loud splash into the nearby water grabbed her attention. "Calpurnia!" she screamed in terror. "Ma fille!" Hoyt raced past her and in a few seconds had leaped into the water after the child. Christine stood on the riverbank, her chest heaving, anguished tears in her eyes.

Immediately she began to plead, "God, punish me but not my child! Please, not my child!" She began to pray to the Virgin as Hoyt swam to Callie, whose sweet face was immersed in the troubled waters of the river.

"Calpurnia! Calpurnia!" Finally Hoyt reached her and turned her upright. The child did not move but floated like a dead leaf on the water. "Calpurnia!" Hoyt struggled against the current but finally reached the muddy shore. Exhausted, he lifted the child out of the water and collapsed on the bank. Christine ran to them, crying and pleading with God to save her daughter.

She peeled long strands of wet hair off the child's face and gasped. Calpurnia's lips were blue, her skin cold and clammy. "She is dead. Oh mon ame! Come back to me, my child!"

Hoyt shook off the weariness and lifted the child up to his shoulder. He patted her back, attempting to force the water from her lungs. He wept as he smacked her tiny back until finally, he heard her wheeze.

"Hoyt!" Christine's face appeared unbelieving for a second, then a smile flashed across it. "She's moving! She is alive! Grace a Dieu!"

"Let's get the child home. She needs some attention. Get the carriage, Christine."

"Yes, of course." She ran back to the lane and appeared in a few minutes with Hoyt's open carriage. Calpurnia had not roused, but she was breathing. She was alive—and that was all that mattered to Christine. They did not talk as they raced back to Seven Sisters. Christine held her water-logged child to her chest and kissed her head repeatedly. "You will be alright, cherie. See? We are almost home, dearest." The child could not open her eyes, but her tiny chest rose and fell. Christine watched each breath with worry. They raced down the red clay lane that led to Seven Sisters. In seconds, tall, gangly Stokes ran out to meet them. Christine handed him the child and said, "Take her to her room."

"Yes, ma'am. Mr. Cottonwood is looking for you in his study." He did not look Christine in the eye but took the damp bundle she presented him.

"I will see him. Take her upstairs to her room and give Dr. Page whatever he needs. I'll come as soon as I can." She searched his face for a clue about her husband's request, but there were none forthcoming. Stokes had been and always would be the master's most dependable slave, faithful above all others.

"Yes, ma'am."

Now that the immediate emergency had been handled, Christine could breathe again. Hoyt would see to it that their daughter would recover. She knew it. Her gown was wet and muddy, and she imagined that her hair was messy, but there was nothing she could do about that now. Jeremiah insisted that she appear like a lady at all times, but surely such an emergency as this warranted a measure of latitude. She went in the house, down the hallway to Jeremiah's study. Nobody came to greet her or attend to her, a sure sign that something was amiss. Jeremiah stood at the window, an unlit cigar in his mouth. He wore no coat; Christine spotted his blue jacket resting on the arm of his chair. Immediately she began to worry. He wouldn't harm her with Hoyt in the house—surely not with Hoyt there. How different he looked from the man she had first met. He had been so accommodating, so eager to please her during their courtship. Christine had never had any illusions that he loved her, or she him, but she would have never dreamed that she would be so unhappy— and he so cruel.

"You wanted to see me, Jeremiah?"

He did not look at her at first, and when he did, he showed no surprise at her appearance. He barely looked in her direction. She might as well have been one of the slaves.

"I would ask you to sit, but your gown would stain my chair, I am afraid." He set the cigar in the massive crystal ashtray that rested on the edge of his desk. "You cannot know how unhappy I am, Christine. I have had a letter from your father today."

"Mon pere?"

"Yes, and please refrain from speaking French. It will do you no good. I am immune to your feminine wiles."

"Wiles?" Christine felt her pulse race. She reminded herself to remain calm. "What do you mean? I have no wiles."

Jeremiah leered at her. He strode to his desk and picked up the letter. "He says, and I quote, 'Make my good daughter aware of my correspondence, and please relay to her my fondness and pride in her situation.'"

She did not know how to respond, still unsure what crime he imagined she had committed. Her inner voice urged her again to remain calm. "I shall go write to him immediately and thank him for his kind words. Thank you for sharing them with me." She turned to leave, holding her breath for luck as she did. In just four steps he was behind her.

Grasping her arm savagely, he pulled her to him. His breath smelled stale, a sickening combination of whiskey and salted pork. "Do not walk away from me, wife! Never walk away from me. Do you understand?"

Her silver earbobs jingled as she nodded. She didn't pull away, for that would only enrage him further. She had to keep quiet until she could discern the source of his rage. Christine prayed that Claudette Page had not been successful in her desire to educate him, to fill his ears with the one thing that could destroy Christine completely. He would kill her—that much she was sure of.

"Why is he coming here? Why, Christine?"

"Who? Dr. Page? Calpurnia fell into the river, and he happened to be passing by and gave assistance. If it weren't for Dr. Page, our daughter would be..." The words began to pour out of her mouth. She detested lying. She never mastered "mensonge discrete," discreet lying as some called it. But for Hoyt, for Calpurnia, she would lie to the holy angels themselves.

"Don't play coy with me! I am speaking of your brother!" He shoved the letter at her and commanded her to read it. Fearful of what he might do next, she hastily began to read. 'Esteemed Son-In-Law...'"

"Damnation! Skip down to the last paragraph. Read it! Convince me that you did not call him here!"

"'In the interest of our mutual benefit and kind relationship, please receive my son Louis with all courtesy when he arrives at the end of this month. I have entrusted him to carry out my business and have requested his assistance in procuring the adjoining lands to the south of Seven Sisters. He has also requested a review of the most recent financial records, and I trust you will accommodate him in this matter.'"

"Louis is coming here? I swear, mon mari—I mean, my husband—I did not know! I have not written him or my father since this spring. He has not come at my request."

He stomped toward Christine and snatched the letter from her, reading it silently to himself. Fighting every instinct in her soul, mind and body, she stood rigidly, almost defiantly. In this she was innocent!

"You think I believe you? I know you swoon and pant after Louis Beaumont. He is the only man you have ever truly loved, isn't he, Christine." He stomped back to his desk and sat in the heavy wooden chair.

"He is my brother, Jeremiah! How dare you suggest such a thing?!"

"Don't play the frightened damsel with me, wife."

She could bear the insults. It was nothing in comparison to the truth, was it? "I swear to you, Jeremiah, on everything I treasure, I did not write to Louis. Whatever he and my father have planned, I know nothing."

"So you say. How can I trust you?" He poured himself another glass of whiskey, tossed it back and closed his eyes. Christine breathed a quiet sigh of relief. He didn't know! He knew nothing about Hoyt! Not yet. Bravely, she continued to stand before him. Eventually he looked up, his eyes bleary and red. "Go, and for God's sake, do something with yourself. No more gardening today, Christine."

With a curt nod, she left the room, closing the doors behind her. As quickly as she could, she ran up the stairs to her daughter and Hoyt. Her heart skipped a beat when she heard her daughter crying loudly.

Just a little longer together, Hoyt! We have just a little longer!

I'm coming, Calpurnia! Mother is coming!

Chapter 13

"Momma?" My eyes felt heavy, and my entire body hurt like I'd been hit by a Mack truck, especially my left side. Confusion and pain collided, and I caught my breath.

"Detra Ann! You're awake! Nurse! She's…" The words sounded muffled and I strained to hear but fell asleep again. Suddenly a beam of light hit my left eye, and I felt my eyes flutter open.

"Momma? Where am I?"

I began to see clearly now. Sunlight peeked through cheap plastic blinds, and the walls were a horrid mauve with grey plastic trim. Medical machines were beeping around me. My mother hovered over me, her pearls dangling from her neck and ears; she was wearing her yellow suit, the one with the tiny yellow flowers at the lapel. She always wanted to look like she'd stepped out of the Sears and Roebuck catalog, she said. How sad that they don't send out those catalogs anymore. Still, my mother could be kind, if a bit overprotective.

"Are you awake again? Detra Ann?"

"Yes, I'm awake."

"You are at the hospital," she said slowly and loudly like I was hearing-impaired.

I tried to sit up, but a sharp, stabbing pain tore through my side.

"Don't move, alright? The doctor is on…his…way."

"I'm not deaf, Momma. Please, can you get me a glass of water?"

"I don't think you're supposed to drink anything yet. Not this soon after surgery."

"Surgery? Please get me some water."

"Detra Ann? You're awake." TD hovered over me now. I ignored Mother's pursed lips and the eye roll that seemed to accompany all her conversations or interactions with him. He kissed my hand—he was as handsome as ever. His hair was slightly longer and messier than I last remembered…I kind of liked it. I touched it as he leaned forward. No matter how lost he was, TD always smelled like sawdust and sunshine.

"Hey, baby. Does this mean we're back together?" Oh Lord! I was never this needy—what was I saying?

"I'm here, Detra Ann, and your mother is too."

I whispered through dry lips, "I need something to drink."

"Be right back."

As he disappeared from my view, I struggled to get my bearings. The pain in my side was excruciating—I had nothing to compare it to. I'd never had children or any major surgery, except for that time I broke my finger on the playground. That had been Ashland's fault, but I never told anyone. He hadn't meant to smash my finger with that teeter-totter. Oh, and I'd had my wisdom teeth removed too. How sick I had been that night. Something about the pain medicine made me sick. Oh my God! The pain was unbearable.

"Listen, dear, the doctor has you on a drip—see the tube? The button is right here. When you start hurting, press the button. You will recover, but it is going to hurt for a while. Don't be a hero, Detra Ann."

"I won't," I said glumly, immediately pressing the button.

"What happened? Why were you in that woman's house?"

"Somebody pushed me, I think." I remembered climbing up the stairs, calling for Carrie Jo... "Carrie Jo...is she okay? Did they hurt her too?"

TD returned with a cup, and I prayed it was water. I could see the IV bag pumping fluids into my body, but I was so thirsty.

"The nurse says you can't drink any water but you can have ice chips, if that makes any sense. Here you go, baby."

I took the cup in my hands as Momma slowly eased my bed up a few inches. "That's good. It hurts too bad to move up any higher. Thanks for the ice." The pain medicine was working again—I felt no pain at all now. I scooped up a few ice chips in my mouth and crunched them. They were the best things I had ever put in my mouth. "Somebody hit me in the stomach and I fell down the stairs. I couldn't see who it was, but it wasn't Carrie Jo. She was in the hallway. Wait, I do remember someone being on the stair with me. What was her name? Why can't I think?" My brain felt like it was wrapped in damp cotton.

"It's the pain medicine," my mother whispered to TD.

"Wait, she's not supposed to be there. She lives at Seven Sisters, right? I wonder why she was at Carrie Jo's house."

"Who, baby?" My mother patted my forehead with a damp cloth.

"Isla. Yeah, that's it."

TD's face turned deathly pale. He said, "What did you say, babe? Isla?"

"Yes, she pushed me down the stairs at CJ's house. Oh, TD! It was the scariest thing I ever saw. She was right in front of me—she just popped up out of nowhere. I found the front door open, and I got worried for Carrie Jo. She'd had a bad night at the house, we both did. Jeremiah Cottonwood tried to get us, but we ran and ran..."

"What are you talking about?" My mother's face reflected her shock. "Is she talking about *the* Jeremiah Cottonwood? Is that who you mean? He is dead, Detra Ann, and has been dead for over a hundred years."

"Cynthia, I think it's the meds talking. Don't take anything she says seriously," TD lied to my mother. He knew that what was happening at Seven Sisters was real—very real.

"How can you say that, TD? I saw her. I know I did." I summoned up her face from my fragmented memory. She had appeared just inches in front of my face. I wasn't sure how I knew her name or how she knew mine, but she did.

Go home, Detra Ann! Her face twisted into a snarl, the voice in my head full of inhuman viciousness. I remembered that she'd startled me and then struck me hard in the gut. "I'm so tired."

"Rest now. I'll be here when you wake up," TD whispered in my ear. "I love you."

"I love you too," I said, at least in my mind.

Then I wasn't in the hospital room anymore.

I found myself standing in the ballroom of Seven Sisters. Shadowy couples dressed in black swirled about me, dancing to a macabre waltz played by an invisible orchestra. The massive chandelier above me shone with amber light that cast living shadows on the walls of the room. The black-clad dancers did not seem to notice me, but I could feel the silk rubbing against my skin as they moved around and around. With escalating alarm, I pushed my way through the couples; their indiscernible faces did not acknowledge me, but somehow I knew they were aware of my presence—and I was an unwanted guest. I didn't belong here. My side hurt and my skin grew cold, the thin hospital gown providing me little comfort. I stumbled forward, terror rising inside me. What if I could not get out?

"Please," I shouted, "please let me out!" I reached out to touch the shoulder of a man who swung by me in a perfect circle. He robotically turned his face to me, but none of his features were clear except his hate-filled eyes.

"Where is your invitation?" he demanded as he and his partner swooped around me.

Sobbing now, I pushed on. My side burned, and I imagined that I felt blood dripping from the wound. Time had no meaning here in this ballroom of specters, but I knew I had walked much further than was necessary to reach that door. Again silk slapped my face and bodies pushed against me as I shoved my way to the exit.

"Let me go! Let me out!"

My cries went unheard over the noise of the scratchy violins. Finally, in the briefest of moments, the couples in front of me moved and I could plainly see the door. I was almost there! Again they shoved against me. Weeping and reaching, I said, "You have no right to keep me here!"

Then the chandelier dimmed as I made a final push to escape the spinning crowd. I extended my shaking hand toward the door with every ounce of energy I had. Somehow I knew this was my last push, my last try. If I wasn't successful now, if I couldn't break free, I would be here forever. I felt the tears welling up in my eyes.

Then she appeared—Isla! Hovering between me and the door. With a kittenish smile and fierce eyes, she floated closer. I had nowhere to go. The dancers whirled behind me in their evil circles—the only way out was before me.

"No, Christine. You can't leave yet. You haven't been properly received, and he's waiting for you. He's been waiting, and now the wait is over. Take my hand, Christine, and it will all be over." She reached her hand out to me, only a few feet away. I stared at it. It was a lifeless, pale thing, so small and childlike. So young, so perfect.

So dead.

I opened my mouth to protest, but all that came out was a scream.

Chapter 14

I woke up to the smells of breakfast and the sound of Ashland calling my name. I stretched like a lazy cat and followed my nose to the kitchen. My husband had taken a shower, set the bar for breakfast and had everything ready for me before I got up. "Morning," he said, "How did you sleep?"

"Great. How is your shoulder? I hope I didn't drool on you."

He laughed. "No but you do talk in your sleep."

Sitting at the bar, I slid my plate his way to accept a few spoonfuls of scrambled eggs. "Did I at least say anything interesting?"

"I'll never tell," he teased.

I sipped the hot coffee and wolfed down my bacon and eggs. It felt like forever since I'd eaten. I had managed to grab some chips from the vending machine at the hospital but had never opened them. "Boy, that was delicious. Anything else in there?"

"Check the fridge. I think there is some fruit salad if you want that."

"Yuck, I'll pass. I better get a shower before we head to Springhill. I assume we're going first thing?"

"I'd like to. I'll tidy up here."

Hopping out of the chair, I kissed his cheek and took my coffee cup with me. "Give me ten minutes."

"You got it."

During my walk up the stairs, I focused on not spilling my coffee, not on the spot where Detra Ann fell or on the tiny hole in the wall from the bullet. I hoped she was going to be all right. As quickly as I could, I rummaged for some casual yet presentable clothing and then headed to the shower. I didn't look in any mirrors or even glance around the room. If there was something here, I didn't want to know. Drinking down the last swigs of my coffee, I took my shower and got dressed in record time. No sense in dawdling and giving Isla a chance to reappear. I stopped for a moment. Nope, nothing. Hmm...things were oddly quiet this morning.

Ashland rapped on the door. "Almost done," I called.

"We have to go. Something's happened to Detra Ann!"

"What?" I flung the door open as I buttoned up my pants. "What happened?"

"I don't know. TD said something about a seizure—now she's in a coma. I don't know. Are you ready?"

"Yes, let me grab my shoes and purse."

"I'll be in the car."

"Okay, be there in a sec!" I towel-dried my hair and grabbed a hair clip. *Not fooling with my hair today.* Two minutes later I ran after him, grabbing my purse off the foyer table as I practically ran out the door. Locking it behind me, I yelled up the stairwell, "You're not going to win, Isla!" I don't know why I did it, but it felt good. I was angry, angrier than I had been in a long time. I didn't hear a sound, not even a giggle.

As Ashland navigated the busy streets, I sent TD a few texts to let him know we were close, but he didn't answer. "Must be with Detra Ann," I told Ashland. "God, I hope she's okay."

"Me too. She's like a sister to me, you know. She is the nearest thing to family that I have. Besides you, of course." His voice shook as he turned into the parking lot.

I didn't know what to say. I rubbed his shoulder as we whizzed down Springhill Avenue. A few minutes later, we pulled into an open spot. It was a good thing we'd gotten here early, as the parking lot was nearly full. A few minutes later we were stepping off the elevator onto the fifth floor of the hospital. When the doors opened Ashland and I both froze—the place was full of women from the Historical Society. A nurse approached our group and asked us to relocate to the waiting room. We complied, but some of the society did not go without some mild protests.

"Ashland! Carrie Jo!" People hugged me like they'd known me all my life. "So sad what's happened! How in the world did she get shot? Now she's in a coma!"

My plan was to let Ashland field these questions. I'd stay in the background until I could see Detra Ann. But Holliday Betbeze had other plans. She found an empty seat beside me and attempted to probe me for more information.

"Were you robbed? Is that what happened? Did Detra Ann protect you from a thief? You know, that is a very dangerous part of town. My own cousin was robbed down there just two streets over."

"I didn't know that," I said, attempting to deflect her questioning.

"Tell me the truth, why on earth did you and Ashland ever give up that big old house? I would have stayed there until they drug me out by my shoelaces."

"You know you don't own a pair of shoelaces, Holliday," another woman chimed in. For a few minutes, they forgot about me and chatted about the tragedy and the "Seven Sisters" curse. After a while, Cynthia came out of her daughter's room and soon became the group's new center of gravity. Ashland hugged her and said something in her ear. She nodded and smiled weakly before patting him gently on the shoulder. After a few seconds, he walked out of the room, leaving me behind without a word. I gave Cynthia a polite smile and tried to follow after him as quickly as I could. It didn't happen.

"Wait, Carrie Jo." Cynthia stepped in front of me. The crowd stopped their chattering, waiting to see what happened next. In a quiet voice she said, "I want to apologize to you. I said some very rude things yesterday, and I regret them. Detra Ann told me that it wasn't your fault—and she told me what she thinks happened. And that lady detective called me to say you aren't a suspect. I was wrong. I jumped to the wrong conclusion, and I am truly sorry for that." Cynthia didn't wait for my response. She scooped me up in her thin arms and hugged me.

I squeezed her shoulders and whispered, "Don't worry about me. We're here if you need us."

She wiped at her eyes with a crumpled tissue. "Is there anything you can tell me? Anything at all? My daughter mentioned that someone else was there. Isla, I think her name was. Is she a friend of yours?"

How should I answer this? "The only person I saw was Detra Ann. I swear to you, I didn't see anyone else."

She touched my arm and nodded. "It must have been the pain medication. She's never been able to tolerate it." She walked away slowly, and I went down the hall in the direction Ashland had gone. I pushed the door open to Detra Ann's room. TD sat in the chair next to her, his long hair tucked behind his ears, his eyes bloodshot and tired-looking. Ashland stood on the other side of the bed staring down at her. Detra Ann's blond hair was spread around her like a golden halo. Her face was serene; she reminded me of Sleeping Beauty. Even though she was the picture of peace, the air around her was not.

Bette popped in the room, and she practically ran into me. "How have you been, Bette? I came by to see you, but you weren't there. Are you okay?"

With tears in her eyes, Bette nodded. I could see that she was a big old mix of emotions right now, but I had no idea why. I had not gotten the idea that she and Detra Ann were all that close. Maybe they were after all. People deal with situations like this differently.

For about the sixth time today I received an unexpected hug. But this wasn't just an "I'm here for you" hug. Bette was heartbroken. "Bette, please. You're scaring me. What has happened? Is it your son? Your boyfriend?"

She looked from me to Ashland, her heart on her sleeve. Her perfect white curls bounced as she shook her head. "Now isn't the right time to share my news. As soon as Detra Ann is better, I will tell you everything. Right now, I just wanted to see you. And I know this may sound strange, Carrie Jo, but I wanted you to know that I love you. And you too, Ashland. I love you both. No matter what happens. Now I have to go help Cynthia. I'm going to make sure she eats, even if it is in the lousy hospital cafeteria. We'll talk soon." With that, she walked out. Ashland's eyes met mine—he looked as confused as I did. What was going on with Bette?

"Ashland, we have to do something." TD sounded desperate. "What can we do? I've been here with Detra Ann, praying for her. Can you believe that? Me, praying? I won't quit, but there has to be something else. I have to do something."

I nodded and said, "I agree. Of all the people in the world, this shouldn't be happening to Detra Ann. She didn't do anything to deserve this. I think we all know that this wasn't an accident. Isla did this, and I can't understand why. I thought her power was broken, but I guess she never left."

"I can't stand sitting back and waiting. I hate playing defense." TD's deep voice shook with a mixture of anger and grief. I could tell he was considering having a drink—or five. I touched his shoulder to remind him that he wasn't alone.

Ashland shook his head. "No, we won't sit back and wait for the other shoe to drop. I'm making the call. Henri needs to be here, and whatever he tells us, we're going to do, right? Everyone agree?"

"I don't know what else we can do," I said.

"If it helps Detra Ann, of course. I'm in." He reached out, took her hand and kissed it.

"I'll go make the call." With a resolute look, Ashland left the room. That was my Ashland, always ready to rescue someone. I sighed, hoping that he was right—that Henri knew more than we did.

I sat next to TD and quietly prayed for Detra Ann. Soon, the room felt and even looked lighter. The bells on her machine rang less and her heart rate was calm.

I knew it. We weren't alone. And maybe this time, we'd get it right.

Chapter 15

An hour later, it was quiet, which was a relief. The ladies had left, deciding to each cook a dish for Cynthia Dowd. It was like a wake lunch, only Detra Ann wasn't dead. It was morbid, if you asked me, but I guessed they did things differently down here in Mobile. Just one of the social quirks that made this place so unique.

I settled on a corner couch in one of the many waiting rooms in Springhill Memorial. I had a water bottle, a bag of dried pineapple from the vending machine and the book that Mia had sent me. Ashland and TD were counting on me to get to the bottom of the problem—find out why Mia and Isla felt they still had a claim on Seven Sisters. When I knew what it was, we could come up with a plan. We needed a plan, big time! I'd deliberately left the ICU floor, at Ashland's urging, in favor of the fourth-floor waiting room. There were more people here but they didn't know me or try to chat with me. I needed quiet to read, but I didn't want to go home. Not without Ashland, and he understandably wasn't leaving until Detra Ann was better.

He'd gone home and grabbed me some snacks, a toothbrush, a pillow and my favorite chenille blanket. I hated the idea of dreaming here in the hospital, but I thought I'd gotten better at controlling who I dreamed about. I'd gotten quite good at calling out names and entering the right dreams. But I was the first to admit that I had a lot to learn about dream catching.

I hunkered down on the couch, which was remarkably comfortable given the circumstances. Kicking off my shoes, I examined the book again. It felt old, small and certainly not magical. It was a plain brown leather book, but hopefully there were some words inside that were going to set us all free. Especially Detra Ann.

I skimmed through the part I'd already read. I flipped through the section about Delilah's time in Canada. Surely, whatever I needed to know about her had to do with her time in Mobile, after the war. No sense in wondering. It was time to find out.

For five years Canada was home even though it didn't feel like it. I missed Mobile, but we were surrounded by people who loved us. The Iverson clan was a hearty lot with plenty of children to keep me entertained during those long, tedious winter months locked inside away from the cold Canadian wilderness. During our stay, I had picked up a bit of our mother tongue and developed a propensity for storytelling, which according to my mother was a family tradition. I got quite good at telling stories and even began to write my own stories and plays.

Uncle Lars and his wife Aida treated me well, but their daughters were far from friendly and liked to refer to me as the "dark bird." I assumed they were referring to my dark hair and eyes, which were so markedly different from their own blond hair and blue eyes. Still, the small children liked me, and many of my male cousins treated me affectionately.

In fact, some of my cousins were so friendly that Adam came to me one afternoon and instructed me to behave less warmly with them. I admit that at the time, I was quite naïve about such things and didn't know why he was making such a fuss. It wasn't until one of my cousins proposed to me that I understood Adam warning. Marriage to a beloved cousin was an honorable thing to my family, and indeed to many people at that time, even though such an idea seems repugnant in today's world. I had no mind to marry anyone at that time, even though I am sure my parents would have found such a match pleasing and acceptable. A year after our escape from Mobile, my mother died rather quickly. Right until the end she worked in the Iversons' store alongside her sister-in-law until the morning we found her dead in her bed. Poor gentle Mother—she had been the sun in our sky, the warm embrace that held us all together.

Adam and I grieved like orphans even though our father was still very much alive. After our relocation, he spent much of his time on the trade routes with his brothers and didn't know about Mother's demise for several months. I had set pen to paper many times, but where would I send a letter? What would I say? After the trading season ended, he returned home to discover her long gone and buried. We found him there at her grave one afternoon, unable to speak or move his left arm and leg. Eating became impossible, and soon he shrank into a husk of the strapping man we knew. He followed Mother into heaven just a month after his return home. And then we were orphans in the truest since of the word.

One would think that such a tragedy, the loss of parents, would drive two siblings closer, but it did not. Adam became sullen, often angry at the mere sight of me. In turn, I did my best to avoid him, spending as much time as I could with my aunt and her many grandchildren. His moods were unpredictable—at times he would leave me bouquets of purple flowers on the sideboard. Other times, he would pore over his newspapers, reading news of the war, and would slam the door in my face if I approached his room. Soon he took to leaving me alone for days on end. I went to him once, begging him to speak to me, but he refused— until one spring evening. He'd been drinking from the brown jug that Father had kept in his desk drawer. I thought that odd because Adam never drank and showed little regard for those who did.

I had retreated to my room, shed my day dress and brushed my hair before braiding it to make ready for bed. It had been a long day. Adam had sold our parents' cabin on the outskirts of town, and we had moved into the rooms above the store as a way to save money. Adam had steady work, with many orders for new tables and chairs coming in all the time, but we had no need for a home with three bedrooms.

"Delilah!" I heard him call me. I didn't go right away, for I dreaded the idea of squabbling with the brother I loved so much. "Delilah, please come see me." Unable to resist his gentler tone, I walked into the other room, waiting to hear what he had to say. I sat in a chair near the hearth. It was chilly in my nightdress, and spring had yet to yield warmer temperatures. Adam's blond hair shone bright in the candlelight, his cheeks were pink from working outdoors.

"I think we should go home."

"We cannot go back. You sold our home, remember?"

"No." He shoved a cork in the jug and set it back in its place in Father's desk drawer. "I mean home to Mobile."

"What? This is our home now, Adam. We have no one to go back for. How can you suggest that we leave our parents?"

"Our parents are dead, Delilah. We have property in Alabama, did you know that? We retain ownership of the carpentry shop and the store—even though they are empty. I had an inquiry from a woman, a Miss Page, who wants to buy them, but I can't part with them. We could do it—we could make something for ourselves."

"What are you saying, Adam? Is the war over?"

"Yes, and Mobile is rebuilding. We should be there to help. I know you miss it! You often talk about it, the warm creeks, the hummingbirds, the blackberries."

"We aren't children anymore, Adam. We have a life here. How can we leave Uncle Lars and Aunt Aida now? After all they have done for us?"

"We have worked and earned what we have. Father left us very wealthy, Lila." He moved his chair closer to me. "Please, come with me."

"You sound as if you've made up your mind already. After weeks of not talking to me, of treating me like a stranger, you have the nerve to ask me to leave with you? What will you do, leave me in the wilderness somewhere?" Tears stung my eyes. How could I leave my parents behind? How could he ask me this? I would never be able to pull the weeds from their graves or visit them whenever I needed to talk.

"I love you, Delilah. With all my heart I love you." His blue eyes were full of pain, and I suddenly felt sorry for him. I squeezed his hand and kissed his cheek. How could I stay mad at my own brother? He was all the family I had now.

"I love you too, Adam. Tell me, what has been the matter? Why have you been so distant? Is it because of the war? You blame me, don't you?"

"It's not that. I can't talk about it. Please don't ask me to explain—I will one day, I promise."

That would have to do for now. Adam was an Iverson, stubborn through and through. Pressing him would only lead to more bickering. "If I agree to this, how soon would we leave?"

He smiled his beautiful smile as if he'd already won the argument. "It would take us a few weeks to settle our affairs here and to find passage south, and I would have to find a solicitor for our legal needs. Probably by the end of May, I would think."

"I haven't said yes yet. Let me sleep on it so that I may keep at least a shred of dignity." He hugged me, holding me close to him. I welcomed his embrace; it had been too long since we had been kind to one another. Suddenly, Adam kissed me tenderly on the neck and then released me. He walked out the door, and I watched him leave. He had never kissed me before, much less in such a personal way, and I hardly knew what to think of it. I still remember that night. How I tossed and turned, how I dwelt upon that kiss.

The next morning, I rose early to prepare his breakfast. I tried not to see the eager look on his face, but I could see he wasn't going to allow me to avoid giving my answer. "Although I am loath to leave our family, I am willing to return to Mobile if you like, at least to settle our affairs there. I want you to promise me that if I choose to return, you will not stop me."

"Why should you return here? Has anyone asked for your hand?"

"No, of course not."

He smiled again and said, "Agreed. I shall tell Uncle Lars this morning after breakfast."

"Adam, if I had said no, would you have left anyway?" What prompted me to ask such a question, I do not know, but I did want to know his answer.

He poured a cup of dark coffee and stared at me. "Does it matter now? To Mobile and to our future!" He raised his cup to me and drank from it cheerfully. He chattered about details that did not concern me. Soon he left to see our uncle. Usually I would dress and go downstairs to help in the store. Sometimes my aunt needed help moving things, and I had a knack for selling. None of her daughters came to the shop except Elsa, the oldest. Her swollen belly kept her from helping now—her new baby would arrive very soon. That morning, I dawdled amongst our things, mentally making a list of what I would keep, what I would give to my aunt and what I truly didn't need.

Walking over to the rolltop desk, I rolled back the lid. My father had built the desk when he was a boy, and it still rolled smoothly. This I would take with me. I sat down on the cushioned chair and stared at the neatly stacked letters. Taking one in my hand, I ran my finger over the script, missing him more than I had in months. I didn't cry, but my heart broke to read his letters even though they were all business transactions. I read them all, and when I was through, I opened other drawers and found other stacks of letters. Again, many of these were business-related, but finally I found one that was not.

It was a worn envelope addressed to me. I had never seen it, nor had anyone ever read it to me.

Dear Delilah,

I call you this because I hear that is what your family calls you. My name is Dr. Hoyt Page. I am a physician living in Mobile, Alabama, and I am writing to inform you that you are my daughter. Forgive me for my bluntness, but as I am ill and not likely to live through the night, I feel a sense of urgency to reach out to my only living child.

As I have stated, I am your father. Your mother was Christine Beaumont Cottonwood..."

I couldn't believe what I was reading! Delilah was the baby! I immediately sent Ashland a text.

Big news in book! I'm going to keep reading, but I will come up and see you in about an hour. You still there??

A few seconds later he responded: *Yes, Detra Ann is stable now but still unconscious. I will be here.*

I scanned the waiting room. I could hardly believe this bombshell I was reading. Nobody paid me a bit of attention, which was great. I tucked in my headphones, tapped on an instrumental song on my phone and continued to read. I couldn't stop now!

Your mother was Christine Beaumont Cottonwood, and she died the night you were born. There is no way, my dear, to pretty up the facts. Christine was a married woman, married to a horrible man, Jeremiah Cottonwood, whom I recently killed. It was quite easy to do, as I have hated him for such a long time. I set upon him as he was riding drunk on his way home again to Seven Sisters. I stepped out of the shadows and shot him dead. Now he had paid for his crimes against your dear mother. The man was a monster and deserved his fate. I have avenged your mother's death, and soon I will join her. Please do not think too meanly of me to have done this deed—how could I allow him to go on living? In the case of your mother, justice moved too slowly for us all.

What else should I say to you except that I am sorry, truly sorry, for the misfortune that fate seems to have dealt you? You are the daughter of a Beaumont. That may not seem like much at the moment, but it is a special thing. You are also my daughter, the child of a prosperous doctor, and I have left everything I own to you. Won't my sister be surprised to learn about you! Your aunt, Claudette, is not a woman to be crossed, so be kind to her. Perhaps you can give her one of the houses I have bequeathed to you.

I wish we had had a different life, Christine and I, but it wasn't to be. We had our moment in the sun, and you are our proof that our love was real. You had a sister, Calpurnia, but she has been missing for nearly seventeen years. I cannot prove this, but I feel sure that Mr. Cottonwood killed her after your own dear mother died, knowing that Christine would have left your sister the heir to her fortune. I hope that somehow you will forgive me, forgive us, for not being the kind of people who could care for someone as special and lovely as you.

I imagine you often. I wonder if you like singing and playing music as Christine did, or maybe you prefer drawing, reading and writing as did your sister. I wish you were here so I could steal a look at you, as I did so many times when you were a child.

Please know that if I had believed the Iversons to be unsuitable people to serve as parents for my daughter, I would have taken you from them without a word or thought. But even I, a man who has never had a wife and family to call his own, could see that you were happy. I saw you many times, working in the shop and sometimes in attendance at church. I had hoped one day that you would return to Mobile to see me or that perhaps, once the war was over, I might go to see you, but such a visit is impossible now.

I love you more than I love my last breath. I love you more than I love even my own sister. I pray that you have a happy life. Think of me not as a vulgar man but as a fallible one who loved your mother and my children the best way I knew how.

Yours truly,

Your father,

Dr. Henry Hoyt Page

Can you imagine, Ernesto, what I felt as I read that letter? Knowing the truth forever changed me! I imagine some might feel betrayed to know that her parents were not her blood kin. Some women might feel angry at being pushed to the side so that her parents could continue their illicit affair undisturbed. Others might begrudge the inevitable title of "bastard," but I felt no shame about it.

No! I was free, Ernesto! Free like the Great Wind that blew through Shakespeare's plays. Free like a young colt that's discovered there is life outside the prison of the corral! Everything made sense now! I clutched the letter to my heart and spun about the room. I did not know this man who claimed to be my father; indeed, I did not even know if his words were true. I did know that now, more than anything else, I wanted to go to Mobile. I had to go and see what my true father had left me. I wanted *to know about him and my mother. I would always love my Iverson family, but I was old enough now to know the truth about who I was! I truly was the "dark bird!" A bird of another flock!*

But what about Adam? What did this mean for him? Was it my property he was thinking of claiming for himself? I tucked the letter in my dress pocket and continued to search. In the hidden compartment under the desk I found three more letters. One was from the Miss Page that Adam had spoken about. With shaking fingers I opened the letter and read it feverishly.

...wish to purchase the sundries store on Royal Street. Please let me know...

Thank God! How would I feel knowing that my own brother would be willing to steal from me, his sister? Wait! I was not his sister. We were raised as such, but there was not an ounce of Iverson blood in my body. And Adam, well, he was a Norwegian through and through. Suddenly, I heard him bounding up the stairs. He must have received a happy answer from our—his—uncle. He came into the room with a smile on his face, but it quickly faded as he saw the letter in my hand and the state of the desk.

"Adam," I whispered, unsure of what I wanted to say. He didn't ask any questions; he tossed his hat on the table and closed the door behind him. I walked toward him, Miss Page's letter in my hands. All of a sudden I knew the truth, the mind-blowing truth: I loved him. I loved him like a woman loves a man. By the kiss he had given me earlier, I knew he felt the same way. He knew the truth and had probably known for some time but had kept it from me.

I didn't know what I should say, so I said nothing at first. Then, with a trembling voice I said, "I know who I am now. I know that I am not your sister."

He nodded, looking relieved, his fair complexion an embarrassed pink. At last, the weight of the truth lifted off of him, but he didn't move. I knew that he would never care that some might call me bastard. He didn't care what anyone thought, and neither did I. For the first time, I kissed him. Chastely at first and then passionately. It sounds strange, doesn't it, Ernesto? That I could so freely kiss a man whom I had previously considered my brother. It sounds strange and unholy to me even now, but I think we always knew.

We did not kiss again after that, not for many weeks. We spent our time packing and preparing for our trip. I asked him one quiet evening while we sat in the nearly empty house how long he had known the truth. He confessed that he had always known, that he remembered the day I came to live with his family, a frail child who cried constantly. But it wasn't until recently that he realized he loved me. He had promised our mother that he would never tell me, but my discovery of the letter had freed him from that constraint.

Adam advised me to refrain from telling the Iversons about our relationship, for they would not approve. In the Old World, adopted children are considered blood kin. So we kept our secret and left with their blessing. I genuinely felt heartsick about leaving my aunt and her grandchildren.

I won't bore you, Ernesto, with the details of our trip. The days were long and tedious with too much riding and not enough walking. Adam treated me well, making sure that I was as comfortable as possible in whatever carriage, train or wagon we found ourselves in. However, he was still changeable. At times, he introduced me as his sister, at other times as his fiancée, although he had not actually proposed. It did not escape my notice that these "sister" introductions were typically made in the presence of other young women, women that Adam might have had an eye for.

Truth be told, I spent half the journey to the Gulf Coast not speaking to him. For two months we traveled and never did he kiss me again.

We arrived in Mobile on a Tuesday. The dirt streets in front of our shops were muddy, but from the wagon we could see that somehow the businesses had made it through the war without any missing walls or fallen roofs. "See! That's a sign!" Adam said excitedly. We looked for lodgings for the next few nights, as our plan was to live again in the apartment above our sundries store. We would have to paint, make small repairs and then set about the task of becoming reacquainted with the community. A daunting task if ever there was one! I shall never forget how hopeful Adam was—how sure he was that everything would be okay.

For my part, I was as nervous as a cat in a room full of rocking chairs! Besides the change in scenery, I faced the prospect of navigating the social community knowing the truth about my own parentage. I had to find my own solicitor, present my letter and proceed with claiming my inheritance. I didn't know Claudette Page, but what woman would want to hear the news that her brother had had a child out of wedlock—two, if you included my missing sister—who would be the heir to the fortune she thought she had inherited? As Adam tended to his legal affairs, I tended to mine. I found a lawyer named Mr. Peyton on Royal Street, not too far from our shop. With some surprise, he listened to my story and read the letter.

"How amazing! To think, I knew the man and never knew that he...well, I never knew he had a daughter."

"Two daughters. He has two daughters, Mr. Peyton."

"Well, technically, just one living heir. Calpurnia Cottonwood was declared dead years ago. Her inheritance from her mother was claimed

by her father, or the man we believed was her father. How incredible!" He
twisted his waxed mustache tips and stared with wide eyes. *"I suppose
you have something that would corroborate your story. A will, perhaps,
or some other documentation."*

The question surprised me. I had not expected that I would need to prove
my identity. I confessed as much to the attorney.

*"Let me speak frankly to you, my dear. This is quite a thing to present to a
judge. He may not believe that this letter is from Dr. Page or that it is a
true document. I am almost certain that before we proceed, we need
something else. At least something that we can use to authenticate the
handwriting."*

"What? Who would make up such a thing? I would never..."

*"I believe you. I am on your side, and I want you to have what belongs to
you, but...well...have you met Claudette Page? Dr. Page's sister?"*

"No, I haven't."

*"There is no way that lady is going to lie down for this. Not for one
minute! I have never met such an independent-minded woman, and she is
most disagreeable. To top it all off, you'll be accusing her brother of a
great lapse in virtue, a topic that is particularly important to the lady.
She is one of our city's strongest advocates for 'greater Christian
morality,' as she calls it. I heard a rumor—it can't be true, though—that
even the local pastors consult her before they preach their sermons.
Apparently, they were becoming too liberal here for her liking."*

"She must be very influential to hold such sway over the community." I
fiddled with my gloves, unsure what to do next. How could the man who
claimed to be my father do this to me?

*"Still, if Hoyt—I mean, Dr. Page—took the trouble to send you this letter,
then chances are he made some record of it somewhere. I'll check with the
courthouse to see if there is anything useful there. My friend Mr.
Schumacher is the director of our bank. I can inquire with him about any
accounts or safety deposit boxes. If we cannot produce supporting
documents, we will have no choice but to meet with Miss Page personally.
I am sure she would want to avoid a scandal, so that should work in our
favor."*

*"I don't wish to cause a scandal, and I'm not here to take anything that's
not mine, Mr. Peyton. I confess I am just as surprised about all this as
anyone else is."* I paused and then asked the question I was dying to ask.
"What do you know about my mother and sister?"

*"Until today, I would have sworn that Christine Beaumont was a saint.
Never had a bad word to say about anyone, and she lived with the devil
himself! I don't blame her too harshly for wanting to find some happiness
in this world outside that cold fish of a husband. However, as your*

attorney, I advise you to keep that letter to yourself. No one, not even Miss Page, needs to read Hoyt's confession."

"I will keep it to myself." He rose to see me out, but I had one more question. "What about Calpurnia? What can you tell me about her?"

"I didn't know her personally, but I did attend her coming-out party. My son Gerald was quite taken with her, but unfortunately for him, she showed no interest. I do remember she was very shy, some might even say bookish, but still a lovely young woman. You look very much like her. Yes, if anyone saw you, they might look twice. That might help your case, Miss Iverson—I mean, Miss Page."

I rose to my feet smiling. I liked the sound of my true name. "I will leave this to you then, Mr. Peyton. My brother and I are staying at the Iverson Sundries Store."

"Oh yes! I'll be in touch soon."

I walked back to the store and set about cleaning the place. What would my parents think about all this? I tried not to think about it. Maybe it was best that I gave it up—left the name behind and spent the rest of my days as an Iverson. It was certainly something I needed to think about. As I swept up the dust, thinking and stewing over the fact that Adam was gone yet again, a shadow darkened my doorway. A woman dressed in black from head to toe blocked the sunlight, her tall, lace-lined bonnet adding height to her already imposing figure. I raised a hand to my eyes and asked, "May I help you, madam? Our store isn't open yet, but if you'd like to place an order for something specific..."

She walked in and untied the bow under her chin. With an unimpressed expression, she looked around the store and then finally at me. "Delilah Iverson, I presume?"

"Yes. May I help you?" I smiled at the sunlit figure.

"I was just getting to know your brother at the carpentry shop. We haven't been properly introduced. My name is Claudette—Claudette Page." She didn't offer me a hand of friendship or even a smile. She held her bonnet to her as if she were afraid that the dust might soil her hat beyond repair. As she stepped out of the light, I could see her features more clearly now. She had pale skin, carefully curled black hair and full lips. I imagined at one time she had been an attractive woman but never one prone to smiling.

"Miss Page, nice to meet you. May I help you?"

"Are you or are you not Delilah Iverson?" So the swords were sharpening, were they? Miss Page did not know me if she thought I would be cowed by her unfriendly attitude. I knew who she was but not why she was here.

"That depends on who you ask, Miss Page."

"You have the look of your mother," she said as she stared around the room at the crates and boxes.

I didn't know what to say. Who was I to argue with such an observation? I had never laid eyes on my mother. I felt my chin rise and I clung to my broom handle, fighting the urge to hit her with it repeatedly. "The nature of your visit confuses me, Miss Page."

"Oh, I just wanted to have a look around."

"I see," I said.

"You know, I wrote to your brother while you were in Canada. I offered to buy this place so you wouldn't have to come all this way. I mean, the economy here isn't what it used to be. You might find it difficult to turn a profit, Miss Iverson. Mobile already has a sundries shop. Do we really need two?"

"A little competition is good for the economy, at least that's what I've read. Do you have a different theory?"

"Yes, I have a theory. I think you're an opportunist, Miss Iverson. Your coward brother ran from the war, and now the two of you are back to exploit the hardworking people of Mobile. But I won't let you do that!"

"How dare you talk about my brother in such an offensive manner! My brother is no coward!"

"So you see how it is then." Her voice was like sharpened steel. "I care for my brother as you care for yours. Why sully Hoyt's name now that he's gone, now that he's dead. Let sleeping dogs lie, Miss Iverson, and I'll do the same for you."

"Are you threatening me, Miss Page?"

Another shadow appeared in the back door. It was Adam!

"Come now. Do I need to threaten such a sensible girl as yourself? Lay down your claim to my brother, and I will do the same for yours."

Adam walked into the shop from the stockroom, shock written all over his face. "What? What claim are you referring to, Miss Page?"

"Isn't it interesting that when the war came to our fair city, you were nowhere to be found?" Adam's face turned beet red, and he walked to the half-open door and held it open. "If Miss Iverson leaves her ridiculous claim at the courthouse door, I will keep my opinions to myself. No one has to know that you were a coward, Adam."

"How dare you!" My voice rose in anger. "Get out of my store! I will make no such promise! Who do you think you are that you can come here and threaten me—threaten us? Get out!" She stomped out, leaving us alone. I turned to Adam, but the damage was already done.

All his hopes were dashed now—his male Norwegian pride crushed like flowers under a bootheel. His worst fears were realized. The gossip had begun—Adam Iverson was a coward. Adam Iverson was yellow. I could hear his imagination at work already.

"Adam!" I called after him, but I didn't see him until late that evening. And so it was for two weeks until I heard again from my attorney...

I forced myself to close the small, worn book. I didn't have time to focus on another mystery like what happened to Delilah Iverson. Detra Ann was fighting for her life, and the gravity of the situation became very real to me. I needed to help my friend.

Finally, I knew how I could do it.

Chapter 16

Cynthia Dowd walked out of the tiny hospital bathroom and gasped.

"Oh, I'm sorry. I didn't mean to startle you. How is she?"

With a worried expression, she glanced at her comatose daughter and whispered, "I think she's doing better. See, she's got color in her cheeks this evening. I think she knows we are here, don't you?"

I politely agreed with her and followed her back to Detra Ann's bedside. I sat in the noisy pleather seat and tried to be quiet. I needed Cynthia to leave—this would be dangerous, but I had to do it. Making contact with Detra Ann could only help. At least that's what I believed. Since Cynthia was whispering, I whispered to her, "Have you seen Ashland and TD?"

"Yes, they went to grab a bite to eat. Ashland told me he wanted to bring you something too. You must have just missed him. They went to Jumpers for takeout. They'll be back soon."

"What about you, Cynthia? Don't you need to eat something?"

"No, I can't eat. Not while she's like this."

I sighed. "Yes, I can see that." I sat quietly again, trying to work out how I could get her out of here. I needed to be alone with Detra Ann, and I needed enough time to fall asleep and make contact with her. I prayed that I wasn't making a terrible mistake by attempting this.

She leaned back in the seat beside me and said with a smile, "Wasn't it nice that the ladies came to see me this morning?"

"Yes, very nice indeed. Bette seems to truly care about you." Bette! As discreetly as I could I reached for my phone and texted her while Cynthia sat staring at her daughter.

Bette, this is Nancy Drew. I need your help. Can you come to the hospital? I need to get Cynthia out of the room.

My "Nancy Drew" reference was an observation that Detective Simmons had made about Bette and me during the Mia incident. She'd called us Angela Lansbury and Nancy Drew. It had tickled Bette tremendously.

On the way. What do you have in mind?

Can't share now but it's crucial. Please help.

Roger that.

Bette added a smiley face and I tapped one back. For the next fifteen minutes, I chitchatted with Cynthia as she talked about Detra Ann's last beauty pageant, how she'd shocked the committee by performing "Dixie" on her flute while leading her white poodle through an obstacle course. It was quite humorous to hear, and I was sure that Detra Ann would be mortified that her mother would tell such childhood secrets.

The door opened, but it wasn't Bette. Ashland and TD were back with food. "There you are," Ashland said. "What's up with not answering your phone?" I checked it and noticed his two messages.

"Oops, sorry. I don't know how I missed those," I whispered.

"Why are we whispering?" Ashland asked me, but it was Cynthia who answered.

"Because she's asleep. She'll wake up when she's ready. Now you boys go out in the hall and let her rest a while."

"Hey, everybody!" Bette missed the speech about whispering, but Cynthia didn't say a word to her. "How is our princess doing, Cynthia? Oh, look at her. I think I see color in those pretty cheeks. I'd say she's on the mend. Have the doctors come in recently?"

"They won't be in until morning."

"You know what? You don't look so hot, Cynthia. I mean, you look pale, darling." I loved the way Bette said "darling." It was the long drawn out version, "daw-lin." It just kind of lingered there.

"I don't care what I look like right now."

"I'm not talking about your gorgeous face, Cynth. You can't neglect your health right now. Not when Detra Ann is going to need you so much. When was the last time you had some fresh air?"

"I don't know. This morning, maybe?"

"I tell you what, let's go for a walk. Maybe visit the gift shop and find her some flowers. She'll like seeing those when she wakes up."

"No, Bette! I can't leave her. What happens if she wakes up and I'm not here?"

"You won't be gone long, and Carrie Jo is here. You can trust her to stay, right?"

"Oh, yes, ma'am. I'll stay. Ashland brought me some food, and I have a pillow and blanket. Take all the time you want."

"I won't be gone long, though," Cynthia said, stretching her back before she walked over to the mirror. She stared at herself disapprovingly. I felt bad for manipulating her, but I needed her to leave. Ashland watched the whole thing quietly and didn't interfere, but he knew something was up. I'd have to explain what I was doing. That would be tricky.

Bette kept her game face on as they left and didn't give a clue that I had called her. Now that was a true friend. I would have to thank her somehow later.

"What's up, beautiful? You're up to something. You might as well tell me now."

"Yes, I am up to something." I arranged the pillow and blanket in the chair next to Detra Ann. I reached over and held her hand lovingly. Through tear-filled eyes, I stared at her perfect pink manicured nails. She'd tried to help me, to save me from something in my house—probably Isla—and now she was trapped, trapped in another world. I had to go help her. Suddenly awareness crept across Ashland's face.

"No, Carrie Jo. This isn't a good idea! What happens if you make contact with her and then you're in a coma too?"

TD broke in, "Wait! Ashland's right. Detra Ann wouldn't want that."

"I have my friend's hand, that's all. I'm tired and am going to take a nap now. If I see her, I will talk to her, maybe get her to come back to us."

"You can do that?" TD sounded unsure but willing to give it a shot if it brought Detra Ann back to him.

"I've never done it before, TD, but I would like to try. With all my heart I will try. She loves you so much. I can't imagine that she'd want to be too far away from you."

"Ashland, I don't want to put her in danger, but if she can find her..."

"I know. Okay, Carrie Jo. I guess it's okay, not that you needed my permission. I know you. You would have done it anyway."

"I sure would have. Now turn out the light, please, and try to keep the nurses occupied for the next thirty minutes."

"Sure, but I am going to be right outside. If I hear something, I am coming in."

"Fair enough."

Ashland turned off the light and held onto the doorknob for a minute. I smiled at him to reassure him and then closed my eyes. Sleep didn't come immediately; there were too many distractions. To make matters worse, I could hear Henri's deep, booming voice in the hallway. He'd come! But I had to focus on Detra Ann.

Detra Ann, where are you? Why won't you come back to us?

I rubbed her hand gently, just like my mother would do for me when I was sick as a child, before she became sick herself. It had always comforted me; hopefully it would help me make a connection with Detra Ann.

All of a sudden, I stepped out of reality and into the dream world, and what I saw terrified me. I wasn't holding the hand of beautiful, tanned Detra Ann—I was holding the hand of Christine Beaumont!

I looked down at Christine, only I wasn't a character in a dream or some ghost from the past—I was me! Wrapped around her arms and legs were black snake-like cords that held her in place. "Help me! They won't let me go!" I stared, but only for a moment. A disturbing sound from the hallway, like a demonic train, shook the building and threatened to bust through the wall. I began to furiously untie the cords and free her from the hospital bed. At first, I didn't think I could release her, but suddenly the cords fell off. She sat up in the bed and put her arms around me.

"You can see me! You have to help me! He won't let me go! Where is Hoyt? Hurry!"

With frightened fingers I untied the last tie. "I will help you, Christine—but where is my friend, Detra Ann? I have to know!" The crashing train noise ceased, and suddenly the room became foggy so quickly that I could barely see Christine. But I didn't release her hand, and she clung to mine. She slid off the bed, her full skirts rustling as she did. The gray fog cleared and she stared at me, then recognition crossed her face. She squeezed my hand even tighter—I thought she would hug me again.

"I don't understand how you are here, my own dearest. How I have missed you! Please help me! Oh no! They're here, Calpurnia—run!" she sobbed. Her brow beaded with sweat, and her dark blond hair became wet with it.

I pulled on her hand. "I'm not Calpurnia. I'm Carrie Jo. What about Detra Ann? Where is she?"

"We have to go now, Isla is coming—my tormentor, the one who tied me here!" The door blew open, and the sound of a thousand angry invisible bees filled the room. It was the same sound I'd heard in the Moonlight Garden the night Ashland, TD and I defeated Isla—or thought we had.

"Christine! Where are you going? I've only just begun to play with you. So happy that Calpurnia could join us," Isla purred, her perfect blond ringlets bouncing against her cherubic cheeks.

"I'm not Calpurnia!" I shouted, but who was going to hear me over the furious noise? Christine tugged on my hand, and we ran pell-mell down the hallway to the back wall. I screamed, preparing for the pain of running into the wall, but nothing happened. Instead I opened my eyes to find myself and Christine standing in the ballroom of Seven Sisters.

A lone candelabrum provided light in the dreary blackness that surrounded us. Catching my breath—I thankfully still had breath—I noticed a figure walking toward us. It was Jeremiah Cottonwood. He wore all black except for shiny silver coat buttons that glittered in the dimness. He looked as if he were going to a funeral, and then it occurred to me that this was how he must have been dressed for his own funeral. Hoyt Page had killed him over a hundred and fifty years ago.

"Christine, daughter...how nice of you to come to my party. More guests will be arriving soon. Come closer and embrace me." He stretched out his arms to us with a devilish smile, and I noticed that the tiny silver buttons weren't buttons at all but spiders that fell off his velvet suit and scrambled across the hardwood floor. I shuddered at the sight.

"Stay away from us, Jeremiah."

His evil smile vanished, his mouth opened and an unearthly scream rose—it penetrated my very bones. "I'm alive! I'm still alive," I kept telling myself. I hoped it was true. How could I be here?

Still, Christine squeezed my hand. "We have each other now, Calpurnia, and nothing will stop us from going to our peace. Nothing! Step aside, Jeremiah! Your curse has been broken."

He did not move but stared at us, his neck bent down, his head tilted up. The evil smile had returned, and his dark eyes shimmered strangely. He observed us like an animal would, an animal stalking its prey.

Fearlessly, Christine continued. She walked around him with sure steps, never letting go of my hand. "Remember the words you whispered in my ear the night you killed me? You cursed me. You said no one would ever love me again, not now and not for eternity." She stepped toward him bravely, ignoring his angry, purple face and the beastly, guttural sounds he made. "You are a liar! I am loved!"

"I loved you!"

She smiled at him. "Yes, I remember how you loved me, Jeremiah. I remember how you slid the rope around my neck. I remember how you tightened it and raised me from the ground until I swung higher and higher. Oh yes, I remember your love! You exacted your revenge and stole my life, and now you think you can keep me in death too? What justice is that? I will be free!"

"What do you know of love, Christine?" He hissed at her.

"You condemned me and then killed me, but what you didn't know was that you set me free. Free from you who cannot love!"

"Don't speak to me about love, harlot!"

"Call me what you will, but I have love. My daughter loves me! The power of our love breaks your curse, Jeremiah!"

"But I'm not..." I started to explain myself, but then the invisible bees began to circle me again. It was Isla, here to serve Jeremiah, to see to it that he exacted his revenge on us for all eternity. Briefly I wondered what debt she was paying by serving him in death, for I knew in life she cared nothing for him. He had been amusing to her and, like most men, a means to whatever end she imagined or schemed.

"What kind of fool do you take me for, Christine? This is not Calpurnia, your bastard daughter."

Suddenly, Jeremiah reached for Christine with a gnarled hand and snatched her viciously from my grip with such force that I fell backward. He slid his arm around her neck. The look of fear had returned to her face, and I could see her surprise. She'd failed. How could she have confused me for Calpurnia?

Whatever the reason, I had failed Christine. And I had failed Detra Ann.

"This can't be," she yelled. "Calpurnia?"

"You are mine, Christine! And now another has come to join our party! Bring in our guest, Isla." Isla stepped out of the outer darkness and with a wave of her hands made candlelight appear around the room—it looked just as it had the night of her coming-out party. Wax candles burned bright, an orchestra played in the corner of the room and black-clad dancers took their places on the floor. My skin felt cold and clammy, as if death were nearby. It was, wasn't it? She wore a purple dress with white ribbons at the sleeves, and her invisible hemline never touched the ground.

I couldn't be here! I couldn't be! How is this even possible?

"Hoyt!" I heard Christine scream with all her might. "Hoyt! Help me, my love!"

I swung my head to the door and wanted to run to him but couldn't get up. I suddenly felt heavy, as if my limbs were covered with concrete. I couldn't move or get up—only helplessly watch whatever was about to happen. *Oh my God! That's TD! Why can't she see it's Terrence Dale and not Hoyt Page?*

"I'm here, Christine." Then, TD wasn't TD anymore. He was taller, thinner with darker hair, and he wore a tailored brown suit. "I failed you before, but I will not fail you now, my love. Come to me. Let her go, Cottonwood. You have no claim on her."

She wrangled free from Jeremiah but only for a second. Grinning, Cottonwood slid his arm around her neck again and said savagely, "She's mine, Page. She always will be mine. You may have her heart, but I have a covenant that cannot be broken, the covenant of marriage. I am on the side of right."

Hoyt stormed toward Jeremiah, determined to rescue Christine, but he ran into the invisible force that Isla seemed to manipulate so easily with just her hands.

"Isla! Stop this! How can you let him use you like this?" I pleaded with her. I was desperate.

She giggled and pressed her hands together, a move that forced me almost flat to the hardwood floor.

"How can you set her free, Page? See, she is mine still."

"You are a murderer! You murdered Christine. You are an unjust man, and you have no right to keep her here! You would have killed our daughter too, if I had allowed it. I saved her, Christine. I saved Delilah!"

"Let me go, Jeremiah. Please I beg you." Christine struggled less now, and I could see that she was giving up. "Don't keep me here anymore. I can't bear it. I want to be with Hoyt and my children."

"Did you think that I didn't know about you and Hoyt, about your bastard children—the ones you tried to pass off as mine? What a fine game player you were, dear! Granted it took me years to discover that Calpurnia was his ill-begotten stock, but once I knew, everything changed. You stole that from me! I will never let you leave, not now—not ever!"

"Christine! Christine! Come to me now! Please! Before it's too late!" Hoyt cried out from his knees. Isla whirled around us, and this time she sailed by so close that I could smell honeysuckle and something else...death. I could feel her excitement as she waited to kill me.

"I can't, he won't let me go! It's no use, Hoyt," Christine cried pitifully. For a second, her face faded—I could plainly see Detra Ann! Jeremiah was holding Detra Ann!

"Fight, Detra Ann! Fight!" My friend struggled with renewed vigor, but it lasted only a few seconds.

Isla growled, but I continued to shout, "Fight! You are not Christine, you are Detra Ann Dowd. You are my friend, and I care about you! Now fight, damn it!"

Jeremiah seemed confused, but then Detra Ann's face disappeared and it was just Christine again, crying hopelessly.

"Let her go, Jeremiah! She's not Christine!" Finally, I could stand. I reached for Hoyt and helped him up too. A swell of terrible music rose in the ballroom, and the once-frozen dancers began to dance around us. The stale air moved like a brewing storm.

"You are a guest in my house now, my dear. Please join the dance," Jeremiah said, squeezing Detra Ann's neck, choking the life from her.

"NO! Detra Ann! TD, do something!" I screamed as a faceless man in a black suit whipped his arm around my waist and spun me about, lifting me a few feet from the ground. We danced in a circle, his invisible hand on my waist, pulling me tighter and tighter.

"Calpurnia, my darling," he whispered. I recognized that voice! David Garrett! He was here too, trapped with everyone else! It took everything I had not to scream my head off as I struggled between my fear of falling to the ground and my terror at being held by this faceless ghoul.

The doors opened again, and the dancers froze to see who else had arrived. It was Bette!

I gasped and then screamed at the top of my lungs, "Bette! Run! Leave before it's too late!" But she didn't appear to hear me. The ghost that held me swirled us back to the ground, and I violently pushed away from him. I made my way through the dancers—I had to get to Bette!

"Let her go!" she commanded Jeremiah. "Now!" Bette stepped toward Christine as he visibly released his hold on her. Then the oddest thing happened—Bette transformed before my very eyes. Her perfect puffs of white curls grew, and her hair darkened to a lustrous dark brown. She appeared tall and thin, like Hoyt. In a flash, her blue capris with the yellow daisies all over were replaced with a flowing pink and white gown and a lovely white hat with a soft ivory-colored feather. She walked toward the center of the room and stood between Hoyt and Jeremiah. The bees went silent, and I noticed that even Isla slid as far away from Bette as she could. Fear, which had been tangible and sovereign just moments ago, fled into the shadows like a wild animal along with Isla and her cohorts. Peace filled the room. I alone stood out from the darkness. Hoyt (or TD, I wasn't sure which) was only a few feet away from me. He watched with a rapt expression of pure love.

Bette wasn't Bette. She was young and beautiful—she was Delilah Iverson.

"Can it be?" Christine's hand flew to her chest, and she took a step away from Jeremiah. He did not reach for her again. I noticed that he too had retreated a little.

"Yes, Mother. I am Delilah, your daughter. I am here to take you home."

In one bold move, Christine covered the distance between them and embraced her tightly. After a moment, Delilah stepped away, touching her arm as she walked toward Jeremiah. His typical haughty expression had vanished, replaced with a look of abject despair and anger.

"My mother doesn't belong to you anymore. You were wrong—she is loved. I love her, just as my sister loves her. We are leaving here now, Jeremiah Cottonwood, and don't think to stop us."

He backed away as a light surrounded her. I couldn't explain it, but love shone through her like a big bright candle. No. Like a star.

Arm in arm, they walked toward the outside door. Another light, brighter and bigger than even Delilah, shone brilliantly. As the door swung open, that light filled the ballroom in a flash.

Hoyt stumbled after them, pleading, "You can't leave me again, Christine. I love you and always will. Don't leave me now."

Christine paused on the garden path and gave him a beautiful smile. She reached out her hand, and he ran to her.

"Wait! TD! You can't go!" I cried out, unsure what to think about what was happening. I watched their glowing figures walk through the Moonlight Garden, Delilah on the right, Hoyt on the left and Christine in the middle. I didn't dare take my eyes off of them, but I could "feel" the others around me disappearing into nothingness.

Instead of giggling, I heard Isla crying. Crying that her life and afterlife were now completely over. She would go down into the grave and be gone forever.

Worm food now, I suppose...

Jeremiah didn't whimper or wail, but simply slid into a small black hole that appeared in the floor. He didn't even make a sound as he slipped away down into the abyss. The hole closed, leaving only a small scorch mark on the floor.

I looked back up and saw the three lights, Delilah, Christine and Hoyt, fading away into the dark night. They were together at last. I wondered if they would simply go to sleep or if they would have time, their time—the time that was stolen from them. I didn't know. I hoped they found Calpurnia waiting wherever they were going.

I sat on the hardwood floor and cried my eyes out.

Epilogue

Ashland and Carrie Jo stepped out onto the dais and faced the excited crowd. It was springtime in Mobile, bright and cool—the perfect day for unveiling the new Bette Marshall Museum and the Terrence Dale House. The new museum housed the extension of the Seven Sisters art collection, while the Dale House was the rebuilt slave quarters, reconstructed according to TD's plans. It had been next on his list after restoring the Moonlight Garden. Ashland and TD had wanted to restore the plantation to be as historically accurate as they could make it, and this addition would do just that. Carrie Jo had commissioned a painting of Muncie that now hung in the foyer of the Marshall Museum. It was one of my favorite places to visit.

I wondered what our missing friends would think about the honors we bestowed upon them today. I wondered if TD remembered me—I liked to imagine that he did. I thought about him every day. At first, he was all I could think about. How could he have simply walked out of the hospital and disappeared? But slowly, the space between the crashing waves of grief grew, and eventually I found the strength to continue. But my future was forever changed by his absence.

Ashland made his speech, and the crowd applauded. I watched Carrie Jo as she stood smiling by his side. Funny how close we were now. She was like the sister I never had. I couldn't imagine life without her, and I would forever be in her debt for what she did.

"But none of this would be possible without the help of Detra Ann Dowd, the director of the Seven Sisters Living Museum. Please make her welcome." The crowd again applauded, and I solemnly took the podium. I closed my eyes for a second and let the sunlight beam down on me. We'd worked like dogs to make this happen in such a short time, but at least it was done. These weren't just important landmarks and museums. They were memorials to our friends.

It was the least we could do.

According to the papers, Bette Marshall had died of a sudden heart attack in her home. TD had simply disappeared. For a while, rumors circulated that he'd fallen off the wagon again, but when he didn't reappear, everyone changed their mind. I knew the truth. So did Ashland, Henri and Carrie Jo. That was all that mattered.

"Thank you, everyone, for your support throughout this process. Special thanks to the Historical Society for your tireless commitment to Seven Sisters...." I read my notes and tried to keep a smile in my voice. I thought I did okay. When my speech was finished, I took a seat on the dais. Carrie Jo reached for my hand and squeezed it. Suddenly, I missed TD so badly that I almost cried. I squeezed her hand back, and she didn't let go. I was glad for that.

When the ceremony ended, we stepped off the dais and I fell into Henri's big arms. He'd become a dear friend to me these past six months. I was glad that he had decided to move back to Mobile. Within a month, he'd purchased the Cotton City Treasures antiques store, and I'd spent a bit of time there helping him set up his displays. It was peaceful work, and he seemed to value my opinion. Despite what some of the wagging tongues might think, we weren't romantically involved. But I cared deeply for him.

We spent the next thirty minutes greeting visitors and answering questions. When it was over, I gave a sigh of relief. I was leaving Seven Sisters at the end of the month. My assistant, Rachel Kowalski, was taking over the directorship. I knew I was leaving the house in good hands. Of that, I had no worries. I'd given enough to the house. We all had.

It was time to leave the past behind...time to say goodbye to Seven Sisters. I took a walk through the Moonlight Garden. I touched the flowers and breathed in the scent of magnolias and roses. I picked a few petals off the ground and walked to the Atlas fountain.

"Goodbye, TD." I tossed the petals into the water and watched them spin wildly and then slowly sink to the bottom.

I turned my face to the sun once more and felt peace wash over me. I couldn't say for sure, but in that moment I believed he heard me.

For the last time, I walked out of the maze and back to the house. Henri, Ashland and Carrie Jo waited for me. We walked through the house and closed the door behind us.

We didn't look back.

~~*

The Stars We Walked Upon

By M.L. Bullock

This book is dedicated to all the fans of the *Seven Sisters* series. Thank you for walking through the Blue Room and strolling down the shady paths of the Moonlight Garden with me.
May you have many dreams, and may they all come true.

O Stars and Dreams and Gentle Night;
O Night and Stars return!
And hide me from the hostile light
That does not warm, but burn

That drains the blood of suffering men;
Drinks tears, instead of dew:
Let me sleep through his blinding reign,
And only wake with you!

—Emily Bronte

Excerpt from "Stars"

Prologue

Mobile, AL, 1851

Sunlight splashed through the tall conservatory windows, and I leaned back in the comfortable parlor chair, a glass of brandy in my hand. I closed my eyes, allowing the music to carry me to places far and away. The sound of the piano lent to the illusion of sanity and comfort, two things perpetually absent from my world of escalating darkness. The notes were light and choppy and full of happiness. If I allowed myself to, I could imagine I was in the music room of some talented debutante hoping to impress me, the elegant Captain David Garrett.

How many times had this been the case? How many musical recitals had been performed for me?

Sipping my brandy, I scanned through the memories with pleasure. The first face I recalled was that of the delightful Katrina Phelps, the daughter of Christian and Mary Beth Phelps of Savannah, Georgia. A pretty thing with light brown eyes, a sharp, clever wit and a sultry voice, a voice too sultry for one so young. Still, as charming as her face and figure were, she had not yielded to my ardent desire despite my best efforts to persuade her. The Phelps family welcomed me into their particular society; that is until that wretched letter arrived. And then Katrina was lost to me.

Ah, but there was always a fly in the ointment. One sour spinster who could not or would not leave the past alone. Yes, the past was my constant companion. I shook the memory of Miss Phelps and her tearstained face away. How she cried over me! At the time, I believed that I loved her—imagine that!

Oh yes, then there was Miss Virginia Lewis. The mother was so keen to make my acquaintance that I barely knew whom to seduce—the mother or the daughter. However, after meeting the woman's husband, I decided that the latter would suffice. Unlike many of the maidens I dabbled with, I had not been able to control myself, so willing was she. I did partake of the young woman's delights and so perhaps deserved the disdain of Red Hills' society, but in the end, what did I care? Red Hills was no Savannah, nor Charleston nor even a Mobile. It was merely a farm community, and Miss Virginia Lewis nothing more than a glamorous wealthy farm girl with hefty arms, pink cheeks and skin that tasted like butter. My cheeks warmed at the thought of her, or perhaps it was the brandy. I smiled remembering our times together in the milk shed, the store cupboard, the floor of the carriage. But I had been a much younger man then, just hitting my prime.

The piano's notes climbed higher and the music became lighter. I yielded myself to the tune, pausing only to sip the decadent drink in my crystal glass. I felt as if the notes could almost carry me to heaven—it was probably as close to that holy place as I could ever hope to reach.

Especially after what happened to Miss Cottonwood. Dear, sweet, gentle Miss Cottonwood. Now she had been a true lady. *That had not been entirely my fault.* The girl must have been out of her mind to seek me aboard the Delta Queen—or been encouraged to do so by someone other than me. With slitted eyes I observed my nude piano player. Loose coils of long blond hair hung down her back and stuck to her skin. How she sweated when we made love! She was no pasty-faced farm girl happy to endure whatever pleased me. No, she was an active participant—curious, hungry and eager to please and be pleased. It occurred to me that I should love her. After all, we were bound together in a dark world of our own making; perhaps I did love her in my own perverse way.

Although I told myself that she was the bane of my existence I admired her ambition, her skilled depravities. How I loved her constant scheming—her spirited aspirations far exceeded mine. She was like that biblical hussy Jezebel, and she deserved to be thrown out of the tower. I was the doomed Ahab.

I knew all this, and yet I was her slave.

Suddenly the piano made a crashing noise as her hands slammed down on the keys. Quick as a flash she was off her tufted stool and standing before me. Her damp tresses covered her goblet-shaped breasts.

"What are you thinking? I demand you tell me!"

As subtly as I could, I glanced at her hands to make sure that they held no object that might injure me, for my love had a deadly temper. Seeing no scissors, knitting needles or any other type of blade, I smiled at her peacefully.

"I think of nothing but you, my love. What else should I think of?"

"You're a fool! Tell me you're not thinking of her!" Her hands went to the curve of her naked hips, and she stared at me with unbelieving eyes.

"Calm down, dearest. Sit in my lap. Let us talk of the future—not the past. You promised, remember?"

I could see the struggle in her eyes as she gave in to my request and smiled that catlike smile. Her arms snaked about my neck, and her frame was as light as a feather as she perched in my lap. With insincere calmness I stroked her hair as she plunged her hand in my open shirt and rubbed my chest lightly. "Now. Where shall we go next, darling?" I spoke carefully in soothing tones. "To Paris? Perhaps to Boston? Where shall I take you?" She kissed my neck with her childlike lips—lips that always tasted of lemonade. How she loved the drink! "Nectar of the gods," she called it as she added ridiculous amounts of gin into her glass.

"I want to see *all* of those places, my darling captain. All of them! But we must wait a little while."

I wondered what plan she had concocted in her feverish brain. Isla Beaumont rarely kept me in mind when she planned a scheme. Why should today be any different? She took my hand with her small one and kissed it. "Good news, my love. I am with child."

I was shocked into silence. I weighed her mood to determine how to proceed.

"Isn't that delightful?"

I responded with a confident smile. "If you are happy, I am happy. I must say I have never considered myself a family man. My, how you have changed me."

She giggled. "Oh no, darling. I am quite sure that I am carrying a Cottonwood. A long-awaited boy for Jeremiah Cottonwood. Won't he be delighted to hear the news that he will finally have a son!" She hopped out of my lap and spun about as if she were in the ballroom.

It was my turn to laugh. The whole thing seemed so outlandish I could not wrap my mind around it. "You and Cottonwood? Tell me, my clever love. How did you ever manage that? It was my understanding that the man had no appreciation for young beauties such as yourself, not of the female persuasion."

She curtsied graciously, lifting the edges of a pretend dress. "Never underestimate my skills. That would be a mistake. He was like clay in my hands." She giggled again and pretended to hide a nonexistent blush.

I raised my glass to her and said, "Well done."

She frowned. "You do not seem as pleased as I imagined you would be. Isn't this the cleverest thing? Just think. In a few months we will have what we wanted—Seven Sisters! Oh, and that is just the beginning! Imagine me with a fat little baby and all that money. Won't that be funny?"

"Not to doubt your amazing ability to make men do whatever you desire, but what makes you believe that Mr. Cottonwood will welcome this news? We all know that man is an evil-tempered drunk."

"I have it all planned out."

"I had no doubt of that."

"You must trust me, dear Captain. I will tell you more later, but now I need a distraction—a 'faveur discrète'. Let us go upstairs and celebrate!"

I swirled the rest of my brandy and tossed it down my throat. The warmth of it invigorated me. Now wasn't the time to consider the meaning of all this. I would do that when she slept—whenever she slept. Sometimes she would not sleep for days. I pulled her close to me and stared down into her cherub-like face. How could such a face hide such a mind?

"You are full of surprises, my sweet one."

"Happy surprises?" Her coy look stirred my loins.

"Are there any other kind?" I scooped her up in my arms. She kissed my neck as I stepped over the body of our hostess. I accidentally kicked her and foolishly offered an "Excuse me."

To that, she giggled again. "David," she whispered in my ear, "Lennie Ree can't hear you. She's dead."

By the time we made it upstairs, I was nearly naked and completely hers.

***

Hours later I slipped out of our stolen bed to go downstairs in search of food. I was thinking not only for myself but also for my beloved, who was always ravenous after a murder. Now that she was with child, I was sure she would be even hungrier. But I needed food myself too. This was no small house—surely there would be something hidden in a larder somewhere. Maybe even some lemonade for my Isla.

Being the lover of the demanding, demented cherub took a lot of energy, and I needed to build my strength. I walked down the stairs holding up my trousers with one hand and whistling. I paused at the bottom step to give a respectful nod to our dead hostess. Just as I stepped over her the front door opened—there was nowhere to hide. The housekeeper, a tall, thin woman dressed in all black, did not see me at first. She set her basket down on the entryway table and left her purse there while she removed her plain black hat. I could see by her demeanor she was not someone to be trifled with—a no-nonsense kind of woman.

I decided to take the bull by the horns. Some women preferred to be charmed into doing whatever it was I wanted them to do; others preferred the direct approach. I chose the second option and hoped for the right results. If she failed to amuse me, then of course we would simply have to kill her too.

"And who might you be?" I asked in a commanding voice.

The woman appeared calm, not shocked in the least by what she saw or by my question. She had not run out the door, which she very well could have. Out of respect, I buttoned my trousers and my open shirt.

"Docie Loxley is my name. I am the housekeeper."

"Well, Miss Loxley, it appears that my hostess has had an accident and died."

"That much I see, and it is a shame. I have not been paid in six months. Who's going to give me my wages now?" She walked toward the stiff body of Lennie Ree Meadows and touched her with the toe of her black boot as if she wanted to make sure she was dead. She needn't have bothered.

Isla said from behind me, "We should bury her. But somewhere where dogs won't find her. You don't want the dead to come back. They smell awful." She hopped on my back as if she were a child and I a child's party entertainer. I did not argue but gave her a piggyback ride up and down the stairs. Isla giggled with pleasure. At least she was clothed now, although her hair was mussed and she smelled of our lovemaking. She slid off my back and stepped gingerly over our hostess. She presented herself to the housekeeper, her hands on her hips. If the housekeeper knew that her life was in the young woman's hands, if she understood that Isla could and would kill her if it pleased her, she gave no sign. She sighed and said to her, "You needn't bother yourself with this mess. I will bury her after breakfast. She's not in any hurry. Are you hungry?"

Apparently deciding the housekeeper should live, Isla bobbed alongside, free spirit that she was, and followed her into the larder. I heard Isla ask her as if it were the most natural thing, "After you bury the old lady, would you mind helping me get my hair in order? It's a rat's nest."

I didn't hear the woman's reply but if she had given the wrong one, I would have heard Isla's angry scream. As they left, I stole a tablecloth from a nearby table and covered the deceased woman's body. "Again, my apologies, madam." Leaving her in Miss Loxley's hands, I walked away from the whole mess in search of more brandy.

Now there were three of us—three savages and all with black hearts.

Chapter 1—Carrie Jo

"Dang it!" I woke myself up again faced with a choice—either put my size-seven foot on Ashland's behind and kick him off our brand new canopy bed or get up and leave. After five nights of unintentional access into his less than faithful dreams I had had about enough. It was too late to get into a knock-down, drag-out fight, so I decided to take the high road. In an angry huff, I sat up like a snapped rubber band and threw back the covers. Naturally, he didn't flinch.

Of course not! Why should he stop dreaming about some curvaceous supermodel while I'm fuming right beside him?

I stared down at the perfectly peaceful face of my sleeping husband, and my heart was a ball of feelings—none of them good. I couldn't decide which I hated more: that I couldn't control my dream catching or that I couldn't stop thinking about what I saw. Maybe it was just that I wouldn't be able to sleep for the rest of the night—God, I was tired! Call me sensitive, but the images of wanton women twisting under my husband in the throes of passion were just a bit more than I could bear. The last thing I wanted to do was fall asleep again and "enjoy" the big finish.

He's lucky we have a housekeeper who likes to cook for him because I sure as hell won't be making him breakfast! Not this morning!

Still, in the back of my mind I knew how this would play out. He'd wake up as chipper as a beaver with a new log without a clue as to why I was so pissed. I sure couldn't come out and tell him. Nope. No way was I giving up the high ground now. I might have issues, but I wasn't the cheater. I'd slap a big ol' fake Carrie Jo smile on my face and pretend that everything was right as rain. Thankfully, he did not have women's intuition. For someone who had extrasensory gifts, Ashland Stuart was none too perceptive—at least not when it came to me.

Swearing under my breath, I got out of bed and walked to the large round window across the room. The moon glowed round and near-perfect above the city of Mobile. A few wisps of clouds passed in front of it, but they quickly skittered away as the breeze blew in and along with it the fog from the nearby bay. According to the weatherman, the temperatures were never this warm in January, but people didn't seem to mind. They liked wearing flip-flops and t-shirts even in the dead of winter. As my old friend Bette used to tell me, "If you don't like the weather in Mobile, just wait a few minutes, dah-ling. It will change!" She'd chuckle and shake her head in amusement, white curls bouncing with every shake. I wondered what advice she'd have for me now. She loved Ashland, that much I knew. I had known her less than a year and she was thirty years my senior, but she had truly become one of my best friends ever. I missed her every single day. She had been a second mom—a confidante, my protector. I loved her.

I leaned against the window with arms crossed and stared down at the quiet downtown streets below. From the top floor of our Victorian home, the view was peaceful, with the exception of the occasional siren from the nearby police station. My friend and assistant Rachel informed me that the quiet façade would quickly fade when Mardi Gras kicked off in a few weeks. Apparently it was such a parking and traffic nightmare that she'd already developed maps to help us navigate traffic and avoid the bead-hungry, moon-pie-seeking masses. We even changed our office hours to accommodate the local parade calendar. I looked over my shoulder at Ashland—he didn't stir. Typical.

Think about something else, Carrie Jo!

I tried to distract myself with thoughts of work. I still couldn't believe I had an office—a real business of my own. Word had gotten out about my role in the restoration of Seven Sisters and the additions to the facility. Those old plantation owners were beginning to see what a lucrative venture restoring these beautiful downtown homes truly was. Of course I could not take all the credit. It took a team, and many of those team members were no longer with us. Like it did so often recently, my mind traveled back to the first time I visited this charming yet dangerous city. Some people called Mobile the Azalea City; others called it the Port City. In my own experience I believed a better name would be the Supernatural City. I had never been to New Orleans, but I was pretty sure that old city had nothing on this one.

I nervously spun the white gold wedding band on my finger and stared at the shiny ring in the moonlight. Tears flooded my eyes. We'd fought so hard to keep it all together, and now here I was staring out the window unable to sleep beside the man I loved. I did love him, and he loved me. I would just have to figure out a way to get my dream catching under control.

Suddenly I felt two hands on my shoulders. I gasped and nearly jumped out of my skin. I turned to find a laughing Ashland standing behind me with his hands raised in surrender. "Sorry! I thought you heard me. I didn't mean to startle you."

"What the hell?"

He laughed again. Normally I would find the sound cheerful, even sexy. Now I just wanted to slap him. He said in a softer voice, "You were deep in thought. I didn't mean to scare you like that."

"Well, you did. Let me catch my breath."

"I've got a better idea. Why don't you come back to bed? Maybe I can find a way to soothe your nerves?" He rubbed my shoulder, but I didn't encourage him.

I stammered for a moment, then stomped to the bed and grabbed my blanket, intending to find sleep elsewhere. "I can't sleep. You go to bed. No sense in both of us being tired." Playfully he grabbed the other end. He still had no clue how mad I really was. He had no idea that I knew about his breast-centric dreams. "Let go, Ashland!"

"What did I do? I said I was sorry. Now come to bed."

I glared at him. Unless I was willing to tell him the truth, I would have to do as he asked. "Fine! I just hope I can sleep. My eyes are going to look horrible in the morning, and I have to meet with Desmond Taylor. You know, you've had me up every night this week."

"What? Have I been snoring? I'm sorry, Carrie Jo. Maybe I should get some of those strips for my nose—the kind that keeps your airways open. You should have said something sooner." I flopped in the bed and turned my back to him, beating my pillow into submission. He tucked the blanket around me and kissed me on the cheek.

Darn him! How dare he be kind! I like being mad at him.

"I promise to pick some up tomorrow, and don't worry about Taylor. You're a genius. He would be lucky to have you work on his project. In the meantime, if my snoring gets really bad I can go sleep in the guest room. Should I?"

I sighed, guilt over my snooping washing over me. "That won't be necessary." As he put his arm around me and held me, I realized I was being a fool. A man's mind was his own territory—it belonged solely to him, and that included his dreams. How would I like it if Ashland saw a few of my dreams? I never planned to dream some of the crazy stuff I did, but it happened. I let him cuddle up to me, and I enjoyed his clean sandalwood scent and his strong arms. *Well, as long as he's only dreaming about it and not acting upon it, then we should be okay. Chances are he doesn't even remember them. Most people don't remember their dreams at all.* Still, I had to do something if I wanted to stay married. And indeed I did.

I glanced back at the clock on the bedside table. It was 4:45. Weird. What were the odds of that happening again? I had woken myself up early every day since Monday. Now it was Friday night—no, make that Saturday morning. As I pondered the puzzle, my eyes grew heavy and I soon fell back to sleep.

I chose to think about something else for a while. Like Delilah Iverson. I'd put her to the side too long. I had promised myself after my friends died (they did die, didn't they?) that I would dig in deeper. If for no other reason than to honor their lives. I hadn't kept my word, which wasn't like me at all.

Conjuring her image from my memory of our ballroom encounter, I whispered her name. It felt right to seek the ghosts of the past. Maybe that's what I needed to do if I wanted to stay out of Ashland's head. Since I could not turn my dream catching off, I needed to learn how to focus on using it productively.

It seemed like a good idea at the time.

Chapter 2—Delilah

Another hot summer day passed by without a single customer darkening the door of the Iverson Sundries Store. A small, greasy-faced child plastered his face on the front glass of the store before he was shooed away by his rotund mother, but that was the closest thing to a customer we had. A stray cat had made his way in the back door, which I'd absently left open, but I showed him the way out with the help of one of my new Shoemaker brooms. Around 4 o'clock, after sweeping the floors for the third time, counting spools of thread and repeatedly climbing the ladder to check the top shelf of my stock, I gave up. Miss Page had been true to her word. Nobody wanted to have anything to do with me or my business. For weeks I had managed to ignore the hisses and unfriendly faces, but now it was all too much. Mobilians had clearly cast their vote for the respectable Claudette Page. Friendless, hopeless and feeling defeated, I decided to call it a day. It was sad to say, but even the newly arriving northerners avoided my store. It was a hard pill to swallow.

In contrast, Adam's woodworking business continued to increase—there was never a lack of activity at his shop. It took hard work to get it moving; I had to give him credit for that. In the beginning nobody had wanted to give him a chance either, but he'd been persistent. And it didn't hurt that he had a handsome face and friendly demeanor. Funny how nobody wanted to have anything to do with me, but my "brother" was perfectly acceptable. But then again, he wasn't an illegitimate bastard, a social usurper. What would my parents say about all this? What would I say to them?

I strolled down the wooden sidewalk, making a right turn toward Adam's shop—I was happy to make the turn off Dauphin Street away from the snooty shoppers who crowded every store but mine.

With a tinge of bitterness, I recalled this morning's conversation with the only other Iverson in this town. "It seems to me that Mobile has far too many aspiring female woodworkers. For God's sake, Adam, don't encourage them."

"What am I supposed to do, Delilah? Close the shop door and forbid anyone to walk inside without your permission? You cannot tell me you're worried about a few silly girls. You know only you have my heart."

We rarely spoke openly about how we felt about one another, and I was beginning to think that he was doing so now only to prevent further argument. Any other time he did not want to talk about our future together, or love, or feelings—except after the lamp blew out. I welcomed the guilt that came with the memory of our first time together. It had been awkward but wonderful until the sunlight streamed into the room and I woke up alone. He barely spoke to me in the days that followed, but he could not keep up the isolation since we lived in the same apartment above the store.

Well, I only had myself to blame. I loved a man who most of the county considered my brother. For the hundredth time I asked myself, "What was I trying to prove?" It's not like I needed money—both Dr. Page and my parents had been generous in their bequests to me—but I enjoyed working in the shop. It was the only life I knew, and now Claudette Page had seemingly put an end to all that. Mounting pressure from the unofficial leader of the local moral society had taken its toll.

The afternoon heat rolled up from the sidewalk like an unseen blanket. I suddenly missed the coolness of Canada; even my unfriendly cousins were not as cruel as Mobile society. Unwilling to witness their collective disdain any longer, I kept my eyes on the path in front of me until I crashed into another pedestrian. My victim was a young woman, slightly taller than me but wearing more fashionable attire than mine—a moss-green dress that flattered her wide gray eyes. Despite her otherwise polished appearance, she had a bundle of tight curly red hair that appeared barely controlled by a diamond-shaped green hat. Before I could mumble an apology and continue on my way, she said, "Miss Iverson? Adam Iverson's sister?"

"I am Delilah. May I help you?"

"Your brother tells me you are an excellent dressmaker. I happen to be in need of an excellent dressmaker." She rocked back on her heels delightedly, as if she were doing me the greatest favor imaginable by offering me a job. The young lady appeared oblivious to the stir our collision had caused. When I did not respond immediately she added, "Oh, my manners. My name is Maundy Weaver. I own the dress shop two streets over." She stuck her lace-gloved hand out to me, and I shook it.

"I had no idea my brother made a habit of visiting dress shops. Thank you, but I don't need a job." I tried to get by her, but she touched my arm.

"If I could have just a minute of your time. Would you join me for a glass of something cool?"

She quietly added, "My shop is just a minute away."

I was curious now, so I nodded and followed behind this mysterious Maundy Weaver. Her shop was indeed just two minutes away. I was surprised I had never seen it, but then again I had not spent much time exploring the area. I wondered how well my "brother" knew the woman and why she believed I needed a job. With a polite smile, she opened the side door and we stepped into a small parlor. She waved me to a seat at a polished two-person table. I recognized the work—Adam had built this. As Miss Weaver poured us a glass of something that looked like iced tea, I looked about me. Through an adjoining door I could see into her store. She had customers, busy dressmakers and an endless sea of colorful fabrics neatly arranged along the walls. In her parlor there was no evidence of her dressmaking business. However, I could see that she was fond of pink roses for her china, and many decorations displayed that painted theme.

"I am glad I caught you. When it gets this hot out, many shops close early. I suppose you find this climate a bit oppressive after Canada." She placed the glass in front of me, and I could not resist taking a sip. The drink was not tea at all but something much more delicious. She laughed at my reaction. "Sarsaparilla. I like the flavor, don't you?"

"Yes, I do. I see quite a bit of Adam's handiwork here in your parlor. I didn't know you were a customer, but I think there's some mistake. I'm not looking for a job. As you know, I have my own store. Iverson Sundries on Dauphin Street."

"Miss Iverson, if I may be direct?" I nodded slowly. "I know all about your story and would like to help."

"Really? How much of my story do you think you know?" I set the glass down and stood. How dare Adam talk to this woman about our private matters!

"Please, sit. I am a woman who appreciates the direct approach. I did not mean to offend you; it's just that I too have crossed swords with Claudette. I know what a vicious adversary she can be, but you can beat her."

"So you think closing my store and coming to work for you as a dressmaker will beat her? I'm afraid I don't follow your logic." I sat back down, suddenly feeling tired.

"Of course you don't. You have no idea who I am or what I can do, Miss Iverson—or do you prefer Miss Page?"

"Delilah will do fine."

"I have just learned that your attorney, Mr. Peyton, has every intention of advising you to withdraw your case."

I could not hide my shock. "He can't do that!"

She laughed dryly. "Oh yes, he can. He's her cousin—and yours since you are a Page too. And as such, you can take him to court. You may not get much, but it will be on record and that might come in handy later. He should've shared with you his connection with her at your first meeting. It's what legal folks call a 'conflict of interest.'" I sank back in the chair. Could this day get any worse? Miss Weaver seemed to pick up on my thoughts. "Are you ready to quit?" She removed her hat pin and her hat and tossed it on the table beside her. She didn't attempt to tame her wild red hair as she leaned toward me with one arm on the table, waiting for my answer.

"I don't quit so easily. Why does my situation interest you so much, Ms. Weaver?"

With a smile she answered me, "Maundy, please. Why shouldn't it? You're a woman. I'm a woman. I believe we women should stick together. This world is an unfriendly place for us, hence my offer. I am not merely offering you a job; I offer you a way to get even. You need something—and you need it very badly. I can help you get it."

Her tone of voice made the fine hairs on the back of my neck stand up. "And what is it you think I need?" The thought that I should never cross this woman flashed through my mind.

She laughed again. "The only thing a woman ever really needs—information."

Surprised by her answer, I asked, "Information? I don't understand. Information about dressmaking?"

"Don't tell me you're dull, Delilah. You can't be dull with that face. No, not dressmaking. You'd be surprised how much you can learn during a dress fitting. There are not many social situations in which the classes mingle so easily. I have been a dressmaker all my life, as my mother was before me and hers before her. None of us Weaver women got into the business because we loved dresses." She cackled at some joke that only she knew. "With just a glance I can take your measurements and see the perfect dress for you or any woman—tall, thin, short, fat. I can make any woman look and feel good. With that ability comes a lot of trust. Women trust me. And when they trust you, they tell you things."

"And what kind of things do I need to hear?"

"Everyone has a secret, and most people don't want those secrets to see the light of day. That includes the high-and-mighty Claudette Page. In fact, I would venture to say that of all the people in the great city of Mobile, she has the biggest secret of all." She sipped her sarsaparilla and smiled at me through her yellow-tinged teeth.

"What secret might that be?"

"Oh, that's for you to figure out. I don't like Claudette Page, but she is not my mortal enemy—she's yours. Your very existence has threatened everything she holds dear. Her reputation, her wealth, her family's name—these are all things she's willing to die for. But if you find out her secret and confront her with it, she'll slink away like a scolded puppy. Now," she said, setting her glass down and smoothing her dress as she stood, "I need a dressmaker. Your business is in shambles, and that's not likely to change. Put a sign on the door that says you're closed for remodeling. Have your brother install some new cabinets or something. While he works on that project, you come help me. I'll make sure you get the opportunity to get the information you need."

"Why are you helping me? I'm not ungrateful, but why?"

"I'll keep my reasons to myself for now, if you don't mind. It's not that I don't trust you, but I would like to wait. Work for me for the next six weeks, and I can promise you everything will be different."

I stood up and extended my hand to her. "You have yourself a deal, Maundy."

She shook it and smiled broadly. "Smart girl. I'm Miss Weaver during working hours. I'll see you at Rose Cottage in the morning."

"At your house? I thought I was to work here, in the shop?"

"Oh no, dear. This little shop is for regular folks like you and me. My most exclusive clients have their fittings and consultations at Rose Cottage. It's a private service that I offer them. For example, I have clients who need help with their Mardi Gras ball dresses, but privacy is an issue. Keeping those dresses secret is a must until the big reveal at the ball. It's kind of a local tradition. It's ridiculous how they try to outdo one another, but if it's pearls they want, it's pearls they will get. Or whatever strikes their fancy. That's not going to be a problem for you, is it?"

"Not at all. And where is Rose Cottage located?"

"Turn left on Monterey Street and follow it to Virginia Street. My house is behind the Magnolia Cemetery. You can't miss it. It's the yellow two-story with the green shutters. Do you have a carriage?"

"Yes, I do."

"Bring it. It will rain tomorrow. It always rains after heat like this. And dress nicely, Miss Page. You'll meet your new attorney tomorrow."

"New attorney?"

"My friend, Jackson Keene. He'll help you get all this sorted out."

"I don't know how to thank you for all this."

"One day I'll tell you." She leaned forward and peered into my eyes. "One day I will ask you for a favor. I will expect you to grant it. In the meantime, keep your eyes and ears open and your mouth closed. Don't ask questions. The quieter, the less intrusive you are, the more likely they'll trust you and the sooner you'll hear something. Something useful you can use to put that old woman in her place. I have had enough of her and her moral society."

With a final handshake I slipped out of the house and walked back home. In one conversation I had lost everything and gained it all again. I wondered about my new partner, Maundy Weaver. What did she want from me? It would do no good to ask. I could tell she was not the kind of woman who would be easily persuaded to do anything other than what she wanted. Still, this was better than any plan I currently had. Once again, life had handed me an unexpected fork in the road. I hoped this time I had chosen the right path.

Chapter 3—Henri

I drizzled the bourbon into the hot pan and watched the flames appear. I worked the pan just like a short-order cook, coating the pecans in the decadent glaze. Turning off the flame, I continued to cook the alcohol out, pleased that I hadn't burned the pecans. At least not this batch. Glancing at my wristwatch, I had a moment of panic—Detra Ann would arrive any minute, and I wanted everything to be perfect. I did not want to stop and think about what I was doing, how foolish I was to even dream that Detra Ann and I would ever be anything more than friends. But I did hope and dream. Although I couldn't deny that I cared about her, I didn't know how she felt about me. Not only that, but we were business partners. What was I doing having heart palpitations over a business partner? "Strike one, strike two," as my granddad used to say.

Walking the pan to the dining room table, I spooned the glaze over the plated roasted chicken. I couldn't help but smile and for a moment felt confident that at least she'd like the dish I'd prepared for her. I tossed my dirty apron across the bar in the kitchen and searched for my lighter. No, on second thought, lighting candles would be coming on too strong. With nervous hands, I struggled to open a stubborn bottle of wine when I heard an unusual noise coming from the direction of the bathroom. It sounded like squirrels scratching at the wall—or someone breaking in! I put the wine aside and slipped quietly into my office. Removing my gun from the desk drawer, I went down the hall to investigate the source of the noise. I paused in the hallway waiting to hear the sound again. I was much more agile than I had been a year ago. I'd spent so much time at the gym—I had never been this fit before. My thirty-fifth birthday was last week, and I hadn't told a soul. I didn't need to be reminded how old I was. I couldn't turn back time, but I could get in shape. And I had.

Scratch, scratch...

Nope, the noise wasn't coming from the bathroom. It was coming from the guest room. As I stepped toward the door, I cocked my gun. I stood sweating in my gold-colored polo shirt, silently counting backwards from three. I heard a thud on the other side of the door and swung it open, my gun poised and ready to shoot the invader.

"Get up now!" I shouted in my most authoritative voice. "On your feet! Put your hands where I can see them!"

The intruder didn't respond right away, but when she did I almost fell over. "Calm down, Henri. It's just me," the crumpled figure complained.

"Lenore?"

"Yep, the one and only."

"What the hell are you doing climbing through the window? I could have shot you!"

"If you shoot me, you better hope you kill me. Because if you didn't, you know I would kick your ass!" She dusted herself off and stood up to face me. Her expression let me know that nothing much had changed. She was still as crazy and defiant as ever. From the way her clothing looked, she didn't need to bother trying to tidy herself up. The only time I'd seen my cousin dressed appropriately or nicely was at our grandmother's funeral, and that had been more than twenty years ago. Today's outfit was red leggings and an oversize pink shirt with black combat boots.

"I'm going to ask again, why are you climbing through my window? You plan on robbing me?"

"I don't want nothing you have, Henri Devecheaux—I never have, and I'm sure as hell not a thief!" A little more apologetically she added, "I couldn't come through the front door. You got a damn ghost on the front porch. You know I don't fool with no ghosts."

I laughed, setting my gun down with a sigh of relief. "What do you mean?" Before I could get an answer from her, the doorbell rang. "Um...just wait right here."

"No, Henri! Don't you open that door! I'm telling you the truth, fool! Don't you ever listen? A ghost is out there!"

"Lenore, have you been drinking? That's my dinner guest, Detra Ann. She's a real person, my business partner—not a ghost." I sighed and pointed toward the screwed-up window. "Just fix my screen. Please. I'll be right back." I couldn't believe my luck. My crazy cousin had to show up tonight of all nights. Once again I felt as if the Man Upstairs had it in for me.

Sliding the gun into the back of my pants, I strode to the front door. It wouldn't do to wave a gun around in front of Detra Ann, considering she'd been shot last year. The glass reflected her slender frame. I could tell from the length of her shadow that she was wearing high heels. That was promising. You didn't wear high heels unless you wanted to impress someone. At least that was true for most women I'd met. On the other hand, Detra Ann wore high heels almost every day. I wasn't sure who she was trying to impress. She was a natural beauty, even with bleached blond hair.

I opened the door with a smile, trying to act as naturally as possible. "Hey! Right on time. Come in, please."

"Oh, Henri. It smells wonderful. Nice shirt." She kissed my cheek and handed me a bottle of her favorite red wine. I pretended I didn't notice the smell of whiskey on her breath. "I hope this goes with what you've prepared." She flashed an empty smile.

"This is perfect." Remembering the gun in my waistband, I pointed to the dining room and excused myself. "Make yourself at home. I'll be right back."

"Are you still fussing in the kitchen? Is there something I can help you with?"

"No. Everything is ready. This won't take a minute."

"Okey dokey." She smiled again and walked to the dining room.

As I was returning the gun to the desk drawer, I heard the shower running in the bathroom. What was I going to do with Lenore? She had always been a lost soul, but her behavior had gotten worse after Aleezabeth disappeared. We had been the three amigos—Peas, Carrots and Onions, our grandma had called us. I was pretty sure I'd been Onions.

Aleezabeth...

How long had it been since I'd summoned up her memory? When was the last time I'd called the sheriff of Dumont and demanded an update? Too long ago. I'd let Aleezabeth down, first by leaving her to walk home by herself and now by failing to find her and bring her home.

I leaned against the doorframe with the wine bottle in my hand. So much for a nice, relaxing evening with Detra Ann. I'd have to explain Lenore before she had a chance to crash our dinner.

"Hey, you coming? I'm going to start without you!"

"Yep, on the way." I stopped by the kitchen for the corkscrew and strolled into join her. To my surprise, Detra Ann had lit the candles and was already digging into supper. I poured the wine and sat down with her.

"Hidden talents, Henri. I had no idea you could cook like this. Are you professionally trained? Did you go to culinary school somewhere?"

I took a big swig of the fruity red wine. "No, but I've always loved cooking. I think it's just a part of my heritage. You know, everyone from New Orleans can cook."

She shook her head as she finished a bite of the chicken. "That's not true at all. I had an aunt from New Orleans, and she was the worst cook on the planet. Every Christmas she'd make us these God-awful pralines and then call us the next day to see if we'd eaten them. It was so funny because my dad would lie to her and tell her they hit the spot. She never knew he had a hole dug in the backyard that he lovingly called 'the spot.'"

"That sounds like something my father would have done. He was kind of a jokester."

"I've never heard you talk about your father. Is he still alive?"

I took another swig of wine and eyed the hallway nervously. "I'm not sure."

"What?" she asked incredulously.

"He kind of slipped away. Daddy liked playing music, or he did before he hooked up with my mother. He was a high school science teacher, but he dabbled in music—mostly jazz. One weekend a group of his old band buddies came around, and when they left town, Dad and his sax left too. I assumed he left with them."

"That must have been so hard on you. How old were you?"

"Fourteen. My birthday was the month before he left."

"And you've never seen him in all this time?"

"No, but that's not unusual for my family—we're all a bunch of wanderers. For example, my cousin Lenore showed up tonight. I haven't seen her in years, and suddenly she's here."

Her dark eyelashes fluttered in surprise. "You should have said something. We could have had dinner another night. I hope I didn't inconvenience you, Henri."

"You're never an inconvenience."

She dabbed her mouth with the linen napkin and smirked. I could tell she didn't believe me. After a year, I knew her facial expressions pretty well. At least I thought I did. We chitchatted about work stuff, like the crate of antiques that had come in that morning, a client that refused to pay us, the noise from the construction on Dauphin Street. When our plates were nearly empty and the conversation died down, I felt more relaxed. I was pretty sure that Lenore had passed out on my bed, but at least she wouldn't be crashing our dinner date—I hoped.

"I have to admit I had an ulterior motive for inviting you here."

She set the napkin on the table, leaned back in the chair and appraised me suspiciously. "Not to steal your thunder, but before you tell me, I have something for you. For your birthday."

"How did you know I had a birthday?"

"I took a peek at your driver's license a while back. Since you didn't mention it, I figured you wanted to keep it quiet. You know, thirty-five isn't ancient." Opening her oversize purse she removed a gold box with a royal blue ribbon wrapped around it. "This is for you." She slid it toward me.

I laughed in surprise. "I can't believe you did that. You're full of surprises, Detra Ann."

"Wait until you open it."

I picked up the box and put it back down. "I am sure this is a wonderful gift, but I really want something else."

She froze for a second and said, "Okay, what do you want?"

"I want a dance. I mean, it is my birthday." I walked to the CD player and hit play. I hadn't planned this, but it felt right. Etta James began her sweet serenade.

At last...my love has come along...my lonely days are over...and life is like a song...

With a sad smile, Detra Ann joined me on the makeshift dance floor. Her arms slid around my neck, and I held her close. Her long blond hair rubbed against my hands, and I did my best to breathe slowly so my heart wouldn't beat out of my chest.

"Remember that day, at the ribbon-cutting?"

"Yes, I remember," I said quietly. I knew it was hard for her to talk about TD, even now.

"I don't know what I would have done if I had looked out into that audience and didn't see you."

"You would have been just fine, Detra Ann. You are strong—stronger than you think."

She squeezed me tighter and laid her head on my shoulder. I couldn't help but touch her hair. "I will never forget it." We danced until Etta sang her last notes. When the dance ended, she stepped back and reached for the gift before I could say or do anything else. "Now open it before I change my mind."

Quickly, I opened it, pulling the ribbon first and removing the golden cardboard lid. Inside was a silver key tied to another blue ribbon. I recognized it—this was the key to Cotton City Treasures. Puzzled, I turned it over in my hand.

"I'm giving you my share of the business, Henri. It's time for me to move on. I've taken a job in Atlanta—I'm leaving at the end of the week."

It felt like someone had kicked me in the gut. I put the key back in the box and replaced the lid. "I can't take this. This is too much, Detra Ann. I can't let you do this."

"It's already done, my friend. I signed the papers yesterday, and it is official. You are the sole proprietor of Cotton City Treasures—you own it all. It's just my way of saying thank you. If it weren't for you, I wouldn't be here today. I mean, I know I'm not a hundred percent yet, but you have been a lifesaver. Truly. Thank you for everything."

Stunned, I murmured, "You're welcome."

She sprang from her chair and hugged me, and I breathed in her sweet smell. Detra Ann sometimes wore expensive perfume, the kind you normally only got a whiff of in fashion magazines, but then there were times when she smelled like sun-dried sheets and wildflowers. That's how I always thought of her. And now she was leaving. "I thought this would be easy, but it's not. I will miss you most of all," she whispered in my ear. After a few moments, she reached for her purse and headed out the door. "I have to go. I'll come by and see you before I leave, I promise."

I watched her car lights disappear down Conception Street, and then I closed the door. I felt like my heart had been snatched out. Lenore was standing in the doorway, her hair wild and damp from her shower. Her olive-colored skin practically glowed in the candlelight.

"Please tell me you weren't intending on telling that ghost you loved her. She's not for you, Henri."

"You don't know what you're talking about, Lenore."

She clucked her tongue, "You've always been a fool when it came to women. Remember Peaches?" As she strolled across the wooden floor, I noticed she was wearing a pair of my socks. She peered through the blinds and said, "She was a nightmare, and she left you high and dry just like I told you she would. Then there was that red-haired stripper, Anastasia…"

"She wasn't a stripper—she was a burlesque dancer, and that was over ten years ago."

"Don't correct me. You've got a bad habit of thinking you're the only one that's right, Henri Lamar Devecheaux. You can't love that girl. She's already dead—she's a ghost. At the very least, she's a shade."

"What are you talking about?" I knew I would regret asking, but I did it anyway. "What the hell is a shade, Lenore?"

"Someone who's been touched by Death. A part of her is already gone. Death only got his bony hands on part of her, but all that's left is a shadow—a shade. He'll come for the rest." She stood closer to me now—she touched my hand tentatively as if she thought I was a shade too. "You know what I am saying is true. I can see it in your face. What do you have to do with this, Henri?" I didn't answer her. I wanted her to leave my home, but I was too polite to say so. She touched my arm again. Sure that I was real, her face softened; her voice was unusually soft and kind. "She's someone who should have died but escaped the reaper's hands. But he'll come back for her. And if you're anywhere around her when he does, he might take you too. She's been amongst the dead, seen them, touched them. Death won't let her go—she's his. She can never be yours, cousin."

"I don't believe a word you're saying. You don't either. You just like tormenting me, don't you? This isn't about Detra Ann at all. This is about Aleezabeth. Tell me the truth, Lenore. Why are you here? What do you want? Money?"

As if she didn't hear me, she walked around the room, examining my pictures and my collection of antique silver spoons. "That's probably why she's drinking and taking those pills. She feels cold Death creeping into her bones and thinks she can escape it. It won't work. It never does. She's a ghost already…"

"Shut up, Lenore! If you don't stop talking like that, you will have to go. I don't believe Detra Ann is the only one drinking too much. You're on dope now, aren't you?"

She closed her eyes and held her breath, tilting her head like she was listening to an invisible voice. Then her eyes sprung open and she said, "I'm here to help you, Henri. I didn't come for any other reason. You're about to see the supernatural like you've never seen it before! I want to help you, cousin. You're the last family I got, and I'll be damned if I just let you go." She pursed her lips and scowled at me. "I lost Aleezabeth. We both lost her—I won't lose you too. I am staying right here until that ghost is gone. Have a care for your soul, Henri. Please."

I rubbed my forehead in frustration. "Listen, if you want to stay for a while, fine. But there are some ground rules. Number one, you aren't just lying around the house all day. You've got to get a job. When I leave the house, you leave the house. No climbing in the windows or kicking down doors. Number two, you leave Detra Ann alone. No talking to her about all this crazy stuff—in fact, you don't talk to her at all. She's been through enough. Number three, if you steal from me, you're out of here. All I have to do is call Detective Simmons at the Mobile Police Department and she'll come pick you up *tout de suite*. Those are the rules. You understand?"

Lenore could see I was serious. She didn't argue and nodded her head. "Can I smoke in here?"

"Not in my house, but there's a chair in the backyard if you want to puff on your cancer sticks. You've got the guest room—that's the room you broke into. Do you have clothes?"

"I've got enough, and the guest room suits me fine."

"I'm cleaning the kitchen and going to bed. There's some leftover chicken in there if you're hungry."

"I think I'll go smoke first." Without even a thank you, Lenore slipped out of the house and into the darkened backyard.

With a sigh I went to the kitchen to tidy up. Corking the wine and removing the dishes from the table, I slid on my rubber gloves and let the hot water run in the sink. I had a dishwasher, a nice stainless steel one, but I liked washing dishes by hand. It was therapeutic. After tonight's turn of events, I needed some therapy. The woman I loved—yes, I could admit that now—was leaving me behind. *Isn't that terrific?* I cracked the window a bit to let some cool air in. It was too early in the year to turn on the air conditioning, but the house felt stuffy tonight.

I squirted the blue dishwashing liquid into the sink and watched the suds build. I caught a whiff of Lenore's cigarette. I thought about asking her to move away from the window, but then I heard her whisper into a phone. "Hey! You ain't going to believe this, but I found one." I froze and turned off the water. It was quiet for a moment. "Sure I'm sure." Another pause. "Yeah, probably, but we'll have to move fast."

Chills ran up and down my spine. For a second it was as if the air stopped moving and I stopped breathing. I knew exactly what—no, who—Lenore was talking about.

Detra Ann.

Chapter 4—Carrie Jo

Desmond Taylor insisted that I meet him at Idlewood first thing in the morning, and I was happy to do so. Off the beaten path, the old house stood off Carlen Street about a mile from Seven Sisters. Another forgotten gem crumbling into the Mobile landscape, Idlewood was in nowhere near the condition Ashland's family home had been. It was in far worse shape. And to think I believed restoring Seven Sisters had been challenging. Still, the old house had good bones, as Terrence Dale used to say. And to top it off, it had a fascinating history. One that I couldn't walk away from.

Idlewood was actually a twin home. The original house was the Idlewild Plantation in Derby, Louisiana. The McClellans visited the home and loved it so much they purchased copies of the original plans and reconstructed it here in Mobile. Idlewild was a raised plantation—a unique construction because of its mix of French and English features. Typical for the wild woods of Louisiana, it had been a rarity during its time here in Mobile. The front facade of Idlewood had three dormers, which gave it a graceful look despite the sagging roof. Rusty, ornamental cast-iron balustrades looked promising but in much need of some skilled attention. But the thing I loved the most were the galleries. This type of house normally had molded capitals, but Idlewood's galleries were lined with gorgeous fluted, Doric columns that begged to be restored to their former elegance.

According to Mr. Taylor, Idlewood's current owner, this Greek revival plantation house had undergone at least a dozen changes since the original construction. But fortunately these had been relatively minor and had not taken away from the original owner's vision. Luckily for me, I knew what Idlewood had really looked like, right down to the paisley wallpaper in the hallway—I had seen it in a dream. Once upon a time, about a hundred and fifty years ago, there had been a grand Christmas ball held here at Idlewood. Dr. Hoyt Page and his beloved Christine Cottonwood rekindled their romance in the upstairs nursery. A little boy battled the flu, and rare Christmas snowflakes had fallen, much to the delight of a pair of cocker spaniels and the gathered party. Unfortunately, I could not revisit the nursery or any of the rooms on the top floor, as the stairs were deemed unsafe.

"Tell me, Mr. Taylor, what did you have in mind?"

The older man thought carefully before he spoke. "I'll be honest with you, Mrs. Stuart. I am not sure what to do with this old house. It doesn't seem practical to me to restore it. My wife and the Historical Society seem to think differently, but then again my wife is a sentimental old gal." He chuckled and continued, "I don't have a bottomless pocketbook, but I do have a heart to restore Idlewood, if that's possible. From what I hear about your work at Seven Sisters, you really put that home back on the map. Maybe we can do that here. I don't know. Believe it or not, I've been offered a substantial grant to begin the restoration. But I'm not a foolish man. I've been in business all my life, and I know this kind of project isn't something to take too lightly. We could be looking at a very long project, and I have a construction business to run. I don't have time to manage all this. Not to mention I wouldn't know where to start."

I chewed my lip and looked around the room at the dusty walls and cracked floors. He was right, of course. Restoration was hard work. It took hundreds of hours of research, and then there were acquisitions. Then there was the reconstruction of the property and meeting all the requirements of the local historical society, which could be a major task in itself. I felt sad thinking about working on a new project without Terrence Dale—and probably without Ashland. Still, this was what I did. What I had always wanted to do. Maybe getting the Seven Sisters job *had* been just a fluke—I'm sure Hollis Matthews knew about my dream catching from Mia, and that's why they wanted me in Mobile—but this...this was an opportunity to prove my abilities as a researcher.

"You are right. It is a commitment, Mr. Taylor. Here's how we'll start. Let me ask you a few questions."

After another thirty minutes I got the bottom line. Mr. Taylor didn't want to be involved in the daily decisions, but he did want monthly updates. He would use his construction company to do the work under my team's supervision. Before anything began or any plans were finalized, we would undertake a lengthy appraisal process. He had a dollar figure in mind, and he wouldn't pursue the restoration if the cost exceeded that amount. His ultimate goal was for the home to turn enough profit so all future maintenance would be self-supported. He didn't want to be stuck managing a "money pit," and I couldn't blame him there.

And one more caveat. He had no idea how to collect antiques, but his wife was eager to help. In fact, he wanted her to help. I agreed to his terms, and we ended the meeting with a handshake. Mr. and Mrs. Taylor were going out of town on an extended cruise in a few days, and he wanted to have a detailed project proposal before he left. Which meant I'd have to work day and night for the next forty-eight hours to pull something together. I agreed to do that but reminded him this was just a preliminary proposal. When it came to restoration, there was always that one thing you hadn't considered—like the cost of taking care of any bodies you uncovered.

I left the meeting so excited that my hands were shaking as I dug my cell phone out of my purse. Ashland should have been the first person I called, but after last night, I still couldn't face him. I thought about calling Rachel and then just frowned in the rearview mirror and tossed the phone back in my purse.

You are being a total jerk, Carrie Jo! You can't get mad about some dreams.

Oh, yeah? Well, why is he dreaming about other women? Is he seeing other women?

Sick of my own drama, I flipped on the radio. Bob Marley sang "Three Little Birds," and for the next fifteen minutes I tapped my fingers on the steering wheel as I sang loudly and completely off-key. By the time I made it to my office at Oak Plaza, I felt more like my old self again.

The first thing I saw when I stepped inside was a ridiculously large vase full of pink roses. There had to have been at least a hundred buds crammed into the white ceramic vase. It smelled glorious, but it did seem a bit much. Unless you were at a funeral. As I slid my coat off, I smiled at Rachel. "Gee, who died? Those can't be from Chip."

"Uh, no. Those are for you, actually." She handed me a card and smiled. "Happy anniversary!"

"Oh." I took the card and smiled sheepishly. "Thank you so much."

"You hit the flower jackpot, I think. I'd be lucky if Chip bought me just a half dozen. He's a sweetie but not big on sentimentalism. Me either, I guess. What should I do with these? Put them in your office? I can't leave them here. I don't think the visitors will be able to see my desk."

"I'll take them. I have a table in my office. Let me put my purse and coat away first. Then I'll tell you the awesome news!"

"No bother. I think I can handle this monster." Rachel wrapped her arms around the massive vase. "So what did you get Ashland?"

I felt a bit woozy for a second but caught my balance easily. I wished I could tell Rachel my secret, but I had to tell Ashland first. If I ever got around to speaking to him again. Just a few weeks ago I thought telling Ashland that we were having a baby would be the perfect anniversary present. Now I didn't know when I would tell him. "I'll be honest with you. I've been so busy with our new office that I haven't even thought about it."

"Carrie Jo! Are you kidding me? It's your second anniversary—you have to do *something*." As if she could fix my problem, she asked, "What did you give him last year?"

"Okay, now who's being sentimental?" I helped her position the white ceramic vase on the table and arranged the flowers. Touching the soft petals, I remembered our first kiss. I would never forget that night. It seemed like a lifetime ago.

"Let's see...last year I got him a first-edition copy of *The Jungle Book*, believe it or not. He's a huge Kipling fan."

Shoot! I must be the worst wife on the planet. Spying on his dreams and forgetting our anniversary. Yep, I'm batting a thousand.

Before she could ask me anything else, I told her the good news about Idlewood. Immediately we fired up our computers and began grabbing the research we needed for the proposal. Of course, we had the Seven Sisters model to go by, but each job had its own challenges. Ashland called me sometime around lunch, but I let it go to voicemail. Rachel's eyes widened, but she didn't ask any more questions. We ordered Chinese and kept working. By the time five o'clock came around, I needed a break from numbers and plans and debated on whether or not to head home.

Just then, Chip arrived to pick up Rachel. I'd already asked her to work on a Saturday, and I couldn't very well insist she work past five. She had a life—it wasn't her fault I was trying to avoid mine. "Have fun, you two."

Chip waved goodbye and walked out the door, but Rachel lingered behind. "Carrie Jo, it's your anniversary. Go home, for goodness' sake. Whatever you two are going through, you can work it out. I just know it. We've got a handle on this now. Go home. I'll come and help you tomorrow."

"I appreciate that. I'll go home soon, I promise."

"No need, apparently...your husband is here! Have a nice night! Don't do anything I wouldn't do."

"Which is what?" I asked with a laugh.

Ashland walked in, his expensive cologne filling the room before his arrival. God, that man always smelled so good. And he looked great, of course. I could see he'd bought a new shirt, light blue like his eyes, and he had taken the time to get a haircut. My emotions surged again—on one hand I wanted to feel his hands on my skin, but on the other hand I wanted to slap the smile off his face. This was indeed a dilemma.

Where had even-tempered, reasonable Carrie Jo gone? When would she be back?

"Hey, I tried to call you. Did you get my messages?"

"Were there more than one?" I picked up my cell and saw he'd called three times. "Oh yeah, I've been slammed here. It's been kind of crazy. Sorry about that." I shuffled the papers around on my desk and avoided eye contact.

"You haven't been in business for more than a week. You're slammed already? What do you have going on?" He sounded a little irritated, as if he didn't quite believe me. He picked up the sheaf of papers on my desk and scanned them. A slow smile spread across his handsome face. "You got Idlewood? That's amazing, Carrie Jo."

Snatching the papers away from him I answered hotly, "I haven't got anything yet. I'm working on the proposal, and I have less than forty eight hours to get it to Desmond Taylor. This might be my only chance to work on the Idlewood restoration. I don't want to blow it."

"Oh, I see." He noticed the flowers on the side table and pointed to them. "You like the flowers?"

"Yes, they are very nice. Thank you, and happy anniversary. Your gift isn't here yet. It might be a few days late."

"Carrie Jo, what is going on? You've hardly talked to me all week. I get the feeling you're mad about something, but I don't know what. Please just tell me what's on your mind."

"I don't have time for this right now, Ashland." I added more gently, "When I finish this proposal I swear we'll talk all you want. Okay?"

"Fine. Why not let me help you? I'll cancel the dinner reservations I made, and we'll work on this together. Who else, besides you, knows more about restoration projects than me? What are you in the mood for? Chinese? Italian? I could call Mama's and go pick up something."

The idea of food made my stomach feel queasy. All I wanted was a bottle of water and some oranges. I'd always heard that pregnant women had strange cravings—I didn't want much of anything except oranges. I couldn't get enough citrus fruit lately.

"Are you okay? You look a little pale."

"Yes, I'm fine. I've just been staring at these computer screens all day. You don't have to stay, Ashland. I am sure you're just as tired as I am. Go home—I'll be there in a couple of hours." I sat behind my desk and didn't wait for an answer.

"Damn it, CJ! It's our anniversary! Can't you at least pretend you want to spend it with me?"

Leaping out of the chair I yelled back at him, "Can't you give me some space?"

"Tell me what's going on!" His voice grew louder and I could tell by his body language that he was none too happy with me. I couldn't deny he'd been patient about the proposal, but I still couldn't shake the feeling of betrayal.

"Alright! You want to know so much." I flew to my feet. "You've been dreaming about women—lots and lots of women! You don't even care that I am lying right beside you! Every night it's someone new, Ash. I can't remember the last time I got to sleep without being forced to watch my husband make love to someone else! You tell *me* what the hell is going on!"

"Are you seriously mad about some dream? Like I get to pick what I dream about? Is this really what you're mad about, Carrie Jo?" He laughed bitterly and put his hands on his hips. "All this time I thought I'd done something wrong, and this is why you're pissed? I can't believe what I'm hearing!"

"You better believe it!" Fat, salty tears welled up in my eyes. I felt another wave of nausea. "Why are you all of a sudden dreaming about other women? Are you having an affair? With that brunette you're fantasizing about?"

"Who? What the heck are you talking about—I don't even know how to answer that. You know..." He raised his hands and walked toward the door. "When you're done being crazy, call me."

I stared in shock as he walked out the door, making sure to slam it behind him. I fell back in my seat and cried my eyes out. He was right, I was acting crazy. What the heck was wrong with me? I suddenly missed Bette. I needed someone to talk to, someone who could help me navigate this ball of confusion that I'd wound myself up in. Detra Ann had quietly stepped out of my life, and Rachel and I didn't have the kind of relationship that I felt comfortable sharing my problems with her. Most people had a mother to talk to. Not me.

Ugh, I don't have time to feel sorry for myself. I wiped my face with a tissue and continued to work on my project. Work was probably the best thing for me right now. If I were home, I would just wallow in my misery. At least at work I could focus on something else. I struggled with the spreadsheets for about an hour and then gave up. My mind wasn't here, and neither was my heart. I wasn't going to get anything done tonight except cry all over my paperwork. I grabbed my purse, hoping Ashland had gone home. He was right, we did need to talk, and I would have to start with an apology. I got behind the wheel of my BMW, slid the key in the ignition and turned it.

Click, click.

And that made me cry too. After a few minutes, I rubbed my red face with my now soppy tissue and decided to walk home. At least I'd get some fresh air and have time to rehearse what I would say. It was only four blocks from the office, and I hadn't worn heels. A light winter wind blew, but the temperatures were only in the fifties. It had been a long time since I'd gone for a walk through the streets of downtown Mobile. I thought about Seven Sisters and how hard it would be to get there. *No, you've got enough problems, Carrie Jo.* I kept my eye on the broken sidewalks and tried to enjoy the scenery. This was a particularly nice block, with lovely old homes and cast-iron fences with fleur-de-lis perching atop the occasional posts. I walked past a house with thumping music and excited young people. When was the last time I'd been to a party?

Halfway there now. Just ahead I saw the low-hanging sign that marked one of Mobile's most significant landmarks, the Magnolia Cemetery. Often referred to by locals as the City of the Dead, some of the city's earliest citizens were buried here, along with hundreds of Civil War soldiers. There were even huge mausoleums that housed the bones of entire generations of families. I approached the open gate and slowed my walk. I had always meant to explore this place but had never gotten around to it. I tugged my purse up on my shoulder as if some nefarious purse-snatcher hovered near me in the shadows of the great oak trees.

A flash of light caught my eye. *Must be the night watchman making rounds.* I paused at the open gate. *Hmm...that's odd. I thought they closed this place at dusk.* Well, I was here, and there was a good chance that Ashland would need some time to cool off. Shoving the squeaking gate open the rest of the way, I headed toward the light. I'd let the security guard know I was here, have a quick peek around and then head home. No harm done, right?

The light bounced through the trees, and it was difficult to keep up with it as I navigated the maze of graves. I hoped to avoid tripping over the roots of the massive oak and magnolia trees that littered the cemetery. I couldn't help but squint at the grave markers of some of the cemetery's older residents. Some of the tombstones were so old that the names were hard to read. Since the beginnings of Mobile, bodies had been laid to rest here— neatly at first, and then much more haphazardly as the centuries passed and space became an issue. Everywhere I looked I could see sentimental stonework like weeping angels and broken columns. Besides the children's markers, I found the broken columns the saddest. They represented the last person in a family line. During the Civil War there were a lot of broken columns installed in the Magnolia Cemetery. How many sons had died during that horrendous war?

This was no time to be distracted. Shaking myself out of my reverie, I called out to the security guard. "Hello! Excuse me!" The cemetery was getting darker by the second, and there were no lights besides the bouncing light I had chased from one side of the grounds to the other. Peering through the dim light, I tried to discern a figure. I stepped out from under an old oak covered in Spanish moss into a clearing and watched the light. The air suddenly felt thick and, for lack of a better word, sparkly. It occurred to me that what I was seeing was not normal at all. That wasn't a flashlight! What had appeared to be the beam of a flashlight suddenly changed color to a soft amber glow that bounced ever so softly off the ground about three feet.

"What in the world?" I thought perhaps it could be children or teenagers playing in the cemetery, but that didn't make sense either. I leaned against the oak and called one more time. I had to be imagining things. "Hello?" The light stopped bouncing, expanded and then shrank to half its original size. "Oh my God!"

Yep. This was something supernatural.

Suddenly the light shot across the cemetery toward the gate to the left. Without thinking, I took off after it. It didn't move as I got closer to the gate; it just hung in midair, still bouncing a little. I'd heard of orbs before but had never actually seen one. If that was what this was. Many people thought these were some type of ghost, but I had no idea. Most of the ghosts I saw were in dreams. Well, before Seven Sisters.

It was completely dark now and a chill crept into the air, a chill that had not been there before. Another warning sign. Clutching my purse, I ran ahead, stopping to hide behind a moldy mausoleum wall. I held my breath and silently counted to ten before slowly peering around the corner to take a peek at the light. The reasonable part of my brain told me to call someone, but who would that be? I watched as the light hovered in midair just this side of the gate. Maybe it wanted me to follow? Why else would it hang around?

I looked around the cemetery and saw no one else—no one living, anyway. I was by myself except for whatever entity this was I was chasing. Terrified, I leaned flush against the marble, the cold creeping through my clothing. I heard a noise I couldn't identify—it started as a low moan and quickly became a screech. A small, dark shadow launched itself from the top of the mausoleum and landed on the ground beside me. It was a damn cat! A gray cat with an attitude, upset at the invader who had appeared in his playground. After my heart stopped pounding in my chest, I peeked around the corner again and took a deep breath. It was now or never.

I stepped out quickly, as if I could surprise it. As I did, the light flared and passed through the closed gate, disappearing into the dark Alabama night. I decided to follow it—I'd come this far. The gate was stubborn and didn't give way without a fight. I gripped the cold cast-iron bars with both hands and pushed as hard as I could, and the gate swung open. I felt the chill again, and the hairs on my arms stood up.

Here I was again, completely surrounded by the supernatural with nowhere to run. Still clutching my purse like it was some sort of fashionable life preserver, I took a deep breath and stepped through the gate.

That was the last thing I remembered.

Chapter 5—Ashland

My wife never ceased to amaze me, but lately the surprises weren't anything good. To think she'd been spying on my dreams and accused me of cheating. I couldn't believe this was the Carrie Jo I loved and married. When I first saw her, she took my breath away. The more I got to know her, the more I was amazed at her knowledge, but it wasn't just that. She had a deep compassion for people, even though at times she doubted her own ability to help them.

I will always remember the first time I saw her—a beautiful woman standing at the foot of the stairs of my family home. She wore a red blouse with slightly puffy sleeves and a red and white skirt with a tiny rose pattern all over it. Her legs were tanned and lovely, her face even lovelier with amazing green eyes and wild curly hair. I could tell instantly that she had a sense of humor and that she would not be easily impressed with my southern-boy swagger.

Seeing her there that night was like a sign, or at least I thought it was. But now I didn't know what to think. I stuffed some clothing in my overnight bag and headed out the door. I didn't leave a note for her—why bother? It sounded like she thought I was a disgusting letch. Didn't she know I loved her more than any woman on the planet? Hadn't we been through enough together for her to know that I was hers forever? Apparently not. Locking the door behind me, I looked down the street to see if I could spot her car. I made a deal with God: if I saw it in the next sixty seconds, I would know she wanted to work it out and I would stay. I tossed my bag in the truck and waited. When she didn't come, I sighed, pulled out of the driveway and drove to the marina. I'd stay on the Happy Go Lucky tonight and figure out what my next move was. It would be cold as heck on the water this time of year, but it would have to do. I stopped by the grocery store to grab a few things for supper. I was starving. And to think I had planned on giving Carrie Jo an anniversary gift that she would never forget. I shook my head, did my shopping and headed to the boat.

About an hour later, I was sitting on the deck chewing an overcooked hamburger and watching the moonlight splash on the water. This was not the way I had planned to spend my anniversary. Wiping my hands with a napkin, I checked my phone yet again for a text or voicemail from Carrie Jo. Nothing. Not a peep. I stared off into the distance, sipping my beer and wondering what I could do to fix our current situation. We'd been through too much, seen too much to give up now, but this wouldn't work if only one of us was committed to seeing it through.

To make matters worse, I was seeing ghosts again. Not family ghosts this time, thankfully. Most were strangers, faded people who glared at me from curtained windows and sailed past me at inopportune moments. Even at home. Having other people around seemed to keep them away, though. Thank goodness for Doreen. When Carrie Jo wasn't there, Doreen was. The more living souls in the house, the merrier. People told me my "sight" was a gift, but I wouldn't call it that. I'd hated psychics and mediums when I was growing up, and now I'd become the thing I hated. Yeah, seeing ghosts was never fun. It always surprised me, and unlike on those stupid television shows, they never wanted anything or asked for anything. They didn't speak to me or ask for my help "finding the light." They were always unhappy or fixated on something. And likewise I never spoke to them or tried to communicate with them. Maybe I was going crazy like my mother.

To keep my mind straight, I decided to keep a diary. I wrote down what I saw, where I spotted the ghosts and the dates I saw them and for how long. I noticed that my ability to see ghosts was heightened during the full moon. What was I? Some sort of psychic werewolf? The only place I really found peace was on the water. I never saw anything out here. Once I thought I did, but it turned out to be nothing. And nobody had ever died on my boat—I'd bought it brand new just to be sure. Thank God for that.

Now I really thought I was going crazy. I saw a ghost yesterday, but it wasn't a true ghost—it was Detra Ann, who I knew for a fact was alive and well. What made it stranger was the ghost appeared in my home, on the stairs where she had been shot—probably by another ghost. I had called out to her, but she disappeared, shimmering for a second and then fluttering away like the end of an old movie reel. Her appearance had surprised me so much that I yelled. Doreen had stepped into the hallway to check on me. She swore that there was no one else in the house. I couldn't understand it. Maybe tomorrow I would go by the shop and see Detra Ann and Henri. I missed my friends. I missed my wife. How on earth had my life gone completely nuts?

I checked my phone one more time before I took it below to plug it in. I cleaned up the galley and headed to the shower. Carrie Jo wasn't going to call me. My wife was a stubborn woman but normally not this unreasonable. Why not just call it a night? After my shower, I fell asleep reading a book on mastering extrasensory perception. I woke with a stiff neck to the sound of someone calling my name.

"Ashland! You there?"

"Carrie Jo?" I tossed the book to the side and walked out on the deck. Libby Stevenson, a former schoolmate and my new attorney, stood on the dock with two cups of coffee. Her long dark hair shone in the sunlight. I had never seen her in casual clothing before, but today she wore blue jeans with a purposeful hole in the knee and a comfortable-looking blue t-shirt that read *LA: City of Dreams*. "May I come aboard? I come bearing gifts."

"Sure," I said, running my hands through my wild hair. My eyes felt sticky and my brain was tired—I must have stayed out later than I thought. "How did you know I was here? Did you talk to Carrie Jo?"

"I just happened to be riding by and saw your truck here. I know it's not a workday, but I figured I'd come take a peek at the infamous Happy Go Lucky." She handed me a cup of coffee.

I took it from her with a smile. "Infamous? I wouldn't say that."

"Well, it's the talk of the office. Roger Bosarge says that this is the boat you caught that prize-winning fish in—he thinks either this boat is lucky or you cheated. That was at the Deep Sea Fishing Rodeo a few years ago, right?" I nodded. "Someday you'll have to take me fishing." Pretty white teeth gleamed at me, and I couldn't help but smile back.

"You like to fish?"

"Big time. Growing up that's all we did. My dad believed in teaching us how to fish. I have to admit it's been a while since I've tossed a hook in the water, but I think I remember how to catch one." We sipped our coffees and sat in silence for a few minutes. "How did Mrs. Stuart like her gift?"

"I haven't given it to her yet."

"Oh, I see." Libby's blue eyes widened, and she clamped her lips for a second. "Sorry to hear that."

"It's no big deal."

"For what it's worth, I'd love to get a gift like that. Any woman would. I hope she knows how lucky she is."

"Truth be told, I'm the lucky one." I meant every word. I did love Carrie Jo. Despite this minor glitch, we'd gotten on very well considering the supernatural forces that continually arrayed themselves against us. She had helped me unravel my family's sordid past and set us free from a variety of self-inflicted curses. I was indeed a lucky man.

"That's sweet. You're just too good to be true."

I decided to change the subject. "So how is Jeremy? I heard he started his own veterinary clinic in Clarke County. Has he gotten over Kelly yet?"

Libby pursed her lips and rolled her eyes. "You know how my brother is. He's been in love with Kelly about as long as I've loved—" She stopped short, and I thought I saw a blush rise on her face. Taking another sip of her coffee, she continued, "Well, it's been a long time. At least she didn't leave him standing at the altar. He's got his animals so I think he'll be okay."

"He's got a terrific little sister—I'm sure he'll be fine."

She laughed dryly at the idea. "Relationship advice is truly not my field of expertise. If you need to evict a deadbeat, then I'm your girl. But I'm sure you're right. My brother is kind, handsome and successful—like you. He won't be lonely for long. Frankly, I would like to see him play the field a little more. Get out there and mingle. I think his biggest problem is he doesn't know what he's been missing."

I smiled at the idea of Jeremy mingling. He had been an excellent receiver, the best football player on our team; the guy was fearless on the field, but when it came to women he could hardly put two sentences together, at least before he met Kelly. I was bummed that the two of them had split up, but that kind of stuff happened.

"Which brings me to my next question...what made you get into an all-fired rush to get married? I thought you would be single forever."

"What makes you say that? I have never been a player."

Libby took a seat beside me and carefully removed the plastic lid from her steaming drink. "Oh, come on. It's me you're talking to. The unofficial little sister to the entire Bulldogs football team—I know the truth, Ash. Let's see, there was Shay Dawson, Aimee Wilkinson, Jenna Daughtry..."

"Shay and I are just friends, always have been. Aimee...I did like her, but she moved senior year. And Jenna wasn't the kind of girl to stay with one guy for too long."

"You know, Jenna's changed a lot. Can you believe she married Tony Merritt? Better her than me. I don't think I could ever be a preacher's wife. And then there was Detra Ann. I always thought if I didn't marry you, she'd be the one to put a ring on your finger. Y'all were inseparable."

My phone rang, and I unplugged it from the charger. "This is Ashland."

"Morning, sunshine! Is Carrie Jo coming in today? I told her I'd be here this morning, but she hasn't showed up. If she's going to be late could you ask her to bring some breakfast when she comes in? I'm starving." Rachel Kowalski always talked like that. She threw whole paragraphs at you without taking a breath. Young, ambitious, and completely loyal. I felt guilty that I didn't know what to tell her.

"I'm not at the house right now, so I'm not sure."

"Did she mention coming in? Because that was the plan yesterday. Here I thought I was late. You two must have stayed up too late last night. Oh, the married life."

"Actually, I stayed on the boat last night."

She was silent for a moment. "Sorry, Mr. Stuart. Didn't mean to be nosy. Well, I'll call the house phone again. She's not answering her cell, and her car is here."

"Her car is there? Tell you what—I'll head that way and bring you both some breakfast."

"Sounds yummy. Thanks so much! Bye!"

I dialed Carrie Jo's number, but she still wasn't answering. Her cheery voice asked me to leave a voicemail. I hung up and tried the house phone. Still no dice. Doreen didn't work on Sundays, so I'd have to go check myself. That familiar nagging feeling that something was wrong began to grow in my gut.

"Thanks for the coffee, Libby, but I have to go."

"I overheard the conversation. I hope everything is all right with Carrie Jo. Need me to tag along?"

"No, I'm sure it's nothing. My wife hasn't been feeling well lately."

"I'm just a phone call away if you need me."

"Thanks." I began collecting my things and practically ran down the pier to my car. What a jerk I'd been! I should have stayed home last night instead of pouting on the boat. I haphazardly dialed her phone again as I peeled out of the parking lot slinging rocks and dust. The harbormaster yelled at me, but I didn't have time to explain.

No answer. This isn't good.

Adjusting my rearview mirror as I sped down the causeway, I nearly screamed. For a second it appeared that someone was in my backseat. I saw a face—a man's face. He had pale skin, dark hair that curled around the collar of his crumbling white shirt and empty eyes. I could barely form a thought before he vanished in a less than a second. My car swerved erratically until I got it under control. I swore under my breath as I tried to slow my breathing.

No. This isn't good at all.

Chapter 6—Delilah

I ran as fast as my feet would carry me away from Adam's shop. He shouted my name again, but I didn't stop to answer him. I didn't know where I planned to go—back to Maundy's, I supposed. Where else could I go? Anywhere but with Adam. In my mind I could still see his sweaty back writhing over Blessing Harper, the leatherman's middle daughter. She'd been panting beneath him, repeating his name hungrily, when I walked into the store room of the carpentry shop. I wouldn't have even walked in if he'd bothered to close the door. It was almost as if he wanted to get caught.

Adam came running after me, still shirtless. "Stop, Delilah!" He reached toward me and grabbed my shoulder, spinning me around forcefully.

"Get your damn hands off me!" I shouted at him.

"So now you are swearing? What else has Maundy Weaver taught you?"

"Me? You have no room to criticize me, Adam Iverson! How could you do this?"

Suddenly he stiffened, his chin raised defiantly, and peered down at me with icy blue eyes. "This is your fault," he said viciously as he pointed a finger at me. "You are the one who decided we should no longer be together. Remember the speech you gave me, *sister*? You are the one who wanted to forget about us, and for what? To claim an old name and a fortune you will never have. What would our parents think about you now, Delilah?"

I slapped him as hard as I could right across the face. My hand stung, and his pale skin instantly turned red with the vivid prints from my fingers and palm. He took a step toward me but then froze, his glance riveted to some action over my shoulder. I turned myself, relieved to see Jackson Keene walking toward us, his face dark with concern.

"Here comes your new lover to save you, sister. Now I see why you pushed me out of your bed." I gasped at his insinuation, feeling now as if I had been the one slapped, especially in light of the fact Adam was walking away with bits of straw on his naked back. He didn't wait around to hear my reply, not that I would have given him one. In his mind he would always be right, no matter how wrong he was. He was a fool. His tall, lumbering frame headed back to the carpentry shop.

Some women would have fallen apart; I knew a few who would do just that having worked in Maundy's shop and in her private parlor for the past few months. The stories I'd heard I would never have imagined. Maundy was right—women did talk too much, about too many things and especially about one another. Unfortunately as of yet, I had heard nothing about Claudette Page. But I had heard plenty of tales of adultery, babies born out of wedlock, husbands who asked their wives for strange acts in the bedroom, and it was all proof of what I suspected. Marriage was not so much a thing to be desired as a hardship that crushed the soul—at least the female soul. The more I heard, the less I wanted to be Mrs. Anyone. How could I have ever imagined that I would be Adam's wife?

Instead of weeping like a child, I relished the rebellion that rose up within me. Adam had been the one who wanted to return to Mobile, and I had agreed. He was the one who wanted to come back "home" and make a name for himself, and I had come with him. We had done everything he wanted and nothing else. I refused to live my life according to his whims anymore. I vowed to never be under the control of any man ever again. And I would never surrender my right to my family name and my inheritance. I was going to have everything I wanted in this life—even if that meant living without love! All the passion, all the love I had believed I felt for Adam had been nothing but an illusion.

"Miss Page, may I be of assistance?" Mr. Keene glared toward Adam's shop, obviously ready to defend my honor. If only he knew that I didn't have any honor left. But I did not worry that Adam would tell him. He would rather die than have the world know he had been romantically involved with his "sister." Why? Half the town knew the truth—I was the bastard child of Christine Cottonwood and Hoyt Page. The other half believed everything Claudette Page and her unofficial "morality society" told them. That I was a nobody, an incestuous scam artist bent on destroying the Page family name and with that the City of Mobile. Last week the woman had the nerve to send me a check for five thousand dollars and a one-way train ticket out of town. I ripped up the check and sent it back with a little note of my own.

Keep your money, Aunt Claudette. In the future, please send all correspondence to my attorney, Jackson Keene.

"Yes, Mr. Keene, I believe you can be of help to me. I would like to find a new place to live. I think it's time I moved out of the store. In fact, I would like to sell the whole building." He blinked, his intelligent eyes full of surprise.

"Mr. Iverson may have something to say about that."

"I have full confidence in your negotiation talents. If Adam does cause a fuss, let him know that I am willing to relinquish all the other Iverson properties to him...and remind him that he has as much to lose as I do when it comes to reputation. All I want are the proceeds from this building. I am sure that is what my parents would have wanted."

"I'll make the arrangements, Miss Page, and begin inquiries on a new home. I think we can find something for you...here in town, correct?"

"Yes," I said with a smile, pretending that he didn't look relieved. "I intend to keep working with Maundy Weaver. Maybe something on Florence Street or perhaps Carlen? Is the Winslow home still available? The yellow one with the wisteria out front?" He smiled and nodded. Together we walked back to my shop, side by side on the dusty wooden walkway. I glanced back once to make sure Adam wasn't glaring at us, but I needn't have worried. He didn't show his face again. He wouldn't with Mr. Keene around. Seeing the street now crowded, I decided to take the back way around.

"You know, if you sell the shop, Claudette Page will think she's won."

"Let her think that. What it really means is—what's that poker term? Oh yes, 'I'm all in.'"

He laughed. "I never figured you for a poker player."

"It's a recent hobby I've taken up, and I am told I'm quite good at it."

"I believe that completely," he replied, smiling down at me. "So a small home, like a cottage?"

"Yes, nothing too pricy."

"You know, according to Dr. Page's will, you technically own a few properties near here."

"Yes, and if I step foot near one, his sister will have me tossed out before I unpack the first trunk. No, I don't think I'm ready to go to war. Not yet, Mr. Keene."

"I like your spirit, Miss Page." By his smile, I could tell he meant it. Still, I refused to blush like a teenage virgin. "It is nearly suppertime. Will you do me the honor of having supper with me this evening? We could talk more about what it is you're looking for, in the way of houses. Did I tell you that the judge who will be hearing your case came in on the train today? I have already taken the liberty of introducing myself to him. I think the high-and-mighty Claudette Page may find this new judge less flexible on the law."

"Flexible. That's a nice word for it," I huffed, ignoring his question. "Judge Parker barely even heard our case before he ruled against me." A few people walked down the side street and stared at us, but I had trained myself not to look at their faces. I didn't even mind that some women saw me and crossed to the other side of the street, as if being illegitimate were a disease to be caught. Mr. Keene didn't seem to mind at all.

"You were right to appeal, and you *will* win. Of that I am sure. The morality law that Judge Parker cited is a relic—almost as much of a relic as the judge himself. I feel sure that by this summer you'll be sipping lemonade on the porch of some Page property." He smiled again—it was a nice thing to see.

Jackson Keene was not overtly handsome, not like Adam with his chiseled, Nordic features, impressive height and fit physique. From working in Maundy's shop I could take Mr. Keene's measure without ever putting a tape to him. Barely 5'10", he had a sturdy medium build with flashing blue eyes and a manicured mustache that hinted at pink lips. I knew for a fact that the ladies enjoyed looking at him because anytime he visited the shop there was a wave of excited chatter after he left and sometimes even while he was there. He was five years my senior but had a young face, and I believed if he ever shaved he'd probably look much younger than he was.

He paused at the back door of my shop as I pulled the key from my purse. I thanked him for walking me home, but he didn't leave right away. He stood with his hat in his hand, waiting for my answer to his invitation.

With a polite smile I answered, "Yes, I will have supper with you. Step inside, Mr. Keene. You can make yourself comfortable in the shop. There are some chairs behind the counter. I would like to tidy up if you don't mind. I won't be a minute."

"Certainly, I will be happy to wait." He followed me into the shop, and I walked up the stairs sure that he was watching me. I changed my clothes quickly. Although Adam no longer lived in the apartment with me—he'd moved into the quarter house attached to the shop—it wasn't beyond him to come stomping up the stairs without warning. Tidying myself as quickly as I could, I scowled at myself in the mirror. Hadn't I just sworn off men? Here I was, going to dinner with my attorney. Tongues would wag, but weren't they already? Again rebellion filled my heart.

What did these people know about me?

I dipped my fingers in the water basin and smoothed my hair in an attempt to tidy up the curls that sprang up around my face. I had a new gray dress with a thin black ribbon that ran across the top of the bodice. It had a modest neckline with three-quarter sleeves, a bit old fashioned perhaps but perfectly respectable for a business dinner.

In a few minutes I was ready, but I lingered at the mirror. I was still young and some called me pretty, although it had been a long time since anyone had complimented me on my appearance.

Like I had so many times since I first read that letter from Dr. Page, I studied my face in the mirror. I wondered whose eyes those were, whose nose? Did my mother have a pretty voice? How did she die? I would never know, but at least I had life. I supposed I should be grateful that I wasn't abandoned at an orphanage or drowned in a river. With a frown I reached for my perfume and sprayed my hair once before I rejoined my guest.

I heard Mr. Keene sliding the wooden chair back; it made a hash sound, and I tried not to stare at the scrape on the floor. He walked toward the back door but I stopped him.

"No, not the back door. Let's go this way, if you don't mind." I waved him to the front. I took the key out of my black satin purse and opened the front door.

"As you wish." He followed me out and waited patiently as I fumbled with the key. My black lace glove caught the metal, but I quickly unsnagged myself and locked the door. "You look lovely," he whispered.

"Thank you, Mr. Keene. Where are we dining tonight?"

"Let's take my carriage. Have you been to Patterson's yet?"

"No, I haven't, but I am quite hungry." I climbed aboard the carriage and arranged my dress neatly. Mr. Keene sat beside me, and together we rode through town with our heads held high. As we traveled, he told me stories about the war, how various businesses and families had fared and what he thought about the prospects for the city. He had been born in Mississippi but had been in Mobile since the end of the war. I did not think it polite to tell him I probably knew more than he did about Mobile society, as I was Maundy's friend and was privy to much information. So I listened and nodded appropriately.

We drove at least twenty minutes, passing the cathedral and the expansive oak groves that lined Dauphin Street. I had not been this far down Dauphin since I was a child, and I could barely remember those times anymore. The carriage turned down an unmarked road, and I suddenly felt a bit panicked. Where were we going? The carriage paused in front of a looming plantation at the end of a wide red dirt lane. As we drew closer, I could see that the house wasn't completely empty; a few lamps shone through the windows, and gas lamps flickered along the carriageway. Despite the light it didn't feel like a happy place, not in the least. I shivered and pulled my wrap closer. "Is this Patterson's? I didn't know we were going to someone's home."

"You've never been here, Miss Page? This is Seven Sisters."

I caught my breath. "My mother's home?"

"Yes. She moved here from north Alabama when she married Jeremiah Cottonwood. Truth be told, it was her money that kept this house in the Cottonwood name. It's no secret that her husband could not manage his pocketbook, much less an estate of this size."

In a determined voice I said, "I want to go inside."

"I don't know if that's such a good idea. I had no intention of stopping—I merely wanted you to see the place. I don't think anyone lives there anymore, except for a few of the former slaves and occasionally some obscure relative. And...not to cast aspersions, Miss Page, but the current resident is probably a Cottonwood and thus is less likely to make you welcome. No offense, of course."

"I want to go inside," I said again as I slid clumsily out of the carriage seat. The red clay dirt crumbled into powder beneath my feet, evidence of the long dry spell Mobile had endured recently. Mr. Keene stepped down beside me and offered me his arm.

"Let us go and make our acquaintance." I slid my arm through his and held my breath as the massive front door opened. A tall black man stepped out on the porch. Other faces peered at us from the hallway. My grip on Mr. Keene's arm tightened as we walked up the steps.

The attorney called to the man in a friendly voice, "Good evening. We would like to call on the lady or gentleman of the house. I am Jackson Keene, and this is Miss Delilah...Iverson."

"Delilah Page," I corrected him. I wasn't going to hide my identity like some criminal. He squeezed my hand gently. The tall man showed no emotion one way or another. His dark eyes revealed nothing.

"Please come in, sir, ma'am. My name is Stokes. I will tell Miss Cottonwood you are here. I think she's been expecting you." With a puzzled look, Mr. Keene followed the man into the house and I trailed behind him. Pulling my gray silk wrap even tighter around my shoulders, I nearly fainted at the sight.

The house was easily the biggest home I had ever visited. Maundy Weaver's was nothing in comparison to this place, and I thought her home grand. That was before I set foot in Seven Sisters. Under my feet was a colorful rug with big blue flowers. It looked worn and frayed at the edges, but the floors were neatly kept. A side table held a vase full of dying flowers, the shriveled petals the only flaw in the scene. The place smelled like soap and magnolias. Stokes had walked up the wooden staircase, leaving us to wait in the foyer.

I saw a small fire burning in the room to my left, and like a moth to a flame I walked toward it. Mr. Keene did not follow me, and I did not seek his permission to go. I still couldn't believe I was here—at Seven Sisters. *This may be the closest I'll ever be to my mother!*

So many fine things, and yet an overwhelming sadness pervaded the room. It almost made me cry. A small collection of books lay on a round cherrywood table near the fireplace. I couldn't help but touch them. I thought Miss Cottonwood must like to read, a hobby that I had not taken up faithfully. I read quite well but found that reading for long periods of time made me sleepy. After glancing at the books for a few minutes, I warmed my hands at the fire.

I heard voices in the foyer but didn't turn to look. I stepped back from the fire and saw a large portrait hanging on the wall. I couldn't imagine why I hadn't noticed it when I first came in. The frame was painted gold, and I could see the artist's signature in the corner: *R. Ball.*

It was a portrait of a young woman dressed in a beautiful coral gown. Her shiny brown hair was arranged in a complicated yet flattering hairstyle, and dainty earbobs dangled from her pretty ears. She had a faraway look in her eyes, and on her lips was a hint of a smile. I wondered who she might be. My mother? Some relative I would never know or be able to claim? As if someone were reading my mind, a voice beside me answered my question.

"That is Calpurnia Cottonwood—the daughter of the late Jeremiah and Christine Cottonwood. From what I understand she was the beauty of the county. She disappeared some time ago, before I was born."

I wanted to continue to stare at the portrait, especially now that I knew the woman's identity. To think this was my sister Calpurnia, and not just a half-sister or a stepsister but my true blood sister, if Dr. Page's account was to be believed. She was riveting. Still, I couldn't be rude to my hostess; I had not been invited into this room. The least I could do was be polite.

Pulling my attention from the portrait, I faced the new lady of the house. Younger than me and not as tall, her voice didn't quite match her face. Although she was young, she had a deep voice and intelligent hazel eyes. I could tell she didn't give two figs about her appearance: her clothes were smart but not too stylish, and she wore her dark blond hair in a simple bun. My hostess did not extend her hand or offer a smile. I could sense that she was suspicious, but who could blame her with two strangers showing up at her mansion uninvited? If she did know who I was, then she must think I was crazy or an upstart. Honestly, I didn't know why I had wanted to come inside. Visiting Seven Sisters had not been on my list of things to do. The idea had never crossed my mind before we arrived there this evening.

My attorney cleared his throat and offered an explanation. "Please pardon the intrusion, madam. We were just passing by, and the house is such a lovely Mobile landmark that we could not resist visiting it. Let me introduce myself properly. I am Jackson Keene and this is my friend, Delilah Iverson-Page." I thought I saw her eyes widen a little, but Miss Cottonwood did not comment or ask questions. In fact, she ignored Mr. Keene entirely.

"Yes," she said as she stepped toward me, "you have the look of her. I have seen you before—at Miss Weaver's fitting parlor. Now I remember. But you don't remember me? My name is Karah Cottonwood."

Embarrassed at the slight I stammered, "We see many women on a daily basis. Forgive me if I don't. Did I work on your dress?"

She smiled, and I was reminded of that phrase, 'the cat that ate the canary'. I had a feeling I was the canary. "No, you didn't work on my dress. I came to place an order with Miss Weaver. We have not been introduced, not officially." She turned her attention to the portrait. "Is this why you are here? To assess some claim on Seven Sisters?" She finally spoke to Mr. Keene. "You are an attorney, correct?"

With a courteous wave of his hand, he shook his head. "As Miss Page's attorney, I can assure you that my client has not expressed any desire to make a claim on Seven Sisters. She was merely curious to see the place, and I must confess she had no idea I was bringing her here. Please accept my apology. It was not my intention to inconvenience you." Miss Cottonwood listened, but her gaze didn't leave my face. I felt compelled to speak.

"I have no such desire."

The young lady must have been satisfied with that answer, for she took a deep breath and a sincere smile crossed her face. "Have you had any supper? I was about to take mine, and there is more than enough. Would you two be my guests? I never knew your sister, Miss Page, or the late Mrs. Cottonwood, but I will be happy to answer any of your questions if I can."

Now it was my turn to smile. "Oh, yes. Thank you very much."

"Follow me." Miss Cottonwood walked with her hands in front of her. Wherever she was from, she was certainly trained to behave like a lady. An evil thought crossed my mind. What if I did claim the house? Shouldn't it be partly mine? Miss Cottonwood was living in grand style in this grand house, enjoying my mother's wealth while I was laboring in the dress shop. Then I instantly felt guilty. My current situation was not Miss Cottonwood's responsibility or anyone else's. She had not wronged me.

We walked down the broad hallway, and I tried not to stare at the oil paintings that filled the walls. We walked to the door and stepped into the most beautiful room I had ever seen. With some pride Miss Cottonwood said, "This is the Blue Room—it is my favorite room in the house. The servants tell me it was once a place for musical concerts and spiritual readings. I think it's a delightful space." For the first time I heard youthful excitement in her voice. "Please make yourself welcome while I go tell Docie to set two more plates." With a polite nod she left us, closing the door behind her.

"Mr. Keene, have you ever seen anything like this place?" I explored the room, curious to examine every nook and cranny. On one wall a built-in shelf displayed a collection of ceramic puppies. I longed to pick them up and hold each one in my hand. I imagined they felt cool and smooth, but I did not dare. My hostess would not appreciate strangers destroying her property.

"I can't say that I have. I have been in some grand old homes, but I have to admit this is the grandest. I hope you hold no grudge toward me because I brought you here without warning. On reflection perhaps this was not a good idea. Perhaps it is wrong to show you all this knowing that you could never claim it."

"I am grateful that you did. I would never have had the courage to come here myself. I suppose I could press the issue if I wanted to, but I am happy with what I have—or will have." Tapping the spines of a collection of books by some obscure author I added, "It's never been about the money, Mr. Keene. I hope you know that. I want my name. My real name. I want to hold my head up high and introduce myself as Delilah Page. It is what my father wanted, or else he would never have written to me."

"Yes, the letter." His voice dropped. "Let us keep that letter to ourselves, if at all possible."

"Why? I'm not ashamed. I am who I am. I'm not less of a person despite my unhappy situation."

"No insult to you, Miss Page, but let me remind you that your father confessed to murder in that letter. In fact, I suspect that he did indeed murder Miss Cottonwood's father."

My face paled at the reminder. "I haven't forgotten that, Mr. Keene."

"Please call me Jackson."

Before I could argue with him, I heard yelling in the hall. Curious to discover the source of the disturbance, I walked to the door and opened it slightly. The young Miss Cottonwood was arguing with an older woman—a woman I had never seen before. "Just stop it! Do what I ask!" The older woman raised her head and stared at me. Miss Cottonwood spun about and saw me standing there. With a swish of her skirts she left the old woman in the hallway and came toward me, her face a mask of determination.

"Come, Miss Page. Let's sit together. Dinner will be here soon." Leading us to a round table in the corner of the room, she sat as if she were a queen at court. She had a natural elegance, an elegance I admired but did not have. As she and Mr. Keene exchanged pleasantries and talked about Mobile, I stared around the room, silently comparing myself to Miss Cottonwood. I was taller by at least a foot, and my dark hair was prone to curl, while hers was smooth and not as dark. Could it be true that we were related somehow? I wondered what Mr. Keene thought about her. I knew nothing about her, but I was dying to know where she was from and who she was related to. As if she read my mind, Miss Cottonwood said, "I suppose you are both wondering about me."

"We do seem to be at a disadvantage. Excuse me for asking, but is that an English accent I detect?"

"Yes, Mr. Keene. I spent quite a bit of time abroad with my mother before coming to Mobile."

I finally asked the question I had been dying to ask, "Who is your mother, Miss Cottonwood?"

With an even, steely gaze she answered me, "My mother is Isla Beaumont, daughter of Olivia Beaumont, sister of Christine Cottonwood."

"Are we related then in some way?" I asked her, my voice shakier than I expected.

"I think we are cousins, Miss Page."

"And your father?" I asked, ignoring Mr. Keene's scowl. It wasn't the proper thing to ask, but people asked me all the time, didn't they?

"Jeremiah Cottonwood. Unfortunately I never knew him." We three sat in silence for a full minute before she spoke again. "It seems there are a great many secrets here in this house. Don't you agree, Miss Page?"

"Yes, I do." A flurry of questions filled my brain. What happened to my mother, to my sister? What did my mother look like? Did she leave me anything? A note or a letter? But it was too soon in our acquaintance to bombard Miss Cottonwood with those queries. I had already broken protocol with my rude question once, but I had to know for sure. The servant, the older angry one with the slick dark hair, came in with platters of food and plunked them down unceremoniously on the linen-covered table.

"Thank you, Docie. Now please bring the wine for our guests."

She glared at Miss Cottonwood, who tried to ignore her. Our hostess placed her linen napkin in her lap, and I did the same. With a shiny gold fork she pierced a piece of ham and placed it on her plate. I helped myself to a piece of warm bread and a pat of butter. It was a simple but delicious meal. As she cut her meat into tiny pieces, she asked, "What are your plans, Miss Page? Do you intend to stay in Mobile?"

"I do indeed. This is my home. Granted, I have legal battles ahead of me, but I don't plan to turn tail and run. Mr. Keene is helping me adjudicate my case with the court. I am sure you have heard all about it."

"Where would I have heard anything like that? Do you think me a gossip?"

Her question surprised me. "I didn't mean to imply that," I said defensively.

Docie returned with a glass pitcher full of burgundy wine. She poured the young woman's drink and set the pitcher on the table. She didn't offer to pour ours or wait to be dismissed but glared at me again before leaving us alone. Aware of her servant's rudeness, Miss Cottonwood's cheeks reddened. She stood and poured our drinks, and then returned to her seat. Mr. Keene kept silent, watching the two of us. I thought I spotted a hint of a smile on his lips.

"I think what Miss Page means is that she is aware her situation is the source of quite a bit of gossip amongst certain quarters of Mobile society. It would not surprise either of us if you had heard something negative about her. However, having enjoyed her acquaintance these past months, I can vouch that she is a kind lady with a good many fine qualities." He sipped his wine and said seriously, "You know, it might be beneficial to you both to form some kind of alliance. Even an unofficial one. After all, you are family and face similar situations."

Ignoring the last part of his statement, she asked, "What sort of alliance?"

"Because of your unique social positions, it might be wise to make a united front against anyone who would deny either of you your heritage. At least you could stand up for one another, if the situation called for it." I watched the candles on the table flicker as I sipped my wine. My lips felt dry, and my heart pounded.

"I agree—if you are so inclined, Miss Page." She set down her fork and knife and watched me.

"Very well, I agree. Do you have an attorney, Miss Cottonwood?"

"Karah, please. If we are to form an alliance, then we should call each other by our given names, I think. And no, not yet."

"Please call me Delilah. And if you don't think it out of place, I would like to recommend Mr. Keene. He's been a great help to me. I am sure he could help you too."

She smiled broadly. "Would you be willing to take me on, Mr. Keene? I have had no luck with finding adequate counsel. At first lawyers were calling on me nearly every day to offer their services, and now I can't seem to find any help. I confess I feel somewhat desperate. If it weren't for my mother's nest egg, I would have nothing at all. While she's away, all I can do is wait—it's most frustrating."

I knew exactly what had happened—Claudette Page. The woman held a lot of influence here. There was no doubt she was using that influence to force us both to leave Mobile.

Mr. Keene nodded. "I would be happy to do some research for you. Let's meet again to talk about the particulars."

His answer pleased her. She raised her glass to me and said, "To new friends."

It must have been the wine, but I smiled and added, "To family."

When we left that evening, I felt happy, happier than I had in a long time. Karah and I had plans to meet the following week. I was to return to Seven Sisters for tea, and my cousin promised me that I would be given full access to my mother's belongings. I could hardly believe it. As the carriage rolled down the long driveway, I looked back just to prove to myself that I wasn't dreaming.

I saw the curtains move in an upstairs room of the house. A dark face peered down at me. It was an old woman, much older than the angry Docie. Even from this distance, I could see her expression clearly: she was afraid. She shook her head and mouthed some words, but I couldn't understand them. I felt troubled and turned to ask Mr. Keene to stop and turn around, but when I looked back the woman was gone. I pulled my wrap closer.

I didn't look back again.

Chapter 7—Carrie Jo

I woke up to a rough tongue licking my face. A friendly cat meowed at me before he stalked off. At least he was friendlier than the furry bag of claws that had assailed me in the cemetery. I sat up, wondering where I was. Cold, stone floor, wooden pews, high vaulted ceilings—I was in a church. I stood and dusted off my clothing. Morning light filtered through the stained glass windows. Under normal circumstances I would've found the imagery beautiful, but these were not normal circumstances. I picked up my purse from the ground and looked around to make sure I hadn't lost anything. Checking my hands and legs, I didn't see any injuries, but the side of my face stung. I touched a ragged scratch on my cheek, probably delivered by the evil cat.

Have I really been here all night? How did I get here? And where is here?

I heard the sound of a key ring jostling; the metal security gate screeched and then the side door of the church swung open. The emerging air felt fresh and warm, and I was thankful for the sunshine. I didn't know whether to call out or to hide. My indecisiveness had me frozen to the spot.

"Well, good morning. Have you been here all night? Get a bit of prayer in?" an older gentleman in a black suit called to me as he shoved the keys in his pocket. His head was semi-bald; white wisps of hair poked out from his temples, and the morning light surrounded him like a halo.

"I'm not sure," I confessed. "I must have fallen asleep. If you'll excuse me." Great. Now I was lying to a priest. In a church, no less.

"No need to rush off. Is this your first time visiting the basilica?" The more he spoke, the more I discerned a heavy French accent. Odd to find a French priest in Mobile, wasn't it?

"Um, basilica?"

"Yes, young lady. You are at the Cathedral Basilica of the Immaculate Conception. I am Father Portier." After a moment he asked, "Are you sure you are all right?"

"Yes, I am. I just...I'd better go. Thank you, Father."

"Very well, thank you for visiting. I must go ring the bells. Can't be late."

"Yes, of course." I strolled toward the open door. The downtown streets were becoming busy now with morning traffic. Then I thought if anyone could answer my questions about the supernatural, surely it would be a priest, right? I glanced at my watch. It was nearly eight o'clock, just two minutes till. "Father if you don't mind, I do have a question."

He smiled pleasantly. "And I will be happy to answer it after I ring the bells. I shall return in a moment."

I sat in a back pew and waited as he began to climb the narrow stairs that led to the belfry. In just a minute the bells began to chime, sure to wake up any nearby residents who were still asleep. It was a beautiful sound. The old man returned to the sanctuary and walked toward me. "Ah, still here. I was hoping you would not change your mind. Not everyone likes the sound of bells, you know."

"I think they're lovely."

"That's nice. Now what is your question, my dear?" He sat in the pew across the aisle from me, resting his gnarled hands on the back of the wooden seat in front of him.

"It's probably going to sound strange, especially coming from someone you don't know, and...I must confess I am not a Catholic."

"We are all children of God. What do you want to know?"

"Thank you for saying that. I am not sure God knows who I am, but it's nice of you to say so."

"I have a feeling He knows all about you, young lady."

"Do you believe in the supernatural, Father? I mean, the world of ghosts and supernatural activity. Is it all evil? Maybe figments of our imagination?"

He considered my question for a moment, then pointed at a nearby statue. It was the Virgin Mary holding the baby Jesus. The statue was painted in bright colors, and on her breast was painted a purple heart. "Do you see that statue?" I nodded. "Do you see the rose she's stepping on?"

"Yes, I do."

"Whenever you see a rose in a painting or statue of the Blessed Virgin, you should look for the secret."

"Secret? I don't understand."

"Look carefully at her hands. Do you see anything unusual?"

I got up from my seat and walked toward the statue. I studied Mary's hands for a moment, then caught my breath. "She's holding something in her hand...it looks like a pearl! What does that mean?"

"That is the question." He rose from the pew, walked toward the statue and studied it with me. He stood looking up at the artwork and then smiled at me. "Not even church scholars can agree on the reason for that pearl. Some say it's a symbol of the purity of the Virgin, while others say it represents the Parable of the Pearl, and there are other more fantastic opinions with which I won't bore you."

"That's interesting, but I'm not sure what that has to do with..."

He chuckled. "Ah, to be young again. So impatient to know all the answers. That is my point. The truth about the pearl's meaning is a mystery. It is there, we can see it, we know it is an unusual thing and this statue is very old. Much older than even me, and that is quite old." He smiled pleasantly. "But we don't know what it means. You see, the world is full of mysteries, not the least of which is the subject of the supernatural. Like this pearl, it is something to be discovered and defined by each man, each woman."

I stared at the pearl and considered his words. He asked kindly, "Does that help you at all, or have I confused you more?"

"Yes, it does help." I did feel more peaceful. He didn't answer my question, not directly, but perhaps he was right. This was a subject that had no answer, no black-and-white definition. "I'd better go now. My husband will be looking for me."

"I am sure he will be. Take care, and mind those steps. I would hate for an expectant mother to trip on the cathedral stairs."

"How did you know?" My hand flew to my stomach protectively.

"When you get to be as old as I am, dear lady, it is easy to spot the glow on a young mother's face."

I smiled and touched my flushed cheek before I turned to walk out of the church. Such a nice old man. Almost made me wish I were Catholic. I walked down the steps and out to the courtyard. I was on Conception Street near the intersection with St. Anthony. Yes, I knew this church; I just never knew the name. I turned around to get a better view of the old building and caught my breath. The place had two huge towers flanking the massive sanctuary. Round domes sat atop the towers, which must have housed the church bells. To my surprise, the gate was locked again. I couldn't believe Father Portier had managed to close it so quickly and so quietly.

Curious now, I walked back to the church, but it was locked up tight. A red-haired gentleman wearing green coveralls walked toward me whistling. "Need to get in there? I was just about to open up. Sorry I'm late. Hey, you're new."

"Yes, I'm new, but I was just in there talking to Father Portier."

He pushed up his thick glasses. "What are you talking about?"

"I was just talking to your priest, Father Portier. Older man, balding, with white hair?"

He looked around as if someone might jump out at him. "Is this some kind of joke, lady?"

"No joke. I swear it's the truth. Just ask him yourself. He's right inside."

With a skeptical look, the man opened the gate and stepped inside. There was no one around.

"He rang the bells a few minutes ago. Are you going to tell me I made that up?"

"Those bells have been on a timer since the early '90s. Listen, I don't know what you're into, drugs, booze or whatever, but you need help, lady."

I backed away and walked out of the church. By the time I made it to the end of the sidewalk, I was already running. I didn't stop until I reached Conception Street. When I got home I wasn't shaking anymore. I was tired and hungry, and I had butterflies. Mostly, I was happy to have something else to think about besides Father Portier and the weird experience I'd just had.

I walked up the sidewalk, happy to see Ashland's truck in the driveway. What was I going to say to him, coming home in yesterday's clothes? *Sorry, babe, I passed out in a church.*

As if he could hear my thoughts, he bounded out of the house. "Thank God! Are you okay? Where have you been, Carrie Jo?" Before I could answer him, he put his arms around me and pulled me to his chest. "You had me so worried."

"I am sorry. I'm a jerk." I clung to him, feeling ashamed that I had not told him the news about our child. Now was as good a time as any. "I will explain everything, I promise, but first I have to tell you something. I can't go another minute without telling you. I should have already told you, but I was so angry. I know it was stupid. I'm so sorry."

"What is it?" His bright blue eyes searched mine, and he held my hands. "Are you sure you're okay?"

"Ashland Stuart, you are going to be a father."

He dropped my hands, and his eyes widened. "Are you serious?"

"Absolutely. But if you don't believe me, you can wait six and a half to seven months and see for yourself."

A big, beautiful smile crept across his face. He picked me up and kissed me passionately. Before I could say "Boo," he carried me into the house. His worries had clearly vanished.

"We'll need a bigger house. And furniture." He put me down and kissed me again.

"Okay, calm down. I've had a rough night. That was the good news. Now I have something else to tell you. It's about Delilah Iverson, and something else happened. I was at a church. Well, it was a gate and then a church. But Ash, I'm starving. I would love some of your cheese grits."

"I can take a hint. Why don't you call Rachel and tell her you're going to be late? She's been almost as worried about you as I have. Why is your car at the office?"

"It broke down. Brand-new BMW, and it won't start. Food first, Mr. Stuart. I'll go change if you don't mind." I touched his hand. "Are you sure you're happy? We've never actually talked about having kids."

"Of course I'm happy. Aren't you?"

"Yes, I am."

"Good. Then you go change, I'll cook, and we'll meet back here in ten minutes."

"Yes sir," I said playfully as I walked up the stairs.

Chapter 8—Carrie Jo

At 9:45 p.m., I finally pressed the send button on the proposal, shooting it off to Desmond Taylor with a weary smile. I couldn't have done it without Ashland and Rachel. Even Chip helped out by picking up the takeout and pulling up old purchase orders from our Seven Sisters job. It was definitely a team effort, and that felt good. Hopefully we would hear something positive from Mr. Taylor soon. I leaned back in my chair and sighed. What a weird forty-eight hours this had been! I'd been so busy with finalizing the prelim proposal I hardly had time to mull over my supernatural encounter with the cemetery light and the friendly priest. When I retold the story to my husband over breakfast he didn't question my sanity.

Looking as tired as I did, Ashland began picking up our dinner remnants, empty takeout boxes and half-empty water bottles, while I closed up shop on the computer. With bleary eyes I closed the folders, remembering to save our work one last time. I was just about to shut the whole thing down when my inbox dinged. I hoped it was Mr. Taylor emailing me back to confirm that he received the file, but it wasn't my prospective client. The email was from Alice and Myron Reed.

"Uh-oh."

"What is it?"

"I just received an email from the Reeds. I wonder what this is about." I could tell from Ashland's raised eyebrows that he was as suspicious as I was. Nothing good ever came from chatting with the Reeds. Since their daughter's arrest they barely spoke to me, but I suppose I couldn't blame them. A few months after Mia's commitment in the state mental hospital, I got a notification from the Reeds' attorney of a pending civil action, but then they suddenly dropped it. I had no idea what they were thinking—then or now.

"Babe, why don't you wait until tomorrow to read that? I'm sure it's not anything super important."

I tapped my finger nervously on the mouse pad. "You are probably right, but if I don't check it I'm going to spend all night thinking about it. I mean, what if Mia somehow got free? Wouldn't you want to know if she might be lurking in the bushes?" I said with a sad smile.

Ashland sat up straight and tossed the leftovers in the garbage can. "If for some reason that ever happened I'd be on the phone to the governor." With a worried expression he added, "There's no way that woman should be let loose on the public. Here, I can bag this garbage up in a minute. Let's open the message now and see what is happening."

I waited for him to join me, and then I clicked on the email.

Dear Carrie Jo,

We are writing to tell you some sad news. We lost our daughter Mia this morning...

I gasped at what I was reading. This couldn't be true!

Services for Mia will be held Tuesday at Grant Funeral Home in Birmingham, Alabama. We thought it was only right that we invite you to speak on her behalf, as you were her closest friend. If you cannot attend her service we understand, but please know that you always hold a special place in our hearts.

For my part, I cannot claim to understand what my daughter was thinking when she reportedly attacked you...

"Reportedly?" Ashland said with a scowl, but I kept reading.

I will always remember you two as the closest of friends and sisters of the heart. Please know that Myron and I love you and hope for the best for you.

If at any point in the future you find information about Mia's claim, please let us know. I'm sure any light you can shed will go a long way in explaining to us what happened to our daughter.

Please call us when you can.

Love, Alice and Myron Reed

"I can't believe this." Ashland's hands were on my shoulder. I clicked off the computer and leaned back in the chair, looking up at him. "Can this be possible? Is she really gone?"

"What I can't believe is that they would ask you to speak at her funeral. Who are these people?"

"That does seem weird—so it's not just me."

He shook his head and said, "Nope. In fact, I bet my attorney would tell you that it could be a trap. Whatever you said could be used as evidence if they chose to try and sue us again."

"You're right. I'm stunned that Mia is dead. I thought she was dead after she attacked me at the house. I thought they were both dead—there was so much blood and..."

"It's okay. You're safe now, and she's really gone this time."

I knew what he was saying was true, but it still didn't seem real. "I don't mean to sound morbid, but I wonder how she died."

"Let's get out of here. Things might get crazy now, especially if the press hears about this. It's best to prepare for whatever publicity firestorm this might create."

"It could get nuts. If Mia was still in that facility, then only one thing could've happened to her—suicide. I would never have imagined that kind of ending for her. She was always so strong-willed, strong-minded. I swear to you, the girl you met wasn't the one I knew. Something happened to her, and I'm not sure what."

"It's no mystery to me, Carrie Jo."

"What?"

"The house got to her. Anyone who comes in contact with that house has had something happen to them. It's like it's cursed or something."

"You don't believe in curses, Ash."

"Two years ago I would have agreed with you. Now I am not so sure." He shook his head. "Are you ready to go home?" I grabbed my purse and followed him to the front door. Chip and Rachel were long gone, so I locked up the building and headed to the car.

"Where are you going? Your car is dead, remember? I'll have the mechanic pick it up tomorrow."

"Yeah, I forgot all about that." Determined to give it a try just once more I said, "Let me just try it." I didn't wait for his answer; I hopped in my BMW and to my surprise it cranked right up. Either there was some glitch with my car or unseen forces were indeed at work—perhaps it wasn't a coincidence that I ended up at that cemetery gate after all.

Ashland pulled up beside me with a frown. "See you at home."

***

When Ashland fell asleep I slipped out of bed. It had started to rain. From the sound of it, the drops were heavy and fat, not the typical pitter-patter drops you hear in spring. Low rumbles of thunder warned of an approaching storm, and I felt an urge to watch it roll in. Mobile had no shortage of springtime storms, but we'd been in kind of a drought recently. Tonight, I could smell the rain in the air.

After having made up from our big blowout about his dreaming, I didn't want to risk invading his privacy again. And I couldn't trust myself not to look. In fact, I really couldn't help it. Just like he couldn't control his dreams, I couldn't control my wandering into them. Gathering up my favorite white quilt, I walked down the hall to the guest room. I flipped on the small lamp by the door just so I didn't trip over anything, I didn't need a lot of light to watch the storm. I shuffled across the wood floor in my socks and plopped in the comfy chaise lounge that overlooked the backyard. It wasn't a fabulous view; there were too many trees and tall buildings to see too much below, but I could see the sky perfectly.

I hunkered down in the chair, wrapped my blanket around me, leaned back and watched the lightning light up the sky. At first the blasts of light were subtle, just flashing through black clouds along the distant horizon. It was a beautiful sight. Then the lightning became more defined. It shot through the massive cloud deck, hitting the dark waters of the bay first and then various spots along the edges of the Port City. Thunder rolled and as it boomed and shook the house, sleep seemed impossible. As I enjoyed the scenery, I protectively rubbed my still flat stomach. I was going to be a mother. Was I ready for that? Well, ready or not, I was going to find out soon. I had no doubt that Ashland would be a good father; he was such a good person. "Good night, little one," I whispered to my stomach. Then I thought about Mia, the sane Mia, the one who would have been delighted to be an aunt. Maybe my husband was right—somehow Seven Sisters had gotten to her, had driven her crazy. Strangely enough I couldn't muster up a single tear.

I rubbed my tired eyes and yawned. The gold-toned pendulum clock on the mantelpiece began to chime. I couldn't believe it was midnight already. I was tired, but I also felt unsettled. I glanced at the side table and the worn copy of *THE STARS THAT FELL*. Could I really afford to stay up half the night reading a book? Well, I *was* the boss. I could call in if I wanted to. I had no appointments that I knew of, so I could certainly sleep late. I tossed my wild curls behind my shoulder and out of my face, picked up the book and turned to the worn silk bookmark.

Okay, Delilah. Help me out here. What's going on in your world, and does it have something to do with mine?

Chapter 9—Delilah

My second trip to Seven Sisters was no less impressive than my first. The more I thought of it, the more inconceivable it was that I had lived in Mobile most of my life and had never seen this house. But then again that may have been by design. I would never know if my parents, the Iversons, knew about my true identity; however, it did stand to reason that they would want to protect me. Even though my Iverson family would not have cared about what the upper crust of Mobile thought, I did care. I was left alone to fight for my future. Of course, I had choices. Nothing prevented me from moving away from Mobile and its stuffy social circles. At least I had a small fortune that I could fall back on thanks in part to both my families. Still, as I told Jackson Keene, money had nothing to do with my return to Mobile. I came to claim my name and my family. I was secretly heartbroken to learn they did not want to know me at all.

In a strange sort of way, I felt compelled to pursue my name. Partly because, by all accounts, my mother had no choice but to send me away. She was the unhappy wife of a cruel man, a woman who had found some stolen joy in the arms of my father. I liked to think that whatever her flaws were, she loved me deeply and apparently wasn't afraid to stand up to her tormentor when pressed to. I was hoping to learn more about her, my sister and my cousin this afternoon. I pulled up in the carriage and handed the reins to Stokes, the big man who had met us the other night. He was a man of few words and didn't even walk me in, pointing toward the door with a grunt.

Here in the light of day, I could plainly see that Seven Sisters wasn't quite as grand as she used to be. She'd survived demolition during the war, but she hadn't escaped the effects of time and all those stormy summer afternoons. The rain and humidity had left green mold on the columns, and there were loose boards on the porch and missing side rails. Still, it wasn't anything that couldn't be mended if someone had a mind to invest something in the place. I was curious to hear exactly what plans Karah had. Did she plan to sell the house? Deed it to a cousin? I absently wondered if I could afford to buy the place, and if I could (which was doubtable) would I be allowed to do so? I sighed as I climbed the steps carefully.

I did not invite Jackson, as he now insisted that I call him, to return with me. My cousin and I had much to talk about—some privacy should be expected. Better to leave these things within the family. I walked through the open door and followed the sounds of breaking dishes or something. A woman screamed in anger, and I heard another crash. The idea of someone deliberately breaking the beautiful things in this house starched my collar. I stormed down the hall and walked into the Blue Room like I owned the place.

"Put it down now, Docie. I will not tell you again." Karah said, somewhere between tears and anger. "Do not break another thing! You are mad! Just like her!"

Docie grabbed another ceramic dog from the white painted shelf. I looked at the ground in horror. Several other ceramics had already been destroyed; the evidence of Docie's crimes were scattered all around in piles of broken figurines and ceramic dust.

"You don't tell me what to do! I am not your servant but hers!" She raised her hand and prepared to destroy another pup, but I grabbed her arm.

"You break another thing, and I will have you arrested! Put it down now, madam."

So surprised was she that she did as I told her. The ill-tempered Docie dropped the toy dog on the carpeted floor. Luckily for her it did not break. "Now find a broom and dustpan and clean these things up."

With a sneer she brushed past me, pushing her way out of the room. I doubted she would return, but at least her tantrum had ended. "What happened here, Karah? Is she mad? Are you harmed?"

I walked to her, removing my gloves and tossing them and my hat on a nearby settee. "Let me look at you." She seemed frozen and was staring at a spot on the floor. I followed her eyes. She appeared transfixed by one particular ceramic, a cocker spaniel with a red ball in its mouth. "Karah, are you all right?"

She pulled her eyes away and stared into my face. I don't know what I expected to see, but it wasn't the big black bruise around her eye. "Oh my goodness, Karah! Did Docie do this? You need to see a doctor!"

Finally, realization shone across her face. "Delilah?"

"Yes, it's me. You told me to come, remember. What has happened here, Karah?"

"Cousin?"

"Yes. Here and in the flesh." I tried to sound jovial. I still wasn't sure what I was dealing with here. Suddenly she flung her arms around me.

"Thank God. I prayed that you would come. Don't leave me here again. You must stay with me, cousin. I do not think she wants me here, but I want to stay. I have to wait for my mother. She promised she would come! She always keeps her promises! But she...she..." She pointed to the destruction and then sank to the carpet, crying. Yes, there was more here than met the eye.

"Karah, shhh...all is well. See? She is gone, and I will not let her harm you again. Come sit on the couch." Wiping her face on her brown silk dress sleeve she agreed and let me help her up. Before I could question her further, I saw the face of an old, dark-skinned woman peeping in at the door. When she saw me, her yellow eyes widened, and she did not waste any time getting to me.

"I knew that was you, Miss Calpurnia. I said that you would be home soon, and here you are! I am going to have to tell your mother. She will be surprised to hear that you're home—are you home for good? Would you like some tea? You and your friend? Let ol' Hooney get you some tea, just like you like it." So surprised was I that I did not correct her.

"Yes, Hooney. That would be wonderful. Thank you."

She pinched my cheek with her gnarled finger, and I thought she would hug me, but then her face changed. "You ain't Miss Calpurnia." She stepped back in surprise. "Oh, excuse me, miss. I didn't mean to touch you. I just thought you were my mistress's daughter come to see me. I feel like an ol' fool. I guess I won't need to wake up Miss Christine after all."

"No, I am not Calpurnia. But I am her sister, Delilah. Miss Christine was my mother."

Karah had stopped her crying and watched us.

"Oh Lord, can it be true?" Hooney said. "Hannah told me you was okay. But I thought she dropped you somewhere or maybe laid you in the woods. Was you with the doctor? He was a good man, bless him."

"No, he sent me to the Iversons. I had a new family to take care of me, but now I am back. Karah is my cousin." Then inspiration struck me. "What happened to her eye, Hooney? Did the other lady, Docie, do this?"

"Child, I don't know. I heard the commotion and came to see. It could have been her...she's got a mean streak as wide as the Mobile River. But then again, it could have been someone else."

I sat next to my cousin. "Tell me what happened, please."

"I...I..." She started crying again.

I turned to Hooney. "May we have that tea you offered us, Miss Hooney?"

She chuckled. "Oh, it's not Miss. Just Hooney. Yes, ma'am. I'll make you some tea just like the kind your sister liked. Lots of honey."

As she scurried off, I slid the Blue Room door closed behind her and then returned to the settee.

Without waiting for me to ask again, Karah said, "You will never believe me, Delilah. You do not know what has been happening here. It is like the house does not want me here. Things happen. Strange things, and Docie only makes it worse by doing the things she does. She deliberately instigates them."

"Them? Who?"

"The ghosts. The ghosts of Seven Sisters. They don't want me here, but I have to stay. I promised my mother I would wait for her."

I didn't know what to make of her confession. She had been abused, that much was obvious, but ghosts? I never believed in such things. I suspected that if there were any evil entities in this house, they were all very much alive. I sighed and smiled at my cousin. "I'll be here as long as you need me. We will face these ghosts together."

"You promise?"

Trying to bring a lighthearted moment into a very depressing conversation, I raised my hand and said, "I do so promise and swear."

"Very good. We will have Stokes pick up your things, and you can take your sister's room. Let me show it to you. Nothing has been moved since she disappeared. You may find some clues about her there." To my surprise Docie returned to the room with a broom and a dustpan. She did not speak to us but went about her business tidying up the room. We rose to leave but not before I stopped in front of her.

"Everything you have destroyed here today you will replace. You had no right to do so; these belong to my cousin and to me. If you cannot control yourself and keep your temper, then I am sure my cousin can find someone much more suited to this type of home service." Without a word she continued her work and promptly left us. Karah's eyes were wide as she watched me. Suddenly she smiled, which made her face appear much younger. I had only met her a few times but always thought of her as solemn and serious. Her smile was a good reminder that she was young—that we were both young and had our lives ahead of us. "Now come show me this room. I hope it is close to yours."

"It is very close. I am staying in Uncle Louis' room. I must show you his picture—he was a beautiful man. Quite popular with the ladies in Paris and New Orleans. Maybe one day he will turn up with a new bride. Wouldn't that be wonderful?"

"I have never heard of him. You must tell me everything." For the next few hours, we walked through the house. Our tour began in my sister Calpurnia's room. It was a lovely room, but it looked rather sparse without her personal effects in it. Karah told me not to worry and that all of Calpurnia's things were in the armoire. I could look through any of it and keep whatever I liked. Someone in the household, presumably a servant of Calpurnia's, had neatly wrapped up her pretty hair combs, and we found a velvet bag of her necklaces and small rings. My eyes watered just wearing them. To be this close to my sister and now to be with my cousin—the emotion overwhelmed my heart. Next, we went to Louis' trunks and politely peeked inside them. Karah had been correct; Uncle Louis was unusually beautiful, with white skin that appeared to glow, blond hair and beautiful blue eyes. His oil painting likeness portrayed him in a blue blazer with copious blue ruffles, and he looked quite dandy. We put the picture in a respectable place on the downstairs mantelpiece.

"Now, let's go to your mother's room. I am sure you will want to see it."

Suddenly, a quiet reverence washed over me. I nodded and followed her back up the stairs. We walked past Calpurnia's room to the large room on the right. With a sweet smile, Karah opened the door and moved out of the way so I could take in the sight. Instantly I detected the sweet smell of roses. There were none to be seen, but I could smell them nonetheless. "Oh that smell, it's lovely. Where are the roses? Is that a perfume or something?"

Karah sniffed at the air. "I smell nothing, cousin. Perhaps you washed your hands with rosewater earlier. Anyway, I will leave you alone so you can explore your mother's room in peace." Grateful for her thoughtfulness, I nodded as she closed the door quietly. I closed my eyes and then opened them. Here I was at last, in the room where I last saw my mother. I had been an infant then, but now I was a woman. I was suddenly drawn to the bed, my mother's bed. It was large, with a metal rack that hung above it. It was bare now but I was sure that during my mother's time, it had held mosquito netting so the lady of the house could sleep without the incessant buzzing and biting. There was a white cotton quilt on top of it now, and I rubbed my hands across it.

Like a child, I crawled in the bed and clutched the pillow. Loneliness overwhelmed me. They'd all left me. My mother, my father, the Iversons and even my sister Calpurnia. Death had taken them all, except for my sister. I refused to give up hope for her. She would return one day, surely. I cried hot tears of grief, and the loneliness of my soul felt so deep it was as if it were a drum pounding. When I thought I couldn't cry anymore, the smell of roses became stronger and it so comforted me that I fell asleep. I don't know how long I slept, but it could not have been long because the sun was still high in the sky. I heard the sounds of life downstairs, but at least they were happy sounds. No breaking ceramics, no screaming or beatings. It was a happy day.

Suddenly, the light in the room became bright, so bright I could barely see. I shielded my eyes with my hands and tried to discern its source. The light diminished, and in its place was a woman. I knew, somehow I knew, that this woman was my mother. This was Christine Cottonwood.

I sat up and slung my legs over the side of the bed. "Mother?" She didn't answer me. She held a white dress out in front of her and then looked at her reflection in the long mirror. She spun about and laughed. So happy was she!

"Oh! Callie, darling. You startled me. Don't just sit there—come help me change."

"But I am not Callie, Mother. I am Delilah."

"Now, Callie. We do not have time for those kinds of games today. Dr. Page is on his way to take us on a picnic. Come here and hug Mother." I could not resist her request. I sprang to my feet and ran toward her outstretched arms.

"Mother!" The light returned to the room and flared around her body. She smiled still and seemed not to notice the brightness. I shielded my eyes from fear but kept running toward her. She leaned down with a sweet smile, her arms wide, and I ran into them as she disappeared. I was left clutching the air, feeling the last fleeting bits of her leave me alone in her bedroom. The smell of roses faded in a few seconds and was replaced by the smells of a musty old house and my own sweaty body.

"Mother!" I cried out again. The door opened, and Karah stood in the doorway. She looked at me sadly.

"You saw her." It wasn't a question.

"Yes! My mother. I saw her right here. I was in the bed, and then she came in the room with a bright light around her. She thought I was my sister, but I did not care. She tried to hug me. She disappeared." I didn't cry now. I felt comforted, fortunate that I had seen her. I had seen my mother, not just a painting or a photograph. I saw her with my own two eyes, which should have been impossible. My mother was dead.

"They are all here in this house. I see them too. I never wanted to come here, you know." Karah sat on the bed, her feet barely touching the floor. "My mother made me come. She said she would come soon, that I would see her here. But that was four months ago, and I have not heard a word. Not even a letter or a note. I question Docie all the time because I am sure she knows more than she tells me. She is my mother's servant, not mine."

"Well, we shall have to fix that. You are the lady of the house, at least for now. You will have to have your own maid. We can ask Maundy Weaver. She says there are many hardworking French and Irish girls in Mobile looking for work. And I've heard that if you want a secret kept, you can trust an Irish girl. They are extremely loyal."

"I do not have any secrets. Or beaus or anything requiring a maid. I am just the bastard child of Isla Beaumont and Jeremiah Cottonwood. There—I said it! I am a bastard."

Absently I squeezed her hand. "I am too. Let's not use that name anymore. We are more than a name."

She smiled weakly. "Agreed."

I had to ask her more questions. "Tell me, Karah. You say they are all here in this house. Who are you talking about? Who have you seen?" I no longer doubted that she saw ghosts at Seven Sisters.

"Well, I have seen my father in the room across from the Blue Room, I think it was his study. I have seen a young black woman in the downstairs larder. She pulls my hair and scares me to death. Then I have seen other people, people I do not know. I have looked through all the pictures and cannot identify them. Will you help me? Will you keep me safe?"

"I think we need to call the priest. I hear there is a new priest in Mobile now, a Father Portier. No doubt he would come and pray for us."

"I don't think bastard children are allowed to take communion, cousin."

"We won't ask for it. Surely he would not be opposed to offering a few prayers on our behalf. We are after all very wealthy women."

"Perhaps you are right. But just in case, may I sleep with you tonight? Nothing evil has happened here, has it?"

I was quiet for a moment. I felt nothing but peace and happiness in this room. If something evil had occurred here, my mother's love for her children had washed it all away.

"You can sleep in my bed if you promise not to snore."

"Oh, thank you, cousin."

I hugged her, happy that she felt safe with me.

"I do still intend to work with Maundy, though. I hope you understand that I cannot be here every day all the time. I have to keep my commitments, and I will need to explain to my brother—I mean to Adam."

"I see. I would like to meet your brother sometime, cousin."

I blushed at that idea. I was sure that Adam would be charming—too charming for his own good or for Karah's. I determined quietly to never let that happen. I would tell him nothing. Did he deserve anything more from me? "We shall see, cousin."

She smiled, and we spent the rest of the afternoon walking around the house and waiting for Stokes to return with my things. I also jotted off a note to Jackson asking him to wait on finding my house. I now had a place to stay, at least for a little while. The day ended pleasantly, albeit strangely. This wasn't where I had intended to lay my head at night when I woke this morning, but it felt right.

My favorite part of each day would be when she and I lay in bed together and whispered late into the night. We saw no ghosts, not that first night. It felt as if we were sisters, two cast-off sisters who had finally found one another. I was grateful for that. I was grateful for her. She had no reason to show me such favor, but she did. For the first time in a long time, I fell asleep feeling like I was at home—at last.

Chapter 10—Henri

The Stuarts were on their way—I was looking forward to seeing my friends. I intended to tell them about Detra Ann, if they hadn't already heard that she was leaving, and hopefully enlist their help in getting her to stay. Yes, I had selfish reasons for wanting to keep her in Mobile, but I was also worried about her. She was drinking every day—something she had always hated as long as I'd known her.

Now Lenore referred to her as "the ghost," and that really disturbed me. Detra Ann had cheated death in a very real way...what if Lenore was right? What if the supernatural world wasn't finished with her yet? Moving to another city wouldn't prevent any such encounter. Now how to convey that to her?

I didn't cook this evening, but I had made a few appetizers and mixed a pitcher of hurricanes. Not the syrupy red drink that looked like Kool-Aid, but the authentic New Orleans drink. Lenore, in a rare happy mood, offered to help and even wore a dress for the occasion. I said nothing about her out-of-style baggy denim dress or her mismatched socks. No need to look a gift horse in the mouth, right?

"I think I hear a car."

"Okay, I'll go check." I opened the door and saw Carrie Jo's car in my driveway. The couple stepped out, and CJ waved to me. I waved back and stood on the porch drying my hands on a dish towel.

"Hey, Henri!" Carrie Jo bounded up the steps and hugged me tight. "I am so happy to see you."

"Likewise." I smiled and kissed her cheek and hugged Ashland.

"How's it going, Henri? Things good at the shop?"

"More than good. Come in. I want you to meet my cousin, Lenore."

Lenore flashed a friendly smile, and after everyone exchanged pleasantries I invited them to sit in the living room. "Who wants a drink? I made a batch of hurricanes."

"I'll take one," Ashland piped up. "I guess that means you're driving," he said to Carrie Jo.

Carrie Jo smiled. "I think I can handle that."

"You don't want even a small glass? I use a brown sugar base. It's delicious."

"I have no doubt about that, Henri, but I'm still going to have to pass." The smile on her face told me she wasn't telling me something. She looked at Ashland and said, "Can I tell him?" Her husband nodded, and she smiled even bigger. "Ashland and I are going to be parents."

"Really? That is the best news I've heard in a long time. Congratulations, you two. When is the baby due to arrive?"

"Sometime in May. My doctor says we'll know for sure at the next appointment. I still can't believe it—I'm going to be a mom!" Lenore congratulated them, and we celebrated with a toast. Lemonade for CJ and hurricanes for the rest of us.

"And it's going to be a boy. A boy that looks just like his daddy. A fine healthy young man." Lenore wrapped her hands around her crossed knees and nodded confidently at the couple. Carrie Jo was too polite to say anything except thank you.

"Well, whatever it is, boy or girl, we hope it's just one. I don't think I could handle twins. Especially if they were twin boys."

Lenore shook her head as if she had something to say, but I quickly changed the subject.

"Have either of you spoken to Detra Ann recently?"

"Not me. What about you, Ashland?"

Ashland sipped his drink and shook his head. "She's not returning my calls. I visited her mom recently, and she hasn't seen much of her either. I was hoping you could give us some insight. What's going on with her?"

Lenore let out a little hiss, and I shot her a warning look. "We had dinner the other night. She brought me a little birthday gift—it was the key to the shop. She's moving to Atlanta and leaving me Cotton City Treasures. Everything happened so fast I didn't ask her too many questions because she seemed like she was in a hurry to leave. I'm worried about her."

"You should be. The girl is a shade—she's a ghost already."

Carrie Jo set her lemonade on the table and turned to look at Lenore. "What do you mean, Lenore?"

"I mean the girl has touched Death. She's been in its presence, and it thinks it has a claim on her. It took her friends, and it should have taken her too, but somehow she resisted it. I can promise you that won't last—Death will not be denied. I'm sorry for your friend, but it is the truth."

I tried to keep my voice level. "You don't know what you're talking about. I've asked you to stop talking about Detra Ann like that."

"It's not my fault that you love a ghost, Henri, but I can't lie. She's marked, and she'll pass on soon. And there ain't nothing you can do about it. I am sorry, but it's the honest-to-God truth." She took a big swig of her drink and licked her lips. "I haven't had one of these good drinks in a long time. Pour me another one."

Carrie Jo's eyes were wide with fear. "You can't be right about this. I don't mean to be rude, but what are you basing your statement on? I don't know if you know it or not, but we've been battling the supernatural here in Mobile for over a year and a half. We've seen our share of ghosts and we've beaten them—Detra Ann too. I don't think you realize how strong she is. This can't be true."

Lenore surprised us all by scooting closer to Carrie Jo and taking her hand in hers. She patted it and spoke to her in a soothing voice. "I am sorry that I offended you. I know something about battling the supernatural too. I guess Henri hasn't told you that I've been doing it all my life. People think I'm crazy, and maybe that's true, but there are patterns—laws that the supernatural world follows. Death is hard to escape, especially if it knows what you look like. I'm sure that your Detra Ann is a wonderful person, that she doesn't deserve this, but that doesn't change the fact that she is in danger. Big-time danger."

"If what you say is true, that Death will come for her, then it will come for me too because I was with her. We fought this together. I refuse to abandon her now."

"Maybe you should tell me exactly what happened. If you don't mind. Don't leave anything out. Even small things can help."

For the next hour, Ashland and Carrie Jo caught her up. I shared any relevant bits that they missed but otherwise kept quiet. I was learning a lot too. For example, I never knew about Carrie Jo's dream about Jeremiah Cottonwood and his vicious whip. How unusual that she woke up with the stripe of his whip on her leg. Ashland told us about his first encounter with Isla, and Carrie Jo shared her first dream about Calpurnia Cottonwood. Then we talked about the Moonlight Garden, the treasure, the ghosts of Jeremiah and David Garrett. They told her about the loss of Bette and Terrence Dale, how they saw Hoyt Page and Delilah and Christine. By the end of it, she had more questions, and we answered them as best we could.

"Well, it's obvious that Mobile is a hot spot for the supernatural and that Seven Sisters seems to be ground zero. Everything that's happened to you all has centered around that house. But first, let's deal with the practical things." Lenore took Carrie Jo's hands and stared at them. "Hmm...I never was any good at that. Palm reading, I mean. Let me look into your eyes." She didn't wait to be invited. She grabbed Carrie Jo's wrists and stared deep into her eyes. I almost said something, but Ashland gave me a reassuring look.

Lenore continued, "I know what you say is true about the battle you and Detra Ann did, but she's the shade—not you. No ghost in there. I see only you. As far as your dream catching goes, before you go to sleep at night, you have to put the baby to sleep." Carrie Jo laughed, but Lenore pressed on. "Your little one is who is causing you to wander into your husband's dreams. That little boy will have the same powers his mother does, and maybe some of his father's too. He is already dreaming about you and his daddy. You know more than you think you do, Mrs. Stuart. You didn't have any problems before this, did you? I mean, you could sleep with your husband and drift right off to sleep, right?"

"Yes, that's true."

"It's the baby. He can't control his powers—he doesn't even understand that he has them and that he is special. For a good night's sleep, eat something bland before bed, no sodas or sugar, and sing to him. Sing until he goes to sleep. Then you can sleep without worry."

Carrie Jo nodded uncertainly but then smiled. "It's better than anything I've come up with. I will give it a try."

Then Lenore turned her attention to Ashland. "Start telling your wife the truth about the things you see. Like when you saw that man in the car window..."

"I didn't tell anyone about that." Ashland seemed surprised, and pink rose under his tanned skin.

"It's written on your face. You need to tell her, and you two have to work as a team. I don't know what you have going in your life, but you need to make room for your gift—stop being ashamed of it. It's not going away, and it is only going to get stronger, so be prepared for that. Ask God to help you."

"How do I do that?" He looked confused.

"That's up to you. Go out on your boat and reconnect with Him. He'll help you. He will, I promise."

"So there's no way to make this stop?"

She shook her head emphatically.

"Do I talk to these things or what?"

"You can try, but I doubt they will say anything coherent—just look at what they look at. Pay attention to details. You won't be able to help all of them, but you may be able to help some of them find their rest. I don't have all the answers, but I know pretending it's not happening is not a strategy that works." She touched his cheek, and he didn't back away. "One more thing, Ashland..."

"Yes. What is it?"

"You don't know it all yet. There's something you haven't figured out. You haven't seen the complete truth, the whole truth, the so-help-you-God truth yet. Be prepared for it because the truth won't be denied."

She turned to me with sad eyes. "Now I come to you, Henri Devecheaux. It has been too long since you said her name. She wonders why you do not pray for her, talk to her, look for her. I feel her around this place. Can you see her, Ashland?"

"Not yet, but I sense that someone is very near to Henri." He stared behind me and then shook his head. "No, she's gone."

"That's because you haven't been looking for her." It was more than a statement. It was an accusation. I felt ashamed and angry that she would bring up this subject right now. "You have to find her, Henri. Find her and bring her home so she can rest in peace. When you do, you'll have peace yourself."

I stood up and glared at Lenore. "What if I don't want to know what happened? What good will it do? That was over twenty years ago, Lenore. Am I supposed to spend every day of my life looking for her? I loved her, but she's gone now and I have to let her go—so do you. You have to! I have to! I'll go crazy if I think about it. Is that what you want? Me talking crazy, locked up somewhere?"

"Aleezabeth! Aleezabeth! Can't you even say her name? Quit calling her 'she' and 'her.' She was a living, breathing person—someone you loved!"

"Fine! Aleezabeth! Are you happy?"

Ashland waved his hand. "Um, guys. You said to start sharing. You have a visitor. Tall, olive-skinned girl with long brown hair, a pink skirt, pink knee socks and some kind of white school shirt. She's in the corner of the room. She's barely there." He pointed toward the fireplace as if he were pointing at a clock or a picture, not a ghost. "Can you see her?"

"No, I can't," I said sharply, suddenly afraid.

"Say something to her, Henri." Lenore stood beside me and faced the fireplace.

"I didn't know this would happen. I did not mean for this to happen. I should have stayed with you..." My voice broke, and my heart felt like a rock. "I should have stayed with you. I am sorry, Aleezabeth." I sat on the couch and leaned across the arm, crying. Lenore stared at the corner of the room as if she could see her, and perhaps she could. I could not, but I did feel better.

Ashland gave me a sad smile. "She's gone. I guess that was all she needed to hear—at least for now. I am sorry, Henri. I never knew that you lost someone like that."

I rubbed my eyes with a tissue that Carrie Jo stuffed in my hand. I took a big swig of my hurricane and said, "It isn't something I like to think about too much. I have a life now. I want to keep moving forward, not backward."

He nodded. "I am living proof that sometimes you have to look back to move forward."

Someone knocked on the front door, and I excused myself to answer it. I heard a pretty voice on the front porch and recognized it right away—it was Detra Ann. "Avon calling. Are y'all having a party without me?" I opened it, and she nearly fell inside laughing. It was immediately apparent that she was at least three sheets to the wind. "You know, you really would make a lousy boyfriend. You don't call, you don't come over. That's pretty lousy, Henri." She stumbled into the living room, her red high heels in her hand. "Hey, everyone. I know y'all. Except you. I don't know you—but hey anyway! What are we celebrating? Ooh...are those hurricanes?"

Lenore stepped backward, never taking her eyes off Detra Ann, until she left the room completely.

"Was it something I said?"

"No, that's just Lenore. I don't think you need any hurricanes, Detra Ann. How about some coffee?"

"Whatever you say, doctor." She kissed me on the cheek. I could smell bourbon—it must have been tonight's choice at the bar. "Call me doc-tor love..." she sang off-key and loudly.

"Where have you been tonight, Detra Ann?" I heard Ashland ask as I made a quick pot of coffee.

"Dancing, drinking and saying goodbye to Mobile. I am going to miss this place and all of you. I love y'all, but I have to go." I could hear the stress in her voice now. "I can't stay here, or something bad will happen. I can feel it. You wouldn't understand. I know I should have told you sooner, but my heart couldn't handle it. Yep, my heart...I love you all." Then she began to sing again, "I can feel your heart beat—the heart of love.... Hey! Wasn't that one of your favorite songs, Carrie Jo? That guy William could sing—the band covered all his songs. But don't tell Ashland—I don't think he'd like hearing that too much." I cringed as she rambled on, oblivious to the fact that Ashland was sitting right there. "Hey, where did that girl go? Is that the mysterious cousin—is that your cousin, Henri? I don't think she likes me too much."

"Do you want cream and sugar?" I called to her from the kitchen.

"I want bourbon!"

"You aren't getting any," I replied, shaking my head. At least now I didn't have to explain her drinking problem to Carrie Jo and Ashland. Lenore was right, I sure could pick them. But I couldn't help loving Detra Ann. I poured some of the hot chicory coffee in a stoneware mug, walked into the living room and handed it to her. She thanked me with a pout.

"Ow, that's hot."

Carrie Jo was staring at Ashland. I looked too and saw his face was as white as a sheet. He stared at the front door, and my arms began to feel cold and clammy.

"What is it, Ash?" she whispered.

"I am not sure, but come get behind me. The whole doorway is full of blackness—it's crawling all over the doorframe. Can anyone else see it?"

We all looked, except Detra Ann, who was slow to comprehend the increasing danger. She just stared at us. "What?"

"I can't see it, but I can feel something," I confessed. I sat next to Detra Ann and put my arm around her protectively. Lenore was long gone. *Yeah, battling the supernatural. Right. More like running from it.*

"Carrie Jo, Ashland is right. You need to get behind him—better still, go down the hall." Suddenly frightened, Carrie Jo got to her feet in a flash and would have pulled Detra Ann with her, but I stopped her. "No, leave her with us. We can't risk it following her. We'll stay with her. You go!"

I heard Lenore whisper to her, and Carrie Jo disappeared.

Ashland spoke in a low voice. "That's nothing I have ever seen before, Henri. It's a shape now and he's tall, taller than anyone I have ever known and completely inky black. Oh my God! Do you feel that? It's like all the oxygen just left the room. I think Lenore is right—this is Death we are dealing with."

Detra Ann sobered in an instant. She put down the cup of coffee and clung to me.

"You feel it too? I'm not crazy then?"

"No, you're not. What do we do, Henri? Should I say something?"

"Say nothing," I whispered fiercely. "Be still and pray, both of you. Close your eyes and pray right now!" We did just that. Detra Ann whispered some words, Ashland said the Lord's Prayer aloud, and I poured out my heart to heaven. "God please, protect the woman I love and my friends. She cannot leave yet. Her time is not up. Please, if you have to take someone, take me." My eyes wanted to open, and it was a struggle to keep them closed, but I kept praying, probably louder than I intended. Soon the room felt different. The ominous presence vanished, and the air felt alive again. One by one we opened our eyes. Ashland told us the shape had disappeared. With shaking hands, Detra Ann picked up her coffee. When she realized her hands were too shaky to do her any good, she set it back down on the table.

"It doesn't matter where I go, does it? It is going to follow me. It wants me, I know it. Am I going to die, Henri?"

"We are going to fight, Detra Ann. You won't die—I will be with you the whole time. I swear."

"Can I stay with you?"

"Of course you can." She put her arms around me, and for the first time ever I kissed her. A real kiss, not a friendly, can-I-be-your-pal kiss. She didn't run away or laugh in my face. She kissed me back. I had never been so terrified and so happy in such a short space of time.

That was the moment Lenore chose to step out of the hallway. "Well if she's staying here, I'm leaving. I can't stay with a ghost."

"That's fine with me, Lenore. I didn't ask you to move in."

Detra Ann laughed. "I am not a ghost. I was just drunk, that's all. I am sorry you had to see me like that."

"It ain't the booze, sister—it's the specter following you around. He ain't fixin' to grab me. No way, no how." She crossed her arms stubbornly and stared at me with a perfectly arched eyebrow.

Carrie Jo said sweetly, "Lenore, you can stay with Ashland and me. We have a guest room. I'd like to have you around—maybe you can help us learn what we need to know." I could almost hear her say, "And Henri and Detra Ann could have some time to catch up." She smiled at Ashland, who nodded in agreement.

"Okay, then. Let me get my stuff. Be right back." Lenore left only to return a minute later. "This is it. I don't have much."

"That's great. Well, thank you for the drinks, Henri. I think we'll be going home now. Let's talk in the morning. We have to come up with some sort of plan."

Lenore waited on the porch, still refusing to stay in the room with Detra Ann. I hoped she behaved herself during her stay with the Stuarts. With Lenore, anything was possible. And I hadn't forgotten her mysterious phone call.

I found one...

Chapter 11—Carrie Jo

By the time we made it home I realized how impulsive I had been inviting a complete stranger into our home. But I soothed my nervousness by reminding myself that it was for Henri and Detra Ann. I had privately been rooting for them, and it just made sense to see them get together now. Nobody could ever take Terrence Dale's place, but I couldn't help but believe he would want Detra Ann to be happy. Hopefully Ashland agreed with me; he had to see how good she and Henri could be for one another.

Lenore didn't talk on the drive back to our home. I was dying to ask Ashland about what he saw at Henri's, but I wasn't in the mood to hear Lenore declare Detra Ann a ghost again. When we pulled into the driveway, Lenore didn't move right away. I got out of the car and waited on her. "Are you coming, Lenore?"

She was watching the house, her penetrating eyes examining the exterior for God only knew what. Slowly she opened the car door and stepped outside clutching her two Wal-Mart bags that overflowed with her colorful wardrobe. I sighed and walked up the sidewalk. She'd either come inside or she wouldn't. Ashland opened the door and gave me an amused look. "I know, I know," I whispered.

Eventually she did come in and was the perfect houseguest. I showed her the guest room, guest bathroom and kitchen, telling her to grab something to eat if she got hungry. "What are your plans tomorrow? Are you working somewhere? Do you need a lift?"

"No. I have applications out, but nobody has called me yet. I don't suppose you need a housekeeper or something?"

"No. We have a housekeeper. You will probably meet her tomorrow. Her name is Doreen, and she makes an awesome...well, everything. But if you're interested in that type of work, she might be able to tell you where to go. I bet with the approaching Mardi Gras festivities you could find a job easily."

"That might work," she said, looking hopeful.

"I am going to the office in the morning, but you tell Doreen what you're looking for. If she can't help you, we'll look somewhere else."

Her face softened, and she smiled. "Thank you. That means a lot."

"Good night, Lenore."

"Good night."

I closed the door and went upstairs to pass out. It didn't happen—Ashland was keyed up and ready to talk about what he'd seen. In fact, he wanted to tell me about everything he'd seen. If Lenore helped no one else, she had helped Ash. Sure, she was quirky, but underneath I could tell she had true empathy for people. Plus, she claimed to know a great deal about the supernatural world, and Henri didn't dispute her knowledge. If anyone knew the truth about her, it would have been him.

She seemed like a lost child, wandering through the world depending on the kindness of strangers. She was friendly to everyone...except Detra Ann. I wondered why that was. Perhaps she was jealous of Henri's blooming relationship, or maybe she opposed the idea of her cousin involved with someone ten years younger—or someone white.

Ashland continued talking, and I nodded attentively. He described the ghost man he saw in the car, the many ghosts in the windows of the houses along Conception Street, even the creepy one he used to see regularly when his mother took him to Sunday brunch at the Admiral Semmes Hotel. I listened patiently, pretending that I wasn't creeped out. The poor guy. I couldn't imagine seeing stuff like that all the time and then forcing myself to forget it just to keep my sanity.

I stifled a yawn. I seemed to have no energy today. Boy, missing those pre-natal vitamins even for a day made a difference. I undressed as he talked and finally slid on his old football jersey. I had silk nightgowns aplenty but couldn't resist sleeping in oversize shirts—especially ones that smelled like Ashland's expensive cologne.

"That's not fair."

I folded back the coverlet and slid under the sheets. "What's not fair?"

"You...undressing right now."

I rubbed scented lotion on my hands and feigned innocence. "I have no idea what you're talking about."

He was undressing too and was under the sheets with me in a few seconds. "I love you, Carrie Jo Stuart. I can't imagine spending my life with anyone else."

"That's a good thing, 'cause I feel the same way."

"Say it, then."

I kissed his perfect lips and whispered, "I love you, Ashland Stuart."

For the next hour, we lost ourselves in one another, totally uncaring that someone else was in the house. Afterwards, Ashland dozed off to sleep, but our lovemaking had the opposite effect on me tonight—I couldn't close my eyes. I decided a nice long shower and maybe then a snack would help settle me down. If the butterflies in my stomach were any indication, the baby approved of that idea. After drying off and pulling my hair on top of my head in a messy bun, I padded down the stairs to see what treats Doreen had left me. I was happy to see that she left me a container of mandarin orange fruit salad topped with sweetened pecans. It may not have been comfort food for some folks, but ever since I got pregnant I couldn't get enough of the citrus fruit. Taking the whole container, a spoon and a bottle of water, I slipped into my office and quietly closed the door behind me.

After a few spoonfuls of the tasty treat, I flipped on my laptop in hopes of seeing an email from Desmond Taylor. Nope, nothing yet. I deleted a bunch of junk mail until just the important stuff was left. Digging into the fruit salad, I reread the email from the Reeds. Of course I wasn't going to go to Mia's funeral, but it wouldn't do any good to be mean about it. I felt sorry for Alice and Myron, even though they had considered suing Ashland and me. I wrote them back thanking them for the honor but declining their invitation without giving them a specific reason why. That would have to do. I hit send with a sigh and deleted their original email. That was easier than I'd thought it would be. I hoped that would be the end of the whole sad situation.

Goodbye, Mia.

On a whim, I searched for Father Portier and the Cathedral Basilica of the Immaculate Conception. An image of the friendly white-haired priest appeared. It was the picture of an oil painting—a commemorative portrait from 1829 marking Portier's appointment as the first bishop of Mobile. I could hardly believe it. I had a full-on conversation with a ghost, and I hadn't been asleep. I saved the photo and dug deeper into the history of the cathedral. How was it that I had walked through the gate and ended up in the church three blocks over unless I somehow stumbled into some sort of supernatural portal? Was there such a thing? It had been a common practice in the 1700s and 1800s to build churches atop old religious centers. It was actually a common way to show the natives who the new boss was. I continued to read until my stomach was full and my eyes began to glaze.

That's enough. I need to rest.

I closed the laptop, leaned back in my chair and spun around to enjoy the view of the moonlight bouncing around the backyard. Our little house was quiet except for the occasional sounds of a beam creaking. That sort of thing was to be expected in a home this old. But then I heard another sound, someone talking. It was quiet but distinct. As silently as possible, I went to my door and opened it. Lenore was talking to someone, and from the tone of her voice she was frantic.

"No, I can't do that. You don't understand...I don't know what you mean...."

I knew it was an invasion of her privacy, but I crept into the hallway and stood outside her door. If Lenore was going to do something crazy in my house, I wanted to know about it. I held my breath and took a peek. She had the house phone up to her ear and was sitting on the bed in her pajamas. Her hair looked wild and unbrushed, as if she'd just woken up.

"Why are you asking me to do this? You know I love you..."

Hearing her move around the room, I leaned flush against the wall. *That's enough of that, Carrie Jo. Now go to bed and quit snooping.*

I sprinted down the hall in my sock feet and slid through the open door of my office. I closed the container of fruit salad and put the lid back on my water. I paused to slow my pounding heartbeat.

Lenore's whispering continued, and my hand went protectively to my stomach. I couldn't let it go. I had to know what was going on. Who was she talking to at this time of night, and why was she so upset? My hand rested on the old-fashioned princess phone on my desk. Should I? What if she was in danger? It sounded like someone was trying to convince her to do something she did not want to do. As quietly as I could, I picked up the phone just to make sure Lenore was okay.

"I'm not ready...I can't do it...yes...I understand. I know what this means. This is forever, ain't it?"

There was nobody there—just Lenore speaking into the phone, the dial tone buzzing in the background. With a lump in my throat I put the phone down, left the food on my desk and slinked out of the room. All I wanted to do now was brush my teeth, go to bed and cuddle as closely to Ashland as I could.

This couldn't be good.

Chapter 12—Delilah

As the weeks flew by, the excitement in Mobile grew almost to fever pitch. The city's hotels were filling up as dignitaries and curious visitors from the surrounding counties descended on the downtown area. Lampposts were festooned with purple and gold ribbon, but the city held back a bit on some of the festivities, remembering to honor their war dead with the appropriate decorum. The lost "sons of the south" would be honored during the first parade with an Ash Processional. Relatives of the lost would march in silence dressed in black and doused in ashes, and Maundy and I had spent all morning sewing black ribbons to sell to the supporters. According to Honoree Daughtry, the wife of the commissioner responsible for this year's Mardi Gras activities, this event was expected to help the city begin to "heal from its wounds." I thought the whole thing was morbid, but it kept my hands busy and my mind off my situation.

Parade watchers were already lining the streets and covered the walkways like flies on a watermelon carcass prepared to fully enjoy Mobile's Mardi Gras opening spectacle. We quickly sold our baskets of ribbons, and I took the empty containers back to the shop while Maundy stayed behind to watch.

From what she told me, festivities like the debutante auction and the Night of Masks ball were quite decadent. I wondered what the austere Miss Claudette Page would think about those. I was certain that she would be staging a rally against this sort of revelry, but in fact, Miss Page was a former Boeuf Gras Society queen. Although that mystical organization had dissolved right before the Civil War, Claudette continued to work on behalf of many such organizations. To my disappointment, that had been the most scandalous tidbit I had learned about my estranged aunt thus far. As my court date approached, I began to see my chances of persuading Miss Page to acquiesce to my father's will all but disappear. Perhaps Maundy's idea of gathering information on her had been a waste of my time, just a ruse to hire a decent dressmaker. Thus far, Maundy had gotten much more information from me than I had from her. She pressed me all the time about Adam, leaving me with no doubt that she had was interested in him.

As I pushed my way through the crowd, I reflected on the past few weeks. There had seemed no end to the line of women that flowed through Maundy's parlor and dress shop. We worked as fast as our fingers would allow us, sometimes late into the night. Karah had gotten into the habit of sending the Brougham carriage around to pick me up at five o'clock, which was a blessing. But many was the night when Stokes had to wait for me, sometimes for hours. Regardless of the time of my return, my cousin would be there in the Blue Room with a plate of food and a smile, eager to hear about my day at Mobile's busiest dress shop. I often invited her to visit me at the shop, to come get to know Maundy and the other women I worked with, but she always refused, saying that she did not want to miss her mother's arrival. I pointed out that her mother was not set to arrive for a few days, but she said that she wouldn't put it past her to arrive early.

After all these weeks of being with Karah, I knew very little about her mother other than that she was a popular and gifted actress and quite a beauty. Karah showed me handbills with her image and even shared a tiny portrait of her in a locket that Karah wore about her neck. From what I could see, Karah looked very much like her only thinner and not nearly as flamboyantly dressed. I did not feel anxious about her arrival. I assumed that anyone related to Karah would be kind and friendly.

During one of my late nights at work Adam came by the shop, but Maundy sent him away. She told him we were rushed to finish ball gowns and could not be bothered with a social visit. Listening on the other side of the parlor door, I heard the entire conversation. Maundy was polite but firm in her refusal to let him see me, yet she invited him to visit her for dinner after Mardi Gras ended. I said nothing when she returned but tucked the information away for later use.

The following evening I arrived at Seven Sisters as usual, tired and hungry, but I immediately knew something was wrong. Karah wasn't at her usual place at the round cherrywood table that we often used for our late-night suppers. She was thumbing through one of the many books of poems in the ladies' parlor and barely noticed when I arrived. A stack of books was beside her on the table and I could tell she was looking for something important.

"Good evening, cousin," I said pleasantly and reached for the plate that Hooney left for me. The bread was dry and the soup was cold, but I was so hungry it didn't matter. I dipped the bread into the oniony broth and snacked away.

She turned around, her face in a book, then looked up and gasped. "Oh goodness. What time is it?"

"It's nearly nine o'clock. I didn't mean to startle you. I spoke, but you were immersed in your book. Must be an interesting read."

"I was just...well, you're here now."

"Yes, and I think this is the last late night for me, unless Mrs. Broadus brings her daughter's dress back for some reason or another—which wouldn't surprise me in the least. The way that young lady puts on weight is astonishing. Is there something I can help you find?"

She shook her head and placed the book on top of the others in the nearby stack. Docie walked in, scowled at me and walked back out. Looking even more uncomfortable, Karah said, "Please excuse Docie. She's not used to socializing with other people."

I wiped the crumbs from my hands and said, "Why do you keep her, Karah? She isn't only unpleasant, she also is dangerous and has no regard for our family's things. Not to mention how abominably she treats you. I do not understand. Surely you can find another maid."

She shrugged and absently ran her finger across the spine of the book. Since she was content to stare at her hands, I asked, "What is it? I can see that something is on your mind. Is it your mother? Should I leave?"

"No, I do not want you to go. I think when she meets you she will like you, just as I do. But the truth is my mother is very changeable and I am never too good at predicting her thoughts or her moods. That's not what has me puzzled, though."

"Oh? What is it?" My eyes hurt, and my fingers felt stiff and dry, but I waited to hear her revelation.

"Adam Iverson came by Seven Sisters today."

I sat up straighter and began to apologize. "I will speak with him. I promise he won't come back again. Did he behave inappropriately?"

My lovely cousin pursed her lips in thoughtful expression. The ivory candles on the table sputtered on their shiny candlesticks. I felt an unmistakable draft in the room. The flickering flames cast strange shadows on the wall beside us. "He is in love with you, I think." I could not hide my surprise at her observation. "Mr. Iverson is unashamedly flirtatious, but all he wanted to talk about was you. Do you love him, Delilah? He is rather handsome in a rugged, farmhand sort of way."

"I..." I felt my skin warm, and I toyed with my bread.

Karah quickly added, "Perhaps your affections lie somewhere else now, as Mr. Iverson seems to believe."

How would I navigate this turn in conversation? Until tonight, Karah had never asked me about Adam or our relationship, and I was too tired to play parlor games with her. My rebellious heart won over the intelligent part of my mind that encouraged me to tread lightly.

"I loved him as a brother, until I knew he was not my brother. I thought he felt the same way about me."

"So he mistreated you? Took advantage of you?" She tilted her head and folded her hands in front of her on the table. Seeing my hesitation, she poured me another glass of water.

"No, not intentionally. Adam cannot be anything but who he is. I think we were naïve—I was naïve—but there were no promises made. I had no promise."

"You yielded yourself to him?" Karah leaned forward, the tiny lines on her forehead deepening as she whispered. I sipped my water and did not answer her but merely gave her a glum look. She obviously had never been in love. "What about Jackson? Are you interested in him, Delilah? Not to be crass, cousin, but I do not know any other way to ask."

Surprised by the question I unthinkingly blurted an answer. "Mr. Keene and I have a business relationship. I consider him a friend but only a friend."

"Then you would not mind if he called on me?"

"I have no reason to object."

She reached across the table and squeezed my hand happily. "I am so pleased to hear that. Forgive me for being so forward, cousin. I just had to know. If I thought you had your cap set for him, I would never encourage his attention. I have strong feelings on this matter. I never want to be accused of competing with my dear cousin. There are too many men in the world for that."

I smiled back at her, pretending to be happy. Why hadn't I told her the truth, that I was not sure how I felt about Mr. Keene? Now it was too late say so. Quietly I internalized the meaning of all this. Because of my confession, Karah now knew all about my involvement with Adam and she made it plain she had designs on our attorney. Maundy was right—I was too quick to speak my mind.

"Did you hear me, Delilah?"

"Yes," I lied, then took a sip of my water. I did not drink often, but I suddenly felt the need for a glass of wine or some of Maundy's strong drink.

"Really? What did I say?"

"I apologize, Karah. I guess I am more tired than I thought." I stood up and stretched my sore back.

"It wasn't important. We can talk tomorrow. Can I count on you to help me get the house ready for Mother tomorrow? I want everything to look its best. I am sure Maundy can spare you one day."

"Yes, I will gladly help you. I think I will go to bed now. Do you need help finding your lost bookmark?"

"Bookmark?"

"Yes, or whatever it is you are looking for." I pointed to the messy stack of dusty books piled on the table.

"Oh, bookmark. No, I think I will retire too in just a few minutes. It *is* getting late. Good night, cousin."

"Good night, Karah." Feeling unhappy, I left her in the ladies' parlor and walked down the hall toward the staircase. No candles had been lit in the hallway, and the entire top floor was like a yawning black cavern. The hem of my blue dress had torn as I stepped out of the carriage earlier. I would need to repair it, but now I just wanted to prevent myself from tripping over it and tumbling up or down the stairs. I picked up my skirts to climb up to Calpurnia's room when an odd amber-colored light shining in from the glass door to the Moonlight Garden caught my eye. I paused to decide if I should call out to Karah, but the events of the evening still stung. I decided to have a look myself. It was not unusual to see lights on the property at night, but the color of the light attracted my attention. I had never seen anything like it. As I walked toward the door, the light moved away from the garden entrance, but I could plainly see it shining through the trees.

I opened the door and hoped to avoid waking Stokes, who slept in the small room under the stairs. He was an odd man—an empty man who did not enjoy idle chitchat, especially with women. From what Karah whispered to me on the few occasions we had the opportunity to speak without enduring Docie's disapproving stares, Stokes had been Mr. Cottonwood's right-hand man, never too far from his master. I wondered what the former slave thought about me—if he even knew or cared who I was. The door clicked behind me, and I stepped out on the brick walkway.

Karah and I had walked through the garden during my initial tour of the home, but there had been plenty of daylight to see by. In the day it was a marvelous place, full of hidden spots for reading a book or, as Karah put it, stealing a kiss. But it seemed a forlorn place at night. It was completely dark, with the exception of the half-moon above me and the odd amber light hovering on the other side of the trees.

I walked the half circle to the opening of the maze path, pausing to see if I could determine the source of the light. Tendrils from my usually neat bun slapped my face as a blast of wind blew through the garden, almost pulling me down the path. My hand flew up to shield my face from an unexpected shower of damp magnolia leaves. Then I heard my name whispered on the breeze, "Delilah, Delilah."

"Who's there?" I asked in a near whisper. My heart was pounding in my chest as if I had run through the whole garden. My skin tingled, and my lips felt dry. I stopped on the path, my mind torn between the choices—run back to the house or continue my search to determine the source of the unusual light. "Who's there?" I said in a stronger voice. The wind blew steadily, but at least the trees were not pelting me with foliage. Shielding my eyes with my hand, I watched the light bounce further into the maze. Curiosity won the battle with fear, and I pressed on. In the half light of the moon I could at least see the path ahead of me, and the strange bouncing light seemed to have stopped on the path to wait for my arrival. Walking more quickly now, I called out again, "Who are you? Is that you, Stokes?"

I walked deeper into the twisting garden, to the left and then to the right again until I felt disoriented.

What was I doing? This was none of my business, was it? This was not my house or my property. I was only a visitor here. Who did I think I was, policing the grounds as if I were a true Cottonwood? I had no weapon or any other way to defend myself, but I wasn't thinking clearly as I pushed toward the light that now began to pulsate. The amber color darkened, and suddenly the light disappeared. I scrambled down the hedge, scratching myself on a thorny branch. I swore under my breath—it was a word I had never used before, but I had heard Maundy use it plenty of times. Yet I did not stop. I could not explain this compulsion, but I had to find and identify the source of the light. I stepped out of the maze into a clearing and nearly fell over dead.

Standing in the center circle of the maze was a man, a tall man wearing a fine suit with white collars and no hat. Unmoving, he watched me as I approached just as if he were a statue. I had passed many statues in this garden on my journey here, but none were as frightening as the man who stood before me. I paused about twenty feet from him, waiting for some indication that he was a living being. Another breeze blew through the Moonlight Garden, and on the breeze I smelled magnolias, burning leaves and something else...

My hands flew into fists, and I looked around to see if anyone else had joined us. If there were two men I should certainly run, but I saw no one else. What should I do? Should I turn to flee the garden? I stared in disbelief as a whirlwind of leaves blew between us, blasting my gown and hair. In seconds, it had lashed my hair completely free from its pins. As the wind blew past me I could plainly see that the intruder's hair did not move! He was certainly a statue—or something. A feeling of dread filled my soul with horror, and finally I gained control of my legs. As quickly as I had run into the garden, I began to run out.

I took a right turn down the long hedgerow and ran left, traveling under the blooming dogwoods. I took another left and ran the length of the magnolia-lined trail. My eyes were wide, and my breath came fast and hard. I knew I was heading the right way—there were pods and leaves covering the ground, and the white petals shone bright in the moonlight. My forgotten torn hem caught my foot, and I tripped and went sliding across a pile of damp, musky leaves. I skinned my elbow, but I could not really feel the pain.

I heard footsteps behind me on the leaves and knew I was not alone. I was too afraid to move.

Maybe if I remain very still, he will not see me!

Slowly I pushed my hair out of my face and could see a pair of shoes a few feet from me. With complete horror, I looked up...and there he was, glaring down at me. The stranger reached his hand toward me, and his long nails were dirty and gray. I scrambled away from him, scooting back on my hands and climbing awkwardly to my feet. I stood breathing hard as the thing surveyed me. Since I stood frozen, afraid for my life, I stared back. His unearthly pale skin appeared as if it had never seen the sun. He had a thin, narrow nose, sculpted lips and dark eyes—eyes that had no life in them. On closer inspection I could see that his jacket and trousers were dusty as if he slept in the dirt. My soul was offended on such a deep level, but I could barely understand it. Then it occurred to me. This man was not alive—I was looking into the face of a ghost.

As the awareness of my situation dawned upon me, I could see the amusement in his eyes. I knew who he was—or at least *what* he was, and he knew that too. Since he was not leaving or moving I asked him, "What are you doing here?"

He took a step toward me, and instinctively I moved backwards. In an elegant dead voice he said, "I am waiting for someone."

"Who are you waiting for?" I whispered in the darkness. He moved toward me without moving his feet. It was a sort of glide. He was only a few feet from me now, and as I watched his face began to change...the skin became pinker, the dark eyes took on a dark blue color, and he appeared to breathe. The breeze blew again, lifting the hair off of his collar. Despite the amazing effect, I knew it was all an illusion. He wanted me to think he was alive, but I knew he was not. A smile curled on his lips, and I could see his perfect white teeth.

"It does not matter now, Delilah. She is not here, but you will do. Would you like to take a walk with me?" He offered his hand to me as innocently as a child, but I had no intention of reaching for it.

"No, I don't think I will." There we stood facing one another, he unmoving and my feet locked in place. Then I heard a voice, a familiar voice, a living voice calling to me from the house.

"Delilah? Come inside! There is a storm brewing." The garden intruder glanced at the doorway and then at me. He smiled and rudely licked his lips before he disappeared, melting away until his image vanished. Finally free to move, I bolted toward the door, remembering to lift my tattered hem as I ran. I climbed the steps and scurried through the open door and into the arms of my cousin.

"Delilah! Look at you! What happened? You are as cold as ice. Come inside now and I'll make you a hot cup of tea." I wept on her shoulder and clung to her as if she were the only thing that could save me from death. "Docie! Come quickly!"

Kara's servant walked serenely into the hallway, her hands clasped before her. "Yes? What is it?" The older woman was wearing a long flannel nightgown, and her gray hair hung in a long braid over her shoulder.

"My cousin has seen something that frightened her. Have Stokes search the garden, and please bring us a cup of tea. Quickly now!" Karah led me away, her arm about my waist. I glanced over my shoulder at Docie. The woman had not moved. In fact, she stood in the hallway watching us with a smile on her face.

She knew exactly what I had seen in the garden, and she wasn't surprised by it.

Chapter 13—Carrie Jo

Before I left the house, I checked my email and was delighted to see that Desmond Taylor had replied with his answer: the Idlewood project was a go! I had done it—no, our team had done it! I felt excited by the prospect of beginning a new project. It would take a lot of time, probably a few years, but it would be worth it if we could stop the house from rotting into the Mobile landscape and return Idlewood to its proper place in society.

Ashland had left early for a meeting with his attorney about some mysterious project. I wasn't too sure about this new attorney. She seemed very hands-on, but she was a friend of his from high school; working with him would kind of be her big break. I trusted Ashland. He had been unfaithful to me only subconsciously. I had no reason to believe that there was anything funny going on, but my gut still told me to keep an eye on her.

Rachel greeted me and pointed to the coffeepot. "Made some fresh. Get it while it's hot."

Just the idea of drinking coffee made me queasy, and she must've seen the expression on my face. "What? I thought you loved my coffee."

My hand flew to my stomach, and I nodded glumly. "I do love your coffee, but my child? Not so much."

"Oh my God! Are you serious?" Rachel ran around her desk and put her arms around me. "I'm so happy! I'm going to be Aunt Rachel! When is he due? Or she due? Do we know what we're having?"

I laughed at her excitement. It felt good to tell my secret. "Not yet, but I'm sure we will find out soon enough. I have another appointment in a couple of weeks. Maybe by then they can do the ultrasound and we can see something."

She hugged me again, and before I could get to my office the front door opened. A very happy-looking Henri and Detra Ann walked in. "Hey, guys." I greeted them with a smile.

"Is this how you always start your workday, with a group hug?" Detra Ann laughed and hugged me too.

Before I could say anything, Rachel blurted out, "It's so wonderful! Carrie Jo is going to have a baby."

"I heard! I'm so happy for y'all!" Detra Ann hugged me again.

Henri put his arm around me. "I had to tell her. You and Ashland will make wonderful parents. Congratulations again, CJ."

"Thank you. It is pretty wonderful. So what brings you two by? Not that I'm not glad to see you for any reason."

"Actually I came to talk to you about Lenore."

Thinking that Henri would want privacy I said, "Let's go to my office. Rachel made some wonderful coffee if you'd like some."

"I think we're good."

I sat behind my desk and invited them to take the two seats in front of me. I tossed my purse in the bottom drawer and turned my attention to my friends. "You should know she's gone. I mean, she left this morning before Ashland or I got up. She mentioned something yesterday about getting a job as a housekeeper. I didn't ask Doreen this morning, but I think she plans on talking to her."

Detra Ann leaned back in her chair and glanced at Henri. He said, "Lenore has always walked to the beat of a different drummer, even before Aleezabeth disappeared, but her behavior has gotten worse since. I am grateful that you allowed her to spend the night with you, but that is not a solution. I cannot put you guys in the middle of her mess, especially with a baby coming. I am not sure what she's capable of."

"I agree that Lenore is...quirky. But I'm not sure she's dangerous. Then again, you know her better than I do."

"I think I have a way to help her. What if, somehow, we could find out what happened to Aleezabeth? I mean, I would never ask for myself, but...she needs to know or she is never going to move past it. That's why I am here, Carrie Jo. I know you and Ashland both have skills in this area. What if we could solve the mystery, find my cousin and bring her home? I think that would..." Just then, my phone rang. Despite my attempts to ignore it, Rachel poked her head in the doorway.

"I hate to interrupt, but that's Desmond Taylor on the phone. He's on a cruise. I'm not sure when you could call him back. Do you want to speak with him?"

I didn't know what to say to Henri. Was he asking me to dream about Aleezabeth? "Forgive me, y'all, but I have to take this. Just give me a second."

"We can talk later." Henri stood, and Detra Ann just stared at him.

"It's not that you guys aren't important to me. It's just that—"

Henri raised his hand and gave me a dismissive wave. "I should never have asked." He walked out of the office; I could hear the front door chimes, and I sat staring open-mouthed at Detra Ann.

"What did I do?"

"Don't worry about him. He's just worried about Lenore. And no matter what he tells you, he's not over what happened to Aleezabeth. Tell you what—why don't we meet you for dinner and then we can talk."

"That sounds great. Why don't you guys come over about six? I'm really sorry, Detra Ann."

"Nothing to worry about. You leave him to me. We will be there." She walked out of my office in her shiny taupe heels.

"Okay!" I called after her, still puzzled by what just happened. I picked up the phone.

Desmond Taylor might have been on a cruise, but he was certainly in work mode. He had a slew of questions, and I did my best to answer them. After the thirty-minute call ended, I couldn't help but worry about Henri. It was not like him to be short-tempered with me—I knew something was seriously wrong.

The day dragged by, but finally five o'clock came around and I waved goodbye to Rachel as I headed home. Doreen had graciously agreed to cook for our dinner guests, and my stomach was grumbling. I found Ashland in my office using my computer. I dumped my purse and briefcase on the side table, slid my arms around his neck and kissed the top of his head.

"Whatcha doing?"

"Just checking on a few things. You know, I never did give you *my* anniversary present." He turned the wooden chair around and patted his leg playfully.

"You're right." I slid into his lap and wrapped my arms around his neck. "But unfortunately your gift is going to have to wait. We have dinner guests coming, remember? I texted you earlier."

He smiled wickedly and said, "This will only take a minute."

I blushed and scolded him, "Ashland."

"It's not that, and I'm pretty sure that those kinds of *gifts* take a little more than a minute." I smiled back at him and punched him playfully on the arm. "Open the browser," he said.

"What?"

"Open the browser on the computer. I want you to see this."

I reached over and pulled up the browser window he had minimized. It was a website featuring historic Mobile landmarks. I had to admit that I was puzzled. "Okay, so this is Widow's Row. I have seen this before. What am I looking for?"

"Tell me about it."

"This house was originally part of Widow's Row. It was housing for Civil War widows—there were quite a few of them. But there was something of a scandal there around the turn of the century. At the end of this street would have been the Southern Market. Right here." I pointed to a map that showed the layout of the old city. "One row of houses ran east, and the second ran west, that way. Of course, the county courthouse was across the street back then. It's a shame that most of those houses are gone."

"Not all of them are."

"Really?"

"A few have been wonderfully restored, like the Murray House, but there is one that's kind of been left behind. It's on Eslava Street."

"Eslava...it runs parallel to Virginia Street, right?"

"Yes."

"So what am I looking for?"

He reached around me and clicked on another screen. A tiny house, sometimes called a "shotgun" house, popped up on the screen. "It's yours. I thought it would make the perfect office for your new business. You could restore it and really show off your talents. And of course, you'd be restoring a patch of Mobile. What do you think?"

Tears welled up in my eyes. "I think it's wonderful." I put my arms around his neck again and hugged him. "I love you."

"I love you too."

"And I didn't get you anything."

"Nonsense. You gave me the best gift of all." He nervously touched my stomach. I nodded and put my hand over his. I kissed him, feeling so grateful not only for the wonderful gift but for the fact that I had someone as wonderful as Ashland in my life. What a fool I had been to make such a big deal out of his stupid dreams! I felt blessed beyond belief.

I heard voices in the hall. "Oops. To be continued. Our guests have arrived a few minutes early."

With one last kiss I scooted out of his lap, and together we walked out of the office holding hands like two teenagers.

"Hey, guys!" I called to them. "Glad you could make it. I'll check with Doreen on dinner. Be right back." Ashland squeezed my hand, and I went to see if I could help in the kitchen. As expected Doreen was a whirlwind of activity; a sauce pot on the stove filled the kitchen with delicious flavor. She slid the pork roast out of the oven and set the pan on the stove top before she spun around and gasped.

"Mrs. Stuart! You almost gave me a heart attack." She pushed her eyeglasses back to the bridge of her nose and gave me a goodhearted yet disapproving scowl.

"Sorry," I said sincerely. "Thank you for going the extra mile tonight, Doreen. Smells delicious." I stuck a spoon in the sauce before she could object. "Can I do anything?" The sauce was delicious. Not like Bette would have made, but I couldn't wait to dig in.

"No, ma'am. I have this under control. Dinner should be ready in about twenty minutes. I think your guests are a bit early."

"Yes they are, and we aren't in a big rush," I said as I stole a warm yeast roll from the covered basket on the bar.

"You never said if you wanted me to serve. Did you want this buffet style?"

"Buffet style is perfect. We can wait on ourselves." I resisted the urge to hug her. Doreen didn't enjoy being touched—or surprised. I seemed to always do both. Leaving dinner in good hands, I went to join my friends, but Detra Ann caught me in the hallway and waved me into the bathroom. I giggled as she closed the door behind us.

"What's going on? Are you dying to tell me the details?" I asked teasingly. Her distressed look made me change my tone immediately. "Detra Ann?"

"I thought about calling you after we left this morning, but I didn't know what to say."

"You should have. I'm sorry about that phone call."

"You must think I'm a horrible person. I mean, I never meant for this to happen with Henri. It just sort of happened."

I grinned at her. "What? You must be the only person who didn't see this coming. And of course I don't think you're horrible—this is the way it should be. Nobody expects you to mourn forever, Detra Ann. This isn't the 1800s."

Sitting on the side of the tub with her head in her hands, she whispered, "I just don't know. I don't know if this is right. I don't know if this is what I want. That's horrible to say, isn't it?"

I sat on the floor next to her and waited for her to look at me. Sitting this close, I could see the dark circles under her eyes that she tried to hide with expensive concealer. She hadn't been sleeping and was much thinner than she had been last year. She didn't have any extra weight to begin with. "I think it's time for you to think about yourself. Not your mom. Not Henri. Yourself. It's okay to take care of you. And if you're not sure how you feel about him, then slow down. No one will fault you for that."

"I'm leaving, Carrie Jo. I took a job in Atlanta."

"Oh wow."

"He thinks last night changed everything, but it didn't. He doesn't understand what I've been through. I mean, I know he knows—I've talked about it plenty of times—but he doesn't know how I feel. It's just too soon. It's too much. I just can't. And there's this other thing."

"What?"

"Lenore is right. I am a shade, a ghost. I think I am marked. I think—no, I know—that something bad is going to happen to me."

Instinctively I grabbed her hands and said, "No! Don't listen to her. She doesn't know what she's talking about. We beat those ghosts, and it's over. End of subject. Lenore is crazy—I caught her talking on the phone to nobody last night. There was no one on the other end." No way was I telling Detra Ann what Lenore said or what Ashland saw.

Her beautiful eyes widened, but she continued, "You and I both know that with that house it's never truly over. I can't pretend that I understand why all of this happened. I still don't know why Bette had to go and why Terrence is gone. What was the connection—what made me so special that I escaped? It's not fair, and I think I just got lucky. But my luck is wearing out. If I don't leave, if I don't make a run for it, well, then I'm going to join them. I hear things. I see things. Dark things. If I sit still for too long shadows creep in. I can't even close my eyes for very long. Something is coming for me, CJ."

I heard Ashland call me from the hallway, and I scrambled to my feet and opened the door. "Right here. Be there in just a second." I didn't offer any explanation other than that. He'd have to wait. I closed the door and sat next to Detra Ann.

"Listen to me. If you decide to leave, that's fine if that's what you need to do. But if you're leaving just to run away from some phantom, then you should stay. We can fight this, Detra Ann, and we *can* do it if we stick together. That was the mistake I made the last time. I took off half-cocked into that hospital room, and look where it got us. Bette is gone." A sob escaped my throat. "And that's on me. TD's gone. And that's on me. They had no idea what I was doing, and I put them in a horrible situation. You are not alone, and I'm not going to let you fight this by yourself. Let's go in there right now, tell them what's going on and get everyone on board so we can come up with some sort of plan. Enough with working behind the scenes—we need to be honest and put everything out in the open."

"I can't do that to Henri. He is so broken up about Aleezabeth and Lenore. I don't think he can handle one more thing right now. And let me remind you that you have a baby to think about. I can't have you fighting Death on my behalf. I won't do it. I just wanted you to know that I value your friendship. I am glad I got to know you."

"Me too, but don't talk like I'll never see you again."

"I want you to promise me something." I didn't like the sound of this, but I nodded. "Promise me that you will look after Ashland. If anything were to ever happen to me and you ditch him, I will come back and haunt you."

"Of course I will. But don't talk like this. We're sticking together, remember?" Before she could protest, there was a knock on the door.

"What's going on in there? Carrie Jo are you okay?" When did Ashland get to be so nosy?

"Yes. I was just feeling a little sick. I'm okay now. Coming right out." Detra Ann and I hugged, and I emerged from the bathroom with my hand over my stomach. "Must be evening sickness."

Soon the four of us were chatting, but it was impossible to really have a conversation with Doreen coming in and out. She insisted on waiting on us even though we'd agreed on a more informal buffet style. Thirty minutes later, she waved goodbye, and I gathered the supper plates and quickly carried them to the kitchen. I'd tidy those up later, but I had something to do. No way was I going to lose another friend. I decided it was time to take charge. I meant what I'd said about no more secrets. Wiping my hands on the kitchen towel, I marched back into the living room and stood with my hands on my hips. I didn't give a hoot about what they were talking about. I spilled my guts.

"Detra Ann needs our help, y'all. I know that you have something to say, Henri, and I am sorry about this morning's interruption. But this is a situation that can't wait."

Detra Ann scowled at me. "Carrie Jo...stop."

"Nope. You might be mad at me forever, but at least you'll be alive. We have to tell them. So tell them already!" Ashland and Henri stared at me like I had two heads. "I'm not kidding. You tell them or I will."

Detra Ann shot to her feet and glared at me. "I didn't want you to say anything, CJ!"

"Well, I did, and I refuse to lose another friend! You can hate me later, but tell them what's going on."

She slid her hands into the pockets of her fitted sweatshirt and paced the carpet in front of the big window on the side of the house. The streetlight was on out front, but the side of the house looked dark and gloomy. After a few moments, she leaned against the windowsill and stared out into the darkness with her back to us. "Lenore is right. Something is following me. I knew it the day I left the hospital. At first I thought it was the pain medicine. God, that stuff is awful. That's why I prefer drinking. Booze doesn't make my skin crawl or cause me to hallucinate. Pain medication makes me loopy big time, but that wasn't it. At first it only happened once, maybe twice, a day. I was walking down the sidewalk in front of my mother's house on Palladium Drive, and I passed that big oak that stretches almost into the street. You know the one, Ashland, the one we used to climb. As soon as I stepped into the shadow, I heard it groan, like it wanted to devour me." She shivered, turned around and leaned with her back against the window, her hands still in her pockets. "By the time I got into Mom's house I was shaking so bad I thought I would pass out." She began pacing again.

"Then the shadows in my house began to groan whenever I came close to them. You can't know what it's like having to leave the lights on 24/7 like you're a four-year old! I don't dare turn a light off because the shadows don't just groan now—they call my name!" Detra Ann's voice rose in fear. Henri reached for her, but she raised her hand and shook her head. "No. Let me finish." She took a deep breath and continued, "A month after the hospital event, I was in the shower when the light went out in my bathroom. The bulb blew—that's what I told myself anyway. There I was in the shower, naked and soaking wet, just waiting to die. The groans grew louder and louder—I could feel the darkness gathering. I tripped out of the shower and crawled to the bathroom door. A slimy hand grabbed my foot and pulled me back, but I kept struggling to get away. Finally I remembered the Lord's Prayer. I said it, like you did the other night, Ashland. I said it, and it let me go. I reached the door handle and turned it, and I was free. Then I called Henri to change the light bulb for me." She reached out and squeezed his hand. "You have been so good to me. I don't deserve you."

Henri's dark eyes sparkled with tears. "Don't say that. I am the lucky one. I love you, Detra Ann."

"I know," she said sadly. She turned back to the big window. Nobody said a word; I sure didn't know what to say. "Even now, if I stepped into the yard and stood under that tree where the shadows are the darkest, it would take me and I would never escape." She peered out the blinds, and my skin began to crawl.

"Detra Ann, get away from the window," Ashland warned her sternly. He stood in front of me and waved his hand behind him, and I got off the couch and moved to the doorway. I couldn't see anything, but apparently my husband did.

It didn't seem to faze her. "See? I can see the darkness gathering now. It's just waiting for me. I don't know what's in those shadows, but I know if it touches me, I'll die. Tell me I'm wrong! Any of you! Tell me I'm wrong!"

"Detra Ann, get away from the window!"

Tearing her eyes away from the darkness, she looked at Ashland. As she did, the window behind her shattered with a loud boom, and pieces of glass flew across the living room. Ashland fell on top of me to protect me, and Henri snatched Detra Ann's hand and pulled her to the ground. As we lay there trying to figure out who was hurt and what happened, the chandelier flickered.

"Everyone get up now!" Ashland yelled. "Upstairs, everyone!"

We did as we were told and climbed the stairs like four maniacs. I flipped on light switches as we ran so none of the shadows could touch Detra Ann. She wasn't crying or saying anything at all, just running with fear in her eyes. I couldn't blame her. If Death were chasing me and using shadows to reach me, I would be fearful too. When we made it to the end of the hallway, I grabbed her hands. "Don't run away from us, Detra Ann. Stay close, okay?" She bobbled her blond head. Her makeup was running under her eyes, and her hands shook.

Standing on tiptoe, I tried to see the ground floor, but it was completely dark. I imagined that I too could almost hear an inaudible whisper.

"Oh God, it's calling my name. Lenore was right! It is Death. He wants me! I cheated him, and now he wants me. He's come to claim me!"

"Well, he's going to have to fight us if he wants you because he isn't going to take you, Detra Ann! We're safe here. There is light up here, see?" I heard the light bulb pop above us, and the light faded.

"Oh my God!" she shouted and ran into the guest room.

"Stop, Detra Ann! Wait for me!" I ran to her, flipping on every light I could as I went. "Follow me. I have a flashlight somewhere in my bedroom." Grabbing her hand I called, "Ashland! Where is the flashlight?" Coming to himself now, he ran to us and opened the closet. Hidden in the back was a huge Maglite that could light up the neighborhood when fully charged. He turned it on. The light was so bright it was nearly blinding. Henri was holding Detra Ann now, and she was weeping.

"I love you. I love you. I love you," she repeated over and over again.

"Shh...it's okay. Shh, now. It's okay. We are all here together."

Then the guest room lights went out and the lamps popped. We were in total darkness except for the Maglite, which lit up the entire room with harsh white light. So far it wasn't flickering, but who knew how long it would last? We heard a sound, a slapping, crashing sound. The tree limbs from the oaks that surrounded our house were slapping the windows—slapping them so hard they were all breaking! Between the crashing and the groaning, it was a horrible cacophony. Surely the neighbors would hear this! Somebody would come help us! But what if they didn't?

"I love you, Henri. I'm sorry. I am sorry..." Detra Ann was crying quietly now. The whispers became louder and more threatening. Henri held her as if it might be his last chance. Tears ran down his cheeks.

"Ashland," I said fearfully as he wrapped his arms around me.

Suddenly the smashing and crashing of the branches ceased, and the door to the bedroom flew open—a tall figure stood in the doorway. We gasped and waited. A tall figure stepped out of the darkness and into the brightness of the Maglite.

I couldn't believe it—it was Lenore!

Chapter 14—Detra Ann

"You believe me now, don't you? I said you were a shade." She spat the words out like she hated me. Like I wanted to be in this battle with Death itself.

"How did you get up here? Is there a way out?" I demanded, suddenly feeling hopeful.

"The only way out is the way you came in, and it's pitch black outside." She leaned against the doorframe staring at me.

Carrie Jo stood by me protectively. "How did you get up here? Did you see it?"

"I saw nothing but the wind blowing and the house dark. I can feel it, though. It's still very close."

"She's right. We're not out of the woods yet," Ashland added.

"I don't understand why this is happening! Why won't it leave me alone? How do I make it stop? Do you know, or are you going to continue to hate me? Why don't you try to help me since you seem to know so much?" Anger and frustration rose up inside me. She could help me, I knew it, but for some reason she wouldn't. "Why? What have I ever done to you? I don't even know you, Lenore!"

She didn't answer but glared at me with her almond-shaped eyes. Her mouth was a pair of hard lines.

"I know who can help us," Carrie Jo said in a rush.

"Who?"

"Father Portier! He'll know how we can defeat Death."

"What makes you so sure, Carrie Jo?" Henri asked.

"Because he's already dead."

"What?"

"There's no time to talk about this." She waved the flashlight and walked out the door. "Let's go before this thing comes back." She grabbed my hand, and we scrambled down the stairs with lightning speed, the guys following behind us. CJ grabbed her purse off the entryway table, and we headed out the door. We climbed into her BMW, and I was surprised to see Lenore climb in the backseat beside me. CJ slid the key into the ignition and we rolled down the driveway onto the crowded street. Ashland passed me the flashlight, and I held it like my life depended on it. Maybe it did.

"Oh no, it's a parade night," Carrie Jo said as we drove down Dauphin and nearly ran into a barricade. "We'll have to go around to Conte Street.

Maybe that's not blocked off." She turned right and eased down the street slowly. There were people everywhere.

"Where exactly are we headed?" Ashland asked her in a worried voice. "Not to Seven Sisters, I hope."

"No, I don't think this has to do with the house. Not directly, anyway. We're going to the cemetery. That's where the gate is, and that is where I met the priest. This must be why. I didn't put it together until tonight."

"Hold on now. Nobody said anything about a cemetery. We're trying to escape Death, not knock on his door," Lenore said fearfully.

"As you said, he's not looking for you, right? Then you have nothing to fear." Henri snarled at her impatiently. "And nobody asked you to come."

"Someone has to look out for you, Henri Devecheaux." He snorted and looked out the window.

"What are you thinking? How are these things connected?" Ashland asked, his blue eyes full of questions.

"Detra Ann is a spiritual person. She said that she was able to escape it when it came for her in the bathroom by praying the Lord's Prayer."

"Okay..."

"There must be some prayer we can use to make it leave her alone for good. The priest told me to look for the secret."

Ashland's face was filled with doubt, but I piped in, "Listen, it might be a long shot, but I'm willing to go on a little faith here. Even if it means walking through a cemetery."

"What if the gate won't open? What if we can't get to the priest? You said yourself you don't know how you got there."

"It will open. It has to."

Ashland looked at me in the rearview mirror. "You sure you want to do this?"

I nodded, and Henri squeezed my hand. "I'll be right with you the whole time," he murmured.

Ashland nodded and said, "We'll have to park and walk. This is about as close as you're going to get." Carrie Jo pulled the car to the side of the road, claiming the last parking spot on the street. The sidewalks were jammed with revelers streaming toward the parade route. "Let's see. If we cut through that vacant lot, we should come out on Virginia Street, but the cemetery will still be a few blocks away. Keep the flashlight close and stay close to the group, Detra Ann."

"Got it," I replied. Ashland had nothing to worry about. I was never letting go of Henri's hand. "Let's go!" We emptied the car and walked down the sidewalk away from the gathering partiers. I suddenly wished I'd grabbed my jacket before we left. My sweatshirt provided little protection from the frigid night air. My heart hammered in my chest as I scanned the sidewalks for shadows. There were plenty.

"Go ahead and turn on your flashlight. Just point it down at the ground. We don't want to attract attention," Henri whispered to me. With cold, stiff fingers, I slid the button into the on position and breathed a sigh of relief as the shadows around me vanished. Lenore slipped her arm through mine—I didn't pull away, but I clutched Henri's hand tighter. In the distance a marching band blasted "On Broadway" to the appreciation of the happy parade watchers—the sound echoed through the narrow streets of downtown Mobile. I could hear the occasional blast of police sirens. In a strange way it comforted me knowing that the police were so close. As if they could actually help me.

Ashland paused on the sidewalk. "We're getting closer. How are you doing?"

"So far, so good," I stammered. The cold made my teeth chatter. Lenore's fingers were about to freeze me to death. Of all of us, she was the least prepared for the cold weather. She wore thin tights and an oversize, long-sleeved t-shirt. Henri was the only one who'd had the good sense to dress warmly, but then again none of us expected to be visiting a graveyard at night. I waved the flashlight on the grass in front of me and carefully stepped only in the light. For some reason, I thought about TD. I hadn't thought about him as much lately, but the love I had for him had not diminished at all. Some girls had high school sweethearts, and others had college sweethearts. I had neither of those. TD had been it for me, or at least I thought so until he disappeared. In the months following his death, I had a difficult time sorting through my feelings. TD had left me for a ghost. I had been pushed unwillingly into a battle and fought for my life, and all for what? I felt abandoned. Life was completely unfair. I was reminded of one of my favorite quotes from an English literature class. "Life makes fools of us all."

So why was I thinking of TD now?

"This way, here's the street," a Mardi Gras vendor shouted at us. An inflatable fleur-de-lis hat perched upon his head, and his cart was full of parade swag. Before he could begin his spiel, Ashland raised his hand politely and said, "Sorry. Not today." We left the man staring after us as we shuffled down the street. The parade was a few streets over, so there was nobody else on Virginia Street.

I looked over my shoulder and said to no one in particular, "I wonder why he's over here." To my surprise, the man and his cart had disappeared.

"Don't pay any attention to that. He's just having fun with you. Keep that light on and keep walking." Lenore's furious whisper made my heart pound. I knew exactly who she was talking about. I did as she instructed and kept my eyes on the ground, always stepping only in the light.

"There it is!" The Magnolia Cemetery sign swung gently in the breeze. The gate stood open—it was a foreboding sign, as if someone had expected us to visit.

Carrie Jo paused before we walked inside the graveyard. "There are no lights in here, so you'll have to lead the way. Just walk straight toward the back; that's the gate were looking for. Are you going to be okay?"

I swallowed hard. "Oh God, I hope so." Our little group shuffled together down the narrow walkway. I had been here once before in middle school, but that was a long time ago. I certainly wasn't an expert on navigating this massive maze of graves. Immediately to the right I noticed a row of mausoleums. Even though there was very little moonlight, they seemed to have an eerie glow about them.

Lenore shook her head. "I ain't going in there. Too many ghosts. I'll meet y'all on the other side." Before we could argue with her, she was already halfway down the sidewalk.

I chewed my lip as I watched her disappear down the street. I wanted a shot of whiskey, but it was too late for liquid courage. "Carrie Jo, I've been thinking. What if the gate doesn't work? What if only you can go through it? What if it takes us somewhere else?"

"We connected the last time, remember? I think we can do it again. What choice do we have?" She looked so hopeful, but I felt anything but confident. The last time we went "ghost busting," I ended up the prisoner of a murderous spirit who was convinced that I was his dead wife. The wife he hung from a chandelier until she died. Now CJ wanted to go see another ghost. But she was right...what choice did I have?

"Alright. Then let's do this. Wait." I reached for Henri and kissed him on the lips. "Just to remind myself that I'm alive." I smiled up into his worried brown eyes. "It's okay, right?"

He said, "I plan on keeping you alive. I want a second date." Despite the situation, I couldn't help but love him for saying that. I waved the light around nervously, took a deep breath and entered the cemetery. Some of the newest tombstones were located near the entrance. I remembered seeing these on that middle school trip when we came to take rubbings of the tombstones. I didn't like cemeteries even as a child. I'd found the first suitable grave there was, made my rubbing and waited impatiently for everyone to finish theirs. A few feet into the graveyard, a shell pathway began. It glowed in the dim light. I waved the flashlight around again and gasped. Something ran from the light—it looked like a cat. At least I hoped it was a cat. My eyes couldn't stop flitting about searching for anything that moved.

"How far is it, CJ?"

"All the way in the back." The four of us hurried down the pathway together, Henri and I in front, Carrie Jo and Ash right behind us.

Ashland cleared his throat. "Guys, I don't know whether to tell you this or not, but..."

I spun around, waving my flashlight furiously.

"You're going to blind us, Detra Ann," he complained.

"Sorry. What is it?"

"Lenore was right—this place is teeming with ghosts. And they don't look too happy to see us here."

Carrie Jo asked, "Anyone we know?"

He paused and looked into the darkness. "Not that I can tell, but the shadows are moving now. Just like before...when whatever it was appeared at the house."

"Death. It's Death, Ashland. Just say it."

"We don't have time for this, and we can't stop...go now! Run!" He didn't have to tell me twice. I took off running toward the distant gate. Carrie Jo was beside me. I paused for a second when a looming figure appeared on the right of the path. It was a massive angel statue with his arms stretched to the heavens. "Oh Lord!" I whispered and kept running. The light from my Maglite bounced as I ran, and I could hear the whispers collecting around me. Ashland was right. The shadows were gathering, and now there were many ghosts to contend with. In my mind I could see them reaching for me, demanding that I return to their realm to take my proper place among those who had surrendered life.

No! It's not my time!

My chest burned—it had been a long time since I had gone for a run. I was so out of shape, but adrenaline-fueled fear kicked in and propelled me forward ahead of my friends. I turned the corner of the path, and a gruesome-looking cherub sat perched on top of a moldy gravestone. Long ago, some grieving family member had thought the fat-faced figure would be a fitting tribute to their lost loved one. I couldn't disagree more. Ahead of me, I could see a looming shadow that covered the walkway. I waved the Maglite at it, but it didn't disappear. I came to a screeching halt, and my friends piled behind me. All of us were panting for breath.

"Oh my God!"

"Go around it!" Carrie Jo screamed at me.

Clumsily, I tripped up a small round hill, and the flashlight flew from my hand. Carrie Jo grabbed it and reached for my hand, pulling me to my feet.

I heard a swishing sound and felt a disturbance in the air around me. Someone or something was there—I just couldn't see them.

"You can't stop! Believe me," Ashland yelled at me. My friends nearly picked me up off the ground and carried me to the back gate. I was almost in tears and not thinking at all.

"Come on, baby. Almost there," Henri said, looking over his shoulder as he cleared a small row of graves running behind me. It was the first time he'd ever called me baby. I liked it. I suddenly realized that I did love Henri. It was different from my love for TD, but it was love nonetheless.

CJ waved the flashlight at the back gate—only fifty feet away. "Almost there!" she shouted over the growing whispers. Suddenly a flash of light appeared in front of the gate. Then the light disappeared, leaving the figure behind. "Lenore?" she asked.

It wasn't Lenore. I knew that figure just like I knew my own. That was Terrence Dale. I snatched the light from Carrie Jo and shined it at the gate again. He didn't disappear. He stood staring at us, his face not unfriendly or reproachful. It was him! I heard Henri gasp beside me. "Is that..."

"TD..." I whispered, tears filling my eyes. He wasn't dead at all but completely alive. There was even a halo of light around him. Had we gotten it wrong somehow—was he alive but stuck in the past? Maybe he needed our help to break free from wherever he was stuck. I couldn't think straight, and I was freezing. I could see my breath now in the light. He looked directly at me and gave me a heartbreaking smile. Then he vanished.

"No!" I yelled and ran toward the gate. "Terrence!"

Chapter 15—Carrie Jo

Before I could stop her, Detra Ann flew through the gate and disappeared, taking the flashlight with her. The three of us stood in the dark cemetery and stared at the gaping entrance. "She's gone," Henri said. "I was supposed to protect her, and now she's gone." He banged on the gate and walked in circles, his hands on his head. He let out an anguished cry. "Do something! Where is she?"

"She passed through the gate, Henri. She didn't wait for us. She was supposed to wait." I didn't know what else to say. I needed a moment to think.

"What are we supposed to do now?"

"Henri!" A voice called out from the darkness of the adjoining street. Lenore appeared on the other side of the gate. "Where is she?"

"She's gone."

"I was afraid of this." Lenore tapped her lip with her finger. "Well, time for plan B. Do we have one?" Everyone stared at me.

I paced in front of the gate. No, we didn't. My half-cocked plan A was all I had, and now Detra Ann was gone.

"Ashland, what do you see? Are the ghosts still here?"

He peered into the inky blackness and said, "No. They are all gone. There were dozens of them here just a minute ago."

"Shoot! When she ran through the gate, it must have closed the connection."

"How do you know that?" Lenore asked me suspiciously. "You done this before?"

"Kind of. We went through the wall together at the hospital. And when I walked through the gate the other night, I ended up in the basilica. Look, we all saw her. The gate was open, and now it's not and all the activity stopped. That's got to mean something, doesn't it?"

"She's gone." Henri sat on the ground and stared into the darkness.

"We're not giving up. We have to go to the church. Maybe the gate works both ways."

"Sounds like plan B to me. Let's go. I'm freezing."

I walked through the open gate, closed my eyes and half hoped it would work, but nothing happened. Ashland looked glum, Henri wasn't talking at all, and Lenore acted like this was all a joke. As we walked toward the church, the music got louder. We would have to cross the parade route to get to St. Joseph Street. The Order of Polka Dots sailed down the street on vibrant floats, while the crowds roared, pleading for beads, moon pies and candy.

"Carrie Jo? You okay?" Lenore stood inches from my face. "Hey!"

"Yeah, I'm okay." I suddenly realized how lovely Lenore could be if she actually cared about what she looked like. She grabbed my hand and dragged me behind her as we dashed across the street.

"Lenore! Wait! You're hurting me." I snatched my hand away.

She walked toward me and got in my face again. "You don't have time. Death has her, and he ain't gonna wait," she shouted at me over the music. I waved to Ashland and Henri, who were stuck on the other side of the street. A police officer on horseback stepped into my line of sight so I couldn't see them anymore. "Carrie Jo, listen to me. Don't get them involved, please. Trust me when I tell you that it can only be bad. We can do this together. Let's go. They know where we are going, and they'll catch up." A drunken reveler pushed me as he chased after a float. Another one brushed up against me and leered at me. One thing was for sure—we couldn't stand here on the street. Maybe Lenore was right. Could I really put Ashland and Henri in danger? I'd already managed to lose Detra Ann. I looked one more time toward the street, but the crowd was growing and people were pushing and shoving.

"Let's go," I shouted back at her and began following her through the crowd toward St. Joseph and Clairborne Streets. People with painted faces and novelty lighted headbands circled me and shouted, "Happy Mardi Gras!" A man in the parade spun me about playfully as I struggled against him, feeling a surge of panic. Finally I broke free from the crowd and pushed to the edge where I could see the red and white building of the cathedral in the distance. Lenore took my hand, and together we ran as fast as we could. I glanced behind me, half hoping I would see Ashland and Henri close, but they were nowhere to be found. We ran to the cast-iron gates, and I held on to the cold metal as I tried to catch my breath. I could plainly see that the gates and the church doors had been locked. I swore under my breath. Grabbing my hand again, Lenore led me down the sidewalk.

"Give me just a second. I have to catch my breath."

"We're running out of time. This way." Lenore pulled me toward the back of the building. This was the side that faced St. Joseph Street. I'd never explored this area before.

"Maybe we should call someone and ask them to let us in." I knew that was a stupid suggestion, but I was out of ideas. I wasn't sure what I was going to do even if I could get inside.

"Look! We can get in that way!" There were some narrow concrete stairs that led down to the basement of the church. That was unusual in itself, as most buildings in Mobile didn't have cellars. Especially here in the downtown area, as close as it was to Mobile Bay. Yet here it was right in front of me. She tugged on the gate twice, but it would not budge.

I looked over my shoulder again, half expecting to see the red-haired caretaker come running toward me, but the streets were empty. "Let's do it together." Lenore nodded, and we shoved hard on the gate. To my surprise, it worked: the gate rattled open, and we walked down the stairs, closing the gate behind us. The rusty old latch cut my finger, but I managed to wriggle it back into place without locking it. Better to make it look closed so no one suspected anything.

What were the chances that the door would be unlocked? Lenore blew on her cold fingers and then turned the round knob. It opened with a click, and she smiled at me as if to say, "See, I told you this would work." We walked inside the church basement, and I was immediately assaulted by the musty smell. When was the last time anyone had aired this room out? Lenore was fiddling with a lighter she retrieved from somewhere. She flicked the flame and moved it around slowly so we could get our bearings. "Looks like a mission closet or something. Hey! There are some coats!" She walked a few feet away and began digging through a pile.

"We can't take those. They belong to the church, Lenore."

"Okay, you freeze to death, but I'm borrowing a coat."

Standing there shivering while she slid on a warm brown coat was more than I could bear. "Alright, if we're just borrowing them." I grabbed a long black trench with an insulated lining and slid it on. I immediately felt warmer. Seeing a pile of woolen hats, I grabbed one of those too. "Where is that lighter? We have to get upstairs."

Lenore flicked the lighter again, and together we searched for the door. We found it, but it was locked, and no amount of banging would open it.

"Shoot! There has to be another door." I felt along the dusty walls, and Lenore walked in the opposite direction doing the same.

"Hey!" she yelled. "I think I found something over here. Come help me." I ran to her, practically tripping over a box of books that someone had left on the floor. "It's in the floor. Look!" Next to the back wall was a small hatch in the floor with a metal chain attached to it. "Help me." Together we tugged on the chain, and the hatch opened. The smell of moldy earth rose up to greet us. Lenore cast the light around the entrance quickly, but there wasn't much to see beyond a set of dodgy-looking wooden stairs.

"I don't know. Should we be going down those things?"

"It's the only option we have, isn't it?" Without another word, she was climbing down the ladder. I heard the wood creak and complain under her weight, and she was smaller than me.

I heard a thud coming from the entrance of the cellar. It sounded like someone was coming toward us. I hurried down the ladder and reached into the darkness. "Lenore!"

She clicked the lighter, but it wouldn't work. "I'm here. Take my hand." I did, and she clicked again until the lighter released a small flame. "This way."

The historian in me couldn't help but pay attention to the wooden beam that ran along the top of the passageway, the dirty gas lamps that hung from the walls and the random items that I occasionally tripped over like a shovel and a small metal cart.

"What on earth is this place?" she asked as she waved furiously at a cobweb.

"I'd say an underground railroad." I squinted around us in the dim light.

"Are we going the right way?"

"Stop a minute, Lenore. Listen!"

She scowled at me but kept quiet for a few seconds. "What's that?"

I tugged at my coat, pulling it about me tighter. Straining to listen, I heard a voice. It had to be Detra Ann! "That's her! Move faster, Lenore!" We blindly ran until we reached a fork in the tunnel.

"Where now?" she shouted. We stood waiting to hear something.

"Help me! Someone!"

"This way! She's this way!" I took off to the right and stumbled over an unseen obstacle as I ran toward Detra Ann's voice. Shafts of light filtered through the grate above us. I stood under it, looking up into the church, when I heard another noise, a scratching, fluttering sound. "There! Grab that and we'll climb. Maybe push the grate."

"Better idea. Let's go up those stairs."

How had I missed those? We hurried up the curved stairwell and into the church. The only light was dim candlelight. I didn't know when it happened, but somehow we had passed through the "gate" because we were in the old church. The walls were as they had been during my supernatural trip, painted burgundy and gold. According to my online research, the renovations had completely changed the look of the cathedral. In modern times, the basilica had white walls with gold accents.

"Let her go! You have no place here! Leave now!" It was Father Portier, standing in front of the altar. Detra Ann's blond hair swirled around her, moving in an unearthly black cloud that seemed to want to swallow her. "Go, now!" The priest stood rigidly in defiance, but a blast of the black cloud sent him flying backwards into the wooden pews. Horror and dread filled me as I watched the old man collapse into a heap.

"Father Portier!" I yelled, running toward him with Lenore beside me.

At that moment, Detra Ann saw me and screamed, "Run, CJ!" The black cloud expanded, shrank and expanded again. Suddenly it broke into a hundred smaller clouds, and I heard the scratching, fluttering sound again. In the blink of an eye, the clouds became crows that flew straight toward us with deadly focus.

"Get down! Under the pews!" I screamed, dragging the priest to the floor and crawling under the benches. The crows flew above us, diving occasionally to peck and scratch at us. Lenore screamed in pain, and I looked back under the pew toward Detra Ann, who lay on the floor about twenty feet away. "Father Portier! Please! Help us!" I shook him again and again until he began to stir.

The old man turned his head toward me and pleaded, "You have to go. Before it's too late."

"I am not leaving without my friend."

"You have no choice, I am afraid. He will not release her." I peeked out from under the bench at the spinning vortex of birds that threatened us.

"I am not leaving Detra Ann!" My heart pounded in my chest as I crawled under the benches toward the front of the church, crying and praying as I went. When I finally made it to the front of the church, I reached my hand out from under the pew. Just then an angry bird with a sharp beak dipped down and scratched my skin savagely. Crying out in pain, Detra Ann spotted me and shook her head. The black cloud gathered around her thin frame, and a hundred screeches echoed angrily through the church.

Defiantly I slid out from under the wooden bench and stood in the aisle. Lenore and the priest were standing there beside me. The cloud of birds fell to the ground and broke into a thousand pieces of black paper. Suddenly a tall man—taller than any I had ever seen—stood between us and Detra Ann. I could not see his face; a gauzy black fog covered his entire body, and only his pale white hands were clearly visible. He did not speak, but his head rose as he observed us.

"Help us." I said to the priest.

Father Portier said in a sad voice, "There is nothing I can do. He is here to collect a life. If I had one to give, I would gladly give it for your friend. But alas I do not. I am sorry, my dear."

"But it wasn't her fault. She never asked for this! We didn't do anything wrong! For pity's sake, Father. Please do something."

He nodded sadly and said again, "I am sorry, my dear."

I heard Detra Ann crying behind the tall figure, and I walked ahead a few more steps. "You can't have her! It's not her time!" Death did not respond, but neither did he move. Then his answer came. He beckoned me toward him, and I knew what he wanted. He wanted me. He would take me in exchange for Detra Ann. *A life for a life....* I heard the words ringing in my head.

Death waited for my answer. *What about the baby?* Fear washed over me, and tears rolled down my cheeks. Then there was Lenore. "I've got this," she whispered. She stood, hopping up and down in her hand-me-down Reeboks as if she were gearing up for a prize fight. It didn't take a rocket scientist to see she was about to do something stupid.

"Wait! What are you doing?"

"Thinking about someone else for a change!" She grabbed my hands and hugged me. "I knew this was how it was supposed to be. I knew it when I met Detra Ann. She's not the only shade here. I'm one too—I've been one ever since Aleezabeth died. It should have been me that day."

"I don't understand," I confessed. The figure in front of us growled, but Lenore didn't appear moved by it.

"I cheated Death once too. I've been running all these years, but it's time to stop. This is what's right. This is what Aleezabeth wants." She hugged me again and suddenly released me. Then she ran toward the growling figure, screaming, "Aleezabeth!"

I yelled at the top of my lungs, "Lenore! No! Come back!" I watched in horror as she sprang into the air and fearlessly hurled herself toward Death. Then the massive shape vanished, taking Lenore with it. Everything changed. All the coldness, the fear and the dread vanished—even the interior of the church was different. I could smell the freshly painted white walls; the sooty sconces had been replaced with modern-day pin lights that shone from the ceiling. I stood rocking on my heels in shock at the transformation.

I tried to process what had just happened. Lenore had given her life for Detra Ann. My friend lay crumpled on the floor, and I ran to her side.

"Detra Ann! Wake up. Please wake up!" I patted her face desperately. I had to know she was okay.

Her eyes fluttered open, and she looked up at me. "Is it gone?"

"Yes. It's over." We held one another, both of us crying, and then she asked me. "Where is Lenore? I saw her—you came for me. Is Henri okay? Ashland?"

"The guys are fine. Lenore is...she's gone."

"Oh no..." she cried and held onto me as I helped her up from the marble floor. The priest had disappeared too. Detra Ann and I alone stood in the church together, holding one another until Ashland and Henri came up from the basement and ran down the aisle toward us.

"Carrie Jo? Are you okay, baby? Why are you bleeding?"

I glanced down at my hands. He was right—they were bleeding. "It's okay. I'm okay." He put his arms around me and kissed the top of my head.

Henri held Detra Ann tight, tears streaming down his face. "Lenore, where is she?"

"She's gone, Henri," I said softly. "She wanted to be with Aleezabeth. She said it was right."

Detra Ann held him closer and whispered in his ear. I couldn't hear what she said, but I didn't need to know. They had each other now. He nodded and wiped his eyes. This would be hard for him. Lenore was all the family he had. Except us. We were a family. A strange, wonderful family.

Chapter 16—Carrie Jo

The next few days were strange to say the least. I felt like I was walking in a fog. I closed the office while we worked out the details of Lenore's memorial service, then the four of us took the Happy Go Lucky out into Mobile Bay. The only one who seemed truly happy was Detra Ann, and who could blame her? Our first evening out was quiet. The water was like smooth glass, and the air felt warm and welcoming. We were sailing to Point Clear, where we would stay for a few days. With just a quick phone call, Ashland had managed to book two suites at the Grand Hotel. It was a beautiful place with a breathtaking view of the bay. Naturally, I was fascinated with the history of the place and promised myself that sometime during my stay I would explore the older wings and the grounds.

After dinner on the boat, Ashland and I spent an hour looking out over the bay, enjoying the lights and the stars that glittered above it all. We held hands and quietly enjoyed the peaceful view.

"How are you?" he asked softly, his eyes still focused in front of us.

"I'm fine. The baby is too. Everything is okay."

"That's good to hear."

"What about you? How are you doing with all this?"

"I haven't seen anything in forty-eight hours. Any ghosts, I mean. It's like everything went quiet again. It's times like this when I question if I ever saw any of what I thought I saw. But I know I did."

"Don't question it. You did see those things. Just enjoy the quiet for as long as it lasts." I smiled at him and squeezed his hand. Then I asked, "Are you sure you want to stay in Mobile, Ashland? I think the Port City has more than its share of ghosts, don't you?"

"I love Mobile, but I want you to be happy. Do you want to leave?"

I squinted at him in the dim light. "Nope. You're stuck with me, babe. Wherever you are—that's where I want to be. We made a promise, remember?" I slid out of the white leather chair and climbed into his lap.

He kissed me like he meant it. I kissed him back, and I definitely meant it. With a wicked smile, I led him to the shower, stripping off my clothes as I went. I loved this ridiculously large shower stall. It had four shower heads, a smooth stone floor and sultry blue lighting. Just perfect for what I had in mind. I kicked on the wall stereo and turned on the water as Ashland raced to join me. It was a nice way to end the day.

Afterwards, I pulled on a giant t-shirt and climbed into the feather bed and fell asleep almost immediately. For once, I didn't have a worry in the world.

***

I woke up with Hooney's face so close to mine that I could feel her breath on my cheek. She whispered to me, but I was half asleep and had difficulty understanding what she said.

"Your mother wants you to go. Leave this place, Miss Calpurnia. Leave now."

I had given up trying to convince the old woman that I was not my sister. In a perverse sort of way, the misidentification made me feel closer to Calpurnia.

"Why? Why should I go?" I pressed her, but Hooney's tight grimace let me know that I would get nothing else out of her. She had passed on the message and believed it should be enough. "Where is my mother? Why does she not tell me this herself, Hooney?"

"You know good and well why." I heard a noise from the hallway...someone was here! Karah was not in the room with me, and I could see that her rose pink dress was no longer hanging in the armoire. She must have dressed in one of the other rooms because she never dressed quietly. That meant Isla would be here any moment—if she had not yet arrived.

"Tell me, is Karah's mother here? I have to get dressed."

"She is, Miss. But if I were you, I would run the other way. She's the devil, that one." With that, the old woman left me without another word or glance. I flopped on the bed wondering what to do. If Hooney was truly relaying messages from my mother, was I wise to ignore them? I snorted at myself. When did I begin believing in ghosts? Gooseflesh ran up and down my arms. Then I remembered. Probably when I saw the man in the Moonlight Garden...the one whose hair did not move in the breeze!

I dressed quickly and managed to arrange my hair in a decent fashion with the few pins that I found remaining in the bowl on the vanity table. Sliding on my purple heels, I dabbed perfume on my neck and headed toward the stairs when I heard Karah's voice. The sound was coming from the guest room, so I politely tapped on the door and waited. Nobody came, but I could still hear muffled voices. With a frown, I opened the door slowly and hoped it wouldn't give me away. Of course, it groaned as I pushed it open, and I cringed. "Karah, I am sorry to interrupt, but I could not wait to meet your..."

I left off speaking, surprised to see that no one was in the room. There were trunks and packages everywhere; obviously Cousin Isla intended to stay in this room. I heard the voices again and followed the source. I discovered that the sounds were coming from the floor grate. Not wanting to intrude, I turned to walk away, but something in Karah's voice compelled me to listen.

"Please, Mother. You could not be more wrong. She is not your enemy or mine. I like her!"

"You always...take my side for a change...weak, just like your father!" Isla's voice wasn't as clear. It sounded like she was moving about. Where were they? The Blue Room? "Maybe you have already found it. Are you keeping it from me, Karah?"

"Never! I would never do that, Mother. I have searched high and low, and I cannot find it. I swear to you, I do not have it!"

"If that is true, you had better get her out of here before she finds it. Oh, if only you had been a boy. None of this would matter."

I heard Karah's voice, soft and sad, "I am sorry, Mother. I will find it if it takes me..."

"What are you doing there, Miss Page?"

I rose from the floor to find Docie in the doorway, her arms crossed. She wore her usual black dress and severe bun. I stammered, "Well, I thought I heard Karah, but I was mistaken. Nobody is here." I walked towards the doorway, intending to slip out, but Docie would not let me pass.

"You should not be in here without an invitation. This is Miss Beaumont's room, and she is very particular about her things." She suddenly frowned and walked to an open trunk, examining the sumptuous gowns inside. "You have not touched these, have you?"

"No, of course not."

"Good. You will stain her fine gowns. Such lovely fabrics, don't you agree? It would be a crime to damage such an elegant wardrobe."

The voices from the grate had faded; the women had obviously left the room below us. "Very fine. Excuse me."

"Wait, Miss Page."

I froze in the hallway, and Docie purred, "Remember my warning. I hope I make myself clear." I knew that was a threat, and I would be a fool not to heed it. Docie was dangerous, and it sounded as if her mistress had a secret of her own.

Instead of running downstairs to greet Karah's mother, I went back to my room to catch my breath. I knew that Karah had been looking for something, but what? A book, a love letter, a will? The only way I would find out would be to ask her, but I did not want to put my cousin in such a position. Her mother sounded like a hard woman to please. After seeing Isla's gowns, I changed mine, choosing instead a bright yellow dress with plenty of lace and a respectable neckline. I loathed the idea of presenting myself as the "poor cousin" who had nowhere to go. I was a dressmaker, for goodness' sake! I changed shoes and earrings too and then headed towards the stairs for a second time.

There was no one in the ladies' parlor, but I could hear the musical sound of tinkling laughter. The beautiful Isla Beaumont was now holding court on the patio near the Rose Garden. From the half-open door I could see Jackson Keene, Karah and a man I did not recognize listening to a riveting story told as only an actress could. Isla was the most beautiful woman I had ever seen, with dainty facial features and hair like an angel's, blond and perfectly curled. Even though she was Karah's mother, she barely looked old enough to have had a child. Isla paused her monologue and tilted her head toward me.

"Come now. Don't be shy." I immediately felt embarrassed to have been spotted dawdling behind the door like an awkward child. She rose to her feet and neatly arranged her ethereal blue dress before making a beeline for me. "You must be Delilah. I am Isla Beaumont." I felt ill at ease, perhaps because all her attention seemed to rest upon me now. It was as intense as her storytelling had been.

I blushed and said, "I am Delilah Page. And you are Karah's mother. It is very nice to meet you at last." The older woman flinched at my words even though I could not fathom why. Had I offended her already?

"You do have the look of your sister. I am sure you hear that all the time."

"Only since I have been here, but I never tire of hearing it. You knew her?"

"We spoke a few times."

"A few times? Surely you jest, dear Miss Beaumont. You were Miss Cottonwood's constant companion for some time. I've often wondered how she managed to escape Seven Sisters without your knowing anything about it." The man who spoke to her had a round belly, a balding head and an obvious love for sweets. Even now his fingers could not resist plucking sugared grapes from the silver platter on a nearby table.

"Why yes, Mr. Ball, we did spend some time together. But Calpurnia was very shy and not one for social gatherings, and as you know, I spent much of my time out and about getting to know our neighbors. Ah, but that was before the dreadful old war. Tell me, Delilah, do you suffer the same maladies as your sister?"

I blinked at her, unsure how I should respond. "What do you mean? What maladies?"

She giggled and smiled at the audience watching us. "Am I speaking out of turn? Please forgive me, Karah. You know what I speak of, Mr. Ball. But I promised Karah I would not embarrass you, dear girl. Come join us, Delilah. What a lovely name! Have you ever considered becoming an actress? You have the name for it, you know. I wonder why your mother bestowed such a name on you. Not a very proper name, is it, and

Christine Cottonwood was nothing but proper. Or so we all thought." She giggled again as if she knew some great joke and I was the butt of it. Sadness welled up in me. This woman did not like me, and I had so wanted her to. The gathering appeared shocked and embarrassed by her description of my mother, but nobody said a thing against her. My first instinct was usually wrong, as Maundy often reminded me. So I kept my mouth shut and sat quietly listening to Isla's news about the London stage and how wonderfully she had played Claudia DuMont in some play called "The Delight of New York." Everyone nodded and asked the appropriate questions, but I could not help but notice she did not look in my direction again or shower her smiles upon me. Those she reserved for the men and occasionally for her faithful servant, Docie, who was never more than a few feet away from her mistress. Karah appeared to be as miserable as I was, but there was something else there too. I could not understand it. I watched the silent interactions carefully, just as I had been trained to in the dress shop. It was obvious that Docie worshipped Isla and waited on her as if she were the Queen of England. Karah seemed a mere afterthought to her mother. Isla had a way of selfishly stealing all the air out of a room.

Jackson Keene received more than his share of Isla's attentions, and I wasn't the only one who noticed. Karah's pretty face was awash with red color, obviously flushed with embarrassment at her mother's forwardness. Once Isla even touched Jackson's leg as she spoke. Although she acted like it was an accident, I believed no such thing. As quickly as I could politely arrange it, I excused myself; I was eager to remove myself from her presence. But where would I go?

As I walked through the patio door into the ladies' parlor and then down the downstairs hallway, Docie followed me, watching every step I took.

"May I help you, Docie?"

"No, miss." She did not move but stood in the hallway like a sentinel, her hands clasped in front of her. I wanted to go upstairs and hide, but then thankfully Jackson stepped into the hallway.

"Miss Page, may I speak to you for a moment?"

"Yes, of course. Why don't you take a walk with me, Mr. Keene? It's a lovely night, and it's much too stuffy in here."

"Indeed it is."

As soon as our feet hit the path of the Moonlight Garden, I felt the burden lift. "What do you think of Isla Beaumont, Jackson?"

He mulled over his answer and then said, "How can the daughter be so different from the mother? Karah is the picture of virtuousness, but her mother has no such restraint." That wasn't exactly the answer I had expected. I had no idea that Jackson thought so highly of Miss

Cottonwood. He looked about him; when he was finally convinced that no one was listening he said, "I have had a difficult time of proving your cousin's parentage." We strolled down the brick path together, circled the fountain and walked into the garden maze. "Everyone in the county says that her mother was never a respectable young woman. Isla herself was born out of wedlock, and now her daughter shares her status." He glanced over and added quickly, "I mean no insult. I am merely repeating what others have said."

"That is gossip, Jackson, and I am surprised to hear you repeat it."

"No, it is fact. As Miss Cottonwood's attorney, I have a professional duty to investigate these matters. Supposedly, Miss Beaumont took up with a riverboat captain, a David Garrett, but he was murdered a few years ago. By all accounts he was a man of few restraints. I should not like to shock you, but I have it on good authority that this Captain Garrett once had designs on your sister, until he met Miss Beaumont. After that, he cared for no other woman. I am almost convinced that he is Karah's true father, but what can I do?"

"I can hardly believe what I am hearing. No wonder Isla does not like me—I take it she was no friend of my sister's, then?"

"Not in the truest sense of the word, no. And to make matters more complicated, she had an affair with Jeremiah Cottonwood, while he was married to your mother."

"I see," I said as I pondered what he had told me.

"However, I have good news to share. I have had an offer from Claudette Page. Would you like to hear it? Perhaps I should wait until tomorrow to tell you the details?"

"No, please I want to hear her offer now. I need something else to think about." I sat on a nearby bench and waited.

"Very well. Your aunt came to my office yesterday and says she will agree to acknowledge you in name and will not contest any deed you possess if you agree to leave Mobile. She says she will give you everything that her brother wanted you to have but insists that you must leave and remain away from the city until her death."

I shot up from the bench. "How dare she ask me to leave? How can I leave Karah and Seven Sisters?"

"My dear, Karah could always come visit you wherever you reside. Think about what this would mean. You would never have to work again—no more late nights at Miss Weaver's shop. You could travel and see the world. With this act, Miss Page has sealed your future. You are a very wealthy woman now, Delilah. The world is your oyster!"

Exasperated, I stormed off, walking deeper into the garden.

"Delilah! Wait!"

"You don't understand, Jackson! It was never about the money."

"Please, just think about this."

"No! And don't follow me!" I turned to the left, then to the right and then to the left again, slapping branches out of my way as I went. After all this time, Jackson still didn't understand. Yes, I would have money and possessions, but I would still be denied the thing I wanted most—a family! I wanted to belong somewhere...to someone. Claudette Page was willing to sacrifice her fortune to see that I never had that.

I was so angry that I barely noticed the dark-haired man watching me from the other side of the clearing. Yes! There he was—near the Atlas fountain. It was the same man who had followed me the other night. I froze on the spot. He smiled, and my stomach twisted. I turned to walk away and nearly walked into Isla Beaumont.

Her eyes were fierce—she reminded me of a wild animal. One that was trapped inside the body of an innocent sheep and desperately wanted to be released. "Oh, sorry. I didn't hear you," I said. "I think we should go, Miss Beaumont. There is an intruder in our garden."

She stared at me and then turned her attention to the man standing at the Atlas fountain. She could see him too! The wind picked up, sending her ethereal blue dress fluttering. I just watched as she took down her hair and let her blond tresses blow freely behind her. I looked from her to him and felt my unease growing.

She took my hand and tugged on it, dragging me after her. She was walking toward the man and taking me with her! He hadn't moved, but he had an evil smile plastered on his pale face. "Let go of me!" I yelled at her, wrenching my hand free from her deathly grip. She did not seem to notice. She continued toward him as the wind continued to blow.

I ran! I ran as fast as I could all the way back to the entrance of the maze. I ran so fast that I collided with Jackson Keene. "There you are," he said, steadying me. "Have you changed your mind? Delilah, what is it?"

"Didn't you see Isla? She was just here with that man. The evil-looking one with the dark hair. He...she...they are just in there."

"Nobody came out here. Just you and me. I wish you would reconsider Claudette's offer. I do believe she is being sincere."

"Very well. Make the arrangements. I am ready to leave Mobile." With one more glance over my shoulder, I practically ran back into the house. I could hardly believe it...when I passed the ladies' parlor, Isla was still there, regaling her guests, except for Jackson and me, about her experiences on the stage. How could I have seen her just now in the

garden with that evil man? With that ghost? As if she knew what I was thinking, she stopped talking and smiled at me innocently.

Yes, I was ready to go. I would go to my room and pack, and then leave first thing in the morning. I heard Jackson's carriage leave almost immediately, but I went upstairs and asked Hooney to help me pack. I went to my mother's room and plundered her hope chest and treasures. If I was going to leave, I would take something of hers with me. Karah had told me repeatedly to take whatever I liked. She had no need of it. In fact, she hinted that when her mother left Seven Sisters, she wished to go with her. Then no one would live here, except a few forgotten former slaves.

I found a few books, ribbons and sewing pieces that I decided to take with me. Walking back to my room, Hooney surprised me by bringing supper to me. I ate it, hungry now that I did not have to entertain Isla any longer. "Please ask Stokes to come get my things, Hooney. I am going to stay in town tonight."

"It's too late, Miss Calpurnia. Stokes isn't here now. He had to go somewhere for that lady. I suspect he won't be home until late."

I tried to keep the tremor out of my voice as I replied, "Well, I can send for these things tomorrow. I'll just take one bag with me." My hands shook as I sorted through everything. Just as I was ready to leave, Isla walked into my room. Hooney scurried out, making the sign of the cross as she went.

"What's this, cousin? Are you leaving when I just got here? I was hoping we would have some fun, get to know one another. I have so much to tell you."

"I saw you in the garden, Isla. I saw you with that man." I said, nervously clutching my bag. "I think I will stay in town tonight. Stokes can bring my things tomorrow."

"Hmm...you act like you are the lady of the house here, Delilah. You don't command my servants. In regards to what you think you saw, I must confess I am at a loss as to what you mean." Then in a sad, sweet voice she added, "You know, those are just the maladies I was referring to when I spoke about your sister. She had...such an imagination. It must be a trait the two of you inherited from your father. A Beaumont would never go about saying such things."

"How dare you..."

"How dare I what? Tell you the truth?" She sat on the bed and ran her hands across the leather suitcase. As quick as lightning she opened it and began rummaging through my things. She plucked out the things that belonged to my mother. "This is thievery," she said indignantly as she rose from the bed. "Are you stealing from me, cousin?"

"These are my mother's things. You can't stop me from taking them."

"Everything in this house belongs to me." Her voice sounded sharp and angry. *"You put those things back, or I will call the sheriff and he can settle this."*

"You would call the sheriff to report a sewing kit and a few keepsakes? I can't believe it!"

"You should believe it."

Just then Karah poked her head in the room. "Are you leaving, Delilah?"

"Yes, I am afraid I must. Thank you for your hospitality, Karah."

She went to hug me, but Isla prevented it. "You are not leaving with these things. You empty those cases now! I do not make empty threats—just ask my daughter."

"Mother, I told her she could have a few of her mother's treasures. Surely that is permissible."

Isla slapped her across the face. "Get out!" Karah scurried out of the room sobbing.

I grabbed Isla's arms and shook her. "How dare you hit her? You evil woman! Don't ever touch her again!"

To my utter surprise, she smiled and then kissed me. In revulsion I pushed her away and ran out the door after Karah. "Karah! Where are you?" She was not in her room, and Hooney was nowhere to be found. The balcony door overlooking the Moonlight Garden was open, and I walked toward it. "Karah!" I did not see her and turned to walk back inside when Isla stepped in my path.

"Move out of my way!" I said angrily, but she only laughed. Then her beautiful face hardened. She shoved me toward the balcony, and I fell to the floor. "What do you think you're doing, Isla?"

"I am doing what I should have done a long time ago. I should have done it when you were too stupid to know who you were, but it is no matter. You are worm food now, I suppose." She giggled as she brandished an evil-looking knife.

"Oh God, what are you doing?" I lay sprawled on the floor, my mind racing. I looked about me, hoping to find something to defend myself with. But there was nothing, only a chair and a table. "Why are you doing this, Isla? I am your blood."

"Now, now, don't be difficult. Be still, cousin. I don't want to get your blood all over my new dress." The knife arced toward me as I rolled and scrambled to my feet. I was standing now, but she still blocked the only exit. "Very well. If you prefer to jump, I won't stop you. Go ahead." She pointed her knife to the balcony's edge.

"No!" I shouted. "Karah!"

"Leave my daughter out of this unless you want to get her killed too. Now be a good girl and do as I tell you. Keep moving—this will all be over soon." I heard a noise below and saw Karah looking up at me. Isla sliced my arm with the blade, and I screamed.

"No! Go away!" I kicked the chair at her as I cried and moved out of her reach. Blood poured down my arm as she herded me to the edge of the balcony just as she'd promised. "What do you want? Why are you doing this?"

"Since the first day I arrived here, I knew this was mine. My adulteress sister didn't deserve this place—neither did her fool of a daughter. Calpurnia was so stupid—it was mind-numbingly easy to make her believe that David loved her, but he never did. He only ever loved me!" She shouted and waved her knife. "Now there is just one untidy loose end left. You. The forgotten bastard. I told Claudette that you wouldn't be so easily dissuaded, but she was too proper to agree to my solution. But here we are, just the two of us. I sent Stokes away, and Hooney is so old and blind, she'd never hear you even if you cried day and night."

My back was against the railing now. There was nowhere else for me to go. Only down, down, down to my death. I looked down again but only for a second in case she sliced me again. "Help me! Somebody!" I screamed into the fading light. Nobody answered. I turned to see Isla waving her blade again, and this time she tore through my dress and cut my abdomen. I cried out in pain.

"Mother! Stop it!" Karah reached for an old wooden cane that stood in a bucket near the doorway. She raised it high and swung at her mother.

Isla crumpled to the ground and squealed angrily. "Stupid girl!" She clutched her arm and reached for her knife.

"Stop, Mother! You are out of your mind!"

"Such a coward! How could I have raised such a coward? I never wanted you, did you know that? All I ever wanted was my captain—and my home. That's all I ever wanted. Now you want to throw it all away like it meant nothing. Like what I did meant nothing. You stupid coward!" She ran toward us with her knife raised, but Karah struck her again. She fell again, but I knew it wouldn't stop her—she was truly mad.

"Run, Delilah!" My arm was slick with my own blood and I felt cold, but I tried to keep up with her. Then Docie appeared at the top of the stairs, her hands in her pockets and a murderous look on her face.

"Stop them, Docie!" Isla yelled as she tried to stand after Karah's latest attack.

"You heard the mistress. Where do you think you're going?" Karah's face turned white, and I could see fear arresting her reasoning. It was my turn to do something. I snatched the cane and swung it toward Docie, hitting

her square in the stomach. Without a sound she fell backwards down the stairs and landed at the bottom, her head turned at an awkward angle. Karah pulled me out of the way as Isla ran toward her, leaving her knife behind.

"No! Docie!"

"Run, Karah! Come with me!" We scrambled down the stairs and out the back of the house. A half hour later, my cousin and I appeared at Jackson's door, and the last thing I remembered was Jackson lifting me out of the carriage in his strong arms. How I wanted to stay in his arms forever...

***

The first thing I did when I woke up was examine my arms. I had felt every painful slice Delilah had endured, and I was happy to see that those wounds had not followed me into my own life. I tried to still my breathing, and the baby fluttered about as if he too had seen and experienced the drama. I hoped I was wrong about that. I hoped Lenore was wrong.

Shh...sweet little one. It's all right now. We're safe.

As always, I reviewed what I dreamed, remembering details I thought would be important later. That surely hadn't been the end of Delilah—I knew she had become a celebrated actress. But what about her and Jackson? Did they have a happily ever after? It would be nice to know that someone in Ashland's family did. Ashland stirred beside me and put his arm around me. I lay back down and snuggled up next to him.

"Still dreaming, Carrie Jo?"

"Yes, still dreaming."

"How about this once you just dream about us?"

"I like that idea. Now how do I do it?" I sighed, feeling tired but suddenly very peaceful.

With a devilish smile and a twinkle in his blue eyes, he whispered, "Let me help you with that."

With a smile of my own I agreed.

~~*

The Sun Rises Over Seven Sisters

By M.L. Bullock

Dedication

To the ghosts of the South, we remember you.

MIDNIGHT has come, and the great Christ Church Bell
And may a lesser bell sound through the room;
And it is All Souls' Night,
And two long glasses brimmed with muscatel
Bubble upon the table.

A ghost may come;
For it is a ghost's right,
His element is so fine
Being sharpened by his death,
To drink from the wine-breath
While our gross palates drink from the whole wine.

—William Butler Yeats
"All Souls' Night"
Autumn 1920

Prologue—Isla

This morning's chilly air had long since evaporated, replaced by the pungent fragrance of the nearby docks. No cool breeze blew off the water. Not one strong enough to wind through the stale rooms of the Holy Angels Sanitarium. I supposed building the hospital near the Mobile Bay was meant to soothe the facility's patients, but it did not bring that kind of relief for me. The eternal slapping of the water on the shore and the constant churning of the steamboats passing by made me think of my Sweet Captain.

Oh, mon amour! How I miss you! Rescue me, my darling! Take me in your arms once again!

Never had I met a man so beautiful and amiable. So far above all others. Until he failed, and then all of heaven wept at his fall. I was sure some lovely angel with long limbs and golden skin was loving him even now, and the thought of it filled me with anger all over again. Yes, in the end he had been like all the others. Unfaithful to the bone was he, and the fact I missed him so only reflected on my poor character.

Yet, I did miss him. Especially during the quiet moments of the day. Wouldn't any wife miss her husband? Even an unfaithful one?

I could not think of him now. Not with so much to plan.

I would never give up my claim on Seven Sisters. It was mine now, that and the Beaumont fortune. They would both be mine! I clamped my lips together in determination.

One of the dull girls who shared a room with me—Angela, I believe her name was—muffled a cry at the sight of my grimaced face, but she did not speak to me. She knew better. Yes, she had learned that quickly, in spite of her madness. We shuffled down the hall to eat our morning meal, looking like a string of prostitutes, our hair unbound, gowns hanging loosely. The guards made the women here surrender their ribbons and corset ties for fear we might hang ourselves. Who ever heard of doing yourself in with a corset ribbon? I could not imagine ever doing such a thing, but then I was not the kind of woman to take her own life. I might be compelled to take the lives of others. Whenever necessary.

I had a clever mind, but I would remove anyone who stood in my way. It was as simple as that. I tried to explain all this to the physician. When I saw I shocked him, I used my prettiest pout and even twisted my hair playfully, but he was not moved. After a few hours of constant interviewing, I told him what I thought about him and demanded that he release me.

"My dear lady, I did not put you here. You are a ward of the city now and due to stand trial. Only the judge can issue a release, so I suggest you make yourself comfortable. Take time to reflect upon your deeds, and perhaps the judge will have mercy on you." I knocked over his ink well and slapped his papers around before he yelled for the guard. Upon later reflection I realized that I had been foolish to act so rashly, but I felt sure I could persuade Dr. Hannah to petition the court on my behalf. I was still pretty. I had charms and skills that many women did not. From that day forward I did not stir up the staff or the other patients. Not openly, at any rate.

After stuffing a piece of dry biscuit into my mouth and swallowing a few gulps of water, I walked into the open yard looking for a quiet place where I could sit alone. How I longed to have a meal that required a knife and fork. Never would I enjoy that here. I could not abide the company of such madwomen! Even now they were behaving like idiot children. One of them, a tall, thin wisp of a woman, slapped her own face constantly. She had near permanent red marks on her cheeks. Most days, a guard would eventually tire of her self-destruction and tie her hands together. Then she would sit and moan and whine until bedtime. If anyone cared to listen, they would hear her repeat the same phrase, "My boy, Dimitri. My boy, Dimitri." She had a heavy Russian accent; I had heard it before during my travels with my captain!

Oh, David! How I miss you! What will become of me now, my love?

Another patient always pulled at the hem of her sleeve or dress. She pulled away inches of fabric every day and seemed absolutely riveted by the destruction. In the short time I had been at Holy Angels Sanitarium, she had been issued two garments, both essentially sacks made to look like dresses. I did not think she minded much because she quickly unwound them and then sat naked, crying that she had nothing to do. Mrs. Ambrosia, she was called, and she appeared as if she would come sit by me this morning with her missing sleeve and hem to the knees. I hissed at her under my breath to discourage her without making an open fuss. She took the hint and wandered off in the other direction, tugging at the string on her sleeve.

Now, where was I? I said to no one in particular. I stared at the nearby waters of the Mobile Bay from behind the cast-iron bars. I made plans for after this unnecessary excursion. A girl had to have plans, didn't she? I was always a girl with a plan. I would demand, pleasantly, to see the physician tomorrow. I would apologize most humbly and explain to him the great distress I had been in since the death of my husband. He would understand. Men always understood pretty faces.

I frowned into the sun and closed my eyes. Where had Docie been? She had visited me only once, and even then she acted as if she did not want to linger too long. I suspected my former maid had vanished—probably with my remaining fortune. That would be a mistake for her. I treasured loyalty above all things.

The sound of mewing pulled me back to my present circumstance. I had seen the kitten before, but it had not amused me to help it in any way. Fortunately for the lost feline, my situation had changed. I knelt on the ground near the fence and pulled a few biscuit crumbs from my pocket. I knew the guard was watching me, for he always watched me, but thus far he had been careful to keep his distance and had not spoken to me directly. He was a portly man with a bushy brown mustache and thinning hair. Just from observing him I could tell he was secretive and quiet. Those men were the most dangerous kind because they were hard to predict and sometimes hard to please, but he did not frighten me. I pushed the biscuit pieces through the metal bars and spoke sweetly to the animal. Hunger drove it to trust me at least long enough to accept my offerings. It was a sad-looking tabby cat, underweight with missing patches of hair. I did not imagine it would live very long, but anything was possible.

After it got a taste of the biscuit, it naturally wanted more. I pretended I had not noticed the guard step closer to observe me. I held another piece of biscuit out for the kitten to see but put it in my lap. I let the loose gown fall from my shoulder, exposing my skin. Since I was pretending that I did not see the guard, I did not bother to tug it back into place. I kept my eyes on the kitten, who was not cooperating too well. If it wanted something to eat, it would have to take a chance. "It's okay, Mr. Buttons," I purred loudly enough for the guard to hear, "you can trust me."

"What do you plan on doing with that animal? You cannot bring it in here, miss."

Artfully placing my dainty hand over my eyes, I peered into his face with my most innocent expression. "Oh no, sir. I have no intention of keeping him. I only meant to help him along a bit. Look how small and helpless he is."

"Keep that cat out of the yard, miss."

"Oh, have I broken a rule, sir?" I turned my upper body, arching my back slightly, and my hand flew to my mouth as if I were surprised. "Forgive me. May I toss the last of my crumbs to the poor thing?"

He shuffled his feet and hesitated but finally said, "Yes, you may."

"Thank you, sir. Here, Mr. Buttons."

I tossed the crumbs through the gate and stood clumsily, pretending I might trip and fall on my loose gown. His hands quickly went out to steady me, and I did not push them away. "Again, I thank you," I whispered as a small smile spread across my face. I did not meet his eyes but looked at his hand as he removed it nervously. This was too easy. I did not know yet what my plan was, but I felt sure that if I needed to, I would be able to call upon the very helpful guard. Who knows? Maybe Dr. Hannah would not see reason and release me. In that case, I would need help from someone else. I left the guard to watch me walk away, looking back once over my shoulder to give him a demure smile. I picked up the skirts of my untied dress just as I would if I were climbing the steps at Seven Sisters.

He did not follow me. The lady warden, a stern woman named Miss Calypso, came toward me, her shiny black kid boots clicking on the grimy floor. "Miss Beaumont, you have a visitor."

"I have a visitor?" I could not hide my surprise.

"Your mother has come to see you. Straighten your dress and make yourself presentable. As presentable as you get, anyway. The physician has given you permission to sit in the private yard to speak with her. This way, miss."

I thanked Miss Calypso politely and followed her. How clever of Docie to claim to be my mother! Surely she could manage that disguise! She had seen me on the stage for years pretending to be Ophelia, Lady Macbeth and a dozen other characters. I smiled more, thinking of what her choice of disguise might be. Would she have colored her hair? Surely she would not have borrowed a gown, for she did not fit into my clothes at all.

I stepped through the physician's office, and he greeted me briefly. I could tell by his suspicious look and tone that he had not yet forgiven me for my outburst the week before. The lady warden opened the door that led to the doctor's private garden. It was a meager garden at best, but it did have a pleasant shade tree, a young magnolia, two benches and a few scant patches of Bourbon roses. My eyes were on none of these but on the woman who sat on the farthest bench. Her cold blue eyes clamped on my face. This was certainly not Docie, and I could not place her although she was familiar to me in some way. Perhaps she was a fan of my work? I smiled pleasantly, but it was not returned. She studied me as she rose from her peaceful spot in the shade of the tree. She came closer, and the unsettled feeling climbed up my spine.

This woman was my mother.

There we stood appraising one another, not in an overtly threatening manner, just curious. One would have imagined that I would have questions, and perhaps someone other than myself would have been overwhelmed with love or sadness. I experienced none of those things. It did not occur to me to wonder what she might be thinking. Did that matter? I knew one thing—she had been a fool for sending me away. I was beautiful, intelligent and clever at solving puzzles.

Olivia Beaumont had a chiseled, lovely face for an older woman. She must have been at least forty, but she was far lovelier than her sister Christine had been. Olivia had dark blond hair that appeared to have been tinted recently, perhaps to hide silver strands? I smiled at that. She wore it in an upswept, feminine fashion like the women in London. Her hairstyle held plenty of decorative pins, and she wore carefully placed curls at her neck and ears.

I wondered what she would do if I told her about her brother, how he died beaten in the head with a garden curiosity by his brother-in-law's young black lover. *Worm food now, I suppose.* Would she collapse into a pile and whimper as her fragile sister had? I knew she would not. She was not a frail thing but someone with a will and soul of steel, despite her lacy appearance.

Her lips were carefully painted a dark color, but it did not make her look a whore. It made her light blue eyes lovelier and more expressive. At her ears were modest pearls, and her gown was also in the London style with a smaller bustle than the hoopskirts we Southern women were forced to endure. So was she more than a fashion plate? She appeared wealthy and lovely, like a great woman should. I wondered how she came to be here. Who had summoned her to the Holy Angels Sanitarium?

There we were, mother and daughter, standing in a sparse garden and silently staring at one another. I suddenly felt foolish for looking so out of sorts. When had I last bathed? When had I washed my hair? She seemed not to notice those things but instead focused on my face.

"Ah, thank you for waiting, ladies. I did not mean to be so long." It was Dr. Hannah, the tall, fleshy physician with the white hair and the monocle. His pale skin had a touch of pinkness, like a baby's or an albino rat's. I suppressed a giggle at the thought of Dr. Hannah as a rat. Olivia stared at me, her blue eyes like two glass marbles that could see right through me. I quieted and sat with my hands folded in my lap, just as I had learned from Christine and Calpurnia.

"Thank you for coming, Mrs. Torrence. How disappointing that I will not meet your husband. Typhoid, is it? Very nasty illness, that. If I were you, I would keep far away from home until he is completely clear of the disease."

Abruptly she stood and interrupted his speech. "Would you mind if I had a few minutes alone with Isla? As you can imagine, we have many private things to speak of."

With a serious pursing of his lips he answered her, "Certainly, Mrs. Torrence. I will be in the office if you need me. I would like to speak to the two of you together, but there is no need to hurry. Take your time."

"In fact—Dr. Hannah, is it? We will not be speaking with you at all, today or any other day. This is for you." She handed the man a scroll of papers. He could not hide his surprise as he scanned the documents.

"Everything looks to be in order, but I am afraid I haven't yet completed my examination of Miss Beaumont. This is most irregular." His objections availed him nothing, and he knew it after a few more stern looks. "Will you be leaving right away?" Olivia stared at him as if he were the mental patient. He sputtered and stammered, "Yes, of course you will be. Very well, I will ask the warden to collect your daughter's things. Good day to you then, Mrs. Torrence." She did not smile or thank him, just watched him disappear back into the white painted building.

I marveled at the whole thing. I had planned to seduce my way to freedom, but Olivia wielded a power I had never seen before, all without saying please or smiling even once. I wanted to learn how to use this power. I wondered if she would share it with me.

"Now you and I need to talk."

"Yes, Mother," I said sweetly.

"Drop the act. Do not call me Mother. I am not your mother. I am your aunt. You may call me Mrs. Torrence."

Now I felt like Dr. Hannah, completely unprepared to withstand Olivia's stare and authoritative manner.

"Your mother was a common street woman from New Orleans, a woman who convinced my brother that he was your father. He was foolish to believe so, but he did."

"What do you mean you are not my mother? I have always been told that you were. How can this be wrong?" I frowned in suspicion.

"I am not. I would think I would know whether or not you were mine." No smile, no expression of sadness or regret. No expression at all. To her, this was a boring conversation forced upon her by the judge who had summoned her to speak on my behalf. Or so I assumed.

"Then why the charade with the judge and the physician?"

"Why not? It is what they believe, so who am I to tell them different? I refuse to share family gossip with them or shame my family further."

I stepped toward her, uncaring that my gown had fallen off my shoulder again. "What about the shame it brought on you? Having a cast-off child, having me believe you did not want me as your daughter."

"It is my brother who should feel the shame. On the other hand, he is dead, so I doubt he feels much of anything." I gasped at her total lack of concern for my feelings on this matter. "Are you going to cry now? If so, do me the courtesy of waiting until we are in the carriage. I cannot abide public outbursts."

Sniffing away the wash of emotions, I answered her confidently, "I will not make a fuss."

She appraised me again. "I *should* leave you here. I am sure you could finagle your way out if you chose to. Probably already have a plan, don't you?"

I should never have admitted it, but I nodded slowly.

"Yes, you are your father's child. Scheming and planning. Let us go now."

"Where are we going, Mrs. Torrence?"

"To Seven Sisters, of course. I want to see what's become of my sister's fortune. You sure have made a mess of things, haven't you?" She walked toward the door, but I had to correct her. I had done everything—everything imaginable—to keep the family fortune. I would not let this slight pass.

"No! Your sister did that by having two children out of wedlock. Cottonwood knew all about it. However..." I smiled proudly here. I was anxious for her to respect me. *No need to wait. Let us establish the facts now*, I told myself. "He has left everything to his rightful heir, my own daughter, Karah Cottonwood."

Olivia's hard stare elicited another sentence from my lips. It was probably not wise to say aloud, but the words came anyway. "That leaves nothing to the Beaumonts, I'm afraid."

"Is that what you truly believe?" she asked, her face a pretty, unemotional mask. It wasn't really a question; it was more of a challenge. "My carriage is outside." She walked into the office, down the hall and out the door without looking back once. Good thing for her she didn't. I stuck out my tongue at her at least a half dozen times during the trek to the entrance. To my surprise the raggedy-looking tabby cat waited for us as if he too wanted to escape. He rubbed against my leg as if I were his only friend. Perhaps I was. More was the pity for him.

Olivia eyed me as I petted him once. "Your pet?"

"Hardly," I answered as I climbed into the carriage behind her. I was ready to go home and take a bath, eat real food and find a new dress. I watched Mrs. Torrence as she instructed the driver which way to go. Frigidity masked as decorum. Did she think I would be intimidated by her folded hands, her elegant kid gloves? I looked down into my own hands. Broken nails with dirty beds and torn skin. I stared at them intently. I did not hide them. Maybe these weren't the hands of a lady, but they were the hands of a fighter, someone accustomed to fighting for everything.

I could feel her cold eyes on me, but still I smiled at my hands.

No, these hands would not let me down.

We would fight, and we would win.

Chapter 1—Carrie Jo

The tap on the front door woke me from my nap. That was aggravating, as I could just feel myself slip away into a pleasant dream. With my recent influx of nightmares and sleep paralysis, dreaming about something nice would be a godsend. Thankfully I was no longer invading my husband's dreams. I shuddered to think about what he would be dreaming now that I was as big as a house. Although our love and commitment to one another remained strong, Ashland and I argued a lot lately. The worst part was, our disagreements, as he called them, were mostly over insignificant things like who misplaced the hammer or how the puppy got out. As I reminded him frequently, the new dog had been his idea and I never used the hammer. Well, hardly ever. I did hang a baby calendar in my office. And I found some cute wooden monograms to hang in my room.

Ashland's dog, a cute white Maltese, demanded constant affection and attention, and quite frankly he was a lousy watchdog. In fact, he was in full-blown nap mode at the foot of the couch when the visitor came to my door. He hadn't even budged at the knock. *Yeah, right. Big-time watchdog. Thanks, fella.*

Ashland and I would have to talk about that later. Well, maybe not. I think we had fulfilled our mandatory couple's argument quota for the year. Especially after last night. That had been the fight of the century, and I couldn't understand it. Why was Ash being so unreasonable? Apparently the subject of baby names was a hill that both of us were willing to die on. He hated the idea of naming our child anything "old-fashioned." I hated the idea of giving our son or daughter this year's trendiest name. Well, it couldn't be as bad as Carrie Jo. What had my mother been thinking?

"Just a second," I called to the unscheduled visitor who tapped again at the door. I tossed the soft throw blanket to the side and slid carefully off the couch. Navigating life with a big old baby belly had proved a challenge, but I liked being pregnant. Whenever he or she arrived (I still held out hope for a girl) I would miss this experience. The closeness with my child, the feeling of life growing inside me. It was like my love with Ashland had created a bit of magic, and now that magic would become an amazing person. "Whatever, Carrie Jo," I muttered to myself. I had become too sentimental lately. Too many sappy movies.

Peeking through the glass door, I could see the mail lady waiting patiently for me. I arranged my sloppy t-shirt and flyaway hair before opening the door with a smile.

"Good morning! These are for you, Mrs. Stuart." I accepted the bundle of letters and the package she handed me. I dropped a few items, but she graciously picked them up for me. No way was I going to bend down, not without some help getting up.

"Thanks. Anything good in there?"

"More baby catalogs. Almost time, isn't it?" Sharone Pugh and I had become quite familiar with one another the past few months. Too many late nights spent shopping online for baby clothes, furniture and whatever else struck my fancy. Sharone showed up day after day with something new. I gave up apologizing after a while. She didn't complain. Not too much, anyway. I joked with her that I would have the best-dressed infant in downtown Mobile, but at this point the only colors in the child's wardrobe were yellow and white. (Lenore had declared we would have a boy, but I wasn't so sure.)

"Can you believe my doctor says three more weeks? I don't think it's humanly possible to get any bigger."

"I was as big as a hippo when I delivered my first child. Gained seventy pounds too. You look wonderful. I'd better go. I have a ton of mail to deliver, and I can't leave my truck on the street. Have a nice day." She walked away as I said goodbye.

Closing the door behind me, I set the package on the foyer table and flipped through the stack of envelopes. The third letter in, I froze. It was from my mother. I stared at her name written in the familiar handwriting.

Deidre Jardine

Dumping the rest of the mail on the table with the package, I took the letter with trembling hands, grabbed the blanket and plopped back on the couch. As if he or she knew my heart was pounding, the baby turned in my tummy and pressed on my bladder. "Hey, cut that out, kiddo." After a few seconds the baby got comfortable again, and I leaned back on the pillow hoping to get some relief from the dull ache in my side. The clock struck half past the hour. It was 9:30 on Saturday morning, just a few hours before the baby shower. Plenty of time to take a nap. Ashland would not be back from his latest deposition for a while, and lately he had been in no mood to just hang out. I tried to be understanding, but I'd had my own crankiness to deal with. I blamed it on the pregnancy, but I knew it was stress. For the past six months Ash had been battered with lawsuits about the most mundane things, from claims on the estate to an unhappy tenant who claimed he was a slumlord.

And now this letter.

It was just one more thing. What could she possibly have to say to me? We had not spoken, emailed or messaged one another in over two years. Sure, I had stared at her contact info in my phone a few times, but I never actually called. Then again, she never called me either. Feeling tired and tearful, I put the letter on the coffee table and lay down again. The house was quiet, and there were no shadows. Maybe it would be safe to sleep. Safe to dream. I needed the rest. I could read the letter later. I touched it once again and then wrapped the blanket around my shoulders and snuggled into the plush couch. I had so many reasons to be happy. So why was I so unhappy?

I told my mind to be quiet, and after a few more minutes of unhappy rumination I fell asleep.

***

Olivia Torrence had spoken barely a word on our journey to Seven Sisters. Obviously she had been here before. She did not crane her neck out the carriage window or gawk up at the white-painted edifice that shone brightly in the late morning sunlight. She was not overawed by the sheer size of the plantation or the obvious wealth that commanded it. I reminded myself that Olivia Beaumont Torrence was probably the wealthiest woman I had ever met. If I could have her as my ally, then who could stop me? But for that to happen, I would have to show her I was worthy of her partnership. No flattering words or innocent smiles for her. She would appreciate intelligence. I had to show her I was worthy of her trust.

The carriage shifted, and I slid across the seat. I noticed that she had barely moved a muscle. How was that possible? Was she made of stone or marble? She did remind me of the statues in the Moonlight Garden. Elegant, pale and forever frozen in one position. Despite the uncomfortable nature of our silence, I refused to be the first to speak. Instead, I peeked out the window at the house, uncaring that she thought me a fool. Once the carriage arrived, Stokes came to the door and pushed the latch, freeing me from my latest prison. It was good to be home! This was my home! I had broken every commandment in the Holy Bible to have this place, and I would not be denied. Not now and not ever. Hooney lingered in the doorway, but she did not offer a glass of lemonade or a bite to eat.

I frowned at her, and she made the sign of the cross. I laughed and strolled into the house like I owned it. Over my shoulder I said to Mrs. Torrence, "Forgive me, Aunt. I need to bathe and change. It has been far too long since I had a proper scrub."

She slid off her gloves and ignored me, which aggravated me to no end. She strolled into the ladies' parlor with Stokes on her heels. I heard her speaking to him in low tones, and I stomped up the stairs happy to be out of her company. "Hooney! I need a bath. Send someone up here with some hot water." She also did not answer, but I noticed she shuffled her old feet to fulfill my request. What did I care if she carried the water up herself? I doubted she would, though. Soon I heard wood being tossed in the upstairs stove and the sloshing of water. When the water was heated, I would soak my bones and wash away my cares.

I had claimed Christine's old room. Seemed appropriate—this was where the lady of the house slept, wasn't it? To my utter shock and amazement, all my things had been packed in trunks, stuffed away like yesterday's rubbish. "Hooney!" I yelled in my most aggravated tone. She never came.

It was Hannah who came into the room, drying her hands on her yellow checked apron.

"Yes, miss?"

"I am hardly a miss, am I? Why are my things stuffed away? Look at my dresses! Everything is wrinkled. How can I wear these now? They must be pressed immediately."

"Mrs. Torrence told us to pack your things. I tried to pack them proper. I can try again. I am sorry, miss."

"What do you mean pack my things? I am not going anywhere!" I snapped at her. She looked at me, unsure about what I was saying. I shoved her out of the way and stomped out of the room. I suddenly did not care that my hair was a mess or that my dress hung off my thin, dirty shoulders.

In my bare feet I stomped into the ladies' parlor to find Olivia, but she was not there. Angrily I sailed through the Blue Room and yet again found no sign of her. Crossing the hall, I could hear her shuffling around in Jeremiah's study. She sat straight-backed in a cherrywood chair—not the master's chair, but a more petite one. She had shoved Jeremiah's monstrosity to the side as if it were something she could not abide touching. Perched on her nose were a pair of spectacles, and she was sorting through a stack of crumpled papers.

"What do you mean by having the servants pack my things? I have no plans to leave Seven Sisters."

"I am not prepared to speak with a madwoman," she said, barely breaking her gaze from the papers.

Her answer surprised me, and I sputtered for a moment. "How dare you! I am nowhere near mad. I do not know what plans you think you have for me, but I can tell you mine. I am not leaving Seven Sisters. This is my home."

She tossed her glasses on the desk and stood behind it, looking tall and rigid like an oak tree. "Speak to me like that again, and I will put you back where I found you. You are here only by my good graces. The sooner you understand that, the easier things will be."

"Easier? You have no idea what I have endured—the price I have paid."

"No more than any woman has, I am sure," she said flatly. "That is your problem. You think yourself a victim. You are weak, like most women. You are too old to play games like a spoiled schoolgirl."

Feeling the thrill of rage rise again, I smiled at her and stepped closer to the desk. I subtly searched for a weapon. My eyes fell on a letter opener with a black enamel handle.

Her perfect brows rose astutely. "See? Weak. Murder is a common solution for common minds. Imagine that I would waste my time rescuing you when I heard you described as clever! I shouldn't have bothered." Without waiting for my response, she picked up her spectacles and sat back down in the chair. She pretended to read her many papers.

"I am not leaving Seven Sisters, Aunt."

"I don't think you have much choice in the matter, do you? Dead or alive, you will do as you're told."

I stared at my aunt with a ferocious glare. How dare she judge me! Call me old, would she? She who wore a high collar and long sleeves, undoubtedly to mask her age? Should I tell her that the neck and hands were the first to go? There wasn't enough lace in the world to hide those telltale signs. She was entirely too thin, but I still had a young, firm body with plenty of soft curves. As I stood with my head held high, I caught a whiff of myself. I had the stench of the asylum on my skin. It humbled me. For a moment.

I left her without a word and went upstairs to take my bath. I needed to think and not act. How many times had my Sweet Captain reminded me of that very thing, "Think first, then act, my love." According to him, I was too spontaneous, too ready to act without first thinking through a matter. I should have taken his advice. But in the words of old Ben Franklin, it was never too late to try. I had not yet made up my mind about Olivia. Would I kill her? Rob her? Befriend her? I pondered these options as Hannah washed my hair with lemon-scented soap. The aroma was intoxicating. Then she scrubbed my feet with the bristle brush and, when I was dry, rubbed my skin with coconut oil. I felt like a debutante when her ministrations were completed.

"Dinner is almost ready, miss. You want me to help you dress? I think this pink gown is less wrinkled than the others. I promise to finish pressing the others tomorrow. I do apologize."

"No pink. Bring me the dark blue dress. The one with the blue lace on the sleeves."

A few minutes later I walked down the stairs to dine with my aunt. As I walked ever so slowly, I thought about her words. She considered me weak, but she was wrong. Oh so wrong! I had survived when she and the rest of the Beaumonts had cast me off as unworthy. And all this time I had lived. I had nothing to hang my head about. A celebrated beauty, I had traveled the world like a queen with David by my side, sometimes performing, other times watching him win his precious card games.

I took a few more steps, remembering the first time I saw David standing near this bottom step. How direct he had been! How I wanted to stare into those eyes of blue velvet forever! When we failed in our mission to lead Calpurnia into finding the Beaumont treasure, I made another plan and achieved it. My own mind had conceived those plans! None other. Still determined to win, I had a Cottonwood baby. Although she was a girl, I had delivered a promised heir. Could anyone imagine how difficult it was to seduce a man who preferred boys? I had taken great pains to capture his attentions, but I had managed it. It was easy to do with Calpurnia neatly locked away in her prison. And I had been the one who convinced Jeremiah to finish Christine. I watched him pull the rope as her body went up and up. If not for Hoyt Page, the adulterer doctor, I would have the deed to this place and plenty of freedom to find the missing jewels.

Later, when my Sweet Captain considered leaving me, I made another hard decision. Never could I forget the feeling of his warm blood seeping out of his body and into my hands. And he had never known it was me who pulled the trigger. But now he would never leave me.

I reached the bottom of the stairs and stood in the foyer of Seven Sisters. This was mine. I had made a deal with a devil named Cottonwood.

I had paid the price.

I would not be denied.

Chapter 2—Carrie Jo

I saw Lenore's face. Her dark eyes wide, she mouthed a word to me, but I could not understand her. No sound came out of her mouth. I woke with a start. The puppy yelped in surprise as my body jerked awake. "Oh, sorry, little guy. I forgot you were there." I swung my legs around and sat on the edge of the couch, my head in my hands. How was I dreaming about Isla again? I took a moment to "feel" my environment. There were no ghosts, as far as I could tell. I heard no giggles and saw no gray spirits with bloodless lips and ashen hair. But I had learned something, hadn't I? Olivia was not Isla's mother after all. Why was I seeing this now?

I did feel Lenore's presence, but only for a fleeting moment. She was here, or she had been. Warning me about something. The fat puppy whined beside me, and I stared at him. "Need to go out? Come on, chunky boy." He hopped off the couch and trotted to the door, waiting impatiently for me to get up. I glanced at the clock again. Darn! I had only 30 minutes to get ready. I told myself I'd have to think about all this later as I tried to shake off the remnants of my dream.

The puppy (I would have to give him a name sooner or later) wandered around the garden for a while, entranced by flowers, butterflies and anything that distracted him from his potty task. With some coaxing he finished his business and ran back in the house to find a snack. A snack sounded good, but I had to get going. I was sure there would be plenty to eat at my shower. Especially if Henri was involved. Man, that guy could cook! I trekked upstairs and found something mommy-ish to wear. It was kind of Detra Ann to host this shower for me, but I honestly didn't need anything. Still, it would be good to see Rachel, Detra Ann and the rest of the folks in my small circle of friends. We were like a family. We celebrated one another's birthdays and anniversaries, and we spent holidays together. In a sense, we were a band of broken people, a tribe of weirdos, each with their own supernatural power. Except perhaps Rachel, but then again I considered her research skills pretty amazing. I hoped she'd have some updates for me on that project we were working on. I was curious to see the end result. Ashland would be so surprised!

Speaking of, I hoped he remembered to show up at Detra Ann's. This was supposed to be a couple's baby shower, not just a party for me. I hoped the attorney didn't invite herself as she tended to do at times. I didn't care for her too much. She reminded me of someone, someone from my past that I couldn't trust. But I did trust my husband. He wasn't the kind of guy to be unfaithful. He hated that his father had been that sort of man. Ashland Stuart's life goals included being the complete opposite of his father. I can't say that I blamed him. His father was a terrible husband, by all accounts. In fact, two of the recent lawsuits came from two different individuals claiming to be the misbegotten sons of the late Mr. Stuart. I wondered what kind of father-in-law or grandfather he would have been. My phone dinged, and I read the text from Detra Ann.

Come on, slowpoke!

I sent a smiley emoticon back and slid my swollen feet into my sandals. I tossed my wallet, keys and makeup bag into a purse that matched my dress, then scanned myself in the mirror. I suddenly regretted my attire choice. This bright yellow dress made me look like Big Bird, but I couldn't change now. It was sleeveless with white flowers at the collar and along the hem. It was still warm out even though fall was approaching, and I wanted to wear this dress at least once more before the baby arrived. As if he heard me thinking about him—*oops, did I say him?*—he moved a foot or an elbow and jammed me in the side.

"Okay, settle down. We'll have lunch soon. You ready, kiddo?"

As I pulled the yellow purse strap over my shoulder, I heard a nearly inaudible whisper. I froze in the doorway trying to discern where it was coming from. I glanced down at my phone, hoping it was an audio text, but there was nothing on the device. "Who's there?" I called, my voice echoing down the hall of my Victorian home. "Doreen?"

Nobody answered. I walked slowly across the hardwood hallway and stood at the top of the stairs. This was a dangerous place to stand. Isla had tried to kill Detra Ann here in this spot. I did not linger but moved quickly and carefully down the stairs. "Hello?" I called again. The only response was from the curious puppy, who believed I must have had a snack hidden in my hand. His fuzzy round face took the fear out of me, and I smiled at him and inelegantly squatted down to pat his head. "I'll be back. No accidents while I'm gone, okay?" He jumped up and licked me affectionately. I doubted he really understood a word I was saying.

I made the short drive to Detra Ann's house. Well, it was really Detra Ann and Henri's house. The two were nearly inseparable now. It was only a matter of time before they took the big step. I wondered when Henri would pop the question. He sure was taking his time. Detra Ann rarely talked about TD anymore.

Henri, on the other hand, was actively searching for Aleezabeth, as he had promised Lenore he would. He was committed to the task, and he spent quite a bit of time traveling to Louisiana. We'd traveled with him a few times and spent some weekends in New Orleans with him. The food, the people, the beautiful architecture—I could see why so many people loved the place.

I pulled into the driveway of Detra Ann's home and took a deep breath. There were at least a dozen cars, most of which I recognized. It looked like Ashland had made it on time. I smiled, hoping he would be in a good mood. I didn't plan on telling him about my dream, not right now. He had enough to worry about, but I wanted to mention that I had seen Lenore. Maybe he was seeing her too? For some reason, Ashland was always reluctant to talk about the things he saw unless forced to. He was a private man, but he had a warm heart and the most beautiful smile I had ever seen. I was completely in love with him. He had changed my life.

I suddenly remembered the letter from my mother. "Oh, shoot!" I muttered. I had left it on the coffee table at home. I couldn't worry about that right now. Maybe Ashland and I could read it together later.

Grabbing my purse and locking my car, I walked up the brick walkway to the lovely Creole home. Detra Ann had finally bought her own place, and it was chock full of antiques from her store, Cotton City Treasures. She had a flair for displays, and it showed. I rang the bell, and she opened it dramatically. "Should I say surprise?"

I laughed and hugged her. "Not unless you want me to pee on myself."

She laughed too. "I'm just teasing. Come on in here. Look at your belly. That's going to be a big boy! I mean girl. Maybe you'll have one of each."

"Please don't say that," I said, ready to cry at the idea.

She hugged me again, "I'm sorry. I forgot how sensitive preggos can be. I'm sure there is just one baby in there. And he—or she—is perfect."

"Hey, baby!" Ashland walked toward me and scooped me into his arms. "What's this? Are you crying?"

Detra Ann frowned a bit. "It's all my fault, Ash. I'm an insensitive friend. The kind who suggests she's carrying two youngins in there. Just for that, I volunteer to babysit anytime you need me." She kissed my cheek, and I smiled back, wiping away the ridiculous tears. "Y'all come out to the patio when you get ready. Henri thought it would be fun to have this shindig by the pool, and it's only a 'little' hot. He's been cooking, and it's going to be delicious."

"Sounds wonderful. Don't worry about me. I've just got the blues today. And my side is killing me. This kid can kick like you wouldn't believe."

She laughed and said, "I'll get you something to drink and meet you on the patio."

Ashland looked down at me with concern. "What kind of pain are you having? Should we call the doctor?"

With a weak smile and faux confidence, I shook my head. "I don't think it's anything to be concerned about. The last time I mentioned it, Dr. Gilmore said it was probably just my ligaments stretching. I have never heard of contractions in your side, but hey, I'm new to all this childbearing stuff. How did it go today?"

"Nothing I can't manage." He gave a small laugh that didn't sound too cheerful. "Did you hear back from the project manager for the Idlewood house?"

"No. I get the feeling that he wasn't expecting all the red tape. I'm going to back off on the project until after the baby. I'll call him tomorrow and tell him. He'll probably be happy to hear it. Might give him some time to get his act together. Are you sure you're okay?"

He held me in his arms and kissed my forehead. "Stop worrying. Today was just another Monday."

"It's Friday, babe."

"Exactly." He hugged me and whispered, "I love you, Carrie Jo."

"I love you too, Ashland. Please don't make me cry again."

"Ha! How is telling you I love you going to make you cry?"

"You've obviously never been pregnant." I kissed him and released him.

"What's going on that I don't know about?"

With a guilty look I answered, "How did you know?"

"I just know."

"Nothing big, just a dream and a letter. Can we talk about it after the party? Junior or Junior-ette is starving."

He didn't like the compromise, but how could he argue with a hungry child? "All right, but no secrets, remember?" I nodded in agreement. "Oh, wait. I got you this."

He walked to the nearby table and handed me a corsage box with a genuine smile. Ashland was definitely one to shower a girl with flowers. I loved that about him. "How beautiful! Are those Bourbon roses?" I knew they were, but I was enjoying the conversation. This was the first time in recent days that he'd smiled. "Put it on me." I held my arm out, and he slid the fluffy corsage arrangement on my wrist. "I love it, Ashland. It's beautiful."

"Not as beautiful as you, Carrie Jo Stuart."

I rubbed my hands over my belly and turned sideways. "Really? Even with this big belly?"

"Yes, and you get more beautiful every day." I kissed him again, and we walked hand in hand to the patio where our group of friends waited patiently. They applauded as we walked through the open French doors. I smiled at all the faces and accepted hugs from everyone. Chip and Rachel were the first to wish us well. They were on-again, off-again, but I was happy to see them together, at least for the moment. Henri wore one of his many aprons; this one said: *Cooking Up Something Good*. By the smell of it, I knew that was true. Nobody cooked like Henri. And as I predicted, Libby Stevenson, Ashland's attorney, made an appearance. I noticed she recently ditched her long dark hair in favor of a sassy bob. It flattered her angular face. I wondered why she bothered to come when we barely spoke to one another, except in passing. I supposed she came as Ashland's guest. Libby had one of those smiles that never quite made it to her eyes, the kind of smile you couldn't trust.

Whatever, lady, I said to myself. I chose to ignore her but shot Ashland a look. He gazed back at me questioningly. I didn't bother explaining; I shouldn't have to. Less than a minute ago, we were practically making out. Now I wanted to choke him.

Detra Ann spoke up, "Let's get this party started! We're here to welcome Baby Stuart. Thank you all for coming—now let's play some games." For the next 45 minutes we played goofy games and ate crab puffs, gumbo and mini cheesecakes. I laughed about a hundred times and opened a seemingly endless pile of gifts. Jazz played quietly in the background, and Henri surprised me with a beautiful cake.

"Oh my gosh! You bake too?" I dipped my finger into the frosting and tasted it. It was my party, right? Cream cheese frosting so light it tasted like heaven. "When are you going to marry this man? He can do it all." Everyone got quiet, and I felt embarrassed. I hadn't meant to meddle in their business!

Detra Ann just smiled at me. "Funny you should mention that." She held up her left hand and waved her fingers at me.

"What? Does that ring mean what I think it does?" It was almost as big as mine, and it shone beautifully against her tanned skin. "Oh my gosh! That is beautiful! When? Where?"

Henri smiled and put his arm around Detra Ann. "Last week at the LSU game. I have a friend who works in the booth, and they let me pop the question over the Jumbotron. You should have seen her face."

She squeezed his hand and smiled at me. "Only Henri would do something like that. I thought he was pranking me at first. Until he whipped out this big ol' ring. How could I say no?"

"Why didn't you tell me? Ashland, did you know about this?" He smiled sheepishly and raised his hands as if to say, *I had nothing to do with this*.

"We didn't want to overshadow the shower. This is y'all's party. We planned to have an engagement party after the baby arrives. We'll tell the whole world then."

I felt the tears again for about the fifteenth time that day. This was getting beyond ridiculous. "You guys. That is so wonderful. I am so happy for you both." I hugged Detra Ann, thankful that she had made it through her dark times and found someone as amazing as Henri. She hadn't drunk a drop since Lenore's death, and her antiques business was booming. I was so happy for her. She deserved some happiness. Didn't we all?

It appeared that most at the shower had not heard the news, and everyone offered congratulations. "I'm so happy for you both," Libby said in her deep, sultry voice as she hugged Detra Ann halfheartedly. Detra Ann accepted the hug, but I saw her stiffen a bit. She gave Libby an icy smile and moved on to the next person.

I accepted a slice of the cake and sat by the pool listening to Bob Marley and the Wailers and watching my friends. Soon people began to say their goodbyes. Rachel was one of the first. "Sorry, CJ, I have to go. Chip's mother is being a pain in the arse."

"Hey, that's my mom you're talking about," he said defensively.

"And she's a pain in the arse." Rachel rolled her eyes at him and hugged me. "You coming in tomorrow? I have that tree mapped but..." Her voice dropped to a whisper. "I think there's something you should see."

"Really? What is it? Are there pirates in the Stuart tree? I would expect nothing less," I joked.

"It's better to show you than tell you. I promise I'll fill you in tomorrow. I'll be there at 9."

"Call me curious! Of course I'll be there. Thanks, Rachel."

She smiled and left with Chip. I started picking up plates when Detra Ann stopped me. "No, ma'am. No cleaning of any sort. This is your party. Henri and I will take care of this. I think you better figure out where you're going to put all these gifts. Did you drive the BMW?"

"Yep, and Ash drove the Jeep, so we should be okay. I hope. You guys are so generous. I'm going to have to get a bigger house just to have enough room for all this," I said with a laugh.

"No doubt you will." She finished off her glass of punch and observed the remnants of the party. "Wonder why she came?"

"Who's that?" I asked, munching on sugared pecans. She glanced toward Libby. "Oh, her. I don't know. Well, I probably don't want to know."

"Remember when she said, 'I wish you both happiness,' or however she put it?"

"Yes."

"She didn't mean it. My bells went off big time. I mean, why say anything? She's such a liar. Like I said, I don't know why she came. I sure as heck didn't invite her. I don't think she likes anyone here, except Ashland. But then she always was a loner, even in school. Her brother was pretty nice, though."

"Really? I didn't know you guys went to school together. I think we both know why she's here, right?" I rolled my eyes. The young attorney wouldn't be the first woman to have a second thought about my husband. He had practically been a household name before the stranger from Savannah nabbed him. I knew for a fact that half the Historical Society still held a grudge because Ashland married a girl from Georgia and not a "belle from Mobile proper."

"Libby is barking up the wrong tree if she's after Ashland. He's not going to do you like that."

I wiped the sugar from my lips with a yellow napkin. Detra Ann had Ashland's and my initials printed on the napkins, cups and plates. It was a nice touch. I had to remember to keep one for my neglected scrapbook.

As if she heard her name, Libby strolled over to us, her mules slapping on the brick. "Can I help you ladies with something? Need help loading your stuff, Carrie Jo?"

"I think we have it. Thanks."

She stared at me a moment and said, "Well, I guess I'll go, then. Nice party."

As she walked away I felt like a jerk. Not every woman on the planet wanted my husband. Right?

"Nice of you to come, Libby," I called after her. She didn't act like she heard me. Instead, she stood on tiptoe and whispered to Ashland. He leaned down to hear her, and she took advantage of the nearness. Her arms went around his neck, and she hugged him. With her whole body. It was kind of embarrassing. Ash seemed surprised, and he patted her back like she was a child. My raging pregnancy hormones wanted me to slap her into the pool, but I kept my head. *Always listen to your instincts, CJ*, I warned myself.

Detra Ann made a disgusted, snorting sound and yelled, "Ash, we need your help over here."

He said something to Libby, and she left the party. I felt my face flush with embarrassment. Henri sensed the tension and said, "Let's see if we can get this bassinet in the Jeep. If not, I know it will fit in the truck."

"Wonderful party, Detra Ann. Thank you." Avoiding Ashland's eyes, I grabbed a couple bags and headed to the door. I was ready for this day to be over. I felt tired, I had eaten too much, and the green-eyed monster threatened to make an appearance. Detra Ann smiled understandingly and helped me carry the baby's gifts to the car. Thirty minutes later I was headed home with Ashland's Jeep behind me. The way I was feeling, most of this stuff was going to stay in the car overnight. I couldn't imagine hauling it all inside. My puffy feet would never allow that. What made me eat all those crab legs? I felt the sharp pain in my side again, and this time it was so severe I caught my breath.

"Oh God, oh God, oh God," I said as a kind of chant against the pain. Soon it subsided, and I pulled into the driveway. Putting the car in park, I leaned over the steering wheel and waited, hoping it didn't happen again. Ashland seemed oblivious as he juggled pastel-colored gift bags and house keys. When I was sure I was okay, I got out of the car with my purse and a few bags.

Walking up the drive I could feel an oppressive cloud, an unhappy fog unseen by human eye but felt by the spirit. It wasn't a presence, per se, more like bad mojo—or something. I looked up and down the street; the sun was going down now, and the afternoon traffic had dissipated. Compared to my neighbors' front yard, my flowerbeds looked forlorn and forgotten. Even my newly planted mums had croaked. Why did everything in my yard look dead? I walked up the driveway and almost tripped over a cat. It was the largest black cat I had ever seen outside of the zoo.

"What in the world? Where did you come from?" Like a bolt of lightning, Chunky Boy (that's what I'd decided to call him) ran out of the house after it. "Hey! Come back!"

Ashland was out the door and running past me. "Damn! I'll get him."

I wanted to say something smart like, "Serves you right for leaving the front door wide open," but I kept my mouth shut. I shook my head and headed for the front door when I heard a car slam on its brakes. Chunky Boy yelped, and I dropped my bags. As I ran down to the end of the driveway, I could see Ashland bent over in the street. He picked up Chunky Boy as the driver got out to apologize.

"Oh, I am so sorry. He came out of nowhere. Is he okay?"

Even from this distance, I could see he wasn't. His white fur was covered in blood, and he was clearly lifeless.

For the umpteenth time today I let the tears flow. This time I actually had a reason.

Chapter 3—Rachel

"I've been an unofficial member of the Seven Sisters ghostbusting team from the beginning, but nobody talks much about what happened over there," I complained again. Chip nodded as I continued, "I do believe that Carrie Jo is a dream catcher, though. She's not a huckster. In fact, she's one of the most honest people I know."

His eye roll revealed he had a different opinion. *Gee. That's pretty close-minded of you, Chip.* I decided to change the subject a bit. "What have you heard about the house?"

"I know I'm glad to be out of there, and I can't wait until you've finished up with it completely. Then I won't worry so much. Too many rumors about that place. Did you know it's on the Ghost Hunters website? I think those guys are trying to get in there. You know, to investigate."

"Oh really, nonbeliever? If there's no such thing as ghosts, what would they possibly investigate?"

"I never said there wasn't, but dream catching? I thought that was some Indian myth."

"I think the term you are looking for is Native American," I scolded him. Chip always said the most inappropriate things. He was so unsophisticated. I couldn't believe I'd even agreed to go out with him, much less do anything else with him. I quickly added, "But for your information, I'm not afraid of the house. I like helping out the Historical Society, and it's a big deal for Mobile. Besides, if I didn't manage the tours at Seven Sisters, who knows what they'd tell the visitors? I wonder about what they teach kids in school these days. Everyone should know the history of the city they live in."

"You sound like an old lady, Rachel Kowalski."

"Me? Because I believe in the unseen, the supernatural? I think you've got that the other way around."

He squinted at me through his glasses as if he didn't quite believe me. The truth was, he was right in a way. I was kind of an old lady. I did worry about everyone and everything. "You didn't answer my question, Chip. Did you see something in the house?"

He said, "I never saw anything, but more than once I felt like someone was watching me. Especially in the Blue Room. Got worse after Hollis Matthews died. It was more of a feeling, that's all. What about you?"

I didn't know if I was ready to tell Chip about my experience. He might think I was losing my mind, as he clearly thought Carrie Jo was a bit loony. He wasn't a deep thinker at all and certainly not spiritual. Once again I wondered how on earth I could be serious about a guy like him. I was totally a spiritual person. I didn't go to church as much as I used to, but I believed in God and the supernatural world. Why did people separate the two? God was a Spirit, right?

I decided to change the subject to a less controversial one. Chip had a short attention span, and he probably wouldn't notice anyway. "Do you believe in curses? Like family curses?"

"Come on, Rachel. You've met my mother," he joked, sipping the remnants of his Starbucks coffee.

"I'm serious. Do you believe in curses, like the Kennedy curse or the Rockefeller curse?"

"Are the Rockefellers cursed?"

I shrugged, aggravated that he was missing the point again. "Just something I heard. So you admit that you believe the Kennedy family is cursed?"

He snorted at the idea. "I didn't say that. I mean, they've had an unusual amount of bad luck. They might be cursed, if that's what you want to call it. I think it's just luck, though. Some families are luckier than others."

"What makes them lucky?"

"I don't know. It's too early in the morning for philosophical discussions, Rachel. You up for dinner tonight? I'm thinking deep-dish pizza from Mushrooms."

"I'm thinking of washing my hair." I opened the car door and grabbed my purse.

"Hey! Don't leave mad. What do you want me to say?" He got out of the car and leaned over the roof of his Volkswagen.

Chip had money. Not Ashland Stuart money, but he came from a wealthy family. He wasn't the handsomest guy on the block, but he wasn't bad-looking either. My biggest complaint was that he lacked imagination. I knew I shouldn't have hooked up with him the first time, let alone again. We were just too different.

"I'm not mad. I just can't make it tonight. I have some major studying to do, but I'll call you. Okay?"

He believed me. I could tell because he beamed from ear to ear. Boy, did he have large ears. *Come on, Rachel! Stop being so damn picky!* He tapped the top of his car happily and watched me unlock the office door before he drove away, completely oblivious to the fact that we were headed for another—permanent—breakup. I would have to deal with that later.

I flicked on the lights, tapped the security code on the alarm pad and made some coffee. CJ never drank coffee anymore, not since her pregnancy, so I made a half a pot. I was firmly committed to drinking every bit of it. I felt tired this morning. Not so much from Chip's snoring but from my constant work on this family tree project for Carrie Jo. I dropped my purse on my desk and went to the conference room, where I arranged the sheets of paper to show CJ my ridiculously detailed research. I looked at it again. Yep, I wasn't imagining things. An entire page of male ancestors dead between the ages of 30 and 40, and most on the lower end of that time frame. I felt a wave of clamminess hit me. *This can't be right*, I'd thought in the beginning. *This has to be some kind of weird coincidence.*

Then I began digging deeper, and that's when things got real hairy. The Stuarts were plagued by freak accidents. For example, one guy got hit by lightning while fishing; another was working on a car, and the dang thing fell on him. Too weird. Things were okay on his mother's side of the tree, but his father's was an entirely different story.

I knew Southern family trees often had tangled roots, but this was crazy. I had traced the Stuarts back to the Cottonwoods—but not Jeremiah Cottonwood. Ashland was related to Isaiah Cottonwood, Jeremiah's brother. In the words of my father, "That puts a whole 'nother spin on that, Sparky." Sparky. Who nicknamed their daughter Sparky? My brother Andy used to tease me and call me "Sparkly" just because he knew it ticked me off. I'd rain down curses on him for all the good it did. Nothing bad ever happened to him. I was lousy at cursing, and I sure as heck knew something about curses. My mother firmly believed in them, as did her sisters, and as a child I tossed salt over my shoulder, avoided crossing streams while wearing a skirt and never, ever stood on a stump—all activities that could have brought down the curses upon myself and my family. Publicly I scoffed at the idea of curses. I often agreed with my childhood friends—curses were superstitious nonsense for scaredy-cats— but after they went home, I crossed my fingers, said the prayers and did whatever it took to keep the curses away.

I knew that what I was looking at was nothing short of a curse. A straight-up curse. I had to tell Carrie Jo. And if she thought I was crazy, well, she wouldn't be the first friend of mine to think so.

"Good morning, Rachel!" she called from the front door. "Coffee smells great! Have a cup for me."

"I will! You need anything?" I called back, delaying a face-to-face meeting for a few more seconds.

"Nope. I'm peachy keen," she said as she poked her head in the doorway. "Oh, cool. Let me go drop this stuff on my desk, and I'll be right back." As she turned to walk away, she groaned and froze, reaching for the doorframe.

"What is it? You okay?" I sprang to my feet, nearly sloshing hot coffee on my starched white blouse.

Her face was pale, which wasn't like CJ at all. All throughout her pregnancy she had amazing skin. Before that she had a nice warm-looking tan. At the moment she appeared near death. "You don't look so hot, girl. Can you walk? I think you should sit down."

"I think you're right," she gasped, holding on to the door like a wavering drunk. Finally, whatever pain had hit her subsided. "Okay, I think I can move now. Darn! My side is killing me."

"You have to go to the doctor, Carrie Jo. You could be in labor."

"Can't be. This pain is in my side. I thought labor pains were in the back or the front."

"I'm not a baby expert, but if I had pain anywhere and I was pregnant, I'd be on my way to the OB-GYN. Can I at least call Ashland?"

"No. Please don't do that. Let's just keep an eye on it. See? It's easing up now." I gave her a disapproving look, and she added, "I'll call my doctor in a few minutes. Promise."

I watched her as she sat at the desk and the color finally returned to her face. "Wow, that was a sharp one. I wonder if I pulled something."

"What have you been doing?"

"Trying to tie my shoes," she said with a laugh. "I'm fine. Stop worrying about me. The pain is gone now. What did you want to show me? I'd be lying if I said I wasn't super-curious."

"I've got everything spread out in the conference room, but I can bring it in here if you like," I offered.

"No. I'm good." She cracked open a water bottle and smiled up at me. Carrie Jo had a beautiful face, a cleft chin, startling green eyes and naturally curly hair. She was a natural beauty, and I often wanted to ask her the brand of coral-colored lipstick she wore. It really played up her light olive skin. You could easily describe her as the girl next door, but she was also usually the funniest girl in the room. I both admired her and felt a bit envious. She'd had some amazing luck in life, including landing the chief historian job at Seven Sisters. Of course, her bestie had almost killed her, and quite a few of her friends had died. I suddenly felt ashamed for the envy.

"Great. Whenever you're ready, just come to the conference room."

"Okay, be there in a second."

After a few minutes she joined me and sat next to me, looking over the sheaves of paper. "Beautiful work, Rachel. How's it going in school? Ready to graduate?"

"Dear Lord, yes. Did you get the graduation invitation?"

"Yes! And if I'm not having a baby, I'll be there." She laughed and made a face that let me know she was ready to get on with the whole childbirth experience. I didn't blame her. She was all baby now. Her arms and legs were much thinner than before, and it seemed like the baby was stealing all her nutrients. But then again, what did I know?

With a smile I handed her the first piece of paper. I used the Alari software to create the family tree. I thought it would be easy enough, but filling in the slots on the electronic tree had been anything but. Alari verified each entry, and when it couldn't find source records it forced the user to provide verification via GEDCOM, Rootsweb or one of the dozens of other genealogical sites. I sat beside her and allowed her to look through the papers before I spoke up.

"So this is the completed version. It took me about forty hours of research to find all the connections."

"Oh no. I had no idea I was asking you to work that many hours. I expect to compensate you, Rachel. This is wonderful work."

I shook my head. "No way. This is my baby gift. Remember? As you can see, Ashland comes from a long line of tangled relations." I smiled tentatively at her. Maybe I shouldn't tell her anything. She had enough going on now. What with the pain and the baby.

"Hey, what's the deal? Is this right?"

I peeked at the paper she was holding. It was the information about Isaiah Cottonwood and his connection to Ashland. "Yep, it's right."

"So Ashland is not a direct descendant of Jeremiah Cottonwood? I can't say I'm disappointed. I've never heard of Isaiah. Or maybe I have, but I just don't remember him."

"He never came up in our previous research, Carrie Jo. Funny thing is, Ashland is both a direct descendant of the Cottonwoods and a cousin to the Beaumonts. See here? In 1870, Dara Beaumont married this guy, and that's the cousin. Not unusual when families stick close to home. Apparently in this family group, people kind of hung around and didn't move away when they got older. Except Calpurnia, but she didn't have much choice. See?" I pointed to another section of the genealogy.

"I wonder what this will mean for his estate."

"I'm not sure, CJ."

"Here's something even more surprising. There is a codicil to Jeremiah's will."

"Yes, I heard about that."

"You knew?" I asked, surprised.

Her cheeks went pink. "Not until recently."

"Here is a copy of it that I made from the archives downtown. It clearly transfers all property rights to Isaiah. Jeremiah must have been quite a jerk. This codicil was created just a month before he died, and with it he basically took the family fortune away from his daughters and his in-laws and gave it to his brother. Which sucks since most of the money probably belonged to the Beaumonts originally."

"That does suck," Carrie Jo added, still staring at the pages. I promised myself I wouldn't say a word unless she did. The idea of talking about a curse seemed ridiculous to me now. Except for the evidence. I handed her a copy of the spreadsheet that displayed the birth dates, death dates and ages of the deceased. Maybe she would notice it herself. She said, "Good work, Rachel." She scanned the printed sheet down to the bottom.

Carrie Jo stared at Ashland's name for a second and then scanned back up. She saw it too! With wide eyes she looked at me. "And you are sure about these ages?"

"I doubled-checked everything, CJ. It's all accurate. I even had Chip look at it with me. You know he's got a photographic memory."

Carrie Jo didn't say much but kept staring at the page. "Why so young? I mean, I know people back then didn't live as long as we do, but 35 seems very young to die. And it's men only? How many generations does this phenomenon go back?"

"Near as I can tell, right around the time of the codicil. Isaiah's sons, Jacob and Christian, died at age 31 and 34, respectively, but his two daughters both lived into their sixties. Next generation, these three men, all dead before 35. And it goes on until today."

"And Ashland is about to have a birthday." I could hear the fear in her voice.

"I'm sure it's nothing, Carrie Jo. I mean, I noticed it too, but what could it mean? The Cottonwood line has had some bad luck, but a lot of families experience tragedy. Try not to worry about this." I regretted pointing this out; the look on her face said it all. "Don't obsess over this stuff. It's nothing to worry about." *Or nothing you can do anything about, anyway.*

She didn't look at me but kept staring at the papers. She pulled her phone out of her purse. "Maybe not, but I know someone who can tell me what I'm looking at—I hope." I watched her dial the number, and my heart beat faster. "Hey, Henri? You got a minute? I'd like to come see you. I need your opinion on something. Sure, I can be there in a few minutes. Yes, breakfast sounds great. No, Ashland isn't with me. Just Rachel. Great. We'll be there in 15."

She put the phone down and stared at the papers again. I was dying to ask so I did, "How can Henri help?"

"He's a bit of a spiritualist. He knows a thing or two about supernatural subjects. You up for some pancakes? He's got extra."

Happy to finally be included in something beyond answering phones and creating reports, I nodded with a smile.

"Grab your purse and let's go. We need to bring these papers too."

"I've got these. You get your purse. I'll drive, CJ."

"I'll let you." As I slid the papers into the envelope, a shadow crossed the window outside. The sky suddenly seemed darker. Was there a storm brewing? This changeable weather was one of the things I disliked the most about Mobile. You could be lying out in the sun in the backyard one minute and getting drenched the next. A flash of lightning popped across the distant sky. It came from the direction of the harbor.

Yep. There was definitely a storm brewing.

But what kind?

Chapter 4—Carrie Jo

The two of us didn't talk much as we drove to Henri's. I could tell Rachel wanted to say something to comfort me, but what could she say? Suddenly everything I'd been through the past few days made sense. The arguments, the bad luck, the feeling of oppression. Sounded like a curse to me, but I was no expert.

Henri now lived in the apartment over Detra Ann's antiques store, but honestly that wasn't much of a move. Cotton City Treasures was only two streets over from his old digs. And it wasn't a permanent move, now that they were getting married. I loved his apartment, though. It was in an old building with fabulous gargoyles perched at the corners of the roof. A rarity in Mobile. There weren't many such objects in the downtown area. There was an interesting pyramid building with two sphinxes at the door. Some kind of Masonic lodge, probably. I'd never asked about it, but it was on my to-do list. If I ever had the time.

And if I could ever get the supernatural stuff cleared away. Between the ghosts, the dreams and the specter of Death, I'd been a little busy. Now I suspected that something else hung over us, over Ashland and our child. Maybe that was why I had been so resistant to the idea of having a son. Did I somehow psychically know that the Cottonwood boys were cursed? I needed to show the evidence to Henri and let him tell me what he thought. He came from a family who understood curses and hexes, as he had related to us many times.

I did the math while Rachel drove. Two men in that generation, then three, then two, then four more. I couldn't remember the second page, but I would never forget seeing Ashland's name at the bottom. No way could I tell him about this.

"Oh my God!" I said as a flock of crows hovered in front of our car. They hung in the air for a moment, then flapped their wings and flew away. "Holy smokes! What was that about?"

"I...have...no...idea," Rachel said slowly. She was gripping the steering wheel so tightly her knuckles were white.

We pulled in front of the antiques store, and I waved at Detra Ann as I got out of the car. I looked over my shoulder to make sure the evil birds weren't stalking me. She waved back but didn't stop to chat. An excited customer was purchasing a blue and white tray and asking the pretty ponytailed blonde a bunch of questions about other items in the shop. I pointed to the stairs, and she nodded at me as the breathless patron kept up with her queries.

I didn't know how Detra Ann worked with the public, but she loved it. It took someone special to take a public relations degree and use that to run an antiques shop. One of the things I loved about her new business was that every item came with a story. Not just word of mouth, either. No,

Detra Ann had hidden talents. She wrote what she knew about each item and made sure the new owner got a copy of her story. The community and its visitors loved her place. *It's like she was born for this.*

We walked up the narrow stairs to the apartment and opened the glass door that led to Henri's loft. After Lenore died, he had sold his house and moved in here instead. I didn't blame him. It was a gorgeous open space with warm painted walls and to-die-for fixtures and extras.

"So what's up, ladies?" Henri tossed off his apron, which read: *Boo-yah.* "Who wants some pancakes? I made enough for a small army—I had a feeling I'd have guests this morning." He rubbed his hands together as he served us with gusto. He was obviously proud of both his premonition and his pancakes. I took a bite. He had reason to be.

"I'll take a few of these. As always, it smells like heaven in here."

"You want the syrup warmed?"

"Whatever is easiest, Henri. Thanks for this." Rachel blushed as he handed her a plate of hot pancakes. I smiled a bit. I never knew Rachel had a crush on Henri, but then again I had been kind of self-involved for the past few months. I knew she liked Detra Ann, though, so I didn't worry about any shenanigans there.

After he poured the juice and set everything on the table, I handed him the stack of papers. "Take a look at this and let me know what you think."

With a curious look he accepted the envelope and put on a pair of gold-rimmed glasses.

"Glasses, huh?"

"No jokes, CJ. My eyes may be old, but I'm not."

I chuckled and covered my mouth with my hand as I chewed a delicious bite of pancake. I was hungrier than I thought. And to think, I'd walked away from Doreen's omelet this morning. But then again, our housekeeper's cooking didn't stack up against Henri's. I'd often told him he needed to open a restaurant. So far, I hadn't convinced him.

"Okay, what am I looking at?" He stared at the papers and looked up at the light. "Did it just get dark outside? The news didn't say anything about bad weather this morning. That storm is way off the coast." He hopped up and flipped the light switch, and the beautiful fleur-de-lis embellished chandelier filled the dining room with warm light.

"What storm?" Rachel asked.

"Looks like we have a late tropical storm brewing off the coast, but it's pretty far away." He went to the window and looked outside. It had gotten dark quickly, first at the office and now here. As the old folks used to say, it "looked like the bottom would fall out of the sky" any minute.

I loved Henri's place. It had so much New Orleans flair; cool photos from his time there covered the living room walls. A collection of fleur-de-lis candle holders rested on a side table. One of the walls in the living room was painted a dark red, and an elegant gold-rimmed mirror hung in the center of it.

He slid the papers out of the envelope and shuffled through them quickly before he began intently studying them. He didn't ask me what to look for, and I could tell when he spotted it. "So he has a birthday in about a month?"

I nodded, wiping my mouth with the linen napkin and pushing the plate to the side. It was wonderful, but I'd lost my appetite again. "Do you think it's possible that we—that we're..."

"Cursed?" Rachel answered for me.

"Yeah, what she said." If I didn't say the word, then we wouldn't be, right?

"Let's look at the facts, and then we'll look at the rest. According to this, every man in Ashland's family tree—in this particular line of ancestors, anyway—has died at an early age. From these notations about the causes of death, it looks like a string of accidents."

"Some. I can't be sure about a few of the others, so I left question marks beside their names. Even if you assumed that those men died of natural causes, that's still a lot of early deaths." Rachel added in a serious voice, "Men usually died around age 55 to 60 during the early to mid-1800s. There's definitely a trend of men dying young in that particular family."

"No doubt there is. How old is Ashland now?"

"He'll be thirty. We've joked about the baby coming on his birthday. And that's another thing—what about the baby? What if I have a boy? What will that mean?"

"Hold up, let's not jump to any conclusions." Just then a bolt of lightning cracked through the sky and illuminated our faces in blue light. I winced at the closeness of it. The lights flickered, but the power didn't go out. I heard the shop door ring downstairs; we'd left Henri's door ajar on accident. I heard footsteps coming up the stairs. Feeling creeped out about curses, I turned to look and was relieved to see it was Detra Ann.

You are being ridiculous, CJ. All the ghosts have settled down. You're just looking for trouble. If you're not careful, you'll find it.

Detra Ann slid her arms around my neck and hugged me. I needed all the hugs I could get right now. I squeezed her back, and she grabbed a plate. "I'm stealing some breakfast, but help me keep an ear out for customers. I've got the buzzer set. It sure got dark outside, didn't it? I might have to bring my antiques table inside, Henri. I think it's going to flood any minute. What are y'all up to?"

It was just like Detra Ann to talk in a constant stream of consciousness. She plopped down in the empty chair with her plate and dug into the pancakes.

"We've found something weird. It has to do with Ashland. Have you ever heard about a, well, I guess the thing you could call it is a..." Why was this so difficult to say?

"A curse, she's talking about a curse." Henri filled in the blank this time.

"What kind of curse? Like a hex or something?"

"No. More like a family curse," Rachel said. "All of Ashland's male relatives from the Cottonwood line died early deaths. We're just concerned about him since his birthday is around the corner."

"So you think Ashland is cursed? What would make you say that?" She put her fork down and stared at the three of us.

Henri handed her the family tree, and as she flipped through it he questioned me, "What's been going on? He mentioned he's had some legal troubles recently. What else is happening?"

"I don't know. What am I supposed to be looking for?"

Rachel raised her hand. "Um, I can answer that. The women in my family are experts on curses."

"Oh, so like they're witches?" Detra Ann asked innocently between drinking orange juice and nibbling on her pancakes.

"Lord, don't tell them that. No, they aren't witches at all. They're just very superstitious. My mother and her four sisters break curses all the time. They can spot them a mile away too." She snapped her fingers. "I am sure they would be able to tell if you or Mr. Stuart had one!"

"Whoa, let's not get ahead of ourselves here. We don't know if he's—if we're..."

"Cursed?" Detra Ann finished for me.

"Well if you believe in curses—and I've always been taught that you have to believe in them for them to work—a number of things can cause them," Henri began to explain.

"Not to contradict my elders," Rachel said with a smile, "but that's not entirely true."

Henri leaned back in his chair and drank his coffee as another pop of lightning came close to the shop. "What can you tell us about curses, Rachel?"

"Well, they manifest differently, and they can fall on individuals and families gradually. The way I understand it, curses work the opposite of a blessing. You know, when you say a blessing over food or you bless someone for some special reason?"

"Or say, 'Bless her heart'?" Detra Ann joked, obviously trying to lighten the mood.

"Not quite like that, no. Bad stuff happens to people all the time, but when it hits you nonstop it might just be a curse. A curse is basically negative energy that gets bound to a person for some supernatural reason. For example, in our family, we believe that if you steal, you've put yourself under a curse. Negative acts bring curses. Sometimes someone can send a curse to you, but you would have to do them wrong in a major way for them to be able to curse an entire family for generations. I'm talking about a serious curse here."

"What other evidence do you have to support the idea that Ashland might be cursed?" I could tell by her tone that Detra Ann wasn't convinced, and I was glad for that. I still couldn't even say the word.

"You know what? We have had some issues lately. He's had lawsuit after lawsuit, things keep breaking around the house, we argue all the time. It's like we're in this funk and can't get out of it."

Nobody spoke for a minute, and then Henri asked, "What about animals? Any weird encounters?"

"On the way here, a flock of crows nearly caused us to have an accident." Rachel's voice sounded even quieter now, and I shivered when I saw her spill salt in her hand and toss it over her shoulder.

I cleared my throat and made a confession. "That's not all. Some stray cat on our street lured our puppy into the road, and he got hit by a car. He died." I chewed on my lip for a second while my friends stared at me wide-eyed. "Also, things keep coming up missing, like we've got a thieving gremlin in the house. I just chalked it up to me being absentminded because of the pregnancy, but I'm thinking it's something else now. Can this be possible? I mean, everyone here knows that the supernatural world exists, but this kind of thing...a..."

"Curse, Carrie Jo. It's a curse. Saying it won't make you more cursed, I promise." Rachel patted my hand.

"Yeah, well, curses. That's a whole other ballgame. This can't be right."

"But that's the thing about a curse. It's not in your face. It's sneaky. Most people don't even seem to notice they are under one."

"I agree with Rachel. If we can do something to prevent it, break it, we should. If his birthday goes by and nothing happens, then we know we're good."

"Until next year," Rachel mumbled.

"So I'll just stress out for the next ten years every time he has a birthday? No. If Ashland is cursed, I want to break it, right now—today! It's not just Ashland. It's the baby too, if we're having a boy. And there's another thing."

I turned to Henri, who watched me intently with his warm dark eyes. "I saw Lenore, Henri. She was speaking, trying so hard to tell me something, but I couldn't understand her. It was a word."

"If Lenore is involved, then the chances that something is wrong have increased dramatically. She would want to help, no matter where she was. No clue at all what she was trying to say?"

I took a sip of milk and shook my head. "I had a dream and was about to wake up. That's when she came, at that in-between place. I can't explain it any better than that. I could see her pretty clearly, but it sounded like she was trying to talk underwater. Then she was gone and I was awake. It was so fast I couldn't work out what she said."

Detra Ann reached across the table and grabbed my hand. "Hey. We're with you. We all love you and Ashland. If there's a curse, we'll figure out how to break it. But...I have to say this. I think it's a good idea to keep this to ourselves for now. No need to freak him out. We all know how much he hates this kind of stuff. You said yourself, he's been under quite a bit of stress recently."

Rachel's forehead wrinkled with concern. "What? If I was cursed, I would want to know it. I know I'm not as close to Ashland as you guys are, but I wish you'd reconsider that."

I looked from one face to the other, not sure what to say. "I think Detra Ann is right. For now—just for now, Rachel—we don't say anything to Ash. But didn't you say that for a generational curse to work it had to be sent by someone who was done wrong in a big way?"

"Yes, that's what I understand. Let me check with my mom, though. Like I said, she and my aunts are the expert on curses."

Henri put the papers back in the envelope and handed them to me. "While she does that, I'll check with a friend in New Orleans. He's a pastor there. Whenever I need prayer, he's the guy I call on. Let's get him praying over this situation. Maybe he can get some spiritual insight into what we're dealing with. I think the big question is who put this curse on Ashland's ancestors, and how do we break it? It's going to be difficult to make things right if the curser has been dead for over a hundred years."

For some reason I just had to laugh. Like the old-timers said, "You either laugh or cry." Everyone looked at me like I was sure-enough, put-her-in-the-loony-bin crazy. "I don't mean to laugh. I swear. It's just what you said." I stifled more laughter. "About the curser being dead. I mean, these Cottonwoods and Beaumonts don't die. I don't know why you're worried about that." Then the tears came, and Detra Ann put her arms around me. I cried on her shoulder, feeling more tired than I had ever felt in my life.

She whispered kindly to me, "It's going to be fine, CJ. I promise you, I'll stick close to Ashland. He'll think we're joined at the hip. Maybe I'll start by meeting him for lunch today. Keep an eye on him. I can call Cathy in to work the shop for me."

I gave a sigh of relief. Not because I had all the answers. Quite the opposite. I had a bunch of questions. But at least I had my friends. We had friends.

"That leaves me. I'll do the one thing I know I can do." My friends knew what I meant. I'd be dreaming, but with a purpose this time. It had been a while since I pursued the past through the dream world. I'd had plenty of dreams, but those came naturally and were less taxing than dreaming with a purpose. I didn't mention what I had seen about Olivia and Isla. That might not be relevant...oh, who was I kidding? I was pretty sure the evil blonde cherub would be involved somehow. But why bring up Isla to Detra Ann? The dead girl had tried to kill her!

It was always risky going back to Seven Sisters, but now that the spirits had settled down, I was sure it wouldn't be so dangerous.

I hoped.

Chapter 5—Karah

Sitting on the worn blue quilt, I shook my blue silk purse and listened to the sound of the last of my coins. Hoping it was more than it sounded, I loosened the cord and dumped the coins on the bed. This wasn't enough to make it through the week, much less another month in Mobile. Out of sheer embarrassment I had refused to stay with Delilah, but my pride had cost me. I was no charity case, and I refused to allow Jackson to cover the expense of my continued stay here at the boarding house. I had to make plans for my future, but the truth was I had nowhere to go. Mother had sold our home in Virginia, and God only knew what she did with the money. Docie probably knew, but she would never tell me. She was always Mother's creature, although I suspected she had abandoned her and taken Mother's meager supply with her.

This trip had cost me all my savings, but it cost me even more than that. I had been spent emotionally in ways I had not expected. Why had I come to Mobile? Why had I trusted Mother? The small stipend she gave me had long since disappeared, and I had no other means of support. When Mother sent me to Seven Sisters, she assured me that all would be well. Ah, she excelled at lying, and I excelled at believing her. But no more.

She had made claiming my inheritance sound like a mere formality. She had assured me that my father had made provision for me and that local society would not question my parentage. "They will see your beauty and know right away that you are a Cottonwood. No, *the* Cottonwood." But society had not accepted me at all, and neither had my father's family; none had accepted my invitations to visit me at Seven Sisters. I had received a few letters from an uncle I did not know, but I had not been allowed to read them. Docie snatched them up and kept them secreted away until Mother arrived.

"You let your mother deal with this man," she warned me as tersely as possible.

All I had to do was wait for her, care for the house and most importantly of all—find the Beaumont treasure.

But she had been wrong, and no treasure had yet been found. Jackson informed me that the will was very specific and that I needed proof that I was who I claimed to be. I had no proof, only the word of my mother. I wrote her and informed her of the many challenges I faced in Mobile. She wrote me back, but it was only one line:

I will succeed. I am on the way.

I received no more letters, but a short time later Docie returned. She had hard eyes and a cruel grip, which she did not mind applying to my young wrists. Easy enough to hide the bruises. "Wear gloves, Karah," my mother would tell me. She did not care one whit what Docie did to me.

It wasn't until I was almost ten that I understood that Mother went mad sometimes. During those dark times I would be sent away to a nearby girls' home until she recovered. I had a few happy times, though. Especially when Captain Garrett came to us. He insisted that I call him Uncle David, which I liked. I much preferred pretending he was my father, but from my earliest age Mother made sure I knew he was not.

"You are a Cottonwood, my dove. That is much better than being a Garrett." I hated seeing the hurt on the captain's face, but I did not dare argue with her. How I missed the captain! He brought joy into my dim life for a time, and when he left us for good, darkness descended.

I had heard it said that Mother had been a great actress in her prime, but she did not speak of it much anymore. How I loved seeing her standing in the spotlight, although I had to witness her performances in secret. "Theaters are for mature minds," she would say before she stepped into the carriage and disappeared into the night with a wave or a scowl. Thankfully Docie would leave with her and I would be alone.

Occasionally, I would steal into Mother's rooms for a while and read her plays. If the trunks were left open, and they rarely were, I would grab a gown and hold it up to my small body pretending that I was my beautiful mother. Of course I had to be careful to put the dresses back the way I found them.

Once, while we traveled through Virginia, I did sneak into a theater to see her. It wasn't hard to do. We traveled with a company of actors through a string of Virginia cities, and the hotels were often very near the theaters. I crept out at quite a few of them; often I pretended that I had to deliver something to Isla Garrett, as she sometimes called herself. The usher let me pass, but I never made it to the dressing room. I hung back in the shadows of the stage and chewed on my fingernail or a stolen apple as I waited for the play to begin. It was like watching someone I did not know. She wholly transformed herself each night and became whomever she pretended to be. I could not believe this breathtaking, living doll was my own mother. She was a magical creature full of light and laughter. It was almost as if she could change her features, her voice, her body shape. She could have played Hamlet himself if she had taken a mind to.

That seemed a hundred years ago; now she sat in a mental asylum awaiting trial for attempted murder. I could hardly believe it!

The weeks went by and shamefully I had not seen her once. How could I, after what she tried to do? That did not stop Docie from coming to see me. She demanded that I attend my mother, defend her, help her in some way. I refused. I did not know the devil she had become.

But I had found a friend in Adam Iverson. One early evening, when I ventured out long enough to find needed toiletries, I ran into him on the sidewalk outside the boarding house. He was kind to me and offered to help me with my packages. I refused, of course, but he begged to take me to dinner. Overwhelmed with loneliness I accompanied him to a small dining room on the outskirts of town. He was flirtatious, as he had always been, but not too inappropriate. The following day he left a bouquet of flowers for me at the front desk, and I had spent much time with him since that first dinner. I had other visitors too. Jackson came a few times. He carefully let me know that it was Delilah who sent him. It was clear to me that she was the object of his true affection. I cared not, for I had my eye on Adam. He was strong, clever with his ideas and amiable enough. At least for a little while.

But I did miss Delilah, and I was happy to hear that she got stronger every day. The slice on her leg had become infected, but she had recovered and was apparently anxious to see me. I couldn't face her either. I made my apologies to the attorney and promised I would visit my cousin soon. I did not bother to inquire about my own legal status. How could I make a claim now when my only true witness to my parentage had gone mad?

Imagine my surprise when Stokes showed up at my door. My mother had been released and was residing again at Seven Sisters, he told me in his loud, deep voice. Not only that, but a relative of mine, a Mrs. Torrence, requested my presence at the house. I considered calling Mr. Keene, as he had been gone only a few minutes, but I felt better about making this trip by myself. I left a message for Adam with Mrs. Shields, my landlady. I asked him to wait for my return at his shop. I would come see him soon. How could I involve any more innocent people in what could only be considered my family's madness?

Curious now, I collected my purse and followed Stokes to the carriage that would take me to the grand old house. Of course I knew the name, Olivia Torrence. She was Isla's mother and my grandmother, but I had no knowledge of her involvement in our lives at any point up until now, and so naturally I was suspicious of her. If I learned anything from my mother, it was to be suspicious and to question the motives of everyone around me. Especially my mother's.

As the carriage pulled into the long driveway of Seven Sisters, I did not experience the wonder and happiness that I had the first time I made this journey. The white columns used to rise up like a welcoming temple in the promised land. Now the massive home seemed more like a mausoleum, for there was no one about. A massive mausoleum full of secrets and lies. There were only a few lights burning in the windows this evening. The dim light added to the solemnity I already felt. Whatever could Mrs. Torrence want with me? She had cast off my mother as a child; I could not hope for better, could I? Then the likely truth occurred to me: she wanted what all Beaumonts wanted—the return of their fortune. Like my mother, Mrs. Torrence pinned all her hopes on me to be the one who brought her the reward. I would disappoint her too because I knew nothing at all and had found nothing at all. Whatever treasure had been there, it was long gone now. Or hidden so carefully in the house or grounds that it would take ten lifetimes to recover it.

To continue to seek it would be madness.

I made my way into the house cautiously, as if someone or something would jump out at me any moment. I fully understood the phrase "on pins and needles" as I made my way from the open foyer to the ladies' parlor. The first thing I saw was the pale face of my mother as she sailed toward me with a smile.

"Mother? Why are you here?"

Ignoring my question, she said gaily, "Here is my lovely daughter, Aunt."

I raised my eyebrows at both her greeting and her address of "Aunt." I had always thought Olivia to be my grandmother, not my great-aunt. While my mother was animated and showering me with forced affection, the older woman hardly moved. She sat like a thin, tall statue in the largest chair in the ladies' parlor.

"Karah, this is your aunt and mine, Olivia Torrence."

"How did you get out, Mother? I thought you were to stand trial for what you did to us?" I didn't bother with the formalities. We were not a formal family.

"Yes, and little you did to help me! Imagine not helping your mother when she needed you the most! I sat in that jail with all those other women! No family. No friends. Barely any food at all. Do you know what I went through? The guards mistreated me—of course, men only want one thing. That's all they think about. Like your father! You ungrateful—"

Mrs. Torrence exclaimed, "Isla! That is enough! Sit down before I have Stokes tie you to a chair and gag you. You will contain yourself, or you can return to Holy Angels Sanitarium. Now, Miss Cottonwood, please have a seat here at the table."

I cast an angry look at my mother but took the seat across from her. How different the two women were in spirit, though they were very much alike in physical appearance. Olivia stood a near head taller than Mother. That I could tell even though she had not yet stood. They had similar etched features, like two lovely porcelain dolls, but they were made of ice, not porcelain. Olivia dressed more demurely than Isla, but she was older. Old enough to be Isla's mother. I wondered again how this family tree ran.

"You must have many questions for me, and I certainly have some for you."

I nodded but kept my mouth shut. It seemed better to collect information than share it, and I could do that only if I kept quiet. "Are you the daughter of Jeremiah Cottonwood?" Olivia asked.

"I have been told all my life that I am." I held my head high and stared daggers at my mother.

"You have the look of the Cottonwoods. The wide mouth, the colorful cheeks. I would say that you could be."

"She most certainly is! Even Jeremiah acknowledged her."

"Yes, but the courts haven't, have they? And your recent performance makes it less likely that they will. However, all is not lost yet."

"Truly? Tell us, Aunt. What do you have planned?" Isla smiled broadly as if she had been given a long-awaited gift.

"I do not need your help in establishing Karah. You leave that to me."

"She is my daughter!"

"Unfortunately for her. But she is not yours to worry over anymore, Isla. She is my ward and in my care until she is established. The only thing you can bring her is shame and notoriety. Imagine working as an actress! What were you thinking?"

Isla stood up and slung the chair back. It made a scraping sound as it slid across the floor. "I did what I had to do! You cannot keep me from my only child."

Without standing or arguing, Aunt Olivia rang the bell beside her. Stokes came immediately. "Please escort my niece to her room and make sure she stays there until I summon her," Aunt Olivia said coolly.

"You cannot imprison me, Olivia! I will not have it."

"You have nothing to say about it. Now go peaceably, or Stokes can pick you up and carry you. Whichever you prefer." With an angry scowl, Isla did as she was told. It was likely the first time in her life she had obeyed anyone. It was certainly the first time I had ever witnessed such a thing. Even Uncle David had not been able to command such obedience. I immediately feared and liked my great-aunt.

"Will you imprison me as well?"

Olivia poured me a cup of tea and slid it to me. "Come. Let us put the knives away. As the daughter of a madwoman, you will appreciate the honest truth."

I sipped my tea nervously and said, "If you knew she was mad, why did you leave me with her? Why have I never met you, Aunt Olivia?"

She toyed with a sugar cube as if she weren't sure what to say to me. With slender fingers she tossed the cube into the lukewarm tea and stirred it with a golden spoon. "She was Louis' daughter. Who was I to interfere? If he wanted to leave her in a girls' home or send her overseas, I had nothing to do with it. If it pleased him to tell everyone that she was my bastard daughter, then that was fine too. Nobody who knew me believed his stories. Louis was one to tell tales. He and Christine were both such dreamers. I was the practical one. I married a practical man and have lived a very respectable life, all told. It wasn't until I learned what Louis had done with our fortunes that I decided I must do something."

"I see. You gave no thought for me at all until your fortune became involved..."

"This will be the last time I remind you, put the knives away, girl. You are no match for me, and I will not be swayed by your insults. Do nothing foolish; I am the only one who can help you."

"Really? You want to help me now?" I swallowed the anger and resentment that began to brew within me. "How do you propose to do that?"

She leaned back in her chair and closed her eyes for a moment. I watched and waited to see what would happen next.

"When I met my husband, Louis practically disowned me. If it weren't for our mother, God rest her soul, I am sure he would have. You see, he was the son, the heir to all our fortunes, but he was not a wise man. He arranged for Christine to marry Jeremiah, knowing full well that she loved another."

"The doctor?"

"I see you know your family history. Yes, the doctor." She opened her eyes and smiled, but not at me. She was thinking about something. "Louis loved Christine and me, but he was easily influenced. He wouldn't think twice if he needed to use you for something. And as we all loved him so much, we tolerated him."

"Why are you telling me this?" I asked her.

She seemed not to hear me. She stood, walked to the French door and stared out of it. "He cared for Jeremiah, in his way, but he did not love him the way Jeremiah wanted him to. So he gave Jeremiah the next best thing. He gave him Christine. I told our mother all about it. I begged her to stop the marriage, to save Christine, but she believed Louis. Louis thought it would be a good match. The two most powerful houses together, joining their bloodlines and their wealth to establish a dynasty. He had such dreams and hopes."

"But Jeremiah didn't love Christine. He loved Louis. He treated her badly and swore at her in my presence. My own husband tried to stop the marriage, but to no avail. I knew nothing but disaster would come of it." She sat down again. Sitting up straight, her arms on the armrests, she looked like a beautiful queen, a tired old queen reflecting on her life on the last day of it. "Then the gossipers came. Jeremiah was burning through the money. He made poor investments, spent money on new slaves, the kind he liked, and God knows what else. He was a devil of a man.

"At that time, I went to Isaiah, Jeremiah's brother, and pleaded with him to intercede. I told him about the love his brother had for Louis. I told him Jeremiah would ruin us both, but he laughed in my face. He told me to stop interfering in my sister's marriage. If she wasn't complaining, who was I to do so? I almost believed him, but I went to Christine. She confessed to me her love for Hoyt Page. What could I do? Mother died, and there was no one left who could influence Louis to do what was right. Soon he began traveling to New Orleans, and for a time, I thought he fell in love. Unfortunately, she was a whore. Imagine how I greeted her when he brought her to our family home. I turned her out before she could put her feet up. How he hated me for that!"

She sighed sadly and straightened her dress. "After that, he had nothing for me. No more brotherly love. We were estranged. I stayed out of his business and tried my best to salvage whatever was left of the family fortune. Then your mother came here. She made things worse. She got pregnant with you and complicated things even more. Somewhere, she says, there is a codicil that names you as sole heir to Seven Sisters and the other Cottonwood properties. Without it, everything will go to Isaiah, Jeremiah's hateful brother. Now my sister is dead, my brother is dead, and I am left to clean this mess up! How cruel fate can be!"

She slammed her fists down on the table, causing the candles to flicker in their heavy brass holders. It was the most emotional thing I had seen her do.

"Fortunately, niece, my husband has a great amount of influence in the government of Alabama. One stroke of his pen, and he can make you legitimate. You will inherit Seven Sisters, as the late Mr. Cottonwood wished. You will have your own money, so you can live comfortably. And best of all, your mother will not be around to steal it from you. I plan on taking her back to north Alabama when I leave, provided you agree to my terms."

My mind swam at what she offered me. I would be legitimate—at least legally. I could be free from my mother's shadow and her ever-reaching hands. I knew there must be a catch.

"Why would you do this for me? I know there is a reason. Please do me the courtesy of telling me what that reason is, madam. I deserve to know the truth."

"You will allow my investigators to locate my missing property. If they are unable to do so, you will sell whatever lands and assets you possess to provide me with the return of the Beaumont money. Minus this house, of course. I would not dream of claiming your family home. And one last thing. You will testify against Miss Page and refuse to recognize her as your relative. Neither she nor her sister, if she should reappear later, will have any claim on this place or the Beaumont fortune."

I shot to my feet, boiling with anger. How dare she demand anything at all! Of all my so-called family, only Delilah had been kind to me. In fact, she loved me. That much I knew, even though I had not been as kind to her recently. I felt even more ashamed that I had not seen her or spoken to her in weeks. "You cannot demand such a thing. Why would I renounce the only family I have for your gain? You ask too much. I am nothing without loyalty."

Olivia rose to her feet, but her voice stayed calm and cool. "If you want my assistance, those are the terms. I have everything I need with me. We can visit the courthouse to see the judge whenever you like. Think what this could mean for you, girl. Think about yourself for a change. I will give you a day to think about it. If you refuse, then you will never see me again. And you will have no one to support you."

How was it that I could be denied love so frequently? Was I not worthy of love? I had not chosen to be born, and I had not chosen my parents. Yet, everyone rejected me again and again. Except Delilah. She alone had accepted me. Without her, I would have no family at all. I had not wanted this fortune, and I was not willing to pay the price that my mother and aunt apparently were. Such beauty. Such cold hearts.

"I am glad to hear that you are taking my mother with you. I have long since known that she needed the care of someone skilled at managing her. I do hope you know what you are undertaking. As far as this house goes, I have no attachment to it. I do not care if you burn it to the ground. And as for my cousin, I will not deny her, either privately or publicly. She is the only family I have, and I will not disown her, even if it means I will be penniless. I would like to say it was pleasant to meet you, but it hasn't been. Good day to you, Aunt Olivia. You promised me I would not see you again—it is a promise I hope you keep." I swung my skirts out from under the table and walked toward the door.

"Where are you going? Do you intend to walk back to the boarding house? How long do you think you will live on the change you have in that purse? I suppose you could earn a living on your back. Maybe that is a talent your mother can teach you."

I did not take her baiting. I walked into the foyer and out of the house. I could hear my mother screaming upstairs and feel my great-aunt's cold eyes burning at my back. I kept walking. If I had to walk all night, I would.

I would never go back. Not now. Not ever.

Chapter 6—Carrie Jo

I woke myself with a scream of pain. The contraction was so powerful that it took my breath away. I had no doubt I was in labor. I had no time to dwell on what I had dreamed. No time to consider Olivia's threats or Karah's emotions. I reached out and suddenly remembered that Ashland wasn't there. He had left early this morning to secure the Happy Go Lucky. Against all odds, Tropical Storm Jasmine was growing and heading our way. Catching my breath, I reached for my cell phone as I tried to sit up. Sweat beaded on my forehead, and I gasped for air. Thankfully the pain eased and the muscles relaxed. I looked at my alarm clock, remembering somehow that I needed to time these contractions.

"You can't come now, baby. You have a few more weeks before you make your appearance. Stay inside where it's safe." My child did not respond as he usually did. He lay quiet and still. And that bothered me. "Hey! I know you hear me. Let Momma know you're okay." Still nothing. Not a kick. Not a punch. He—or she—was as still as...

No, I'm not going there. The baby is fine. I am fine. Everything is going to be okay. Tears of panic welled up in my eyes. Everything *would* be okay, wouldn't it? Only one way to find out. I was going to the hospital. I dressed as quickly as I could in a voluminous summer dress. As I slid it over my head, the next contraction hit me.

"Agh!" I doubled over and managed to ease myself back on the bed. I looked at the clock. Five minutes. These were really far apart. I was in the early stages of labor. I gasped and focused on breathing. I swore at myself for not taking those Lamaze classes when I had the chance. Ashland wanted to go, but I thought it was dopey. I just wanted to get through it with as much dignity as I could and have a healthy baby. Breathing as calmly as I could—*that's what you're supposed to do, right?*—I waited for the pain to ease. When it finally let up, I slid my feet into my sandals and grabbed my overnight bag and purse. By the time I made it to the bottom of the stairs, nearly five minutes had passed. I sat in the foyer chair and waited for the next contraction. I grasped the corner of the table as the pain hit me again. It seemed stronger this time. Oh God! Should I call an ambulance? It would take me at least ten minutes to get to the hospital. There was no way I could drive. Knowing that Ashland probably wouldn't have a signal out on the water, I called Detra Ann.

"Hey, girl!"

Breathing heavily, I said, "Girl, I need you to take me to the hospital."

"Oh my God! Where are you? Is it the baby?"

"Baby, yes. Home. Please come now." My breathing came quick, and I forgot again how I was supposed to breathe.

"I'm on the way now! Henri! Bring me the keys, babe! It's CJ..." She hung up the phone, and I didn't call her back. I scribbled a note for Doreen and left it on the foyer table where I hoped she would find it. I panted through the pain and waited patiently for Detra Ann to show up. When I heard the car screech into the driveway, I opened the door and stood leaning against the doorframe.

"Oh my God! Help me, Henri." She said slowly and loudly, "It's go-ing to be all right, Carrie Jo!"

The pain eased up a bit, and I growled at her. "I'm not deaf, Detra Ann. I'm having a baby."

She didn't seem to mind my snappiness. "I'm calling Ashland now."

"He's going to tie up the boat. He doesn't have a signal out there."

"I'm try-ing any-way, o-kay?"

"Fine!" I said as I rolled into the front seat. "I told you I'm not deaf!"

"Your seat belt!" She reached for me, and I swatted her hand away.

"Oh my God, Detra Ann. If you put that seat belt on me, I'll kill you." She danced around me and climbed in the back, ignoring my crabbiness like the true friend she was.

Henri put on his flashers and drove us to the hospital in record time. "You're right. No answer."

I didn't respond. I stared at my watch and waited for the contraction. I could feel it building, and I knew it would be a strong one. I suddenly prayed I didn't pee on myself. I had to go, and I didn't want to pee in Henri's car.

"This sucks so bad!" I yelled as I clutched the dashboard. We pulled into the ER driveway of Springhill Memorial, and Detra Ann bounced out of the car and inside to get a wheelchair.

A nurse chased her, and together the two women managed to get me into the chair. Henri yelled at us, "I'm going to the marina to get Ashland. I'll be back soon."

"Okay, thanks!" I yelled at him like I was crazy.

"Breathe, Carrie Jo, breathe. It's all right. You are going to be all right. Oh my gosh, I'm going to be an aunt."

"This your sister?" the nurse asked as she pushed me through the double doors.

"Yep," I lied. I knew they wouldn't have let her stay with me if I'd said no. She was like a sister to me. That had to count for something.

For the next fifteen minutes a swarm of nurses worked around me, hooking me up to intimidating machines that supposedly monitored the contractions and my heart rate. The on-call doctor was coming to check my dilation. When she arrived, I cried, "It's too soon. The baby isn't supposed to be here yet. And he's not moving. What's wrong?"

"It's okay. Babies sometimes get still before they are born. If he's in the birth canal, there isn't much room for him to move around. Let's just check." The doctor moved her stethoscope over my stomach and listened intently. As she moved the cold round piece over my stomach, my panic grew. Shouldn't she have found him by now?

"Ah, there he is. He's fine. You want to hear him?" I nodded and accepted the stethoscope. Yes, I could hear his heart beating strong and evenly. I knew he was a boy. I had known it all along. I didn't know why I'd tried to deny it. I tried not to think about what that might mean.

"Let's take a look now. See how far you have to go."

Detra Ann stood at the head of the bed holding my purse and my hand. I looked at her, and she smiled down at me like a cheerleader-angel.

"Hmm...not that far along after all. Only dilated two centimeters."

"That's bad, isn't it? Is the baby going to be okay?"

The doctor smiled patiently. "Yes, he is fine. Early labor happens to many women. Your doctor is on the way. We'll consult, but if the due date is three weeks away, then he'll probably want to stop those contractions for a while." She looked at her watch and said, "If your doctor isn't here within the next half hour, I'll write the order myself. Either way, you'll have to stay overnight so we can keep an eye on you and the baby. We don't need the baby to come today. He needs to wait a bit longer, if possible. Would you like something to help with the pain?"

"No, I think I'm okay for now. I'll wait."

"Okay. I'll be back soon. Hopefully with the orders for that drip. It will stop the contractions. Let the nurse know if you need anything."

She smiled at me and rearranged my blanket before leaving us alone.

Detra Ann put our bags on the nearby table and sat beside me. "Don't worry, CJ. It's going to be fine. You heard the doctor. This happens sometimes. I have seen it in my own family. My cousin Lanie came to the hospital four times before she actually had the baby. She just about wore us out."

"I don't mean to be an inconvenience to anyone."

"That's not what I meant. I hope you know that."

"I'm sorry to be such a jerk. I want the baby to stay where he is because I know he'll be safe in there. What happens when he comes out? What about this curse? I can't stop thinking about it."

"Well, you need to. That baby needs you to think happy thoughts. All right? I mean, think about this in the light of day. Are curses even real? What if it's all just a big coincidence and you're worried over nothing? Lots of people die young. It's not a reason to believe in curses. I think you should tell Ashland and let him worry about it."

"But you were the one who said we shouldn't tell him," I said, frowning at her as I prepared for the next contraction.

"Well, I know, but I changed my mind. If it's going to make you go into labor and make you sick, then you need to tell him."

"Carrie Jo?" I heard a voice call from the doorway.

"Yes?" I answered and froze. It was my mother. "Momma?"

"Yes, it's me. Your housekeeper told me where to find you. I hope it's okay that I came."

It wasn't, but I didn't want to argue with her. I was so shocked at seeing her that I didn't bother to introduce her. She wore a neat dress that came past her knees. To my surprise, it didn't have long sleeves and it wasn't black. It was cobalt blue and completely out of style; she probably bought it at one of her favorite secondhand stores. The dress had a conservative neckline and three-quarter sleeves. She wore cheap shoes and carried an even cheaper black purse. Deidre Jardine had once been a pretty woman; today she wore light pink lipstick and a bit of mascara, which made her look prettier than usual. How long had it been since I had seen her wear makeup? I thought it was against her religion. She had gotten ultra-religious about seven years ago and given up worldly things like makeup and jewelry. I was surprised to see she wore gold stud earrings, like the kind girls wore when they first got their ears pierced.

Before I could say anything else, a wave of pain hit me. I closed my eyes and focused on making it through the agonizing half minute. The machine beside me sputtered out paper and beeped. A nurse appeared and studied the paper. "That's a good one. If you decide you need pain medicine, just yell."

"Breathe, baby," my mother coached me patiently.

"Mom is here too? That's great. Between your sister and your mother, you will do just fine." Thankfully Deidre didn't make a fuss, but when I opened my eyes I could see her looking at Detra Ann questioningly. My friend shrugged and didn't say anything.

"What are you doing here, Momma?"

"Didn't you get my letter, Carrie Jo?"

"Yes, but I haven't had a chance to read it yet. I've been a bit busy."

"I see," she said sadly. "It's not important. What can I do for you?"

"You can tell me why you're here, Deidre." I said curtly. Detra Ann's eyes widened, but she kept her mouth shut.

"I wanted...I didn't know you were having a baby. Your housekeeper told me you were going to the hospital. I didn't mean to interfere. I'll go now." She sounded on the verge of tears. She picked up her purse and headed out the door.

As she disappeared, Detra Ann scowled at me. "I had no idea you could be so mean, CJ. I know y'all are estranged, but she is that baby's grandmother."

"You don't understand," I said woodenly, offering no further explanation.

"You're right, I don't. I'll be right back." She stomped out of the room after my mother and left me alone. I instantly felt guilty. Of course she was right, but she didn't know what I'd been through with Deidre. The humiliating childhood. The horrible teenage years when I couldn't keep friends. Coming home from school to find a circle of strangers praying over your bedroom, touching your things, rebuking the devil. She had done that. Not me. If Detra Ann wanted to be mad at me, so be it.

I lay in the bed, tears sliding down my face, when another contraction came. My phone rang in my purse, but I couldn't reach it. Feeling desperation rise within me, I said a prayer. "It's me, God. I know we don't talk as much as we should, and that's totally my fault, but I need your help. Please protect Ashland and our baby. Help me know what to do because I haven't got a clue."

Just then, Detra Ann came back in. My phone rang again, and she dug it out for me. Without waiting for permission she answered. "Hey, Ash. Sure, she's right here. Everything is fine."

She handed me the phone, and I took it with shaking hands. The contraction was passing, and I felt like myself again. "Hey, babe."

"You okay? I'll be on the way soon. Henri found me."

"Sorry to mess up your day."

"Stop that. You just hold on, okay. I promise you it's going to be all right. You just do what the doctor says and listen to Detra Ann. We'll be together soon, the three of us."

"All right." The tears sprang up again, against my wishes.

"Hey, hey," he said in a low and comforting voice, "don't cry. You can do this. I promise you I'll be there soon."

"I can do this," I repeated obediently. "Be careful."

"Will do. Talk to you soon. Let me speak to Detra Ann."

"All right." I handed the phone back to her. A nurse hustled in the room and reviewed the paper. She let me know my doctor was coming down the hall now. Detra Ann smoothed my hair and kissed my forehead after she hung up the phone.

"That's from Ashland. And me. You know I love you, CJ."

"I love you too." I leaned forward and fell into her arms. We hugged until the next contraction came.

"Is she still here?" We both knew who I meant.

"Yep. She's in the waiting room, crocheting and praying."

"That's good. For once in my life, I'm glad to hear that. I can use all the prayers I can get."

Chapter 7—Ashland

Everything went wrong that morning. I fell off the boat for the first time ever. The engine didn't want to start, and when I finally thought I would be able to get her going, Henri came running down the pier. I knew right away it was about CJ, and that made the weight of the day feel even heavier.

"Baby is coming, Ashland. She's at the hospital."

"He's not supposed to be here yet." I couldn't help but worry. This wasn't normal, was it?

"Somebody better tell that to the baby because he's absolutely determined to arrive. You want to ride with me?"

"No, I better take mine."

"You sure?" he asked, studying my face.

"No, I'm not sure."

"Get in. I'm driving. You look like you need a minute to think."

"Yeah, probably so." I left the boat where she was, climbed into his Dodge Charger and put on my seat belt. We didn't say much as we drove out of the marina parking lot, but I was glad for his company. I sensed he wanted to say something, but he didn't. I wasn't one to push someone to talk. It was a trait that drove my wife batty.

The dark clouds gathered above us and seemed to increase as we drove. "I can't remember when I saw the sun last. Weather seems weird lately."

"Yeah. You can't ever tell about the weather down here."

"What's going on, Henri? Is it the baby? I can tell there's something you aren't telling me. Don't hold back now. I want to know what's happening. Is Carrie Jo sick or something?"

"As far as I know, the baby is fine. Carrie Jo is fine too. I swear." He was trying to play it cool, but I knew he was holding back. I started to ask him again, but something caught my eye. It was a lone figure standing at the edge of the road. For a millisecond I thought he was alive, but as we approached him I saw that I was wrong. He was a ghost, and if he didn't move, we would drive right through him. His black suit was covered with dust, and it looked like something from the early 1900s. His hair had a dingy white tinge, but his skin was even whiter. Then he jumped into the road as we drove through him, and instinctively I gasped and tried to move out of the way like a wild man. His face lingered in front of mine for a long, agonizing moment, and he grinned at me. His dry, dead lips pulled back from his yellowed teeth. I screamed as he passed through my body, and Henri screamed too. The soul-sucking phantom pulled all the warmth out of me.

Henri slammed on the brakes. "What the hell was that about?" he demanded. "You seeing things?"

"Hell yes!" I said, trying to calm my breathing. I wiped my face furiously with my hands as if I could wipe away the ghostly residue from my soul. "I guess you didn't?"

"No, but I felt something. Coldness. Gone now. It is gone, right?" He glanced over his shoulder into the backseat, and I followed his lead. Nothing there. Thank God.

"Yes, it's gone."

"Anyone we know?"

"Nobody I have ever seen. And I hope I never see him again." I kept my eyes glued to the road ahead and tried not to look around me. So that's why I had been out of sorts this morning. The spirits were back. "I don't think I'll ever get used to this. I thought by talking about it and, you know, embracing it and all that jazz, it would get better. But it hasn't."

"What do you mean?"

I didn't have time for this right now. I had to get to my wife. Why did I even bring it up?

Henri glanced at me and said, "What's up?"

"It's been months since it happened last, so I thought it went away. I've seen things at a distance, but that just now was right in my face. It's like he was taunting me. Laughing at me. Something isn't right."

Henri's jaw clenched, and I could see him struggling with something. We were just ten minutes from the hospital now. "For the love of God, tell me what you know, Henri."

"The girls didn't want to tell you, but there is a rumor...no, that's not it. There is some concern that you might be cursed."

"What?" I said, laughing.

"Carrie Jo wanted to surprise you with a family tree print. You know the swanky kind you hang in a picture frame? During the research, Rachel noticed something strange about the date of expiration for some of your relatives."

"Date of expiration? Rachel is involved with this?"

"I don't know what else you would call it."

"Sorry, go on. You were saying?"

"The bottom line is the men in your family never live past forty. CJ wants to make sure that doesn't happen to you or your son."

"My son," I said, enjoying hearing that. Carrie Jo had been so insistent that we would have a girl. I always knew that was wrong. Even Lenore knew. I wished she were here now to tell me if I was going crazy or not. "Cursed? How can a whole family be cursed? Is that even a legit concern, or is my wife finding things to worry about?"

"I saw the genealogy, and she's not exaggerating. It is a real phenomenon. Your family never talked about this?"

"Not to me. My dad died when I was a kid, and my Uncle Robert...damn. He died too. Both before they were forty. Great. Does that mean at age forty I'm going to keel over?"

Henri said nothing but kept his eyes on the road. Finally, he said, "Stop holding out. Tell me the truth."

"Most of them died right after they turned thirty. Very few made it to forty."

The car hit a pothole and made a crunching noise. It seemed appropriate. Here we were talking about curses, and Henri's car was tearing up.

"So what's the cure?" I asked. "I mean, how do I get rid of this bad mojo or whatever it is? I can't deny I've been in a kind of funk lately, but I chalked it up to being a new dad. Sometimes crap just happens, and up until now it seemed I had no problem with luck. Now I guess that's all changed?"

"It has to have something to do with your gift. Curses are supernatural, and you have a supernatural ability. Where did you get your gift from? Do you know where it started? Did your mother see ghosts? Your father? Anyone give you clues about where this supernatural stuff came from? Maybe if we knew the answers we could trace the curse."

"Not really. My mother talked to the air all the time, but I didn't chalk it up to ghosts. I thought she was just pretending, playacting. I was a kid, so that kind of stuff didn't bother me. Later, though, she really pursued the supernatural, always dragging me to séances and whatnot. I couldn't tell you about my father. He didn't really share things with me."

"Too bad we can't ask your mother."

"Yeah, I know she'd love being a grandmother. She loved children."

There was an awkward silence as we zipped through a yellow light on Government Street. "We could ask her. If you'd be willing."

I bit my fingernail. I had my elbow on the window ledge. It made me feel ready to act if I needed to. Why did I think I could run from a ghost? Hopefully we wouldn't drive through any more of those.

"What are you talking about?"

"A séance would do the trick. I'm sure we could contact her."

I ran my hands through my hair. "I can't even begin to tell you how opposed I am to that idea."

"I figured you would be. CJ mentioned it, but considering what you're up against.... I'm only trying to help."

"I know it, but there has to be another way."

"You're probably right." Henri banked the vehicle to the right. We were close now, just a mile away. I was so anxious to get there I unbuckled my seat belt in anticipation.

"You'll be a great father."

I couldn't help but smile. "You think so?"

"I know so. Here we are. I'll drop you and then follow you up. Don't wait for me."

"Don't worry, I won't," I said with a smile as I practically jumped out of the car. As soon as the smoky glass door slid open, I knew I was in trouble. There in the lobby were two ghosts, and both of them knew I could see them. "Oh great," I muttered to myself.

"Can I help you?" an older lady with a nametag that read 'Dot' asked me. She must have thought I was talking to her.

"No, ma'am. I know where I'm going." I didn't tell her that an old man and a young boy were standing behind her. Why creep her out like that? The two ghosts weren't frightening like the roadside apparition had been. They whispered to one another, and the younger one pointed to me. The boy's hand passed by Dot's ear as he nudged the man. Dot patted her hair-sprayed hair as if she could feel it. Without much more notice to me or her hair, she answered the phone in a bright, cheerful voice, "Springhill Memorial Hospital. How may I direct your call?"

I sailed past her and caught the elevator. The baby floor, as it was affectionately known around here, was the fifth floor. I stood in the elevator with four other people and a ghost. He had a slack jaw, and the remnants of yellow hair circled his large head. Suddenly as if a magnet drew him, he moved closer to me. He stared at me with his empty gray eyes. "You know, don't you? You know where she is. Tell me," he pleaded with me. I tried not to fly across the elevator and scare the other passengers. As soon as the door opened I jumped ahead of the ladies who stood closest to it. "Tell me!" the ghoul screamed after me. I had gotten off on the wrong floor. Two more levels to go now. I flew past a crowd of people; I wasn't sure if they were dead or alive, and thankfully none of them followed me into the stairwell. By the time I made it to the fifth floor, I was so panicked I had to stop and catch my breath. I heard a sound behind me. Peering down the railing above me was another specter, a ghostly janitor with bloodless skin. His phantom mop plunked to the ground, and he eased down the steps toward me.

"Oh God, oh Jesus!" I prayed loudly. To my relief the words seemed to repel him enough to give me time to slip out the door. I pushed open the door from the stairwell and stepped onto the fifth floor. The atmosphere was very different here. Instead of lingering spirits and angry black clouds, there was an abundance of light and a thick, peaceful feeling. I breathed a sigh of relief as I walked to the nurses' station.

A young nurse with a dazzling white smile greeted me. I said, "I'm here to see my wife, Carrie Jo Stuart."

"Yes, Mr. Stuart. Follow me." She stood to show me the way. She wore yellow scrubs with tiny rainbows all over them. Very cheerful.

"No need to bother yourself. Just point me in the right direction."

She smiled and waved to the left. "She's that way. Room 542."

I glanced down the hall, making sure I had the right direction, and then turned back to her to say thanks. "Thank you..." The nurse was gone. She'd vanished in just a second.

Another woman walked up. "May I help you?"

"No, I know the way."

All I could think of was getting to my wife and son. I needed this day to be over soon. I couldn't take much more. The window at the end of the hallway suddenly clouded. The sunshine departed. Storm clouds were rolling in.

Somehow, it seemed appropriate.

Chapter 8—Ashland

Detra Ann hugged me and, as she typically did, fussed over me and brought me endless cups of coffee. Carrie Jo looked beautiful, but I didn't bother telling her so. She wouldn't believe me, and it didn't seem like the most sensitive thing to say during this painful and stressful process. Thankfully her doctor finally ordered the medicine that would stop the contractions. Carrie Jo had been in pain for several hours. She didn't complain, but I hated seeing the woman I loved suffer. The drip took effect quickly, and her contractions weakened. I breathed a sigh of relief knowing that Baby Boy would be indoors a little longer.

Baby Boy. Funny name, but I liked it. If my wife and I couldn't settle on a mutually approved baby name, I'd be forced to call him that. Now that his arrival was closer, I wondered how important names were anyway. I kissed CJ's hand and didn't say too much. I let the nurses do their work and tried to keep out of the way. I kept my eyes trained on my wife and not the creatures that occasionally sailed past the door or popped in to stare at me.

Seeing ghosts wasn't like the movies. Not at all. The spirits weren't trying to communicate with me or convince me to help them. Not in any kind of coherent way. Most of the ghosts I saw were a little eccentric—a bit mad, really. It was more like they sensed I was different, and that difference drove them even crazier. I got the sense that when you died, if you didn't pass on to wherever you were supposed to, you were left to amble about the spirit world trapped in your own nightmare. It wasn't a fate I wished on anyone. Especially someone I loved.

I used to believe that like Carrie Jo, I would get better at my "gift" or whatever you wanted to call it. But it hadn't happened for me, no matter how many books I read or how much I practiced. The appearance of a ghost scared the hell out of me every single time. Regardless of how much I prepared to see one, they always caught me by surprise. I prayed constantly, more so than I ever had before, but so far my prayers appeared to be unanswered. At least I had my friends, and until this latest session of ghost-seeing passed, I would keep them close. The more living beings around me the better.

Here we were all crowded in the room together now. The living collective appeared to repel the majority of the ghosts. Of the six of us, CJ and me plus Rachel, Chip, Detra Ann and Henri, only Henri and I knew what was happening. He looked at me encouragingly but like a true friend kept his mouth shut. One nurse complained about the number of people visiting, but I assured her it was okay. I was pretty sure I hadn't heard the end of her unhappiness, but let her try and run them out.

Suddenly everyone got quiet again. The machine bleeped to life as Carrie Jo squeezed my hand and sweated through another contraction. "I'm good, babe. Promise. I'm good," she whispered as she turned in the bed trying to find a comfortable spot. Miss Henrietta, the name I gave the unhappy nurse, came back in a deeper frown on her face.

"Okay, everyone. I have to insist you step out. The doctor is coming to check Mrs. Stuart again. If she hasn't dilated any more, he'll probably send her home. Clear the room," she said with a wave of her hand.

CJ frowned at her. "It's not like I haven't been trying," she sassed back at her. "Go ahead, babe. I'll be fine."

I kissed her forehead and walked out with a growing feeling of dread. Henri stayed close. "I've got your six, Ashland," he whispered as we stepped outside.

"Detra Ann, is she going to be okay? What's going on?" A petite brunette stood between us and the waiting room. Her dress hung off her small shoulders, and her lips quivered nervously.

"Oh yes, she's fine, Mrs. Jardine. I don't believe you have met Carrie Jo's husband yet. This is Ashland Stuart."

If she'd told me the woman was the pope, I wouldn't have been more surprised. I extended my hand to her and studied her face. Now that I knew she was CJ's mother, I could see the resemblance. "I didn't know you were here. I'm sorry. I would have come to speak to you sooner had I known."

"I'm sure it's not something my daughter would want everyone to know. We haven't been on the best terms, but I do care about her," she offered as a kind of apology. Her bright hazel eyes glossed with tears, but I was suspicious. I knew what Carrie Jo had been through with this woman. The nervous lady before me hardly appeared threatening, but looks were almost always deceiving.

"Her doctor is with her right now. Maybe when he completes his exam you can see her. If she's up to it," I said carefully.

"I saw her earlier, but only for a few minutes. I'll see her when she's ready. As long as she's okay. I had no idea she was having a baby."

As she spoke, a young spirit sailed past, holding a bundle of blankets in her arms. I tried not to stare at the ghost, but she stared at me, her pale face too close to mine. Mrs. Jardine turned around to investigate. I couldn't be sure, but as she faced me again I thought I saw her eyes widen a bit. Could she see the girl too? The spirit paused to listen to our conversation, but when no one acknowledged her she began to fade away. That was something else I had learned about the spirit world. The more attention you gave the creatures, the stronger they became. In some cases simply ignoring them was enough to send them back to wherever they came from.

I shivered involuntarily, and Henri touched my shoulder. "You need anything?" he asked.

"Coffee?" Detra Ann offered me.

"Please, no more coffee. I'll be up for the next two days if I drink another cup," I said as she frowned at me.

"Mr. Stuart, the doctor would like to talk to you." The crotchety nurse waved me back to CJ's room, and I excused myself from the gathering. Chip and Rachel crowded around Mrs. Jardine and asked her about her stay in Mobile. I was glad to see it. I didn't have a bad feeling about her, regardless of her history with Carrie Jo.

"Mr. Stuart, nice to see you."

"Dr. Gary. Good to see you too. Are we having a baby tonight?"

"I was just telling your wife that she's made some progress. She's dilated to four centimeters now, but I'd like to wait if the baby will allow it. She isn't due for a few more weeks, and that time is crucial for good lung development. I know you're miserable, dear," the older man said to Carrie Jo as he squeezed her hand, "but if you two can hold out a little longer, it will be better for both of you." He turned to me and continued, "Mrs. Stuart appears to be responding well to the medications; the contractions have diminished, and that's a good sign. I'd like to keep her overnight, just to watch her. If all goes well, I'll send her home in the morning, and then we'll see what Junior decides to do." Relieved, I hugged the doctor. He good-naturedly patted my back. "I know it's a nerve-racking process for both of you, but I assure you that you will get through it and everyone will be fine. The baby's heartbeat is strong and steady. Mother's health is good too. I see nothing to worry about."

"Thanks, doc. That is good news."

"I'll see you two in the morning."

"Thank you, Dr. Gary," CJ called as he walked out the door. "Sorry, babe. Didn't mean to make you worry about me," she said with a small smile.

I kissed her forehead again and sat in the chair beside her. "You had nothing to do with it. You heard the doctor. It's up to Baby Boy, not you."

She wrinkled her nose at me. "That's the name you want?"

"Well, no. It's just a nickname I came up with."

"You're convinced he'll be a he, aren't you?"

I couldn't help but grin. This moment was the happiest I had been all day. I nodded and confessed, "From day one."

"All right, so what names do you have in mind?"

"Really?"

"Yep, whatcha got?"

I squeezed her hand and said, "I was thinking Richard or James."

"Aren't those Bible names?"

I laughed aloud. "I don't think there were any Richards in the Bible."

She laughed too and wiped tears from her eyes. "We're going to be okay, right? No matter what?"

"No matter what. Yes, we will be fine."

I held her until we heard a knock on the door. It was Carrie Jo's mother. "Hi. I just wanted to say goodbye before I go back to the hotel. It's getting dark, and I don't really know my way around here. I'll be praying for you, Carrie Jo."

CJ looked at me, and I smiled at her as if to say, *It's okay. I'm right here.*

"Stay for a minute, Momma." That delighted the older woman to no end, and she dropped her purse in the chair and walked to the bedside. As she and CJ talked, Henri and Detra Ann stepped in the room to watch us. Detra Ann waved me over, and we walked outside for a minute.

"Listen, I know they have a rough history, but her mother is telling the truth. She didn't know CJ was pregnant, and she really does care about what happens to her. Let Carrie Jo know, okay?"

"Yeah, I will."

"Henri told you, didn't he?"

"I knew anyway. I just didn't know what to call it."

"So you think you're cursed?"

"Who's cursed?" Mrs. Jardine asked, standing a few feet away.

Detra Ann piped up, "It's just a figure of speech. Ashland's had some bad luck lately is all."

Without waiting for an invitation, Carrie Jo's mother grabbed my hand and began to pray, "Dear God, break this curse on this young man's life. No weapon formed against him will prosper, just as your Word says. Keep him safe as he fights the good fight. Amen."

Surprised by the impromptu prayer, I murmured "Amen" and thanked her.

"No need to thank me. I can't have my only son-in-law cursed. I'll keep praying. That's something I know how to do." She smiled brightly, and I had to admit, I did feel better. My space wasn't ghost-free, but the spirits had diminished a bit and none were in my face. Always a plus. "Your friend said he'd take me home. I'll come back in the morning, if that's okay."

"Sure. Carrie Jo is supposed to go home in the morning, but I'm not sure what time. Are you sure you're comfortable at the hotel? Which one are you staying at?"

"Don't worry about me. I am very comfortable in my room. You be with your wife."

"Hey!" Detra Ann said. "I'll ride too. Here comes Henri now. See you in the morning, Ash." She kissed my cheek, and I could feel her glossy lipstick on my skin. I waved goodbye and hurried back to CJ's room.

She'd snuggled up in the blankets and had her eyes closed. She stirred and made sure I was there, then went back to sleep. A few hours later I hunkered down in the chair and thought about the simple prayer that Deidre had said over me. It comforted me, and soon I fell asleep.

Chapter 9—Carrie Jo

Before nine o'clock, Ashland and I were headed home. I'd made it through the night with no other contractions, and we both breathed a sigh of relief. I think everyone thought I would be disappointed that the baby's arrival had been delayed, but I wasn't. Not at all. As long as Baby Boy stayed close to me, I knew I could protect him. *Oh no! Did I just call him Baby Boy?* I smiled at Ashland and shook my head.

"What?" he asked innocently.

"You. You've got me calling our son Baby Boy."

"You're okay with a son, then?"

I leaned back against the seat and smiled even bigger. "Yep, I'm okay with it. I don't know why I was so dead set against having a boy." We pulled into the driveway and weren't a bit surprised to see cars already there. Doreen's old truck was on the street, and of course Rachel's and Detra Ann's vehicles were in the driveway.

"I know why. And I know what you think."

Suddenly all the brightness of the day seemed to vanish. One of my well-meaning friends must have told Ashland what we discovered, and now he was going to say it—the word I didn't dare say.

"I know about the curse, Carrie Jo."

There. He said it. Now it was real.

For all three of us.

I couldn't meet his eyes, so I stared at the yard. It was so sad-looking, with dead flowers and moldy sidewalks. How did they get moldy? We had the place power-washed just two months ago. It sure as heck didn't look like it.

"Now what, babe? How do we break it?"

"*We* can't break it, Carrie Jo, but you can help *me* figure it out. This is my deal. And I want you to promise me something."

"What's that?" I asked suspiciously.

"I don't want you to do anything that will put you or our son in danger. Our son...yeah, I like that." He squeezed my hand. "I couldn't stand it if I knew you two were in danger. I mean it, CJ. Nothing. No visiting the house. No stirring up spirits. You let me do this. Okay?"

I bit my lip and searched his face for any kind of softness. There was none to be found. He was dead serious about this. "If you won't promise for me, do it for Baby Boy."

My hands rubbed my stomach as our son adjusted his foot, shoving it deeper into my ribs as if to say, "Yeah, I agree with Dad."

"Okay, I promise not to do any of those things."

It was his turn to be suspicious. "And don't do anything else I haven't thought of yet, okay?"

"Scout's honor." I held up two fingers. "Now let's go in the house before the bottom falls out. It looks pitch black out here. The weather is so unpredictable."

"This has got to be from Hurricane Jasmine—the storm is on the way, but it's only a Cat 1. We'll be okay." He chuckled at Rachel waving from the front door. "Looks like we're home base this time around. I guess that's fair since we camped out with Henri for the last tropical storm. Do I need to send everyone home?"

"No, I like having our friends around. This storm will be like the last one, I'm sure. It will fizzle out before it gets here."

"Looks like we have an extra guest."

I could see my mother's petite figure through the big bay window. How did I miss her? I sighed and nodded. Ash didn't need me losing it right now, and so far Momma had behaved. I promised myself I would get to the bottom of her appearance here right away, though. I couldn't have my baby around someone so judgmental, so unpredictable.

Stop being so negative, Carrie Jo. What if she's changed?

I had given her chances before. I loved her, no doubt about it, but it was easier not dealing with her. Not talking to her. Not hoping things would change. Yeah, that was way easier than seeing her, daydreaming about a "normal" relationship. Here we were, dealing with a curse, and she showed up out of the blue. What was up with that? She did seem different, but maybe that was also a ploy. The old Deidre Jardine would have recited at least five Bible verses at me by now. I wondered what she was up to. I hoped and prayed this wasn't about money.

Doreen came barreling out the door. "Here she is! Mrs. Stuart! I am so glad to see you. You had me worried! No baby yet, huh? No worries. He will come in his own good time. I stocked your pantry for the storm, but I didn't know all these people would be here. Do I need to make another trip to the store?"

I smiled at her and followed her into the kitchen. "Hey, everyone!" I waved to the rest of the group camped around the widescreen television in the living room. "No, Doreen. This is fine. You didn't even need to do that. If we need something else, I'm sure one of these guys will go. I hope you made me some fruit salad. I'm starving."

"Of course. Right on the top shelf. Just for you."

"You go home and be with Stephan. Are you staying in Mobile?"

"Oh no. I never stay for these storms, and I wish you would go too. We go to Stephan's mother's house in Evergreen. No storms there." I smiled at her and insisted that she go home. The skies were darkening, and according to the local weather reports that blared from the next room, Hurricane Jasmine would be bearing down on us in the next few hours. I didn't know what it was about hurricanes that made my friends want to gather around a television. But I imagined that was the way it would be for the next few days. I was glad. I wanted them close to me right now. And close to Ashland.

"I am sorry about your puppy, Mrs. Stuart. He was a sweet dog."

"Thanks, Doreen. Me too. You go to Stephan now. I'm fine. We'll see you when this is over."

With a nervous wave, she grabbed her purse and left out the kitchen door.

Doreen's powder blue Ford backed out of the driveway, and I waved at her as she pulled into the frantic street. Pretty busy out there. Hm...maybe I did need to pay attention. It was dark enough for the streetlights to come on already. Yep, this was going to be a doozy of a storm.

"Hey, babe. I have to go to the boat. I never did get her secured, and I'd hate to lose her. We've had some happy memories there."

"Ashland...shh..." I said, giggling and kissing him. We had long speculated that we'd conceived during an overnight trip on the Happy Go Lucky.

"Relax. No one can hear me." He kissed me back. "Henri's going with me. Won't be gone but about an hour."

"Sure, but hurry back. No hanging out on the boat."

"In this weather? No way, crazy lady." He laughed and shook his head. "Be back in a bit."

"Better be," I said, kissing him square on the lips before smacking his behind playfully.

"Be kind to your mother," he said to me before he walked out the door. For a second I thought I heard Chunky Boy whine after him as he always did. Chunky Boy and Baby Boy. What a pair they would have made! I sniffled and felt someone beside me.

"You want a cup of tea?" That someone was my mother.

"Yes, but could you make sure it's herbal? Caffeinated drinks make the baby very active."

"Good idea. I was hoping we could talk. Your friends went upstairs to put your shower gifts away. Looks like you were really blessed with all those gifts."

I followed behind her. My back felt sore, but I reasoned it was from the hospital bed. That had been one long night and one stiff mattress. "I have to ask, Momma. Please don't take this the wrong way, but why are you here? I haven't heard from you in over two years. Now you're here?"

She put the lid on the teapot and set it on the stove. "Cut to the chase, hmm? Sometimes you remind me of your Aunt Maggie so much."

"I don't want to talk about Aunt Maggie, Momma. I want to talk about you. And me. It can't be like it used to be. I won't let it be. That's not what I want for my child."

She nodded and looked me square in the eye. She didn't argue or get defensive. "Okay, cards on the table." She sat across from me at the small, round breakfast table. "About a year ago, I had what they called a cardiac event." I waited to hear what else she would tell me. I would hold my sympathy until after I heard the rest of the story. Not that she would lie about such a thing. Deidre Jardine was many things but not a liar. "I am fine now. They put two stents in me, but I can do everything I used to do."

"Sorry to hear that. Does heart disease run in our family?" I wasn't asking for me. What about the baby?

"Not that I am aware of. I know it's a bit of a shock seeing me after so long, but I've come to realize something." Just then the teapot screamed and Deidre got up to pour our cups. I didn't hurry her, but I was dying to hear what she had to say.

Setting the cup in front of me, she stirred in a cube of sugar and put her spoon down. "I don't blame you for not trusting me. For wanting to keep me away. I needed help, Carrie Jo, and I didn't know how to ask for it."

"What kind of help, Momma?"

She laughed nervously. "I'm still not sure. But I have made peace with the Big Man Upstairs. That happened when I thought I was going to die. You know how you hear that your life plays before your eyes when you are dying?" I nodded, unable to sip my tea or even move. I couldn't distract her now, just when she was about to tell me something significant. I could feel it rising, like the crest of a wave. "Well, that's not what happened to me. I didn't see my life—I saw yours."

"Really?"

"Yes. And I had no idea. It was like I could feel what you felt, see what you saw. I realized that while I thought I was protecting you, loving you, saving you, Carrie Jo, I was terrorizing you instead. Every incident. The time I came to the classroom to get you after Ginny's stepfather...I walked through that whole thing as you." When she met my eyes, the hazel color appeared a bit green now. I had forgotten they changed color like that. "You needed someone to protect you from me. I hurt you. In my desire to shield you, I did the thing I dreaded. Please believe me, protecting you was really all I wanted to do."

"Protecting me from what?"

"From who I was. And who I was afraid you'd become."

"I don't know what you mean." The baby moved around, and I rubbed my stomach to still him. "Tell me what you mean."

"Where do you think you got your dream walking from?"

"Dream walking?"

"Yes, that's what my mother used to call it."

"Used to call what?" I asked incredulously.

"Going back in time and sometimes forward, through dreams."

I heard a puppy whine somewhere. Must have been the neighbor's dog. A vehicle with a screaming siren whizzed past my home and down the bumpy street. I held my breath as she whispered the truth at last.

"You, my daughter, come from a long line of dream walkers."

Chapter 10—Ashland

"Ash, you have to call me back. Like ASAP!" Libby's voicemail sounded urgent, as if someone's life hung in the balance. As Henri navigated the traffic, I dialed her office number. I had enough stress in my life right now without Libby losing her mind on me. She wasn't the one being sued. By multiple people.

Without saying "Hello" or "How's your wife?" she immediately began throwing a tantrum. "It's like I said! Someone opened the floodgates. It's open season on Ashland Stuart. What the hell did you do? Post your net worth on a forum? We have another lineage claim! Myron and Alice Reed, whoever the hell they are! And just to make it worse, plaintiffs Rhodes and Hines have teamed up and are asking for nothing less than half—of everything!"

"Hello to you too, Libby. In case you haven't noticed, we are in the middle of a hurricane right now. Can't this wait? I can't imagine the wheels of justice moving so quickly that I need to head to the courthouse right this minute. That has never been the case."

"Screw the hurricane! Aren't you listening? You are in major trouble, Ashland." She was talking too loud in my ear; I held the phone away from my head and seriously considered throwing it out the window into the gray, choppy waters of the Mobile Bay. I should never have hired Libby. Once again I let my loyalties to friends and family get me into trouble. And my track record with lawyers wasn't the greatest. Henri shook his head in surprise at Libby's tone but kept his eyes on the dangerous roads.

I put the phone back to my ear. "Okay, reality check, Libby. You work for me, remember? Bring your voice down and breathe between sentences. I don't need this right now, so say what you need to say and be done with it. Now what happened?"

"I got a phone call about a half hour ago from a clerk in Judge Carmichael's office."

My phone beeped, and I glanced at it quickly. It was Rachel. Probably wanting me to pick up something for Carrie Jo, like those chicken-flavored crackers she snacked on constantly. I'd have to call her back after I handled this situation. "And?"

"It's true. All of it. Those jerks down at Rodney and Waite came up with this idea—no doubt about it. It's bad, Ash. Whoever drew up your mother's will left a lot of loopholes for crazies to jump through. Unbelievable! The only thing you can do now is settle with these people, and quickly. Then we can make the changes to the original document official and stop the bleeding. I think you need to start thinking of a number you can live with, and let's get them to the table. It's the only way you'll be able to walk away with at least the shirt on your back."

My blood boiled as I listened to the not-so-surprising news. Who in the world sues someone just because they share some DNA? Now the Reeds too? This was unreal. "What? Listen, I'm not prepared to talk about this today."

There was suddenly a deafening silence. "This isn't like you, Ashland. How can you be so blasé about being sued? Don't you understand what I'm saying? Come see me now, and we can get the prelim stuff squared away. I'm sure Carrie Jo would understand. How can I help you if you won't let me?"

"I'll come to your office Monday, after this storm blows through. My wife comes first, Libby. In case you weren't paying attention, we are about to have a baby."

"Well, I *know*," she said with an extra edge of snark to her voice. "I was at your shower, remember? But I would think you'd want to protect your child from all these lawsuits. And I doubt this storm is anything to worry about. It's down to Category 1 status now. Just come by. I've got lunch."

"Goodbye, Libby."

I hung up the phone, shaking my head, turned on the radio and stared at the rising water. We had time to make our trip to the Fairhope Pier and back, but beyond that would be sketchy.

High winds are expected. Hurricane Jasmine has produced gusts up to eighty miles per hour, and she's just getting started. Let's go to Meg, who has an update on this surprisingly powerful storm...

"When it rains, it pours, huh?" Right on cue, fat raindrops slapped the windshield and soon covered the car in sheets of water.

"Literally. If there was any doubt about it before, there isn't now. I've definitely stepped in a streak of bad luck. Are you sure you want to be riding in a car with me?" It was a joke, albeit a bad one, but Henri didn't laugh.

"Stop making that your confession, Ashland. You'll only make a curse stronger by agreeing with it."

"Yeah, whatever." I paid no attention to the spirit that stood in the waters off the causeway. We were driving too fast for him to reach us. At least, I hoped.

"Curses aren't bad luck. Bad luck happens to everyone. That's not the same thing as a curse."

"I'm listening."

"Curses that affect generations of people have to have some weight behind them. You can't just speak a few negative words about someone and hope it hurts them. For a true curse to work and affect a family for generations, there had to have been some major wrong done to someone. Its source must be a great injustice. A wrong that needs to be made right."

"I get that, and I believe it, but how am I supposed to know what that is?"

"Do you believe in God, Ashland?"

We sloshed along the causeway and turned off the bridge onto Highway 98. The watery streets were nearly empty, except for a few people making last-minute provisions. I thought about his question; it was important to answer truthfully. "I've always believed there was, and I still do, but I have a lot of questions for him. If I ever get to see him."

"Do you talk to him at all?"

"Are you asking me if I pray? Sure, I pray." My mood went from bad to worse. This wasn't the time to be having a heart-to-heart about my spiritual life. "What's your point, Henri? Cut to the chase."

"Well, I'm trying to say that I don't have the answers, and even if Lenore was here with us, she wouldn't either. Carrie Jo can't find out, because she's in no shape to perform her 'dream' detective work. Rachel knows about curses but nothing specific about your case. Yet you say you're seeing ghosts again, right?"

"Yep, unfortunately."

"I think God is trying to talk to you, Ashland. I think you have to trust him to show you the truth. If you haven't already, ask him to reveal the source of the curse to you. Tell him you are willing to make right whatever wrong has been done. That's what I would do, if I were in your shoes. Because when you boil it all down, it's about you. This is your battle, and it always has been. From the finding of the Beaumont treasure to the battle in the ballroom. You've been the focus of all this spiritual activity, although it's not always been in an obvious way. God sent you Carrie Jo, and us, if I may say so, but this battle has been for Ashland Stuart."

The car came to a stop at the marina, and we sat in the parking lot. The windshield wipers sloshed back and forth, slinging the water onto the already soaked pavement.

I knew every word he said was true. It had been about me. I'd spent all my time trying to protect Carrie Jo, but Seven Sisters had been *my* house. The Beaumont treasure was also mine. The ghosts had been from *my* past. Now this curse threatened my son and someday my grandsons. Unless I stopped it.

"Pray with me, Henri. I don't know what to say."

He nodded and grabbed my hand. "Lord, nothing is hidden from you, for you see all things—everything in the past, present and future. I know you can see this man's heart and his desire to break this curse over his life and his family. Please, Lord, speak to Ashland. Speak in a language he will understand. Show him what he needs to know. Show him what to do. Give him what he needs to set himself and his family free. We put this in your hands and trust that you will give the answer. In Jesus' name, amen."

"Amen," I whispered. I wiped my eyes and stared at my boat rocking in the marina. I hoped he was right. "Well, no time like the present."

"Need some help?"

"Sure, come on. Let's move her away from the floating dock—that's the worst place to leave a boat during a hurricane. Hey, actually, you should move the car to the other side of the marina. That's where I'm taking the boat. I'll meet you over there."

"All right."

I got out of the car and was soaked to the bone before I'd taken two steps. I walked quickly to the Happy Go Lucky and dug for the keys in my wet pants pocket. I untied the boat and turned the key.

Click, click.

"Come on, are you kidding me?"

I adjusted the throttle and turned the key again.

Click, click.

Smacking the dashboard in frustration, I tapped the gas tank gauge. How the heck was I out of gas? I went below deck and grabbed a half-empty can. It wasn't much, but it would be enough to get me the few yards I needed to travel. The boat rocked and rolled in the rough water of the Mobile Bay. My phone rang in my pocket again, and I suddenly remembered I needed to call Rachel back. I climbed the steps, shielding my eyes from a spray of water with my hand.

I couldn't answer the phone now. Suddenly the wind became so savage I could barely stand up. I waited until the blast of wind passed, then raced to the tank. With clumsy hands I poured the gas into the tank and replaced the gas cap. Closing the outer cap, I stowed the empty can under the railing, latching it secure with a bungee cord. Just as I stood up, the boat lurched, sending me hurtling across the deck.

As I struggled to get up, I thought I saw someone standing near me. It wasn't Henri. It was a woman—it had to be. She wore a moldy dress with a torn hem. I tried to look up to see her face when I felt and heard the sound of wood hitting the side of my head. *Wait!* I thought as the blow came. The boat tilted again, and this time I rolled into the water.

The shattering pain overwhelmed me. I slipped down, down, down...

Chapter 11—Olivia

As I waited for my host to join me in the garden, I watched a line of black ants steal sugar crumbs off the top of a forgotten cake. I felt no need to interrupt their work, nor did I feel a great deal of sympathy for the person who would leave such a treat unprotected in a den of ants. I did not accept the mint tea offered me or eat any of the sweet delicacies before me. Isaiah took his time. I knew it was his way of toying with me, reminding me who had the upper hand.

Of all the confrontations I could have hoped to avoid in this life, and I was not one to fear anyone, this would be the one I dreaded the most. I was about to face the man I rejected to marry another. Why did men believe that a woman who possessed a modicum of attractiveness could not possibly be sensible? That a woman must always be guided by the heart or its inclinations?

I was and had always been a sensible woman. I had not come in tears, as I was sure my sister would have done if she had been in my shoes. And I had not come as a servant—I had come as a Beaumont, the last Beaumont, unless God saw fit to give me another child, which seemed unlikely considering my age. In my world, women who were twenty and five and had not had a child were considered old maids, barren, cast-off spinsters. They were whispered about and never invited to social events. Useless dried husks without value.

I had a child, a girl-child, whom I had summarily given up to have the marriage alliance I preferred. I lied to her and told her that she belonged to my brother; it was better for her to believe that. Better for everyone. But Isaiah would not likely be willing to ignore the truth. Our daughter, Isla, had seduced her own uncle Jeremiah, and from that unholy union had come Karah. No, I doubted that Isaiah would be pleased at all.

And I knew he would never let me forget my change of heart, especially now. Not when he heard the whole truth. But still I was here, despite my better judgment, and I had a purpose.

Isaiah must make this right.

The fool girl, our own daughter, convinced her uncle to sign a codicil that named only her children as his heirs. If she'd just left things alone! Claudette and I had arranged a settlement for Christine's youngest daughter, Delilah, and God knew where poor Calpurnia was, probably at the bottom of the Mobile River. My personal investigation into the matter had revealed nothing. It was as if the girl had disappeared from the face of the Earth. Everything had been perfectly arranged until Isla and her schemes interfered. Since there was no male heir between her and Jeremiah, and Karah's parentage was being questioned by the courts—also thanks to Isla—the Cottonwood property, including the missing Beaumont fortune, would go to Jeremiah's brother, Isaiah.

All of it. The irony of the situation did not escape me. He would have what he had lost. But he would never have me.

I had not seen my former lover in ages. For the first five years, he would send me the occasional vague letter asking again why I had rejected him. I never responded.

In the first pleading correspondences, he shared the depth of his despair and pledged his undying love. "I shall never feel again what I felt with you, my darling. Oh, have mercy on me and let me hear you call me that once more. I could have any wife I choose, but my only desire is for you, my own Olivia."

I would admit this to no one, but I kept those letters. On the many nights when I was alone, I would unfold them and read them again and again, pretending that I would write him back. How could I explain to him why I did what I did? I could not, so I never picked up a pen.

Lost in my silent reverie, I did not hear the dogs barking at first, but then I saw Isaiah approaching. He leaned on a silver-headed cane and wore a finely woven black suit that had obviously been made for his trim body. He wore no hat, and I could see that time had been kind to him. He had all his beautiful dark hair, now flecked with white. I did not ask why he used the cane. I still had my manners when I wanted them.

Without a word, he sat down across the small table from me. Spotting the ants, he snapped his fingers and the dogs came running. He put the china dish on the ground, and the nearest hound devoured the food. Isaiah did not seem to care that his dog's pawing and excited eating broke the fine dish.

I raised an eyebrow but said nothing. With some swagger he leaned back in his chair and stared at me. I could see he was taking in every line, every change, every less than firm inch of my skin. He did not hide his amusement at my appearance or my situation. He had the advantage, and he enjoyed it.

This was not going to be easy, I feared. It was he who spoke first.

"This business with the codicil. Did you plan this, Olivia? Was that your plan all along? To use our daughter to seduce her uncle?"

"What kind of woman do you think I am, Isaiah?"

He spun his walking stick and said, "The kind of woman who leaves her intended at the altar while she runs off to marry another. The kind of woman who refuses to tell me where my child is or what's become of her. That's the kind of woman you are, dear Olivia."

"You can't think that I..."

"Can't I?" He smiled at me, rubbing the silver horse head atop his cane.

"To what end? I am not clever enough to dream up such a scenario. I can only assume it was Fate that caused these things to happen."

"Ah." His eyes looked playful. "As do I. It was Fate that left me the inheritance, all the inheritance, Olivia. See, you should have married me, for it was always mine anyway. And I would have loved you without it. That is the truth. Now I will have the fortune without your love. Things change, my dear, and so have I. I found peace with my wife, Virginia, and she has given me many sons and even a daughter. So you see, it was the Hand of Providence that led you away from me to marry Calloway James Torrence, that well-known adulterer. How is life with the old man now? Is he even still alive? My wife tells me you have no children. Well, besides our child."

"You have no right to speak so personally to me! I am not a child anymore, Isaiah." I stood, ready to leave immediately. "You have not changed at all. You are a small man, ruled by your pride and ambition, and obviously I cannot reason with you. Do the right thing, Isaiah. You must set this codicil aside and leave Christine and Jeremiah's original will to stand."

"Too hasty, my dear. You always end things too hastily. I am sure you want to hear me out on this. I have something to say to you, Olivia. Or rather, I have someone you should see."

He rang a little silver bell on the table, and to my utter surprise our daughter walked down the leaf-covered path to our outdoor dining space. She mocked me with a curtsy and sat next to Isaiah in an outfit that was obviously intended for the stage. She showed far too much cleavage, and I kept my face a mask as she leaned forward and kissed her father on the mouth like a wanton.

"Isla, I told you to stay home! What are you doing here?"

"Imagine my surprise, Aunt Olivia, to learn that this man, Isaiah Cottonwood, is my own father. Imagine my great surprise! For I am *truly* surprised! And an even greater surprise, *Aunt* Olivia, is that you are my *mother*! Can you imagine how surprised I was to learn this? You tricked me, Mother! What can that mean for my daughter, Karah? That her father was also her great-uncle? We are one big happy family now, aren't we?" Isla walked toward me with a rare, serious look on her face. "And I want what belongs to me. I will not let this go. You should know that by now."

She got in my face and smiled. "You left me with the general, and he took his liberties with me, Mother. His hands were all over my body. When he got bored with violating and hurting me himself, he invited his friends to do the same. I learned many tricks from the general. Cruel to the last was he, but in the end, I took care of him. One last time. And there were others too, all except my sweet Captain. And even he failed me like all the rest. But now I have my own father!" She walked over to stand beside him, her hand on his shoulder. "He will make sure I get what I deserve. Won't you, Father?"

She slapped the table and yelled at me, "I told you that you would never take Seven Sisters away from me! That it was mine. That it belonged to me. Now we know why, don't we? I will live there until the day I die. Then my daughter..."

"No, you are coming home with me. I have left you too long in this world." I masked my shock, regret and revulsion. I would deal with those later.

"You cannot command me, Mother," she said in a mocking voice.

"Maybe not, but I have legal custody of you until your next court appearance. You *will* go where I command you."

"She can't, can she, Father?" Her sickeningly sweet voice was too much to bear. I left the two of them at the table, her giggles in my ears. Isaiah did not call after me, nor did I wish him to. I left his estate at Park Hill and headed back to Seven Sisters. This was too heartbreaking. I decided I would retrieve my ill-begotten daughter tomorrow and go home. That would be that. I would tell my husband the truth about our fortune and let him do what he could to solve the problem. He might even abandon me, as would be his right. I had failed to deliver a fortune or a child. I was doubly cursed.

As I finished dinner alone, Stokes came in. I could tell by the way the old man shuffled his feet that he wanted to announce someone. "Who is it, Stokes?"

"It's Isaiah Cottonwood."

"I see. Well, let him in, please."

Twice in one day. Apparently, Isaiah had thought of something else to hurt me with. What would he do now, bring Karah before me?

"I am sorry to call on you so late. I realize this is most inopportune of me."

I did not rise. I wiped my hands on a thick linen napkin and waited for him to get to the matter at hand. "Why have you come, Isaiah?"

"I come because—I wanted to tell you—she's not..."

"Ah, Isla," I said, smiling at him sadly.

"I do not know how it happened, but it did happen. I was asleep, and the next thing I remember was her naked body on top of mine. I hardly know how to say this to a lady, but when I woke up, we were... she was...." He shuddered, and I could see he was overcome with disgust and shame. "Once I knew it was not some sort of bizarre dream, I threw her off of me. She laughed at me, her own father! Our daughter is mad, Olivia! Mad and dangerous! I threw her out of the house, and I do not know where she has gone. Perhaps to this captain she speaks of."

"He is dead, Isaiah. She shot him. In Roanoke. He has been dead for three years now."

"That's impossible, for I saw him earlier at my home. He stood outside the door waiting for her. She went to him when she left me. I locked the door behind her."

I took a sip of the dark claret. "Then you saw a ghost."

His eyes were even wider. "That's not all. She said—she cursed me, Olivia. Already I feel it taking effect. I am sick now, and I fear I shall die."

"You are being dramatic, Mr. Cottonwood. An angry woman—a madwoman—assaulted you. That is all. Do you really believe in curses? What woman has the power to do such things?"

"Don't talk to me about women, Mrs. Torrence."

"You expect me to help you after you confess to me that you have had carnal knowledge of our daughter? You expect me to assist you at all?" I smiled at him and watched the low light of the candelabra flicker. The candles burned low, and their red wax dripping made the moment that much more somber.

"You don't understand. I feel—my heart—the doctor says I am not supposed to have— Ahh...help me, Olivia."

I stood up as Isaiah slumped over the table, panting for breath and pounding at his chest. "I do understand you—and I curse you too! How dare you molest our daughter. How dare you refuse to help me! You thought you'd take advantage of my situation, but it has turned on you, hasn't it? Fate is a cruel mistress, Isaiah. This is why I did not want to marry you. You have always been unsteady. How does the saying go? 'A double-minded man is unstable in all his ways...'"

I rubbed his shoulder with my pale hand and whispered in his ear, "You are that man, and you are unstable in all your ways." All the emotions I had locked away, had carefully forbidden myself from feeling, rose to the surface. And despite my sudden tears, the emotion I felt most strongly was anger. All of it fell on Isaiah. My reasoning renounced its position as my chief counsel. Raw anger took control, and for the first time in my life, I welcomed it and allowed it to flow through me like dammed-up water through a pipe.

I sobbed, "I curse you, Isaiah—and your sons too. May you die, may they die in the prime of their life! May they feel happiness but have it stolen from them before they can fully possess it! I curse you for stealing my soul! You never cease to disappoint me, and now you would do this to me. You will not have what you seek. No peace for you or any of the Cottonwoods! Just as you did this to my blood, I curse your blood!

"I leave you now, Isaiah. I will never see you again. Except when they bury you. And they will bury you soon. Probably tomorrow."

Just then another guest joined us. It was Isla. "Mother, I can explain."

"What is there to say? I have cursed the man who hurt my daughter and stole my fortune. Now he is doubly cursed. See, he is dying. Leave him be, Isla. Why don't you go be with your captain in the Moonlight Garden before we have to leave this place?"

"You know about my sweet Captain?" Her voice sounded frail, quiet, pretty.

"The Moonlight Garden has always been a special place. Go now and leave your father to me."

***

I sputtered the sea water out of my lungs. How long had I been lying on this piece of foam, floating around the harbor? I'd woken up long enough to throw up, and now I was dying of thirst. Thankfully the storm had been during a warm season, or I was sure I would have died.

"Hey! Somebody! Help me!" I shouted about a hundred times. I heard nothing but the winds roaring and the waves crashing in response. Yelling into a storm was futile, so I waited for the waves to diminish and then tried again. The sun was rising now. How long had I been out here?

Long enough to know that Henri's prayer had been heard. God showed me what I needed to know, how the curse began and how I could break it. I had no doubt I would be found, because this had been his plan all along.

When the Coast Guard ship sailed in my direction, I cried. Not just because I had been found but because I knew how to break Olivia and Isla's curse. I would live to break it.

Carrie Jo! I love you! I know what to do now! I'm coming to you, baby!

Chapter 12—Carrie Jo

"I spent my whole life trying to prevent this dream walking, to prevent it from developing in you, but I failed—and I caused you great pain in the process," my mother said earnestly. "Please believe me when I tell you that I begged God a hundred times to take it from us. To take it from you. If you had seen the things my mother went through...she got so obsessed. All she wanted to do was sleep, and then one day she didn't wake up. I think the dreaming killed her, and I didn't want that for you. I thought if I followed the rules, you know, went to church, lived a holy life, if I became pure in the eyes of God, I could save you. I can't explain my reasoning. It all seems so crazy now."

"I can't believe this." The pain in my back worsened, but I didn't move. I stared at her. "You mean you knew what was happening to me and you didn't tell me? You knew all this time? I thought I was crazy. I thought you hated me!"

"I'm sorry, Carrie Jo. I am very sorry that I let you grow up not knowing what I knew, even if that wasn't very much."

A blast of wind moaned around the eave of the house. I heard the television bleeping a weather alert in the other room, but I was frozen to the spot. Rachel and Detra Ann were upstairs, laughing about something. The surreal moment lingered and I said, "How could you do that?"

She wrung her hands and covered her mouth. Finally she said, "All I can say is I am sorry."

"And I'm supposed to do what now?" I stood up. "Act like a 'sorry' makes it all better. That it erases it all? You're wrong, Momma. I'm not going to forget and..." I felt the need to get away, but I wasn't done giving her a piece of my mind. Kind Carrie Jo warned me to watch my mouth—that I would regret it if I said something stupid—but as sure as I was pregnant, I didn't listen to the voice of reason.

"I'm not asking you to do anything, Carrie Jo. Nothing at all. It's up to you if you want to accept my apology or not."

My hands were clenched into fists. My ponytail felt limp and my back pain kicked into high gear, but the tears were coming. There would be no stopping them now. "With Ginny, you knew I wasn't crazy? And that time when I kept seeing that old man in my dreams—the one who hurt himself? You knew those dreams were real and you let me sleep in that house anyway?"

"We had nowhere else to go! It was that or the street. Your dad left us high and dry. I had to take whatever we could get." Her eyes narrowed in frustration. "I'm not proud of what I did, the decisions I made. Not proud at all. I know it's too late to ask you to trust me now, but I could not let one more day go by without telling you that I am sorry. I am sorry about it all."

"What about my father? How come you never wanted to tell me about him? You know what that's like when you're a kid? What it's like now? He hates me, doesn't he?" The pain in my back grew more intense, and I could see flashes of light around the corners of my eyes. I put my hand on the table to steady myself.

"No! No, Carrie Jo. He doesn't hate you. He was afraid of us. Afraid of me. He's not a bad man, just a fearful one."

Angry words were poised at the tip of my tongue, but they didn't spring forth like I wanted them to. To my surprise, a splash of water landed on the floor between my legs. It felt warm and sticky. It didn't stop. My sandaled feet were all wet now. All I could think to say was, "Momma?"

She jumped out of the chair. "It's okay, Carrie Jo. This is normal. Your water broke. The baby is coming soon. We've got to get you back to the hospital." She put her arm around me and led me to the side door. "Oh, shoot! My car isn't here. Detra Ann? Rachel?" The girls bounded down the stairs, still smiling until they saw me.

"Does this mean what I think it means?" Detra Ann asked.

"Yes, her water broke. We've got to get her back to the hospital right now."

"Why did they send her home? I knew that was a mistake. Let's take my car." She ran to the living room, grabbed her purse and came back. "Let's do this, CJ. You've got this! Rachel? Would you mind cleaning this up?"

"Sure, I'll clean up and turn everything off. I'll meet y'all up there. Should I call Ashland and Henri?"

"Yep, that would be great." I hated the way everyone was talking so calmly. Like one of us had a baby every day. "See you there. Oh, and grab her suitcase by the front door!" Detra Ann said as she hurried me down the steps.

"Can't I change my clothes first? I look like I peed on myself."

"Um, no, girl. You don't have time for that. Once your water breaks, labor could start any—"

Just then I screamed. If I thought yesterday's contractions were anything to brag about, I was sorely mistaken. "Shoot! Shoot!" I said as I tried to remember how to breathe. I kicked myself again for not taking those Lamaze classes. "What do I do? What do I do, Momma?"

"Take slow, deep breaths when you can. I ain't gonna lie. It's gonna hurt like hell, but you'll survive."

"That's one hell of a pep talk, Deidre," Detra Ann scolded her.

"Well.... Oh, and don't push yet. For the love of God. It's not time to push. Let's get to the hospital first. We'll start timing the next one."

"Okay, okay," I said, breathing as slowly as I could. It was hard as heck to do with my heart pounding and my pulse racing. Detra Ann practically shoved me in the backseat and began backing the car down the driveway like a wild woman. *Should I tell her my purse is hanging out the door? Breathe, breathe, breathe!*

"Too bad it's not a girl. We could call her Jasmine, in honor of the storm," Detra Ann said, smiling at me in the rearview mirror.

"Never," I promised her. "But Ashland would love that. I hope Rachel got a hold of him."

"Don't you worry about it, CJ. He'll be there." Detra Ann shouted at me as she ran a red light.

Deidre gasped and grabbed my hand. "Sweet Lord!"

"Get your watch ready. I feel another one coming. I'm sorry about your backseat, Detra Ann."

"Son of a b! Did you see that guy? I don't care about the backseat, but don't have the baby in my car! Jasmine deserves better."

Between pants and twists of pain I panted, "I'm—not-calling-her—Jasmine. Oh God, oh God!"

Detra Ann hit a curb trying to avoid a car. It was like being on a painful bumper car ride. My mother prayed beside me the whole time. Detra Ann grinned like a maniac when she wasn't honking at someone or threatening to cut their body parts off.

"Here we are! Pulling in the driveway now!" she yelled, forgetting once again that I was pregnant and not hard of hearing.

"Great! Perfect timing! Here comes another one!"

"Three minutes apart! That baby will be here soon!" My mother opened her door, rescued my purse and practically dragged me out of the backseat. "Hey! My daughter is having a baby! Like right now!"

"Momma! That's an ambulance guy. Not a nurse!"

It didn't matter. She was going to make sure someone helped me, and all I could do was hold my breath and hope the pain quit. A dark-haired young man squatted down in front of me. "What's your name?"

"Carrie Jo. It's Carrie Jo."

"Okay, Carrie Jo. I've got a chair here. Think you can stand so we can get you in it?"

"In just a second." I held my breath and waited for the contraction to let up.

"Don't hold your breath. Try to breathe through them. It will help with the pain. That's better. Take your time. I'll wait." Over his shoulder he told the approaching nurse what was happening.

"I think I can stand up now."

"They are three minutes apart," Deidre told the nurse as she pushed me through the hospital doors. "And her water broke."

"Sounds like we have a baby on the way. If it's a girl you could name her Jasmine."

I rolled my eyes at Detra Ann, who ran along beside me. "Never," I mouthed to her.

My clothes were drenched, my forehead was covered in sweat, and I was exhausted already. "Detra Ann, call Ashland, please. I need him here."

"I will. Deidre you stay with her while I find out what's going on."

Before I knew it, the nurse had me in the elevator and we were headed to the fifth floor. No long registration process for me. "Got no time to waste. The doctor says to bring you up now. Baby's coming! It's going to be okay. We're going to get you an IV started, he'll check to see how far you've dilated and then we'll go from there. How does that sound?"

"Like a dream. I'd like to wait for my husband."

The nurse, a young woman with pretty, soft-looking brown hair, smiled sympathetically. "Hopefully he will make it in time. But either way, I think you will meet your baby soon." Sure enough, another nurse came in quickly and had me rigged up to the IV in no time.

Dr. Gary arrived, apologizing that he had sent me home. A quick examination confirmed it. "Eight centimeters dilated. It's almost time."

"I know!" I practically screamed at him as another contraction, the strongest so far, took my breath away.

"How about an epidural to help with the pain?"

"Please? I would love one." All my pledges to "go natural" went out the window. I wondered if breast-feeding would hit the chopping block too.

"Be right back," Dr. Gary said as he pulled the blanket back down.

"Momma, please find out where Ashland is—he needs to get here."

Detra Ann walked back in, her phone in her hand. I could tell by the look on her face that something was wrong.

Something was dead wrong.

"Ashland is missing. Henri saw him fall in the water. He's with the authorities. They are looking for him now." She flew to my side and rubbed my hand. "You listen to me, Carrie Jo Stuart. We are not going to entertain anything negative about Ashland, you hear me? He is going to be fine. Right now, you have his baby to think about! I know you want to cry and fall apart, but you can't! You don't have that luxury! Let's have this baby so we can find out what's happening."

"Detra Ann, no! I can't—you have to go be with Henri! Help him find Ash! Please!"

Dr. Gary heard the shouting and came in; a nurse was tying on his face mask. "What is this? What's going on in here? Trying to have a baby, people."

"You don't understand, Dr. Gary. Carrie Jo's husband, Ashland, has disappeared off his boat. He's in the water and they haven't found him. But they will!"

"You had to tell her that now?" He sat on the rolling chair and rolled to my side. "I know you wish you could be doing something else right now, but this child needs you. Your son needs you. Let's welcome him into the world and make sure he's healthy. That's the number one thing right now, got it?"

Still in shock from the news about Ashland, I said, "Yes, that's the number one thing. Ashland's baby. Oh God, please protect him. Momma!"

"Yes, darling."

"I know you wanted to be in here, but I need you praying for Ashland. Let Detra Ann stay with me, and you go pray. When Rachel gets here, get her praying too. Please, Momma. Pray your very hardest!" I cried as the sweat poured off my forehead.

"What's the air on?" Detra Ann asked the nurse. Without waiting she checked the room thermostat and immediately dropped it. It didn't do any good because just then the lights went out. In the momentary silence I could hear the winds rattling the windows of the hospital like moaning ghosts demanding to be let in.

"I've had enough of ghosts! You hear me? Enough!"

Dr. Gary stared at me. "Carrie Jo, are you with me? Nurse, check her IV bag. I did not order anything that would make her hallucinate."

Detra Ann assured him I was fine, that I was just worried about Ashland, and then the labor began in earnest. "Okay, let's check. Yes, fully dilated. That was fast once you got started. That's a good thing. Some people have the worst time opening up. Let's see...oh yes, I see a little head already. Now it's important that you push when I tell you to push, okay. Are you in pain?"

"No pain, just a lot of pressure. Can I push yet?"

"Let me get in position. Okay, let's push."

I sat up and held my knees, pushing with all my might. *This isn't right. This shouldn't be happening. Not without my husband. Ashland, I love you. Where are you!*

I need you right now!

Chapter 13—Carrie Jo

"Of course you know this will open you up to a ton of lawsuits now, right?" Libby said, frowning at Ashland. "And that you've just signed away seventy-five percent of your net worth? That's a big deal, Ashland. I'm not sure you understand how far this decision reaches. This could haunt you for the rest of your life."

Libby couldn't know how apropos her choice of words was. "We hope so," he answered cryptically.

"I just can't believe this. You're normally so level-headed. Is this because of your son? Or something else?" She glanced at me as if I were the culprit. I kept my face completely expressionless.

"Yes and no," he said. "That's all I can tell you. I appreciate your help with all this."

"I still don't get it. I don't get this whole thing. I need a vacation." She tapped her head with her pen in frustration. "It might be the last one any of us take."

"Don't tell us you're breaking up with us, Libby," I said with a smirk. Ashland laughed, and boy, did that sound good. Money was all Libby really cared about. Well, money and stealing my husband. Now she would lose on both counts.

"Two of these claimants can't even prove they are related to your family. You do know that, right?" He nodded, and I could tell he was starting to feel a bit aggravated about this whole conversation. "This sets a bad standard, Ashland. Not just for you but for many of the older families here in Mobile. You haven't heard the last of this, I'm afraid. Not by a long shot."

"This is the right thing to do, Libby," he replied. "Not just for us but for everyone involved. I know you don't understand my decision, our decision, but this is it. This is how it should have always been."

Libby shook her head, her stylish bob swinging as she did. With perfectly manicured hands she stamped the documents and folded them up neatly. She placed them in the thick manila envelopes and looked at us like we were both out of our heads.

"As long as you know what you're doing. Who am I to say?"

Ashland and I walked out of the building and stepped into the warm sunshine. It was hard to believe that a major storm had blown through here just two weeks ago. Most of the fallen oaks had been removed, but there were plenty of houses missing shingles, windows—you name it. I closed my eyes for a moment as we stood outside the car. I felt lighter, like an unseen weight had been lifted off my shoulders, and I was sure Ashland felt the same way. After a minute, I poked him in the side. "One more stop before the event, babe. Can't daydream now."

"I'll leave all the dreaming to you."

"As well you should. Speaking of which, Deidre says she'll meet us at Seven Sisters with Baby Boy. Did Mr. Chapman from the city call you? He said the sign arrived and they'll be installing it in front of the house today. I can't believe Seven Sisters won't be called Seven Sisters anymore, but I like the sound of the Beaumont-Cottonwood Manor. It sounds...right. Oh, I almost forgot. Doreen and Rachel are coming too. I can't believe this is going down without Henri and Detra Ann. Are you sure we can't wait?"

"We'll throw them a huge party when they get back. And yes, I'm sure this can't wait. You know, I've heard people talk about getting married in Vegas, but I've never actually met someone who did. Can't believe they went without us," he said with a smile.

I laughed. "I can. Those two don't need us there. They'll have Elvis and Marilyn Monroe as their witnesses. I promise you this, though, Detra Ann's mother is going to have a nervous breakdown when she finds out they got hitched. She's the only girl in that family, and I'm sure Cynthia's always dreamed of throwing her a big wedding."

"Probably so."

He turned the car down the forgotten road. His Jeep found every bump and pothole, but it didn't matter. We were on a mission. It was hard to believe fall was here, with the way the sun beamed down on us. The balmy weather made me want to slip off my shoes and prop my feet up on the dash, but now wasn't the time for that. The Jeep came to a stop, and in the distance I could hear the river lapping against the sandy riverbank.

"This is about it," I said. "I remember seeing this place in a dream. There was once an old oak tree that stood there. Isla used to climb it and watch the boys swim. The Delta Queen used to roll along here, and just a way down was where she embarked the night Calpurnia landed in the water."

"When we ceded the house to the city, I thought that would be the end of all this. I hope this truly is the end. Do you think it will be?" he asked me, grabbing the roses out of the backseat.

I slid my sunglasses up to the top of my head. "No matter what happens, this is the right thing to do. I am proud of you, babe, for wanting to make it right. I think the ghosts of the past will know that you've tried, that we've tried, and they'll accept that."

He squeezed my hand, and we walked down the steep hillside to the riverbank. "I don't know how we managed to talk the city into changing the name of the house. Usually this kind of thing takes years. The Beaumont-Cottonwood Plantation. That has a nice ring to it, doesn't it?"

"Yep, it does." He handed me some roses. Thankfully, the florist had been nice enough to clip the thorns from the stems. I took the flowers, and we stood by the water with our heads bowed. "You ready?" I asked him quietly.

"Yes, I am. Finally." With his eyes closed, he tilted his head up toward the blue sky.

"Dear Lord, my wife and I ask you to lift the curse that was placed upon my family all those years ago. I know that wrongs were done, many wrongs. I know that many people were hurt as a result of those wrongs. Although I did not personally do these things, I take responsibility for them as the current representative of our family. I repent, Lord. We stole from others, we made our brothers slaves, we hid our secrets and refused to repent of them. Many of us did murder and many other sinful things in your sight. But I, Ashland James Stuart, do repent, Lord, on behalf of my sinful ancestors. I am sorry." I squeezed his hand as a tear rolled down his cheek.

As he wiped his face with his hands, his eyes looked even bluer through the tears. Still speaking to God, he said, "I have given the moment to the people who deserved it. I have a clean conscience, God. I have given the house the name it deserves. I hope this is enough. But if it's not, please tell me what to do and I will do it. If not for me, Lord, for my son and my wife. She is innocent."

"No, I am not so innocent either," I said to Ashland. Then I spoke to God as Ash had, toward the blue sky. "I have been bitter and unforgiving toward the people I love. I had no idea that you were trying to help me, that my mother was doing what she thought she should. I was wrong to hate her. For that I am sorry. I do not know how I am related to Muncie yet, if at all. But if I am, I will not be ashamed to call him my cousin. Or uncle. Or whatever he may be. I accept him. Thank you for keeping Ashland safe. Thank you for our family."

It was my turn to cry now. I put my face in Ashland's chest and cried my heart out. When my tears had flowed, I prepared to throw the flowers in the water as a kind of tribute to the many Cottonwoods, Beaumonts and others caught up in the centuries-long curse, but I froze. Standing on the water, just as she would have described Reginald Ball as walking out like "Holy Jesu," was Calpurnia. She was not the sickly, defeated girl I remembered from my dreams but happy and smiling. She walked toward us, the hem of her coral gown skimming the water.

"Ashland, do you see her?"

"Yes," he whispered without looking at me. She floated closer, and the bright sunlight sparkled in her intricate hairstyle. With shaking fingers, Ashland handed her a red rose. Her fingers never touched his, but she accepted the flower from him. "Be at peace," she whispered to him. She smiled at me too, and the coral earrings bobbed at her ears. Suddenly, Muncie stood beside her. He was no longer Muncie the boy but Janjak the man, the teacher in a three-piece suit. He took her hand, and I held out a flower to him with shaking fingers.

"Be at peace," he said to me in a soothing, rich voice. Together they stepped back on the water and soon faded away with smiles on their faces. We breathed a sigh of relief, but then there were others, walking to us across the river.

Isla came next. She wore her powder blue gown with the full lacy sleeves. I could feel Ashland tense beside me, but he offered her the rose. "Forgive me, cousin," he said in a sincere voice.

"Be at peace," she said. She accepted the rose and vanished immediately. Others came too, Christine, Delilah and finally Olivia.

I had seen Olivia only once in a dream, but I knew Ashland had seen much of her, either in dreams or as a ghost. He handed her a rose as she drew close, her hair still upswept with not a hair out of place. She looked at the flower for a moment and leaned closer to his face. "So you are the curse-breaker? Be at peace, cousin." She too vanished as Isla had done.

We tossed the rest of the roses on the water and watched them float away down the Mobile River.

"The curse is broken, Ashland. It is over, at last!"

"Yes, I believe it is. Thank God!"

"I was so nervous. I hardly expected to see Janjak or anyone!"

"Me too!" We were all smiles.

"We better get going. Little AJ will be missing you," I said with a smile.

"I can't believe you named our son Ashland James."

"Well, if it was good enough for you, it's good enough for him. At least it's not Jasmine."

"What do you have against Jasmine?"

"Nothing, really. Maybe we'll consider it for our daughter."

"Daughter? Whoa! We just gave away all our money. Maybe we should slow down on growing the family for a while."

"No way. We've got to restock the family tree, babe." I put my arms around his neck and kissed him.

"And what good stock it is too," he purred playfully. As I kissed him I pretended I didn't hear a giggle or two coming from the direction of that old oak tree.

"You hear anything?" I asked cautiously.

"Nope. Let's go."

We drove out of the woods and down the bumpy, beaten path, back to the road that would lead us to the future. Our good future. It *was* going to be a good one. A curse-free one.

I felt overwhelmed with gratitude. "Thank you," I whispered to no one in particular. I knew everyone who was supposed to hear it would.

Author's Note

Thank you for taking this journey with me. When I wrote book one of the Ultimate Seven Sisters Collection, I had no idea I would end the series with six books! What is even more surprising to me is how much you all love Carrie Jo, Ashland and all the folks at Seven Sisters. Seven Sisters was my first book, and it will always hold a special place in my heart. From the Blue Room to the Moonlight Garden, I know every inch and visit it myself often in the books.

I am often asked if Seven Sisters is a real place. I am sorry to say that no, it isn't. But then again, who really knows? So many of the old houses have been lost, and I am sure somewhere down the line there was a house like it, complete with a creaking staircase and plenty of ghosts. We have an abundance of haunted houses in the South. I based the house on a combination of houses you can find in Mobile, Alabama including the Historic Oakleigh House and the Bragg-Mitchell Mansion. Mobile is a lovely city with plenty to see and do. If you haven't been, come on by!

I get other questions as well, like, "How is Mia still alive when Carrie Jo said she was dead?" The answer to that is Carrie Jo was wrong. She has been wrong before—but in the end, it all works out.

Because we all love this series so much, I've begun a spin-off series. Carrie Jo and the gang need a new house to explore, so we are headed off to Idlewood. The Ghosts of Idlewood is Book One of the new Idlewood series. It will be available sometime in 2016.

If you love historical fiction, check out my Desert Queen series. It's about Queen Nefertiti and her ill-fated love with Akhenaten.

I've also begun a series set in Dauphin Island, the Sirens Gate series. My heroine, Thessalonike (called Nik by her friends), gets into plenty of trouble. It's an urban fantasy with a touch of humor and snark.

I have other series planned too, many featuring ghosts and great Southern families. I would be honored to have you follow me on Facebook. Just look up Author ML Bullock or sign up for my mailing list at www.mlbullock.com and get updates on new releases right in your mailbox. I don't send spam, and I only email about new releases.

Thank you again for every kind email, Facebook post and message. I appreciate you.

All my best,

M.L. Bullock

Read more from M.L. Bullock

The Seven Sisters Series

Seven Sisters
Moonlight Falls on Seven Sisters
Shadows Stir at Seven Sisters
The Stars that Fell
The Stars We Walked Upon
The Sun Rises Over Seven Sisters

The Idlewood Series

The Ghosts of Idlewood
Dreams of Idlewood
The Whispering Saint
The Haunted Child

Return to Seven Sisters
(A Forthcoming Sequel Series to Seven Sisters)

The Roses of Mobile
A Garden of Thorns
All the Summer Roses
Blooms Torn Asunder
A Wreath of Roses

Cotton City Antiques
(A Forthcoming Seven Sisters Spinoff Series)

A Voice from Her Past
The Haunted Letter
Henri's Ghost Light
Missing Time in Mobile
Phantom Photos of Tomorrow
The Weeping of Angels

The Gulf Coast Paranormal Series
The Ghosts of Kali Oka Road
The Ghosts of the Crescent Theater
A Haunting on Bloodgood Row (forthcoming)
The Legend of the Ghost Queen (forthcoming)
A Haunting at Dixie House (forthcoming)
The Ghost Lights of Forrest Field (forthcoming)
The Ghost of Gabrielle Bonet (forthcoming)
The Ghosts of Harrington Farms (forthcoming)
The Creature on Crenshaw Road (forthcoming)

Storm Castle Series (forthcoming)

The Haunting of Joanna Storm
The Disappearance of Joanna Storm
The Ghost of Joanna Storm

The Sugar Hill Series

Wife of the Left Hand
Fire on the Ramparts
Blood by Candlelight (forthcoming)
The Starlight Ball (forthcoming)

The Sirens Gate Series

The Mermaid's Gift
The Blood Feud
The Wrath of Minerva
The Lorelei Curse (forthcoming)
The Island Jinx (forthcoming)
The Fortunate Star (forthcoming)

The Southern Gothic Series

Being with Beau

The Desert Queen Series

The Tale of Nefret
The Falcon Rises
The Kingdom of Nefertiti
The Song of the Bee-Eater

To receive updates on her latest releases,
visit her website at MLBullock.com
and subscribe to her mailing list.

Made in the USA
Middletown, DE
20 August 2017